TRANSCENDENCE

THE COMPLETE HUMAN++ TRILOGY

DIMA ZALES

♠ MOZAÏKA PUBLICATIONS ♠

Copyright © 2018 Dima Zales and Anna Zaires
www.dimazales.com

Published by Mozaika Publications, an imprint of Mozaika LLC.
www.mozaikallc.com

Cover by Najla Qamber Designs
www.najlaqamberdesigns.com

e-ISBN: 978-1-63142-338-3
Print ISBN: 978-1-63142-340-6

MIND MACHINES

HUMAN++: BOOK 1

ONE

THE GARGANTUAN SYRINGE APPROACHES MOM'S NECK. GRANDPA squeezes her hand and tries not to look at the rapier-sized needle as it breaks his daughter's skin.

"Misha," Mom tells me in Russian. "This hurts."

I take a step forward, my hands balling into fists as I glare at the white-masked surgeon.

"Why is it going into her neck?" I demand.

I see no hint of empathy in the doctor's reflective eyes, and I seriously consider punching him in the face. Since distracting him might worsen Mom's situation, I settle for a calming breath, though all I really get is a lungful of sterile, Clorox-filled air.

The operation room has bright surgical lights and torture-chamber surgical equipment sadistically displayed throughout.

"Why are all these frightening things around us if it's just a simple injection?" I stammer, taking it all in for the first time.

The doctor's knuckles whiten as he presses the giant plunger. A disgusting gray liquid whooshes out of the syringe into Mom's neck.

"Why do the nanocytes need to be delivered in such a terrible way?" I ask—mostly to prevent myself from fainting.

"They shouldn't be," Grandpa says in English.

Mom's round face is contorted with the kind of horror and desperation I've only seen on it once, when a scrawny mouse scurried into our living room in our first Brooklyn apartment. Just like on that day, an ear-piercing scream is wrenched from her throat.

I take another step forward. Maybe I'll just pry the doc away from her.

The bald spot on top of Grandpa's head is beet red, and I wonder if he's about to kill the doc with his shoe, employing the same violent swat he used against the culprit mouse.

The doctor steps away from us.

Mom's screaming turns into gurgles and fades away.

Gray liquid starts pouring out of her mouth.

I feel paralyzed.

The same liquid streams out of her eyes, then her nose and her ears.

"It's the nanocytes," I yell in horror, my vocal cords finally working. "But they can't be replicating!"

Mom's head disappears, replaced by a vague liquid shape of the replicating gray goo. In a violent heartbeat, the rest of Mom's body turns into the same fluid grayness.

With two gurgling screams, Grandpa and the doctor also melt into puddles of squirming, colorless protoplasm.

The enormity of these losses doesn't fully register before the substance creeps over my own foot.

A savage searing pain spreads through my body, and I know it must be from the nanos breaking my flesh into molecules.

This can't be real, is my last thought. *This has to be a dream.*

———

I jackknife into a sitting position on the bed. Either the gruesome deaths or the realization I was dreaming woke me.

My bedroom is darker than a naked mole rat's lair. Going by feel, I locate my phone on the nightstand and light up its screen.

When my eyes adjust and I can decipher the time, I fight the urge to toss the phone at the wall. That would be like killing the messenger—fleetingly therapeutic, but pointless. It's 3:00 a.m., which is probably my least favorite a.m.

I take a deep breath the way my yoga-obsessed ex-girlfriend taught me, and surprisingly, I feel a bit calmer. I guess things aren't so bad. If I calm down enough to fall asleep again soon, I can doze for another five hours and probably still be functional during the day.

Getting up, I go to the bathroom. The AC chills my naked body as I walk, so the first thing I do is vigorously wipe away all the cold sweat.

My breath evens out further.

As I make use of the facilities, I chide myself for freaking out over that unlikely dream scenario. Grandfather's been dead for two years, and even when he was alive, he didn't speak flawless— or any—English. Also, the nanocytes we're using on Mom are the non-replicating kind, which is partly why each dose costs an obscene amount. Future replicating nanotechnology will build itself out of raw materials, so it'll only cost as much as those materials do, but that's not the case with this experimental batch. Finally, the injection procedure is noninvasive and *won't* require a surgeon, or even a doctor, to be present. This nightmare was just a manifestation of my irrational anxieties.

What I need now is sleep. As one of my family's favorite Russian sayings goes, "Morning is wiser than evening."

Yawning, I get back into bed and fall asleep half a second before my head touches the pillow.

TWO

"A CURE FOR DEMENTIA AND ALZHEIMER'S?" UNCLE ABE'S GRAY EYES pulse with excitement, the way Mom's often do.

"It's not exactly a cure," I say at the same time as Ada says, "It's mostly a treatment for the symptoms."

"How cute," Uncle Abe says in Russian. "Your chick is already finishing your sentences."

As though she understood the Russian words, Ada's face lights up with an impish grin.

"We're not a couple," I tell Uncle Abe in Russian.

"Yet?" He gives me a knowing wink.

"It's not polite to speak in Russian in front of Ada," I say in English.

"I'm okay," Ada says. Only the shadow of a smile lurks in the corners of her eyes now, making her look like a punky version of the Mona Lisa.

"Still, I'm sorry," Uncle Abe tells her, his accent softening the *t* and the second *r*.

As we stroll through the hospital corridor, Ada takes the lead. She's a typical New Yorker, always twitchy and multitasking. I surreptitiously look her up and down, my eyes lingering on one of my favorite assets of hers—that special spot between the soles of her Doc Martens boots and the tips of her spiky hair.

Ada glances over her shoulder, her amber eyes meeting mine for a second. Did she feel me gawking at her just now? Before I can feel embarrassed, she stops in front of a green door and says, "This is the room."

The three of us walk in.

Unlike my dream, this isn't an operating room. It's spacious, with big windows and cheerfully blooming plants on the windowsills. At a glance, it's reminiscent of my stylish Brooklyn loft—if a mad scientist's wet dream was used as inspiration for the interior design.

Staff members from Techno, my portfolio company that designed the treatment, are already in the back. Mom is sitting on an operating chair in a white hospital gown, with a plethora of cables attaching her to a myriad of cutting-edge monitoring tools. Completing her getup is a headset—something straight out of the old *Total Recall* movie. It must be the "latest in portable neural scan technology" that JC, Techno's CEO, mentioned to me. I make a mental note to define *portable* to him.

I hear a "hi" from the farthest corner of the room. The person who spoke must be hidden behind the wall of servers and giant monitors. The other Techno employees keep working silently, though it isn't clear whether they didn't hear me come in, or if they're being antisocial.

Many folks at Techno could stand to improve their social skills. A psychiatrist might even label some of them as borderline Asperger's. Personally, I find those types of labels ridiculous. Psychiatry can sometimes be as scientific and helpful as astrology —which I don't believe in, in case that's not clear. A shrink back in high school tried to attach the Asperger's label to me because I had "too few friends." He could've just as easily concluded I had Tourette's based on where I told him to shove his diagnosis. Then again, maybe I'm still sore about psychiatry and neuropsychology because of how little they've done for Mom. Pretty much the only good thing I can say about psychiatry is that at least they're no longer using lobotomy as a treatment.

I look around the room for JC. He's nowhere to be found, so he must be in a similar room with another participant of the study.

Mom turns her head toward us, apparently able to do so despite the headgear.

My heart clenches in dread, as it always does when Mom and I meet after more than a day apart. Because of the accident that damaged Mom's brain, it's feasible that one day she'll look at me and won't recognize who I am.

Today she clearly does, though, because she gives me that dimpled smile we share. "Hi, little fish," she says in Russian. She then looks at her brother. "Abrashkin, bunny, how are you?"

"Mom just used untranslatable Russian pet names for us," I loudly whisper to Ada and wave hello to the still-uninterested staff in the back.

Mom looks at Ada without recognition, and I inwardly sigh. They've met twice before.

"Who's this boy?" Mom asks me in English. "Is he an intern at Techno or something?"

"She's not a boy, and her name is Ada," I respond, trying my best not to sound like I'm talking to someone with a disability, something my mom deeply resents. "She's not an intern, but one of the people who programmed the nanocytes that'll make you feel better."

"Nice to meet you, Nina Davydovna," Ada says as though they haven't done this before.

Mom's eyebrow rises at either the girlish resonance of Ada's bell-like voice or her proper use of the Russian patronymic. She quickly recovers, though, just like the last time, and also like the last time, she says, "Call me Nina."

"I will. Thank you, Nina," Ada says.

I realize Ada addressed my mom so formally on purpose—to lessen Mom's stress—so I give her a grateful nod. Of course, if Ada wanted to go the extra mile, she could've worn different clothing or changed her hairstyle to eliminate Mom's confusion about Ada's gender. Then again, Mom's confusion might be part of her condition, because to me, despite the leather jacket and black hoodie obscuring much of her body, Ada is the epitome of femininity.

"Is she his girlfriend?" Mom asks Uncle Abe conspiratorially in Russian. "Have I met her before?"

"I'm not sure, sis," Uncle Abe says. "From the way he looks at her, I suspect it's just a matter of time before they hook up."

"Oh yeah?" Mom chuckles. "Do you think she's Jewish?"

Blood rushes to my cheeks, and not just because of this "Jewish or not" business. It's something that became important to Mom only after the accident—unless she's always cared but only started voicing it after the brain damage lowered her inhibitions. My grandparents certainly often spoke about this sort of thing, going as far as blaming the situation with my father on him being non-Jewish—something I consider to be reverse anti-Semitism.

It's unfortunate, but their attitude was forged back in the Soviet Union, where being Jewish was considered an ethnicity and used as an excuse for government-level discrimination. Since one's ethnicity was written in the infamous fifth paragraph of one's passport, discrimination was commonplace and inescapable. My mom was turned away from her first choice of universities because they'd hit "their quota of three Jews." She also had a hard time finding a job in the engineering sciences until my father helped her out, only to later sexually harass her and leave her to raise me on her own. Even I was affected by this negativity before we left. When my seventh-grade classmates learned about my heritage from our school journal, they told me that with my blue eyes and blond hair (which darkened to brown as I got older), I looked nothing like a Jew. Though they used the derogatory Russian term, they'd meant it as a big compliment.

What makes the topic extra weird is that in America, where Judaism is more of a religion than an ethnicity, we're suddenly not all that Jewish. I mean, how can we be if I learned about Hanukkah in my mid-teens and when I had a very non-kosher grilled lobster tail wrapped in bacon last night?

Yeah, I also learned what *kosher* means in my mid-teens.

Either way, I couldn't care less about Ada's Jewishness—though, for the record, with a last name like Goldblum, she probably is Jewish. I don't know what that term means to her either, since she's just as secular as I am. I think my biggest issue with Mom's question is that I simply loathe labels applied to entire groups of people, especially labels that come with so much baggage.

"It's hard to say," Uncle Abe says after examining Ada's dainty nose and zooming in on her pierced nostril. "With that hair, she's definitely not Russian."

Here we go, another label. To my grandparents, the term *Russian* was interchangeable with *goy* or *gentile*, but I don't think my uncle is using it in that context. Though in Russia we were Jewish, here in the US we're Russian—as in, the same as every Russian speaker from the former Soviet Union. I'm guessing my uncle is saying that Ada doesn't look like she's from the former Soviet Union, since a certain way of dressing and grooming typically accompanies that, at least for recent immigrants.

I decide to stop this thread of conversation, but before I get a chance to put a word in, Mom says, "When I was young, that kind of haircut was called an explosion at the noodle factory."

They both laugh, and even I can't help chuckling. I know the haircut Mom is referring to, and it's an eighties hairdo that may well be a distant ancestor to what's happening on Ada's head. The bleached, pointy tips make her look like an echidna with a Mohawk—an image reinforced by her prickly wit.

The door to the room opens, and a nurse walks in.

Seeing her scrubs raises my blood pressure, though I'm not sure if it's from the standard white coat syndrome or a flashback to my earlier nightmare. Probably the former. There was no anesthesia in Soviet dentistry when I was growing up, so I developed a conditioned response to anything resembling dentist clothing.

Anyone in a white coat gives me a reaction akin to what someone suffering from coulrophobia—the irrational fear of clowns—would experience during a John Wayne Gacy documentary or the movie *It*.

The nurse walks over to Mom and reaches for a big syringe lying stealthily by Mom's chair.

The Techno employees in the back collectively hold their breaths.

The nurse doesn't seem to understand the auspiciousness of the occasion. She looks like she wants to finish here and move on to something more interesting, like watching a filibuster on C-SPAN. Her nametag reads "Olga." That, combined with her circa late-eighties haircut and makeup, plus those Slavic cheekbones, activates my Russian radar—or Rudar for short. It's like gaydar, but for detecting Russian speakers.

I bet Mom is insulted by the hospital assigning this nurse to her. It implies she needs help understanding English. Having earned a Bachelor of Science in Electrical Engineering after moving to the States in her mid-thirties, Mom takes deserved pride in her skills with the English language—skills the accident didn't affect.

In the silence, I can hear Mom's shallow breathing; her fear of medical professionals is much worse than mine.

Olga grips the syringe and raises her hand.

THREE

UNCLE ABE LOOKS AWAY. I'M TEMPTED TO FOLLOW HIS LEAD BUT decide against it.

To my relief, instead of Mom's neck, Olga connects the syringe to the port below the IV bag. This makes sense, since it's the easiest way to access Mom's vein.

Reality further diverges from my nightmare as I note the clear liquid carrying the nanocytes and the fact that Mom doesn't even wince throughout the whole ordeal. And she's operating on senses heightened by fear, so if there was a reason to wince, she would have, and she probably would've screamed as well.

The people scanning the monitors murmur amongst themselves, but no one sounds alarmed. Excitement permeates the air.

The nurse double-checks the vital signs and makes a Grinch-like face. In a Russian accent that confirms my Rudar's suspicions, she says, "I'll be around if I'm needed."

Without waiting for anyone to respond, she exits the room.

"How are you?" I ask Mom.

She shrugs, clearly overwhelmed by all this activity.

"You'll be fine, Nina," Ada says. "I'm sure of it."

I've read through countless reports and studies on the treatment, so I should be as confident as Ada is. But I worry, because as the poem goes, I only have one mother.

"I feel a slight burning in my arm," Mom says. "But it's not too bad."

"That's normal with intravenous delivery." Ada plays with the silver stud pierced through two spots in her ear cartilage. "It would've been worse if you'd gotten all the liquid at once. You might've felt nauseous."

I wonder where Ada learned all this medical info. Her background is in software, like mine, though I haven't written a line of code in a decade. In contrast, Ada is the most genius programmer I know, and that's saying a lot. As part of my job, I meet tons of talented software engineers—not to mention I'm besties with a world-renowned techie.

As though she read my mind, Ada says, "I was in the room with a few of the other participants, so I know what to expect."

This is yet another example of Ada's strange behavior around me, which began when I broke up with my ex a few months back. Is she hinting that she disapproves of my apparent lack of interest in the other participants? If so, she might actually have a point there, but she has to understand that all this—from investing so much of my own and my venture capital fund's money into Techno, to getting my friends in the industry involved in the Brainocyte research and development—is to help my mom. At least, that's my primary motivation. Of course I'm glad this technology will also lead to great things for other people, but I hope Ada can forgive me for focusing on the most important person in my life.

"How are things looking?" Ada asks loudly enough that the people in the back can't ignore her.

David, part of Techno's army of engineers, gives her a thumbs-up and says, "So far so good."

Ada nods at David, then looks at me. "Don't worry," she says. "Nina is still set to be the first participant to proceed to Phase One."

Looks like my suspicion was right. It must irk Ada that I'm not showing interest in any of the others. Once I make sure Mom is doing well, perhaps I'll pay some of the other participants a visit, starting with Mrs. Sanchez.

"What exactly is this treatment?" Uncle Abe asks and sits down on the couch—the only surface not covered by wires.

Ada looks at my mom, who doesn't reply, leading me to believe she forgot the details of the treatment. Usually, that would upset me, but since we're doing something to fix this very problem as we speak, I remain optimistic.

"That liquid contains Brainocytes," Ada says when she's sure neither my mom nor I want to take the lead. "They're the product we're testing."

My uncle and, sadly, Mom look at Ada with blank expressions, and Mom mumbles a paraphrase from a Russian proverb about how eggs are about to teach the hen.

"Okay, let me start over," Ada says and takes a seat on the other end of the couch. "Brainocytes are a type of nanocytes designed to penetrate the blood-brain barrier and create the most powerful brain-to-computer interface—BCI—ever made."

The blank looks don't change, so she says, "How much do you know about nanotechnology and neuroprosthetics?"

At the mention of nanotechnology, Mom's eyes shimmer with recognition. "After I finished college the first time, we had a scanning tunneling microscope where I worked, so the idea of molecular machines was often discussed, especially when the translations of Eric Drexler's work became available."

"Why do I have a feeling I'm about to regret my question?" Uncle Abe mutters.

In his defense, he must've heard Mom talk about her old job more often than I have. That old job is closely intertwined with the whole affair involving my father, so those memories are like emotional dynamite for Mom. Since I can tell my uncle is about to say something that might really upset her, I stop him by plopping down on the couch between him and Ada.

14

Smiling at Mom, I say, "The simplest way to explain Brain-ocytes is to say that they're a bunch of super-tiny robots. They're currently swimming through your bloodstream into your brain, where they'll plug into your neurons. This will allow for all sorts of interesting interactions."

I've seen this exact expression on Uncle Abe's face when he tried uni sushi and learned that *uni* is Japanese for a sea urchin's gonads. Once he's won the yuck battle with himself, he says, "That sounds pretty invasive and creepy, but if anyone was going to agree to such a treatment, it would be our Nina."

It's true. Mom is more adventurous than her brother in every way, including her choice of foods. She loves uni.

Through the couch cushion, I feel Ada stiffen as though she's preparing to spring into action. I'm not surprised. The topic my uncle hit upon is Ada's pet peeve.

"It's not invasive at all," she says, her tone veering dangerously close to patronizing territory. "Nina is getting the safest neural interface of its kind. By not requiring the opening of the skull, as other similar technologies do, we avoid the risk of infection, not to mention leakage of cerebrospinal fluids—"

"This isn't the first time someone's tried to work directly with the brain," I interject before Ada can smack my uncle with a technical treatise. "Parkinson's and epilepsy patients already receive special brain pacemakers. Other products on the market—like retinal implants, for instance—allow the blind to regain some rudimentary sight, and cochlear implants allow the deaf to hear. Some implants turn thoughts into computer commands so quadriplegic patients can control their prosthetic limbs. Brainocytes can replace all these brain-implanted devices and, as Ada was saying, in a much safer way."

"I understand," Uncle Abe says, but his tone makes me doubt that he actually does.

Pretending I'm still explaining things to him, I continue for the benefit of Mom's failing memory. "The Brainocytes are the hardware. They'll lodge themselves all over Mom's brain, and once that's done, we can use the right software"—I incline my head toward Ada, acknowledging her key role in the creation of the necessary apps and interfaces—"to treat Mom's condition by stimulating the correct neurons in the carefully selected portions of her brain, all with the aid of external supercomputers. The idea is to simulate brain regions to supplement any missing functionality in the heavily damaged parts."

Ada sighs, and under her breath, she murmurs something along the lines of, "So this is how much you have to dumb things down for investors?"

"Sorry." I gently poke Ada with my elbow. "Do you want to take a stab at explaining Phase One to my uncle? I'm sure you can go over it without insulting anyone's intelligence."

"Don't mind if I do," Ada says, "especially since Phase One is very easy to explain. We'll primarily be working with neurons responsible for vision, specifically the ones within the ventral stream. My Augmented Reality Information Overlay suite of services will evoke Einstein's API—"

Uncle Abe chuckles, interrupting Ada, and even Mom's eyes appear glazed over. Despite all of Ada's prodigious cognitive abilities, adjusting to her audience isn't her strong suit.

Sighing in defeat, Ada says, "Why don't you have a go at it, Mike? Meanwhile, I'll make myself useful by checking the monitors."

She gets up and trudges to the other side of the room.

Unpeeling my eyes from the tightness of Ada's black jeans, I say, "Ada had one thing right. Phase One *is* really simple to explain, especially in comparison to the other stages. In a nutshell, you'll see text boxes hanging in the air, like thought bubbles in cartoons or dialog in comic books. These notes will be provided to you by an advanced artificial intelligence called Einstein, which is like Siri in your phone"—I look at Mom—"or Cortana in yours"—I look at my uncle—"only a thousand times more versatile and way smarter. By the way, Mom, Einstein was designed by my friend Mitya. You remember him, right?"

"Yes, I do," Mom says in Russian, and I see the grateful smile she adopts when her memory works like it should. "He's such a good boy and a wunderkind to boot."

"If you say so," I say, feeling a pang of jealousy at my mom's unabashed admiration for my friend. Though she thinks very highly of my mental capabilities, Mom is biased toward people whose work results in actual products. She calls them "doers." As a result, she admires software wizards like Ada and Mitya, since she can see the apps they write. Because I merely invest money in companies, I'm not a doer and thus don't make her as proud. Never mind that without me, a lot of doers wouldn't get their ideas into the market at all.

"You didn't see the debauchery your good boy Mitya partook in at MIT," I tell her, then stop, realizing I almost incriminated myself. Mom might correctly deduce that as Mitya's former roommate, I was also involved in said debauchery.

"Everyone does something stupid in American colleges," Mom says, not missing a chance to brag about her personal experience with this venerable institution. "Now can we please get back to explaining what's happening in my head?"

"Right," I say. "At first, you'll have extra information about everything around you, consisting mostly of notes on new people you meet or new places you visit. It won't be that different from me walking around with you, giving you reminders. Of course, we wouldn't give you Brainocytes just for this phase, since special glasses or contact lenses can be used for this type of memory assist. Another company my fund's invested in is actually aiming to do just that. But Phase Two takes things in a far more interesting direction, one that can only be achieved with Brainocytes."

"We're ready," Ada says excitedly. "Just waiting for JC to join us."

The door opens, and JC prances in.

"I always thought CEOs were like the devil," Ada tells him. "I was just talking about you, and here you are."

I inwardly smile. JC's lucky Ada isn't Russian, since the equivalent of "speak of the devil" in Russia is "remember the shit, and here it is."

"Hello, Adeline," JC says, using Ada's full name as a small retaliation.

Ada hides her face behind the screen, but I can tell JC won this round. Ada hates her full name almost as much as she loves her nickname. The latter honors her namesake, the Countess of Lovelace. Ada Lovelace designed the first-ever algorithm for a mechanical computer that Charles Babbage was planning. The machine was called the Analytical Engine, but sadly, Babbage didn't actually build it, so the historical Ada never saw her programs run on it.

JC ignores Ada and gives my mom a creepy smile that, combined with his red hair and rounded face, makes him look like a lecherous leprechaun. Well, the smile is creepy in my opinion. Mom glows in response, so as icky as it seems to me, she appears to like it. Again.

In his late forties or early fifties, JC is the oldest employee at Techno, a place where some people call me, a thirty-five-year-old guy, "sir." But his age isn't why JC is the CEO. He's the CEO because he has an uncanny knack for motivating the people around him. JC's weapon of choice is getting folks as excited about technology as he is, a technique that doesn't work on Ada because she doesn't think JC is excited enough—which, compared to her, he isn't. I wonder if Ada would make a better CEO because of that. Not that she would want the job; she doesn't like managing people. Just getting her to lead a team of super-bright software engineers was an epic effort that required bribes and pleading.

"Your name is JC, isn't it?" Mom says.

"Yes. May I call you Nina, then?" JC walks up to her and touches her IV-free elbow.

"Please do," Mom says.

Maybe it's me, but her remembering him when she forgets most other people makes JC look smug, and I'm tempted to tell him my mom's favorite saying about men: "To a Russian woman, a man needs to be only slightly more attractive than a gorilla."

"Can we please start Phase One?" Ada asks.

Interesting. Ada interrupted this weird exchange. Maybe that means I'm seeing things that aren't there? Ada is no expert when it comes to social interactions, but she isn't rude. If she noticed older people flirting, she wouldn't have intruded. She must not have picked up on the same vibes.

"If Nina is ready," JC says, "I think that's a great idea."

"I'm ready," Mom says.

JC nods at her solemnly and walks over to stand next to Ada.

I get up from the couch and join them.

"Okay, when I press this button"—Ada brushes her finger against the Enter key—"Phase One will begin."

"Do it," Mom says and closes her eyes.

Ada's finger dramatically hovers above the key for one long moment. Then she presses the button with a flourish.

FOUR

Mom opens her eyes and blinks so fast I wonder if she's trying to communicate in Morse code.

At first, the screen displays only static.

As Ada frantically types on the keyboard, the picture becomes clearer. Soon after, I see a ghostly outline of the room from Mom's point of view.

"This part will be encrypted shortly," Ada says to no one in particular. "For now, it'll help us get an idea of what Nina sees."

I make out shapes that correspond with the people in the room. Since this is Mom's neural data we're looking at, I half expect to look taller and handsomer—and maybe even have a halo over my head—but I'm just a shapeless blob, same as everyone else on the screen. I think that's from our algorithms, though, and not my mom's true perception of me.

The metadata shows up next to the shapes, just like the thought bubbles I expected. I don't know about Mom, but I find these bubbles helpful. They make me recall the names of a few of the shyer engineers in the room.

Mom attempts to remove the brain-scanning contraption from her head as she looks around. Uncle Abe rushes in to help her.

Some of the nearby monitors go berserk, but no one seems worried about it.

"This is so weird." She waves her hand next to where her brother's nametag data must be. "I feel like the Terminator."

Uncle Abe helps Mom gain a greater range of motion by removing more monitoring equipment.

"Can I change what these subtitles say?" Mom asks after a few seconds. "Can some of them be in Russian?"

"You'll have to learn how to use the mental computer interface first," Ada says. "That's something we'll work on for the rest of the day." When Mom frowns, she adds, "If you want to change a couple of them manually right now, you can. In fact, it'll give us a small head start since we were going to have you type on a keyboard during the interface portion anyway. Let's remove that IV and the rest of the gear so you can be more comfortable."

"I'll go get the nurse," Uncle Abe says. "It's safe to take all this stuff off, right?"

"Quite safe," JC says. "Most of that equipment is meant to collect data for us, but we have a dozen more subjects to go. We'd need to remove all those devices to take the brain scans in a few minutes anyway. Besides, the Brainocytes are now collecting the most important data."

When my uncle leaves, Ada tells Mom, "We'll teach you how to keep your Einstein database up to date. It uses face and voice recognition technology, and it'll know when you meet someone for the first time. From there, you'll learn how to store a new person's information. Relatedly, for future phases of your treatment, your Brainocytes will start monitoring your brain activity at crucial moments, such as when you interact with people you know well. Should your condition worsen, the Brainocytes will help your brain by recreating these healthier brain states when you meet that person again."

"She means you won't just see text, but also feel the right feelings," I chime in.

The door opens, and the nurse, Olga, lumbers in, followed by my uncle.

She frees Mom from the IV, the blood pressure monitor, and all the other medical equipment. With a lack of curiosity bordering on the pathological, the nurse once again leaves the room.

Mom shuffles over to the monitor.

"Here," JC says. "Touch the text box you want to edit and type in your custom information."

"Wait," Ada says. "If she's going to use the keyboard anyway, why don't I start the BCI learning algorithm?"

"We won't gain much by capturing these few keystrokes," JC says, "but go ahead if you want."

Ada's fingers dance over the keyboard, something pings, and she gives Mom a thumbs-up.

Mom proceeds to edit the metadata bubbles.

"That's not funny," Uncle Abe says when he sees the bubble she changed above my head. She replaced "Mike Cohen" with Russian text that roughly translates to, "Dear self. If you ever need this reminder and can no longer recognize Misha, your only son, it's best for everyone if you arrange for yourself to be euthanized."

Above Uncle Abe's head is something similar.

After I read JC's bubble, which says, "Interesting young man," I realize we're literally intruding on Mom's private thoughts.

"When will you turn on the encryption?" I ask Ada.

"Now, actually," Ada says and presses a few keys. When the feed from Mom's vision goes static, she adds, "The data going to Einstein and other servers was already encrypted, so there's nothing to do there."

"You didn't have to do that," Mom says. "If I need to sacrifice my privacy to help with the study, I'm more than happy to do so."

JC and Ada exchange looks. I strong-armed everyone into letting Mom into the study because she's my mom, but I also knew she'd make an outstanding participant—as her willingness to let us spy on her demonstrates. Not that I would've done anything differently had she been the worst patient in the world; when it comes to Mom, filial loyalty trumps all.

"You don't have to do that, Mom," I tell her. "We have a protocol. After the initial setup is complete, we want to make sure the participants enjoy the privacy they deserve."

"Are you ready to work on the BCI?" Ada asks, looking eager to change the subject.

Mom glances at me questioningly, so I decipher the Ada-speak for her. "She means learn how to use your new Brainocytes as a computer interface."

"Right," Ada says. "Though I think Nina understood me." Facing Mom, she says, "To be more specific, you'll work on learning how to type with just your mind. It'll be easy. First, we need the Brainocytes to observe you typing for real for a few hours. Afterwards, you'll learn to type mentally, using your imagination. If all works as planned, my team's algorithm will catch your imaginary keystrokes, since mental actions light up the same parts of the brain as physical actions."

The door opens, and a big, dark-skinned man in scrubs walks in, pushing a wheelchair along.

"I'm here for Nina Cohen," he says.

"That's me," Mom says.

"You're scheduled for an MRI," the guy explains and steers the chair toward her.

Mom leans away and says, "I'm not getting into that."

The guy looks confused.

"She can walk to the MRI," I tell him. "You can leave the chair here. Will that be a problem?"

"No," the guy says, "but Dr. Carter said—"

"Such an overly litigious country," Mom cuts in. "These doctors like to cover their asses to the point of insanity." She stubbornly folds her arms and gets up. "I won't be a part of this foolishness. Please lead the way, young man."

The guy folds the wheelchair and leaves it by the wall. Under his breath, he mutters, "Okay, but the doc said to use the chair."

"When will she be back?" I ask the guy.

"In about an hour and a half," he says.

"Do you want anything to eat afterwards?" I ask Mom.

"A turkey sandwich," she responds, "with extra mayo."

"You got it," I say and suppress a smile at the look on Ada's face. I could've predicted she'd cringe at Mom's food choice.

Mom and her disgruntled guide exit into the corridor.

"A sandwich sounds good," my uncle says. "Especially one with extra mayo."

Ada takes this one in stride. I guess she's more invested in my mom's health.

"Anyone else hungry?" I ask, looking around the room. "I'm buying."

Pretty much everyone takes me up on the offer, supporting my theory that most people—even if they're fasting or on a strict diet—will gladly gobble down free food.

When we get to the cafeteria, I realize the staff in Mom's room must've texted or emailed the majority of the other Techno employees, because most of them are here. Grinning, I extend my offer of a free lunch to them as well.

Grabbing a tray, I pull my uncle along and stand behind Ada.

She loads her tray with a salad, an apple, two bananas, and a heap of steamed vegetables.

Uncle Abe gives her tray a dubious onceover. "What about meat and bread?"

JC chuckles, and I fight a smile of my own. For the second time today, my uncle is about to regret his question.

To Ada's credit, this particular optimum nutrition lecture is the shortest one I've heard her deliver. It only takes her a couple of minutes.

"So the easiest formula," Ada concludes, "is to maximize your micronutrient intake while eating as few calories as possible. The best route to that is whole, unprocessed, plant-based foods."

My uncle demonstrates how little Ada's spiel influenced him by getting a very processed and not very plant-based ham sandwich.

He believes in the Russian proverb that states, "Bread is the head of everything," and worships meat to the point that ham is probably enshrined in his kitchen.

As I make my own selections, I wonder why Ada decided to trim down her pitch. Is she finally learning to adjust to her audience? She didn't even go into her reasons for eating this way—reasons that have little to do with vanity. She wants to maximize her lifespan so she can, and I quote from having heard this a dozen times, "catch as many transformative paradigm shifts in technology as possible and, hopefully, live long enough to catch mind uploading."

Ada's nutrient logic must've rubbed off on me, because my meal contains half the calories I might've chosen otherwise. I also get Mom's extra mayo in packets instead of slathered on the bread. This way, Mom can decide for herself how junky she wants her meal, leaving my conscience somewhat clean.

We sit down and start eating. Inevitably, the conversation returns to the topic of Brainocytes, and Ada says, "As much as I try, the implications of this technology are difficult to wrap my head around."

"If it's hard for you, imagine what it's like for us mere mortals," I say.

"We can help so many people," JC says, his green eyes shining fervently in his freckled face. "We can restore vision to the blind, hearing to the deaf, and memory to those who've lost it."

"All wonderful, but just scratching the surface of what's possible," Ada says. "Eventually, we'll be able to take a regular person and enhance the very thing that makes us human—intelligence, memory, empathy. Can you imagine the impact on the world if much smarter human beings populated the planet?"

JC bites into his burger, Twix-commercial style. Like me, he knows and understands Ada's transhumanist views. I agree with some of them, as do three quarters of Techno employees. JC probably also agrees, but he doesn't like these ideas bandied around in front of laymen. According to him, talking about human enhancements is bad for business, thanks largely to Hollywood's obsession with cautionary tales about human hubris.

"Fine, if you want to keep things prosaic," Ada says, "just the virtual and augmented realities alone could revolutionize the entertainment and educational systems. Once people start seeing the internet in their minds and watching movies and playing video games in their heads, the daily life of the average person will be unlike anything in history."

"Right," JC says. "We'll turn into a completely self-centered society. I can't wait."

"You're wrong," Ada says, though she knows JC likes to play devil's advocate. "When text and email will be done in people's heads, we'll end up with technology that's indistinguishable from telepathy. Being able to communicate through thought will connect the human race more than ever before. Though all that is short term. Having this unprecedented look inside the brain will lead to—"

"—brain simulations," I say, imitating her voice. "Which will lead to better AI and brain uploading."

"Which will also lead to fear," JC picks up, though his voice sounds like Yoda's instead of Ada's. "Which will lead to anger, which will lead to hate, which will lead to suffering, and all this leads to the dark side of the Force."

"That's not the exact quote," Ada says, and I have no doubt she's right. She has an eidetic memory when it comes to pop culture references.

Everyone except my uncle laughs at JC's joke, but it's nervous laughter. They all know this work really *is* scary to some people. This is why JC wants to keep the focus on correcting debilitating conditions for the time being. Even the worst luddites wouldn't deny Alzheimer's patients the chance at living a normal life, or quadriplegics the ability to control their environment, or blind people their vision. But as soon as the topic veers into Ada's favorite territory, improvement of normal function, things get thornier.

My uncle's pocket rings.

He gives us an apologetic look before taking out his phone and glancing at the screen. Whatever he sees there makes him frown. Getting up, he explains, "It's my son. I have to take it. Misha, I'll meet you in Nina's room."

With that, he walks away from our table. As someone who knows his son, I shudder and mentally wish Uncle Abe good luck.

The rest of us talk shop for the remainder of the meal, and I learn that Mrs. Sanchez is the next person scheduled to get Phase One enabled. We all know how little this first phase will help her, so the plan is to expedite her treatment and see if the phase that simulates missing brain function will help her more. Ada says she wants to oversee the beginning stages of this, so I volunteer to join her, in part to prove that I do care about the other participants, but also because I don't have to fake it. Given Mrs. Sanchez's situation, I genuinely do care about her.

Like Mom, the reason she's in this study is because of me. In fact, her life was affected by the same event as my mom's—that fateful car accident. Mom doesn't remember what happened, so I had to read about the crash online and in police reports. That's how I learned that a mentally unstable man was waltzing across the Belt Parkway highway. Mom hit the brakes in an effort to spare his life, and she succeeded in that. Unfortunately, she traded hitting the man for hitting the metal curb. What's even worse is that an SUV swerved to avoid colliding with Mom's car.

It was Mrs. Sanchez's son, daughter-in-law, and two grandchildren in the SUV. Instead of hitting the guardrail on the left, their car went down the hill on the right side and flipped multiple times. They all died, but the poor woman, Mrs. Sanchez, still doesn't truly know this. Her Alzheimer's was already in full swing by that time, and the tragic news about her family doesn't register when someone informs her of what happened. The problem with *not* informing her, however, is that she repeatedly asks for her son and his family. She's a widow, so after the accident, the only family she had left was an older brother who passed away a few months ago.

I've been paying her bills ever since, and when I got the chance, I convinced JC to include her in the study despite her poor health.

"Let's get Mrs. Sanchez something that's safe for her diabetes," I suggest.

Ada gives me an evaluating look. "She likes her junk food, so that'll be tricky."

"We'll get something healthy and something fried, but only show her the healthy choices first," I say. "We used to do this with Grandpa."

"Sounds like a great plan," JC says. "You two go do that, and the rest of us will run ahead."

I get up, and Ada follows.

"It *is* a good idea," Ada says. "Why don't I get the healthy choices and you get the rest?"

"Sure," I say.

"Just don't get her anything with too many carbs," Ada warns. "She could go into a coma."

"Deal," I say and walk back over to the tray line. "We'll drop off Mom's sandwich in her room on the way."

———

"This tastes like hospital food," Mrs. Sanchez complains as she eats Ada's healthier choices.

It *is* hospital food, but since Mrs. Sanchez doesn't recall where she is and hates hospitals on top of that, I see no need to remind her. She'll realize she's in a hospital when she looks in the mirror and sees her outfit, which is the same white hospital gown Mom was wearing earlier today.

Making a face, Mrs. Sanchez looks at Ada. "Are you sure they didn't have ice cream?"

"I'm sure," I lie. "But they did have Jell-O."

If I left the answer up to Ada, she might've blurted out the truth. She's almost pathologically honest, a bit like young George Washington, though I have my doubts about him. In Russia, we have an identical story about a young kid never telling a lie, only in that version, it was Lenin, the communist revolutionary leader.

"Is the Jell-O sugar-free?" Mrs. Sanchez's kind, chubby face twists in disgust at the very idea of sugar substitutes.

"No," I lie again. "So don't eat too much of it."

The real reason I said she shouldn't have too much Jell-O is because Ada might have an aneurism from watching Mrs. Sanchez eat something chock-full of aspartame, or whatever the name of the "evil" artificial sweetener is in Jell-O.

When Mrs. Sanchez tastes her gelatinous treat, she rubs her lips questioningly, and I'm ready for her to catch me in another lie, the way she did with the soda earlier. In that case, she got suspicious because Ada had peeled off the label; misleading someone doesn't count as lying in Ada's book. Fortunately, Mrs. Sanchez doesn't say anything this time and continues consuming her Jell-O.

I study Mrs. Sanchez as she eats, and worry overcomes me again. She and Mom are the same height and age and have similar apple-shaped body types. According to Ada, this increases my mom's risk of diabetes. Sure enough, Mom's sugar has been creeping up. Sooner or later, I might have to unleash the full wrath of Ada's dietary philosophy on her in the hopes that she starts eating healthier—unless the Brainocytes can be used to curb cravings?

While I'm pondering that, a nurse comes in carrying a syringe and a tray of food.

"Didn't Mrs. Sanchez already get her Brainocytes injection?" I whisper to Ada, then realize the syringe is too small.

"She did," Ada replies. "This is probably her insulin."

"Oh, good. You're already eating," the nurse says to the older woman and nods gratefully at Ada. "I'll be back in a few minutes to give you your insulin."

Mrs. Sanchez looks as excited at the prospect of getting a shot as a toddler would. She nervously twists her giant emerald ring, a treasured gift from her older brother, who, shortly before his death, gave her a much better gift in the form of his consent for her participation in this study. I hope the ring doesn't make her ask about her brother again—a topic as painful for her as the inquiries about the rest of her family.

My phone vibrates, and I see it's a text from Uncle Abe telling me my mom is back from her MRI. I want to hurry back, but I decide to stick around a little longer.

"If it's your mom, you should go," Ada says, and to my shock, she gently brushes her fingers against my elbow. "My minions are working on the BCI with her, and it'll be useful if someone with a brain is there."

Ada is a Team Lead for the software developers at Techno, and she refers to them as minions, even to their faces. Contrary to Ada's statement, they have more than enough brains and are paid triple what they'd earn at a hedge fund, the usual path for New York experts of their caliber.

"Good luck, Mrs. Sanchez," I say. "I hope this treatment helps you in the long run."

Mrs. Sanchez nods, and I head over to Mom's room.

As I walk through the white corridors, I pass the rooms occupied by the other participants. I continue to Mom's room without stopping because I want to catch her before she finishes her lunch.

"Hi, kitten," Mom says in English. Though her English is good, sometimes she overlooks certain subtleties, like the fact that this literal translation of what sounds cute in Russian comes off as fairly emasculating in English.

David, one of Ada's brightest minions and a second-generation Russian immigrant himself, gives me a sympathetic smirk.

Mom is sitting on the couch with a keyboard on her lap, so it looks like she's done with lunch after all.

"Your uncle left," she says, "and you should go too. David tells me I'll be typing for hours and learning how to control an imaginary dot for the rest of the day after that."

"That's nonsense, Mom. I'm not going anywhere."

"Surely you have some important business to deal with? Or a girl to take out?"

"If you insist, I'll check in with my secretary and maybe read up on some companies on my phone later," I say, knowing if I don't give in to this Jewish mom business of "don't worry about me" at least a little, she'll keep it up for a while. Besides, my mom is right. A multibillion-dollar fund doesn't run itself. As good as my analysts are, I still have to vet all investment ideas, not to mention deal with the investors. I cleared my schedule to be with my mom for this treatment, but there's always work to be done.

"Good," she says and picks up her keyboard. "So, David, what do you need me to do?"

The rest of the day passes the way Mom said it would. Under David's tutelage, she masters the art of typing with her mind. Sometimes, her fingers twitch as though she's really typing, but most of the time, it looks pretty eerie as text shows up on the screen without any outward action. She simply has to imagine herself typing the words.

The "mental mouse" portion of BCI training is a lot trickier for her, but David assures her she's doing well and that she'll have it down in a day or so.

"Why do I have to sleep here?" Mom asks after everyone's done eating dinner.

"Just in case," David says. "Dr. Carter agreed to assist our research on the condition that we take every safety precaution."

"I haven't even met this Dr. Carter," Mom says, "but when I do, I'll give him a piece of my mind."

She has met him, and I know because I was there. She actually gave him more than a piece of her mind, which is probably why he stayed away today.

"It'll be fine, Mom. I'll be around if you need me. Everything will be fine."

"You're not staying in the hospital." Mom takes her ultimatum stance, planting her hands on her hips. "If you stay here, I'll leave, Dr. Carter or not."

"I won't stay in the hospital," I say, knowing this is a fight I can't win. "But I'll be here first thing in the morning."

Mom considers this for a moment, then shows her approval by removing her hands from her hips.

What I left unsaid is that I'll be nearby. I booked a room at the HGU Hotel so I'll be within walking distance, just in case something goes wrong tonight. If Mom knew this, she'd be upset, especially since I booked the six-hundred-dollars per night King Suite, the only room they had available on short notice. Though she knows I make insanely large sums of money, she can't turn off her legitimate concern over finances, a response she developed when we first moved to the United States. Since I was thirteen then, I didn't internalize the situation as much as she did. I understand her feelings on the matter, though. We came to the US as refugees with a few hundred dollars in savings, if that. Between the help from Uncle Abe, who let us stay with his family in the beginning, the special immigrant-aid program called NYANA, and the very generous help from the American welfare system, we had just enough to survive while we got settled. Eventually, though, Mom felt uneasy about receiving "government charity" and found a home attendant job on Brighton Beach. Juggling English lessons and a Bachelor's degree with her grueling job must've been a nightmare. I still can't believe she went through it all. To me, the idea of picking up my stuff and moving to a place where I don't speak the language and don't know anyone or anything—say, Spain or Japan—is unthinkably frightening.

What's even more impressive is that Mom essentially did it for me. Besides the possibility of new pogroms, Mom's biggest fear was the looming prospect of me getting drafted into the nightmarish institution that was the army in the former USSR. It was a place where being Jewish would've made the already horrific hazing practices borderline deadly. I'm glad I didn't have to go through that. The NYC public school system isn't the army, but the bullying I experienced there has led me to believe I have very little tolerance for humiliation and pain.

My reminiscing is interrupted by a pair of guys who wheel in a bed for Mom to sleep in. David and the rest of the Techno peeps take this as their cue to leave for the day.

I stay for a bit to chat with Mom about anything she might've been embarrassed to bring up in front of strangers. When she demonstratively yawns for the fifth time, I get up, kiss her cheek, and say in Russian, "Bye, Mom. I'll see you in the morning."

"Yes," she responds with a yawn. "Morning is wiser than evening."

"Indeed it is." I smile at her and leave.

When I make my way down to the first floor of the hospital, I consider moving my car from the hospital parking lot to the hotel. I decide against it, since the hotel probably has valet service, meaning I'd have to wait to get my car if I needed it in a hurry. Besides, I'm just three measly blocks away, and the hospital has better security.

It's a new development, me worrying about a car. I was never into cars, and I'm still not, but I've grown to love mine, even though it started off as a joke. My car's nickname is Zapo, short for Zaporozhets, in honor of a horrific Soviet-era car my grandpa was constantly lying under and repairing when I was growing up.

Zapo isn't an authentic recreation of that ugly car, of course. In terms of energy efficiency, they're actually polar opposites. I'd say they're spiritually connected by their fugly exterior designs. Zapo is a Prius, but the inside is modified so drastically that it cost me almost as much as an entry-level Bentley. Additionally, Zapo has a beta prototype of the Einstein navigational system that Poisk, Mitya's company, is working on, plus other mods and an engine that would make the cars from *The Fast and the Furious* jealous. I half-jokingly call Zapo my "super-expensive gold-digger repellent."

Exiting the large automated doors, I turn onto 30th Street and spot Ada trying to hail a cab without any success.

Now I'm truly glad I didn't decide to drive. I rarely get a chance to talk to Ada outside of work.

When she sees me, she lowers her arm and says, "David emailed me about Nina's day so far. She looks to be the furthest along. I'm very pleased we're making such swift progress."

"You can take most of the credit for this," I say. "You and your minions wrote such an intuitive user interface that even my grandpa would've mastered it—and he had trouble working the VCR."

"Everyone had trouble with those clunky VCRs," she says, but I can tell she likes the praise. I think she's even blushing, and I've never seen her blush.

"Do you want to stay at the hotel with me?" I ask. Her eyes widen, and I realize what I just said. "I mean, in the same hotel as me. In a separate room."

"Right." Her shock turns into a grin so wide her eyes almost close. "I'm sure that wasn't a Freudian slip."

My face feels hot enough to cook an egg on. Trying to lessen how foolish I look, I say, "I just pictured you schlepping all the way back to Williamsburg and wanted to offer a better alternative."

"I get that, and thank you, but I can't," she says. "I have to feed my rats."

"Your what?" I ask, wondering if it's possible to mistake the *c* in cats for the *r* in rats.

"I adopted a bunch of rats once they weren't needed for experiments anymore," Ada explains. "A lot of the Techno folks did. My cuties aren't as needy as a bunch of dogs, but I can't *not* show up without notice or setting up a long-term feeder for them. Plus, it's bath day today, and they love it so much. Rain check?"

"Sure," I say. Would it be impolite to ask her how many rats she actually owns and how many it would take for her to qualify as a rat lady? "I'll put you up in a hotel room of my choice some other day then."

We look at each other and laugh.

Ada sees a cab in the distance and waves at it. The cabby stops in front of us, and I hold the yellow car door open for her. "I'll see you tomorrow at nine, right?"

"Yeah," she says, getting inside the cab. "I'll check on Mrs. Sanchez first, and then go to your mom's room. I'm sure we'll get to Phase Two with her, and I'm excited."

"Yeah, me too," I say and shut the door.

On the way to my hotel room, I wonder if it was just my imagination, or if Ada was a little friendlier toward me. For a few months now, Ada's been acting a bit distant around me. Since the start of this behavior coincided with when my ex dumped me, I figure Ada is just dreading the uncomfortable conversation where I ask her out and she has to turn me down. Since our working relationship is hard to define—as a major investor in Techno, I'm someone her boss, JC, answers to—I've been wary about pursuing anything. Not only am I sensitive about the issue of workplace sexual harassment, but Ada is the most irreplaceable person on the Brainocytes project. I knew she was bright when she first joined Techno, but around the time she started growing distant, I noticed how much of a genius she truly is. Maybe it's my infatuation goggles at work, but the leaps she's singlehandedly made with the Brainocytes software shaved off at least six months of work from the project.

I think about Ada on and off for the rest of the evening. As I fall asleep, I decide that once the study is complete, I will ask her out, consequences be damned.

FIVE

I WALK DOWN THE HOSPITAL CORRIDOR, MUNCHING ON AN EGG-AND-cheese croissant. In my free hand, I'm holding a bag with a breakfast sandwich for Mom, oatmeal for Ada, and a diabetes-safe omelet for Mrs. Sanchez.

Figuring I'll leave Mrs. Sanchez's food with her, I make my way to her room.

When I enter, I realize I'm the first one here and look at my watch. It's 8:50 a.m., a little before the usual workday starts, even for a bunch of workaholics like the folks at Techno.

Then something odd becomes apparent. Though it looked like Mrs. Sanchez was in her bed at first, she actually isn't.

I look around the room as though she might be hiding behind all the hardware in the back.

Obviously, she isn't here.

I exit the room and bump straight into Ada.

"Hey," I say. "Do you know where Mrs. Sanchez is?"

"She should be in her room." Ada looks at Mrs. Sanchez's door. "She isn't?"

"Excuse me," an unfamiliar nurse says, approaching the door. "I need to get through."

"Are you here to see Mrs. Sanchez?" I ask, not moving out of the nurse's way.

"Yes," she says. "I'm here to give her her insulin."

"She's not in her room," I say. "I was just there."

The nurse looks at me doubtfully, so I ask, "Do you have any idea where she could be?"

"She's supposed to be in her room," the nurse says.

"Could she be in the bathroom?" I ask.

"The nearest one is in her room," Ada says and goes into the room.

"If she left the room to use the bathroom, it's two doors down," the nurse says.

I head down the corridor and find the bathroom empty.

When I get back, Ada and the nurse are walking toward me.

"She's not in the room bathroom," Ada says.

"And she isn't in the one down the hall," I respond.

"She couldn't have wandered off too far," the nurse says. "They would've spotted a patient at the nurses' stations at each end of the floor."

"Maybe she walked into one of the nearby rooms?" I ask.

The nurse shrugs.

"Why don't you go check," I suggest. "Ada and I will make sure Mrs. Sanchez didn't somehow join one of the other participants in our study."

The nurse leaves, and Ada and I split up to search the rooms of the two nearest participants.

I enter Mr. Shafer's room.

He isn't in his bed.

I check the bathroom and find it empty.

On a whim, I walk up to the bed and touch it.

The scratchy, over-starched hospital sheets are still warm. Wherever Mr. Shafer went, he left recently.

Ada is waiting for me in the corridor, looking worried.

"Mrs. Stevens is gone too." Ada runs her fingers through her bleached Mohawk.

"So is Mr. Shafer. Maybe it's something JC organized? Maybe he's giving a lecture or something to the whole group? Or maybe Dr. Carter—"

"No," Ada says. "I would've been notified if someone from Techno had planned anything. I don't see how Dr. Carter could be behind this; he clears everything with JC. Besides, he knows Mrs. Sanchez needs her insulin."

I consider her words carefully and find no flaw in her logic. There's no reason these three participants should be missing from their rooms. If only one person was missing, especially Mr. Shafer, we could maybe brush it off as him going for a walk despite us explicitly telling him not to. That the relatively sedentary Mrs. Stevens is also missing is a lot stranger, since she wouldn't go for a walk to literally extend her life. And the fact that Mrs. Sanchez, with her foot problem, is also gone pushes this incident firmly into the realm of the impossibly anomalous.

My mind leaps to another thought. Are the others missing as well? Though it's not completely rational, my gut turns into tundra-like permafrost, and I quickly say, "Check on the others. I'm going to Mom's room."

Hoping I'll feel like a paranoid fool in a minute, I sprint down the corridor and stab the elevator button with my finger.

The elevator doesn't instantly open, so I dump the food I'm still holding into a nearby garbage bin and punch the button again.

Then I notice the elevator has a light indicating where the car is, and that happens to be on the fifteenth floor. The number changes to fourteen far too slowly, so I decide to run down the two floors instead of waiting.

The staircase is musty. It probably doesn't get used much. I whoosh down, trying not to inhale too much stale air as I take the stairs two at a time.

When I exit the staircase, I get strange looks from the nurses at their station. Ignoring them, I zoom down the corridor.

My breath is ragged by the time I reach Mom's room. As I twist the handle, I will Mom to be there, going so far as picturing her reaction to seeing me disheveled and out of breath.

Cracking the door open, I'm confronted with a bizarre view.

Mom is sitting in a wheelchair, eyes closed as though she's asleep.

She's being wheeled by a guy I've never seen before—though now that I have, I won't soon forget him. The hands holding the wheelchair handles are covered in tattoos, as is all the skin peeking out from under his scrubs. With his nearly seven-foot bulky build, protruding forehead, and quarter-pounder jaw, he's living proof that humans are closely related to apes, and maybe even bison.

"Where are you taking her?" I ask loudly, hoping they'll hear me at the nurses' station. "Who are—"

I register a whirlwind of movement, and a tattooed fist crashes into my cheekbone. The shock of pain sends me reeling, and the playing cards tattooed on the ape-bison's knuckles dance in my vision as the world starts to fade.

SIX

Fighting unconsciousness, I attempt to curl my hands into fists.

All I accomplish is gaining enough self-awareness to feel an oversized arm grab me and throw me.

My back slams into a small table, and air wisely decides to vacate my lungs. Gasping, I slide down. Junk clatters on the floor around me, releasing the powerful stench of medicine.

With a monumental effort of will, I struggle to not pass out.

The ape-bison guy slams the door shut behind him.

I keep gasping for air and fighting for lucidity.

Pushing up with shaking hands, I wonder if this is how boxers feel when they try standing after getting knocked down. If so, why didn't they pick another profession? For me, this decides it here and now: I'd prefer a career as anything else, even a politician, to that of a boxer.

Slowly, I gather my legs under me. I figure the boxing referee would've counted to nine by now.

Fighting nausea, I tentatively put weight on my jelly-like legs. Instantly, vertigo seizes me, and I fall on all fours, losing my break-fast on the floor. In a detached manner, I wonder why I've never heard of a boxer throwing up during a match. On a positive note, despite the acidic taste in my mouth, I feel a minuscule dose of relief.

Struggling to my feet again, I stumble toward the door. By the time I grasp the doorknob, I feel like I've regained some rudimentary hand-eye coordination.

When I exit the room and look around, I see my attacker at the end of the corridor to my right. He's blurry, as though I'm seeing him through a fog—like the hedgehog from the Soviet cartoon of my childhood.

"Stop him," I yell, or try to. The sound comes out raspy and weak. Worse, the attempted yell messes with my already unsteady breathing.

Holding on to the wall as I stumble forward, I will my breath to stabilize.

When I feel like I can survive expending the air, I yell, "Stop that guy!"

This time, my voice carries better, but I hear the elevator doors *ding* at the end of the hall.

My adrenal glands go into overdrive, and I jerkily increase my pace.

A nurse looks up at me from her desk. "Are you okay? Why are you screaming?"

Unable to yell again, I close the distance between us and choke out, "That large man with a wheelchair?"

"He got into the elevator before you started yelling," the nurse confirms. "What's going on?"

"Call the police," I gasp. "Someone kidnapped my mother, Nina Cohen."

The look on the nurse's face reminds me of a squirrel facing a bicyclist in Central Park.

I don't stop to calm her down and stagger toward the elevator.

One car is on the twentieth floor, while the other is already on the ninth.

I quickly assess my options. I can summon the elevator, or I can walk down. It's nearly nine in the morning, and I don't know if that means the rush hour for the elevators has begun, especially when it comes to going down. On the other hand, am I in any condition to attempt the stairs?

I punch both buttons and turn toward the stairwell, figuring I'll go down to the next floor before making a decision. If I can't get down on foot, at least I summoned the elevators closer to the floor below.

"You're bleeding," the nurse yells when I'm halfway through the door. "You should let me—"

Whatever she said I'll never know, because the door closes behind me as I begin my descent.

I'm feeling slightly better, though I suspect it's from the adrenaline. I can't take the stairs two at a time like I did a few minutes ago, but at least I don't stumble and I can let go of the handrail once in a while.

When I get to the eleventh floor, I'm still not sure whether I'll be better off taking the elevator. I hurry to the door and stick my head out. One elevator is on the fifth floor, and the other made it all the way to the twelfth. I decide it's definitely worth the wait and jab my finger against the elevator button, wishing it were the ape-bison's eye socket.

Milliseconds stretch into ages, and I decide to multitask so I won't go crazy. I command Einstein in my nifty phone to dial Ada before I even take it out of my pocket.

"Mike," Ada shouts as soon as the call connects. "I didn't find a single participant. I'm talking to JC right now, and he has no clue—"

"Someone's kidnapped them," I blurt out. "I saw a man taking my mom. Call the police. I'll try to get you more information."

"Wait, who—"

The elevator doors open, and I rush inside, ignoring the call for the moment.

I have a new choice to make. What floor do I press? Given the wheelchair the guy had my mom in, and since Ada said everyone else is missing too, I can only assume the kidnapper is putting all the participants in a large vehicle, maybe even a bus. Given Manhattan rush-hour traffic and hospital zoning rules, it's safe to assume he wouldn't park near the front doors. No, doing something as nefarious as loading unconscious people into a vehicle is best done in the relative privacy of the parking lot. Thus decided, I press the basement-floor button. There could be flaws in my logic or other variables I'm missing, like they, whoever "they" are, might have an ambulance or diplomatic plates, but I have to act on my best guess.

The doors close, and my call disconnects.

I keep my thumb on the close-door button as the elevator starts moving. Supposedly, holding this button will make the elevator travel without stopping, an express feature designed for emergency personnel. When I first heard this, I didn't really believe it and was never selfish enough, or in a big enough rush, to test it. I do know that pressing the close-door button doesn't shut the doors any faster and might just act as a placebo, like those walk buttons at pedestrian crossings in NYC.

The elevator crawls past the tenth floor, then the ninth. I look at the door's reflective surface and see the nurse was right. My shirt is covered in blood. Fortunately, most of the blood is from a nosebleed. I've been prone to nosebleeds since I was a kid, and I've learned not to worry about them. At MIT, I used to get nosebleeds from the dry air caused by the dorm's central air system. Mitya, my then roommate, used to tease me about it, saying the reason I get so many nosebleeds is because I have such a large schnoz. I'd retort that big noses are considered a sign of virility in many cultures and that they also accurately correlate with a certain part of a man's anatomy, similar to shoe and hand sizes.

Besides the blood, the right side of my face has a bruise so big I think it might develop a few bruises of its own. On the plus side, the nausea has subsided, or maybe I'm just getting used to it. Overall, the pain in my body has gone from agonizingly burning to unpleasantly pulsing.

I pass the fifth floor without stopping and start thinking the elevator might make it all the way down without interruption. Is this trick with the close-door button actually true? Or is everyone coming to the hospital at this hour going up? Whatever the cause, I hope this continues.

I pass the fourth floor, then the third. When the elevator passes the second floor, I let go of the button and all my muscles tense, ready for action.

As soon as the door opens, I try to sprint but end up staggering out of the elevator. Ignoring the returning lightheadedness, I hurry toward Zapo and look around.

I don't see anything, but I do hear a large-vehicle engine starting in the distance.

Fishing my car keys out of my pocket, I press the Start Engine button that was originally meant to warm up my car in the winter.

Most Priuses start so quietly I wouldn't be able to hear my car from where I'm standing, but Zapo isn't a typical Prius. I can make out its tricked-out engine quite distinctly.

I also hear the sound of screeching tires from the same place I heard the other vehicle's engine start.

Picking up speed, I swallow my heart back into my chest and say to both the AI on my phone and in the car, "Einstein, I'll be driving on manual."

"You asked me to remind you to never drive drunk or tired," says Einstein's voice. For the sake of understandability, the AI's German accent is subtler than the one the famous physicist actually possessed.

I fight the urge to curse at the AI, as that would simply waste valuable seconds. Besides, worrying about my safety *is* something I usually want Einstein to do; it's just that today, it would be better if Einstein were smart enough to worry about my mom instead, a task that's still too generic for Einstein to tackle, no matter how much I anthropomorphize the AI by calling it a "he."

At least, as always, Einstein saves me a few precious seconds by pulling my car out of its parking spot and sliding the door up. Yes,

Zapo's door opens vertically, like the DeLorean from *Back to the Future*.

"I'm not drunk or tired," I say as I leap inside. "I'm in a big rush."

Before I can get a lecture, I buckle up.

"According to my settings, you also asked me to be wary of you being in a rush," Einstein says.

A cartoony version of the famous old man with fluffy white hair shows up on the large dashboard screen and looks at me with carefully calculated grandfatherly concern.

"Activate manual drive," I demand. "This is an emergency override. Code red. 911."

One of the code words must work, because Einstein says flatly, "Manual controls activated."

I grab the wheel and slam on the gas pedal.

"The speed limit in this parking lot is eight miles per hour." Einstein stares at me with unblinking disapproval from the screen. "You're going twenty-one miles per hour."

"Get used to it," I say, though I know full well he won't. "This is why I needed the emergency override."

"It's not safe." Einstein's white hair seems to get wilder as he frowns. "Please consider slowing down."

I swerve toward the exit, all my focus on catching up with the bigger car I heard.

When I see the parking lot exit a few moments later, I become the first New Yorker in history to be grateful for traffic.

A line of four cars is waiting to leave the lot, and the second from last is a large black minibus I strongly suspect is the vehicle I'm after.

I try to see its license plate, but the Honda behind it is blocking my view. I text Ada what I know about the car so far, typing out, "Tell the cops the perps are driving a Mercedes Metris minibus. I'll text you the license plate number when I have it."

The cars move, so I pull up close to the Honda before clicking send.

45

"One out of every four car accidents in the United States is caused by texting while driving," Einstein says. As always, his German accent is almost undetectable when he's doing his favorite task—quoting stats.

"I'm not driving now." I try not to sound defensive. "I'm sitting in traffic."

"Texting while driving causes a four-hundred-percent increase in time spent with eyes off the road," Einstein retorts. In many ways, he's just an advanced version of those annoying customer service answering machine AIs, and his arguments can be just as circular.

"What are the statistics of accidents caused by people who are arguing with their navigation systems?" I move forward to take the space created by another car moving up.

"No data," Einstein says.

"I bet once more people have something like you in their cars, those stats will be high." I drum my fingers on the dashboard.

Einstein doesn't argue—yet another bit of proof that he isn't that clever. If he possessed a generalized intelligence, he would've noted that it's him, not me, who usually does the driving, and since an AI can multitask better than I can, no accidents would occur.

When the minibus pulls up to the exit, my whole body tenses and I forget about Einstein. As soon as the Metris starts moving, I do the most dickish parking lot maneuver I've ever done. I floor the gas and circle around the Honda, pulling my nose into the opening the minibus just left.

I can practically hear the woman cursing over her blaring horn, but I don't care. Mom's safety trumps social mores. As soon as the Metris moves a few inches forward, I boldly cut in front of a Crown Vic, following my prey. This time, it's a guy who curses at me, so I keep an eye on him in my rearview mirror. If he's aggravated enough, he might exit his car to start a fight with me, and that's the last thing I need.

The guy doesn't get out, but about a dozen cars behind him join in on the honking, their joint blaring synchronizing with my pounding heartbeat.

Ignoring the noise, I orient myself. This is First Avenue, and all four lanes are jammed. At least I'm right behind the minibus, even if neither of us can move.

I use this chance to text the license plate to Ada. I also consider leaving my car and running up to the Metris. Before I can do so, the cars inch forward. The left lanes are moving a bit more freely, causing everyone from the right lanes to make matters worse by trying to switch over there.

A few cars up, I see the source of the traffic—a double-parked car. I've lived in this city long enough to loathe people who double-park. This particular offender is a Poland Spring water delivery truck, as evidenced by the paint job on the sides and the man wheeling an empty water container into the vehicle.

I've never wished for a cop to appear this badly. First, this imaginary cop would help me stop the kidnappers. Then, once my mom was safe, he'd write this idiot a juicy ticket, since even commercial vehicles aren't allowed to double-park and block traffic in Midtown. Then I remind myself that this Poland Spring guy is why I'm able to follow the minibus, so in a way, he's doing me a favor.

When the Poland Spring truck starts moving, so do all the other cars.

"The speed limit is twenty-five miles per hour," Einstein chimes in.

"That's my speed."

"You're going twenty-six miles per hour," he says.

Since we're approaching an intersection, I ignore the AI and tighten my grip on the wheel.

The Metris turns right onto 34th Street and cuts off three cars as it slots itself into the leftmost of the three available lanes.

Tires screeching, I attempt to duplicate the minibus's rude maneuver and pass a Lexus and a Hyundai. When I screech by a super-aggressive NYC yellow cab, I'm not surprised that the idiot scrapes my bumper. At least the touch is so light it doesn't impede my turn.

"You've been in an accident," Einstein says. "You should pull over."

I contemplate hitting the LCD screen, but figure it's best to just ignore him, especially since the Metris cuts across traffic again to get to the rightmost lane.

I follow him, and we pass by the ever-present orange cones that seem to proliferate in Manhattan. When I spot the nearest green directional sign, my stress level climbs. I can guess why the Metris turned into the rightmost lane. In a few feet, it's going to make a right to get onto the FDR Drive, one of the Manhattan highways. I should've thought of this back in the parking lot—not that it would've helped. Langone Medical Center is right next to the highway, so any kidnappers worth their salt would take advantage of that fact. On some level, I hoped to chase them through the congested streets until we passed a police car. It doesn't matter, though. I'll follow them into the surrounding ocean if I have to.

My knuckles go white on the steering wheel, and my calf muscle tenses as I hit the gas again. In an instant, I catch up to the minibus, and our bumpers nearly kiss.

"We're too close," Einstein whines and blurts out more safety minutia, but I ignore it all because my already hyperactive heart is threatening to jump out of my ribcage, *Alien* style.

In the tinted glass of the Metris's back window, I see the protruding forehead of the ape-bison asshole.

He locks eyes with me and shouts something toward the front of the car.

With smoke coming out from under the minibus's tires, the vehicle shoots forward and makes a sharp right turn, ignoring the red light in front of us.

SEVEN

I NEARLY FLOOR THE GAS PEDAL AS I TURN THE STEERING WHEEL ALL the way right.

The tricked-out motor roars to life, and Zapo accelerates like no other Prius before it.

"You're passing the red light at double the speed limit," I hear Einstein say over the screeching tires and the pounding in my ears.

I ignore him and focus on the road.

The minibus is already merging onto FDR, and I fly onto the highway after it.

The middle and fast lanes are unusually free today, though the rightmost lane is beginning to clog up.

The kidnappers cut in front of a black Jeep Wrangler in the middle lane.

I let the Jeep pass and look in my rearview mirror. A red Cadillac is gaining on me on the left. I normally wouldn't dare switch lanes in this kind of situation, but today, I signal the turn, say a prayer to the Cadillac's brakes, and swerve into the middle lane.

The Cadillac's burning tires make an unhealthy squeal, but nothing hits me.

Einstein spews a laundry list of infractions, but I tune him out so I can focus on the minibus as it switches lanes again.

After successfully swerving in front of the Cadillac, I decide to really push my luck with the Honda Accord in the fast lane. Though it's at least a couple of feet closer, I'm hoping the driver saw my earlier stunt and started driving more cautiously.

I signal again and swerve.

There's a loud thump as the Honda's bumper crashes into mine.

EIGHT

"You've been in an accident," Einstein complains again.

"No shit," I grit out and push the pedal harder. Something clangs behind me, and a look in the rearview mirror confirms what I already suspected. My back bumper fell off.

If I had time for caution, I'd probably pull to the side of the road. Instead, I slam on the gas.

My tires squeal. The car pulls left, and Zapo leaves its paint on the shoulder of the highway. At least I didn't go over the rail and fly into the ocean.

"The car alignment is off," Einstein says.

"Now you tell me," I say and do my best to adjust to the constant leftward drag of my ride.

For the next few minutes, the minibus continues to speed up and jump from lane to lane. I follow, and given my lack of bumper and the car's misalignment, the fact that I only lose my right mirror is some kind of miracle. Einstein doesn't agree with my assessment. Throughout the chase, he unleashes a torrent of complaints about my driving. The highlights include going triple the speed limit, leaving the scene of multiple accidents, not signaling when switching lanes, and driving in a damaged vehicle.

As we get closer to downtown, I feel a glimmer of hope, and when we pass the Brooklyn Bridge, the hope congeals into a possible plan. The kidnappers are likely heading into the Battery Tunnel. Their only other option is to get off the highway and face downtown traffic. If I'm right, after they exit the Tunnel, they'll encounter the tollbooths, and with any luck, there'll be cops around. Even if the cops aren't present, I can make a big scene once we get there, maybe by crashing into the minibus or one of the booths—whatever it takes to get attention. There's even a small chance I won't need to do anything. If Ada gave the police the minibus's license plate, the cops at the toll stop—assuming there are any—may simply do their jobs.

My target goes around the diminutive Smart Fortwo car in the middle lane, so I swerve after it, hoping the environmentally conscious hipster chick inside that tiny coffin doesn't get a heart attack. The minibus whooshes into the Tunnel on the left side, and I nearly crash into the wall as I squeeze in behind it.

Handling my damaged car was difficult up to this point, but it'll be particularly tricky in the enclosed space up ahead.

When my eyes adjust to the Tunnel's darker environment, I blink repeatedly, as though that'll change what I see.

The left-side window in the minibus is open, and the now-familiar ape-bison hybrid is sticking his head out. Then his tattooed hand pulls out a gun as big as my head—which is where the weapon's barrel is now pointed.

On pure instinct, I duck in a move worthy of a Ninja Turtle as a shot rings out.

The Tunnel must somehow amplify the sound, because this is what a cannonball would sound like if it were fired directly into my eardrum.

Scenes from my early childhood don't flash before my eyes, and I'm not hit with the pain of getting shot—all good news. Somehow, the guy must've missed, though I have no idea where the bullet ended up.

When I look up, he's still there, aiming the gun in my direction.

A new spike of adrenaline rekindles my body's last reserve of energy, and the world gets sharper and clearer. Trying to make myself a more difficult target, I turn the wheel toward the orange cones that separate the lanes inside the Tunnel. The nearest cone flies up behind me and hits the green Ford Mustang on my tail.

Alas, my reprieve only lasts seconds. The shooter leans out of the right-side window, and without much ado, he fires at me again.

My ears ring and my windshield explodes, raining tiny shards of glass all over me.

I slam my foot on the brake so hard I hurt my ankle. Or at least the brake is what I meant to slam. In the heat of panic, I must've pressed on the gas, because Zapo suddenly lurches forward.

I hear another shot.

My shoulder feels like it was hit with a burning-hot baseball bat, then skinned with a potato peeler and sprinkled with alcohol and salt.

At the same time, the steering wheel jerks in my hands, and I register the weather-beaten wall of the Tunnel rushing toward my face with the inevitability of tax season.

Somehow, in that brief moment, many thoughts rush through my head, but the highlights are: "A bullet must've hit my tire" and "I'm going to die, and I haven't saved Mom."

Zapo smashes into the wall, and I see it start to pancake before the world becomes one violent explosion of whiteness, followed by the nothingness of unconsciousness.

NINE

"WHERE AM I? WHAT THE HELL IS HAPPENING?" I TRY TO SAY, BUT my lungs are empty.

I gasp for air, but something is obstructing my nose and mouth. It feels like someone is smothering me with a pillow after an elephant sat on my face.

I hear the creaking of plastic and metal as someone's thick-gloved hands grab me. Pain explodes throughout my body, and oblivion reclaims my consciousness.

———

I feel like I'm inside a meat grinder. I open my left eye a sliver and close it before the blinding light can ruin my retinas.

"Damn," I attempt to say, but my lips feel stuck together. "How much did I drink last night?"

"You're going to be okay," says an unfamiliar voice. "We're taking you to the hospital. I gave you something to make you more comfortable."

I feel warmth spread from my arm, an itchy sort of warmth that takes the pain away.

A splinter in my brain doesn't let me enjoy the relief. My mind resembles scrambled eggs, but I remember the problem and try to say, "No, I need to stay conscious. My mother was kidnapped. They shot at me—"

Realizing I'm just mumbling, I focus on not letting the drugs put me under, but the warmth spreads above my neck and my awareness slips away.

————

I try opening my eyes, but I feel like I'm too stoned. What the hell did I smoke?

"Will he be okay?" asks a familiar female voice from somewhere far away. "What's wrong with him?"

"He was shot, but the bullet only grazed his shoulder," an unfamiliar male voice responds. "He was also in a car accident, so he has a mild concussion, bruised ribs, whiplash, and a slew of other minor injuries."

Even in my confused state, I know that list isn't complete. With pride, I recall that I also got punched in the face and didn't cry afterwards or anything.

"He looks like aged steak," the female voice says, and through the haze, I feel like her name is on the tip of my tongue, along with the iron taste of blood and medicine. Something tells me this woman doesn't eat meat and wouldn't compare me to steak, or any other non-vegan dish, as a compliment.

"The police officers want to ask him a few questions," the male voice says. "Maybe you can shed some light on this situation for them instead? I don't think he should be disturbed."

"I already spent a few hours talking to them in circles," the woman replies, and I'm finally clearheaded enough to connect the dots and name her as Ada. "I just wish the cops would focus on looking for Nina and the rest of our test subjects instead of hounding us. The last thing Mike needs is an interrogation."

I will my eyes to open, and they grudgingly oblige, though I immediately close them again when the bright hospital light pounds the rods (or is it cones?) in my eyes like a sledgehammer. Trying again, I manage to keep my eyelids open long enough to glimpse a disheveled Ada standing next to some guy in a white coat—the sight of which instantly triggers my dentist/doctor phobia.

During my next eye-opening attempt, I take in my surroundings. The sterile whiteness reminds me of my recent nightmare. I try to focus my thoughts but find it much harder than controlling my eyes.

My throat feels like sandpaper, but I still try asking, "Where am I?"

This is when I realize a mask is covering my face and muffling my words.

"I think he's awake!"

Ada's exclamation is too loud for my hurting brain to deal with, so I mutter, "Too loud."

"He tried saying something again. You should take off that oxygen mask," Ada tells the doctor.

The doctor studies me skeptically.

Ada steps closer to me and softly says, "Mike, Mishen'ka, how are you feeling?"

That assault on my ears must've made my mind fuzzier, because I don't believe the gentle way Ada is touching my hand is normal, and I've never heard an American properly use the diminutive Russian form of my name before.

The white-coat man finally feels the need to remove the obstruction from my face.

I try speaking again, almost instinctively. "Where's Mom?"

Once the question leaves my lips, I realize that's the reason I'm fighting the drugs or whatever it is that's making me want to nap.

"The police and FBI are looking for her," Ada says, and I note that her tone is indeed uncharacteristically soothing. "They've been grilling me and the other Techno employees about everything. They've also collected information on every study participant and even asked about the research."

A wave of disappointment crashes against the sudden tsunami of nausea. My breathing speeds up, and I overhear Ada say, "I think he's in pain. Give him something. Please."

The doctor must agree with her, because he does something and a new wave of pleasurable warmth arrives.

Ada leans in and strokes my hair.

"Wait," I say. "I don't mind the pain. I want to—"

Before I can finish the sentence, the drug knocks me out.

———

This time, I wake up remembering everything. I guess it's an improvement. I lie there trying to master my mind before I let anyone know I'm awake, lest they knock me out with painkillers again.

Somewhere, Ada is having a heated discussion with who I assume are members of law enforcement.

"He might know something critical," a man says. "His own mother is—"

"I'm awake," I half moan. "And I want to help in any way I can."

I pry my eyes open and see Ada's face as though through a haze. Her forehead is creased in worry, which I find both comforting and surprising.

Next to Ada are two vague shapes that must be the cops, though they aren't wearing NYPD uniforms.

"Mr. Cohen, if we could ask you a few questions," says the guy on the left, and I can't help but think he looks like a German Shepherd.

"This is very important," adds his partner. This one, perhaps inspired by my foggy brain, reminds me of a root vegetable—something between a beet and a potato.

"Of course," I say and swallow to clear the needles from my throat. "Ask away."

So they ask. With the combination of drugs and adrenaline in my system, I feel like a captured spy pumped full of truth serum. Constantly fighting for lucidity, I answer all their questions as accurately and methodically as I can, which in my condition isn't saying much. Eventually, I ask my own questions and learn the authorities haven't made any headway in locating Mom and the others. No one stopped the minibus outside the Tunnel. There weren't any cops there, and the tollbooth clerks were out of their depths after hearing the gunshots.

"We think they changed the plates shortly after passing through the tollbooths," says the German Shepherd guy.

"But rest assured, we will stop every black Mercedes Metris driving in the New York metropolitan area," says the beet-potato guy.

They're interrupted when my old pal, the dread-inspiring white-coat guy, walks in and says, "Gentlemen, you said this would take two minutes."

Ada puts her hands on her hips and gives my interrogators a look she usually reserves for people who don't bother getting their code peer-reviewed.

"I'm okay," I say, but even to my own ears I sound like an anemic anorexic.

The doggie guy gives me an unsympathetic onceover and says, "If we can just have one more moment."

His veggie partner brings something up on his phone, places it in my hands, and says, "We got these from the hospital security footage."

To my relief, I can lift the phone to my face, though it feels like it's filled with osmium, an element denser than lead.

When I see the screen, I forget the strain of holding up the phone and fight for the energy to look through the photos in front of me.

There's a different person on each of the three images. Two are caught at very odd angles, but it doesn't matter since I already know I haven't seen them before. The remaining photo is distinguishable, and the mug on it is very familiar.

It's the guy who punched me in the face.

"Have you seen any of these men before today?" the second guy asks.

I shake my head but don't stop looking at the ape-bison asshole.

I guess the beet-potato guy notices me burning holes into the screen with my eyes, because he leans in and looks at the image. "Is that the man who attacked you?" His voice is almost soothing.

"Yes." My arm stings, and I realize I've clenched my fingers around the phone so hard the IV entry into my arm got messed up. "But I don't think I've seen the others, and I'm sure I've never seen him before today." I tear my eyes away from the screen and look up at the man leaning over me. "What about you? Can't you look them up using facial recognition software?"

"No," says the canine policeman. "I mean, yes, we tried. Two of the images didn't capture enough of their faces to allow a lookup; the picture of the man who attacked you did allow for a scan, but he didn't pop up in any of our databases."

I shake my head and wince at the agonizing throb in my skull.

I hand the phone back to its owner, and he takes it. He must see the despair on my face, because he looks questioningly at his partner. It's as though he's trying to telepathically check if he should say something.

His partner gives him a slight nod. The beet-potato guy clears his throat and says, "The tattoos on the man who shot you are common within certain Russian criminal elements…"

Now that he mentions it, I realize he's right. I'm no expert, but I've seen enough movies featuring the Russian mob—almost all the action flicks nowadays—to notice certain patterns when it comes to the ink Hollywood puts on its villains. It's possible there's a correlation between the tattoos in those movies and the ones in reality, at least if the studio people did any research. The latter isn't a given, since everything else related to Russians in American films is far from accurate. The vast majority of the time, the atrociously spoken language doesn't match the subtitles, and the actors who play the Russian characters don't look remotely authentic, like the stereotypically Swedish-looking Dolph Lundgren from *Rocky 4*. And yes, as much as I don't like terms like Slav, Aryan, Semite, and so on, I believe a movie should look realistic.

In any case, armed with this idea, I see that my attacker could easily be Russian; he has a rounder face with a brick-like jaw similar to my elementary school janitor. I can't believe I didn't pick up on it earlier, but I guess my Rudar isn't impact resistant.

The German Shepherd guy takes me out of my musings by saying, "You mentioned your uncle was there at the hospital, but you never mentioned your cousin."

Finally understanding why they've been tiptoeing around this Russian-crime connection, I say, "Joe wasn't there at all. Do you actually think he could have any connection to this? You think he would kidnap his own aunt?"

"Or someone who wants to get to him might've taken her," the vegetable guy mumbles defensively. "We need to think of every possibility. Your cousin is—"

"Thank you for your time," his partner interrupts. "Here." He hands Ada a business card. "If either of you recalls anything of note, please give us a call. We have your information, and we'll stay in touch."

"Wait," I shout at them, but they're too far away to hear me. To Ada, I say, "Why would Joe's enemies, if that's whom they suspect, take a dozen strangers and Mom?"

Ada shrugs. "Your cousin did call your uncle when we were having lunch…"

"What are you saying? That my uncle is part of this?" I stare at her. "That's crazy. My uncle adores his sister. In fact, that reminds me. He needs to know what happened."

"I believe they already talked to him," Ada says. "They spoke to everyone who was at the hospital and the families of every participant. I guess they're still trying to reach your cousin."

"Look, Ada, about my cousin…" I pause, searching for the right words, then end weakly with, "He's a complicated person."

Okay, so maybe that's the understatement of the century. The labels people use when referring to my cousin are *psychopath* and *sociopath*. Though I hate those psychological terms, in this case, it's quicker than saying, "He who flouts the law while being prone to aggression, and who shows little remorse over any of the atrocities he's committed."

Gathering my thoughts, I start over. "Okay, he's not a nice person—maybe even a horrible person—but I believe he has a code, or something that passes for ethics, and in his own way, he has deep respect for my mom, who helped him—"

"I didn't mean to imply anything," Ada says. "I'm sorry."

I nod, accepting her apology, and wonder if I'm giving Joe too much credit. Past events replay in my mind. The time I found him beating a bird with a rock when we were kids. The time in Sheepshead Bay High when he put that big kid in the hospital with five broken ribs for using the funny Russian nickname of *Josya* instead of *Joseph* or *Joe*. Then again, I also recall Joe's face at the hospital after Mom's accident. He looked like he might strangle one of the nurses. At the time, I took that to mean he didn't like his aunt being in that situation.

"I think your conversation is too stressful for Mr. Cohen," the white coat suggests to Ada, and I remember he's still here.

I shift in the bed and grimace, unable to fight the rush of pain made worse by my dread for Mom.

"Do you want me to give you something for the pain?" the white-coat guy offers.

I look at him and finally get around to reading his nametag. His name is Dr. Katz.

"No more painkillers," I say. "I want to clear my mind so I can focus on the kidnapping."

The doctor looks momentarily surprised. I guess he thought I was too wimpy to refuse painkillers. In the next moment, however, he returns to that professional detachment they teach in medical school. "You'll have difficulty breathing without medication. Your ribs are—"

"I'm actually feeling much better," I lie. "When and if I'm in pain later today, I'll take something."

To create the illusion of vigor, I try to sit up, hoping it'll also help with my sudden bout of lightheadedness.

I have to almost literally bite my tongue to keep from screaming in pain. When my head stops spinning, I glance guiltily at the doctor. He either didn't notice or doesn't care—no doubt another thing they teach in medical school.

Ada grabs the remote control for my bed and helps me get into a half-sitting position. When I'm more upright, I'm surprised that I don't projectile vomit, shout obscenities, or lose bowel control. The performance must be convincing enough, because Dr. Katz looks mollified.

Pushing my advantage, I steady my voice and say, "Thank you, Doctor, for all the help so far. I really don't like hospitals, and I hope I can get out of here as soon as possible. For now, maybe you could give me a few pills I can take as needed? Perhaps Percocet?"

Dr. Katz considers this. His expression implies he doesn't approve of his patients deciding what painkillers they should take, but since I must have suggested the right one, he simply says, "Sure. I'll write the prescription," and walks away.

As soon as Dr. Katz is out of sight, I let my shoulders stoop slightly, but for Ada's benefit, I don't slouch in proportion to the agony I'm feeling. She's staring at me with the intensity of a jeweler pricing out a diamond, so I say, "I'll need your help getting out of here as soon as I can walk."

"What good will that do?" Ada crosses her arms. "Besides make things worse."

I hold her gaze. "I might come up with a way of locating everyone."

She looks away for a moment, then touches my IV-less left elbow. "Look, Mike," she says softly. "I can't even imagine how you must be feeling, but you have to realize the cops are professionals at this, and you—"

"I care about this more than they do," I say. I know it's an illusion, but I feel healing energy spreading through my arm from where Ada's tiny hand is resting. "More importantly, I can approach this analytically, like an engineer."

It might be another drug-induced delusion, but as soon as I say those words, an idea forms in my head. It must illuminate my face like the proverbial light bulb, because Ada pulls her hand away and looks at me intently. "What is it?"

"The engineering approach," I say, stressing every syllable. "I think I know how to find Mom."

TEN

I must've given Ada a clue, because she looks thoughtful for a moment. "If it's what I think—"

"Do you know where my phone is?" I pat down my gown-clad body, realizing for the first time that I'm naked under the thin layer of cloth.

Ada grabs my phone from a random pile of objects on the side table and hands it to me.

"Wow," I say as I examine the sleek device's flawless surface. "There's not even a scratch on it."

"You were overdue some good luck," Ada says. "Let's hope it holds."

"The sense of relief I feel is disproportionate," I say, the phone shaking along with my hand.

"You could be projecting something onto it," Ada suggests.

"Maybe. Then again, I did nickname my phone 'Precious.' I bet you didn't know that."

For the first time since I woke up, mirth twists the corners of Ada's lips. "I like that," she says. "Only you do realize that instead of prolonging your lifespan the way Precious did for Gollum, yours just shortens your attention span?"

"It's a prototype," I say and unlock Precious. "The first wave of super-smart phones from SandoMobile, a firm my fund is invested in. These puppies will cost two grand when they come out, and not because they have any gold or diamond bling built into them, like other luxury cellphones. The cost is all due to its fancy hardware, most of which I can't even leverage because of the lack of proper software."

"If you want me to write software for this thing, you can forget it." Ada's smile touches her eyes. "Brainocyte apps will keep me busy for a couple of years."

I mumble that it wasn't what I meant and check the screen. Precious is already on the hospital's Wi-Fi.

Einstein's tiny face looks at me from the screen, his cartoon eyes wise and patient.

"Einstein," I enunciate, "start a video call with Mitya."

"Done," the AI responds in his German-accented voice, and Mitya's company's video conferencing app launches.

"Let me hold that for you," Ada offers and leans in so close I can smell her coconut shampoo.

"Thank you." I hand her the phone, and our fingers touch for a second, generating a spike of oxytocin that goes from my hand straight into my brain.

She sits on the bed next to me and holds the phone as though we're about to take a selfie.

To my relief and surprise, it only takes twenty seconds for the app to indicate that someone has picked up the call. Considering we're about to chat with a multibillionaire C-level honcho of multiple corporations, I'd say I just got lucky.

The rest of the world knows Mitya as Dmitriy Levin. Unlike my name, Dmitriy isn't easy to Americanize, but it does have two short forms—Mitya and Dima. My friend prefers the less commonly used version of the two. As I look at him now, I recall how people thought we were related back at MIT, calling us the M&M brothers. I'd like to pretend it's because of the same keen intellect in our eyes, but I suspect it's really because we have the same brown hair, which we still keep equally short, and the fact that we're both allegedly immigrants from Russia—even though that last part is inaccurate, since Mitya is from a part of the former Soviet Union that's now Ukraine.

"*Zdorovo.*" Mitya's booming voice sounds like he's here in person, thanks to Precious's fancy new speaker technology. "I can't see you yet."

"That's 'hi,'" I whisper to Ada, and to Mitya, I say, "Hey, I have Ada here with me."

Mitya stares at his screen intently. He's sitting in some cushy conference room, wearing his signature blue hoodie. The video must finally turn on on his end, because he exclaims, "Wow. What the hell happened to you?"

"You won't believe it," I say and explain the events of the day to him, occasionally letting Ada fill in the gaps on parts I didn't know, like the total loss of my poor Zapo.

"Bro," Mitya says at the end of the tale. "What can I do to help?"

"I have an idea," I say. "It requires leveraging the servers you've been donating to the project."

Mitya is hugely invested in Techno, second only to me. Besides money, he's also given Techno a lot of technology and other resources, the most expensive of which might be his time. And, naturally, he's provided the servers that the Brainocytes communicate with. Who else has custom-designed supercomputers lying around?

Mitya must understand where I'm going right away, because he says, "Are you forgetting the privacy stuff? My people worked with hers"—he nods at Ada—"to make all the connections completely anonymous. JC didn't want people feeling like we could track their whereabouts from the backend—"

"I'm not a noob like JC." I tilt my head. "I know you can hack whatever crypto Ada's minions and your peeps put together. You got into—"

"Hey," Mitya interrupts in Russian and looks meaningfully at Ada. "I got this," he adds in English. He looks thoughtful for a moment, then starts typing on his very loud mechanical keyboard. Judging by his focused expression, he's no longer looking at Ada and me. He probably minimized our image to go through the privacy code.

"They did a good job," he mutters, his eyes scanning the screen. "Someone's getting a promotion."

"That's nice. I'm glad you're happy with your peeps." I have a hard time taming my sarcasm. "Now can you please help me locate my mother?"

He doesn't respond for a few minutes, but his keyboard sounds like machine-gun fire. I half expect to see smoke surrounding him.

"I can probably do it," he finally says. "In a few days, if I'm lucky. A week in the worst case."

"I don't have a few days." A wave of nausea hits me, causing the room to spin. "It needs to be minutes, or hours at the most."

"I'm sorry." He grimaces. "Locating people using Brainocytes wasn't in the specs. Quite the opposite, actually. All I can say is that *something* is running on those servers, so at least it's proof of life."

"That something could be the backups," Ada whispers. "Or even my—" She stops talking and looks at us sheepishly, probably feeling bad over shattering my "proof of life" hopes.

I fight the urge to scream in frustration, partly because I don't think it'll help, but also because I don't have the strength for something so strenuous. Inhaling deeply, I let out the breath and say, "Is there something we can do to locate them? You two are the smartest people I know. Can't you think of something?"

I stare pleadingly at the phone, then lock eyes with Ada.

"Well." Ada looks away and nervously rubs the buzzed part of her head. "When you first brought this up, I thought you had a more complicated idea in mind. It, too, would require some coding, but not as much as what Mitya quoted. I think I could write this app in a few hours or so. It's just that it kind of goes against every Techno policy we have."

"I promise if those idiots fire you for this, you can come work for me." Mitya's green eyes blaze with avarice. "What did you have in mind?"

"Dude," I say. "You promised not to poach her, remember?"

"Wait." Ada looks from me to the screen. "You guys talked about me?"

Mitya does a poor job suppressing a snicker, and I give him a warning glare. We have talked quite a bit about Ada, but almost never in a professional context. Usually, I just tell Mitya how close I'm getting to maybe, probably, possibly asking her out, and he tells me how much of a wuss I am.

"That's not important now," I say. "Tell us your idea."

"Fine." Ada moves the phone to her other hand. "We can use the backups."

"Yeah, you mentioned those before," Mitya says. "What do you mean?"

"In computer science, a backup is the practice or a set of procedures for making extra copies of data or hardware in case the original gets lost or damaged," Ada deadpans.

"This is serious, Ada," I say. In case she wasn't kidding, I add, "We obviously know what a backup *is*, just not what you mean in this context. Is there a backup of the secured data that's easier to hack?"

"No, it's the Brainocytes themselves," Ada says. "Doesn't anyone ever read the documentation?"

"I think I understand," Mitya says. "The hardware is redundant."

"Exactly," Ada confirms. "If any one Brainocyte goes out of order, an identical one can replace it."

"And you've kept double the Brainocytes, meaning for every test subject that was injected, you have an extra batch on standby." Mitya pushes his amber-tinted computer glasses up his nose—his poker tell.

"I know all that," I say, not caring if I sound defensive. "I don't see how those extra Brainocytes can help us, though."

"If we activate any of those backup Brainocytes," Ada says, "there won't be any security issues, because these Brainocytes all share the same IDs. So I can write an app that will leverage your mom's backups to locate her primary Brainocytes, or her, in other words."

Even with my less technical know-how, I recognize the simplicity and elegance in this solution. I also see the problem. "I thought Brainocytes only activate when inside a subject's brain."

"Hence the procedure issues I mentioned earlier," Ada says. "Not to mention privacy—"

"I volunteer," Mitya cuts in. "We don't have to tell anyone about it if you think you'll get in trouble."

"Wait." My head is spinning again, but this time, it's not just from the concussion. "It can't be you, Mitya. Even with your private jet, wouldn't it take you about a day to get here from the West Coast?"

"I can cut that down to—"

"No," I say firmly. "I need you in your office, helping write the app Ada mentioned and working on hacking the security in case this new Plan A doesn't work."

Mitya nods disappointedly. I've always known that my friend was helping with this project because he, like Ada, wants mature Brainocyte technology inside his head. I can't even blame him, since I've thought about it myself. It doesn't take much of a leap to picture how cool it would be. I mean, I have techno-orgasms just using Precious. Brainocytes integrate with your *mind,* so it would be like my phone on steroids and amphetamines. It's just that I never allowed myself to dwell on this because it makes me feel like a selfish, lousy son—like I'm investing in Techno for reasons other than helping Mom get better.

Thinking of Mom tightens my chest. I wonder if the kidnappers fed her and whether they're treating her okay.

I'm pulled out of my thoughts by Ada loudly clearing her throat.

I expect she's about to volunteer to receive the Brainocytes, but she doesn't. She just looks at me expectantly while tapping her steel-toed boot.

"It should be my head," I say with a confidence I wish I felt. "It's my mom we're trying to save."

"You just went through an ordeal," Mitya objects.

"Which just means I'm already under a doctor's supervision," I counter. "I even have an IV in my arm and everything. If we want to do this on the down-low, it doesn't get any stealthier."

"I think it'll work," Ada says. "The Brainocytes are pretty harmless. If I thought they could hurt Mike, I'd veto this plan, but I think this is the best resource distribution. Mitya works on a secondary solution, and I go get Nina's backup batch and start writing the locator app in the cab."

Her confidence unknots my stomach. "Thank you," I say, touching her hand.

"Fine. I'll take a crack at this security for now." Mitya says. "Keep me posted on your progress, and let me know if there's anything else I can do to help."

"We will," Ada says.

"*Spasibo*," I say, thanking him in Russian.

"Don't mention it," Mitya replies in Russian. "Good luck, guys," he adds in English and disconnects.

Ada hands me my phone and says, "Do you want me to get you anything on the way?"

"No. Just get me a batch of nanotechnology, the less tested on humans, the better."

Ada chuckles. "Try to get some sleep while I'm gone. I'll pick up your Percocet prescription as well."

Without waiting for my response, she leans in and gives me a loud smooch on the forehead.

I'm so stunned I only recover from the kiss once she's gone. Her lips are officially the softest things to ever touch my forehead —not that I make a habit of checking textures that way. I wonder what the kiss actually meant. Was that more than a friendly kiss, or does Ada always act that way when a male colleague is in pain in the hospital?

The nap idea is a good one, so I let myself close my eyes, just for a second. My breathing evens out, and I'm about to drift off when I hear someone approach my bed.

I open my eyes, and blood drains out of the big bruise I call my face.

"Hi, Mike," my uncle says. "I'm sorry if we startled you."

"You didn't," I say, staring at the person accompanying my uncle—the guy I used to think of as a friend, until he scared the shit out of me with his antisocial behavior.

"Hi, cousin," I say in Russian, meeting Joe's lizard-like gaze.

ELEVEN

"WHERE'S MY AUNT?" MY COUSIN DEMANDS WITH AN INTENSITY THAT implies I'm the one responsible for my mom's disappearance. "Speak. Now."

"The cops were here," I reply tersely. "They thought *you* might know where she is."

Joe steps toward the bed. His blue eyes glint with ice that reminds me of Hannibal Lecter's signature stare. I glance at my uncle for help, but he's clearly petrified.

"They also hinted that this could be the work of an enemy of yours." I wait one frantic heartbeat, then ask, "Is it?"

My cousin stops his onslaught, considers the idea for a moment, then confidently shakes his head. "No. They got it wrong. No one who knows me would dare fuck with my family."

The words aren't spoken with any bravado, but his sheer calmness is what bothers me. He's just stating a fact. Of course, there's a subtext to his words, a threat to whoever the kidnappers are. In this moment, it's all too easy to picture Joe going complete Keyser Söze on their asses and killing their kids, their spouses, their parents, their cats/dogs/parrots/goldfishes or whatever.

"How bad is it?" Uncle Abe asks, studying my face. His voice is so kind it's hard to believe he and Joe share half of their DNA. "Does that hurt?"

"Not much," I reply. I probably would've sounded more sincere if my voice hadn't cracked and if I hadn't cringed.

"Are you ready to tell me who did that to your face?" Joe asks. It might be my imagination, but did his intensity dial down from eleven out of ten to a mere ten?

"It was this big Russian guy," I begin and tell my uncle and cousin the whole story, only without going into the nitty-gritty details of the Brainocytes—specifically that they'll go into my head. Instead, I say there's a technical solution.

My uncle looks petrified as I go on, while Joe's features simply darken, an impressive feat given his semi-permanent somber expression. I fleetingly wonder if this whole situation is bringing back memories for them of how they lost Aunt Veronica. She had a heart attack before I came to America, so I don't know many of the details surrounding her death, but I suspect both men were forever changed by it.

"This technical mumbo jumbo," my uncle says. "Do you think it'll help us find her?"

"It sounds promising," I reply. "Plus, there's this other solution Mitya is working on."

"I don't have much faith in these solutions," Joe says, his expression unreadable. "And I don't have any faith in any solution that involves the pigs." He looks me over; then, perhaps deciding it's too harsh to compare me to the cops, he adds, "Especially the pigs."

"So what do you suggest?" I do my best not to sound challenging, since I need to keep my head to put the Brainocytes in.

"I'll look into this myself," my cousin says. "Whoever these fuckers are, they're making me—" His jaw muscles spasm, and he stops talking. Taking a calming breath, he pulls out his phone.

His face is back to its expressionless state, but I think I briefly glimpsed some emotion there. Was he about to say, "They're making me mad" or "They're making me look bad"? I don't mind if it's actually the latter. Maybe if he thinks these criminals don't respect him and are about to ruin his reputation by taking his aunt, he might be more motivated to help her. Or maybe I'm being unfair, and he genuinely cares about his aunt.

"You mentioned there was a Russian nurse at NYU Langone," Joe says. "Her name was Olga, right?"

"Yes," I say cautiously. "Why? Do you think she had anything to do with this?"

"Put in your number," Joe says instead of answering and hands me his iPhone.

I take the phone and note he created a new contact in his phonebook, calling me "bro2." I doubt it's because he's particularly fond of me. It's far more likely he used that term because there's no word for *cousin* in Russian. Instead of cousin, you use the word *brother*, but add a degree of separation to it. For example, Joe and I are *secondary brothers*, because our parents are brother and sister— kind of like how the term *first cousins* gives the same information. I wonder if this nomenclature results in cousins feeling more like family in the Russian-speaking part of the world. I certainly felt like Joe was my brother when we arrived in the US, but that quickly changed. Having said all that, Joe speaks English much better than Russian, having arrived here when he was just a kid. So maybe he meant "bro" as a kind of English slang, since he has another "bro" in his phone already. Still, even that suggests a closeness we don't really share, at least as far as I know.

Seeing the irritation on my cousin's face, I focus on the task at hand and put in my phone number.

"Check if you got my text," he says and types something into his phone.

"You have a text from Joseph Cohen," a German-accented voice says from my phone.

My uncle raises an eyebrow. "Should I read it?"

"No," I respond and tilt the phone toward me. Joe's message is just an ellipsis. "Einstein, please save this as a new contact and rename it Joe."

"I'll be in touch," Joe says and turns on his heels. When he's almost by the door, he says over his shoulder, "I expect updates on the technical solutions when you have them."

Before I get a chance to come up with some witty but safe reply, Joe is gone.

My uncle is left standing with an uncomfortable expression on his face. I know this isn't the first time his son has put him in an awkward position. Probably more like the millionth time. I can't even fathom what it must feel like to be the father of a guy like Joe, especially when you're as chill of an individual as Uncle Abe is. In that family, the apple fell so far from the tree it didn't even land in the same garden.

"I think he'll help," my uncle finally says. He looks like he's trying to think of the right words, but he ends up only adding, "Just be careful."

I nod, ignoring the throbbing in my temples.

"Did you eat?" my uncle asks, and I recognize an attempt to change the subject.

"No," I say. "Think you can bring me something light?"

Looking relieved, Uncle Abe asks me what I want, and I request fruit and Jell-O. In truth, I don't think I can stomach something even that low-cal, but I'm too exhausted for any more conversation and could use a moment to close my eyes.

As soon as he leaves, I fumble with the bed controls to make the mattress flat and doze off.

———

I wake up to voices and a sharp pain enveloping my whole body. Breathing hurts, shifting on the bed hurts, and even thinking hurts. All remnants of the pain medication must've gotten flushed out of my system while I was sleeping. As a cherry on top, I also feel my bladder starting to complain.

"He's been sleeping since I left to get food," my uncle says. "Dr. Katz suggested I let him sleep, so I stepped out to buy him some clothes to replace the ones he bled on."

Ada nods. "Good thinking. He might want to be awake for this, but maybe we should let him sleep a little longer."

"I'm awake," I croak and open my eyes. "How did it go?" I give Ada's messenger bag a meaningful look.

"I'm almost done with the app," Ada says. "I submitted the code to my own personal Git repository and asked Mitya to review it. Do you want to take a look? I can walk you through it."

"Yes, please. Anything I can do to help."

Ada gets her laptop out, and I put my bed into a sitting position. She places the computer in front of me, and I examine her code.

Now, I'm no programing novice. My MIT Bachelor's degree was in Computer Science, and they don't give you that without forcing you to get your hands dirty. More importantly, my very first job was as a C++ developer at a startup. I did that for a few years before I made enough money to start my venture capital fund. Though I was a good programmer, I admit the money had less to do with my coding skills than luck—or rather my uncanny skill at picking good companies, as I prefer to think of it. That startup gave me a load of stock options, which went through the roof when they had an IPO.

This is all to say that when I think Ada's code looks too clever, it doesn't mean I'm too dumb to get it, though I guess someone too dumb might say something similar. It's just that, like with some of her speeches, Ada didn't bother making this code easy to read. To be fair, as a bit of code that's meant to be used once and thrown away, its illegibility might be excused, especially since she wrote it in a rush. But part of me cringes whenever I see her use the more obscure "?" format for her conditional statements instead of "If, else." Call me lazy, but something like "if statementVar==true, consequenceOfTruth, else consequenceOfFalsehood," reads much better to me than "statementVar?consequenceOfTruth:consequenceOfFalsehood." She also didn't include any comments explaining her code. Yet despite all these minor gripes, I get the feeling I'm looking at the work of a genius as I review line after line of the app.

I get so engrossed in the code that I automatically accept and eat the fruit salad my uncle brought me and then gobble down the Jell-O.

"I don't know what any of the APIs you invoked do," I say at the end. "But aside from that, this all looks good to me."

What I don't say is that I'm slightly disappointed by how error-free it all is. Had I found something wrong with her code, I could've shown off my skills. Then again, since this stuff will be running in my head, and since its purpose is locating Mom, Ada's competency is a good thing.

"Great," she says. "While we wait for Mitya's feedback, should we proceed with the next part of the plan?"

She glances at my uncle. Her unasked question is obvious. Do we want to do the Braincyte thing in front of him?

"Uncle Abe, can you please get me more food?" I ask. "Maybe mashed potatoes?"

If my uncle caught on to our scheme, he doesn't show it. He simply says, "Ah, you're getting your appetite back."

In the Russian culture, having a good appetite and, relatedly, being slightly overweight is a sign of health. As a result, my grandmother had always tried to overfeed me.

"Yes," I lie. "Starving."

"How about you, Ada?" my uncle asks. "Can I get you anything?"

"I had a smoothie on the way, thanks," she says. She watches my uncle leave before retrieving the giant syringe from her bag.

"Ready?" she asks and approaches my IV bag.

"I guess." I look at the needle in her hand with distrust.

"Look, Mike, I can see you don't like hospital stuff. I understand. I don't like it either. After my mom got sick..."

Ada's eyes look distant, and it's clear she's reliving the day her mom succumbed to cancer. I want to jump up and give her a comforting hug, but since I don't think it would be appropriate, I just say, "It's okay. Let's do this."

"You sure?" she asks, regaining her composure.

"Just one question," I say. "Do you know what you're doing?"

"Yes, I've done something like this before." She rubs the corner of her eye with her finger. "You'll be fine. I promise."

She puts her hand on mine and gives it a gentle, reassuring squeeze. In an ironic turn of events, she's the one comforting me.

I wish I knew where Ada got her unshakable optimism from, but I do feel a modicum better. Capitalizing on this, I remind myself that what's about to happen is critical to locating Mom. I also tell myself that my fear of all things medical is irrational, a condition I developed from getting my teeth drilled without anesthesia—something that isn't relevant to my current situation.

When I feel like my voice won't quiver, I swallow and say, "Yes, I'm ready."

Ada doesn't give me a chance to change my mind. In a swift, confident move, she sticks the needle into the IV the way I saw the nurse do to Mom what feels like a year ago.

The clear liquid fills the bag, and the Brainocytes start their trek up my veins.

TWELVE

As soon as I picture the stuff swimming in my bloodstream, my already bad nausea intensifies.

"It's making me lightheaded," I gasp. "There are also all these odd sensations in my body."

"Lightheadedness is normal, but I doubt you can feel more than that. It's not possible to actually feel the nanobots swimming through your bloodstream," Ada says. "But you might feel a slight burning at the entry point."

As soon as she says it, I notice there's indeed a burning sensation around the spot where the IV connects to my arm. And then my lightheadedness evolves into something worse, and the hospital room spins around me faster than my dorm room did on the morning after I drank half a bottle of vodka with Mitya.

"You're turning white," Ada says worriedly. "Breathe."

I take quick, shallow breaths, in and out, figuring what works for panic-attack victims should work for me. The breathing helps a little, though I can't inhale too deeply without feeling pain in my ribs.

"That's good," she says. "Keep doing that. It'll be okay. Trust me."

I keep breathing and try to relax. When I put Mom through this yesterday, I didn't stop to think how I would feel about tiny machines messing around with my brain. Now I realize I'm terrified, but of course, it's too late.

"When can we test the app?" I ask, desperate to distract myself.

"After Mitya is done reviewing the code," Ada says. "But before we get to that, there's something I need to tell you. Something important. I—"

She stops talking when my uncle enters, carrying a tray of food.

"You were saying?" I say to Ada.

"Later." Ada's lips press together in a slight, but surprisingly adorable grimace. "You should eat first."

I look at the tray of food and realize my appetite is also similar to that hangover incident. Nevertheless, I reach for the mashed potatoes and valiantly swallow as much of it as I can, figuring food should help me heal faster. I wash it all down with a little square box of whole milk while Ada mutters something negative about dairy consumption.

"I want to try standing," I say when I can't ignore my bladder anymore. "Uncle Abe, can you please give me a hand?"

Ada frowns. "Is that a good idea?"

"I need to use the restroom," I explain. "I wanted to try getting up anyway."

"The doctor said it was okay." My uncle looks at Ada to see if she'll contradict him, and when she doesn't say anything, he extends his hand to me.

I lean on him and place my feet on the floor. My head is pounding with agony, and the pins and needles in my legs join the already crowded party of unpleasant sensations in my body.

"I think I need a nurse or a doctor," I say, realizing I'll have to pull the IV with me to the bathroom otherwise.

Ada walks off to get someone, and I use this chance to wince in pain.

"Maybe you should use one of those metal bucket things instead?" my uncle suggests. "I can see you're hurting."

"I'll be fine," I grit out through clenched teeth and attempt to put the least amount of weight on my uncle's hand as I stand up.

Just as swiftly, I sit back down again.

"I'm just warming up my legs," I say defensively. "They fell asleep."

The second attempt hurts more, but the room doesn't spin as fast and I can stand straight for a few beats before I need to rest again.

"What are you trying to prove?" my uncle asks in Russian. Then, more conspiratorially, he adds, "Are you trying to show off in front of the girl?"

"To help Mom, I need to be on my feet," I say and get up again.

Grabbing the IV stand, I take a shuffling step. The worst pain is coming from my side, as if something isn't letting me take in a full breath. Must be the bruised ribs. My left elbow hurts too. I don't recall why, but my shoulder and face are particularly painful. My face is also burning from the blood that, for some reason, rushed to my head. On top of that, I feel like I'm about to lose both the food I just ate and my bladder control. Otherwise, I'm feeling great.

A male nurse I don't recognize comes in with Ada. With unprofessional surprise, he says, "You're standing."

"Yep. And please tell Dr. Katz I'm checking out. Also, can you take this out?" I shake the IV tube.

The nurse looks at me suspiciously but does as I requested.

"Help me get him to the bathroom," my uncle says and grabs my right elbow.

"I don't need help," I say and take a firm step.

My next step is far less firm, but I make it anyway. The less I shake, the better I seem to feel, so I shuffle forward slowly.

By the time I make it to the bathroom, I'm ready to spill national security secrets just to make the pain stop. Though I only need to go number one, I do my business sitting down so I can catch my breath.

My nose decides to bleed again, or, more specifically, my left nostril. I stuff it with rolled-up toilet paper, a trick I learned when I was a teen.

"Is everything okay in there?" the male nurse booms from outside the door.

"Loving it," I yell back. "I got this."

Cutting short the toilet rest, I get up and wash away any sign of my nosebleed, which has already stopped.

I examine myself in the mirror and chuckle humorlessly. My face looks way more purple than it feels.

Leaving the restroom, I refuse the nurse's help again. The trip back to my bed hurts a tiny bit less—maybe because my brain is adapting to the constant pain.

"Where's my uncle?" I ask when I lie back down.

"I'm not sure," Ada answers. "I think he left to make a call. I tried explaining how we'll find your mom, and he seemed excited."

"Well, we're not waiting for him to return," I say, "assuming we can use the app already. Or do I need to call Mitya and hurry his ass up?"

"No," Ada says, her forehead wrinkling. "He finished the review."

"But?"

"No buts." Ada clears her throat. "It's just that I only have the most rudimentary tools on this laptop. I'd be far more comfortable if we could get you to the Techno headquarters or the NYU Langone Center, though the most optimal option is my apartment. This way, I'd get to keep my job in the end."

"Are you saying you don't have what you need to make the app work?"

"No, I can make it work," Ada says, "but just barely. You'll get the most vanilla build of the interface, and you'll have to use the laptop inputs to work with it. No debugging will be available, and the worst part is this version doesn't collect much data. I figured since you're doing this anyway, we might as well learn as much as we can about—"

"Time is of the essence," I remind her. "No offense, but I

couldn't care less about Brainocyte research right now. Once we locate my mom, you can collect all the data you want."

"Okay," Ada says and sits next to me on the bed. "Here goes."

She does something on the laptop.

"Did it work?" Ada asks after a few seconds of silence.

"I feel *something*," I say. "Like the world is getting a little clearer."

"I think that's a purely psychosomatic response," Ada says, waving dismissively. "Can you see it?"

She points at the screen, but I can't tell what she's pointing at from my angle.

"See what?" I ask, but then I do see it.

The "it" in question is a golden sphere floating in the middle of the room. It doesn't look like a hologram or a computer image. It looks solid and very real.

"I see it," I say. "What is it?"

"Just an icon you need to click." She puts her computer on my lap and points at the trackpad, saying, "You'll be able to do this with your mind after some training, but for now, you should use that."

I drag my middle finger across the trackpad's cold surface and notice another artifact move next to the base of my bed. This object looks like a square piece of white marble the size of a matchbox. When I study it more closely, I realize it has a triangular shape that leads its movements.

It's a three-dimensional version of those classic computer arrows I've used all my life, only bigger.

"The pointer," I say. "It looks so real."

"We're dealing with your vision center," Ada explains. "It doesn't take a lot of effort to make things look solid."

Determined to locate Mom, I suppress my awe and use the trackpad to move the white arrow toward me, then away from me, then left and right. It looks kind of spooky when it passes through my body like a ghost on its second trip toward me, but that's how it should be since the arrow is simply in my mind.

"Use the up and down key to make it move vertically," Ada suggests.

I do as she says. The process reminds me of flying my Phantom 3 drone or playing some kind of video game.

"Press the Enter key or left-click to initiate the icon," Ada says before I get a chance to ask her what to do.

"Okay." I navigate the white pointer to the middle of the room so it touches the golden sphere. "Done."

As soon as I press Enter, the room disappears and the world falls into a bright tunnel of static and colors.

The tunnel ends abruptly, and I'm back in the room. A text box that resembles a street sign hangs in the air. I guess this is how Mom's Phase One reminders must look from inside her head. The box says, "Connection failure."

I explain what happened and see Ada's face drain of color. I know what she's thinking—I saw the code after all—but given the gravity of the situation, I say, "Please tell me what this means."

"A connection failure message can mean many things." Ada's voice is unsteady. "It could be a problem with the hospital Wi-Fi, for example."

"My phone is on the same network, and it's working fine," I counter. "Besides, doesn't cell connection kick in when Brainocytes aren't on Wi-Fi?"

"You're either on Wi-Fi or a cell network, and when on Wi-Fi, the firewall can still create this situation," she mutters. "Let me try a different port."

She appropriates the laptop, changes a variable in her code, recompiles the app, and—I'm guessing—reloads it into my head.

"Let's try again," she says. "The new icon should show up in a moment."

The golden sphere returns, and I repeat my earlier actions.

The result is the same: connection failure.

"It's happening again," I say, a heavy feeling growing in the pit of my stomach. "What else might be causing it?"

"It could still be the hospital firewall," Ada says. "But it could also be an issue with the connectivity on the other end. It's hard to say. I doubt it's because your mom's Brainocytes are disabled."

The hairs on the back of my neck stand up as though I got electrocuted. "Ada... the only way the Brainocytes can be disabled is if the host brain is dead, right?"

This is when I notice my uncle is standing there. I'm not sure when he returned, but judging by the stark paleness of his face, he at least heard the last thing I said.

I stare at him, icicles floating in my blood, and he stares back at me. Through all the mishaps of the day, I didn't let myself consider the possibility that my mom might not survive her kidnapping. Yes, it would've been a rational thing to worry about, but I just couldn't dwell on it, maybe because the idea is too unthinkable. Now that I'm forced to consider it, though, dark specks dance in my vision.

Despite Ada's reassurances, the evidence we have points to this horrific possibility.

Mom might already be dead.

THIRTEEN

Seeing our faces, Ada quickly says, "Those are just a few possible explanations. Instead of speculating, let's rebuild the app with debugging capabilities and maybe expand it so we can see where the connection is going awry."

I swing my legs off the bed. My aches and pains somehow fade into the background, perhaps because I'm so terrified.

"Okay," I say, grasping at the thread of hope Ada gave me. "We have to get to your place to retry this, right?"

"Ideally, yes," Ada says. "Though it might be closer to—"

"I don't want to get you into trouble," I cut in. "So as long as you have all the tools you need at your place, that's where we'll go."

"I might be even better equipped there than at Techno," Ada says. "I was going to tell you—"

I make a slicing gesture through the air. "I'm already sold on going. Uncle Abe, did you drive here?"

"Yes," my uncle says.

"Can you give us a lift to Williamsburg?"

"Of course," he says. "But—"

He stops and I follow his gaze to the somber countenance of the law enforcement official I labeled as the beet-potato guy. Now that my mind is no longer under the influence of drugs, I see that he doesn't really look like either one of those vegetables, per se. He looks more like the Mr. Potato Head toy—which only vaguely resembles a potato—and his complexion is a lighter shade of red than a beet.

"Detective Sawyer," my uncle says, his voice turning hopeful. "Do you have any new information for us?"

At the detective's expression, my hands and feet turn colder than when I nearly got frostbite in Moscow.

He's got bad news, I can feel it.

"There's something I want you to look at," Sawyer tells my uncle, and his tone intensifies my fear. Taking out a large phone from his jacket, he approaches Uncle Abe. "We found the black Mercedes Metris minibus," the detective explains. "There was one body discovered inside it, and I'd like you to take a look at it. My partner is on the other end; he'll point the camera for you."

My uncle takes the phone and looks at it for the ten longest seconds of my life. Then he screams the Russian equivalent of bloody murder, drops the phone on the floor, and covers his mouth with both hands as he doubles over. I look incredulously at my tough-as-nails uncle as he whimpers softly. This is a man who fought in Afghanistan, and the Soviet version of that conflict was a nightmare.

I jump to my feet, a surge of adrenaline turning the pain into a distant buzzing.

Before I can bend down, Sawyer retrieves the phone and hands it to me. "I'm sorry," he murmurs.

I look at the screen.

The camera scans the inside of the car, and I see a body sprawled on the seat in an unnatural position. It's a woman dressed in a white hospital gown—a woman who possesses an achingly familiar apple shape.

"No," I whisper. "It can't be."

The camera only captures the body up to its shoulders, so

despite my uncle's reaction, it could be someone else. Of course, denial *is* one of the major stages of grief.

"Move the camera up," I instruct Detective Sawyer's partner on the other end. "Let me see."

The view begins to move.

With all my might, I will this person not to have Mom's face. I feel like I'd make a deal with the devil for it to be anyone but my mom.

The phone's owner finally lets me see her upper body, and I feel myself getting welded to the ground.

This body has no face.

Of any kind.

I blink, horror clouding my thinking.

It's not just the face that's missing.

It's also the scalp and the ears.

This body has no head.

FOURTEEN

Hypnotized by the atrocity on the screen, I can't look away.

My fingers loosen for a second, but I tense my grip before I can drop the phone like my uncle did.

I feel the half-digested mashed potatoes in my throat.

The person on the other end of the phone must understand the reaction the headless upper body generates in people, because he lowers the phone again, and this is when I see it.

On the body's right hand is a ring.

A giant emerald ring that changes everything.

"This is Mrs. Sanchez," I say hoarsely. "That's her ring."

I hand Ada the phone since she's seen the ring as well. Ada looks at the screen and nods. Then the phone on the other end must move again, revealing Mrs. Sanchez's headless body, because Ada turns translucently pale and clutches at her mouth as though she's about to lose her smoothie.

"It's not Mom," I say, this time in Russian, because I think my uncle is so lost in grief he didn't hear me identify the body. "It's this poor lady who was part of the experiment."

Relief relaxes the worry lines in my uncle's face. I realize I, too, must look relieved and feel a pang of guilt. A better person wouldn't be so glad to see Mrs. Sanchez dead in Mom's place.

Detective Sawyer takes out a notebook and pen and says, "Tell me about Mrs. Sanchez."

A half-coherent conversation follows, where I tell him about the poor woman, her family situation, her Alzheimer's, and her diabetes.

"Maybe she went into a coma," Ada says in a shaky voice. "She didn't get her shot this morning, and I doubt the kidnappers brought insulin with them."

"You're right," I say. "They might've finished her off, not wanting to take a comatose patient with them."

"But why take the head?" my uncle asks. "Is this some crazy cult? Or terrorists? Is there going to be a beheading video on YouTube?"

As soon as he asks this, a piece of the puzzle falls firmly into place.

Ada beats me to verbalizing my suspicions. "It's about our research," she says. "They took the head because that's where the Brainocytes are."

I've been too busy to think about the kidnappers' motives until now, but what Ada suggested is the best explanation, especially in light of the missing head.

The detective must also see it, because he asks us to explain the research to him again. I let Ada handle it while I take my uncle aside.

In Russian, I whisper, "Can you get rid of the cop for me? I want to go to Ada's house and retry the technological solution, but I have a feeling he might insist I identify Mrs. Sanchez in person or something. Afterwards, tell the hospital people I checked myself out and that they can send me my bill whenever it's ready. And don't worry, whatever Ada and I uncover, I'll keep you in the loop."

My uncle bobs his head, and as soon as Ada finishes her explanation, he turns to the detective. "Can I buy you a cup of coffee?"

In a lower voice, but still loud enough so I can overhear, he adds, "There's a private matter I'd like to discuss with you."

The detective's eyebrows go up in an uncanny imitation of Mr. Potato Head. He probably thinks my uncle might tell him something about his son. The proposition is tempting enough that the detective says, "Sure. Thank you."

As soon as they walk off, I tell Ada, "We're leaving. Now."

Ada looks a little shell-shocked. She might still be processing Mrs. Sanchez's demise. Figuring she can sort out her emotions on the way, I grab the clothes my uncle got me and go into the bathroom.

Again, I'm amazed at the effects the adrenaline is having on my pain sensitivity. I almost feel normal as I take off the hospital gown, but when I put on the street clothes, the pain breaks through with such vengeance that I consider taking a Percocet. In the end, to keep my mind as clear as I can, I decide to tough it out.

"Let's go," I tell Ada when I leave the bathroom. "We'll have to cab it."

———

"Please, come in," Ada says after unlocking the reinforced door to her apartment.

I follow her, wondering if she was the paranoiac who installed it. Since her building is smack in the center of the most bohemian, and thus costly, part of Williamsburg, the neighborhood should be pretty safe, though I guess this door might predate the gentrification. I'm not surprised Ada chose to live here. She fits the neighborhood's flair perfectly, and her exorbitant salary is proportional to her brilliance.

Personally, I don't see the benefit in living in trendy neighborhoods unless they come with great restaurants and improve the commute. If I were in Ada's shoes, Williamsburg wouldn't work for me. Though it does have great food options, it's much too far from the Techno headquarters.

I myself live in Brooklyn Heights. It isn't the cheapest place in the world, but since I can afford a penthouse in NoHo (and thus anywhere in Manhattan), I rightfully consider my current multi-million-dollar brownstone a humble abode. In fact, I often feel like I'm following the advice in the book *The Millionaire Next Door*, which talks about self-made rich people living below their means. In my case, I'm more like a billionaire living next door to million-aires, but that's still below my means and within the spirit of the book, I think.

"My office is this way," Ada says and leads me through a sleek kitchen with modern-style cabinets and appliances that look like she got them at the MOMA museum. When we pass through the long, high-ceilinged corridor, I note a strange mix of punk bands and sci-fi movie posters occupying every inch of wall space.

"This is it," Ada says proudly as we enter a room that was origi-nally meant to be the living room. What Ada created here looks a lot like a cross between a data center, a gadget lover's wet dream, and a mad scientist's lair.

In the cool air conditioning of the room, racks of servers hum computations and two enormous TVs are hooked up to the latest Xbox and PlayStation. A row of about a dozen different monitors occupies the wall to my right. At the center of it all stands a desk with five monitors and a keyboard that's split in half, with each half about a foot apart. A large trackpad sits in the middle, with a mouse to the right and a trackball to the left. A giant pair of headphones hanging over one of the screens completes the picture.

"Well, you got your input and output devices covered," I say, noting the row of video game controllers sitting on a large computer tower by the desk.

"Please, have a seat." Ada points to a large beanbag chair that could just as easily serve as a dog's bed.

I sit there, and she plops into a blue Herman Miller chair designed for ergonomic work. It's identical to the ones they have at the Techno offices.

"Give me a minute." Ada puts on the ginormous headphones and starts typing.

Her keyboard must be mechanical, with either blue or green switches, because every keystroke is loud enough to make me daydream about Percocet.

I might've dozed off, I'm not sure, but she startles me when she clears her throat and says, "I'm going to give you a custom-made environment I designed to work with the Brainocytes. I dubbed it AROS, which you can pronounce as Eros. It stands for Augmented Reality Operating System."

The room around me momentarily brightens, and a bunch of floating holographic images appear in the empty and, in some cases, not-so-empty space.

"Don't worry about the unfamiliar icons," Ada says. "Here"— she hands me the Xbox controller—"control the arrow with this."

Sometimes I get depressed when I think about how many video games I've played in my life. It's especially sad when I consider it within the context of, "Time is money." I feel like I'd be twenty times richer if I'd worked instead of playing Xbox for hours. Then again, I could say the same thing about binge-watching TV shows and other entertainment.

The controller sits comfortably in my hands, as only an object held for thousands of hours could. I twiddle the right stick, and the familiar white arrow appears, only this one is ghostly like everything else in this so-called AROS. It also moves much faster than the one at the hospital. Using the right stick, it takes me only a second to fly the pointer to the familiar sphere icon in the middle of the room, which also isn't solid in this instantiation.

I click it, and the result is the same as back in the hospital, only the "connection error" sign is see-through.

"Okay," Ada says without turning. "I traced it this time. The packets definitely left your head and reached Mitya's LA datacenter. There are no problems with the security there as far as I can see. The issue is that the server can't shake hands with your mom's hardware."

A cold fist grips my heart again. "So she's either not connected, or she's dead?"

FIFTEEN

"I DON'T THINK SHE'S DEAD," ADA SAYS. "I PIGGYBACKED ON HER ID and tried to ping the other participants. I got the same results each time."

"Which could just mean they're all dead, like Mrs. Sanchez," I say, but the tightness in my chest loosens at the ray of hope.

"That doesn't add up." Ada turns her chair to face me. "Why leave only Mrs. Sanchez's body behind? If they killed everyone, they would've taken their heads too and dumped the bodies. Heads are easier to transport."

Thanks to Ada's logic, I feel like I can stop hyperventilating a little and gather my thoughts. Getting an idea, I ask, "Is there a log somewhere on the server? Something that can tell you where my mom was at any given point? As they drove around, she probably got onto a couple of Wi-Fi spots before switching back onto the cell network. Wouldn't those events be logged somewhere?"

"Of course." Ada smacks herself on the forehead, swivels her chair back around to face her monitors, and clicks away for a few long minutes.

"You'll have to run the app again," Ada says when she stops working. "I'll be able to access the log afterwards."

The sphere icon shows up, and I click it.

"Yes," Ada says excitedly and attacks her keyboard once more. After a few minutes of frantic typing, she says, "Come take a look."

On the biggest monitor on her desk is a zoomed-out map of New York and its boroughs, with dots spread across it.

"You're a genius." Ada looks up at me. "Whenever Wi-Fi was available, the event was logged, with timestamps and GPS coordinates. That right there"—she indicates an area on the outskirts of Long Island—"is the last location that was logged."

She plays with her trackpad, and the map zooms in on the area, switching to satellite view.

"It's a private airport," I say, examining the greenery, the runways, and a couple of sleek planes.

"This explains why there isn't a connection." Ada swivels toward me again. "They must be in the air without a Wi-Fi connection."

Though I should feel relieved, the idea that someone is flying my mom to who-knows-where is deeply unsettling.

"We have to tell the police," I say. "They might be able to narrow it down to which plane and when."

"Maybe." Ada pinches her bottom lip. "It's certainly worth a shot."

"Can you write a version of this app that'll keep trying to connect and notify us when it succeeds?" I ask. "This way, when they land or drive into an area with cell service or Wi-Fi, we'll know right away."

Ada's dimple shines in full force, and she says, "I was just thinking along those same lines. I've got to say, I'm impressed you thought of it. Unlike me—" She suddenly stops, her dimple disappearing, and looks at me guiltily.

"Thanks, I think," I reply, frowning.

"I didn't mean to make that sound like an insult." Ada looks at her hands. "I've been trying to tell you something, but it can wait until we do this."

Before I can inquire further, she pointedly turns around, puts on her headphones, and begins writing code.

While she's working on that, I get in touch with the detective, explain why I had to leave the hospital in a hurry, and share the airport information. At the end of the call, I don't get the warm, fuzzy feeling that my extra bit of information might magically solve anything. Still, I promise to keep them in the loop on our end, get a reciprocal commitment in return, end the call, and contact my uncle to give him an identical update.

Before I get a chance to check if Ada is done, my phone lights up from an incoming video call.

A jolt of adrenaline hits my already overloaded system.

It's Joe.

He wanted me to keep him posted, and I forgot to do exactly that. Did Uncle Abe tell Joe what he just heard, and does my cousin now want to berate me, or worse?

"*Privet*, Joe," I say, though the Russian "hello" and the very Americanized "Joe" go together about as well as an American eagle and a sickle and hammer. Although, strictly speaking, an eagle (albeit a double-headed one) *was* the main coat of arms of the Russian Empire before it went all Soviet, and I think they brought it back later in the nineties, but that was after I'd left. Some think of bears when they think of Russian symbols, but I've never understood why. There aren't any bears on any of the Russian or Soviet regalia, and if any nation should be associated with bears, it's probably China, given their fascination with pandas.

"Hey," Joe responds tersely. "Is this the Olga you told me about?"

The screen switches to the front-facing camera, and the face of the nurse who was working with Mom at NYU Langone fills the screen.

Instead of her usual uncaring expression, Olga looks disheveled and terrified, like a pigeon facing a rabid tomcat. She's standing in a dingy hallway, and I see a door broken off its hinges to her left.

"Yes," I say, doing my best to disguise my unsteady voice. "That's her."

My cousin perches the phone on something—probably a shoe rack, judging by the boot blocking part of my view. Then he walks into the frame and up to Olga and grabs her by her throat. "Tell me who took Nina Cohen if you want to live," he growls at her in Russian.

I'm almost too petrified to notice the *Terminator*-ish line Joe accidentally quoted. If my cousin were sane, he'd wait for an answer before blocking her speaking apparatus. But this is Joe, and he squeezes her neck until the woman's eyes bulge out of her head. When he lets go, she gasps for air but doesn't scream out answers the way I would have in her place.

Suddenly, a man sticks his head into the open doorway of the apartment. He's big, and his face is contorted in fury.

"What the fuck is going on here?" the guy says in accented English. "I'm calling the—"

Without a single word, Joe leaps at the newcomer.

In a smooth motion, my cousin punches the guy in the stomach. He must catch him straight in the solar plexus, because the big guy doubles over and gets a knee to the face.

"*Nyet*," Olga screams as she looks down at the fallen guy, and I realize Joe just took down her husband or boyfriend.

My cousin must realize this too, because he cruelly kicks the man in the ribs and says, "Speak, bitch, or you're scrubbing him off the floor."

Olga looks too stunned to speak, but Joe doesn't care and gives the guy another vicious kick, this time in the face.

Blood pours from the man's face. Seeing it, Olga frantically cries, "Stop!"

She starts speaking quickly, stress making her mix English and Russian together.

"*He spoke Russian,*" I puzzle out, "*but he had an accent, like he just arrived from there. He paid five grand for the information about the Russian woman, Nina Cohen, and the rest of the people. I don't know who 'they' are. I'll give you the money he gave me. I'm sorry. Please don't kill me. Please don't kill Grisha."*

"I want a name." Joe's hand is back around her neck. "Give me a name, or I'll break your fucking neck."

"He said to call him Anton," Olga gasps. "I don't know his last name. I don't know anything else."

"Describe Anton." Joe loosens his grip on her neck.

She frantically describes a man who sounds suspiciously like my attacker. Joe, who heard the description from me, must recognize that, because he's convinced enough to let go of her neck and pull out a bunch of computer printouts from his pocket.

"Which one?" He shows her the images.

My guess is he has the pictures the cops showed me earlier. I wonder how he got them. Joe's official line of work is private security, so maybe he has connections on the force? At least I hope that's what it is.

Olga points at an image, and in a gesture of uncharacteristic thoughtfulness, Joe turns it my way.

"That's the guy I saw," I say, disguising my voice again.

"Okay," he says to the woman. "Are you sure you don't know anything else? If I find out you do, if I think you lied to me, I'll come back and—"

"I told you everything," Olga whimpers. "I swear on my mother's health."

She rambles some more until Joe stomps on Grisha's leg, causing a loud crunch, and says, "Shut the fuck up."

Olga stops talking, and the silence is broken only by the man's ragged breathing from the floor.

"If you speak to the cops, everyone you know dies," my cousin says with as much emotion as someone complimenting her kitchen. "I'll start with him." He gives Grisha another kick.

Tears stream down Olga's face, but she keeps quiet and simply nods.

Satisfied, Joe steps over the broken body and looms over the phone. Then his palm gets huge, which I take to mean he grabbed the phone. He walks out of the apartment, and the screen shows blurry movements for a while.

The glimpses I get of the building's hallways and windows have a distinct grayness about them. That, combined with Olga's nationality, screams to me "somewhere on Brighton Beach."

My nausea makes a comeback and not just because I'm seeing the world spinning on the screen.

Taking in deep breaths, I unpeel my eyes from the phone and glance at Ada. She's still wearing her headphones and clicking away as though nothing's happened.

I turn off the video on my side so Joe doesn't spot Ada and say, "Joe, you realize I'm still on the line?"

My cousin stops walking and says, "Looks like that was a dead end."

I resist the urge to yell, "It almost literally turned into a dead end, you maniac." Instead, I say, "Not really. The fact that they paid for information supports our earlier suspicion that they want the technology. I was actually about to call you with an update of my own."

In the heavy silence that follows, I tell Joe what I know so far and finish with our airport findings.

"A private airport." He grunts. "They have money. I don't like the sound of this at all. Do you know who owns that place?"

"No."

"Fine. I need to talk to a few people. I'll call you back. Let me know if you find out where they flew to."

"Okay, I will," I say. "But before you go, can you email me the pictures you showed Olga? The ones with the kidnappers?"

"Sure," my cousin says and hangs up without so much as a goodbye.

SIXTEEN

I PUT MY ELBOWS ON MY KNEES, CRADLE MY HEAD IN MY HANDS, AND wait until my breathing evens out.

This is exactly what I needed on top of everything else, to become an accessory to a crime. The righteous part of me wants to call the cops, but a more practical part vetoes that idea. First, if Joe found out—which is likely—he wouldn't hesitate to do something worse to me than what he did to that poor schmuck. Second, rightly or wrongly, Joe had good intentions, or at least intentions that will benefit my mom, and Olga certainly wasn't innocent in this mess. Plus, Grisha looked like he could've kicked Joe's ass, so that makes the beating somewhat defensive. Of course, the latter rationale is more of a rationalization, since self-preservation is more than enough to persuade me against ratting on Joe.

I briefly wonder if I should at least call an ambulance anonymously, but then I remember I don't even know where to send help. Olga can call 911 herself. Plus, since she's a nurse, she can give Grisha first aid if he needs it.

My conscience more or less appeased, I check my phone for the kidnappers' images and find that my cousin came through. I recognize the pictures from earlier, particularly Anton's, the guy who attacked me. Encouraged, I call Mitya and give him the rundown—minus Joe's interrogation of the nurse.

"So I can stand down?" Mitya's desk is filled with unopened bottles of Red Bull, bags of Cheetos, and a jar of green M&Ms, reminding me of our MIT days. "Sounds like you don't need the Brainocytes' privacy bypassed anymore."

"Yeah, that's the main reason I called," I say. "I didn't want you pulling an unnecessary all-nighter."

"I appreciate it," Mitya says. "Let me know if there's something I *can* do."

"Is that Mitya?" Ada asks from her desk, pulling off her headphones.

"Yep," I reply. "I was about to let him go."

"Wait a minute." She walks over, kneels next to me, and leans in close so the phone camera can see her. "Hi, Mitya. I need a favor."

"What's up?" Mitya clearly noticed Ada's proximity to me, and I can see he's itching to say something, so I surreptitiously show him my fist while pretending to rub my chin. He notices, winks, and just says, "What can I do for you, Ada?"

"You know the brain simulations we run on your STRELA servers?"

Strela means arrow in Russian, though I believe Mitya has a clever acronym behind it. Next to his personal time, the STRELA servers is the most generous resource he provides to the Brainocyte project. As of last year, this stupendous hardware topped the list of most powerful supercomputers in the world—or it would have if Mitya had disclosed the exact specs to anyone, which he hasn't. However, he did hint that it's multiple orders of magnitude more powerful than China's famous Tianhe-2, and that behemoth can do a whopping 33.86 petaflops. The plan is to use STRELA to run brain simulations that will allow Brainocytes to make the rest of the brain think the damaged tissue is up and running. It's at the core of Mom's later treatment.

"Yeah," Mitya says, his eyes glinting curiously. "Pricey buggers. What about them?"

"Can you double our allotment?" Ada asks.

"Mind if I ask why?" Mitya pushes up his glasses, and I know that means he's excited.

"Would you *not* do it if I refused to tell you?" Ada tenses up next to me.

"I'll do it since it's to help Mike," Mitya says. "But if you don't tell me why, I'll be pretty disappointed."

"I want Mike to hear the reason why first," Ada says. "Then, when things calm down a bit, I promise I'll explain, especially if you promise to keep quiet about it."

"Mike knows I can keep a secret," Mitya says. "Regarding more STRELA resources, consider it done." He grabs a handful of M&Ms, chews noisily, and adds, "Because it's *already* done. My old mentor at MIT gave up his research with their neuroscience department about a week ago, and since that was the only thing sharing your STRELA servers, those cycles are yours in one, two..." He starts typing on his computer—way too long for a three count, if you ask me—and finishes with, "Now."

"Sneaky." Ada's shoulders relax. "But thank you anyway."

"Yeah, thanks, dude," I say, pretending I'm not completely clueless about the reason for Ada's request. "I owe you big."

"We'll continue this conversation when I see you in person," Mitya says. "Now if you'll excuse me, I'm going to jump into my limo and read the thousand emails that have piled up thanks to you."

"Wait, what do you mean in person?" I nearly shout, trying to catch him before he signs off.

"Oh, I've had my private jet prepped, and my driver is on standby. In less than ten hours, I'll be in NYC."

"I really appreciate your help, but it's too much. You're—"

"Your best friend, and I didn't say I was flying out just to help you," Mitya says. "There's some business I need to take care of on the East Coast, and I want to visit Gramps, so don't worry about it."

"Still. Seriously, thank you," I say. "Is it possible to reach you in your jet?"

"I had to spend a quarter mil, but I now have Gogo's Wi-Fi on my plane." He gives us a smug grin. "And even if I didn't, didn't I show you this?" He takes out a clunky satellite phone and dangles it by its long antenna.

He didn't, and he knows it. When it comes to gadgets, Mitya loves showing off.

"Happy flight," I say, translating the traditional Russian farewell for Ada's benefit. "I owe you so big I don't even know where to start."

"I'll take your *Tales of Suspense* #39 and call it even," Mitya says. "Or your Kamakura katana."

"They're both yours," I say without hesitation.

"You know I'd help without any rewards," Mitya says, his tone turning unusually ceremonial.

"Of course. I know that," I say.

"Oh, and there's actually something Ada can do for me when I arrive," he says, his voice back to normal.

Jealousy floods me in a kind of "protect Ada's honor" alpha maleness that makes me want to reach through the phone and flick my friend on the nose.

"Get your mind out of the gutter," Mitya says when he sees my expression. "I mean she can give me the Brainocytes too. That lady who died, her backups are now useless, so..."

I feel a slight pang of disappointment. He really meant it when he said he's not just coming here on my behalf. *This* is probably what he wants most out of the trip. I should've guessed. With Mitya, everything he does has layers of benefit for him, but—and this is key—also for the people close to him, which includes me.

"We'll discuss that when you get here," Ada says evenly.

"Sounds good," Mitya says. "You should know that I already figured out why you want those extra STRELA servers. If it's for what I think it is, did you know I have more where those came from? In a matter of months, I can do better than double those resources; I can put a couple of zeroes behind what you have today."

Ada's eyes shine so brightly with avarice I bet Mitya can see it through the phone. She'd make a terrible poker player.

"It sounds like we do have things to discuss," she says, her voice betraying her almost as much as her eyes.

"We sure do," Mitya says and signs off.

I look at Ada, who only now realizes how close she is to me. Or I assume that's what happens, because she jumps to her feet and returns to her chair.

"That *Tales of Suspense* is when Iron Man first shows up in the comics, and it's in pristine condition," I explain. "And that katana is from the thirteenth century."

"I knew all that, except for the condition of the comic," Ada says, and I'm not sure whether she's boasting.

"Anyway," I say. "Let's get back to the reminder app."

"Right, that," Ada says. "To make my life easier, I'll give you a different build of AROS that will, among other things, include that app. Afterwards, we'll talk."

Before I can reply, she clicks Enter and I feel that slight "disturbance in the Force" that happens every time she reloads the software in my head.

More icons fill the room. In the middle of it all is the same sphere.

"Load it." Ada gets up and hands me the Xbox controller again.

I do as she says and tell her, "Nothing happened."

"And nothing *will* happen until your mom connects to a cell tower or a Wi-Fi hotspot," Ada says. "Once she does, not only will you get an alert, but so will I."

"Good. Is it loud enough to wake us up?"

"Oh yeah," Ada says mischievously. "It won't be easy to ignore, I assure you."

"Okay," I say. "Now tell me whatever it is you've been teasing me about."

Worry replaces the mischief on her face. "You must be hungry," she says. "Let's talk in the kitchen. You can press the A button to dismiss the icons."

I press A, and all the AROS images go away. When I get up, my legs and body want to scream, but I don't let Ada see it. She leads the way, and I scramble after her into the modern-artsy kitchen.

"You can sit there." She points at the metallic barstool.

After I sit, I tell her, "I'm still not that hungry."

"I have something very light in mind," she says. "Banana ice cream. You'll love it."

I raise my eyebrows at the idea of ice cream being light, especially for a health-obsessed vegan like Ada, but I don't say anything. I'm determined not to get sidetracked from whatever secret she's been building up to.

Ada goes to the freezer and takes out a plastic-wrapped packet filled with frozen, peeled bananas. The freezer is actually chockfull of these, making me wonder if she has a monkey living in her apartment somewhere. Ada takes out four bananas, walks up to a big blender, and puts them in. Before I can object, she starts the machine, and its roar sounds like it has either a chainsaw or a Harley Davidson motor inside. My brain tries to jump out of my skull, and I cover my ears as tightly as possible.

The noise stops, and Ada worriedly says, "I'm so sorry. Your concussion—I didn't think. Are you okay?"

"Sure." I cautiously let go of my ears, though they're still pulsing in pain. "Please don't do that again, or at least not for a couple of years."

"Sure," she says. "I don't know if it'll be worth the literal headache, but here you go." She scoops two-thirds of the smoothly blended banana into a pretty bowl. It looks a lot like ice cream, and I reach in with my finger, curious to taste it.

"Wait," she says and rummages through a cupboard. She pulls out a bag of mixed nuts and sprinkles them over the ice cream.

Before I can use my finger again, Ada places fancy spoons into our bowls and nods approvingly.

I taste the dish. The texture is spot on, but I'm not sure I'd go so far as calling it ice cream in terms of taste. Then again, it could easily pass for some kind of gourmet banana-flavored gelato, and given the simplicity and healthiness of the recipe, that's pretty impressive.

When she looks at me questioningly, I say, "It's yummy, but I think you've danced around the subject you're hiding long enough."

"All right." She licks her spoon nervously. "I'll just come out and say it." There's a long pause, and then she solemnly says, "I have Brainocytes in my head."

I nearly choke on a walnut, cough, and then stare at her, unable to shake off my incredulity. Of all the things I expected to hear, this wasn't on the list. In all honesty, some part of me was hoping she knew something about the kidnapping and was about to tell me Mom was safe and sound. I guess I'm kind of single-minded that way.

Clearing my throat, I put my spoon down and ask, "How? Why?"

"Early on, during primate testing, I stashed a prototype set before we added all the ID security stuff to them." Ada looks down at her quickly melting ice cream. "I guess that makes me an embezzler. I used my position to—"

"Look, Ada," I interrupt. "If you're feeling bad about this, you shouldn't. I don't care about the costs. I'm one of the primary investors, so whatever you took, it was mainly my money. But if you wanted Brainocytes, all you had to do was talk to me."

She looks at me, her eyes glinting with hope despite the suspicious moisture there. "I was impatient, and I didn't think anyone would understand."

"So you put hardware that was meant for a chimp inside your head?" I chance another small spoonful of dessert.

"Aside from security, the Brainocytes haven't changed since then," Ada says with a sigh.

Epiphanies explode in my head, and I say, "So that's why you kept insisting how safe the treatment is." I rub the bridge of my nose. "You already went through it."

"It's also where all these advanced apps and the custom OS for the Brainocytes came from," she says. "Or did you think what I gave you was just meant for your mom?"

"I wouldn't know the difference," I say, but realize that it does explain why her home office is set up better than the one at Techno. "When exactly did this happen?"

"A few months back, right before Kathy broke things off with you. The timing was poor." She looks at my bowl and says, "It's melting."

I shove a couple of spoonfuls of ice cream into my mouth and ignore the resulting brain freeze. So this is why Ada was acting so strangely around me. I was wrong when I thought it was because she was wary about me asking her out; it must've been her guilt about the Brainocytes. I swallow the pulverized banana and say, "Okay, I guess I get the how part, and I can probably guess the why, but I want to hear you say it."

"That part's simple." Ada looks at me steadily, almost challengingly. "I did it for the same reason Mitya is helping us, for the same unspoken reason everyone at Techno is working on this technology. I simply didn't want to wait." She takes a deep breath. "I did it so I can transcend being human."

SEVENTEEN

Maybe I expected Ada to use slightly less pompous verbiage, but I did suspect that transhumanism was behind it all.

"Can you be more specific?" I scrape the bottom of the bowl for the last bit of ice cream. "What exactly did you do to yourself?"

"Well, for starters, I can almost seamlessly do anything that usually requires a computer with just my mind, at nearly the speed of thought," she says. "They say a modern cellphone allows its owner to have access to more information on the internet than President Clinton had during his presidency. My abilities are those of this modern cellphone owner, only taken much further. I can do advanced calculations, access Wikipedia, and Google any question, all in my head. You get the idea?"

The implications are truly incredible, but I put all that aside and say, "Okay, it's not *that* far removed from Phase Three, which Mom and the others were about to get."

"True. Working on my own, I never really went far beyond what we were going to do for your mom. I just expanded on it," Ada says. "But it was enough of a starting point. Mind-computing access aside, when you combine our brain region simulations with a healthy brain, you get a boost in intelligence, and not the metaphorical kind based on apps like I was just talking about. A much more literal one. You know, the topic JC never likes to talk about."

"Okay, neuroscience isn't my strong suit, but I get the gist of how we can simulate certain key brain regions to bypass my mom's trauma," I say, thinking out loud. "The Brainocytes will make the right neurons think a healthy version of that broken brain tissue is in place and firing. I knew enhancement was theoretically possible, but—"

"It'll use that same basic premise," Ada interrupts, "but it'll essentially provide the brain with extra brain regions, as well as faster versions of the original regions. Eventually, neuroplasticity will kick in, and the brain will learn how to really use the extra power. Though even out of the box, I was able to give myself a certain boost—"

"Wait," I say. "I just realized something. This is what's been behind your off the charts coding lately, isn't it? I was just thinking about it earlier today."

"Probably. The brain boost helps with everything, but in this case, my coding improvements might also be due to the integrated development environment—aka AROS IDE—that I've developed. I can literally write code in my head." She beams at me. "I'm so glad I can finally share this with someone. It's so amazing. After a while, typing mentally and using the IDE turns spooky, and I almost feel like the apps get written by me just willing it."

"Hold on." I cross my arms. "So why did you use that super-loud keyboard today?"

She bites her lip. "I was waiting for a good moment to tell you. Sorry. I didn't do it just to fool you. I use the thing for practice sometimes, and for cover at the office. In any case, it's good for me to stay sharp with older tools, because who knows what could happen one day. In general, this enhancement does have a small flaw—you have to be on Wi-Fi or a cell network, though the latter offers reduced capabilities."

"That's true." I uncross my arms and study her with wonder.

"So you'd get dumber if you went camping? But how does the keyboard help you with that? I don't see why you'd ever need a keyboard again—once you come out to your coworkers, that is."

"It's like eBooks versus paperbacks." She picks up our bowls and puts them in the dishwasher. "Some people like one or the other. I still like both, even though I can now read books without any devices at all. Still, even when I used the Kindle, which I loved, sometimes I'd want to read a paperback, and I still do. There's something about the feel of paper in my hands and the smell of ink on the pages. Using a keyboard is like that—a sentimental activity, I guess. As to getting dumber if I'm not around a cell tower or connected to Wi-Fi, you're not that far off. I hate not being on the internet. It's more debilitating than being drunk or stoned, and it's why I never take the subway anymore—even above ground, the reception is abysmal."

"Wait a minute." I decide to voice a concern my mom once raised when I explained the brain simulation stuff to her. "These simulated brain regions aren't simulating your own brain, right?"

"Right," Ada says. "In theory, the Brainocytes can be used to map out my brain, but that isn't what I did. I just used the more generic simulations based on the ones your mom was going to utilize."

"So this is like having parts of someone else's brain in your head?"

"Sort of, I guess, but that isn't an issue. I think of it as having extra neurons supplementing my brain," she explains. "The simulated regions adapt and learn to work together with my biological brain, which means I'll make them my own over time. But I see where you're going with this. Are you worried about the slippery question of identity? Like what happens when the supplemental brainpower gets more powerful than my biological brainpower? Will I be a mind running on a computer server using my body as an avatar? Are you worried about what will happen if I lose connection in that scenario? If I will feel as dumb as a rock in comparison to my normal self?"

I didn't mean to ask her any of the interesting questions she just raised, but since we're going down that road, a big question pops into my head. "What about consciousness? Given the scenario you're describing, if you had more of a simulated brain than a meat one, would you still be conscious?"

"If the brain regions are properly simulated, you won't be able to tell the difference between them and the biological versions, so why wouldn't the whole be conscious? I imagine the resulting Ada would be *more* conscious than I currently am, with her mind expanded and all that. Anyway, we don't need to worry about all these philosophical questions, since the hardware required for even a fraction of the human brain is enormous. The STRELA servers are the best hardware in the world, and they can only simulate small regions. So yeah, so far, I can assure you I'm still conscious." She winks at me.

"But wouldn't it have been better to have these answers before you jumped in and used the technology on yourself?" I ask.

"No." Ada's forehead crinkles. "Doing this now will actually help me bring about more powerful advancements, since the smarter I am, the more capable I am. I see each future mind boost as an incremental update, akin to what's already happened to me. It's not scary at all. So in the future, say when the STRELA servers' capabilities double or triple, I'll easily be able to imagine how things will turn out. The bigger and better-simulated brain regions will adapt and integrate with my brain just like this first batch did. Same thing will be true down the line, when hardware and simulations that are ten or a hundred times better come about. Each boost will become part of me, the same way new neurons do. The resulting Ada will still be me, and obviously conscious, even if she doesn't fully understand the how of it. It's not that different from how a baby turns into an adult over time."

I consider her incremental vision and realize she's right. The "baby me" reached my current state by growing new neurons in a process called neurogenesis. Even as an adult, I have neurons that die and get reborn as part of a slower neurogenesis process. Yet, from the moment I was born until now, I've always been *me*, no matter how much brain tissue got added. If my brain grows more neurons or a new region, I'll still be conscious and feel like myself. I'll just be smarter and more capable of interesting feats. The same is probably true for this virtual brain extension.

"But what if Mitya shuts down the servers?" I ask.

"What if I got a lobotomy right now? What if Stephen Hawking lost that special chair and his voice synthesizer? What if I got an infection and there weren't any antibiotics around?" Ada retorts. "It would obviously suck, but I won't hold back my potential over what-ifs."

"Going back to the scenario where you have the hardware that allows the non-biological half of your brain to exceed the biological half," I say, getting into the spirit of things. "Wouldn't that lead to a purely simulated version of you? And what's to stop that creature from spawning a whole race of Ada copies and taking over the world?"

"A girl can only hope." She fluffs up her Mohawk. "But seriously, as more hardware becomes available, such implementation details can be fleshed out. I can think of ways to keep myself a singleton, if that was what I wanted."

I sit in silence, pondering all this. I can picture these brain extensions morphing into something like brains in the cloud over time. Such technology has the potential of redefining the human condition so completely that the resulting beings would barely be recognizable as *Homo sapiens*.

Ada looks at me anxiously, and I realize I've been silent too long. Figuring we can discuss the future consequences in more detail later, I turn the conversation toward a more pragmatic direction. "I take it you asked for double STRELA cycles to do this brain boost for me?"

"Of course." Ada's unease disappears, and her eyes gleam. "It would be silly not to take advantage of the situation."

I now understand the reason for her sudden candor. Okay, maybe I understood halfway through eating my ice cream, but I no longer have any doubts. She wants me to become like her. She wants to give me all these apps and the intelligence boost. Actually, she already gave me some of it—hence her earlier statement of "here is a new custom OS, but I can't tell you why yet."

"It's already in my head, isn't it?" I say, looking at her.

"Yes," she says. "But it wouldn't work without Mitya's help, and you still have to launch an app to get it started."

"And the other icons?"

"Some are what your mom was going to have," Ada says. "I had help from my minions on those. A bunch of the others are utility apps I wrote for myself. I branched off some open-source projects when I had to, and now you have the basic necessities like a web browser, terminal emulator, email, texting, as well as a videoconference app, word processor, and the IDE I mentioned earlier—just to name a few apps off the top of my head."

"I think I want to go back to your office now," I say and get up. "Thanks for the snack."

"You're welcome." She leads me back to the beanbag chair I've started to view as mine.

Sitting down, I grab the controller and click the A button. The transparent shapes reappear, each representing one of the apps she just mentioned. They form a circle around the room, and I can guess their functions just by looking at them. Zooming in on one to my right, I ask, "That small sphere surrounded by tricolor swirly lines is your version of the Chrome browser, isn't it?"

"I actually branched off Chromium, the project Chrome draws its source from, so you're close," Ada says. "The codebase is mainly C++, my strong suit, so I figured why not make my life easier?"

"Let me try it," I say and use the controller to hover the white arrow over the 3D Chromium logo.

A slightly see-through screen shows up in front of my face.

"I think the folks who made *Minority Report* might sue you," I say, marveling at the apparition. The ghostly screen is the size of my seventy-inch TV. On the screen is an empty page with an address bar in that minimalistic style I associate with Chromium's popular progeny.

I use the remote to move the screen closer to my face and direct the cursor to the address bar, but then I realize I have no way of typing text.

"You'll have to learn how to control all this stuff with your mind," Ada says after I raise this issue with her. "For now, you can use this." She walks over to her desk drawer and fishes out a wireless keyboard.

After she does her magic to hook it up to my AROS, I put the keyboard on my lap, type *techno.com* into the address bar, and press Enter.

The official Techno website looks glorious in this version. The colors are sharper and the text is crystal clear, which makes sense since I'm not really seeing this stuff. The Brainocytes are making my visual center think I am, so the resolution can be anything the eye can see.

"Damn," I whisper after browsing the internet for a few minutes. "This is already better than Precious."

"Yeah," Ada says. "I now use my iPhone for video calls only, and then only for cover. For everything else, I use my head."

"I can't blame you. What do these other icons do?"

She walks me through the apps, and as we go, I log in to things like the email client, the calendar, and so on. Throughout, I feel something between kid-on-Christmas excitement and whatever a crack addict feels when scoring a new fix. This is a thousand times cooler than setting up a new computer or smartphone, even one as prodigious as Precious.

When we get to the music player, I ask, "Does hearing work the same way as vision?"

"The principle is the same. The brainocytes stimulate the right brain area," Ada says. "Oh, and by the way, you're stuck listening to my music library for now."

I browse through her eclectic collection until I find a song called "Where is My Mind?" by The Pixies and press play.

The song starts, and it's the next best thing to being at an actual concert. I again marvel at the entertainment possibilities of this technology. When Techno goes public, all its employees will be rolling in money, and my bank account might finally measure up to Mitya's. Actually, no. Mitya invested so much into Techno that if it grows, he's going along for the ride too. Oh well. It's never been a competition between us anyway, since he would've won many times over already.

"I don't envy the lawyers who'll have to figure out if having songs in someone's head violates copyright," I say. "Loving the music, by the way."

As I say it, I feel a spurt of guilt for enjoying music while my mom is suffering who-knows-what. With the guilt comes sickening worry, and the throbbing in my head comes back with a vengeance, as does the pain from all my injuries.

Taking a breath, I slowly release it and push the worry and guilt away. What I'm doing will help Mom; I have to believe that, or I'll go crazy.

Leaving the song playing in the background, I move on to more apps, trying to feel the enthusiasm this technology should generate.

"So," I say when there are only two unexplained icons left, "I take it the brain-looking thingy launches the brain boost, or whatever you call it, but what's this sphere with a half-moon shape and white halo around it?"

"That's a tongue and gray hair," Ada says, mischief returning to her face. "Just use it and you'll see. You'll like it, I promise."

I click the app and a figure appears, floating in the room. This time, it's the Star Wars franchise Ada is ripping off, because a blue-gray holographic version of the cartoony Einstein, the AI assistant, says, "Hello."

His German-accented voice is as clear as if he'd spoken from where he's floating.

"Einstein," I say. "Remind me to get a new car in a few weeks."

"He can't hear you," Ada says. "I haven't gotten around to

hooking him up with speech recognition like I did with the VOIP stuff. But you can type to him, and I can tell you from experience, once you can do it mentally, it'll be better than speaking."

I type my request and watch Einstein walk over to the calendar app and launch it. The reminder is instantly filled out, though I guess Ada didn't bother creating an animation of Einstein actually writing it out, which would've been neat.

"Okay, Einstein, please go away," I type, and the hologram fizzles out.

"I'm officially impressed," I say, "and I haven't even boosted my intelligence yet."

"Strictly speaking, just using these tools boosts a person's intelligence significantly. But you're right. You're currently doing the same things someone with a very nice smartphone could do, but much faster—which is an important difference." Getting up, she walks over to me and puts a hand on my shoulder. "I think it's time to try the boost," she says with a smile.

Her hand on my shoulder seems to spread warm energy throughout my body, making it hard to concentrate on what she's saying. Straining to focus, I wonder if I want to try the boost. Part of me shouts a resounding yes. The appeal is the same as the reasons I went to MIT and continue to read scientific journals and pursue intellectual self-improvement. More important to the situation at hand, the smarter I am, the higher the chance that I'll figure out where Mom is, as well as who took her and why. I tell myself this as I hover the 3D pointer over the brain icon.

"You can turn it off if you don't like it," Ada reminds me and squeezes my shoulder before dropping her hand. "But I doubt you ever will."

I try to think of something appropriate to say and decide to use the legendary phrase uttered by Yuri Gagarin, the first Russian cosmonaut.

"*Poyekhali*," I say. I'm about to translate it as "let's go" for Ada, but she surprises me yet again.

"I think Armstrong's 'one small step' is more apropos," she says, smiling.

I think back to all the Russian I've spoken behind Ada's back and redden. "You speak Russian now?"

Her smile widens. "Just what I've been able to learn in the last few months. The boosted intelligence has helped."

"And how much Russian is that?"

"I little Russian speak," she says with a horrendous accent. "I better at understanding than speaking."

Shaking my head in disbelief, I repeat Gagarin's statement and activate the brain icon.

EIGHTEEN

NOTHING HAPPENS.

I count to twenty and say, "I don't feel anything."

"Well, yeah," Ada says. "What did you expect to feel, exactly?"

"Smarter," I mutter, feeling like maybe the intellect boost went in the opposite direction. "Or at least something."

"I told you, your brain needs to adjust to this new state of being," Ada says. "The effects are subtle at first. Even as early as the second day, I did better on a slew of cognitive ability tests, even though I felt the same, aside from a certain sharpness that's hard to describe. The only noticeable thing was those weird pre-cog moments I had in the beginning."

"Pre-cog moments?" I frown at her. "As in, psychic?"

"No, but sort of. It was very strange." She chews on her lower lip. "It's like a vivid daydream or hallucination. You see what's about to happen." I look at her incredulously, so she clarifies, "I don't mean literally. The vision can easily be inaccurate. It's a side effect of the not-yet-integrated portions of the simulated brain regions anticipating the result of a decision or action but serving the information to your normal brain too quickly. Thanks to neuroplasticity, they later learn how to work together, so don't worry. It took a day or so before I stopped having these episodes, and since then, I suppose I've simply made better decisions, so no visions required."

"Still sounds strange," I say. "Are you sure you didn't eat too many magic mushrooms or peyote?"

"The effects of mescaline and psilocybin are very different from what I'm talking about," Ada says without blinking. "If you think about the brain's primary function in nature, this phenomenon isn't that odd. The brain tries to predict what's about to happen in its environment. If bushes rustle, the brain might predict a lion is lurking behind them and send the rest of the body into a fight-or-flight response. This is similar, only it's the new brain regions that are shouting 'lion,' and since your regular brain isn't used to it, it shows you a quick dream of a lion as a way to cope with the new experience. That's my theory, anyway."

"Having done neither of those drugs, I'll take your word for it." The nagging aches throughout my body and my overall tiredness make it hard to hide the hint of irritation in my voice as I add, "But this would've been great information to have *before* I enabled this thing in my brain."

"I didn't think it would matter." Ada takes a tiny step back. "It went away for me, and you can disable the whole thing at any moment."

I instantly feel bad for putting her on the defensive. "Sorry if that sounded accusatory." I blow out a breath. "I've had a long day."

"It's not a problem," she says, though I can tell she's still miffed.

"How can I make this process go smoother?" I ask, knowing that letting Ada geek out might improve her mood.

I was spot on with my question. Her bad mood forgotten, Ada rattles out, "My advice is to put a load on your brain. The bigger, the better. Double your reading material, check out those startup financials or whatever it is you do as a venture capitalist. Try your hand at programming again. You can create your own apps that'll run inside your head, and my IDE will make coding easy, even for a noob like you. At the very least, use games like Brain Age; they stimulate all sorts of brain regions and help you see your progress as you go. My Brain Age is 20, which is very good. Take IQ tests or the SATs and the GRE test repeatedly, and you'll see daily gains, for whatever that's worth. In general, any new intellectual pursuit is a good idea."

"Got it. I'd say I'm covered for a while, since just playing with this new toy in my head should keep my brain stimulated on multiple levels."

"You're one hundred percent right," Ada says. "To that end, I advise you to start getting rid of your reliance on the keyboard and controller."

"Sure," I say. "What do I do?"

Ada sets things up for me to learn how to use my mind instead of the keyboard. The protocol is identical to what the people in the study were doing yesterday, but because I can type around a hundred words per minute, the process is quicker and easier for me. I start by typing out predetermined text while the Brainocytes keep an eye on what happens in my brain. Afterwards, using the same text, I mime typing in the air, and the Brainocytes report to Ada an extremely high degree of correlation between "real" and "mimed" typing. I progress to needing less and less physical involvement and eventually just mentally pretend to type. Again, the Brainocytes prove something neuroscience has known for a while: many regions of the brain that activate during regular typing still activate when I mentally type. It's a lot like how athletes can mentally run through their exercises and achieve actual gains.

When I can type by thought alone, I picture what this aspect of the technology will do for people with disabilities and swell with pride at being a small part of it.

Dealing with the controller is even easier since I'm more proficient at video games than I am at typing. Ada isn't surprised and jokes that our generation of gamers might actually have a large portion of our brain dedicated to video game controllers.

"You know, it's possible," I say and mentally bring up the email app. "I read about neuroscience experiments that found the brains of pianists were noticeably different from the average person's."

"Anything you do changes your brain." Ada yawns the most contagious yawn ever and adds, "But yeah, very absorbing and challenging activities have an even bigger impact, and video games can certainly be that."

Unable to suppress my retaliatory yawn, I use the email client window hovering in front of my face to mentally type out an email to Ada, writing, "So is this that technologically enabled telepathy you spoke about?"

She looks distant for a moment, then gives me the widest grin I've ever seen.

In utter silence, I hear a ding in my head and check my email, finding an email response from Ada that says, "Exactly."

"The only issue is that the NSA can, in this case, intercept our thoughts," I joke out loud.

"Sure, having part of your thinking in the cloud could indeed expose your private thoughts to the NSA. That's a potential worry if you're the paranoid type," Ada says. "I say we can cross that bridge later, probably by using heavier encryption."

A text message arrives in my head in the form of a jumping green sphere with a little text balloon icon next to it. I mentally click on it, and the message reads, "I prefer using texting for telepathy rather than email, if you don't mind."

I notice Ada sometimes closes her eyes when she works with her version of AROS. For some reason, that makes her look even cuter, which I didn't think was possible.

Closing my eyes is a great idea, so I do it as I play with my mental apps for a few minutes. What I end up experiencing is icons hanging in the darkness without the distraction of the surrounding room. It's definitely a good way to use the system, but having my eyes closed has one big flaw: I instantly feel the weight of the crazy day press against my eyelids, and another yawn creeps up on me.

"Okay, I'll take that as a hint that you want to go to sleep," Ada says through yet another yawn. "I can't blame you."

"Let me call a cab," I say, opening my eyes and glancing around uncomfortably.

"Nonsense," Ada says. "You should stay here."

"Are you sure? I don't want to impose on you."

I'm deathly tired, so I was actually fishing for her to extend this exact offer, but now that she has, I find myself wondering what it means, if anything. Besides, where would I sleep? Her apartment is big, but—

"There's a couch in the library room," Ada says, and for a moment, I get the creepy feeling that the Brainocytes somehow let her glimpse my private thoughts.

"That'll work," I say, perhaps a tad too quickly. "Thank you."

The adrenaline that was covering up the pain from my injuries must be fully out of my system, because my shoulder's killing me and my legs feel so wooden I can barely stand. I contemplate taking pain pills but decide that might make me miss the alarm Ada set up for Mom's locator app. I just hope I can fall asleep as is.

"Alternatively, you can take my bed and I'll take the couch," Ada says, playing the role of mind reader once more.

"No." I step toward her. "I can't let you do that. I'll take the couch."

"I fall asleep on it with a book all the time," Ada says, looking up at me. "You're what, six-one, six-two? You probably won't even fit on the couch without having to fold your legs under you."

"Can you show it to me?" I shift from foot to foot. "I'm sure you're exaggerating."

She leads me into the library, and I realize she might've actually downplayed how unsuitable this sleeping arrangement is. The so-called couch is a glorified loveseat. Even with her barely above five-foot petite frame, she might feel cramped on it.

"It's fine," I fib and try to hide my disappointment by looking at the rows of books in the room. The subject matter varies greatly. There's a big philosophy of science tome on the shelf to my right, and adjacent to it are a bunch of science fiction novels that I've either read or always meant to. A row of computer science books sits below that. Sadly, I've read these or similar ones before. I have a flashback to the college years I'll never get back as I glimpse exciting titles like *Design and Analysis of Algorithms* and *Data Structures and Other Objects*. I chuckle when I spot the *Introduction to Ada* textbook, a volume that teaches Ada's namesake's programming language—not how to pick her up.

Ada doesn't buy my lie or my avoidance strategy of looking at her books. She waits until I catch her gaze and softly says, "Neither of us has to sleep on this torture device if you promise to be a gentleman."

Stunned, I notice her eyes are the same translucent smoky brown as the thousand-dollar cognac bottle I have sitting in my bar at home. I stare into them for a few moments before I remember she's waiting for a coherent response. "I can pretend to be a gentleman, sure."

She smiles, steps closer, and brushes the backs of her fingers over the extra swollen side of my face. "You poor thing."

I catch her hand and hold it. It's small in my hand and almost painfully warm against my battered face.

Ada waits a couple of beats, then steps out of my reach, pulling her hand away. "Let me use the shower first. I'll put some towels out for you," she says. "Do you want to wait here or go to the lab?"

"I'll wait here," I say, gesturing at the couch.

Ada leaves, and I take a seat, my world whirling from that brief touch.

As the pleasant haze of excitement fades, I feel all the aches and pains of the day again. It's as if I'm one hundred and seventy. Closing my eyes, I call up the AROS interface and use the apps I didn't get a chance to fully examine. When I tire of the apps, I set the alarm app to make sure I don't oversleep tomorrow and dismiss the interface.

Before I can open my eyes, I feel something moving on my leg, followed by a crawling sensation on my shirt, followed by a sudden stop and a small pressure on my chest.

Something just scurried up my body.

"What the—?" I exclaim in panic and open my eyes.

A giant pair of creepy pink eyes are staring me down.

And they look hungry.

NINETEEN

OKAY, SO ON SECOND THOUGHT, THE EYES AREN'T GIANT. THEY'RE actually pretty beady, and they're not that creepy either, just those of an albino.

A white lab rat is sitting on my chest. Upon closer inspection, besides hunger, I also notice a glimmer of intellect in its gaze, though maybe that's just my jittery imagination.

"Mr. Spock," Ada says sternly from the doorway. "How many times have I told you to be mindful of my guests?"

The rat looks at Ada, then back at me, its eyes seeming to say, "I can read your thoughts, Mike, and I'm warning you, here and now, don't try any funny business."

Ada scoffs at Mr. Spock and comes toward me.

I ignore the rat long enough to notice what Ada is wearing, or more specifically, what she *isn't* wearing, which is pretty much anything other than a large towel. The towel is wrapped midway around her chest, and her breasts are perkier and lovelier than I imagined—and my imagination has worked overtime in this area. Even more interesting is the fact that the towel only extends a few inches past her bikini area.

I suddenly feel like I'm in a banya—a steam bathhouse Russians like to visit in winter. It's as if the temperature in the room just tripled.

Seemingly oblivious to my reaction, Ada gently takes the rat off my chest, and I glimpse even more of her flesh. To avoid breaking my promise about being a gentleman, I try not to gawk as she walks away. Still, I'm only human, and I can't help noticing her shapely legs and the dancer-like muscles of her back. I also spot a brightly colored tattoo on her shoulder.

"Let me feed you, my furry troublemaker," Ada says to the rat in a voice people usually reserve for babies or dogs. In a normal, or perhaps slightly playful tone, she tells me, "Come if you want to watch."

I'd watch her do her accounting, knit, or perform any other boring activity as long as she was wearing that outfit. I get up, suddenly feeling spryer, and follow her into the kitchen.

Putting her little charge on the floor, Ada reaches into a drawer and pulls out a box.

"These are lab blocks," she says, forestalling my question, and gives the box a shake.

I hear the scurry of many little feet on the floor as Ada takes out some blueberries and spinach from the fridge.

She pours the brown pellets from the box onto six teacup saucers and then adds a little fruit and veg. Each plate is instantly taken over by a white lab rat.

As I watch them eat, I notice the rats' fur isn't perfectly white. Someone, probably Ada, added colorful streaks on top, like a Mohawk. There's a green-streaked rat and a blue one, while Mr. Spock's streak is a very un-mister-like pink, though I guess the color does match his eyes.

"That's Kirk, McCoy, Uhura, and Scotty." Ada points at each rat. "That there is Chekov, and I bet if he could speak, his accent would be stronger than your uncle's."

"That's kind of racist, specist, and maybe ratist." I snicker, then add seriously, "They all had Brainocytes in their heads?"

"Not *had*. They still have them," Ada says and pours water into a big bowl. "It's all still up and running. Why do you think my babies are so smart?"

I examine the rat crew with renewed interest. When developing Brainocytes, Techno initially experimented on so-called brainbow rats—rats that were genetically modified to have a spectrum of florescent colors added to their neural cells, making them ideal for study under a confocal microscope. To see real-life versions of these famous critters, plus ones with a brain boost to boot, is a big surprise. It also makes me wonder if maybe I didn't imagine the intelligence I saw in Mr. Spock's eyes. Maybe he took better advantage of his rat version of the intelligence boost than I did.

"Can I pet him?" I ask, looking at the pink-streaked rat.

"He'd love that," Ada says. "But not while he's eating."

As though on cue, Mr. Spock stops eating, drinks from the water bowl, and scurries over, giving me an uncannily cat-like stare that seems to say, "I'll tolerate you, mortal."

I gingerly reach out and rub the fur. Spock graciously allows it, or at least he doesn't bite me, which I think is the rodent equivalent.

I guess I never inherited my mom's deep-seated fear of rats. Quite the opposite, I find this little encounter kind of soothing, and I wonder if rats can be employed as some sort of pet therapy. Then again, given the day I've had, it wouldn't take much to lower my blood pressure.

"Where's the shower?" I ask softly, afraid I'll spook Mr. Spock.

"I'll show you," Ada says and leads me down the corridor, past her office, and to the bathroom all the way at the end.

Since I'm still trying to be a gentleman, I primarily study Ada's tattoo as we walk. Unfortunately, I have to give up and look elsewhere, because the towel is hiding most of it.

"You can use those towels and wear those boxers once you're done." Ada points at the pile of fluffy towels and the pair of purple shorts.

"Where did you get those?" I ask cautiously. I don't want to come across as ungrateful, but if they belonged to her ex-boyfriend, there's no way I'm wearing them.

"I like sleeping in boxers," Ada says, and I worry I might start drooling at the image. "They're clean, and I don't have cooties."

"I definitely didn't mean to imply you have cooties."

The Enterprise crew in the kitchen might have something worse, but I don't mention that.

"Do you need help?" Ada asks, her expression unreadable. "With all your injuries, is it hard to undress?"

"I should be fine," I say quickly. Inhaling a breath, I discreetly swallow and add, "Thank you."

She nods toward the kitchen. "I'll go hang out with the gang. See you in a few."

"One moment," I say, and Ada stops in the doorway.

"What's your tattoo supposed to be?" I ask, and maybe it's my imagination, but I think I see slight disappointment flit across Ada's delicate features. Maybe she hoped I'd ask for her help undressing?

"It's the donkey and the dragon," Ada says. "I got it after watching *Shrek*. It's also why I never mix pot with alcohol anymore."

She turns around and lowers the towel just enough for me to get a good look at the ink. Now that she told me what it is, the big pinkish-purple head and the small creature next to it make perfect sense.

Then I realize something else, and a nervous chuckle accidentally escapes me.

The towel goes back up, and Ada gives me a stern look. "Are you laughing at me?"

"No," I say, but a new bout of laughter is on the tip of my tongue, itching to escape. "Don't you see what this makes you?" I gesture at her short haircut, which isn't sticking up as usual since it's wet. Then I mime typing on a keyboard.

"No." She narrows her eyes at me. "What does it make me?"

"The girl with a dragon tattoo," I say, grinning.

"You're clearly tired," Ada says, but her sneaky Mona Lisa smile touches the corners of her eyes again. "Shower so we can go to sleep."

She closes the door behind her, and I hear her chuckling down the hall.

Taking off my clothes is painful, but I manage it. Maybe I should've said yes to her offer.

The shower only hurts where my shoulder is stitched up, but the pain's tolerable. It might not have hurt at all if Ada had helped me get soaped up—assuming that was even on the table. I decide that the coconut shampoo is Ada's trademark scent, so I opt to wash my hair with baby soap instead.

After I finish and towel off, I put on the boxers. They're snug, and I wonder if that means Ada and I have approximately the same butt size. Given our height and weight differences, I figure my heinie is proportionally small, which is manly, while hers is rather curvy, which is awesome. I wisely decide not to discuss this with Ada, especially since I'm in her apartment and she could unleash her rats on me, like that Willard guy from the old horror movie.

Ada meets me outside her room, wearing comfy-looking PJs. Part of me hoped she'd decide to sleep in a pair of boxers, but I can respect her more conservative choice. Besides, it might help me be a gentleman as promised.

Her bedroom is dark, but I can still make out the stripper pole by the closet. I fight the urge to rub my eyes as they widen at the mental images of Ada using that thing.

The queen-sized bed is mixed news. At home, I sleep on a California king, and I've been contemplating getting an even bigger bed. Then again, a smaller bed means we'll be huddled closer together, and that has a certain appeal.

Ada gets under the blankets, and I get in from the other side of the bed.

"Good night?" I say, unsure what the gentlemanly protocol would say about me trying to kiss her.

"Will you hold me?" she whispers and wriggles under the blanket, nestling backward into me.

"Sure." My throat is suddenly too dry to talk.

In the next moment, we're in the classic spooning position.

My mind is whirling. She smells like summer and feels just as warm in my embrace. An almost healing energy spreads from her body into every injury I suffered today. Placebo or not, all the pain disappears as though I took a Percocet.

"Do you mind if we fall asleep like this?" Ada murmurs. "Does it hurt lying on your side?"

"No," I whisper. "Not at all."

After a few minutes of blissful peace, my eyes adjust to the dark, and I notice Mr. Spock and his kin lying in strategic positions around the bed.

As sleep steals over me, I have the eerie sensation that if I hadn't been a perfect gentleman, a pack of rats would've attacked me. Maybe it isn't called a pack, though, but a swarm or maybe a colony? Or perhaps a pride, or possibly even a plague? Knowing the question might keep me up for needless minutes, I use my newfound power to Google stuff in my mind and learn the proper term is actually a "mischief of rats." As odd as it sounds, it's kind of fitting.

I don't think I even turn off AROS before I drift to sleep.

TWENTY

I'M FALLING DOWN A NEVER-ENDING SKYSCRAPER IN SLOW MOTION.

Frantically, I look through every window, searching for something or someone.

Suddenly, I spot my target, and instead of falling, I float in one place and squint through the window.

Inside is a white medical room, and I see Mom sitting on an ancient dental chair. She looks horrified as she stares at the dentist. He turns toward me, and I realize he isn't a dentist at all.

"I know him," I scream at Mom through the window. "His name is Anton."

Mom can't hear me, and neither can Anton. With an abrupt motion, he grabs one of those frightening metal picks and leans toward Mom.

One moment I'm floating outside the window, and the next I'm crashing through it, jagged pieces of mirrored glass flying everywhere.

The sound of breaking glass continues as I leap forward, just as Anton is about to stab Mom in the chest with the dental pick.

My enemy turns in time for me to punch him in the face, and I hope my desperation and hatred give me the strength required to break his monumentally large jaw.

I hear the distant sound of a phone ringing, but I ignore it and focus on my fist, which feels like I just hit an iron plate instead of a human face.

Before I can even think of throwing another punch, a giant fist connects with *my* face in a vaguely familiar arc, and I fly backward through the window.

Looking down, I see the pavement approaching at the speed of light. Though I should be terrified for myself, I'm more worried about leaving Mom alone with that monster.

The pavement approaches even quicker, and I brace for the impact.

TWENTY-ONE

Instead of hitting the pavement, I wake up and realize it was a dream.

Just like in the dream, I hear a phone ringing in the distance. Maybe that's what woke me up from that completely illogical Superman-like nightmare that only a sleeping mind wouldn't question.

I open my eyes and note the room is only beginning to brighten from the rising sun peering through the gaps in the shutters. I dismiss the AROS interface that I left on last night and wonder why I didn't see it in my strange dream. The ringing is coming from down the hall. I have to assume it's Precious, unless Ada also uses "I Like to Move It" as her default ringtone.

I get up, careful not to step on any members of the mischief of rats.

Precious is with my clothes in the bathroom, proving how fickle my love for my phone has become; once I got something better in the form of Brainocytes, I left the poor device in a moisture-rich environment.

According to the phone, it's 6:45 a.m., and it's Joe calling.

My sleepiness evaporates, leaving me feeling like I just downed a venti cup of coffee. "Hey. What's going on?"

"I talked with a few guys who work at that airport." Given the time of day, Joe sounds surprisingly alert. "You won't believe where that plane is headed."

By "talk," does he mean needles under nails or just waterboarding? I don't interrupt him to ask since what's about to follow must be extremely important, and I don't want to have a "talk" with him myself.

"Where?" I ask, trying to sound calm. "I know it didn't get there yet, so it must be really far."

"It's going to—"

A blast of noise that sounds like a computer notification cranked to the level of an air siren drowns out his words.

To avoid going deaf, I raise my hands to cover my ears. My phone slips out of my hands. My heart in my throat, I watch Precious hit the tile floor with a bang and shatter into little pieces. Glass from the phone flies everywhere, and a shard punctures my bare calf.

I stare at it, wanting to reject what I just witnessed. My phone is supposed to be impact proof.

Suddenly, I'm standing there again, not holding my ears, and the phone is inexplicably back in my hand. The pain in my calf is gone too, but the noise is still assaulting my eardrums.

Given how holding my ears turned out, I don't repeat the action. Instead, I tightly clutch the phone. Needless to say, it doesn't fall and I don't get cut.

The noise abruptly stops.

"Location application execution halted," a mechanical voice says, booming loudly enough to have come from Zeus or some other thunder deity.

Through the fugue of confusion, I understand what happened, or at least part of it.

The horrendous noise was from the alarm Ada coded as per my

request. I asked for it to be hard to ignore, and she made sure of that. This means the noise brings good news.

Mom must've blipped on the app's radar.

The second thing that happened, which I'm a bit less sure about, tempers the flood of relief. What was the deal with the phone falling out of my hand, breaking, and then being back in my hand, unbroken? Am I going crazy? Because that felt like jumping back in time.

Then I recall Ada's warning about pre-cog events. She said something about seeing events that her simulated brain regions anticipated, so that must've been my first episode. Maybe the brain-boost regions realized I might drop the phone if I grabbed my ears the way I'd been about to do and gave the biological brain the input, which got turned into a vision of what might happen. Just like Ada explained, this wasn't a psychic prediction, but more of a forecast, and a faulty one at that, since my phone is impact resistant.

"Are you there?" Joe demands from the phone's speaker.

"I'm here," I say, trying to catch my breath. "I'm sorry, Joe, I almost dropped my phone. Where did you say Mom is?"

"Fucking Russia," Joe grits out.

I nearly drop my phone again, or for the first time—or whatever the proper terminology is, given that pre-cog moment.

The last thing I expected was for my mom to be in Russia. Then again, given how long the flight took, it does fit.

"Where in Russia?" I ask, sounding hollow.

"I just found out it's in Russia. I have no fucking clue where specifically." Joe's words are clipped.

My heart sinks deeper.

Russia has the largest area in the world. It's just shy of being double the size of the US. My mom is not a needle, but a grain of sand in a haystack.

Then I remember the alarm and say, "Thanks for letting me know. I was just working on a way to track her on my end, and if I'm lucky, I might have a clearer fix on her location."

"Oh?"

I do my best to describe what Ada and I cooked up with the app. After I finish, Joe asks a few surprisingly insightful follow-up questions. He ends with, "Sounds promising. Go get the data and call me back right away."

The line disconnects, which I guess is Joe's version of goodbye.

I stare at the bathroom mirror in confusion.

My face looks just as swollen, but the pain is more tolerable today. I feel it now that I'm focusing on it, but not as intensely as yesterday.

"Russia?" I ask my bruised reflection. "Really?"

I'm not my grandparents, in that I don't practice their reverse anti-Semitism. Having said that, if I were ever guilty of disliking a country wholesale, that country might be Russia. I mean you don't escape with a refugee status the way we did without developing some irrational—and maybe even rational—negative attitudes.

Thinking about it more, I realize I don't dislike Russians, and I have plenty of Russian friends whom I respect. I also find many famous Russian people admirable and very likable. I guess disliking a country can, paradoxically, be different from disliking its people.

"Mike?" Ada says groggily from down the hall. "The alarm went off."

This is when I realize a ringing is coming from somewhere else. I guess Ada didn't take any chances. Besides the crazy alarm going off in my head, she also created something external to make sure she'd know when the app did its job.

"Coming," I yell. "Can you put the GPS coordinates onto the map, like you did before?"

"On it," she shouts back. "Come to my office when you're done in there. I left out a toothbrush for you last night, in case you didn't notice."

I look at the edge of the sink and confirm there's indeed a sealed toothbrush there, the type dentists give out after a cleaning.

I quickly prioritize and use the toilet first; then I wash my hands and brush my teeth.

I don't bother dressing and leave the bathroom wearing only my boxers so I can quickly learn what the app found out. I do bring Precious with me, though, just in case.

"You'll never believe this," Ada says when I enter her office.

I don't share what I already know, hoping against all hope that Ada says my mom is in Russia, but that Russia happens to be an oddly named town in Florida. It's not impossible—Florida has a city called St. Petersburg and another one called Odessa.

"This"—she taps the screen that's zoomed in on an image of a small airport—"is in Podmoskovye... as in Moscow Oblast... as in Moscow in *Russia*."

The tiny hope bubble bursts, and I feel the need to sit down.

"My cousin just called," I say and grab onto the back of Ada's chair. "His findings corroborate this."

She looks at me worriedly. "You should eat something. You're too pale. At least the parts that aren't purple."

"I'll be fine," I say, my injuries aching at the reminder. "What else did the logs reveal?"

"The cell service in Russia isn't compatible with Brainocytes," Ada says. "But that isn't a shock, since we didn't exactly expect these things to go roaming in the alpha stage of the project."

The cell service we currently use belongs to a company in Mitya's portfolio, and they don't have any cell towers in Russia.

"We can fix this with something like a firmware update," Ada says, "but only after I do some coding on my end and if your mom is on Wi-Fi, which she isn't right now. The log is full of connection attempts, and once she does connect to Wi-Fi, we'll get a new data point. Problem is, they must have fewer public Wi-Fi points in that part of Russia, or she's outside civilization at the moment."

"Of course she's outside civilization," I mumble. "She's in Russia."

"This is all the data we have." Ada brings up a map with a single dot. "She got onto Wi-Fi here." She points at a place on the map.

The town is called Khimki, and the street is named Babakina. On the satellite view, I see gray Soviet-era buildings and a forest in the middle of the town. The public Wi-Fi my mom joined appears to be coming from a school imaginatively named "Number 2."

"That's something," I say, lifting my phone. "Let me call the detectives and give them all this information."

"Yeah," Ada says, "you do that, and I'll go make you a smoothie. Here, take my chair."

Ada leaves while I dial Detective Sawyer's number. He doesn't pick up, so I leave a voicemail describing the situation in detail.

It is only 7:00 a.m., which is on the early side for some people. I contemplate calling 911, but it might be too difficult to explain this emergency. Instead, I call Mitya and cross my fingers. If anyone can give me good advice, it's him.

"What?" Mitya sounds exactly the way he did back in the day after one of his all-nighters. "It's four in the morning."

"It's actually seven. You're on Eastern Standard Time now," I say, wishing I video-called him instead so I could see his expression. "I had to talk to you. I just learned more about Mom."

"Of course." Mitya sounds instantly awake. "What's up?"

I explain the situation, and as I expected, Mitya mutters curses when he learns where Mom is.

If I'm conflicted about my feelings toward Russia, Mitya is very secure in his open dislike of the place. As he told me in college, "You have to live there during your formative years to really get the taste of it."

I can't blame my friend. His bitterness is justified. When he finished the top lyceum in Russia, his parents sent him to get the rest of his education in the US, which is how we met. The Levin family was part of the emerging class of so-called New Russians— people who made their wealth after the fall of the Soviet Union. That status came at great peril, and before Mitya completed his junior year at MIT, he learned of his parents' murder. He doesn't like to talk about it, but the one time he did, he told me the reason he was gone a whole summer as a senior was because he went back to Russia—and now he can never go back there again. I presume he got some kind of revenge on his parents' killers, but I don't know for certain, and I'm not sure I want to know.

"The official route will be too slow," Mitya says after running out of choice words—a process that took a while since he moved from English cuss words to Russian, a language that prides itself on its rich profanity.

"So what do I do?" I ask, afraid I already know what he'll suggest and preemptively dreading it.

"I think you should go there yourself," Mitya says.

"Yeah?" Coldness spreads throughout my body, as though I'm in a Russian winter. "I don't know anyone there. What can I actually do?"

"I know someone there who can help you," Mitya says. "His name is Sasha, though he prefers to go by Alex. You might've heard of him. His last name is Voynskiy."

"As in Alexander Voynskiy?" I ask, not hiding my shock. "The one guy who's actually richer than you?"

"That's not a fact," Mitya says dismissively. "Have you seen the ruble-to-dollar conversion rate lately? With all the sanctions and embargoes, it's pretty bad."

I try to recall everything I've heard about the eccentric Russian. Aside from Mitya, who might come close, we don't really have Voynskiy's equivalent here in the States, but I guess he's like Steve Jobs, Bill Gates, Mark Zuckerberg, and Jeff Bezos all rolled into one. I heard that like Ray Kurzweil, one of Ada's heroes, Voynskiy takes a hundred and fifty supplements per day, some intravenously.

"I don't know," I say. "I mean, it's Russia."

"We both know you'd go to hell for your mom," Mitya says. "This is just a little worse."

"The center of hell in *Dante's Inferno* was very cold." I laugh, but there's no mirth in it.

"Luckily for you, it's summer, so unless she's in Siberia, you'll be warm," Mitya says.

"But how—"

"I'll arrange it for you," my friend says. "My jet can make the flight if it stops to refuel."

"When—"

"I'll need a couple of hours. Will that be enough?"

"I guess." I try not to sound as overwhelmed as I feel. "But don't I need visas and stuff?"

"I have a pricey team of lawyers who can do all the paperwork. I also know whom to bribe in Russia, and even in the US if need be. Don't worry. At the airport where you'll land, you can bring anyone to and from Russia, no questions asked. Hell, you can even kidnap some Russian citizens—say, the culprits—and bring them here, and my guys will still figure out a way to get them into the country, even if we have to issue them each an H-1B visa and give them a bullshit job at one of my companies."

I swallow. "What about talking to the authorities?"

"Do it from the cab or let your uncle handle it," Mitya says. "Don't worry. Ada and I can support you from here, and I promise to pull some strings with my connections in the government, as well as the media. Is your mom a US citizen?"

"Yeah, for many years now. You should've seen her study for that test."

"Good," he says. "That will help if the American government needs to get involved. I'll also contact my friends in the media, so the headlines will be screaming about US citizens being kidnapped and brought to Russia. The pressure will be on."

"Fine." I'm beginning to accept my fate. "Let me ring my cousin so I can let him know all this."

"Your cousin? You mean the psycho you told me about?"

I sigh. "Do yourself a favor and never call him that to his face. But yeah, that one."

"All right," Mitya says. "I'll text you where to go and meet you there."

"Thanks. I might run out of collectible items to repay you with pretty soon."

"Don't mention it," Mitya says. "See you soon."

I close my eyes and bring up AROS. The green box icon that represents text messaging dings with the address Mitya promised.

I dismiss AROS and realize I'm feeling a little different today. My mind is clear, as though I had a bunch of coffee and a ton of sleep—except I had neither. Maybe the intelligence boost is kicking in? I'll have to check with Ada about that.

Unable to delay the unpleasant task any longer, I call Joe and tell him what's going on.

"Your friend's right," Joe says. "We need to get there as soon as possible."

I nearly drop my phone for the third time today.

"What do you mean, *we*?" I try to sound casual.

"I mean I'm obviously going to Russia to get my aunt," my cousin says. "And it sounds like you're going too. Therefore, *we*."

TWENTY-TWO

I HOLD THE PHONE IN SILENCE FOR A MOMENT, THEN SAY, "OKAY, Joe. Let me text you the address."

"Good," he says and hangs up.

Stunned, I make my way to Ada's kitchen.

Only the sight of Ada in her PJs takes me out of my daze. Well, that and the sight of Mr. Spock sitting on the counter.

I think I see recognition in the rat's eyes. He even seems friendly. If he could talk, I bet he'd say, "Hey, I know you. We've slept together."

"Take this," Ada says and hands me a gigantic plastic cup with something thick and green inside.

I sip the liquid gingerly and get hit with a surprisingly refreshing taste. The liquid is cold, sweet, and exactly what I needed.

"Yum," I say after I swallow my third icy gulp. "It tastes a lot like a milkshake. What's in it?"

"Frozen banana, silken tofu, and a little spinach for color." Ada pours herself another cup and looks me over approvingly.

I follow her gaze and remember I'm only wearing boxers.

Oh well. Since she doesn't seem to mind, I decide I'll get

dressed after breakfast. I tell her what I've learned, concluding with the fact that Joe will be accompanying me on this trip to Russia.

"I can see why you don't want Joe joining you," she says. "But I think he might actually be of some help. His job is providing people with security, after all. What I don't get is your problem with visiting Russia." Ada takes a small sip of her green drink. "I'd love to see Russia if I could."

"You're not going," I say firmly, in case she was hinting at it.

"Of course not. I need to provide backup, and I'm best equipped to do that here," Ada says. "It still doesn't explain what your problem with Russia is."

"How can I explain it to you?" I savor my drink and say, "Picture every Russian movie villain."

Ada demonstratively closes her eyes and smiles.

Taking that to mean she's using her imagination like I instructed, I continue. "So, I bet you're picturing a Russian drug lord, or a weapons dealer, or a crazed Soviet spy, or an ex-military mercenary—"

"Actually"—Ada's eyes open, glinting amber in the morning light—"I was thinking of the guys who kidnapped and threatened to cannibalize the yellow M&M candy in that Super Bowl commercial."

"You know, that 'Boris the Bullet Dodger' actor in the ad is actually Croatian. His Russian was barely coherent during his monologue, but yeah, that'll work as far as the point I'm trying to make. Now, take that guy and his crew and picture all these villains multiplied millions of times and located in a spot roughly double the size of NYC."

"Okay." Ada's tone is serious, but her eyes roll slightly upward.

"You now have Moscow in your mind's eye."

"Sure I do. I can trust you, the guy who hasn't visited the motherland since the early nineties."

She has a semi-decent point. I don't watch Russian movies or shows like Mom does, and I haven't read a book in Russian for two decades. As a result, I don't have a clue what's really going on in Russia, outside of American news, and they definitely put a spin on things. So I know the picture I painted for Ada might be irrational, but it doesn't change how I feel.

"I hope you're right," I tell her. "And even if you're not, it's not like I have much choice."

"If it's as bad as you think, it's even more important that you get your mom back as soon as possible."

Either Ada's words or the air conditioning makes me shiver, so I say, "I'll go get dressed."

"Me too, and then I'll prep a bunch of stuff for you to take with," Ada says and reaches inside her fridge.

I leave to go put on some clothes, and by the time I return to the kitchen, Ada has already changed out of her PJs and is holding a backpack. She's wearing skinny jeans and a t-shirt with an internet meme on it. The meme is of Patrick Stewart next to a quote that says, "Use the force, Harry," with an attribution to Gandalf.

"This is for you." Ada hands me the backpack. "I made you sandwiches for the flight and also put in some items that might aid in your brain development."

I take the backpack, thank Ada, and together, we leave her apartment. As we walk down a flight of stairs, I mentally activate Einstein and ask him to get us a car on Uber.

The car arrives a minute after we exit the building, and I get to play the gentleman once again by holding the door open for Ada.

"I'll work on a few apps for you," Ada says and whips out her laptop as the car pulls into traffic. "You should make sure to set up a mobile hotspot on your phone, and double-check you'll have cell coverage in Russia. This way, your Brainocytes will be able to connect to the internet through your phone."

Appreciating Ada's advice, I spend the next twenty minutes sorting out my phone. The whole process feels like it takes hours, but in the end, I'm satisfied. I even surprise the otherwise uncaring customer service rep by telling him their outrageous roaming prices are "fair enough."

Once I'm done, I look over Ada's shoulder to see what she's coding.

After I watch for a while, I can't help mumbling, "That's even less readable than before. How's it going to pass code review?"

"You can review the code on the plane if you want. Since this is just a little video game I'm writing for your entertainment, the review is optional," Ada says without looking away from her laptop. "Tell me something, does Russia have the same expression about looking a gift horse in the mouth?"

"There's a mare and teeth in the proverb, but yeah, there's something like that," I say. "Do you mind if I keep watching?"

"Why do you think I'm not writing this in my head?" she responds via a mental text message. "I want to encourage you to be able to do this for yourself someday."

"Thanks," I mentally type back.

My focus on Ada's work is so intense I don't notice the car stopping and get startled when the driver coughs to get our attention.

We're standing by an airport entrance gate. After a call to Mitya, we're escorted to a special golf cart that takes us to the plane.

Before today, I've only seen Mitya's custom version of the Boeing 747 on his Facebook page. Driving up to it now, I'm amazed at its sleekness and size. I've always pictured something smaller, but this is almost as big as a commercial jet.

My admiration is interrupted when Ada closes her laptop and says, "Okay, I finished and loaded the game into your AROS environment."

"Thanks," I say and resume gawking at the airplane.

When we stop moving, I get out of the vehicle and run into yet another surprise.

My cousin is already here.

"Hey, Joe," I say as Ada and I walk up to him. "How did you get through security?"

Joe doesn't respond, his lizard eyes boring a hole into something over my shoulder.

I follow his gaze and see a posh limo pulling up. It must be an electric, because I didn't hear it arrive at all. "It's probably my friend Mitya," I say. "This is his plane."

Joe crosses his arms over his chest and watches the limo with the same determined mistrust.

When the door opens, it's indeed Mitya who gets out.

I approach and reluctantly give him a Russian-style man hug, a gesture I reserve for close friends I haven't seen in a while. "Good to see you, man. Sorry we won't get a chance to hang out face to face."

Mitya assures me we'll get to chill once I return, and I make the introductions. Ignoring my cousin's suspicious glare, Mitya asks his driver to take my backpack up to the plane, but I protest, saying I'm still capable of carrying twenty pounds strapped to my back.

As we walk up the fancy airstairs, I can tell by Mitya's eager stride that he wants to show off his pimped-out air ride.

The place doesn't disappoint. We pass a high-tech 3D movie theater setup and a huge collection of parachutes and wingsuits. After he shows them off, Mitya leads us past uber-comfortable beds and lets us park our butts on couches that look twenty times more expensive than what I have in my apartment—and I splurged.

Happy his efforts to impress us succeeded, Mitya really pushes it by hollering for the two stewardesses who will accompany us on the flight. The women come out wearing cutesy uniforms that emphasize their ridiculously long legs and model-like facial symmetry.

I notice Ada frowning at them, but I don't feel comfortable reassuring her she has nothing to worry about, in case she's feeling jealous. They're not my type—not that it makes a difference, since I only have one woman on my mind these days, and that's Ada. Besides, if she was going to worry, it should be about the Russian girls I'll meet once I step off the plane. I've heard crazy stories of debauchery from almost everyone who's gone to Russia. In fact, I know men who go to Russia primarily for the effect they have on the country's female population. Vic, one of the analysts at my fund, got married to a Russian girl while visiting there—a girl who's so out of his league the rest of us are convinced she just wants him for his green card.

"Any problem with the Wi-Fi?" Mitya asks when Joe and I take our seats.

"Nope, all set," I mentally text him.

Mitya's phone plays Black Sabbath's "Iron Man" intro as his text notification. He looks at it and says, "Ada, can I get the Brain-ocytes as soon as we're done? Mike just convinced me I'd give my left kidney to have them."

"Sure," she says. "We'll need to get the backups first, but afterwards, we can do that. I assume you know or have access to a nurse?"

"No problem. Anything you need." Mitya pushes his power specs farther up his nose with his middle finger, a gesture that someone might mistake for getting flipped off. "Okay, Mike, anything you want to discuss before we leave?"

I'm tempted to tell Mitya in Russian to keep his grubby paws off Ada, but since she understands Russian now, I'd only sound like a jealous idiot, so I opt for something more practical.

"I have some app ideas that'll be useful when we're in Russia, particularly this gun app I have in mind," I say. "Can you guys help me out by developing these apps once Mitya gets what he wants?"

They wholeheartedly agree, and I feel a tiny spurt of guilt mixed with relief. The big coding project I gave them is, in part, to keep them busy so they don't get too chummy with each other. The rational part of me trusts Mitya. He knows I like Ada and wouldn't stab me in the back. However, the irrational, primitive part of me thinks no one can resist Ada. Either way, the apps will be useful, and if the request has the added bonus of girl-theft prevention, that's just gravy.

"So this is goodbye," Ada says as she comes up to me.

She looks like she wants a hug, so I stand up to give her one. I usually find this type of human interaction a little uncomfortable, but since it's Ada, I might actually enjoy it.

Ada glances at the blond stewardess, then at me, and then she suddenly rises on her tiptoes. She's looking directly into my eyes, and I feel like a fly caught in amber.

Ada's lips touch mine.

TWENTY-THREE

I HAVE TO ADMIT, UNTIL THIS VERY MOMENT, I FULLY EXPECTED something like a peck on the cheek. As I savor the reality of Ada's lips on mine, my eyes threaten to jump out of my head.

In contrast, Ada's eyes are closed, the skin around them creased in smile lines.

I return the kiss, noting she tastes like a strawberry vanilla milkshake. This is odd, since she's a vegan who avoids dairy. More random thoughts like that fly through my mind. I wonder if this kiss is how Ada always says goodbye to her friends. As unlikely as it is, there are precedents. In the Russian culture, even men will sometimes smooch each other on the lips. Brezhnev, the communist leader when I was a little kid, was famous for it.

I almost send Ada a mental message asking, "What does this mean?" but I'm glad I refrain, because at that moment, Ada's tiny tongue locates mine, dispelling any illusion that this is some kind of platonic gesture.

I close my eyes and enjoy the kiss. However, my Zen quickly turns into something primal as blood rushes from my head into other parts.

Somewhere far away, I hear someone, I assume Mitya, chuckle

uncomfortably, and I realize my hand found its way onto Ada's bottom—and might be grabbing said bottom demonstratively.

Grudgingly, Ada and I part. Her face is flushed, and I imagine mine would be too if it weren't purple from all the bruises.

"We have to head out," I say hoarsely, my tone apologetic.

I hear a chime indicating a mental text arrival. It's from Ada, and it says, "To be continued."

"Let's go," Mitya says and leads Ada off the plane. Mitya's butler/driver bows and follows his employer.

I take a seat next to Joe. He reaches into his jeans pocket and takes out a small box with medicine.

"Ambien." He pops two pills into his palm and extends his hand to me.

Since I just woke up about an hour ago, I'm tempted to refuse the sleeping pills. However, I might change my mind mid-flight, so I take them and say, "Thanks."

Not wasting his breath on niceties like "you're welcome," or even a shrug, Joe dry swallows his pill and closes his eyes.

I pocket mine and spend a few minutes speccing out the apps I want my friends to work on. When I finish the email, I decide to check out the game Ada wrote for me, hoping it'll distract me from the departure—my least favorite part of air travel, aside from turbulence, landing, and being in the sky in general.

Closing my eyes, I bring up the AROS interface. The new icon is vaguely familiar. I launch it, and as soon as I hear the music, I recognize the game. I probably should've known it from the code I glimpsed.

The music is a Russian folk song called "Korobeiniki." I've heard it performed with the original lyrics about a thousand times as a kid. Now, though, since Gameboy borrowed the song for this game, it's much more famous and familiar to me as the theme for Tetris. I guess Ada thought a game originally developed in Russia while I was growing up would be a fitting gift for my trip back to the motherland.

A three-dimensional rectangle appears in my field of vision, reminiscent of the typical playfield in Tetris, except it's as big as the Empire State Building. The tetriminos—the pieces in Tetris—are the size of gas tankers as they fall from the top at speeds approaching fifty miles per hour. Though all this looks three-dimensional, I can only manipulate the tetrimino across the same axes as regular Tetris. The scope, colors, and movement are way over the top, and I think I prefer playing the game on my phone. Still, this just demonstrates the videogame potential of the tech—not that I had any doubts about that.

On the bright side, my scores are the best I've ever gotten, though I can't tell if it's from the intelligence boost or just a side effect of controlling the game with my mind, which is obviously more efficient. Another bonus is that I indeed missed the departure.

I write Ada a thank-you email in my head, dismiss AROS, and open the backpack she gave me to see what else I can find to entertain myself.

At the very top of the pile is a Rubik's Cube. I guess Ada really wants me to play with geometric shapes today. The cube is an interesting coincidence. Mom brought one, or its Soviet knockoff, on our momentous trip to the United States. I remember this because I was so bored on the flight that I decided to give the puzzle a shot, a decision I regretted after a few hours. Solving the cube intuitively requires patience, and patience was an alien concept to me as a teen. Now, though, I hope I can do better since I'm around the same age Mom was on our trip to America—a mind-boggling fact in itself.

I take the cube and begin twisting it.

An hour later, I decide that solving this thing intuitively will take way too long, and I still don't have the necessary patience. Bringing up my trusty mental browser, I search "speed cubing." I quickly learn it's possible to solve the cube in under a minute. Intrigued, I read some more and learn the most popular method for solving the cube is called the Fridrich method, sometimes referred to as CFOP. It's perfect for my purposes, since you only have to use intuition to make the cross on the bottom of your cube. After that, thinking is reduced, and you rely more heavily on pattern recognition and muscle memory. Though I don't know which skill sets got boosted for me, if any, pattern recognition should be the most basic thing to improve, since that's what brains are best at in general.

Following a cheat sheet from one of the websites, I solve the cube in ten minutes for the first time in my life. A few solves later, I halve my time. Eventually, I can do it in four minutes, but my hands ache so much I'm forced to stop.

Massaging my hands, I come to the depressing conclusion that speed-solving the cube won't tell me whether my intelligence got boosted, a question I'm pondering more and more.

I reach into the backpack, hoping Ada packed something I can use to better gauge my new and improved mental skills.

I quickly come across a manila folder, on which Ada neatly wrote "Tests" with a thick black sharpie. I take the folder out and spread its contents on the cushion next to me. As the label suggested, I find a slew of tests that include the SAT, the GRE, the MCAT, and a bunch more I don't even recognize.

I grab a pencil and the SAT test, figuring it could be useful since I can look up my old score for comparison. Then again, I scored very high to get into MIT, so my boosted intelligence doesn't have much wiggle room to show off.

I take the test, minus the essay. My first shock is how long it takes me to finish. I initially figured time flew by because I was busy, but as it turns out, it took me less than two hours to complete the test, which is nearly half the time you're given. The second shock is how many questions I messed up.

None. I made zero errors.

My test score to get into MIT was very good, but I still got a couple of English questions wrong, as well as a math one. What's key is that I took the SAT after my mom convinced me to take a year of Kaplan prep courses, which really helped, despite the SAT allegedly being an aptitude test.

So did I do so well because of Ada's boost? It sure looks that way. I understand my English score might've naturally improved over time; after all, I've been in this country longer now and learned my second language on a deeper level. A better math score is trickier to explain. If anything, I expected it to drop since I haven't used any math outside of tip calculations since my last calculus class back in college. When I do have to calculate something more complicated, I resort to Excel, the calculator app, Mathematica, and other similar tools. Yet instead of dropping, my math score improved. Then again, it only improved by one question, so I could argue that the one question I screwed up in high school was a fluke and not statistically significant anyway.

The solution is obvious: I need to disable the brain boost and take another SAT.

Hesitantly, I mentally click the brain-looking app icon and examine myself. I think I'm the same, but it's hard to tell right away.

I grab another SAT test, and as soon as I read my first math question, I can tell things won't go as well for me this time around. I find it difficult to concentrate on the question, and I have a hard time caring about solving the problem. I push through my reluctance and do my best to focus.

Halfway through the math section, I decide I've had enough. The English section doesn't fare much better, and I only end up doing about a quarter of the questions. This, in itself, proves something about the boost.

When I check my answers, it turns out I messed up three math questions and a whopping six English questions. So the boost is real and can, at the very least, have an impact on tests.

I bring AROS back up and enable the boost.

This time, I can actually feel the difference in my state of being. It's subtle, but my surroundings seem more solid, the edges of objects sharper and all the colors brighter. It might be an illusion, but I also feel as though I understand certain things that previously eluded me. I have a eureka moment when I think back to that tricky math question I stumbled on a few minutes ago. It's obvious to me now that a silo consists of a cylinder and two cones.

Another difference is that I no longer feel that strange mental fatigue when it comes to intellectual pursuits. To test out that theory, I decide now is a good time to do a little programming.

I mentally open Ada's pet IDE program and spend the next few hours reading the necessary documentation and mucking around with it. Once I feel up to it, I start writing my first AROS application.

The result is just a few lines, most of them dedicated to including the right API libraries. Still, I feel a glimmer of pride when I mentally press the compile icon and don't get any error messages. I build the app and send it into my head space.

A gray icon appears in my apps list, and I launch it.

A text window shows up in the air in front of me, just for a fraction of a second. I grin as I glance at its message. Honoring the tradition of all introductory programming tasks, it boldly states, "Hello, World."

I'll be the first to admit that the utility of the program is nonexistent. Still, it's a step toward almost literally expanding my own mind.

I check out the MCAT test next and decide I could do very well on it, especially if I cheat by Googling all the biological facts and other things beyond my educational background. Since I can do the searches lightning fast in my head, I could probably get a super-high score within the time limit. I don't actually take the MCAT, though, because I'm getting tired and hungry from all this mental work.

I contemplate summoning the stewardess but decide to check Ada's backpack first, since she said she packed me some sandwiches.

It takes me a second to spot the cardboard box at the bottom. As I pull it out, I notice there's a strange heft to it.

I place it comfortably on my lap and open the lid. I'm lucky I can't drop the box now, because if I could, I probably would have.

Two very non-hungry pink eyes stare up at me from inside the box.

TWENTY-FOUR

"MR. SPOCK?" I SAY, SPOTTING THE PINK STRIPE ON THE WHITE RAT staring up at me from the box. Inside is some sort of veggie wrap with a couple of rat bites in it. "What the hell are you doing here?"

Mr. Spock's whiskers move back and forth, and his perceptive little eyes seem to say, "What does it look like? I had some lunch and now I'm chillin'."

Taking out my phone, I get onto the plane's Wi-Fi and video-conference Ada.

"Mike?" she says. "I see you're using your phone like a person without Brainocytes."

"I need the camera so I can show you this." I point my phone at the box.

"Mr. Spock?" Ada sounds more incredulous than I feel, an impressive feat given how shocked I was to find the stowaway. "Baby, what the hell are you doing there?"

"That's what I asked him a second ago," I say. "But I didn't call him baby."

Ada looks distant for a moment. "He's not scared. Best I can make sense of this is he likes you. Likes you enough to decide to go with you."

"How do you know how he feels?" I study the rat, wondering how he'd look if he was scared, or, for that matter, how he'd look if he liked me. "You don't think he came with me by accident? I mean, he ate the food you prepared for me. Maybe he was in the box when—"

"I get where you're going with this, but I highly doubt it," Ada says. "I can review his data in a bit, but I think he followed you willingly."

I look at Ada and then at the rat, hoping one of them will explain what she's talking about. Neither of them enlightens me, so I ask, "What data? How does a rat have data?"

"Okay, please don't judge me." Ada bites her lip. "It has to do with experiments I've been performing on my little darlings. More specifically, with the apps I'm running inside and outside their heads. These things are easier to implement in rats since their brains are extremely well studied and simpler to boot, plus their privacy is less of a concern."

"I'm not judging," I say when I see how distraught she looks.

"The data I mentioned is what I collect from Mr. Spock's sensorium. I store everything he and the others see and hear. I even have access to their whiskers' perception—"

"You can see everything the rats see?"

"Yes, and I can map out their basic emotions, as well as some of their bodily needs," Ada says. "And I have a way of communicating with them that's better than using verbal commands. I can also control their behavior using Augmented Reality constructs —"

"Wait, what?" I look at Mr. Spock again. "You created Virtual Reality for rats?"

"No. Though I could, in theory, create VR for them, I only augment their reality. For example, I can make them see the walls of a maze that isn't there. The tech is very similar to the way you see the AROS icons. This way, I can get them to run where I want them to, though I don't use it since they're now bright enough to avoid trouble on their own. Their brain boosts are far more advanced than ours—"

Ada keeps talking, but I don't hear her. Dread grips me, and it's not because I've had an animal rights activist awaken inside me. The Brainocyte technology is in its infancy, but Ada's already implemented the basics for perfect surveillance, as well as mind reading—not to mention mind control. All this would be very scary if done to a human brain instead of a rat's.

"—in any case, we are where we are," I hear Ada say when I bring my attention back to her. "Please, take care of Mr. Spock. I'll make sure to include some of the apps I mentioned to assist you."

"Of course," I say, shaking my head to clear the remnants of my paranoia. "Are you sure you don't want me to leave him here, on the plane?"

"No," Ada says. "Take him with you. He'll be lonely on his own or with strangers."

"Fine," I say. "I will. Now can you please explain why he's always chewing on something?" I point at Mr. Spock's jaw. It's moving up and down, and his nose is crinkling.

"He's just bruxing," Ada says. "He does it when he feels safe."

I mentally Google the word and find at least a dozen YouTube videos of rats serenely grinding their teeth.

Spock stops bruxing to clean his snout with his front paws.

"Okay, that's cute," I tell Ada. "But I hope he can hide. As cool as it would be to look like a pirate with a rat on my shoulder, the Russian people, or any people, might not understand."

"Mr. Spock," Ada says, her tone switching to baby talk. "Please hide in Mike's pocket."

Before I get a chance to raise any objections, the rat scurries up the side of the box into my lap. Then he jumps into my tweed jacket and hides inside the inner pocket.

"Wow," I say. "Can you give me the app that displays his emotions?"

"I'll get you that, along with one of the first apps Mitya and I put together for your trip," Ada says and closes her eyes—I presume to work with her AROS.

The world around me flickers in that signature AROS-update fashion. I bring up all the icons and see a couple of new ones.

"The one that looks like a mood ring is the one I call EmoRat," Ada says. "Try it."

I enable the icon, but nothing happens.

"Mr. Spock," Ada says soothingly. "Come out for a second so we can see you."

Spock peeks his head out from his hiding place. There's a subtle green aura around his head, like a halo.

"The basics are the same as a mood ring," Ada says. "The highlights include green, for average wellbeing, blue-green for somewhat relaxed, solid blue for relaxed and calm, and violet for very happy. Just like with a mood ring, you want to avoid amber, which means he's unsettled, the gray of anxiety, and especially the tension of the black moods."

I use a notepad app to create a mental reminder for the rat mood colors and say, "I'll try to avoid those."

"Oh, and there's special emoticon-like stuff you'll sometimes see. Like this one"—a circle with a toilet in the middle shows up as a bubble over Mr. Spock's head—"means the little guy needs to go to the bathroom."

"Got it," I say gratefully and take Mr. Spock to the bathroom.

"Now for the next app," Ada says when I return. "I want you to strap on the camera I left in the bag for you."

I rummage through the bag and locate one of those GoPro chest setups for people who are into extreme sports. "You mean this harness?"

"Yeah, that getup is to make sure Mitya and I can see what you see and hear what you hear," Ada explains. "Since you're a human being and not a rat, I figured you'd prefer a camera. I didn't realize you'd have Mr. Spock with you. The camera's less important now, since I can hear your surroundings through his ears, and if he peeks out of your pocket, I'll see through his eyes. But having him peek out could be problematic, and since we coded the camera solution already, we might as well test it out. So please, put that on."

I carefully take off my jacket and put on the harness.

"I probably look ridiculous," I say as I put the jacket back on without buttoning it.

Mr. Spock pops his head out to check what's happening. I think he decides I indeed look ridiculous, because his color changes from anxious to relaxed.

"You look fine," Ada says. "Now, launch the camera icon and the one that looks like an angel."

I locate the two icons and enable them one after the other.

"Awesome," Ada says from both my phone and to my right. "I can see through the camera and hear the roar of the plane."

I look toward the new source of her voice and nearly drop my phone again.

A small figure is floating in the air to my right. She looks like Ada—if Ada were ten times smaller and dressed as a Valentine's Day cherub. She has a halo, a white toga, and a pair of wings. Only the bow and arrows are missing.

"What's happening?" I ask.

"It's an Augmented Reality interface," the angelic Ada says, and I confirm that her voice is coming from the creature's mouth. "I can hear you through the camera just fine."

I study her closer and realize her outfit and facial expressions aren't as realistic as in the video conference. Still, they're pretty darn good, especially for a 3D hologram or whatever the proper term is.

"This is far too sophisticated even for you guys to have put together in a few hours." I try grabbing the flying Ada, but, obviously, my hand goes through her.

"Have you heard of Centaur censors?" Ada asks.

I nod, things already becoming clearer. She's talking about Mitya's company that developed special cameras optimized for reading facial expressions.

"Well, we combined it with something he still has in development and voilà." Ada flies a circle around me. "I can control the avatar with my mind, like a video game, but the facial features work via the Centaur interface and mimic mine."

Punctuating her point, she winks at me and licks her lips salaciously.

"Please don't do that," I say. "My mind just got flooded with the weirdest imagery."

"Oh." Ada's expression becomes foxlike. "If Mitya wasn't sitting next to me and privy to this conversation, I'd put worse ideas into your head."

"But I'm here," Mitya says from a distance. "So stop it. Now."

"Okay," Ada says with a pout. "I guess it's only fair for you to launch the little devil icon. And while you're at it, launch that instant messenger icon that looks like a tiny penguin wearing pince-nez."

I launch the icon and hear Mitya say from my left, "Before you ask, that instant messenger is based on Pidgin—"

"Dude," I interrupt, looking to my left. "Do you really think *that*'s what I was going to ask about?"

On my left, I see Mitya, only like Ada, he's ten times smaller than normal. Also like her, he's floating in the air and has wings that aren't actually beating. The difference is that Mitya looks like a little red devil with hoofed feet, horns, and a tail.

"Ada picked the theme," he says defensively. "I just kind of went with it."

"You guys are having way too much fun with this," I mutter and log in to the instant messenger, figuring I might as well test it out.

Making sure I have my friends added to my buddy list, I start a chat room and mentally type, "We can talk through this when I don't want people thinking I've gone totally insane."

"Sure," Ada says and flies closer to my right shoulder. "We'll play along with that deception if you want."

"I think she should've been the devil," Mitya says in Russian in the IM window. "That *Bedazzle* movie got the gender right."

"You look more natural when horny," Ada says out loud.

I snicker at Mitya's dumbstruck expression, then mentally type, "Ada learned Russian."

The angel giggles as the devil mutters Russian and English curses under his breath.

"So," I type into the chat, "what app are you working on next?"

"You guys already have a basic face recognition app," Mitya says out loud. "Your mom even used one. Ada is working on tweaking the app to pull data from a backend that Alex, the guy I mentioned earlier, provided. He helped us get access to Vkontakte and other popular Russian social network platforms, and he's now trying to get us access to all the major Russian criminal databases—a perk of having good connections."

Something clicks in my brain, but before I can say anything, Ada says, "I'll expand it to show you more data than what your mom would've had access to. Our work will take some time, and I think you should spend that time sleeping."

"She's right," Mitya says. "Eastern Standard is seven hours behind Moscow time. It'll be early morning when you land."

Crap. They're both right. I've been too busy to think about jetlag.

"My cousin gave me Ambien," I say.

"Take it," Mitya says at the same time as Ada says, "Be careful, those are addictive."

"Now you guys are getting into your roles," I say and push the button overhead to summon one of the hot stewardesses.

"I'm going to ask her for food and water," I find myself needing to explain to Ada.

In the distance, I see the blonder and longer-legged stewardess walk toward me with the grace of a ballerina.

"Just a reminder," Ada whispers next to my ear. "We can see and hear what you're doing."

I ignore Ada and make sure Mr. Spock is hidden as the woman approaches.

The stewardess gives me a thousand-watt smile. "How can I help you, Mr. Cohen?"

"I asked them to call him that," Mitya types inside the chat.

"Like he wasn't already full of himself," Ada responds.

They type more snarky remarks back and forth, but I ignore them as I ask about food and drink. This being Mitya's plane, I'm not surprised when the stewardess whips out a menu with obscene options that include escargot and lobster tails.

I choose a simple cheese sandwich and tomato juice for myself and a bag of trail mix and bottled water for Mr. Spock—without explaining there's a hungry rat in the equation. As the woman leaves to get the stuff, I have Ada teach me how to disable the mental app windows and icons I don't need, as well as how to disable her and Mitya's angel/devil avatars.

"Thanks," I say when I master the skill of manipulating the mental windows. "It's distracting having that stuff around when I'm talking to people, but I don't want to dismiss AROS entirely."

"I'm so jealous." Since I disabled his avatar, Mitya's voice is now disembodied. "I haven't even learned how to type with my mind yet."

An idea that was swirling in my brain since we talked about face recognition suddenly jells, and I excitedly type, "Mitya, this Russian database Alex provided for you, can we use it to look up the kidnappers?"

"Well, yeah," Mitya replies, "if you have a picture—"

"I have three." I forward the email my cousin sent me and cross my fingers.

"I got the images," Mitya says. "Running the first one now."

I'm on the verge of biting my nails when he says, "Sorry, the first one isn't working. Not enough of his face is showing for the algorithm to do its job." After a pause, he says, "Same problem with the second one."

I hold my breath because I know the ape-bison image is discernible.

"Finally," Mitya says. "This last one worked—and the first name is indeed Anton, as the nurse said. I'm looking at the data, and it's not pretty. You're lucky to be alive. I'm sending you the details."

In the silence that follows, I read the dossier on my new nemesis, whose full name is Anton Pintarev. His criminal career began when he murdered his elderly aunt, but because Anton was a minor at the time, he was sent to a special camp for violent underage criminals. According to what my mom told me about those institutions, they might as well have been called Crime Universities, especially since having a criminal record instantly disqualified you from active duty in the army and made it nearly impossible to find a job. Having a record was a more public affair in the Soviet Union than it is in the US. My understanding is that a criminal got a special stamp in his passport and an entry of "prison" in a special worker diary that functioned like a detailed resume back in that system. A year after Anton got out, he was promptly arrested for stabbing a man, tried as an adult, and placed in a real jail. When he was released in the post-Soviet Russia of the early nineties, he found himself in an environment where some of his unsavory skills were valuable, so he got to work and managed to avoid recapture and even thrive. There's a list of crimes he allegedly committed, but the authorities couldn't prove it was him.

As I read, my stomach churns with worry for my mom, because even if one percent of this list is true, she's in the company of a genuine monster. When I reach the graphic details about Alina Petrova, a fourteen-year-old Anton is believed to have brutally beaten, raped, and killed, I stop reading and take a couple of calming breaths.

"This is bad," I mentally type into the chat.

"I know," Mitya says. "But keep in mind, they need the people they took hostage, so your mom should be safe."

"Right," I murmur to myself. "Like Mrs. Sanchez was safe."

"Here you are," the stewardess says. I didn't even notice her approach, thanks in part to my dark mood. She pulls out the table expansion and sets down the tray with goodies. "Let me know if you need anything else."

"Thank you," I manage to say. "I will."

The sight of food lifts my spirits by a fraction.

"Tell her you want her to stop flirting," Ada says in a very un-angelic tone. I'm not sure if she's serious or trying to get my mind off Anton's file.

"Victoria gives an outstanding shoulder rub," Mitya says, staying in his devil character. "She's also an expert—ouch!"

Ada's angel avatar doesn't show it, but I bet Ada either kicked or punched Mitya in the real world. Somehow, even that kind of touch makes me jealous, which is ironic since jealousy led to Ada hitting him in the first place.

In an effort to reassure my friends I'm fine, and to take my mind off Anton, I type into the chat, "All right, kids, tell me about the other apps you're going to write."

Ada and Mitya give me the rundown as I start in on my meal.

"I have an idea outside the apps you requested," Mitya says as I chase down the sandwich with a gulp of tomato juice. "I think I can improve on Ada's brain boost stuff by creating a scheduling algorithm that would allow the three of us to better utilize the STRELA servers."

He proceeds to explain his idea, which reminds me of when I took the Operating Systems course back at MIT. In that course, the hardest part was learning about the clever ways people come up with for sharing limited computer resources. Those resources can be shared between processes running on the system, or, more applicable to our server problem, cleverly allocated between different human users so the users are unaware they're sharing anything at all.

"We should be able to test it on my babies first," Ada says toward the end. "Once we do, keep an eye out for any oddities in Mr. Spock's behavior."

"Great," I say disingenuously. I can tell she's impressed with Mitya's smarts, and I don't like it. "If you don't mind, I'm going to take my pill."

"Good day—or night," Mitya says.

I take my Ambien and give Mr. Spock his food and water.

As the rat eats, I decide to take a Percocet for the pain as well—no need for mental acuity while I'm sleeping.

Feeling properly medicated, I navigate my way to Amazon and use their cloud eBook app to do a bit of reading. I want to get the horrors of the dossier out of my head to avoid another nightmare. It only takes me a few chapters to realize that reading this way is yet another revolution the Brainocytes will bring to personal entertainment.

About ten minutes into the book, my lids grow heavy. I don't fight the drowsiness, opting instead to dismiss AROS altogether and close my eyes.

Despite my earlier attempt to chase away the bad thoughts, my sleep is interrupted by horrific dreams that feature Anton Pintarev committing atrocities against Mom and me.

TWENTY-FIVE

I WAKE UP SLOWLY. IT TAKES ME A MINUTE TO REMEMBER I'M ON A plane and to realize that the motion I'm feeling doesn't mean my bed decided to move on its own.

Actually, for a plane, the ride does feel rather bumpy.

I open my eyes to a surprise. Instead of flying in a plane, I'm riding in a car. At least that explains the shaking—Russian roads are infamously bad.

I reach into my pocket to check on Mr. Spock and feel reassured when he gently nibbles on my finger. Satisfied I didn't lose the rat, I look around.

I'm in the back seat, and there's a gigantic bald woman sitting next to me—or at least I assume she's a woman based on her semi-feminine round features and D-size bosom. She's staring intently at the neck of an unfamiliar black-haired guy sitting in the front passenger seat. The only person I recognize is Joe, who's sitting behind the wheel.

In the back window, far in the distance, I see the airport I assume we landed at. On either side of the road is a bucolic Russian landscape, with its signature birch trees, oaks, and some pines. I spot a red squirrel climbing a tree—a sight that finally evokes something like nostalgia. I've always found the gray squirrels in NYC unsatisfactory compared to their cuter, pointier-eared, and more colorful cousins back in Krasnodar.

As I turn away from the window, I catch the woman looking at me with a stony expression. Now that I'm studying her closer, her lack of an Adam's apple and the hint of makeup on her face assure me she really is a *she*, though I can probably be forgiven for having doubts given her shiny shaved head and muscle tone that's about triple mine. A spiderweb tattoo adorns the rightmost side of her head, evoking stories of spider females feasting on their males during mating.

Without any emotion, in a voice you can only get after at least a decade of smoking unfiltered Russian cigs, she says in Moscow-accented Russian, "Looks like Sleeping Beauty is up."

"What happened?" I try not to gag as a wave of garlic breath mixed with stale nicotine assaults my nose. "How did I get here?"

"You walked," Joe says, his blue eyes glinting in the rearview mirror.

"I told you he was sleepwalking," the woman says.

Though I don't recall being woken up, I bring up AROS and do a quick search on Ambien side effects to confirm my hunch that my memory loss is due to the drug.

"Where are we going?" I ask, rubbing my eyes.

"Levin texted me the location of Voynskiy," Joe says, and it takes me a second to understand he means Mitya texted him where to meet Alex.

The front passenger guy turns around and grins at me. Looking at his weather-beaten face, I can right away tell he isn't Russian. With his hawkish nose and Stalin-inspired mustache, he looks Georgian—which in this context isn't the US state, but a country in the Caucasus mountains.

"I'm Gogi," he says in Georgian-accented Russian.

If his accent weren't enough, that name solidifies my theory on Gogi's nationality. "Gogi" is as common a name in those parts as

Ivan is in Russia. In fact, a fictional Gogi is often the butt of derisive Russian jokes about Georgians.

"I'm Mike." I shake the man's hairy hand. "Though you can call me Misha if it's easier."

"Good to meet you, Mike," Gogi says, pronouncing my name as *meek*. "I can see the familial resemblance." He tilts his head toward Joe.

"I'm Nadejda," the woman says, but only after Gogi and I look at her expectantly for a few moments. "Regardless of whether it's easier, you can't call me Nadya, Nadyusha, or any other variant."

Nadejda means hope in Russian, a fitting name since hope is probably what everyone feels when they look at her—as in, they hope to never piss her off.

"How do you know my cousin?" I ask, aiming the question at no one in particular.

They look at each other. Gogi must lose the staring match, because he's the first to speak, saying, "It's a long story."

My prodding appears to have lessened their enthusiasm for socializing, and Gogi turns back toward the front while Nadejda resumes hypnotizing the back of his neck.

Re-enabling the avatars, I type into the mental chat window, "Are you guys up?"

Since it's 8:14 a.m. here, it must be 1:14 a.m. in NYC.

"Of course we're up," Ada says as she materializes near Nadejda's shoulder.

"Did you notice the new icons?" asks Mitya, who materializes outside the car window—not that it matters for his devil avatar.

I look closer at the AROS interface.

"There are new icons here," I mentally type into the chat window. "Where do I start?"

"Try the face recognition app on her," Ada says, pointing at the large woman next to her avatar. "You'll need to launch that googly-eyed emoticon that Mitya designed as an app icon."

I locate the icon and start the app.

Instantly, white ghostly lines crisscross every nook and cranny of Nadejda's face. I've seen this sort of animation in crime procedural movies and TV shows, and I suspect this is Mitya's flourish and has nothing to do with the actual way this face recognition app works.

Next, a box shows up in the air. It lists information, along with its sources, and I recall how Mom was reminded of the Terminator films when she had a similar process run inside her head two days ago. Thinking of Mom threatens to overwhelm me with worry again, so I focus on the information I acquired about my new acquaintance, Nadejda Vedrova.

Nadejda was born in Latvia, but according to her social media profile, she's "of Russian heritage," whatever that means. From the data in the Russian law enforcement databases, I learn she served in the SUV, a Latvian special tasks unit I've never heard of, where she was a sniper—something that surprises me, since she doesn't seem like the type who likes working from a distance. I also learn she's worked as a private security consultant all over Russia since 2009. In this context, it means she's been a bodyguard for oil oligarchs and the like. That might be her connection with Joe, since he runs a similar business in the States, at least officially. From the Russian Wikipedia, I'm impressed to find out that at the age of twenty-three, Nadejda won gold in Greco-Roman wrestling, which explains both her physique and the "I can crush you" attitude she's sporting. Finally, I discover she's thirty-seven, widowed, and that her husband was killed by a criminal kingpin, who was later shot dead by a high-powered rifle under mysterious circumstances.

"Gogi?" I say in an effort to capture the man's face. When he turns, I say, "Do you have any food scraps or water? I need to feed my little friend."

Mr. Spock takes that as his cue to poke his head out of my jacket.

Joe sees the rat in the rearview mirror and just raises an eyebrow, as if he's met people with white rats in their pockets before but didn't expect me to be one of them.

Gogi's reaction isn't as calm. His eyes visibly widen, and he looks on the verge of asking a dozen questions.

The face recognition lines scan Gogi's face, and a bio shows up in a comic-book balloon above his head. I don't get a chance to read the details, though, because I'm deafened by a noise that sounds like a rabid hippopotamus picked a fight with a horny cow.

Mr. Spock swiftly hides back inside my pocket, and I get the urge to join him as the screaming continues.

"Nadejda," my cousin grits through his teeth. "Shut it."

The woman stops screaming, but her feet stay up off the floor and her eyes bore a hole in my pocket. There's terrified fascination on her face, an expression that looks completely unnatural on her.

I note she stopped screaming as soon as Joe commanded it, so she might fear or respect him more than her rat phobia, or whatever that was.

"Here." Gogi hands me a handful of sunflower seeds, a very traditional Russian snack. "Just make sure you keep your pet away from the lady."

If looks could kill, Nadejda's stare would've slayed Gogi, perhaps after torturing him first. However, her pride must win out over her irrational fear, because after a moment, she places her feet back on the floor and crosses her arms high over her chest.

I drop the sunflower seeds into my pocket, and as soon as I feel Mr. Spock eating them, I study the information the face recognition app found on Gogi—which turns out to be very little. He was part of the elite Georgian Special Forces, and in the early nineties, he participated in the War in Abkhazia. Apart from that, he was discharged after something he did during the conflict in South Ossetia in 2008, but the Russian databases don't know what that something was, just that it was, and I quote, "an atrocity." He's deemed extremely dangerous and is on the Russian version of the no-fly list—only here, again, no explicit cause is given. Finally, no personal information is known about him, and not surprisingly, he has no social media footprint of any kind.

"Your cousin has nice friends," Mitya says, his avatar flying about a foot outside the car window.

I'm about to chastise my friend for goofing off when something happening outside the car window catches my eye.

Actually, it might be more accurate to say my mind scans our surroundings and tabulates what it sees at a speed so blinding I can only assume it's due to the brain boost.

Point number one is that we're currently on a narrow part of the road cresting a hill. Point two, there's a big ditch on either side. Point three, the critical one, is that despite these road conditions, a car is trying to pass us on the left.

Perhaps an unenhanced or less paranoid mind might dismiss all this and think the driver of the offending car is an idiot, but I don't think that's the case, so I let my mind continue with its assessment.

Point four and five are that the car is a large black Mercedes M-Class with four men wearing sunglasses in the middle of a cloudy day.

Then point six happens. The car in question turns its wheels toward us, and it doesn't take a brain boost to know what's about to happen.

The car is going to intentionally ram into us.

TWENTY-SIX

"Joe," I shout. "On your left!"

My perception seems to sharpen, and everything becomes more vivid. I watch the approaching car and try to swallow my heart back into my chest. From somewhere, I recall my body is currently experiencing the Law of Inertia; if we hit the other car, my body will attempt to keep moving in our car's original trajectory. With uncanny mathematical precision, possible scenarios play through my head, down to the number of tons of force I'll experience in different outcomes.

At the same moment, I see my cousin grip the wheel so hard his knuckles whiten. His head turns toward the offending vehicle, and he jerks the wheel.

We swerve.

I start calculating our chances of survival as I glimpse Gogi reaching into the glove compartment.

Nadejda is already holding an Uzi, though where she got it from is beyond me. She slides down the backseat toward me and aims the gun at the window.

Before I can blink or do another calculation, the big woman grabs me roughly by my neck.

"What—" The rest of my question is cut off by her pulling my head down in some sort of wrestling maneuver.

Though I would usually find humor in the way my face ended up in the crotch area of Nadejda's jeans, right now I'm too petrified for levity. I only have one overriding thought in my head.

I'm going to die.

A thunderclap booms above me.

Shards of glass fly everywhere, but Nadejda's body blocks me from the worst of it.

"I think you're being shot at," Ada says, her avatar visible to me even though my eyes are squeezed shut. Her face looks as shocked as I feel.

"No shit," Mitya says, his avatar sounding distraught despite his bravado.

"Shut up, guys," I inadvertently say out loud, but my voice is muffled by the mounds of flesh below my face.

More shots are fired from right next to me. I assume it's Joe and his friends, but I can't be sure since all I can see is Nadejda's zipper. Then again, it's a safe bet she's shooting, because I can feel the tension in her beefy thigh muscles with my cheek.

The car squeals to a jerky stop.

My position prevents whiplash, but I still feel woozy.

In a whirl of action, Nadejda extricates herself from under me, and before I can react, she's gone from the car.

The shooting resumes.

I try to peek through the rear window, but it explodes into shards.

Determined to at least see what's going on, I unhook the GoPro harness from my body and grip the camera tightly.

In the mental chat, I type, "Guys, can you feed me the camera input?"

"Of course," Mitya says. "Done."

I prepare to get shot in the arm and raise the camera like a periscope.

My friend delivers on his promise, and I stare at the video of what's going on outside the car.

Nadejda is still holding on to her machine pistol, while Gogi and Joe have slightly smaller guns. They're all aiming at the black car and walking toward it menacingly.

I point the camera at the vehicle and see that the bad guys' car looks like a pasta strainer.

Though no one is shooting back at my allies, the crew cautiously approach the vehicle. Then Gogi and Joe rip away the front and back doors and unload the rest of their bullets into whatever they find inside.

"All dead," my cousin says, and I detect a note of disappointment in his tone. Maybe he wanted to question the assailants but didn't get a chance to?

Well, I can learn something even if he didn't. I put the camera harness back on and exit the car on legs that feel like jelly.

"You should probably stay in the car, young man," Gogi says as I approach them. Then, probably figuring I didn't understand his Russian due to shock, he adds in broken English, "If you not see death up front like this, it can be very bad."

"He's probably right," Ada says in my right ear.

"At least get close enough for facial recognition to kick in," Mitya says in my left ear.

Gingerly, I take another couple of steps.

A strange kind of numbness overcomes me as I scan one shot-up man after another. I only stop once the face recognition data turns up. As I take it in, the numbness dissipates, and I find myself bent over, dry-heaving violently. My ribs ache with renewed fierceness, and my head reminds me it's only been a couple of days since the concussion.

"At least he hasn't eaten anything in a while," Mitya says from somewhere. "He'd lose it for sure."

"Shut up," Ada says. "Mike, sweetie, are you okay?"

I don't respond either vocally or mentally.

Gogi places a comforting hand on my shoulder, but I don't know how to respond to that either.

Eventually, I straighten, pulling away from Gogi's touch, and lumber back to our car.

Both the local and virtual crews follow me.

The car doors slam behind Gogi, then Joe, then Nadejda.

I just sit there, breathing heavily. Despite the cool air outside, sweat drips down my spine, and my ribs ache dully.

Gogi puts the gun back into the glove compartment without saying anything.

I gather some strength and look at Nadejda. She already hid the Uzi someplace, and in my current state, I don't care to guess where. As though feeling my gaze, the woman looks at me with a strange expression that might be compassion. On second thought, it could be worry about my rat, or maybe she's simply constipated.

Joe's expression, or lack thereof, is easier to read, since it's as emotionless as usual. Seeing he has my attention, he nonchalantly says, "How much do you trust them?"

"Who?" I ask, wondering if he means Nadejda and Gogi.

"Levin and your girlfriend," Joe clarifies.

"They know where we're heading," Gogi chimes in.

"And that didn't seem like a random attack," Nadejda adds.

"I trust them more than I trust any of you," I blurt out. When I see my cousin's blue icicles-for-eyes narrow, I swiftly clarify, "I trust them completely, Joe."

"If we wanted to hurt you, we'd use the Brainocytes to do it," Mitya says.

"Sure, tell them that," Ada says sarcastically. "Better yet, tell them we implanted a nuke inside your head that we can detonate at any time. That should relax everyone."

Glad only I can hear my friends bickering, I tell Joe, "Let's focus on the attackers. I can tell you who they are."

"You can?" Gogi's bushy unibrow tilts right.

"Don't tell anyone in Russia about the Brainocytes," Mitya

warns. "Or else you might join your mom, and not in the way we want."

"I'm not an idiot," I mentally reply. Then I gesture at the camera on my chest and say out loud, "This took images of their faces and sent them to my friends. They looked them up and were about to share the information with me."

Gogi grunts approvingly, and even Nadejda looks a little less solemn.

Reassured, I take out my phone and pretend to read the bios from there instead of the Augmented Reality text boxes.

I rattle out the ages and the criminal records of the dead and finish with their personal connections, such as family members, friends, and other things gleaned from social media. Though my listeners don't seem to care, the social media information I read makes my chest tighten in empathy. I even feel a dash of remorse, an odd reaction since I wasn't the one who killed those men. I guess seeing pictures of their kids, wives, brothers, and sisters humanized them in my eyes, making their deaths register as the tragedy they are. True, this slaughter was in self-defense, but that doesn't make me feel better. I wonder if murders would still happen if everyone knew such intimate details about the people they were about to kill? Could this be yet another way the Brainocytes might improve the world? As soon as the thought occurs to me, I dismiss it. The likeliest suspect in a murder case is usually the spouse of the victim or some other acquaintance, so that rationale doesn't hold.

"They sound like your generic guns for hire," Gogi says, interrupting my inadvertent moment of silence.

"I agree," Nadejda says. "They could've been working for anyone with a large bank account."

"This is why you should've kept one alive." Joe throws out the words as an accusation, as though he wasn't doing a huge chunk of the killing.

Nadejda and Gogi don't respond, and after a moment of sullen quietude, my cousin starts the car and expresses his frustration by slamming on the gas pedal so hard we leave a streak of black tire marks behind us.

As we make our way to Alex's home, I mentally ask Ada and Mitya about improving the face recognition app based on some ideas I've come up with.

"I really like that," Mitya says after I explain what I want. "We can pick out certain markers in the person's profile and have Einstein alert you as needed."

"We can also give them a red halo," Ada says, getting into the spirit of things. "It'll let you spot any dangerous people in a crowd."

"Obviously, we'll leave you with the ability to use face recognition manually the way you do now," Mitya adds.

"You guys don't need to sell me on this," I mentally type. "I was the one who wanted the improvements in the first place."

"All right then," Mitya says. "We'll start coding."

"Okay." I draw in a heavy breath. "I'll just sit here alone, I guess."

"You have three other people in the car with you," Mitya says. "I'm sure they can keep you entertained."

Emphasizing that our conversation is officially over, Mitya's devil visage goes away.

"Don't mind him." Ada's angel avatar flies up to my face. "I'll go code a bit too, but I'll keep an eye on the chat window if you want to get in touch."

She flies even closer to my cheek, mimics giving me a kiss, and evaporates. I'm left marveling at how even a fake kiss from Ada has the power to make me feel all warm and fuzzy.

As the car ride continues, I take in the sights. We're passing through villages and fields of sunflowers and corn. After the dozenth sighting of herds of cows and horses, the rural vista begins to bore me, and I loudly yawn.

I surf the net with my mind for a while before realizing the sun outside isn't fooling my body's circadian rhythm. Somehow, it knows it's nighttime back home. Seeing no reason to fight the inevitable, I instruct Einstein to wake me up when we get to Alex's location and close my eyes.

———

From my perch on the second floor, I see Mom sitting on a metal chair in the middle of an abandoned factory. She's wrapped in duct tape from head to toe like a strange modern mummy. Anton—the ape-bison asshole—is standing next to her with a blowtorch.

I grab onto the rusty hook attached to a gigantic chain and swing toward Anton in a perfect imitation of Tarzan.

Anton turns to me and round-kicks me off the chain.

"Wakey-wakey," says a German-accented voice from far away.

Confused, I fall from the chain and land with a loud splat.

As I lie there, trying to catch my breath, Anton walks up to me and applies the blowtorch to my temple.

My head begins melting, and I realize I'm dreaming.

TWENTY-SEVEN

"Wakey-wakey," Einstein's German-accented voice booms. "Eggs and Schnitzel."

As I struggle to regain my senses, I overhear Nadejda ask, "Does your cousin do anything else besides sleep?"

Joe says nothing, and Gogi chuckles.

"I'm awake," I mumble and rub my eyes, ignoring the twinge of pain in my ribs. "What did I miss?"

"We're almost there," Gogi says and points at a fence in the far distance. The fence looks inspired by the Wall of China.

"Alex calls this his Palace," says Mitya, his devil appearing almost on my left shoulder. "I call it the Monument to Alex's Ego."

I use my phone's GPS to pinpoint my location. Alex's house—or mansion or palace or whatever—is located close enough to Moscow proper to be stupendously expensive, but far enough to allow for a plot of land of this outlandish size.

"I can't see past the gate yet," I mentally respond. "Have you guys updated the face recognition app?"

"We finished that a while ago," Ada says, her angel showing up on my opposite shoulder.

"And we had time to sleep too," Mitya says.

"But not with each other," Ada clarifies hastily.

Instantly feeling wide awake, I launch the new version of the face recognition app. I'm prompted on whether I want to see Einstein's holographic image, and I decide against it; two illusory versions of my friends is enough Augmented Reality for now.

The gate we arrive at wouldn't look out of place in a medieval Russian castle. As we approach, it opens with a metal-on-metal screech.

"Sketchy person alert," Einstein says as soon as I glimpse the armed guards manning the gate. "Sketchy person alert. Sketchy person alert. Sketchy person alert."

"Sorry," Mitya says. "I set up the app so Einstein says that phrase every time he detects a new face that matches the predefined criteria. Those four guards are probably dangerous."

"I bet Mike could've figured that out just by looking at them," Ada says, her wings twitching nervously. "The AK-47s and the Neanderthal foreheads are dead giveaways."

"Mitya," I mentally type. "Does your friend know we're here?"

"I just texted him," Mitya replies. "And he's not my friend."

"He's not?" Ada asks as I type the same question.

"He's an old acquaintance who owes me a bunch of favors," Mitya explains. "If you knew Alex like I do, you'd know that's better than being his friend."

The burly security dudes examine each of us closely and suspiciously check their handhelds, but eventually, they allow us to proceed through the gate.

We slowly drive in and are greeted by a bunch of armed people. All but one raises the "sketchy person" alert. I look at the one man without a red halo and wonder how he ended up here. One manual face recognition scan later, I learn he's a cop.

"Not always a big difference between goons and cops in Russia," Mitya says. "The likes of Alex can hire cops just as easily as they can hire goons, and it's worth having a few on the payroll."

I shake my head and take in our surroundings. As we crest the big hill, we bear witness to the majesty of Alex's Palace—a name that might actually be an understatement. This thing is monstrous and dwarfs most mansions I've seen. It reminds me of a double-sized Winter Palace in St. Petersburg (the Russian city, never to be confused with the one in Florida), except it has many more gold-plated surfaces. Unlike the tsar's former residence, though, this place has some embellishments that seem tacky, the worst offender being the colorful peacocks roaming the gardens that are way too tropical for Russia.

We park on a driveway the size of a modest football stadium, and two armed men escort us to the Palace doors. For people carrying machine guns, their manner is very polite.

A girl who looks like she stepped off the cover of Russian *Maxim* magazine greets us in the vestibule. In passable English, she says, "Hello, Mr. Cohen. I'm Anna. Mr. Voynskiy asked me to take you to the Lounge."

Nadejda gives Anna her signature Ice Queen stare, while Gogi checks her out appreciatively.

"We'd like to speak with your boss *now*," Joe says, and I get the impression he's itching to grab the girl by the neck to emphasize his point.

"He'll meet you in the Lounge shortly," Anna responds, unperturbed. "It's this way."

She turns and starts walking. As we follow her deeper into the Palace, I decide that Alex has a fetish for bling. The heavy chandeliers look like they're made of gold and diamonds, while the paintings and the ancient Russian icons on the walls are set in gold frames—adorned with copious amounts of jewels, of course.

"This sometimes happens when low-class people get money," Mitya whispers conspiratorially from my left. "It doesn't make it any less painful to look at."

"I didn't realize you came from old money," Ada says with a heavy dose of sarcasm. "And don't you own a race horse ranch?"

"Exactly," Mitya counters. "That just proves I know what I'm talking about."

I ignore their banter as we finally reach the Lounge. It's the size of the Bellagio hotel in Vegas—assuming that venerable place decided to turn itself into an opulent restaurant—and has the same feel.

"Please, take a seat." Anna points at a giant table, and we accept her offer.

On the table is a bottle of *Stoli Elit: Himalayan Edition*. A mental search reveals this brand of vodka costs three thousand dollars per bottle. The hors d'oeuvres include black caviar blinis, some strange golden fish roe on a tiny plate, little salmon roe sandwiches, and a slew of other high-end Russian culinary delights.

"May I get anyone anything?" Anna asks politely, and I get the eerie impression she included herself on the list of possible items she can deliver.

"Voynskiy," Joe says firmly.

"Tea if you could," says Gogi.

"Some plain water," I add. "And some nuts."

Nadejda gives me a panicked stare. She probably figured out that the food is meant for Mr. Spock.

"I'll be right back," Anna says and backs away. "Meanwhile, please try the gold caviar. It's Almas, from an albino Iranian Beluga sturgeon."

"Hello." A man emerges from behind one of the giant columns. "I'm Alex."

The man in front of us bears only a vague resemblance to the sharply dressed Alex Voynskiy I've seen in *Forbes Magazine*. In real life, he looks like a hybrid between Steve Jobs and Bill Gates. His clothes, particularly the black turtleneck, remind me of the Apple founder, while his kind face and the shape of his glasses are more reminiscent of Microsoft's former CEO.

"Except he wishes he was ten percent as brilliant as either man," Mitya says after I share my thoughts in the chat. "Alex is a poser. He can't code to save his life. Just another person in the right place at the right time."

"You mean next to you?" I type.

"Exactly," Mitya says. "Listening to me was the smartest thing he did, and this being Russia, he was able to monopolize the market."

A robotic contraption consisting of wheels, a stick, and an iPad on top rolls out from behind the column. I recognize it as one of those telepresence robots.

"That's me," Mitya explains. "So I'll turn off my avatar for now."

"Hi, everyone," Mitya says from the iPad on top of the robot. "I'm Mitya."

"Hi, Mitya. Thanks for letting us use your plane," I tell the robot, pretending I can't just mentally talk to my friend via the chat. Turning to our host, I say, "Nice to meet you, Alex."

After I introduce everyone around the table, Alex says, "Mitya filled me in on the situation, but I want to hear your version if you don't mind."

"We don't," I say, even though it looks like Joe feels otherwise. Between mouthfuls of multicolored fish eggs, I explain the situation, sticking as close to the truth as I can while omitting all mention of the Brainocyte technology.

Halfway through my story, Anna returns with the requested water and nuts. I combine this with the grapes and salad already on the table and sneak a meal to Mr. Spock.

"Just as I thought," Alex says when I finish. "We'll have to get help from Muhomor."

Nadejda and Gogi look shocked, while my cousin and I exchange blank stares.

"I take it he's not talking about the regular meaning of the word *muhomor*?" I type into the chat.

In Russian, muhomor is the name of a poisonous mushroom called *Amanita muscaria*, sometimes referred to as fly agaric. It's a toadstool with a bright red cap speckled with white, and I was always told to avoid it as a kid. A nifty mental Google search informs me this mushroom actually has hallucinogenic properties I wasn't previously aware of. This might explain why the caterpillar in *Alice in Wonderland* was so fond of sitting on it (and maybe why Alice needed to eat so many shrooms).

"No," Mitya replies from inside the chat. "It's a person. I didn't think he was real, let alone someone Alex might know." From the iPad, out loud, Mitya says, "Alex, stop building the suspense. Why don't you tell everyone who Muhomor is?"

"I don't like repeating rumors." Alex pours a shot of vodka with the air of someone who's certainly looking forward to sharing this particular rumor. "I'm sure you've seen certain articles in *Wired*, such as the one about Russia hacking into Pentagon emails, or Russia hacking the Democratic National Committee, or the one about the Russian Dark Net marketplaces that allow one to buy illegal drugs, weapons, and stolen credit cards..." He downs the shot and chases it with a pickle. "If those stories have any foundation in reality, it's Muhomor behind the curtain pulling the invisible binary strings."

"And you know him how?" Mitya asks as the teleconference robot moves closer to Alex.

"Is it really relevant?" Alex pushes his glasses higher up his nose. "He owes me a few favors, just like I owed you."

"If this Muhomor helps Mike, we won't just be even," Mitya says. "I'll owe *you*."

"I can't guarantee he'll help." Alex sits down and faces the iPad. "I can only try to arrange the meeting."

"Fine." Mitya rolls the robot even closer to Alex. "Get in touch with him."

Alex pulls out his phone and types at a speed a tween would envy.

"Why do you assume Muhomor is a him?" Ada asks in our private chat window. "What if it's a her?"

"You have much to learn about the Russian language," Mitya types back. "The word *muhomor* is a masculine noun. A lady hacker would've called herself something like *lisichka*."

"I guess," Ada says. "But those are chanterelle mushrooms, right? They're way less cool than fly agaric."

"Ah," Mitya types back, "but that Russian word is also a diminutive of fox, which makes it kind of foxy, don't you think?"

"I think *muhomor* is cooler," I chime in. "It's a rare Russian word that can be written with letters that occur in both the Cyrillic and English alphabets."

Before anyone can comment further on options for hacker aliases, Alex looks up from his phone and says, "Okay, I should hear back from Muhomor shortly. Now, let's all just relax for a minute." Holding on to the bottle, he walks over to Nadejda. "May I take care of the lady?" Without waiting for anyone to reply, he pours her a shot of vodka and asks, "Can I get you more chicken liver pâté?"

Nadejda looks at him as though he's about to harvest a liver from a chicken that's sprouting from his head. Then, to my utter shock, she smiles as coquettishly as her formidable frown lines allow and says, "Maybe a little."

"Such chauvinistic behavior," Ada comments.

"You're reading way too much into it," Mitya objects. "It's a Russian dinner table tradition for the gentleman to—"

I don't read the rest of the exchange because I notice how my cousin is looking at Alex, who's blissfully adding morsels of liver pâté to Nadejda's plate. His stare reminds me of the ice ball special move the character Sub-Zero enjoys throwing in the *Mortal Combat* games. In a voice as cold as his stare, Joe says, "We didn't come here to relax."

Nadejda, who must know Joe well, turns white, but I have to hand it to Alex. He doesn't flinch and just calmly says, "I understand and respect your position, Joseph Abramovich. The problem is there isn't much I can do. Muhomor is very eccentric. He'll take as long as he wants to reply. Also, I might as well warn you that it'll take even longer to set up a meeting with him."

"Will it?" I ask as Alex puts the *blin*—Russian crepe—that Nadejda refused into his own mouth. "Care to explain why?"

"Take it easy," Ada warns me in the chat. "Your voice shows an unusual amount of irritation."

"Well," I mentally type, "Joe is on the verge of either choking or torture-shooting our host to get answers, and that would be a bad move in this well-defended facility, no matter how tempting it might be."

Alex swallows his food and glances at his phone. Apparently seeing nothing on it, he looks up again and says, "Muhomor likes to include puzzles in his dealings, and that crap usually takes time to crack."

"So let's work with someone else," Gogi says, and I can tell he's also worried Joe might act out his displeasure.

Alex shakes his head. "He's the only such person I know," he explains. "Perhaps there's something we can do in the meantime? Did you want to change your clothes after your long trip? Or take a bath?" He looks longingly at Nadejda. "Or anything else?"

"We could use some weapons," Gogi says, and his unibrow does a jig on his forehead.

"That would be nice," Nadejda agrees and smiles widely, revealing a golden crown on her left canine tooth.

Alex looks like he's about to refuse, but then Joe stands, fists clenched and eyes set on homicide.

"Okay," Alex says a bit too quickly. When Joe unclenches his fists, our host smiles weakly, his relief apparent, and looks at Nadejda. "How can I resist, Nadechka?" he says in a smarmy tone. "Come, let me show you my armory."

To my utter shock, Nadejda lets Alex get away with the diminutive form of her name, and she's the first one on her feet, following him out of the Lounge. She walks next to him, eagerly chatting him up about something I can't quite hear. The rest of us follow with less enthusiasm.

"I'll disconnect now," my friend says from the telepresence robot behind us. "Don't worry about me."

No one shows the slightest hint that they heard Mitya as they continue through the maze of corridors after our host.

"It's in here," Alex says as he opens the large door to his left.

Gogi enters first and whistles loudly.

"It's bad luck to whistle in the house," Nadejda says, but then she whistles too. Even Joe looks pretty impressed, and with good reason.

The room reminds me of that iconic scene from *The Matrix*, when Neo is asked what he needs and he says, "Guns. Lots of guns."

The shelves in the hangar-sized space are overflowing with weapons of varying degrees of destruction. Some of these items look so deadly I suspect even the NRA might not want them in civilian hands. I estimate that about ninety-eight percent of these weapons are illegal in Russia and seventy percent would be illegal in the most gung-ho states in America. To my New Yorker eyes, these guns are obscenely shocking yet fascinating—like a porno scenario you think is sick but can't stop watching.

I walk through rows of plastic explosives, rifles, shotguns, and rocket launchers. Finally, I stop next to a few rows dedicated mostly to handguns, figuring I might as well pick one up while I'm here.

"I don't think you should get a gun," Ada says, appearing as an angel on my shoulder.

"If you're against him using a gun, why did you help me with the gun app?" Mitya asks, appearing in his devil form. "I think he totally should get a gun, maybe even a few. I recommend one of those 9mm Glocks." He points at the nearest shelf. "That one right there is something only cops and soldiers can have in the US."

"I only did the code review for that app." Ada tugs at her Mohawk. "That's far from actually helping, and it certainly doesn't mean I approve of gun use."

"I'm sorry, Ada," I type into the chat, "but I have to side with Mitya on this one." I pick up a gun for the second time in my life—the first time being when I went to a gun range in New Jersey about a decade ago.

"Does this mean the app is done?" I type into the chat. The app in question was the lowest priority on the list I specced out for them before flying out, and with all the other awesome software, I completely forgot about it.

"It's done," Mitya says. "I just sent it to your AROS."

A little 3D gun icon shows up in the air in front of me. The idea behind the app is to assist with aiming, so even a novice like me can actually hit a target. Since I now have access to a gun, I launch the app and grab a Glock to see how it'll all come together.

"Enter the gun model and make," a window asks, and I do.

"The app is querying several good gun databases," Mitya says as though he can see what I'm doing. "If it doesn't recognize the make and model, choose another gun."

"No, it has it," I say as the window spits out the exact data on my gun and disappears.

Faint lines appear and crisscross the gun, slowly zoning in on the rear and front sights. Eventually, a narrow line materializes in my vision. It comes out of the gun's barrel and goes straight into the floor where I'm currently pointing the weapon.

I wave the gun around, and the line moves with it. The theory is if I want to aim at something, I just need to point the tip of the line where the bullet should end up.

"We can market this to the army one day," Mitya says. "We'll call it Augmented Reality Aim Assist, or something."

"Great," Ada says sarcastically. "Our work will be used to take lives."

"Someone will come up with this anyway," Mitya says. "I think you're letting your angel avatar go to your head."

"How is this better than a laser sight?" I type into the chat, partly to stop them from bickering.

"Laser sight isn't perfect and only works up to a certain distance. This optimizes your accuracy at any distance," Mitya explains. "Plus, only you can see the AU sights, so it's stealthier as well."

Making sure the gun isn't loaded and that the safety's on, I aim the Augmented Reality pointer at Alex's head, who's about twenty feet away.

The line makes aiming ridiculously easy, and if the bullet really did fly down that path, the app would indeed make a marksman out of me.

"Hey, Alex," I shout as I close the distance between us. "Do you have a holster I can use?"

"And a couple of duffel bags," Gogi says.

"And a rucksack," Nadejda adds.

"I'll go ask Anna to locate whatever you need," Alex says, a little too eagerly, and leaves the room.

I take in the others' weapons. With my one Glock, I almost feel naked. Everyone else looks like they decided to star in an action movie, especially Gogi, who appears ready to singlehandedly start a small war.

Seeing that I'm armed, Gogi approaches me and gives me a few pointers so that I, in his words, "don't shoot his left nut by accident."

Alex returns and hands me a shoulder holster, telling the others, "Anna will bring the rest of your items shortly."

"Don't go near that," I whisper to Mr. Spock after I cover the gun with my jacket. "If I reach for it in a hurry, I don't want to end up grabbing you instead by accident."

Pink eyes glint from inside my jacket, and I get the feeling that if the rat could speak, he'd say, "Got it, boss. What am I, a Guinea pig?"

In the distance, Alex resumes his conversation with Nadejda. He tells her she's the quintessential Russian woman, straight from ancient poetry. He goes as far as quoting a verse from Nekrasov that roughly translates to, "A Russian woman can stop a galloping horse and enter a burning hut."

His flirting is interrupted by his phone's very nostalgia-inspiring ringtone—a line from the Russian cartoon *Nu, pogodi!*, the Soviet answer to *Tom and Jerry*, only with a wolf and a hare.

"It's Muhomor," Alex says after a brief glance. He then frowns. "As I feared, he's sent another one of his dumb hacking puzzles."

TWENTY-EIGHT

ALEX ANGRILY PRESSES A COUPLE OF KEYS ON HIS PHONE AND SAYS, "I sent the puzzle to a team of experts on my payroll. It usually takes them a few hours to crack Muhomor's assignments, though last time it took a whole day."

Joe slams a fresh magazine into a ginormous black gun. I take it as a bad sign and say, "You mentioned puzzles before. Can you elaborate?"

"Sure, though there isn't much to explain," Alex says. "Muhomor never tells you the meeting location. He encodes it using a different method each time. Once, I got a cryptic text that was encoded; another time, he sent me a username and a server in Turkey to log in to. Though the details vary, the basic premise is the same. He wants you to do some work before he meets with you."

"But why would he do that?" Gogi asks. "I thought he owed you a favor?"

"I have no clue," Alex replies a bit too defensively. "Maybe it's his way of making sure it's me he's communicating with, or maybe he's just weird."

"He could be using you to hack stuff he's too lazy to hack

himself," I suggest. "That Turkey thing sounds like it."

"Whatever the reason, I'm as annoyed with this as you guys are. Probably more so since I have to go through this more often." Alex glances nervously at Joe.

"Can I take a look at the problem he sent you?" I ask. "I'm good with puzzles." In my mental chat window, I add, "At least I hope I am, thanks to my brain boost."

"Sure," Alex says. "What's your email?"

"It's bigcheese@cohencapital.com," I reply.

Alex has me spell out the email and then plays with his phone some more.

I look at his message on Precious, mostly for appearance's sake, since I'd rather do it through the AROS interface in my head.

All the email contains is a picture of an attractive and very typically Russian girl with blond hair and blue eyes.

Now that they saw me look at it on my phone, I figure it's safe for me to close my eyes, so I do. I bring up the same image and maximize it in the AROS interface. When the face is nice and big, I apply the face recognition app to it. According to the results, her name is Lyuba Trupova. She has no criminal record, and most of her data comes from her Vkontakte social media account.

I forward the pic and my meager findings to my friends, and in my mental chat, I type, "Check your emails if you're willing to help me with this puzzle."

"I'm already trying some common passwords to get into her Vkontakte account," Mitya says.

"Good," I say. "Try things like her boyfriend's name, followed by a one or a zero."

"I just tried that," Mitya says. "I also tried 'password,' both in Russian and English, as well as 'god,' 'Minsk'—her city of birth—and 'Belorussian State University,' the school she attended."

"Try 'letmein,'" Ada suggests. "As well as 'love' and 'money.'"

"She wouldn't use love," I say but try it anyway to no avail. "Her name, Lyuba, is short for Lyubov, which means 'love' in Russian."

"Hey, that's actually a good clue," Mitya says. "Notice her last name is Trupova, which sounds like *trup*—Russian for corpse."

Even before Mitya has finished his sentence, I try "necrophilia" as a password and get in. Alex wasn't kidding when he said Muhomor was eccentric.

"Now that I'm in her account, I can see her email. It's skaz-ka@mail.ru," I mentally type. "But I can't log in using the same password."

My friends suggest some very clever guesses for this new password, both based on their research into statistically common passwords and in a more targeted form by trying to backward engineer what someone with Lyuba's social connections would use. None of it pans out, though.

As we chat, the picture of the girl keeps staring at me, and I eventually notice something odd about it. "Guys, do you see something blurry or pixelated about this image?" I say. "I can't quite put my finger on it, but—"

"You're right. I think it's steganography," Mitya interrupts. After a pause, he adds, "Here's what I get when I remove all but the two least significant bits of each color component and perform a normalization. Check your email, Mr. Grandmaster."

Confused, I open my mental inbox. He sent me a picture of a chessboard with pieces arranged around it, which explains why Mitya called me a grandmaster. When I was a kid back in Russia, I belonged to a chess club for a few years, and I've made a habit out of beating Mitya in chess.

The board setup is oddly familiar, and after I stare at it for a few seconds, I remember where I've seen it. That makes me wonder for a second if Ada's brain boost is aiding my memory, but I decide that's unlikely.

A quick mental Google search confirms my recollection, and I type into the chat, "This is the next to last position of the conclusive match between Anatoly Karpov and Garry Kasparov in the World Chess Championship game in 1985. We covered it in the club ad nauseam. I bet the password is 'horseD4.' Horse is what the knight piece is called in Russian, and D4 is where the knight ended up during the finishing move of the game."

I then try the password, but it doesn't work.

"Maybe it's Kasparov?" Mitya says. "I just looked up that game, and that's who won."

I try Kasparov, then Kasparov with horseD4 before and after it, but it doesn't work. I then try a bunch of variations on the same theme, including the color of the last piece, black, and using the English word *knight* instead of *horse*—all without any luck.

"Wait a minute," Mitya writes in the chat. "Could he have done this again? The email was *skazka*, Russian for 'fairy tale.'"

"You're a genius," I type back. "Karpov comes from the word *karp*, Russian for—not surprisingly—carp, which means the password probably contains something along the lines of golden fish or maybe goldfish."

I try my earlier permutations again, adding the word goldfish into the mix, and when I try goldFishHorseD4, I finally get in.

In the chat, Mitya explains for Ada's benefit, "You see, there's a Russian fairy tale written in verse by Pushkin, who was a Russian author of Shakespeare's caliber. The story deals with a fisherman and a golden fish that grants him wishes, kind of like an aqua genie. And, of course, goldfish is a type of carp, so—"

"I'm in," I type and share the password with them.

"I'm in too," they both answer.

I scan Lyuba's emails but don't see anything that looks like a coded message.

"I've got it," Ada says out loud. "In the junk folder, the email from gyromitra@esculenta.com."

"Of course," Mitya says. "The guy's nickname is a type of mushroom, so he sent the email from an account that's the name of a mushroom that looks like a brain."

I Google "gyromitra esculenta," and it indeed looks eerily like a brain. Then I look at the email, dreading another roundabout.

To my relief, the message isn't encrypted. The email contains a Moscow address, instructions for what to tell the bouncers once we get there, and a reminder for Alex not to bring his mercenaries. Since there's nothing about *my* crew, I assume Muhomor will be okay with Gogi, Nadejda, and Joe coming along. I search the meeting place via Yandex (the Russian equivalent of Google), and it turns out to be Dazdraperma, a very exclusive establishment that's a blend of a casino, a strip club, and a nightclub. It even has a banya—the Russian sauna—on the premises.

I share my findings with my friends. Then I open my eyes and announce, "I know where to go."

I realize my mistake instantly. "I told you I was good with puzzles," I say in an effort to cover it up.

People are still looking at me with a mixture of suspicion and disbelief, especially Alex. Since Mom's rescue is on the line, I find it hard to care what they think, so I just explain where we're going.

"I know the place," Alex says after a long pause. "Sounds like somewhere Muhomor might be. I'll go make preparations so we can leave as soon as possible."

He exits the room, and I reflect on how this whole thing must've looked to him and the others. He emailed me; I glanced at his message, closed my eyes, probably had a look of concentration on my face, and then I opened my eyes a few minutes later and blurted out the answer to a puzzle his special team usually takes hours to crack.

"Make sure you get all the weapons you'll need," I tell Gogi, Nadejda, and Joe. "I'll go wait at the table."

No one says anything, so I plod back to the Lounge, cursing myself for not leaving before my friends and I started solving the puzzle.

"They probably just think you're wicked smart," Ada says when I complain about it in the chat.

"You shouldn't feel bad for fooling them." Mitya chuckles. "On a more serious note, and on the topic of getting smarter, I'm done with my STRELA resource allocation project, and the code is going to Ada for review. As soon as she's done, it'll be ready for testing."

"Then let me focus on it," Ada says. "I'm not as good as you at multitasking."

I don't get a chance to jealously check whether she meant Mitya or me when she said "you" because a new email arrives in my inbox.

I read the subject line, and my heart rate spikes.

It says: *If you don't go back to America, this will happen to your mother.*

There's no text in the body of the email, only a file named "play_me.mov."

As I forward the email to Joe, Mitya, and Ada, I pinpoint the icy, deadweight sensation in my stomach. As a kid, this was how I felt when I went to get my vaccine shots.

I start the video.

The camera is zoomed in on a shaved head, and because there aren't any objects around, it's hard to gauge the size of the person in the video, or their identity, or even something as basic as whether the head belongs to a man or a woman.

Then a hand appears in the frame.

The hand is clad in a blue latex glove, and it's holding a large yellow cordless DeWalt drill. A spindly sword-like drill bit is sticking out of its tip.

"No," Ada whispers out loud.

"This can't be heading where I think it is," Mitya echoes.

I suppress the urge to stop watching and brace myself.

TWENTY-NINE

THE DRILL BIT SPINS.

The video has no sound, maybe because the microphone wasn't enabled on the recording device used to film this atrocity.

I feel like I'm rooted to the floor and my roots are filling with a hundred pounds of ice every millimeter the drill gets closer to the back of the person's head.

When the tip of the drill bit penetrates the skin, my cursed imagination fills in the details not available to me, like the person's scream and the horrible bone-crunching buzz and the smell of—

I get violently sick on Alex's marble floor.

When I'm done heaving, my ribs sing in agony, but the video is over.

My friends are saying something, but I just stand there, gulping in air until I get sick again.

"Oh my," says Anna, Alex's model housekeeper. She must've witnessed me losing all that super-expensive caviar I ate on her earlier recommendation. "Are you okay?"

I get sick again. Both my ribs and my skull feel like they're breaking apart. "No, I'm the opposite of okay."

Anna grabs my elbow and starts dragging me away, saying something along the lines of, "Let me walk you."

She leads me to a bathroom to freshen up and rinse my mouth. Afterwards, she takes me somewhere else, and as I follow her, I'm truly glad I can communicate with my friends via the mental interface, because I don't think I can gather the strength to speak.

Into the chat, I type, "It must've been someone from the study."

"I'm so sorry," Ada whispers out loud.

"Yeah, man," Mitya echoes in a subdued tone. "Hang in there. Don't fall apart."

As they continue saying supportive nothings, I take out Mr. Spock and stroke the pink part of his fur, hoping a little pet therapy will help me pull myself together—something I have to do for Mom's sake.

Mr. Spock closes his eyes, which I take as a sign of pleasure. Confirming my guess, he begins bruxing and gently nibbling on my skin. All of that, combined with the violet aura he has from the app, means he's very happy and at ease. After a while, I also feel more relaxed and start thinking rationally enough to notice my surroundings. It turns out the whole gang is around me, with Nadejda staying far outside the rat-leaping range.

"Did you see it?" I ask Joe. "The email I forwarded?"

He nods, his expression unreadable. "Do we know who sent it yet?"

"I have my people on it," Alex says. "But I wouldn't hold my breath. It's from a free provider, so anyone with a Tor Browser could've created the account, sent the email, and remained anonymous as can be."

"Is that true?" I type into the chat. "We can't track it?"

"I'll take a look, but I'm afraid Alex might be right," Mitya replies.

"I don't know what to do," I say out loud to no one in particular.

"You should probably consider going back to the United States." Alex walks over to the nearby table, pours a shot of vodka, and offers it to me. "I saw the video. Those people aren't kidding around."

I shake my head, refusing the vodka (which is very rude in Russia, but I don't care), and grab a handful of grapes instead.

"Looks to me like they're showing their weakness." Gogi adjusts the shoulder strap on his heavy duffel bag. "They know we're on their trail, and they got scared enough to execute one of the hostages."

"But it's such a desperate move." I put all but two grapes in my mouth and feed the rest to Mr. Spock. "It worries me. Desperate people do irrational things."

"I agree," Alex says, knocking back the shot he offered me. "What if Mike's mother is the next victim? What if—"

Alex stops speaking because Joe demonstratively takes out his gun, flicks off the safety, and places the loaded weapon on the table in front of him. In the silence that follows, he stares at Alex until the billionaire looks away. With lethal finality, my cousin says, "We're going to Dazdraperma."

He doesn't need to add any niceties such as "and that's it" or "no more debate" or even "or else I'll shoot you," because it's clear he'd shoot anyone not on board with his plan.

Funny enough, I don't think I disagree with him. It doesn't take a brain boost to realize that if we fly back home, Mom's death is a certainty. True, it might involve something less drastic than a drill to the head, but her chances are slim nonetheless. On the other hand, if we stay, there's a possibility, however remote, that we might save her.

Thus determined, I carefully put Mr. Spock back in my pocket, grab a handful of food from the table, and say, "Let's head out."

———

As we drive through the congested Moscow streets in Alex's tricked-out Land Rover, I can't help gawking at the sights that range from the colorful onion-like cupolas of the Orthodox churches to monuments from both tsarist Russia and the Soviet days. When I was here as a kid, I didn't appreciate any of this, and I still don't, given my state of mind. But I glimpse enough wonders to understand why the real estate prices in Russia's capital are on par with those in New York, Shanghai, and Paris.

Dazdraperma isn't located in the center of the city for the same reason Alex's Palace isn't—it's huge. There's a block-long line, which is crazy in daytime. Lines in Russia shouldn't shock me, though. They're what I think of whenever I picture this country. In Krasnodar, around the late eighties and early nineties—when most of my perceptions of Russia were formed—you had to stand in line to get everything, even something as basic as bread or milk.

We bypass everyone standing in line and waltz up to the bouncers. Gogi tells them the password we got from Muhomor —*shmakodyavka frikadel'ka.*

"That's 'shorty meatball,'" Mitya types into the chat.

"I'm still reviewing the code," Ada replies. "Let me be."

Wanting to focus on my surroundings, I put away the chat window as I pass through the heavy doors.

The first thing we see upon entering is the casino, and it's themed to match the name of the establishment. In Russian, and to some degree in English, the word *dazdraperma* sounds funny, and not just because it sounds a bit like *sperm*. It comes from an infrequently used female name that only the most ardent communists or accidentally abusive parents gave their daughters during Soviet times. It actually stands for "*Da Zdra*(vstvuet) *Per*(voye) *Ma*(ya)," meaning something like "Long Live the First of May." That date was a big made-up holiday in honor of International Workers' Solidarity and reminds me of one of those Hallmark holidays in the US, like a sort of commie Valentine's Day. Incidentally, the Russian version of Valentine's Day is March 8th, though it's known as International Women's Day and kind of incorporates Mother's Day as well. When I was growing up, there were parades on May 1st, and I was often forced to participate in them with the other kids. In Moscow, the parades included soldiers marching down the Red Square alongside rolling tanks, and I believe they recently reinstated the whole practice, though I can't be sure.

The casino has photos of Lenin, wheat husks, sickles and hammers, and other paraphernalia you'd see back in the day on May 1st, but I think it's meant to be ironic, since casinos were illegal back in the Soviet Union. Actually, speaking of legality, I'm not sure gambling is legal in Russia today. Then again, neither is marijuana, and I detect its telltale smell in the cloud of smoke I pass through.

"What do we do now?" I ask my entourage. "Every second we waste is a chance for them to figure out we didn't react to their threat."

"It's still not too late to leave," Alex says. Noticing Joe's jaw muscles tighten, he adds hastily, "Muhomor will send someone to approach us. That's how he always operates."

To stop myself from going crazy, I walk over to a table where a card game is taking place. There's a dealer and six players already at it, and it takes me only a couple of rounds to develop a theory about the rules—in part because it's a variation of poker. Curious if I'm right, I run a mental search. I learn I'm very close to knowing the rules and that this game is called Russian Poker—though I guess they might simply call it "poker" in Moscow. Based on what I've seen so far, I think I could make a killing if I played, though I don't know if it's because I've always had a propensity for poker or if my brain boost is striking once again.

I share my thoughts with Mitya via chat, and he warns me, "Don't even approach the table. Yes, you could make a figurative killing, but then it could turn into a literal killing—of you. You don't want the house thinking you're cheating, and casinos all over the world define being very good at a game as cheating. Even in Vegas you can get something broken for being too lucky—or at least that was the case in the past. This is Russia, so the bone they'll break is your skull."

"Hi," says a soft feminine voice. "You're Mike Cohen."

I turn around and see a familiar Russian face looking at me

with a barely detectible smirk. It takes me half a second to place her as the girl from the puzzle picture Muhomor sent Alex.

"Hi," I say. "Is your name really Lyuba?"

"Why not?" the girl whose name is probably not Lyuba says. "It'll work for the purposes of my current assignment."

"Let's go then," I say. *Lyuba.*

"No funny business," Nadejda adds, her deep voice carrying over the pinging noise of slot machines.

Lyuba takes a good look at the former wrestling champion, and her smirk disappears. She turns on her heels, briskly walks through the casino, and opens a door into the next section of the club, which happens to be the dance floor.

Instantly, trance music envelops us, nearly deafening me, and I marvel at how good the insulation must be in the walls and doors. Just a moment ago, all I heard was the ambient casino noise. Still, I like the super-loud song enough to get Einstein to figure out what it is—"Resurrection" by a Russian group called PPK.

Lyuba pushes through the sweaty bodies on the dance floor and heads toward the giant DJ booth in the farthest corner. The DJ is wearing a shiny cosmonaut helmet, but as it turns out, he—or she —isn't our destination. To the side of the DJ's big podium is a door, and that's where Lyuba leads us.

A short corridor later, we stop at a big metal door, and Lyuba knocks.

A buzzing sound blares, and Lyuba pushes the door in.

Once we've all entered, she says, "He's inside," and slams the door behind us.

Joe reaches out and locks the door.

"Is it me, or is this a bit ominous?" I try typing into the chat but discover I can't.

I'm not feeling so great, and the AROS apps are shouting connection errors at me. My mind feels as though I just woke up with a hangover *and* a sleep-deprivation headache.

Teeth clenched, I look around the room for answers.

THIRTY

THE ROOM IS ALL BUT EMPTY, WITH THE EXCEPTION OF A SLEEK DESK and an office chair. In the chair sits a man with a haircut that could give Ada's hairdo a run for its money.

The walls have an odd metallic sheen to them, and I begin to suspect the cause of my mental state, as well as the reason for AROS bugging out.

I take out my phone to verify my theory, and sure enough, there are no bars or any hint of connectivity.

"Does your phone work?" I whisper to my conspirators.

One by one everyone checks their phones, confirming my suspicions.

So the errors of my AROS interface are due to a lack of connectivity. I got so used to the brain boost that without it, I actually feel like something is missing. I guess that makes sense since, in a way, it's as though an extra part of my brain suddenly went away.

"This room is a Faraday cage," the man behind the desk says without turning. "Hence why I use this." He dangles the network cable that snakes into one of those rugged, briefcase-looking laptops the military likes to use.

"A Faraday cage is an enclosure that blocks electromagnetic energy," I explain in case Gogi or Nadejda aren't familiar with the term. "Put your phone in a microwave oven, and it'll have the same effect. Microwaves have a Faraday cage built in to prevent—"

Alex puts a hand on my shoulder, interrupting me. When I turn, he simply shakes his head at me and says, "Muhomor, let me make the introductions."

"One moment," Muhomor says and types something so fast I wonder if he's just banging the keys randomly to look cool. The keyboard is arranged in JCUKEN (or ЙЦУКЕН in Cyrillic) formation, the Russian answer to the popular QWERTY layout. If Mitya could still communicate with me, he'd probably brag to Ada about his bilingual typing skills, which I lack.

Finally, Muhomor stops the banging and swivels his chair to look us over.

The guy has all the signs of being on a computer for more than twelve hours straight, the most telling of which are his red-rimmed, crusty eyes. Maybe to mask the wear and tear, or maybe to increase the air of mystery around him, he moves his dark shades from atop his head onto his nose. From the front, his spiky hair looks less like Ada's and more like he came out of an anime or Japanese RPG, a feeling heightened by the hint of Asian—likely Mongolian—heritage in his features. He's thin and clad in something like pajamas, which lend him a distinctly nonthreatening air, especially for the super-hacker/criminal Dark Net tsar I expected to meet.

Alex finally gets to the introductions, and Muhomor nods at each of us from his perch, but he doesn't get up to shake our hands.

"So," Muhomor says after Alex introduces the last person, me. "What can I do for you? And, more importantly, what can you do for me?"

Since he's looking at me, I say, "Whatever Alex usually pays you, I'll double it."

"Alex can't afford to just pay me." Muhomor toys with the arm of his sunglasses. "We barter in favors."

"So I'll owe you a big favor," I say evenly. "Time is of the essence here."

"I hear you pick winning companies for a living," Muhomor says, ignoring my plea for urgency. "Is that true?"

"It's an oversimplification, but yeah, that's roughly what I do."

"Good," Muhomor says, and I note some untraceable accent in his Russian. "How about I give you a portfolio of fifty Russian startups to check out, and you tell me which one you'd invest in if it was your money on the line?"

"Deal," I say confidently. "If your information leads to us rescuing my mom, I'll review your portfolio."

"Your mom?" Muhomor raises an eyebrow from under his shades. "I'd also like a million American dollars in addition to the investment advice."

"Done," I say, and low growls come from Gogi and Nadejda's direction. I wonder if they're rethinking how much they should've charged Joe to help him—assuming they're charging him at all.

"Okay then." Muhomor loudly cracks his knuckles. "Tell me how I can help you."

I take this as my cue to give him an edited version of the story, one that excludes any mention of Brainocytes. I finish with, "Maybe you know people who might know something? Or did anything in my story give you a clue about where my mom might be?"

Muhomor drums his fingers on the arms of his office chair for a few seconds, his forehead creased in thought. Then he rattles out, "I'd like to see the photos of all the people you've mentioned—the one called Anton Pintarev and the two you couldn't identify—as well as photos of the men who attacked your car."

"Sure, but I don't have any way of emailing you." I wave my disconnected phone.

"Here." He gets up, takes out a CAT-5-to-micro-USB adapter

from his pajama bottoms, unplugs his laptop, and plugs the freed-up Ethernet cable into the converter.

I take his seat and plug in my phone. As soon as it gets on the network, my mind gets sharper, as though I just drank a triple expresso or popped an Adderall (something I'd done a few times back at MIT).

I restart the chat app and type, "Did you miss me?"

My friends begin speaking at the same time, and I tell them about the Faraday cage and that I don't have any time to talk because I need to email pictures to our helper. Not for the first time today, I notice how seamless this sort of mental typing has gotten for me in such a short time. It almost feels like a psychic phenomenon, like the words show up in the chat because I'm willing them to, and I love that. When it comes to using apps, the feeling is even stronger. The mental effort I exerted while using the imaginary video game controller has fallen away, and I feel like the emails go to Muhomor simply because that's want I want.

"Done," I tell him when the emails leave my outbox.

"Let me plug back in." Muhomor gets inside my space.

I warn Ada and Mitya that I'll be offline for a spell and internally cringe as I disconnect.

The dumbness, for lack of a better term, is much sharper this time, probably because I know what's happening to me.

Muhomor pulls the shades up on top of his head and plugs his laptop back in. I catch him looking at the photos first and then at the bios. He stares at the screen for a bit and then blocks my view as he begins frantically typing again.

I look at everyone else in the room. Joe looks stony, Gogi shrugs, and Nadejda and Alex seem to be two flirtatious words away from holding hands.

The typing stops, and Muhomor turns around and puts his shades back on.

"I'm sorry," he says, not sounding at all apologetic. "Given how little information I have, I can't help you."

"You what?" Joe takes out a gun and steps forward.

"Threatening me won't change the facts," Muhomor says so calmly you'd think Joe's gun shoots water instead of bullets. "Maybe if your cousin told me the whole story—"

"I did," I say.

"No, you did not," Muhomor says. "Nothing in your story even hints at why anyone in Russia would want a bunch of crippled Americans. There wasn't a ransom demand. This whole thing makes no sense."

"Tell him," Joe tells me. "Everyone else will wait outside."

Since he was present in New York, Joe knows about the technology part of the story, though even he doesn't know about the Brainocytes in my head. Still, he must've noticed my earlier omissions, and I bet he understood my need for caution. I also see why he made this suggestion—or more like demand. Given the gruesome video I received, I can't afford to play games with Muhomor. I have to risk telling him the truth.

"Thanks, Joe," I say as he unlocks the door and herds everyone out. "I'll be quick."

Joe closes the door, locking Gogi, Nadejda, and Alex out, and stands by the door like a sentry, arms crossed and face an emotionless mask.

"How much do you know about nanotechnology?" I ask Muhomor.

As it turns out, Muhomor knows quite a bit, so explaining the technology part of the story is pretty easy, though I still leave out the part about my own Brainocytes.

"I think I now have a better idea about what's going on," Muhomor says. "And I have a new deal."

"What?" I glance at Joe, who uncrosses his arms and balls his hands into fists. "We already have a deal."

"That was before you told me the whole story." Muhomor takes off his shades and rubs his eyes. "I have a theory now, and if it's correct, I have to either withdraw from our current deal altogether or ask for a new one."

I catch Joe's gaze. He seems to be offering to soften Muhomor up to make him more agreeable. Imperceptibly, I shake my head. It would be better to get Muhomor to cooperate willingly. Despite strongly suspecting what he'll request, I ask, "What do you want?"

"I want the Brainocytes," says Muhomor, confirming my guess.

I fleetingly consider letting Joe have him, then decide against it, at least for the moment. "For that, you'll have to do more than provide a theory," I say. "To get the Brainocytes, you'll have to basically hand-deliver my mom to me."

"Agreed," Muhomor says, his expression dead serious. "I'll do everything in my power to help you. How does that sound?"

"You'll also have to come to the US to get the Brainocytes," I say. "After this, I'm done with Russia for good."

"That's not a problem. I'll probably need to stay in the US afterwards anyway." Muhomor pulls out a pack of cigarettes, sees my horrified expression at the thought of second-hand smoke, and puts them back in his pocket. "If my theory is right and I help you, I'll have outlived my welcome in Mother Russia. In fact, I'll be lucky if they don't poison my sushi with polonium one day."

Stunned, I stare at him. "Wait a minute," I say slowly, wishing Ada and Mitya could overhear this conversation. "You don't mean it's the KGB that kidnapped my mom?"

For the first time in my life, Joe's expression approaches something remotely resembling concern.

"There's no more KGB." Muhomor cleans his sunglasses with his t-shirt. "But there *is* SVR."

"And you think they're behind this?" I ask incredulously. "Some Directorate T or whatever the modern equivalent is?"

Scenes from one of my favorite TV shows, *The Americans*, flit through my head. It's a show about KGB spies in the US during the eighties, and I love seeing the American side of that decade, since I was living in the Soviet Union at that time. It also helps that the Russian-speaking actors are outstanding, allowing me to enjoy the show on a level that non-Russian speakers miss out on. What's key, though, is that this show is the sole source of my knowledge about the former Russian intelligence agency, and there was definitely a

Directorate T featured as an arm of the KGB that was interested in American advancements in science and technology.

"There's no official modern equivalent on the books." Muhomor looks at Joe for confirmation, gets none, and adds, "But old habits die hard."

"And you think they—"

"No." He gets up and starts pacing the small room, staying at least a leap away from my cousin. "Though this technology seems right up their alley, it sounds like this was done by someone who was looking to gain SVR's favor, or a group only remotely connected with them. Probably something like a subcontractor, if I were to use your American terminology."

"Why do you think that?" I ask, hoping he's right, since KGB subcontractor sounds less scary than KGB proper.

"Those brutes"—he waves at the laptop, where the pictures of Anton and his gang are still up—"aren't your typical agent material."

"True," I say, "but then, wouldn't they have to use people like them? No intelligence agency would want to get caught kidnapping people in the United States."

"The fact that you're alive tells me we're not dealing with the might of the agency itself," Muhomor says in a tone that has me wondering whether he's trying to convince himself as much as me. "I think someone somehow got a whiff of the tech you're working on. That person explained the possibilities to a more connected person and got the job—unofficially, of course."

"Who in Russia could 'get a whiff' of what we're doing?" I ask. "And how?"

"The who is a question for you to answer," Muhomor says. "As to how, I bet you filed papers with the FDA? Applied for a patent, maybe? You Americans are so cavalier with such information."

He's right. Off the top of my head, there's the Investigational Device Exemption filed with the FDA, as well as a million patents that add up to some useful information. Still, it would take someone watching everything from the start to piece it all together, and no one in Russia—or anywhere—should have paid Techno that kind of attention, unless they were tracking all the research and development of every startup company in America, and that seems hard to believe.

Muhomor makes the mistake of getting too close to Joe while pacing, and in a blur of movement, my cousin catches the hacker's slim upper arm in a vise-like grip. "I suggest you get back on your computer," he says softly, almost politely. "You have your new deal. Now tell us where my aunt is."

"Of course." Muhomor unsuccessfully tries to pull free from Joe's grip. "All you had to do was ask nicely."

Joe gives the thin man a push perfectly timed with him releasing his arm, and Muhomor violently plops into his chair. To his credit, he recovers quickly and opens his keyboard to resume that same frantic typing.

After about five minutes, I look at Joe questioningly. My cousin shrugs almost imperceptibly. I nod at Muhomor, and we approach the desk, something Joe manages to do quite menacingly.

"No point in standing over my shoulder," Muhomor says without a break in his typing. "If anything, you're distracting me."

"How much longer do you need?" I ask, fighting the urge to shut the laptop to get the guy's full attention.

"A couple of days," Muhomor says, his eyes never leaving the screen. "Three at most."

Joe slams the laptop cover shut, and Muhomor barely manages to save his fingers. Seems I wasn't the only one with that violent urge.

"Hey." The hacker glares at us. "If you break that machine or my hands, you'll just slow things down."

"We don't have a couple of days," I say. As gently as possible, I put my hand on Joe's shoulder to stop him from doing any more damage. "The video warned me to go back to the US. If I don't..."

Joe gives me a look that says, "Remove that hand or lose it."

I put my hands firmly inside my pockets.

Muhomor looks thoughtful for a couple of seconds and then

asks, "Why don't you bluff them out? Go back to your plane. I'll email you an airport to fly to. We'll choose a backward town with nineties security, and I can make it so they won't know you landed there. We can then meet somewhere safe when I'm done."

"What do you think, Joe?" I ask. "It sounds doable to me."

Joe gives the hacker a onceover and says, "If you cross me, I'll lobotomize you." Matching his actions to his words, Joe pulls out a sharp, thin blade he must've borrowed from Alex's arsenal and jams it a few inches into the desk, a mere hair's width from Muhomor's elbow.

Muhomor visibly pales as he examines the blade. I bet he pictured the thing entering his brain.

Noisily removing the knife from the desk, Joe walks to the door.

"Try to hurry," I urge the hacker as I follow my cousin. "If something happens to my mom, the deal is off and you'll probably have to deal with the SVR—if Joe doesn't get to you first."

Not waiting for his response to that motivational threat, I slam the door behind me.

The world instantly feels richer, and I feel more alive. I have my brain boost back. I fleetingly wonder how long it'll take before I become as reliant on internet connectivity as amphetamine addicts are on their drugs, and decide it probably won't be long.

"Are you okay?" Ada asks worriedly.

"Seriously, what's going on?" Mitya echoes.

Though the music is back to an eardrum-shattering level, I can hear them perfectly well. I guess it makes sense since the Brainocytes are working directly with my brain, giving me the illusion of hearing.

I restart the chat window, and once it's ready, I mentally type, "I'm totally okay, but I'll explain everything in a minute."

Since Joe just started walking away, I take it upon myself to use gestures to explain to Gogi, Nadejda, and Alex that we want to exit the club before we discuss our plans. They understand, and we all follow Joe. By the time we come out by the DJ's podium, I have all my apps back up, with the AROS icons surrounding me in a surreal tableau that blends surprisingly well with the strobe lights reflecting off the nicely dressed people grinding on the dance floor.

Suddenly, I hear Einstein's voice, and I freeze, trying to make sense of the phrase the AI is repeating over and over.

"Sketchy person alert. Sketchy person alert. Sketchy person alert. Sketchy person alert…"

Einstein repeats that statement over and over, as if he's stuck on a loop, but then I realize the face recognition app must've scanned my surroundings for people with criminal profiles. Einstein is warning me there's a bunch of dangerous people around.

At first I wonder if they're Alex's people, but as much as I'd love for that to be the case, it's unlikely. Muhomor forbade Alex from bringing anyone, and Alex told us Muhomor takes that instruction very seriously. Also, I don't get repeat alerts, meaning I've never met these people before, and I'm certain I met the majority of Alex's guards when we were at the Palace.

Still, I have a small hope that the app is bugging out after getting disconnected, so I carefully scan the thousand faces around me.

The heavy music beat seems to grow distant, and despite the sweat gleaming on many faces, I feel like the temperature in the club dropped by several degrees as I note all the men with red haloes sprinkled around the room. Not a single one looks familiar, but I can tell they're dangerous men, hardened by life in ways I can't imagine.

The nearest one looks at me, then at his smartphone, and then gestures in my direction.

On instinct, I leap for Joe. Grabbing his arm, I scream into his ear, "Joe, we're being ambushed!" To highlight my words, I point at the guy who's gesturing.

For a second, I'm not sure Joe heard me, but then two things happen at once. Joe looks at the man I pointed out, and almost instantly, there's a gun in Joe's hand.

Before I can blink, several red-haloed men are holding guns as well.

"They can't start shooting in here," I type into the chat, almost instinctively. "It's too public. It'll be all over the news with a headline like 'Shooting in a Nightclub.' It'll draw too much attention and—"

I don't get to finish my thought, because the loud music is interrupted by a thunderous clap that causes my heart to jump into my throat.

I was wrong in the assessment I just gave my friends.

Someone just fired a gun in the middle of the dance floor.

THIRTY-ONE

ALL AROUND ME PEOPLE BEGIN SCREAMING, SHOUTING, AND running in random directions.

Another shot is fired.

I freeze in place, unsure what to do.

Joe grabs me by the front of my shirt and throws me backward. Before I can hit the floor, strong, hairy hands grab me and shove me behind the DJ's podium. I recognize Gogi as the owner of the hands. As soon as he's done with me, he pulls out two guns with the speed of a gunslinger and fires.

I duck behind the podium and, in morbid fascination, watch Gogi aim his guns again. Dazedly, I wonder if his laser sights are useless in the ambient laser display in the club.

My question is answered instantly.

One moment I see two red dots on the forehead of the red-haloed man who first noticed me, and in the next, two shots blast out and the guy's head explodes like a brain-filled piñata.

Amidst the screaming, the people closest to the dead man freeze in place, and a few smarter ones drop to the ground, protectively shielding their heads with their arms.

Another round of shots follows.

Doing my best to stay hidden from our assailants, I examine my entourage.

Like me, Gogi and Nadejda are using the DJ's podium as cover. He's methodically aiming his two guns while she's preparing her Uzi. I don't know if it's the same one she used in the car or a newer, better model she got from Alex's armory.

Alex is crawling on the floor toward the hallway that leads to Muhomor. It occurs to me we got lucky the assailants didn't ambush us while we were in that room, as was probably their original plan.

I seek out Joe on the dance floor. He's using Gogi's cover fire, as well as the bodies of panicked people, to execute another gunman.

As I take it all in, I realize my allies have a big problem.

Unlike me, they don't know who the bad guys are, and they have to rely on visual cues, such as people holding guns and looking threatening. However, a few assailants are trying to blend in with the crowd, with only their red haloes giving them away.

I form a quick plan to deal with this problem and decide to shut down the music so my allies can hear me share my superior knowledge with them.

Taking out my gun, I approach the dumbfounded DJ.

"Take that off," I shout over the noise and wave my gun (with the safety still on) at the cosmonaut helmet in an up-and-down motion. In the curved, reflective surface of the visor, my face looks like a frightened caricature.

The DJ reaches for the headgear, but it suddenly explodes, shards of glass and plastic flying everywhere. A piece of glass nicks my earlobe, but the pain barely registers. Instead, I watch in horrified shock as the DJ's dead body crumples in front of me.

"Duck!" Mitya screams. "That bullet was meant for you."

My legs fold under me as if of their own accord. Finding myself on the floor, I start pulling cables out of the DJ's laptop, figuring one of them will cut the music. Thanks to Murphy's Law, the cable

I need is the last one I pull, and the music stops, the sudden silence amplifying the terrified screams and the gunfire.

I sneak a peek at the mayhem and spot a red-haloed dude within a couple of feet of my cousin. Grabbing the DJ's microphone, I yell, "Joe, behind you!"

My voice booms across the dance floor, and Joe begins to turn. At the same time, the man pulls out his concealed weapon.

It's clear my cousin won't make it.

"Joe!" I scream, and then I hear the *rat-tat-tat* of the Uzi.

The man behind Joe falls. While I was dealing with the music, Nadejda exited the safety of the podium and got close enough to the action to put her Uzi to use.

Joe gives Nadejda the barest nod as thanks and runs toward the main exit, where the crowd is thicker and will provide him with good cover.

For the next minute, I use the mic to warn Joe and the others where the less obvious red-haloed guys are.

My gaze falls on Nadejda. A red-haloed man must've crept up behind her, because he has her in a headlock. I think I see Nadejda turning purple, though it's hard to tell from this distance and especially with these lights.

"Joe, Gogi, help Nadejda," I yell into the mic, but they have their own problems. Gogi is exchanging fire with three men, and my cousin is dealing with two assailants.

"You should shoot that guy yourself," Mitya suggests urgently. "Use the aiming app."

Something inside me snaps, and I don't even notice how I start up the gun-assist app. My weapon just suddenly has the aiming line. Just as automatically, I take the safety off the gun and use the assist app to line up the barrel with the leg of the guy behind Nadejda.

"If your hand shakes," Ada says, "or if the app doesn't work the way we hoped, you could hit Nadejda."

"If he doesn't shoot, she'll die anyway," Mitya retorts.

I wish I had time to think this through, but I don't. Going off my instincts, I squeeze the trigger.

The bullet bites off a chunk of the big man's thigh.

To my utter amazement, he doesn't let go of his victim's neck. Still, the wound weakens him enough to give Nadejda her chance. In what must be a wrestling maneuver, she rips free from the guy's grasp, and in a continuous motion, she lifts the wounded man into the air. To my eyes, he seems to hover over her head for a moment before his back lands over Nadejda's knee. I can almost hear his spine cracking from all the way behind the podium.

A bullet whines past my ear, and I switch focus from Nadejda to the bullet's origin.

The shooter is a blond guy, and he's still aiming at me.

I touch his right shoulder with my aim-assist line and pull the trigger.

The guy falls. He's twitching on the floor, so I assume he's alive.

"Stop shooting to maim," Mitya yells at me. "Shoot to kill."

"Don't listen to him," Ada retorts.

"Don't speak to me right now," I type into the chat. "I'll do what I have to."

What I don't say is that I'm siding more with Ada's viewpoint. I can't picture myself killing anyone, even though these people deserve it, both for trying to shoot us and because they're working with whoever kidnapped Mom. I'm not sure if it's the bios provided by the face recognition app or something ingrained in me, but I stick to shooting arms and legs, figuring I can analyze my reluctance to kill at a more opportune time. On the plus side—assuming it's a pro and not a con to be cold-blooded—I have zero qualms about the wounds I inflict.

I shoot the arm of a long-haired man aiming at Gogi while a speaker to my right shatters into small bits of metal and plastic.

Unperturbed, I hit the shoulder of a bald guy who was about to get Joe.

An odd sense of flow overcomes me, and I spend the next

couple of minutes in a blur of aiming my Glock, pulling the trigger, rinsing and repeating, over and over again.

When my gun clicks empty, the concentration leaves me, and I take a look at the blood-soaked dance floor. Thanks to our joint efforts, the number of red-haloed men left standing is reduced to just a few individuals.

Since my extra magazines are in Alex's SUV, along with duffel bags full of other tools of war, I decide to leave the rest of our enemies to my cousin and his crew. It's time to get Muhomor and Alex and tell them we have to get as far away from this place as possible. It doesn't take a brain boost to realize a shootout in a popular nightclub means half of Moscow's police department is on their way. Dealing with the cops could easily turn deadly, and even in the best case, it could lead to a huge delay in rescuing Mom.

I turn and instantly get hit with the most intense fight-or-flight response of the last two days—a feat I wouldn't have thought possible until that very moment.

There's a guy behind me.

A guy with a halo and a comic book balloon with his bio above his head.

His gun looks like a medieval cannon, and its massive barrel is pointed squarely at my head.

THIRTY-TWO

OPERATING ON PURE ADRENALINE, I DROP MY GUN AND RAISE MY hands. "Don't shoot! I give up."

My reaction seems to confuse my attacker for a moment, but then his face calcifies.

He's about to pull the trigger.

Suddenly, there's a whirl of motion.

The shooter grabs his head, and his gun flies into the air, landing two feet away from me.

Muhomor is standing behind the guy. Despite the sunglasses, I can make out the terror on the hacker's face. As I take in his tight grip on the briefcase-like laptop, I understand what happened.

Muhomor used his computer to club my attacker on the head.

The red-haloed man recovers and punches Muhomor in the stomach.

Muhomor doubles over, his sunglasses flying to the side.

I dive for the gun and bring it up, but there's no time to enter the gun's information into the aim assist app.

I have to shoot now, without hitting Muhomor.

Fortunately, I'm only a few feet away. Unfortunately, you could run a small town on the adrenaline in my veins.

"Shoot!" Mitya and Ada yell together.

The red-haloed guy sees my dilemma and pounces on Muhomor.

In a second, they'll be too intertwined for me to shoot safely, so I pull the trigger.

The gunshot reverberates through every cell in my eardrums, and the recoil makes my hands jerk.

A red stain on the man's leg proves I hit my target.

The pain must be bad, because the guy starts screaming, bends over, and clutches his leg.

Muhomor uses this moment to kick our opponent in the face. Blood sprays from the guy's nose, and he falls to the ground with a muffled grunt. Muhomor kicks the body a few more times, then looks at me, eyes wild. "What? Who? How?"

"No time," I say. Into the DJ's mic, I add, "We have to get out of here."

Muhomor closes the distance between us and unhooks the DJ's laptop. "It has a network card," he says.

I shrug and hobble away. Even with the adrenaline-induced numbness spreading through my mind and body, I feel a zillion aches and pains.

Joe meets us at the bottom of the podium. He's dragging Alex by the back of his shirt. The shootout must've been too much for Alex, because he has the composure of a ragdoll cat.

As we cross the dance floor, I focus on looking where I step and fighting my gag reflex.

"Is there another way out of here?" Gogi asks Muhomor. "Not through the casino?"

"Yes," the thin man replies. "The banya. Follow me."

He starts running, and we all follow as fast as possible without slipping on all the blood.

We exit the slaughterhouse of the dance floor through the southern door.

The once pearl-white tiles of the spa are covered in crimson footprints thanks to the mob that preceded us. We follow the grisly markers to a staircase on the opposite side of the large pool.

I move almost mechanically, occasionally fighting strange urges, like a desire to clean the blood from my shoes in the hot tub we pass.

A swift sprint later, we reach the stairs, and just as quickly, we find ourselves outside.

Muhomor clearly knew where he was going, because we're in a nearly empty parking lot.

When we reach the Land Rover, Joe says, "Alex, get in the back. Gogi, you drive."

Since I wasn't instructed where to go, I get into the middle seat, and Muhomor joins me. He puts his military suitcase on his lap and stacks the DJ's laptop on top. He then pulls out a sealed smartphone and unwraps it. He must be creating a hotspot for the DJ's laptop so he can get online, not unlike how I've been staying online all this time. I don't mention I have my own hotspot already available. The last thing I want is a hacker anywhere near a connection hooked up to my Brainocytes.

Gogi floors the gas pedal, and our tires violently screech as we surge forward.

As we approach the parking lot's exit, I make out the sound of police sirens.

"The cops are almost here." Muhomor confirms my guess about the hotspot by typing on the laptop in front of him. "And that includes OMON."

OMON is the Russian version of SWAT, so if they're here and see us as a threat, we're toast.

Muhomor opens a terminal session using Putty—a tool I'm familiar with from my programming days. I watch his bony fingers dance across the keyboard, and after a moment, he grins. "This should distract them," he says and presses the Enter key. Alarms suddenly blast from the Dazdraperma club.

Unfortunately, when we hit the street, only some of the cops are looking at the noisy building, and at least two heavily armored

OMON officers are blocking our way, their assault rifles pointed at us.

"Over them," my cousin says, though I don't think Gogi needed urging given how confidently the SUV is torpedoing forward.

The officers in our way fly apart, and automatic gunfire rains down on our SUV from every direction.

I duck, but not before I see two police cars blocking the road ahead of us in a makeshift blockade.

Glass shards, bits of plastic, and metal fly all around me. Bullets whoosh by, and the only reason I don't tuck my head between my legs is my morbid curiosity over our possible cause of death. There are so many options.

We hit the fronts of the two cars with a world-shattering clang.

My head jerks back, and I wish I had tucked my head between my legs after all. It feels like my whiplash from the Zapo accident just got its own case of whiplash.

Straining to breathe, I realize my left nostril is bleeding again. I ignore it and check on how the others are doing. Gogi's knuckles are white on the wheel as our car surges forward. Alex is whimpering something unintelligible from the back. Muhomor's laptops are on the floor, and he's hugging himself and shaking like a frightened five-year-old. Nadejda split her shaved head on the dashboard. For whatever reason, she didn't buckle up when we left the parking lot.

Nadejda's reason for not buckling up soon becomes apparent. Oblivious to the blood trickling from the nasty cut on her forehead, she opens the window, leans out, and shoots at something behind us.

Muhomor calms down enough to execute my earlier idea for dealing with the surrounding violence; he tucks his head between his knees. Then he comes back up with both laptops, sets them up like before, and, to my amazement, begins typing again.

I chance a look back. The rear window is gone, allowing Joe to shoot at the swiftly approaching police cars. As I expected from the whimpering, Alex is on the floor in a fetal position.

The strange concentration I felt back in the club overcomes me again, making me wonder if adrenaline stimulates the brain boost in some positive way. With calm, methodical determination, I locate a magazine for my Glock and load it in with a click. I then turn all the way around so my knees are on the seat and my elbows are resting on the headrest. I aim the gun, and the Augmented Reality sight line appears. As I move the gun around, the AU assist continues uninterrupted, even when I point the barrel at faraway targets, like the nearest pursuing car half a block away.

I struggle to hold the line on the tire. Gogi must've just dodged another car or a pedestrian, because the car jerks and I lose my target.

"Can you drive smoothly for one second?" I say without turning.

Gogi grunts and we stop zigzagging, so I guess he's trying to accommodate my request.

I hold my breath, place the line on the tire again, and gently squeeze the trigger.

The cop car swerves off the road and crashes through the glass of a storefront.

Now that the lead car is gone, I see an even bigger vehicle behind it, and this one belongs to OMON, who are shooting at us with automatic weapons.

"Wow," I hear Mitya say as though from a distance. "I wonder if his shooting skills improved from the brain boost or just the aim app? Hand-eye coordination is—"

I don't hear any more of Mitya's musings, or even the gunfire erupting all around me, because my attention zeroes in on my gun and this bigger car's tire. The state I'm in is amazing. With the absence of all other stimuli, I realize how many distractions were around me. My wrists are no longer aching from the recoil, and I've stopped gagging from the smell of gunpowder. And though the smoothness of the ride is gone, I don't really notice it.

I intuitively raise my elbows off the headrest, adjusting to the back-and-forth motion of the car.

My finger waits for the right moment.

I don't know how I know it's time to take the shot, but when I fire, the faraway tire explodes and the OMON car violently veers off the road.

I keep the gun steady, ready to shoot more tires if I have to, but the road behind us is clear. Still, the sound of sirens is close, so I don't let myself relax. I do, however, pat my jacket pocket and confirm that Mr. Spock is within it.

"Are we safe?" Alex croaks, his voice so small it's barely recognizable.

"No," Muhomor says. "But I'm in their network." He raises the DJ's laptop from his lap. "Anyone without a line of sight on us will have a hard time keeping up. Still, we must switch cars as soon as possible."

"Great," Gogi says. "I'll just find the nearest car dealership."

"No need for sarcasm," Muhomor says after another few seconds of frantic typing. "Everything's been arranged. Take a left on Youth Street. There should be a Gastronom parking lot there."

I realize I'm still in a shooting position, and Joe is looking at me with what must be curiosity on his austere face, though it could just as easily be disapproval. Then he gives me a faint nod that seems to say, "Good shooting. Thanks, Mike."

I face forward again and buckle up, and it's a good thing I do. Gogi must've spotted the necessary street at the last second, because we nearly flip over on the turn.

With no reduction in speed, we fly into the parking lot of a big supermarket, and I reflect on how tragically ironic it would be if we got killed in a car crash right after escaping a war zone.

"Over there," Muhomor says. "The white minivan."

We screech to a tire-smoking halt next to the minivan, and I spot the familiar face of Lyuba, the girl from the puzzle, behind the wheel.

As our crew moves our stuff into the minivan, I calm down enough to pay attention to Mitya and Ada's conversation, and I overhear him say, "That's a Ford Windstar. It's clever using something like that. The back windows are tinted, and the car is so dorky the cops will think it's just a rich soccer mom behind the wheel."

As though to confirm his idea, Muhomor says, "Mike, as the least threatening-looking person, you should sit in the front."

I could argue that my bruises make me look tougher than his skinny ass, but I get into the front seat anyway. My hope is that a family car like this might have a passenger side airbag, a handy device in case Lyuba drives as dangerously as Gogi.

My cousin practically drags Alex into the back of the minivan and stays with him as Gogi, Muhomor, and Nadejda sit in the middle. I buckle up before Lyuba starts driving, but I quickly see I won't need that airbag. If anything, Lyuba drives annoyingly slow.

Her strategy pays off; the couple of police cars we pass simply drive by.

"The Gadyukino hideout," Muhomor says from his middle seat.

"On it," Lyuba says and makes a signaled, super-careful, almost slow-motion right turn.

Once I no longer hear sirens, I let myself breathe normally and reach into my pocket to check on Mr. Spock again.

When I take him out, the poor creature's mental aura is black. According to my notes, that means he's tense, nervous, or harassed. This time, I don't even need Ada's app to tell me he's frightened. His general haggard appearance is surprisingly telling.

"Does anyone have any snacks?" I ask and gently stroke the rat's soft white fur.

"Glove compartment," Lyuba says, reacting to Mr. Spock with a lack of curiosity bordering on indifference.

I open the drawer in front of me and see it's full of Russian-style junk food, which is actually a bit healthier than the American variety. I give Mr. Spock a few pine nuts and a piece of Alyonka chocolate bar. Spock gratefully eats his share, and I follow his example by consuming a much bigger handful of nuts and the rest of the candy. Once the worst of my hunger is satisfied, I gobble down a Tula Gingerbread—a treat from my childhood that tastes like pure nostalgia.

"He looks much better," Ada says when Mr. Spock's aura turns the blue-green color associated with a moderately relaxed state. "And he seems to be acting normal, just like his recently enhanced brothers and sisters."

"Wait," I type into the chat. "You already tested that resource allocation rigmarole on them?"

"I applied it when you went incommunicado in that room," Ada says. "Mitya and I flipped a coin, and I'm about to become the first official human test subject."

"Be careful, guys," I reply and watch Mr. Spock for any deviance in his behavior.

The little guy's color turns blue, and the only strange thing I notice is how intensely he's looking at the cup holder.

"Are you thirsty?" I ask him out loud, and again, Lyuba doesn't bat an eyelash, as though talking to your pet rat is as unremarkable as whipping one out of your pocket.

It could be my imagination, but I think Mr. Spock gives me a barely perceptible nod.

"Ada, do your rats know how to nod?" I mentally type into the chat. "Because I think he just did."

"Well," Ada says, "while I haven't observed that behavior before, I figure with the brain boost and all this human socializing, they might be learning things like that."

"May I?" I ask Lyuba as I reach for the water bottle.

"There are unopened ones in the back," the woman says. "But of course, you can also have mine."

Before I can retort something hopefully clever, Gogi's hairy paw shows up, holding a sealed bottle, and I take it from him.

Water bottles clearly weren't designed for rats to drink out of, and more water spills onto my jacket than into Mr. Spock's mouth. However, it must've been the final thing my furry friend needed, because his aura turns violet—the nirvana-like rat state.

I drink the rest of the water, and we drive contentedly for a while.

When the area turns rural and we're the only car on the road, I overhear Joe talking, which is strange, because he usually only speaks when he's about to hurt someone. When Joe falls silent, Alex says something, his voice sounding beyond terrified.

My heart rate speeds up.

Picking up on the same vibes, Mr. Spock scurries back into my pocket, and in the next instant, the car is filled with an inhuman shriek, followed by the smell of human feces.

I recognize the shriek as Alex's.

As far as I can tell, he just soiled himself and is screaming like a psychotic banshee.

THIRTY-THREE

A LIST OF GLOOMY POSSIBILITIES FLASHES THROUGH MY MIND, EACH more unrealistic than the other. Are the cops shooting at us again? Or is Alex watching another video where a hostage is brutally murdered?

I turn around and see it's something else.

Something to do with Joe towering over Alex and moving his arms around.

"Please, stop!" Alex shrieks. "Please, don't!"

I glimpse the point of Joe's knife piercing the tip of Alex's finger. Alex howls.

I finally comprehend what's happening, if not the why of it.

My cousin is torturing Alex while questioning him about something. The exact questions are hard to hear over Alex's screaming.

Muhomor's face is as contorted in fear as mine. In contrast, Gogi and Nadejda look utterly placid.

"Give him a chance to speak," Gogi says academically in the brief silence between screams. "He's probably ready."

Joe stops his grisly work, but it takes a few minutes for Alex to downgrade from shrieking to helplessly crying.

"You better talk," Nadejda says, her pseudo-friendly voice making me wonder if she's trying to capitalize on their earlier flirtations. "That isn't even a fraction of what Joe will do to you if you don't start speaking."

"Oh boy," Ada's angel form says. "If she's the good cop, I don't envy poor Alex."

"Yes," Alex whines. "It was me, but I didn't have a choice. Govrilovskiy has things on me. I had to tell them where you were landing and about the club, but I tried to stop you from going, remember? That's why I made the video—"

Joe slams his fist into Alex's head, cutting off the rest of his sentence.

My cousin's face is filled with more emotion than I've ever seen from him, but unfortunately for Alex, that emotion is wrath.

I cringe as I watch Joe deliver blow after hard blow, inflicting the kind of damage Alex might never recover from.

I know that I shouldn't be watching this, that I'll have nightmares for the rest of my life, but I'm hypnotized by the cruel precision of each strike and the sound of bones breaking.

In a surreal underscore to the violence, Muhomor starts typing on his keyboard again.

I'm in a strange stupor as the car pulls over to the side of the road, and Nadejda and Gogi restrain Joe. To me, it feels as if only a moment passed between Joe beating on Alex and my cousin's people holding him cautiously.

Slowly, my daze clears, and I process what happened. Just to make sure I'm not crazy, I share my revelations with my New York allies via the chat. "Alex confessed. He told someone, a guy named Govrilovskiy, where we were landing and about our destination—his residence. That was enough information for them to figure out what path we'd take. They also had enough time to dispatch the car that nearly drove us off the road. Since we survived that first encounter, Alex shared our plans to visit Muhomor at Dazdraperma. That's how the squad knew to ambush us there."

"I'm afraid you're spot on," Mitya says. "I'm so sorry I put you in touch with this traitor. I didn't think—"

"It's not your fault," I reply. "This Govrilovskiy was blackmailing Alex, a common occurrence in this country."

"But I should've figured this out," Mitya says. "The club thing could've had several explanations, but I should've considered that first attack. Besides you, me, Joe, and Ada, only Alex knew where you were going to land. True, there were your cousin's people to consider, but they seem very loyal to him, and they're also outsiders in Russia, so that only leaves Alex as the traitor—something Joe must've realized."

I recall Joe asking me if I trusted Mitya and Ada after the first attack and decide Mitya is right. Joe's paranoia made him realize the truth first.

"I just can't believe Alex could eat and drink with you in his home while planning to lead you to your deaths in the club," Mitya says in disgust.

"I don't mean to defend Alex," Ada says, "but he did try to stop you from going to the club. Before, and especially after the video, he insisted—"

"The video," I say out loud as another part of Alex's confession registers. "It was fake?"

"Yeah," Muhomor says. "Now that I had reason to suspect it, I checked it out and verified it's a clip from an obscure Russian horror flick called *The Handy Man*. Also, because we now know both the sender and the receiver, I should be able to link the email to Alex, though that would be overkill since he already confessed."

So this is what the thin man was doing on his computer during the beating. I feel a sense of relief mixed with a desire to punch what's left of Alex for making me think someone might put a drill to my mom's head. I also realize this is why Joe went berserk. In his own way, my cousin must've been worried about my mom, and when he learned Alex had created that video, he acted on the same impulse I'm currently suppressing.

"Let me go," Joe orders his allies, "or you're next."

Gogi releases Joe, and Nadejda follows.

They calmed him down enough that he doesn't resume beating Alex's limp body. Instead, he pointedly draws his gun and says, "Take him out of the car."

Gogi and Nadejda grab Alex and begin dragging him out.

"Wait," Muhomor says frantically. "Alex is a very high-profile individual. You can't just shoot him and leave him on the road. It's better if he disappears, and I know people who can make that happen. I can also make his digital trail look like he took a long vacation in Australia or some other faraway place."

Nadejda and Gogi stop, but Joe looks unconvinced.

"There's also your mission to consider," Muhomor adds. "We might still need Alex for that. If I don't get any hits when I search for this Govrilovskiy character, I might need more names."

"Fine," Joe says and gets into Gogi's seat. "Ride next to him."

The Georgian gets in the back, checks Alex's pulse, and says, "Alive for now."

Lyuba restarts the car, and we ride in sullen silence all the way to the village.

"This place isn't actually called Gadyukino," Mitya tells Ada when she comments on the discrepancy. "I realize why you thought so, given Muhomor's comments about the 'Gadyukino hideout,' but Gadyukino is just a nickname we Russians sometimes give to hole-in-the-wall places like this little community."

Gadyukino, or whatever the real name of this place is, is at its core a former *kolkhoz*, the dysfunctional Soviet collective farm. There aren't any paved roads here, and the village houses look exactly the same as when I visited a similar place all the way back in the eighties—poor and impossibly drab.

One structure stands out, however: the really worn-down and abandoned-looking warehouse we're heading toward.

"How do you feel, Ada?" Mitya asks in the chat. "Any insights?"

"Hold on," I interject. "You already got the resource allocation thing to increase your intelligence boost?"

"Yes," Ada replies. "Right before your psycho cousin went all Vlad The Impaler on Alex's ass."

"And?" I mentally type. "How do you feel?"

"I'm fine," Ada says out loud. "I feel a lot like when I first got the original boost."

"So, like nothing at all," I say. "At least that's how I felt."

"I wouldn't say nothing at all," Ada says. "I feel the potential, and the fact I'm feeling fine is a significant result in itself."

"I guess I'm next," Mitya says.

"Shouldn't it be Mike?" Ada asks. "He might need it more."

"Fine," Mitya mumbles, almost under his breath. With an exaggerated sigh, he adds, "I guess I can wait a little longer."

"You up for it, Mike?" Ada asks.

I think about it, then decide whatever extra advantage this boost might offer is welcome. "Okay, hit me."

"I'll set it up and let you know in a sec," she says. "You might want to pay attention to your surroundings for now."

I catch myself sitting with my eyes closed—a bad habit I'm developing when using the AROS interface. I open my eyes and realize we're already inside the warehouse and Lyuba is parking the car.

I look around.

If a twister decimated a couple of high-end datacenters, plus a RadioShack and maybe the computer department at Best Buy, the aftermath might look like the inside of this "hideout."

Muhomor exits the car, hands the DJ's laptop to Lyuba, and says, "The machine needs to disappear completely, and Alex needs to be kept alive for the moment."

Without waiting for Lyuba to reply, or even inviting us to follow, Muhomor prances toward the big wall of monitors.

Gogi shrugs and heads in the same direction, and the rest of us follow.

"It's all set," Ada says. "Just click on that little blue brain when you're ready."

"I'm crossing my breath and holding my fingers," I mentally jest while locating the icon in question. Initiating the app, I say, "This is it."

THIRTY-FOUR

PART OF ME THOUGHT THIS TIME WOULD BE DIFFERENT, YET I FEEL almost nothing again.

My vision might be slightly sharper, but that could be from the lights Muhomor just turned on. Also, my hearing seems keener, almost like I can tell which keys Muhomor is banging on his keyboard, but this could be an illusion as well. I guess I'll feel more as my brain adjusts to its new capabilities, like before.

"It might help if you get on a better connection," Ada says when I complain to her. "I had more effects than you described."

"Okay," I say, "but I'm not sure I want to get on Muhomor's Wi-Fi."

"Speaking of the devil, I think he has something," Mitya chimes in.

I look over and see everyone huddling around Muhomor as he turns around and says, "Govrilovskiy was a solid lead and proves I was right about the intelligence community connection."

At his audience's blank stares, he asks me to explain and resumes typing. I go through his SVR-contractor theory for those who had to leave the room and for my NYC friends. Since Muhomor is only paying attention to his computer, no doubt working on this lead, I guesstimate the answers to all their questions. I even go as far as proposing theories about the sinister applications the Russian government—and especially the KGB's offspring agency—might have for the Brainocyte technology.

I'm in the middle of discussing the benefits of having telepathic-like coms and various Augmented Reality overlays on the battlefield, when Muhomor stops typing and says, "Like I thought, Govrilovskiy is the head of a group that acts as a contractor for the agency. He has connections in the government, in business, and particularly in the criminal underworld. The good news is I just got into his organization's systems and located a few facilities where his people might keep important research subjects." He works on his computer for a few seconds, and maps of different parts of Russia appear on several screens. "The bad news is there are twelve locations." More maps show up on the screens. "The worse news is that each and every location is pretty much a fortress."

"Can you locate this Govrilovskiy?" Gogi strokes his mustache with his index finger and thumb in a movie-villain manner. "If we had him, we could find out where our quarry is."

Bile rises in my throat as I picture the methods they might use to find out this information. Alex's ordeal is still very fresh in my psyche.

"Let me try," Muhomor replies without turning. "This might take a while, so why don't you all stretch your legs a little?"

Given Joe's body language, it's clear he's considering making Muhomor work faster by putting a gun to the thin man's head. He doesn't actually get his weapon out, though, so maybe he decided that's not the best motivational tool at his disposal.

I locate a dingy chair a few feet from Muhomor and close my eyes for a second. It's a mistake, because it makes me realize how utterly tired I am. There's jetlag, and then there's jetlag combined with the crash you experience after a monstrous release of adrenaline. Despite all this, a spark of an idea—something that might avoid more torture and improve our chances at a successful rescue

—keeps gnawing away at my weary brain, keeping me awake. I rub my temples as though trying to physically jumpstart my brain, and in a jolt of inspiration, a way to locate Mom comes to me.

Hopefully, Muhomor is as good a hacker as I think he is.

Before I speak up, I mentally share my idea with Ada and Mitya. When I'm done, Ada says, "See, the boost might already be working. That's a great idea. I'm ashamed I didn't come up with it myself."

"I feel like I would've suggested it with time," Mitya says, his avatar bashful. "I'll send you the specs you'll need."

"I have an idea," I say, walking back to Muhomor.

"This guy is very careful when it comes to his whereabouts," Muhomor tells me over his shoulder, and I suspect he didn't hear my soft-spoken proclamation. "No obvious calendar entries, no—"

"I know how to locate Mom without him," I say firmly. "Can you look at me, please?"

Muhomor turns around, and for the first time since the shootout, he looks like himself. He even located another pair of sunglasses, and they're back in place, sitting on his nose.

"According to an app I wrote with my friends," I begin, "my mom's Brainocytes aren't currently on any network, either Wi-Fi or cellular."

"Understood," Muhomor says. "Otherwise, we'd know where she is."

"Right," I reply. "But think about it. The Brainocytes are probably trying to connect to the Wi-Fi at these locations you mentioned. The network must be secure, and thus her connection requests keep failing."

Muhomor's eyes widen with excitement. "Of course. But if I hack into the Wi-Fi and leave the right ports open—"

"She'd connect and we'd know her location," I finish. "I'll send over the ports and the specs for the logins."

"Actually," Mitya mentally chimes in, "we could also communicate with your mom once she's on Wi-Fi. Given enough time, I can write something to piggyback on her current interface."

I don't mention what Mitya said to Muhomor because the hacker is already working on the problem, and I don't want to delay him. Instead, I walk around his hideout, collecting parts for another, much less defined idea I have.

It takes me half an hour to locate a small night-vision camera, and a few more minutes to find something I can use to make a tiny harness.

"I can modify this stuff into a camera like the one I'm wearing and turn Mr. Spock into a spy," I mentally type.

"Sure," Ada says. "That'll work great at night. During the day, we can capture what Mr. Spock sees through his Brainocytes."

"Yep," I reply. "I remembered that. I just know that rats have poor night vision, so—"

A noise that must've originally been meant to signal the start of a nuclear bombardment fills the hideout. Oddly, it sounds familiar, like the ding of a computer notification, except obscenely loud.

Then it hits me.

It's the alarm Ada put together to notify me when Mom gets online. The app was running in the background all this time. The fact that it just went off means Muhomor must've hacked the bad guys' Wi-Fi and opened a port for Mom's Brainocytes.

Confirming my realization, Muhomor yells, "Eureka!"

"I have the location." On her avatar, Ada's relieved eyes look as tired as I feel. "Sending it to you now."

I summon Joe and the others and send the location to Muhomor. Then we all huddle around the wall of monitors.

"They're in the Chelyabinsk facility," Muhomor says disappointedly. "It's one of the heavier-fortified locations."

On the screens, we see schematics of the buildings on the compound, as well as a very discouraging satellite view. This place is to a fortress what a fortress is to a wooden hut. Five thousand acres in size with barbed-wire-topped walls surrounding it, the place looks like a military base.

"This"—I point at a building in the middle of the facility—"is where Mom is."

Joe looks at Gogi expectantly, and the Georgian nods, saying, "I think I can devise a plan, but I'll need more details."

Muhomor provides Gogi with a ton of information about the facility and some of the resources we can use.

At the end of it all, Gogi explains the plan he formed based on all our data, and as he goes on, he breaks many of my expectations. I always thought when I located Mom there'd be something like a heist to get her out. If not a heist, then maybe a hostage negotiation. But what Gogi is proposing is neither.

It's more along the lines of a SEAL Team Six black op—something a venture capitalist like me can't even imagine participating in.

"You can take a nap en route," Gogi tells me when the preparations begin. "It's an hour drive to the supermarket, and half an hour more to get the other supplies from Muhomor's shadier connections. From there, it's forty minutes to the plane, and then a two-and-a-half-hour flight to Chelyabinsk."

———

Lyuba is driving again; this time, we're in a station wagon. She transferred all the weapons Alex provided into this car, but not the man himself. Him, she tied up and left behind. I don't dare ask what her plans are for him, because I probably won't like the answer.

As we leave the bumpy dirt road of Gadyukino behind, I try to sleep, but the remnants of adrenaline in my system thwart my attempts.

When we get to our first stop, the supermarket, I look around and can't help but be impressed by the very American abundance of items. Back in the late eighties, when the empty store shelves held only canned seaweed, Russians couldn't have even dreamed of this.

What's extra impressive is that the supermarket contains a

bunch of businesses inside, similar to a Wal-Mart. Purely on a whim, I walk into the hair salon.

"How can I help you?" the hairstylist asks. Styles in Russia often lag behind, so she has a poodle-like eighties hairdo that reminds me of the cashiers from my childhood. However, her smile is genuine, unlike the horrific customer service back in the Soviet era.

"I'd like you to color him gray-black," I say in Russian and take out Mr. Spock.

The woman's composure cracks, and her eyes widen. Before she can decide to kick me out, I take out a thick roll of hundred-dollar bills.

Her eyes threaten to pop out of her head, but the cash does its job. Without a hint of hesitancy, she gently takes the little guy from my hands and asks, "Do you want me to leave this pink streak on top?"

"No," I say as seriously as I can. "He'll be doing something stealthy at night, so the pink won't be right for that."

If the woman thinks I'm dangerous or crazy—a fairly reasonable assumption at this point—she hides it well and proceeds to color Mr. Spock, who endures the whole process stoically, almost as though he understands the reason behind this human madness.

With the rat disguise complete, I get Mr. Spock a bunch of treats and head back to the car.

Once we start driving, I go over Gogi's plan in my mind and find that the very first step makes sleeping nearly impossible. I settle for trying to relax, using all my willpower not to think about the inevitable.

When we get to Mitya's plane, all my attempts to relax evaporate. I'm so terrified of what's about to happen I don't even notice the departure—what I used to think was the worst part of flying. That was before I knew what we're about to do.

Realizing I can't clench my teeth during the whole two-and-a-half-hour flight, no matter how justified that would be, I keep my eyes shut and do my best to stop myself from panicking. It's impossible, though, given what I know.

When the plane is over the Chelyabinsk facility, I'm going to do the craziest thing I've ever done in my life.

I'm going to jump out of the plane.

THIRTY-FIVE

I open my eyes and see Gogi looming over me, all geared up.

It's that time.

"You ready?" he asks and hands me a mess of harnesses, polypropylene-knit undergarments, warm clothes, and a slew of other gear.

"As ready as I'll ever be," I say, forcing the tremor from my voice.

To my right, Joe's already begun his prep, while Nadejda is as ready to go as Gogi.

Hands trembling, I let Gogi help me put all this crap on. He then examines and adjusts every belt and harness on my body and rewards me with a satisfied grunt.

In a panicked daze, I let him lead me toward the airlock.

"Breathe through this." He gives me one of those mask-hat things I've seen jet pilots wear in movies, and I put the contraption on.

As I breathe the slightly sweet air, I realize this must be pure oxygen. Just like after my car crash, I don't feel the high promised by Tyler Durden in *Fight Club*. Quite the contrary, this time around, I'm lightheaded and borderline dizzy.

The others also put on oxygen masks, and the atmosphere in the plane turns somber.

To distract myself from gloomy imaginings, I mentally research the purpose of this step. In the context of high-altitude parachuting, breathing pure oxygen for a half an hour flushes out the nitrogen from your bloodstream, helping to prevent decompression sickness.

"So, I guess I'll be nitrogen free as I plummet to my death," I mentally type into the chat. "Great."

"Don't be a wuss," Mitya writes back. "You're about to do a tandem HALO jump. I paid four thousand dollars for mine a couple of years back."

"Right, but you're crazy," Ada says out loud, her voice soothing. "Mike isn't."

"And you should be working on the piggybacking app anyway," I mentally chime in.

Since no one replies after that, I sigh and masochistically read more about HALO—high altitude low opening—jumps.

The more I learn, the more I question why I insisted on participating in *this* part of the plan. Gogi originally suggested I help Muhomor and Lyuba in their separate efforts and that only he, Nadejda, and Joe do the dangerous part. But no, I wanted to be there in person to make sure Mom's rescue went as smoothly as humanly possible. Now, thanks to my damn bravery and initiative, I'm thirty thousand feet in the air, mentally preparing for something completely insane.

When Gogi gets enough pure oxygen, he walks up to the airlock, mask still on, and opens it.

The noise is beyond deafening, and the cold air hits us like an icy sledgehammer. It must be negative fifty outside, and I'm unpleasantly reminded of that winter trip to Yakutsk—a visit that made me realize the most biting Krasnodar winters are like a trip to the banya in comparison to the weather near Siberia.

"Take deep breaths," Ada says from somewhere. "Don't panic."

"You'll be fine," Mitya echoes. "Once you're in free fall, the fun will begin."

I ignore their chatter. Every part of my body is frozen in terror, especially my amygdala, the region of the brain responsible for fear.

"Can Brainocytes de-stimulate someone's amygdala?" I mentally type into the chat, more so as a distraction. "Can we use them to make someone less afraid?"

"In theory, yes," Ada replies out loud. "In practice, though, it would be very tricky, and I haven't tried it on the rats."

"But that sort of brain stimulation is something I've been thinking about," Mitya says, his devil avatar shaking with pent-up enthusiasm. "Fear is small potatoes compared to figuring out how to increase attention span or trigger neurogenesis."

The implications of this train of thought would usually excite me, but under the current circumstances, they barely distract me from my overwhelming apprehension.

Gogi waves his head toward the black void that's our destination.

I nod, but my feet don't move.

As though leading me through icy molasses, Gogi drags me closer to the airlock. When he deems the distance right, he attaches us together for the tandem part of the jump.

I know I shouldn't, but I look into the dark night outside the plane, and my adrenal glands manage to produce another tsunami of adrenaline.

Before I even realize how it happened, I'm flying through the air.

At first, I do my best to suck my heart back into my chest, along with copious amounts of oxygen; then I can't help screaming into the oxygen mask.

If my Brainocytes hadn't disconnected from the plane's Wi-Fi, I would've told Mitya where to shove his promise of fun during free fall. If I survive this, I vow to tell him that people like him, who do this for fun, are insane.

Going from hypoventilation to hyperventilation, I begin feeling fainter than before and wonder—possibly with hope—whether I'm on the verge of passing out. The welcome blackout doesn't arrive, though, and we just keep plummeting.

The altitude meter on my wrist reminds me of a digital countdown clock in a movie, when the big explosion is only seconds away. Below me, the darkness is so complete I can barely make out the tiny specks of light that must be Gogi's destination.

Rationally, I know our free fall will last about a minute, but as often happens in near-death experiences, it feels like I'm falling a hundred times longer than that, reminding me of the time I got my teeth drilled by a Krasnodar dentist back in the no-Novocain Soviet days.

Suddenly, I'm violently jolted.

Scenes from my life flit before my eyes, and I'm in the middle of saying farewell to the world when I realize the jolt was due to Gogi deploying his parachute.

Now that the chute is open, the speed of our descent reduces about a millionfold, and I get a chance to figuratively pull myself back together.

The distant lights grow bigger, and I stare at them as I practice every relaxation technique I've ever learned. Below us is the whole compound, as well as our impossibly small destination—a meadow inside a park/forest reserve in the center of the compound.

Despite my efforts to calm down, the next few moments of the jump happen in a haze of anxiety.

The forest gets nearer and nearer.

The treetops are almost under our feet, and I fully expect a branch to impale us.

In the last second, Gogi corrects our descent, and we glide toward the edge of the meadow. When we're just a few feet off the ground, he pulls on the parachute with a conductor-like gesture.

I brace for the pain of impact, but it doesn't come.

Gogi's feet expertly anchor us to the ground, and my feet touch the grass with about as much force as if I simply jumped up and down. Still, my knees feel weak, and I have to lock them to stop myself from sinking to the ground.

When I recover a little, I look around the meadow. This greenery is probably meant to look pleasing for the scientists and goons who work here, but right now, in the middle of the night, the place looks like an enchanted forest from a grisly Russian fairy tale—an effect enhanced by the pale moonlight that provides the only illumination.

Gogi takes charge and helps me remove all the equipment. He then ransacks his backpack for Mr. Spock's specially oxygenated cage, as well as our mission clothes and gadgets.

I'm halfway to having everything on when Nadejda and Joe land on the other side of the meadow. She must not be as good at landing as Gogi, or had bad luck, because their parachute is tangled up. The Georgian has to go over and cut them loose.

As the new arrivals join us in suiting up, I use the credentials Muhomor provided to get onto the compound's Wi-Fi.

The instant I connect, what feels like a surge of soothing, focusing energy spreads through my mind. It must be how my brain is learning to react to the presence of its cloud extension. The feeling is stronger because I now have more resources and a higher bandwidth than on the cellular network. If we survive this, I can totally imagine becoming a sort of techno-hermit—someone who has to be within reach of the fastest connections at all times.

"Hey all," I type into the chat, and as I wait for my friends to answer, I check on Mr. Spock to make sure he's feeling good after our ordeal.

The rat starts off amber, for nervous, but as soon as I pet his dyed fur, he moves onto happier green and blue hues, though not all the way to violet. When I think he's calm enough, I pull out the night-vision camera and put it on him.

"See," Mitya types in the chat. "Isn't skydiving fun?"

I don't dignify his question with a response. Instead, I ask, "Is everything ready for the recon part of the mission?"

"Yep," Ada says from my right, and when I glance at her, I see that her avatar looks like her normal self. She's wearing a t-shirt with a red anarchy symbol, and this time, her jeans are tucked into Converse sneakers instead of boots. I guess she thought this situation was too dire for the angel avatar. "All set. Just press the icon."

I make the AROS interface visible and locate the new icon, which looks like a rat wearing spy-like goggles.

After the app loads, three big screens show up in my field of vision. One shows what the camera sees, the second what Mr. Spock sees with his own eyes, and the third one looks surreal, so I ask Ada about it.

"It's my best attempt at displaying whisking—the way rats use their whiskers to navigate in the dark," Ada explains. "As you can see, it's a work in progress."

I put Mr. Spock on the grass and let him run around. The whisker screen looks like something out of *Daredevil*. I can see 3D outlines of the grass Mr. Spock's whiskers touch and a map of the world he thus develops, but it's really disorienting. I have to agree that Ada needs to develop this part of the app some more before it becomes useful. What's more interesting is that I see yet another potential for Brainocyte technology—providing people with brand-new senses. It wouldn't be that hard to give someone a bunch of instruments to wear or carry and get the Brainocytes to feed their inputs to the brain, mimicking something like the echolocation of bats, or the sense for electricity sharks have, or heat vision, and so on.

Speaking of sensory expansion, though Mr. Spock's vision is poor even in the bright moonlight, he *can* see some things we humans can't, such as the ultraviolet spectrum. That allows him to spot an otherwise invisible puddle of something, most likely the urine of a small creature, possibly another rat or a squirrel.

The night-vision camera is the most useful view of the three and looks just like one would expect, green hues and all.

"You can send this URL to everyone," Mitya says. Copying Ada, he also looks like his usual hoodie-wearing self. "This way, they can see through the night-vision camera as well."

I do as he says, and shortly after, Joe, Gogi, and Nadejda are staring at their phones with varying degrees of curiosity.

"Are you sure you can control where your pet runs?" Gogi asks after a few moments. "If the guards see a rat with a camera stuck to its back, they'll raise an alarm."

"Absolutely," I say out loud, feigning confidence. Mentally, I ask Ada, "Are you sure you can do this?"

Mr. Spock springs into action and runs circles first around me, then Gogi, then Joe. Nadejda cringes, so Ada doesn't have Mr. Spock approach the big woman, highlighting the control she can exert over Mr. Spock.

The rat's movements are so precise, the circles so perfect, that Gogi raises his unibrow and says, "We could've used this kind of rat in Ossetia."

On my end, in the screen that shows Mr. Spock's vision—or more correctly, an interpretation based on the activity of his visual center neurons—I see how Ada is accomplishing this. As she explained before, virtual walls show up in Mr. Spock's vision in a makeshift maze. These illusory walls are what prompts him to run, which tells me she conditioned him via mazes and treats. What's really odd is what I see when Mr. Spock looks up at me. Through his blurry vision, I can sort of make out my face, only I look eerily ratty.

"He must see you as the alpha rat," Ada explains when I point this out. "I've noticed this quirk as well. My guess is it's a bit like when humans anthropomorphize other animals by seeing grins on dogs and stuff like that."

"He's rattumorphizing me?" I type and add a smiley face emoticon.

"No," Mitya says. "*Anthropo* in the word *anthropomorphize* is based on the Greek word meaning man, not Latin, since that would be *homomorphize*. Since rat in Greek is *arouraíos*, the term should be *arouramorphize*."

"I think you guys need to tweak Mitya's Brainocytes for pedantic side effects," I reply.

"I don't care what we call it," Ada says. "But when my babies look at my face, it usually appears even more like a rat's."

"Start the recon." My cousin's stern voice brings me out of the virtual chat window, precluding further wonderment about rat vision.

"We're on the clock," Gogi says, just as sternly.

"Should we get through some of these trees first?" I ask. "Then Mr. Spock can scope out the rest of the area."

As one, they start walking. Taking that as a yes, I pick up Mr. Spock and cautiously lead the team toward the edge of the reserve.

The others walk so quietly I have to turn a few times to make sure I didn't lose them.

Eventually, Gogi places a hand on my shoulder, silently telling me to stop.

I put the rat down, pet him, and whisper, "Go."

"Got it," Ada says and does whatever she needs to do to make Mr. Spock scurry forward.

As soon as Mr. Spock is a few feet away from me, I can no longer see him with my naked eye—a good thing since that means the guards won't see him either.

I can, however, see his digital mood aura, and a few moments later, it turns the blackest color of anxiety I've seen so far.

Scanning the screen, I see what he's frightened of, and I get scared both with him and for him.

On the rat-vision screen, the source of our angst looks like a true monster, a mountainous blur of teeth, fur, and muscles.

In the night-vision screen, I see the obstacle for what it truly is —two hundred pounds of running dog.

THIRTY-SIX

"Ovcharka," Gogi whispers.

"That's Caucasian Ovcharka," Mitya tells Ada pedantically. "But I guess a man from the Caucuses can be excused for just saying Ovcharka. And in case you aren't up to that point in your Russian studies, Ovcharka means Shepherd dog, though these doggies don't just herd sheep. With their five-hundred-pound bite force and deadly ferociousness, they make lethal guard dogs, and they're so dangerous they're banned in some countries."

I mentally search the breed and see Mitya isn't exaggerating. Though fluffy and cute in some pictures, these dogs have been used to hunt bears and whole packs of wolves.

It's not just Mr. Spock who's in danger. It's the whole team.

The huge dog stops running a few feet from the rat.

Its giant head turns in Mr. Spock's direction, and its snout seems to sniff the air.

Mr. Spock's aura turns a paler color that I don't even have in my notes, though I'm sure it means something along the lines of, "I just soiled myself."

"Don't move," Ada whispers to Spock. "Don't even breathe."

Despite her words, or the Augmented Reality, or whatever

Ada's using to control the little guy, it's obvious he's about to bolt, and if he does, the dog will spot him, leap on him, and probably eat him in a single gulp.

I resist the temptation to pull out my Glock. We're not using weapons during this part of the plan, because even with silencers (which the Glock now has), the guns will still make too much noise. Instead, we're all equipped with air-based tranquilizer guns that were carefully tweaked and deemed silent enough.

I grab my tranquilizer gun, but I'm aware of a problem. Due to the lack of ballistic data on this nonstandard weapon, my friends didn't get a chance to update my aiming app to work as flawlessly as it does with a regular gun. The aiming line appears, but it's worse than a laser point.

Seeing no other choice, I point the aim-assist line at the dog and pull the trigger.

If I did hit the Ovcharka, its thick fur must have protected it, or maybe the human tranquilizer isn't effective on canines.

Mr. Spock hasn't moved. I suspect it's because he's frozen in fear at the towering behemoth of a dog.

In both camera views, the Ovcharka's teeth are exposed, and saliva is dripping from its maw. Mr. Spock is about to feel like Ripley from *Alien*.

To my surprise, Nadejda springs into action.

Her tranquilizer weapon isn't a handgun like mine, but a rifle. She brings it to her shoulder and takes careful aim.

The shot is accompanied by a barely audible pop, but nothing happens.

The dog leaps and lands three feet from the rat.

I wonder if I'll see Mr. Spock's life play across the rat-vision screen as the dog comes toward him.

When the wooly monstrosity is just a foot away from Spock's head, it stops, tilts its head to the side in that "confused dog" manner, and falls down, its giant clawed paw missing Mr. Spock by a couple of inches.

I realize I didn't breathe the entire time, so I allow myself the luxury of inhaling air.

"Phew." Ada's avatar rubs her forehead in an exaggerated fashion.

"I can't believe she saved him," I whisper. "I thought she hated rats."

I guess I whispered too loudly, because Nadejda leans in and says in my ear, "He's part of the team. We came together; we leave together."

"Still," I reply softly. "Thank you."

Nadejda nods and looks back at her tablet screen.

I stop pretending to look at my phone and focus on the AROS screens in the most convenient manner—with my eyes closed.

Using my mind to place the mental screens all around me, I wait for Mr. Spock to resume his recon.

He doesn't.

It takes a few minutes of soft pleading from Ada before Mr. Spock twitches a single muscle. Eventually, Ada has to resort to a stronger motivation and makes a virtual rat appear (probably Uhura), and that does the trick. Mr. Spock starts crawling after his friend.

"It's a rat race," Mitya says.

"For someone who has important work to do, you sure comment a lot," I tell my friend, irritated. "Did you figure out a way to talk to my mom?"

"I figured out how to show her one of those air bubbles with text of our choosing," Mitya says, "but not a way to communicate back and forth. That would take hours to put together."

"We'll have to use what we have," I say. "Anyway, she's probably sleeping right now."

In the quiet that follows, I watch Mr. Spock make his way to the large two-story facility that's our destination.

Step one of the reconnaissance part of the mission is for the rat to walk around the building so we can see how many guards are around and figure out other critical details. Since we now know dogs are in the picture, this part will take ten times longer than we originally planned, but the precaution should be worth it.

We start by having the rat sneak into the facility parking lot, since it's near our current location and there aren't any dogs or guards in Mr. Spock's way. He discovers a large minibus parked there, proof that the hostages are nearby. This is likely how they were transported here. There are a couple of other cars in the lot as well, helping us estimate the number of guards within walking distance.

After he's done with the parking lot, Spock locates as many outside guards as he can. There are ten or so, which is less than what we estimated. According to Gogi, this is good news. I'm less sure, because this could mean there are up to ten people guarding the hostages inside the facility. On the bright side, Mr. Spock doesn't come across any more dogs.

"Let's move on to step two," Ada says and leads Mr. Spock toward the building.

It takes the rat only a minute to get into the drainpipe, but what feels like forever to crawl up it.

Once Mr. Spock is in the drainage system of the roof, Ada has him navigate his way into the air ducts of the air-conditioning system.

The rat is halfway to the first floor when Muhomor finally speaks through my earpiece. "In position."

Touching his earpiece like a Secret Service agent, Gogi replies, "You're behind schedule."

"I figured stealth trumps punctuality," Muhomor retorts. "Now leave me alone so I can do my thing."

The sounds of keyboard strikes are audible through the earpiece, and we listen to them for a minute before Muhomor says, "They don't have much in their systems, but I see purchases for beds and a lot of scientific equipment that has to do with the brain—fMRI and the like. Most of this stuff is in the target facility, so I can extrapolate that the hostages are sleeping on those purchased beds in the highlighted area."

An email arrives on my phone, and when I look at the attachment, I see a blueprint with red circles around a bunch of rooms on the first floor.

"I'll have Spock investigate," I whisper. Into the chat, I type, "Did you get all that?"

"On it," Ada says, and Mr. Spock changes direction in the air duct, crawling toward the nearest room in question.

Even though the room is dark and the vent blocks most of the rat's vision and the camera's view, I can make out the bed.

I squint at the blurry picture and recognize Mr. Shafer's sleeping form.

"You're right," I tell Muhomor in an excited whisper. "Let's locate my mom and complete this mission."

For the first time, I let myself hope Gogi's plan will actually work as seamlessly as he envisioned.

Mr. Spock crawls to the next room, and I recognize another test subject. Then another and another.

With each participant, I'm relieved we found yet another person, but I'm also disappointed that the person isn't Mom.

As the rat discovers more people, my elation and disappointment grow.

When Mr. Spock discovers the next to last hostage, who annoyingly isn't Mom either, I mentally type, "This is it. She has to be in the last room down the hall. There are no other people left."

"I'm so glad everyone's alive," Ada says in subdued tones. "After what happened to Mrs. Sanchez, I feared the worst."

She stops talking because Mr. Spock scurries up to the final air vent.

When I look at the night-vision screen, my blood pressure rises.

"No," I whisper and examine the rat-vision screen, hoping against all hope I'll somehow see a different image.

The result is the same, however.

Mom's bed is empty.

THIRTY-SEVEN

"WHERE IS SHE?" I MENTALLY TYPE INTO THE CHAT. "WHERE'S MY mom?" I whisper for the benefit of the people on the other end of the earpiece, as well as those near me.

When no one responds for a couple of beats, I step up to the edge of the trees, but Gogi's rough hands grab my shoulders, keeping me in place.

"Mitya," I frantically type into the chat. "Do you have a way of speaking with her yet?"

"No," Mitya says. "I can only show her a textbox, but no back-and-forth communication."

More desperate ideas ignite and flicker out in my head, and I say, "Ada, can we pinpoint her location with the help of her Brainocytes?"

"It's a bit like using one of those 'find my phone' apps," Ada says. "We know she's in this building, probably on the south side, but a more detailed location would require a brand-new app. And even if we did develop it, that app would have to run off your mom's AROS, meaning we'd need your mom's cooperation, which is a catch-22 since we have no way of contacting her."

"Muhomor," I whisper into the earpiece. "Is there a lab or

control center in the facility? Maybe they're studying her or questioning her."

I hear a flurry of keystrokes through the earpiece; then an email arrives from Muhomor with a picture attachment. Through the earpiece, he says, "There, on the second floor, is where the fMRI machine is."

The email contains the blueprints with the room in question circled in red. I forward this to Ada and type, "Can you get Mr. Spock over there so we can have a look?"

"On it," Ada says, and the rat starts crawling through the air ducts again, only, to my deepest annoyance, he's moving as fast as a turtle overdosing on Xanax.

"There," Ada finally says. She's stating the obvious since we can all see the large ventilation grill a foot away from Spock. "That'll give us a view into the room."

On my night and rat vision AROS screens, the video changes from a view of the air vent to that of the room. Unfortunately, only a portion of the large room is visible from this angle.

All I can see is a single guard—not a complete failure since a guard indicates *something* is happening in the room. There are also some sounds, but they're even less useful. All we can pick up on are some muffled voices talking in the distance.

I subdue the urge to punch the innocent birch tree in front of me and scan the screens again.

"Muhomor," I whisper a little too loudly in my excitement. "There, in the left corner, you see that camera?" I start to gesture at the screen in front of me before I recall that Muhomor wouldn't be able to see it even if he were next to me, which he isn't.

"I see it," the hacker says, and I hear his crazy typing again. "I'm tapping into their video surveillance system now."

After what feels like an hour, Muhomor sends me a link. I click it and get a view into the room from that camera.

My first reaction is a wave of relief, because I see Mom very clearly, alive and well. But right on the tail of that relief is a flood of adrenaline, chased by a huge dose of anger.

It's the other four men in the room who bring about these new emotions.

In addition to the guard I saw earlier, there's a pudgy, gray-haired man who's busy speaking with Mom. I can't see his face because his back is turned to both Mr. Spock and the security camera. Aside from standing a little too close to Mom, this guy isn't the source of my concern. That would be the two brutes who aren't looking at Mom. I glimpse their faces and right away guess who they are, thanks to the fifth and final person I see.

My blood begins to boil because it's Anton, the man who abducted Mom over my knocked-out body—the man who, if it were up to me, wouldn't survive the night. Logically, the other two guys must be the people whose pictures we couldn't identify.

I run the face recognition app on them and on the guard, and I learn their names are Denis, Yegor, and Ivan. I also glance at their bios, but I'm not sure why I even bothered. In a nutshell, their profiles say, "Highly dangerous dirt bags. Steer clear."

"So, what do we do?" I ask, looking at Gogi as the man with the plan. "We have to get her out of there."

"We could also wait," Gogi suggests. "They'll let her sleep at some point."

"We don't know how long that'll take," Nadejda replies, and it's clear her smoke-damaged vocal cords have trouble whispering. "Why don't we use the gas I brought, like they did in the Dubrovka Theater?"

"No to the gas, unless there's no other option," I say after a quick mental Wikipedia search. The Russians used that solution during the infamous 2002 Nord-Ost siege. "Mom's health isn't perfect, and the gas harmed some of the hostages."

"Some of those damage reports are propaganda," Nadejda says, though she doesn't sound as confident as usual.

"If we can somehow cut the power to the room," Gogi says, "we can come through those windows." He points on his screen at the two windows in the camera view. "If we also storm through the door, we can make this work quietly enough."

What he doesn't need to say is that a single gunshot could alert all the guards in this facility, and that would be the end of us.

"I think I can take care of the lights," Muhomor says, "but they have this annoying redundancy system I'm having trouble with. The best I can do is keep the lights off for about a minute. We're lucky they're still in the middle of setting up the security in this building, or else the lights would simply flicker and come back on."

"A minute is enough," Gogi says and scratches his neck. "Still, I vote we wait."

"They might detect my activity in their system at any moment," Muhomor says. "You know the deal with the plane, and you know about the explosives that are just waiting to get discovered. I vote we go in."

"We also don't know *when* and if they'll let her sleep," I chime in. "Or when the guard might change. I guess we can wait a few minutes, but after that—"

"We're going in," Joe says with a finality that reminds everyone our mission isn't a democratic one. His unblinking lizard stare is focused on his screen, and his other hand is white-knuckled around the grip of his tranquilizer gun.

I think I understand what's going on. As I suspected, he didn't just come on this expedition because of his warm feelings for his aunt. He probably wants to make an example of the people who, as he put it, dared to fuck with his family.

"Right," Gogi says, all hesitation forgotten. "We start by taking care of all the guards we find."

He proceeds to explain the finer details of the plan, and once he's done, Muhomor prepares to turn off the lights at the most opportune moment, while Gogi, Joe, and Nadejda slither away to put tranquilizer darts into the guards Mr. Spock located.

"Can you use Mr. Spock to find the guards inside the facility?" I type to Ada. "Then, given what's about to go down, you should have him evacuate the building."

In response, I see movement on my mental rat screen.

"I can't believe they didn't let me help with tranquilizing the guards," I whisper, both for Muhomor and my New York team.

"The app doesn't work well with these dart guns," Ada reminds me. "And you can't move as stealthily as they can."

Muhomor sends me an email that proves Ada's right.

Using the links, I open mental screens to see what's happening via Joe's, Nadejda's, and Gogi's head cams. Their movements are indeed stealthy, though stealthy doesn't really cover what they do, especially Gogi. His movements remind me of Snake, a badass character from the *Metal Gear* video game franchise, where a master spy has to save the world.

I spread every view around me, using the AROS interface to tame the out-of-control screens, and as my allies work, I forget my other worries.

A guard on the northwestern side of the building gets a dart in his neck; then his southeastern colleague gets a dart in his left butt cheek. Immediately after, Nadejda and Joe run into a problem.

Instead of being at their separate posts, two guards are smoking together by the entrance.

Nadejda and Joe exchange a few hand gestures, crouch, and then slowly make their way toward the guards.

When they're halfway to their goal, I understand their plan. Sure enough, they grab the guards in identical chokeholds, in unison.

Muscles bulge on Nadejda's and Joe's arms, and the two guards don't get a chance to exhale the fumes stuck in their lungs before falling to the ground.

"Mike," Gogi says, intruding on my voyeurism. "There are no more guards around. Meet us in the parking lot."

I knew that before he said it; I just thought they would return to the trees instead of having me meet them out in the open.

"Mr. Spock only found one guard on the first floor," Ada says in case I wasn't following that screen. I was, but only with a fraction of my attention. "I emailed the guard's location to your cousin."

"Thanks," I type back. "Can you get Mr. Spock to the parking lot?"

"I actually started on that when I heard Gogi tell you where to meet him," Ada replies. "You be careful."

Her encouraging words have the opposite effect. Though I know Muhomor disabled all the pressure sensors, laser fields, auto-feeders for crocodiles, or whatever else my imagination can conjure up, an iceberg of fear forms in the pit of my stomach as I exit the relative anonymity of the forest and walk down the large grassy field before me.

Mimicking Gogi, I do my best to stay out of the lamplight and walk far away from the incapacitated dog, just in case. As I approach the parking lot, I decide the walk isn't that bad compared to something like the HALO jump.

When Joe sees me, he puts a finger to his lips, emphasizing the need to be quiet, and I fight the urge to whisper something like, "I'm not a complete moron," because if I did that, I'd disprove my statement in the process of making it.

I glance around and locate Gogi, who's using something like a coat hanger to fiddle with the minibus doors. Similarly, I find Nadejda working on the locks of another car. It takes them less than a few seconds to beat the locks.

Then I catch the familiar glow of Mr. Spock's aura near the drainpipe.

The rat made it out in one piece.

A minuscule dose of tension leaves my shoulders, and I run to him as fast as stealth will permit. I get on one knee, and he eagerly jumps into my outstretched hands.

Getting up, I turn to find Gogi right next to me and have no clue how he snuck up on me so silently. He points at the minibus and leads me to it.

When we reach the vehicle, Gogi gestures at the minibus's glove compartment and then at Mr. Spock. I take that to mean, "Put him there."

I nod and give the rat a quick rub. I then take out a small

handful of sunflower seeds and leave them in the compartment with Mr. Spock.

"Will he be okay?" I type into the chat. "I assume rats don't get claustrophobic?"

"They can live in literal holes in a wall," Mitya types back.

"I can soothe him from here," Ada says out loud. "Don't worry."

Gogi shakes his head as I reach to close the door, and I notice Nadejda left the doors open to the other car.

Gogi puts his bag into one of the cars, and he and Nadejda begin pulling climbing gear out of her rucksack. I swallow hard, picturing them using those ropes to climb onto the roof.

Joe must decide that the prep is done, because he stalks toward the building entrance, and I'm forced to follow.

My cousin slides a worm-like device with a camera on its tip into the small opening between the door and the floor and stares intently at the video feed on his phone's screen. I look over his shoulder and see that the guard Mr. Spock spotted didn't make his way to the entrance. When Joe deems the entrance clear, he quietly pulls the doors open, allowing me to go in. He then slowly closes the doors behind us.

When Joe slithers forward, I try to both follow him and orient myself in reference to the blueprints and Mr. Spock's air-vent recon.

This place looks like a Manhattan loft that used to be a warehouse. It'll take a lot more work to turn it into a full-fledged medical facility, assuming that's their goal.

The first bedroom, the one with Mr. Shafer, is to the right, so that's where I start turning, but at that moment, my upper arm is caught in a crushing hold that sends a blast of pain through my nerve endings.

THIRTY-EIGHT

A HAND COVERS MY MOUTH, AND JUST IN TIME TOO, BECAUSE I WAS about to scream.

I look at my attacker and feel a smidge of relief, because both the hand over my mouth and the claw-like grip on my arm turn out to be Joe.

"Where are you going?" my cousin says in a barely audible whisper. "The stairs are in the opposite direction."

"I'm going to wake up the hostages," I whisper back, my voice shaking. "Where else?"

"The hostages?" Joe asks. He looks as close to confused as it's possible to get while also appearing homicidal.

"Right," I say, trying not to cringe. "To save them."

"Why?"

"Because they're sick, kidnapped people?" I whisper a bit too loudly. "Because they'll get their heads cracked open and die if we leave them here? Because they're Americans stuck in Russia? Because—"

"Shut up." Joe's whisper is like a punch, and I'm fairly sure he would've accompanied the words with a real punch if we weren't related. In a softer but actually creepier tone, he adds, "They don't matter."

I look at those emotionless eyes.

He really doesn't care.

We've been working under a misunderstanding this entire time. I took it as a given that we'd save everyone, but Joe was only thinking about my mom.

"Look," I whisper. "I'll wake up Mr. Shafer. His condition is the least severe of the bunch. I'll tell him to quietly wake the others and put them in the minibus. It'll only take a few seconds and shouldn't affect our plan in any way." My cousin looks unimpressed, so I try appealing to his inner monster by saying, "If something goes wrong and we get shot at, the extra people could provide cover. Also, once we get to the US, the police won't ask questions about—"

"Fine," my cousin whispers, and I'm not sure whether he agrees so he won't have to punch me, or because I actually convinced him. "You have a minute while I walk ahead and deal with that guard."

We split up, and I continue to Mr. Shafer's room, my footsteps barely audible—a pleasant surprise given the good acoustics in this place.

I turn the corner that, according to the blueprints, leads to the first bedroom. The room should be just a few feet away.

A pair of surprised eyes stares at me in the semi-darkness of the hall.

It's the guard.

Looks like he moved from his original location after all.

The blast of terror causes my pupils to dilate, and despite the poor lighting, I can clearly see his arm lifting his weapon.

THIRTY-NINE

My right hand propels the tranquilizer gun up and fires, seemingly before the conscious part of my brain reacts at all.

The dart does its job, and I grab the gun from the man's limp hand as he drops to the floor, afraid the weapon might make an unwelcome clanking sound if it hit the ground. Though I already have a Glock and the tranquilizer gun on me, I stuff this new weapon into my waistband behind my back as a precaution.

Once my thinking catches up with my actions, I wonder if my sudden quick-draw skills are from the brain boost. Could the Wi-Fi, plus the extra brain resources, be behind my faster reaction time? Since I've never been in life-or-death situations like this before, I have no idea what my normal reaction time is, but I doubt it's this quick.

Trying to steady my overly fast breathing, I walk up to Mr. Shafer's room and turn the door handle.

The door is locked, but the solution occurs to me right away, and it's only two feet behind me.

I go back to the guard and search him for the keys, finding them on his belt.

Armed with the keys, I open Mr. Shafer's door.

It takes a gentle shake to wake the old man, and I resort to holding his mouth shut, Joe style, to make sure he doesn't scream once he comes to his senses.

At first, Mr. Shafer looks like he's about to turn a shade grayer, but then I think he recognizes me because the initial desperation in his rheumy eyes turns into a glimmer of hope.

I let go of the old man's mouth, and he instantly whispers, "Thank God you're here. They—"

I cover his mouth again and whisper, "Sorry, we don't have much time."

I proceed to explain what he needs to do, going as far as pulling up the blueprints of the facility on my phone to show him where to go—not that the instructions are complicated. The parking lot is near the entrance, and that's just a corridor away from where we are.

"I know how to get there," Mr. Shafer whispers. "They didn't blindfold us when we—"

"Okay," I interrupt again. "I have to go help my mom. Make sure everyone gets to the car as soon as possible and leave the front seats empty so we can jump in quickly."

Mr. Shafer nods, but then he looks at something behind me and his eyes widen.

The hair on the back of my neck stands up. Spinning around, I aim my gun at whatever Mr. Shafer just saw—and exhale sharply.

It's Joe.

My cousin is in a half crouch, dragging the unconscious guard behind him.

Mr. Shafer cringes at the sight of the knocked-out guard.

I'm not sure if Joe notices the old man's reaction, but he takes out a knife and kneels as if to tie his shoe. Before either of us can utter a single word, Joe slices the guard's throat with all the emotion of someone cutting up a melon.

I forget how to speak for a second and look at Mr. Shafer as though he might explain what just happened. What I actually see raises a warning bell in my head.

The old man is about to scream.

Except Joe is already next to Mr. Shafer, his hand covering the old man's mouth in a much rougher way than mine did.

My cousin wipes his knife with his left thumb, and the blood lands at Mr. Shafer's feet. Joe then whispers something into the old man's ear. Mr. Shafer's lips tremble, and he turns so white he looks like a ghost.

"Will there be a problem?" Joe whispers loud enough for me to hear.

"No, sir," Mr. Shafer whispers, eyes wide. "I'll get everyone into the car. I'll be quiet. You don't have to—"

"Then get started." Joe's whisper sounds like the crack of a whip as he rips the keys out of my hand and throws them at Mr. Shafer.

Ignoring Mr. Shafer's frantic nods, Joe heads out of the room. Numbly, I follow him, trying not to think about the literal blood on his hands. Out of the corner of my eye, I see Mr. Shafer walk determinedly toward the room adjacent to his. Whatever Joe told him was clearly effective.

I hurry to catch up with Joe, and we make our way to the staircase that will lead us to the second floor.

Joe's movements remind me of a stalking predator as he exits the staircase into a corridor.

When we reach the target door, Joe puts his finger to his lips, indicating the need for silence. He then points at the earpiece and then at my phone.

Instead of using the phone, I mentally compose a text message to Muhomor that states, "We're in position."

"Good," Muhomor says in our ears. "Gogi and Nadejda are almost ready, but I need a few more minutes with the lights. Please stand by until I say go."

Joe looks at his phone, checking on the room in front of us. Suddenly, his grip on his tranquilizer gun tightens, and his features contort in animalistic fury. He takes a small step toward the door, but then checks himself.

My heart goes from pounding to thrashing violently as I focus my attention on the AROS view that shows me the video feed from the surveillance camera Muhomor hacked into.

The gray-haired man, the one who was near Mom, is now within touching distance of her.

I stare unblinkingly as he touches Mom's face with the familiarity of an old lover.

She cringes at his touch and tries to pull away, but her action seems to irritate the man, and he steps even closer.

This time, when he reaches out, his hands go for Mom's bosom.

She tries to slap his face, but he catches her wrist and leans in closer.

Though there's no sound, I can see Mom's lips moving. It seems like she's yelling at the other people in the room for help. The guard and the three other bastards act as though they're not even there.

I didn't think I was capable of this kind of fury. The rage clouds my mind. I can barely think, and it's almost impossible to understand what I'm seeing at first, but then I extrapolate the revolting direction this interaction is heading.

"This asshole is trying to rape my mother!" I mentally type into the chat, without even meaning to. "He's so fucking dead."

I don't know what my friends respond with because my blood is pumping in my ears, and the red mist of anger overwhelms every cell in my body.

Teeth clenched, I reach for my Glock and step toward the door.

FORTY

In a blur of rage, I kick open the door.

As soon as there's a wide enough gap, I shoot the tranquilizer gun at Ivan, the guard who's been in the camera's view the entire time.

Then I spin around and aim my gun at Denis, one of the two assholes who assisted in the kidnapping. Using the aiming app, I put a bullet in his right shoulder.

Both men fall, though Denis hits the ground with a lot of screaming.

I hear movement behind me, and in my view through the room's camera, I watch Joe jump in and put a bullet in Yegor's chest—the second of the two previously unidentified kidnappers.

My cousin also spares a dart for Denis, stopping the bigger man's halfhearted attempt at aiming the gun with his left hand and silencing his pained cries.

The older man—the one whose blood I'm truly after—leaps for Mom. Before I can react, he's holding a gun to her head.

For the first time, I see his face—and almost wish I hadn't. It's covered in scars, burns, warts, and open wounds oozing pus. Combined, it makes him look like a cross between Freddy

267

Krueger, Jabba the Hutt, and the right side of the Phantom of the Opera. It's as if he was raised in the heart of the Chernobyl accident.

"Don't move," the monstrosity says through what passes for lips, and green saliva sprays in a fountain around him. "I'll shoot the bitch, I swear."

I freeze at his threat, but in the video camera feed, I see Joe raising his tranquilizer gun. Before I can cry out for him to stop, he pulls the trigger.

The guy tilts Mom's body at the last second, and Joe's dart hits her instead of its intended target.

Mom goes limp in the guy's arms.

Time, which already seemed to crawl, slows further as I watch the monster-faced man squeeze the trigger of the gun pointed at Mom's head.

"No!" I scream over the boom of the shot.

Mom's head detonates from the inside, spraying blood all around the room. It reminds me of the worst parts of the atrocity I witnessed at the club.

A heartbeat later, her body falls to the floor.

I feel a stunned sense of déjà vu, because she looks exactly like the headless Mrs. Sanchez did when I mistook her for Mom back in New York.

Now there's no mistaking whose headless body that is.

Mom is dead.

A tsunami of grief wells inside my chest, but I channel it into something more productive—anger. I force myself to morph my pain into icy revenge.

I raise my hand and shoot Mom's killer with the tranquilizer gun—not because I don't want him dead, but because I don't want him dead *yet*. I want to make sure he lives so I can unleash Joe on him and let my cousin do as he pleases for as long as he pleases. I don't want this man to die from the merciful quickness of a bullet.

Something calls my attention to the camera view, and I see

Anton, the ape-bison fucker who punched me in the hospital, aim a giant gun and shoot.

I expect pain, and almost welcome it as a relief from my grief, but Anton wasn't aiming at me after all.

In the camera view, I see a huge bloodstain cover Joe's chest. My cousin clutches at his wound and crumples to the floor.

Before I even register my intentions, I aim the app-assisted Glock at the very center of Anton's forehead and spasmodically squeeze the trigger.

Anton falls.

Suddenly, another shot is fired.

In horror, I look at where the monster-face guy fell and see my dart sticking out of the wall, not the man.

The man must've pretended to be hit.

Smoke is spreading from the barrel of his gun—the gun that's currently pointed at my chest.

The melting-hot freight train of the bullet finally reaches my chest, and I fly backward.

My heart stops, and I'm dead before my head hits the floor.

FORTY-ONE

INSTEAD OF FINDING MYSELF IN THE AFTERLIFE, I'M STANDING outside the door, my emotions in turmoil and my mind confused.

Joe is standing there too, very much unharmed and looking at me.

In the room's camera, I see Mom is also alive. She pulls away from the monster man's latest harassing gesture.

Stunned, I try to process it all. Didn't we all just die? Wasn't I just in that room?

Then I comprehend what happened.

I never actually rushed into the room. It was that weird brain-boost side effect, like my phone that broke but didn't break in Ada's bathroom—the phenomenon Ada calls a pre-cog moment.

It makes sense. It's only been a short while since I got the newer and better brain boost, courtesy of Mitya's resource allocation algorithm. Plus, to make better use of the new resources, I'm also on a Wi-Fi network. Just like when I first got the brain boost, I experienced a side effect. Ada said the new boost made her feel like she did in the beginning. I bet she got this weird side effect as well, something I can verify later.

My brain's cloud extension must've showed the rest of my brain what might happen if I gave in to my overwhelming anger. It seems my biological brain isn't yet accustomed to this new extension and reinterpreted this overflow of data as a dream-like scenario. Or, more specifically, a part of me warned the rest of me what might happen if I stormed into the room without waiting for Muhomor to disable the lights and for Gogi and Nadejda to assist us through the windows. My brain gave me a vision using the available information and even utilized my existing memories for assistance, causing me to relive that horrible headless Mrs. Sanchez/Mom moment.

"We need to go in now," I text Muhomor, realizing I'm just standing there, wide-eyed. At the same time, I type into the chat, "Mitya, when we go in, show Mom a text box instructing her to run into a corner and lie on the floor. I don't want anyone using her as a hostage or one of us accidentally shooting her."

"I have everything set up to send that message," Mitya types back. "Let's hope she catches on when she sees it."

As I read Mitya's reply, I hear Muhomor respond to my earlier comment with, "I'm not ready yet. I'm trying to make sure the lights don't come back on prematurely, so I need to work on this a little longer."

On the screen, the monster guy is leaning over my mom as she cringes away, and it takes every effort of will to stop myself from repeating the scenario the brain-boost side effect warned me against.

As time crawls onward, I remind myself that the monster guy has to take his pants off before something truly unthinkable can happen, but this line of thinking, even if it's somewhat rational, makes me feel like the lousiest son in the world. I also keep telling myself that my brain-boost vision was probably an accurate estimation of what will happen if I just storm in—and that makes me feel like the most cowardly son in the world.

I spare Joe a glance, and it seems like similar thoughts are battling in the dark place that's his mind. If a look at a phone screen could castrate someone, the gray-haired man inside the room would be squealing in a high falsetto.

"I want to change the plan," Joe whispers through his teeth. "I want to deal with this gray fucker myself."

"Joe," Gogi says softly into our earpieces. "Mike should handle him."

In my rage, I forgot the plan, and particularly the part where, by a stroke of fate, Gogi said I should tranquilize the gray-haired guy when we storm the room. His logic for doing things this way was sound. Even if I miss, since the man might not be armed (while the others are visibly armed), I can shoot at him a second time in relative safety.

At first, I want to tell everyone that the monster guy is indeed armed, but then I realize his gun was part of my vision, which isn't proof he actually has one. I'm not psychic, and the vision wasn't prophetic, but rather a hypothesis with the same validity as my favorite recurring dream where I'm walking naked in the middle of Times Square.

"Fine," Joe grunts. "But we have to go in—now."

"Nadejda and I are set," Gogi says. "We're waiting on Muhomor."

"Muhomor," I mentally type. "If you don't want Joe to do to you what he did to Alex, you'll tell us everything is all set."

"Fine," Muhomor says hesitantly. "I guess you can go in. The lights will turn off in ten, nine..."

As Muhomor counts down, Joe pulls down his night-vision goggles and stands in front of me, ready to kick the door in.

I lower my goggles onto my face and tense as the world turns different shades of green.

"Lights out," Muhomor says, and the lights from below the door, as well as the AROS view through the security camera in the room, go black.

"Go," Gogi says, and through the two views that represent his and Nadejda's cameras, I see them scaling the side of the building, SWAT style.

Joe springs into motion and gives the door a powerful kick.

FORTY-TWO

Joe runs in and shoots a dart into the disoriented guard's neck—as per Gogi's plan.

I follow him and briefly take in the green-tinted room.

As we hoped, Anton and his goons can't see us in the dark, but they don't look as disoriented as would be ideal, and their guns are out.

I turn toward my objective—the asshole next to where Mom was. Thanks to Mitya's message, Mom is in the corner of the room already, only she didn't get a chance to lie down yet, or maybe she isn't planning to because of the darkness.

My mind gets laser-focused on my goal, but at the same time, I'm able to pay close attention to the many events in the room. I wonder if it's from the brain boost assisting me. I also feel as though time slowed to the point where I can think many more thoughts per second than usual. I've heard of time distortion happening to people in stressful situations, but I doubt it was to this extent. What I'm experiencing reminds me of an altered state of consciousness that has more to do with hallucinogens than stress.

In the next instant, the two windows shatter, and Nadejda and

Gogi fly in, spraying shards of glass all over the floor and bringing a draft of fresh air into the stuffy room.

The monster-faced guy isn't facing the back of the room anymore. Reacting to the sound of breaking glass, he turns, and I get a good look at his face.

If I needed proof that my earlier vision wasn't prophetic but a product of my imagination, I get it now. The man's face doesn't have warts and doesn't resemble Freddy's. He looks like an accountant, or maybe, given the context, a scientist. The worst thing I can say about his face is that he has an overbite. The weirdest part is that this guy looks vaguely familiar, but I'm pretty sure I've never met him before. He clearly isn't a thug, or my face-recognition app would've alerted me—assuming face recognition can work in this green-tinted environment.

His identity isn't important, though. As far as I'm concerned, his name is Shoot Me.

I raise the tranquilizer gun and do my best to aim. The assist app must have a problem with the lighting conditions, because even the flawed version doesn't appear.

I pull the trigger unassisted.

All of a sudden, a green sun flare erupts around me, and I can't see a thing.

"Fuck," Muhomor says through the earpiece. "The lights came back on too soon." When the others shout obscenities at him, he replies with, "If you'd only given me time to—"

I ignore the rest of his monologue.

That this green super flare is from the lights coming back on is preferable to what I originally thought—that I was going blind or having a stress-induced stroke.

Though I can't see much with my eyes, I have an alternative. Since the lights are back on, the AROS screen with the security camera feed is no longer black, and my eyes' condition is irrelevant to AROS, which works with the vision center of my brain.

In that camera view, I see I missed my shot at the scientist again, or for the first time depending on whether the vision counts. At least I assume I missed, since he isn't on the ground.

I'm worried I'll find it impossible to navigate my way around the room using only the camera input, so I rip off the night-vision goggles.

The bright light blinds my green-adjusted eyes, so I take my chances with the camera feed and leap for the corner where my mom is.

My plan is straightforward. I'll put myself between Mom and the rest of the people in the room. If anyone wants to take her hostage like in my pre-cog vision, they'll have to get through me. As a bonus, I get closer to the scientist asshole, so once my eyes recover enough, I'll have a better chance at shooting him.

Navigating by camera turns out to be harder than I thought, and I bump into a chair, causing my kneecap to scream in pain. Gritting my teeth, I vow to learn how to walk around rooms based on a security camera video feed.

Suddenly, I see a blur of motion coming toward me in the camera view.

I squint and make out a fist flying at my face.

The punch connects, and the pain in my knee seems like a tickle in comparison.

As somewhat of a developing expert on getting hit like this, I have to say, pain aside, the punch isn't that bad. I think it only hurts this much because my face is already swollen from my previous adventures. I do see a few stars as I drop the gun, but—and this is critical—I'm still standing. As a side benefit, the hit shocked my vision into recovering, and I can see my opponent quite well. It's the damn scientist guy.

"Come on, Mike," Mitya yells. "Wipe the floor with this old fart!"

"Shut up," Ada tells him sternly. "Don't distract him."

I throw a punch at the guy's cheek, but he dodges it.

Either my movements are slow due to the earlier hit, or the old man is spryer than he looks.

"Felix," my mom screams from behind me. "That's Misha you're fighting!"

If Mom's goal was to distract my attacker, she succeeded spectacularly. Wide-eyed, he looks at me as though he's trying to use x-ray vision. I don't need a brain boost to take advantage of this. Seizing the moment, I plant a satisfyingly hard punch on his jaw.

Something seems to break in my knuckles, but it's worth it, because something also seems to break in the guy's face as he reels back.

I don't get to gloat, though, because as he falls, he grabs me by my belt, and I topple with him in a heap of flailing limbs.

Once on the ground, I recover enough to straddle my opponent and smack him with my forehead. Sparks explode in my vision, and the strike goes on my list of movie fight moves to never repeat again. I'm convinced the blow hurt me more than him.

Next, I try punching him with my fist, but he dodges, and I hit the toilet-white floor tiles. If my knuckles weren't broken before, they might be now.

Through the pain, I make myself another promise: once I master moving around using a camera feed, I'll also learn how to fight. Maybe shooting a tranquilizer gun without any apps should go on that list as well.

Though blood is trickling from a cut in his forehead, my opponent's eyes gleam with fear and malice. In general, he looks much too lucid for my liking.

With my left hand, I punch him in the chest, a move that causes my hand to feel as though a mob of angry bees stung each knuckle. Air whooshes from my opponent's mouth, and I get a tiny bit closer to my goal of knocking him out so he's no longer a threat to Mom.

Then the bastard tries escaping from under me.

I hit him in the face this time, then his ear, and then I knee him in the stomach with my still-recovering knee.

In a haze of pain, in the middle of this bout of almost mindless pummeling—and probably thanks to the boost—I take in the rest of the room through the camera view.

Similar to me, Gogi is on the floor. Unlike me, instead of punching Denis—his opponent who's the bigger one of Anton's flunkies—he's wrestling with him. Gogi must've jumped the man to stop him from using his gun and alerting the nearby guards, though I'm not sure whether I know this by using the evidence I see, or if some brain-boosted part of me was paying attention to what was happening to Gogi without me being consciously aware of it. Looking at the big mess of glistening limbs clawing at each other, it's hard to know who's winning the fight. For Gogi's sake, I hope Nadejda taught him some wrestling moves—an activity I decide to add to my quickly growing list of future self-improvements.

I land another blow on my attacker's face and see blood. As the metallic scent fills my nostrils, I realize I can't tell whether the red liquid is coming from the cuts on my fist or a wound on my opponent.

"Misha, stop!" someone yells. It sounds like Mom, but I must be imagining it. It makes no sense for her to defend the guy who was about to rape her.

My fists scream in agony, yet my victim is still squirming underneath me, meaning he's still dangerous and I need to hit him some more.

In the camera view of the room, I spot Nadejda locked in a fight with Yegor. She has hold of his gun hand, and they're struggling for control of the weapon. Her tranquilizer gun is on the floor, and I vaguely recall seeing her lose it via the camera feed, back when Yegor disarmed her when the lights came back on.

"Misha!" Mom's voice intrudes again. "You're going to kill him."

I don't get a chance to tell Mom something like, "That's a sacrifice I'm willing to make," because my attention zooms in on what Anton is doing—aiming his gun at Joe.

"Mike, he's your father!" my mom screams, but her words don't register as Nadejda also spots Joe's predicament and does something I've only seen in a UFC fight.

With her huge muscles rippling under the strain and her neck veins bulging, Nadejda grabs Yegor by the waist and throws him at Anton.

The two Russian brutes collide with the smack of a slab of meat hitting the butcher's counter, just as Anton's gun goes off.

My eardrums feel like they might pop out of my eyes.

A rush of relief hits me when I see Joe is still standing—meaning Nadejda's ploy worked.

Of course, the gunshot also means our attempts at stealth were for nothing. It's now a matter of minutes before an army of guards descends on our asses.

This is when my mom's words finally register.

She called the man I'm currently hitting *my father*.

FORTY-THREE

"Did she really just call him my father?" I hysterically type into the chat, in part as a sanity check, but also to frame the question for myself.

"She did," Ada replies. "I know it's very *Empire Strikes Back*, but you have to pull yourself together and quick."

My mind is a beehive of thoughts as I try to piece it all together. Mom also referred to this guy as Felix. According to my grandparents, that's indeed the name of the asshole who got Mom pregnant all those years ago.

Slowing my punching, I study the battered face in front of me and realize some of his features are similar to the ones I see in the mirror every day. That's why he looked so familiar. Still, to be extra sure, I manually run the face recognition app. Since the lights are back up, the app runs without a hitch and confirms what I already knew.

This is Felix Rodinov, which are the first and last names of my father. I only get a glimpse of his bio. His real family includes kids, my half-siblings, and a wife he's been married to for about forty years, meaning he was married before and during his affair with Mom. There's a laundry list of scientific accomplishments and posts at various Russian universities and agencies.

An insight flashes through my brain—a vague notion of how his presence answers a number of questions I've had about this whole affair—but I put the thought aside.

More confused than I've ever felt in my life, I stop hitting my father and wonder what to do.

My attention is stolen by what's happening in the camera view. Joe makes his move.

With his real gun, he aims in Anton and Yegor's direction. Joe must have switched weapons because stealth is no longer a factor, and he might as well give Anton the piece of lead he deserves.

His silenced shot is much quieter than Anton's, but it's still loud enough to hurt my damaged eardrums.

Unfortunately, Anton doesn't fall, but Yegor does get a bullet in his eyeball, or so I assume given the bloody fountain of gelatinous goo that sprays from his face and the bits of brain matter that fly out the back of his head. The nauseating smell of blood mingled with gunpowder fills the room, followed by something far worse.

As Yegor falls, two last things happen in his life. His bowels release with a sickening stench, and he drags Anton to the ground with him.

The ape-bison Russian doesn't let the fall put him at a disadvantage. He lands in a kneeling position with his gun outstretched and pointed at Joe.

Anton's forearm muscles twitch. He's pulling the trigger.

In a flurry of movement, Nadejda dives and pushes Joe out of the way.

Anton's gun goes off, and the bang scrambles my brain through my ear canals.

The bullet hits Nadejda square in her left breast.

Blood sprays out, and Nadejda clutches her chest as if to force the blood back in.

Eyes wide with horror and shock, Nadejda collapses to the ground, her bald head smacking loudly against the floor tiles.

Despite the push, Joe doesn't lose his footing. Catching himself, he glances at Nadejda, and a frightening, guttural sound escapes his mouth at the sight of her crime-scene posed body. Like a jaguar, he leaps at Anton. His fist connects with Anton's jaw, and their guns clank against the floor.

Joe's attack looks like something out of a slasher movie. He bites Anton's ear, Mike Tyson style, then spits the blood and flesh into Anton's ever-whitening face.

Anton screams like a terrified cornered animal. Almost in slow motion, I watch as his big, sweaty fist lands a devastating blow to Joe's right eye, and my cousin's head ricochets backward.

As someone who received that same blow, I fear Joe might've gotten knocked out. Acting as quickly as I can, I turn and draw my silenced Glock.

In the blink of an eye, I realize my aim assist is back—at least something good came out of the lights coming back on.

I point the oh-so-helpful line at the only place I can without hitting Joe—Anton's right shoulder.

Squeezing the trigger, I feel the gun kick in my wounded hands.

The bullet rips through Anton's shoulder, and he yelps in pain.

Joe manages not to lose consciousness. Instead, he sticks his fingers into the bloody mound of meat I just created and twists them back and forth, as though trying to find the bullet to keep as a souvenir. At the same time, he claws at his enemy's face with his other hand, and I wince as I glimpse Anton's eyes popping like squished slugs.

Anton's cry is no longer recognizable as human.

I fight the temptation to puke and keep my gun on Anton, but after another moment, the precaution isn't needed.

Joe takes out his knife and repeatedly stabs Anton in the chest.

The blood coming out of Anton's mouth garbles his wails and sprays the room like gruesome fire sprinklers as he collapses to the floor.

Holding in a surge of bile, I check the video view to see if I should shoot Gogi's opponent, but Gogi is already getting up, having won the fight.

Something pulls on my waistband from behind, and with a sinking feeling, I realize my father just snatched the guard's gun I stuck there earlier.

A shot rings out, and I expect to feel a blast of pain. Instead, I see Gogi grab his left upper arm.

I spin around to deal with my father, but my mom is already kicking him in the temple. Felix reels back, his head snapping to the side.

As someone who's played soccer with her, I know her kick is freakishly strong.

Felix looks too dazed to shoot again, but I club him on the nose with the butt of my gun for good measure, and I'm rewarded with the crunch of his nose breaking.

My father goes limp underneath me, finally losing consciousness.

I take away the gun he stole and slide the magazine out, mentally noting to do this earlier in the future—if the future involves the type of events we've experienced today, that is.

Gogi offers me his uninjured hand, and I let him help me up.

Though my legs are wobbly, I manage to stand straight.

"Mishen'ka." Mom rushes to me, and Gogi moves out of her way.

I'm caught in a huge mama-bear hug that instantly makes me feel better. In the next moment, however, she begins sobbing, and my fleeting comfort evaporates, replaced by that feeling I've known since I was a little kid—the despair of having to hear my mother cry.

"We have to get out of here," I tell her forcefully in Russian, pulling back. "Can you run?"

"I think I can," Mom says between hiccups and sobs. Her round face is blotchy, and she looks dazed. "I can't believe you're here, in Russia. And Joseph. Please tell me my brother isn't here—"

"Uncle Abe is in New York," I answer as I grab Mom by her

elbow and unceremoniously usher her to the door. It looks like stress sharpened her memory, or at least her awareness of her surroundings.

"Take her outside," Joe tells me. "Gogi and I will go through the window."

As I field Mom's panicked questions, I lead her out of the room toward the stairs.

In the camera view, I watch as Joe walks over to Nadejda's body, kneels, and checks her pulse.

Gogi, who's in the process of bandaging his arm with his ripped sleeve, approaches them and looks solemnly at Joe. My cousin shakes his head, almost imperceptibly. Gogi's shoulders droop, and while Joe's bloodied face is an emotionless mask again, I swear I see sorrow somewhere deep in his icy-blue eyes.

My grief hits me then. I try not to show it since I don't want to burden Mom. Even though I didn't know Nadejda very long, I somehow became fond of the big woman. It just doesn't seem right that such a courageous, tough-as-nails person is dead, that she died saving my cousin.

Joe jumps to his feet, walks up to Anton, and rips out the knife he left in the man's chest with a violent jerk. I mentally zoom in the camera view, trying not to trip on the stairs as I lead my mom down.

Joe approaches Ivan, the guard, and stabs the knocked-out man in the heart.

A moment later, he's looming over Felix's unconscious form.

"Wait, Joe, don't," I mentally text my cousin.

He bends over.

"Please, Joe, stop," I whisper into the earpiece. "He's—"

Joe either doesn't hear me or doesn't care. His knife cuts into my father's neck on the left and slides all the way to his right ear. A pool of blood forms on the floor.

I'm on the verge of losing the contents of my stomach again, but for Mom's sake, I breathe in deep, fighting the nausea. My father, whom I just met, is dead, and I have no idea how to process that. What should I feel for a man who shared half of my genes yet was capable of such evil? How should I view a stranger who did such horrible things? The cocktail of emotions boiling in my chest is overwhelming, but I know whatever I'm feeling is just the tip of an enormous iceberg I'll have to confront at some point, Titanic style.

"What about Joe?" Mom asks, looking confused. Unlike me, she didn't watch the murder on the camera. "What did you not want him to do?"

"Nothing, Mom," I force myself to say as we clear the turn in the staircase. Swallowing the acid rising in my throat, I lie, "I was asking him if I could sit next to you in the car."

"Of course you're sitting next to me," Mom says, frowning. "Why would he mind?"

"Safety," I say as we get to the first floor and head for the exit. "But don't worry. Everything will be fine."

Through Gogi's camera, I see him slide down the rope like a fireman and run for the second car while Joe gets behind the wheel of the minibus.

My jaw drops as I watch Gogi take explosives out of one of the bags he's had with him since the HALO jump. I mistakenly thought all the explosives were in Muhomor's possession, but it seems like Gogi kept some for himself.

I belatedly shudder at what we risked during the jump. If Gogi's parachute hadn't opened, our deaths would've been violent on a much larger scale than I thought.

When Mom and I are halfway through the first floor, Gogi sets up the explosives around the doomed car, shoulders the bag with the leftover explosives, and puts the car into neutral. He then exits the car and pushes it closer to the facility wall.

Making sure his guns are on him, he runs for the minibus.

As Mom and I approach the building exit, Gogi jumps into the car, and I glimpse the rest of the terrified hostages already inside.

"Mr. Shafer came through," I mentally type into the chat.

Before my friends can respond, gunshots ring out outside.

FORTY-FOUR

"Stay behind me," I tell Mom in a hopefully commanding voice.

Mom listens, proving this ordeal must've had an impact on her usual "eggs don't teach the chicken" philosophy. Normally, she never would've let me risk my life on her behalf—not that we've ever been in a situation like this before.

I open the door a sliver to see where the shots are coming from. Two guards are running toward us from the east.

Fortunately, they're shooting at something that isn't me.

I raise the Glock and aim the assist line at the rightmost man's leg. Suddenly, the minibus crashes into my target, causing him and his buddy to fly in opposite directions and sparing me a bullet.

The minibus violently turns in our direction, grass and dirt spraying from under its tires.

I pull Mom through the exit.

Joe stops the van, and Gogi opens the door.

I help Mom inside, and she scoots toward the middle. I jump in after her and sit by the window, behind Joe.

The hostages look shell-shocked, but they're not screaming or panicking.

Our tires spin in place, spitting grass; then we rocket forward.

I hear shouting and engines revving somewhere nearby.

The guards are almost here.

"Muhomor, the plan has changed," Gogi says into the earpiece. "I want you to blow half the distraction. Just make sure the exit point isn't part of that." At the same time, Gogi presses the detonator in his hands and carefully puts it into his bag.

The ground, along with the minibus, shakes violently as the car next to the facility explodes.

The view from the security camera in the room goes static and dies, so I dismiss that AROS window. I'm guessing about half the facility is now in ruins.

About a dozen more explosions ring out in the distance, and Muhomor says, "That's round one, as requested."

We were originally going to detonate the explosives all at once to create a distraction as we escaped the compound. Muhomor and Lyuba snuck around and placed the explosives around the compound's walls. Of course, in that original plan, we were supposed to be next to our exit point when the explosions went off. Now we can only hope the havoc this batch of bombs created is enough to minimize the number of guards about to swoop down on us.

"I'm also trying to mess with their comms," Muhomor says into our earpieces. "Oh, and you guys might appreciate this—it wasn't part of the original plan, but I was able to improvise."

Loud alarms go off from every direction. Muhomor must've hacked into the alarm system. He's clearly trying his hardest to make up for the lights debacle.

"Keep this up, and Joe might not kill you after all," I text him reassuringly, and he mutters a bunch of choice Russian curses into my earpiece in reply.

The literal and figurative ear assault continues as we move from grass onto asphalt.

A pair of confused guards shows up in our way. Joe's hands tighten on the wheel, and he floors the gas pedal. The guards' bodies thump against the front of the minibus, and I swallow thickly as we leave them broken behind us.

As we approach an intersection, a Humvee, or its Russian equivalent, appears on the road perpendicular to us.

Joe speeds up.

The car does the same.

The driver must be truly insane to play a game of chicken with Joe of all people.

Joe grips the wheel firmly.

The Humvee doesn't slow down.

In a chorus of voices, Gogi, my mom, and the rest of the study participants beg Joe to stop or turn or do *something* to avoid the inevitable crash.

"Joe," I scream over everyone, my voice going hoarse, "even if we T-bone him, which is the best case scenario in this madness, we'll all break our bones or worse. We have older people in the car, including your aunt—"

Without any sign that he heard us, Joe rolls the window down further, draws his gun, turns the wheel, and slams on the brakes.

Maybe it's a trick from the brain boost, but I suddenly understand Joe's plan. In case I'm right, I take out my gun and prepare to assist him.

Victim to the laws of physics, the minibus spins almost ninety degrees and skids to a stop parallel to the Humvee's direction a few feet from the intersection.

As the Humvee passes us, Joe sprays it with a torrent of bullets.

Doing my part, I use the aiming app to shoot the Humvee's front tire.

In a fierce jerk, the Humvee veers off the road. Either Joe hit the driver, or I got the tire—or we both succeeded.

When the big vehicle hits the bushes, it flips over and rolls into the ditch.

Joe turns the wheel all the way to the left and floors the gas pedal.

As we get back onto the road, I notice another car far behind us.

Joe drives like a rabid maniac, and at last, I see the wall looming in the distance. Our target shouldn't be far off.

Mom gasps, and I follow her gaze. Several cars are blocking the road in front of us. We'll never get through them.

I guess Joe wasn't planning on driving in a straight line anyway. With a sudden jerk that makes at least eight of our passengers squeal, the minibus veers off the road and heads straight for the part of the wall we originally planned to escape from.

The wall grows bigger and bigger, the moonlight illuminating the rusty barbed wire across the very top.

Driving on dirt is an art Joe hasn't mastered. A big rock causes me to literally bite my tongue, and I taste blood for the umpteenth time today, while the miniature hill we drive over causes me to hit my head on the minibus roof.

Only a dozen seconds pass before someone in the back throws up, and a sour smell permeates the air, which, combined with the sound of someone heaving, initiates a horrible chain reaction. It takes all my willpower not to join the puke circle, and I can tell by Mom's green face that she's in the same boat.

The car that was behind us and a couple of swifter cars from the blockade aren't just following us; they're closing the distance. They must be better equipped for off-road driving than our piece of junk van.

Our destination, the wall, gets ever closer, but it might as well be miles away, because someone starts firing at us from behind.

Gogi opens his bomb bag and fiddles with something inside.

The first bullet shatters the right-side mirror. The second hits the back window, and someone moans in pain.

My heart skips a beat, but then I see my mom is unharmed. I feel a wave of relief mixed with a hint of guilt, partly because I'm glad for someone else's misfortune, but also because of what I prophetically told Joe earlier—that the participants we saved could be used as a buffer if we got shot at.

Gogi finishes whatever he was doing with the explosives. Rolling down his window, he throws the bag out.

I block my ears, expecting to hear an explosion upon impact, but nothing happens when the bag hits the ground.

Another bullet strikes the back window, but the screams that follow don't sound like cries of pain.

His hand clutching the detonator, Gogi looks intently behind us.

"Phase Two, on my order," he barks, his finger on his earpiece.

"Got it," Muhomor replies.

Gogi's jaw muscles tense.

I look behind us and see our pursuers almost level with the bag.

Unfortunately, we're less than a minute from hitting the brick wall.

"Now," Gogi says and squeezes the detonator.

FORTY-FIVE

THE BAG EXPLODES IN A BLINDING FLASH OF FIRE, AND THE PURSUING cars blow up with it, metal shards and glass flying everywhere.

At the same time, a sequence of explosions goes off in the distance.

I look through the front window. The wall is so close and we're driving so fast that I picture us turning into a human/car pancake.

Suddenly, a chunk of wall in our way explodes in a fireball that makes the bag explosion look like a cheap Fourth of July firecracker.

Once my vision clears, I see a jagged, charred gap where the wall once stood, and we fly through the blaze still covering the edges of the hole. The smell of smoke is acrid in my nostrils, and I feel the heat on my face.

We speed up, and the open windows clear the stench of fire, as well as the nauseating fumes of stomach juices from the motion sickness disaster.

Gulping in fresh air, I enjoy the breeze on my face as we drive in silence for a while. Even the wounded person stopped wailing.

We're probably all thinking of the same questions. Will they continue chasing after us now that we're outside the compound?

Did Gogi get all the cars? Was the commotion Muhomor created enough to throw them off our track?

Holding my breath, I look back.

Two bright lights hit my eyes, and my heart sinks.

There's at least one car behind us.

"Wasn't that awesome?" Muhomor says into all our earpieces. "If I had more explosives planted, I'd blow them up right now."

"I assume it's you and Lyuba driving behind us," Gogi says grumpily.

"Of course it's us," Muhomor answers to my utter relief. "Who did you expect it to be?"

As Gogi curses Muhomor in his native Georgian language, I hear a man in the back moan, "My shoulder... I've been shot. Oh God, I'm going to die..."

I recognize the voice.

"You'll be fine, Mr. Shafer," I reassure him. "Here." I rip the sleeve off my shirt and pass it behind me. "Someone use that to bind his wound."

I use a mental search to learn as much as I can about impromptu bandages like this and walk Mrs. Stevens—Mr. Shafer's closest seat neighbor—through the process of bandaging him as best I can.

"No one is following us," Muhomor says, precluding a question I was about to ask. "I'm looking through the cameras, and they're running from one explosion site to another like ants in a squashed anthill."

"Good," I text Muhomor. "Mitya," I mentally type into the chat. "Do the flight attendants have any first aid training?"

"More than that," Mitya replies with unusual seriousness. "Natalia is a registered nurse, and my plane has a fully stocked first aid kit. I already told her to prepare."

"Thank you," I type. "I don't know how I'll ever pay you back."

"Brainocytes are a gift beyond my wildest dreams," Mitya says with the same unusual seriousness. "Even after all this, I feel like I owe you guys."

"If all this madness is over, I think I'll go change my pants," Ada says. "That was some crazy driving, and the fighting before it—" Her voice breaks. "I thought you were a goner, Mike."

I'm in the process of coming up with something suitable to tell Ada, when Mom gently grabs my chin and tilts my head toward her. She says, "Okay, now that no one's tried to kill us for a whole minute, you better tell me what happened to your face. You already had those horrible bruises when I first saw you today."

"Oh, I got those at the hospital," I say in Russian, in part to make sure our conversation remains understandable only to Joe and Gogi. I proceed to tell Mom the whole story, minimizing the danger I was in when I can get away with it, and I don't go into too much detail when it comes to some of Joe's actions, since he's listening and might not appreciate it. I particularly avoid telling her about my father's fate. Thinking of him, I again feel that confusing mixture of emotions: sorrow, rage, bitterness, and resentment. How could my father—a man I only heard stories about—be behind all this?

"Mom," I say tentatively, realizing I have to ask some very unpleasant questions.

She looks at me intently.

Unsure how to proceed, I blurt out, "About Felix. He didn't hurt you before this evening, did he? I mean, do you remember him doing anything—"

"No." Mom's face simultaneously darkens and turns red. "I remember everything, and we just talked, or more like, he talked about himself the whole time."

"So you didn't get—"

"No," Mom interrupts. "Felix is the same as he was all those years ago—an asshole, but not a monster when sober. It's just that he drank vodka today, and he becomes an absolute fucktard as soon as any alcohol enters his system."

What she said is not only a record amount of information about my father, but also a record amount of cursing. If I were to sum up what Mom has told me about my father throughout the years, it would boil down to him not being a good man and me being better off without him. My grandparents used more colorful language to describe him, but the overall gist was the same. Of course, I'm only human, so sometimes I did wonder about the man, especially when I was younger. As I grew up, I thought about him less and less, to the point where, as I now realize, I never even bothered Googling his name, even though it's something I routinely do with mere acquaintances.

"I can't believe I share DNA with him," I say, nauseated at the thought.

"He isn't all bad." Mom rubs her eyes with the tips of her fingers. "You have to realize I wasn't completely insane when I decided to have an affair with a married man all those years ago."

"He was your boss." The words come out harsh, and to make sure Mom doesn't think I'm being hostile toward her, I add softly, "In America, what he did to you is called sexual harassment."

"Well," Mom says sadly, "something wonderful did come out of the whole mess." She looks at me warmly. "You couldn't be more different from Felix if you tried."

"Did he say anything about me?" I ask, wondering if some of my guesses are correct. "Something to explain how he knew about the Brainocyte project?"

"Yes," Mom says. "I already knew he was keeping tabs on me, but as it turns out, out of fatherly pride as he called it, he kept tabs on all your accomplishments too, including your work."

"So my earlier insight about the kidnapping was right," I say, less to Mom and more so to say it out loud. Even as I used the face recognition app on his face, I knew, somewhere deep down, that Felix being behind all this made the puzzle pieces fit together. "This answers the biggest question of all: how did someone in Russia learn about Brainocytes in the first place?"

"I guess it does," Mom says. "To corroborate something your friend Muhomor suggested, your father indeed mentioned the FDA papers you filed, as well as patents, but it was really my memory condition that clued him in."

"So he figured out what we were working on," I whisper. "Hell, he might've understood more about it than most, since you two worked together in that company where theories of nanotechnology were discussed."

Mom nods. "He claimed he wanted to use this as a chance for us to reconnect, but I knew it for the bullshit it was. My guess is, he understood enough about your technology to get tempted by the possibility of fame and fortune. The man has an ego bigger than his head. From there, he must've reached out to someone who eventually introduced him to the right people, and things escalated from there."

"I think you're right," I say. "I think he eventually started working for a man named Govrilovskiy, a man who's still out there, now that I think about it. He's probably a threat to us—"

"About that," Muhomor says into the earpiece, making me realize the conversation is less private than I thought. "Didn't Gogi tell you? I continued searching for this Govrilovskiy guy since that was our contingency plan, and around the time you jumped out of the airplane, I found him and passed the information on to Gogi."

Gogi turns around and hands me his phone, saying, "I called in a favor with some fellow Georgians and told them there's a million dollars in it for them. Joe said you were good for it."

I take the phone, dreading what I might see, but I look anyway, hoping I'm sufficiently desensitized to violence by this point.

Sure enough, a brutally beaten man is sitting in front of the phone's camera. He's staring down the barrel of a gun.

"*Turizmi*," Gogi says loudly in what I assume is Georgian.

The word must mean something like "go," because the gun on the other end goes off, and the man—who I presume is Govrilovskiy—falls to the ground with a substantial hole in his head.

Mom must see me flinch, because she puts her hand on my arm reassuringly.

I hand the phone back to Gogi, and Joe says, "A couple more million will take care of his associates. I can put up a portion—"

"No," I say, catching my breath. "I'll cover all that too. I like the idea of no one being left to try this again."

As soon as the words leave my mouth, I realize what this offer is—a commission for assassinations. It makes me, the person paying for it, directly responsible for ending their lives. Nevertheless, my conscience doesn't raise any alarms. I feel as much guilt as I would if I offered to pay for Joe's medical or legal bills.

"There's still your father," Mom says, taking me out of my ruminations. "If anyone might try this again, it'll be—"

She notices my expression and stops speaking. I take in a breath, unsure how she'll react, and say, "I don't think he survived, Mom. I'm sorry."

"I see," Mom says, her voice even, but her face is paler than I've ever seen it. Her throat works as she swallows; then she mutters, "I guess he dug that hole himself."

She looks away, and I spot her wiping tears from her eyes.

We ride in silence for a while, and I wonder if the fact I'm not crying over my deceased father and all the people who died today means I'm morally bankrupt or empty inside.

As I try to sort through the tangle of emotions again, I discover the most prevalent one is numbness. It blankets me, covering everything in a soothing fog. Behind that layer of numbness, I feel like I've been shattered into pieces that someone put back together the wrong way. I have no idea if I'll ever be the same again, but I suspect I won't—not after seeing so much death and violence up close.

Determined to escape my dark thoughts, I decide to get some pet therapy and ask, "Gogi, can you please pass me Mr. Spock?"

As a bonus, this distracts Mom from her brooding. When I told her about Mr. Spock's assistance during the rescue, she reacted well—at least on a purely intellectual level. Now, though, she'll have to tackle the reality of having a live rat in her proximity.

"Hmm," she says, catching me looking at her expectantly. "If he's going to be your pet, I'll try not to freak out around him." Her uncertain tone doesn't match her words, and she ends weakly with, "Especially if he's as well behaved and clean as you claim."

As though he waited for her to be okay with it, Gogi opens the glove compartment. Before he can grab the rat, Mr. Spock jumps onto Gogi's arm, then scurries up to the big man's shoulder and leaps right into my outstretched hands.

"He looks a bit like a squirrel, or maybe a guinea pig," Mom says, sounding like someone unsuccessfully trying to convince herself of a falsehood. "I hope it's okay if I never touch him."

"I don't think he likes anyone but me and Ada touching him," I say, though I don't know if that's actually true. "So it's preferable if you don't touch him."

"Good," Mom says, as though touching the rat was an important debt she had to pay, and she's relieved she doesn't have to pay it.

"Now for the most important part," she says, her tone suggesting she's about to teach a big moral lesson or complain about a grievance. Once she has my full attention, she firmly says, "If I'm ever kidnapped again, I want you to promise to let law enforcement handle it. That goes for you too, you hear me, Joseph?"

Joe grunts something unintelligible, and I say, "I'll make sure your Brainocytes allow us to consult with you if you're ever kidnapped again. How does that sound?"

"Oh, about that," Mom says. "I almost had a heart attack when I got your message in my Terminator interface."

"We call that the AROS interface, Mom," I say, finally managing a smile. "And you can thank Mitya for that message when you meet him."

"Speaking of Mitya... is that his plane?" Mom points into the distance.

Her eyes are wide, and I can't blame her.

Mitya's plane is a sight to behold, and where it's parked is just as awe-inspiring as the aircraft.

There's a huge abandoned Soviet-era warehouse by the road,

with a parking lot covered by cracked, winter-beaten asphalt. It looks like it was originally meant to store trucks and the like. The shiny new plane is standing on the lot, looking as out of place as fried chicken liver inside a birthday cake.

It takes ten minutes to load everybody onto the plane. As soon as everyone is on board, we roll out of the parking lot to use the empty highway as a runway—one of the million reasons why our mission had to be done in the dead of night.

Natalia, the flight attendant nurse, tends to Mr. Shafer first, Gogi second, and me last. As I look at the bandages on my hands, I have to hand it to Mitya's wisdom, assuming there was wisdom involved in hiring her. Having a model-hot nurse tend to injuries cuts down on male whining considerably, even from me, a person who isn't interested in Natalia's charms.

"Do you want us to fly you back to Moscow?" I ask Gogi and Lyuba.

"Actually, if it's possible, I'd like to visit the United States," Gogi says.

"I need to go back to the Gadyukino hideout," Lyuba says.

"Okay, I think that can be arranged," I tell them, trying not to think too hard about what Lyuba needs to do back there with Alex. Getting up, I walk over to the pilot's cabin and make the appropriate arrangements. As I come back, for Mitya's benefit, I mentally type into the chat, "Your lawyers need to start working on those H-1B visas."

"Already on it," Mitya replies out loud. "I'll give them real jobs too if they want. Gogi can be your bodyguard or mine, and Muhomor—"

"No more business talk," I mentally reply. "Need sleep."

As though on the same wavelength as me, Joe hands out his Ambien to anyone who wants one, like it's candy. I bet my cousin's generosity is calculated and meant to incapacitate this rowdy bunch so he can get some sleep. I ask for a pill too, but I don't take it right away, because I need to call Uncle Abe and tell him Mom's okay. After that conversation, I call the authorities and explain everything as well as I can, promising that yes, we'll come down to the station to make a statement, that we'll obviously bring everyone wherever they want us to, et cetera, ad infinitum.

The one good part about the unpleasant phone calls is that they sufficiently distract me from the much worse unpleasantness of the liftoff. When I'm done with all the calls, and since Mom and the others are already in Ambien dreamland, I swallow my pill and wait for the drug to kick in.

Instead of counting sheep, I think about everything that's happened and examine the scabby wound that is my biological father's fate. For now, my turmoil has settled into a deep numbness. Given how little I thought or cared about the guy before I met him, that might be a normal reaction. Alternatively, this could be a psychological defense mechanism hiding a deep sense of loss of something I never thought I'd value. It's hard to introspect the truth. What I do know is that I'm the least qualified person to examine my feelings. I was never good at it, even under better circumstances. Maybe, despite my negative view of psychiatry, I'll give therapy a shot after things settle down. I might need it to properly deal with the gruesome things I've seen these last few days.

On the bright side, given my experience with Brainocytes so far, I have no doubt this technology will help Mom's condition. If she wants, she can even end up with a mind superior to the one she had before the accident. Judging by her extremely lucid behavior since the kidnapping, Phase One might've already had some positive effects.

As for me, even though I haven't fully adjusted to the bigger brain boost, I already feel like I could never go back to not having it. In fact, I want more. I guess I'll need to speak with Ada and read up on transhumanism, because in the very near future, I foresee us getting smarter and more capable than the smartest human being currently alive.

"Good night," Ada's voice says softly in my ear, interrupting my sleepy musings. "When you wake up, I'll probably be there in the flesh."

I'm not sure if it's Ada's soothing words, the drug, or the post-adrenaline crash—or even the feeling of a warm rat bruxing next to me—but my eyes get pleasantly heavy and I close them, sinking into sleep.

————

I wake up to people leaving the plane.

"I was worried," Mom says. "I called out to you, but you didn't answer."

"This is nothing." Gogi chuckles. "Upon his arrival into Russia, I helped him sleepwalk to the car."

"Whatever," I say groggily. "I'm going to the bathroom. You're welcome to sleepwalk me there if you want to hold something for me."

Gogi and Mom laugh, and then she says, "I'll meet you outside."

They follow the rest of the research participants off the plane, and I head in the opposite direction to one of the dozen bathrooms.

By the time I wash up and use the facilities, I feel like a slightly more lucid approximation of myself, though a triple espresso wouldn't hurt.

As I exit the plane, I feel like I've aged a couple of decades on this trip. Every bone and muscle in my body is aching all at once. Then I see Ada, and all my discomfort evaporates. It's as though I drank that triple espresso, and it was spiked with a shot of vodka to boot.

Maybe to make an impression on me—at which she succeeded —or maybe as a trick to make sure my mom doesn't think she's a boy again, Ada is wearing a strappy pink summer dress. It still manages to look punky somehow, though that could simply be from her attitude.

I increase my pace and Ada does the same, but she's forced to hold down her skirt, Marilyn Monroe style, because of the wind.

"Oh, you poor thing," she says when she sees my mummified hands. "And your face." She touches my left temple, probably my only non-swollen part. "I didn't think it could get worse than the injuries you had after the accident, but I was obviously wrong."

Instead of replying, I gently clasp her waist and pull her to me.

"Wow," she whispers as she looks up at me. Her amber eyes twinkle, giving her the charm of a mischievous puppy. "All that danger must have—"

I press my lips against hers, channeling all my gratitude for her help, as well as all my longing for her, into the kiss.

She responds with an unexpected fierceness, and to my surprise, her small hands grab my buttocks, giving them a noticeable squeeze.

We're at it for what feels like hours, and I fully expect someone to say, "Get a room, you two," but no one dares.

After the kiss, I take Ada's hand and let her lead me to the limo, where Mitya, my uncle, Muhomor, my cousin, Gogi, Mom, and JC are waiting for us. To my shock, JC is holding my mom's hand—a development I'll have to process later. My friends and family smile at me knowingly, and I know a lot of girl talk—and teasing from Mitya—is coming my way. I don't care, though. My steps are light, and despite the lingering tightness in my chest, I feel like I'm floating on post-kiss endorphins and oxytocin.

The numbness is still with me, shielding me from the worst of the turmoil, but underneath that, I'm aware of a strange contentment, a feeling I never expected to experience after all the horrors we've been through. For that matter, I didn't think I'd feel this hopeful after being repeatedly beaten and shot at and having the person closest to me kidnapped. Yet, paradoxically, that's exactly how I feel—hopeful. Hopeful for my future. Hopeful for Mom's future. Hopeful for the future of the study participants, and that of Alzheimer's patients, paraplegics, and other people we'll soon help. I even feel ambitious enough to feel hopeful for the future the

Brainocytes will bring to the whole human race—though that might be a delusion brought on by my post-kiss high.

In a gentlemanly fashion, I let Ada enter the limo first and then follow, ready to share my feelings of hope with these people, who, in one way or another, for better or worse, are now my closest companions in the world.

"*Poyekhali,*" I say to the driver, echoing the Russian cosmonaut again for Ada's benefit. Then, on the off chance Mitya's driver doesn't speak Russian, I clarify, "Let's go."

CYBER THOUGHTS

HUMAN++: BOOK 2

ONE

I walk through Times Square with the unsubstantiated conviction that someone is following me. This has become an ongoing issue for me. Wherever I go, I think someone or something is there, lurking at the edge of my awareness.

It's like a canker sore you can't help but touch with your tongue. No matter what, I can't just chill and stop worrying about secret surveillance. The problem with this situation is that I know the name of the condition—paranoid schizophrenia—and the knowledge scares me more than my unseen stalkers.

I glance up at the flashy billboards, but the models in the ads aren't the culprits. Next, I look around and see thousands of happy tourists staring at the Naked Cowboy and taking selfies with all the unauthorized Disney and Marvel characters. I decide these aren't my mysterious followers either—which is fortunate. If I thought Mickey Mouse or Spider-Man were after me, I'd commit myself to an institution this very moment. Nor do I think it's any of the multitudes of annoyed New York natives who are following me, because all they want is to get through the hive of people and return to their offices.

Then I freeze in place because, for the first time since my paranoia began, I think I spot one of my stalkers.

It's a man whose face I can't discern. The only detail I can distinguish about this guy is that he's dressed in a perfectly tailored designer suit.

As soon as I spot one guy, I see a dozen more—all dressed in identical black suits.

When the Suits notice I'm aware of them, they abandon stealth and begin pushing through the crowd, eager and ready to grab me.

Since it will take too long to escape through the dense human fog on the street, I hurry toward the road instead. My walk quickly turns into a sprint toward 6th Avenue, and I push and elbow my way through to the car-beaten asphalt.

A black limo screeches to a stop, blocking my way. The limo window rolls down, revealing more Suits inside it.

Backing away, I glance in the direction of the traffic and spot a slew of cars descending on me—all driven by the Suits. I turn to look down the street and see an impenetrable traffic jam.

I turn back, only to face a wall of running Suits—except now I notice something about these men is horribly wrong.

As I attempt to register what I'm seeing, the ever-present bustle of Times Square quiets, creating the feeling that all the people and cars around me have frozen in place, perhaps as shocked by the Suits as I am.

There is a reason for that.

The Suits have no faces.

No, that's not exactly accurate.

They have no eyes, nose, or lips, and where the face should be, I see a smooth mirrored surface instead. Their hands are also reflective, as though their skin is made of aluminum and covered in glass.

What shocks me more is my reflection in their spherical mirrors. I look crazier than the homeless guy with Tourette's syndrome I often see on the ride to Techno's offices. My hair is long with a year's worth of grease in it. I'm missing teeth, my bloodshot eyes with the pupils the size of nickels are darting in random directions, and my face is concentration-camp thin.

The Suits approach me, and I have no choice but to assume a fighting stance.

Before I can land a single strike, however, strong arms grab me and throw me at the One Times Square building. As the impossible arc of my flight takes me toward the fortieth-story window, I again question my sanity—because every person in Times Square now lacks a face, their features replaced with smooth reflective surfaces.

I hit the window, and the glass shreds my skin with a million shards.

More Suits are waiting for me in the room.

They raise their hands, and mirrored blades eject from their fingers.

A dozen of them approach me.

I punch the nearest one in the stomach and wish Gogi were here to see the perfection of my movements, because he would be proud. Unfortunately, I don't have time to dwell on that for long. Instead of doubling over in pain like a normal human, the Suit slices my face with his shiny claws.

The pain is exquisite, and I realize something I should have long ago.

I'm having a nightmare. Again.

———

"You have been unconscious for four hours," Einstein reports somewhere in my groggy brain. "Current time is 4:37 a.m."

I'm about to mentally say something snarky to the AI but decide against it. I asked him to keep track of my brain awareness because I had a half-baked idea of dealing with my nightmares by asking Einstein a question along the lines of, "Einstein, am I sleeping right now?" The problem is that it's hard to remember about Einstein while inside a nightmare. Also, if my nightmare were extra creative, I could potentially dream up Einstein's answer.

My eyelids fly apart, and I'm faced with the pools of amber that are Ada's eyes.

"Another nightmare?" she whispers and cups my face in her hands, her delicate features contorted in a worried frown.

"*Da*," I whisper, trying to fight the grogginess. Then, realizing I just spoke Russian, I say in English, "Second one tonight. Must be some kind of a record."

"Are you being followed again, or did your dad try to kill you?" She sits up, and the sight of her perky upper body distracts me from the nightmare better than anything she could've said.

"Being followed." I force myself to refocus on her face. I know what she's about to say, but truth can be an annoying habit, so I also add, "I've been feeling like this a lot lately."

"Then will you finally go see a professional?" As she did during those few earlier pleading attempts, Ada uses the puppy-eyes tactic to make it extremely hard to say no.

"Shrinks did nothing for Mom when she needed help," I remind her. "Besides, what if I *am* being followed?" We've had this argument before, and it doesn't take enhanced intelligence to know I'm about to lose this battle.

"Gogi doesn't think you're being followed." Ada spikes her limp hair into a sad mockery of her usual Mohawk. "And the nightmares about your father are—"

"Fine," I say. On some level, I've been preparing to give in and see a shrink for a few days now. "I'll see him."

"Her," Ada corrects. "Dr. Golovasi."

"Of course that's her name." I snicker because the psychologist's name sounds like the Russian word *golova*, meaning *head*. "Your doctor is lucky she's not a proctologist."

Ada chuckles weakly. Her Russian has improved over the last five months, so she undoubtedly understood my joke. "Your appointment is at 11 a.m. later today. Now let's go back to sleep so you can get enough rest."

That she already has the appointment scheduled doesn't surprise me. She either just made it using her AROS—Augmented Reality Operating System—interface, or, more likely, she made it earlier in the hope (or certainty) that she could convince me to go. In fact, she probably scheduled and rescheduled this appointment every day for months while she was chipping away at my reluctance.

We both yawn and get into our routine spooning position, her petite frame a perfect fit in my embrace.

As though on cue, I feel a small, warm body cozy up to me from behind my neck. It's Mr. Spock. He's peacefully grinding his teeth in a monster bruxing session, which tells me he's in rat nirvana. I launch the new version of the EmoRat app, and it allows me to feel what my furry friend is feeling—a blissful, in-the-moment calmness that us humans, at least the New York types, can only envy. He's happy to be in bed with us and his fellow rats for the night, though the others are cozying up in front of Ada.

"Good night," I say. I almost add, "I love you," but I stop myself.

Before moving in together, Ada and I said we loved each other, the first time either of us has felt this way about someone. Sadly, I also learned that Ada is peculiar when it comes to the L word. She wants to see actions that show love rather than hear the constant repetition of those words. For some unfathomable reason, she finds them corny. I suspect this whole issue is something *she* should see a shrink about, but if she doesn't want to hear me wear out the phrase, I'll play along. This way, when I do say it on some auspicious occasion, like our twentieth anniversary, it'll feel more powerful—and I think that might be Ada's point.

Feeling more relaxed, I focus on breathing evenly, and after about thirty more inhales of Ada's coconut-scented hair, I fall asleep.

If I have any more nightmares that night, I don't remember them.

TWO

"Dr. Golovasi will see you in a moment." The plump receptionist blows a bubble with her chewing gum. "Fill these out for now."

I take the forms, but before I fill them out, I locate the Wi-Fi and switch over from the slower cell connection. My whole world brightens, and I inwardly sigh at yet another confirmation that I've become as reliant on Wi-Fi (and connectivity in general) as a severely nearsighted person on their glasses. It's gotten to the point where I would've canceled this visit if they didn't have Wi-Fi —a purely hypothetical scenario since Ada made the appointment and she has the same quirks in this regard. Plus, this is a doctor in Manhattan, so Wi-Fi is pretty much guaranteed.

I mentally instruct Mr. Spock to stay in my pocket in case they don't allow pets at this office, and then I make quick work of the paperwork and hand it back. Once I'm back in my chair, I take out two Rubik's cubes and busy myself by speed-solving both puzzles simultaneously. Once I solve and mix the cubes a few times, I try the same feat blindfolded, after first memorizing the state of colors on both cubes. This second way of solving the Rubik's cubes is more interesting, but it only keeps me busy for a few minutes, plus the receptionist gives me weird looks. Bored with the physical world, I remove the blindfold, close my eyes, and launch the Telepathy app.

Ada's pride and joy, the Telepathy app is like a text messenger on steroids and amphetamines. The app uses Brainocytes to activate the areas in the brain that give the message receivers the eerie feeling that the thought they're getting from the sender is making an audible sound in their head. The sender can also imbue the thought with a range of preconfigured emotions—like emoticons, but way cooler since you can feel them. On top of that, Mitya, Ada, Muhomor, and I developed a statistically optimized language to express ourselves quicker and more effectively via electronic communications, and that includes the Telepathy app.

We call the new language Zik, short for *yazik*—Russian for *language*. Zik is as terse as we could get away with, so, like in Russian, articles such as "a," "an," and "the" don't exist in Zik. The Zik alphabet, if you can even call it that, is simply numbers in base two, also known as binary. We took the most commonly used words in Russian and English and represented them using binary numbers according to usage. The least commonly used words get bigger numbers, and thus longer strings of binary, while the most commonly used words get smaller numbers, and thus shorter representations. For example, the word "have," statistically the ninth word in our usage, is simply the binary for nine—1001. Something like "ossify" (turn into bone), though relatively short in English, becomes the binary for thirty thousand (111010100110000) in Zik. The number would be higher if it weren't for Mitya's penchant for boner puns raising the odds of that word getting used. Just for contrast, the original English "have," when represented in ASCII form (one of the ways the alphabet can be encoded in computers) is a whopping 01101000 01100001 01110110 01100101. It might not seem like a big deal to a layperson, but using smaller binary numbers greatly speeds up communication for people with a brain boost.

In any case, now that we have Zik, speaking with people in the outdated verbal manner is a chore. I'm constantly tempted to interrupt the slow-motion speech of my investors because I usually know what the person will say thirty percent into their sentence.

"Hey, sweetie," Ada greets me telepathically in Zik. A warm, fuzzy emotion that's the Telepathy app's equivalent of the smiley face emoji (with the little heart emoji thrown in) accompanies her words.

Emojis are also numbers in Zik. That might sound cold, until you remember the standard smiley face emoji everyone texts to each other is merely the characters ":" and ")" or the number 00111010 00101001 in binary. In fact, in Zik, we can add intensity to our emojis, allowing for a wide range of subtlety in the emotional subtext we use.

"Hi, babe," I reply, imbuing my message with the Zik equivalent of a confident wink. "I'm here at the shrink's office, in case you thought I'd flake out at the last minute."

Ada's avatar appears in the air in front of me. She opted to look like a mischievous imp, so it must be another Monday.

"Do you mind sharing?" she asks and waves her hand around her body.

She's requesting that I launch the relatively new app we call Share. When running, this app allows Ada to see what I see and hear what I hear—not unlike the rat version she developed for Mr. Spock and his kin.

I activate the app, and the imp looks around the room.

"You're not in the office yet." Ada's voice rings throughout the waiting room. Obviously, her speech isn't really here; it's merely the Brainocytes stimulating the auditory center of my brain. More specifically, it's a Zik message that our newly advanced version of the Teleconference app converts into speech experience. This is how we now "speak," even when within earshot of each other and not in public. In public, we speak out loud so people don't think we're a couple of weird mutes who don't even use sign language.

"The appointment is for eleven. It's 10:58 on the clock here." I nod toward the digital wall clock. On Ada's end of the conversation, my avatar looks like Misha, the Russian Bear mascot of the 1980 Summer Olympics in Moscow and my namesake. "I guess the doctor is punctual."

"Awesome, we have two minutes to kill. Time enough for a chat," Ada says out loud, but she must've also used the Telepathy app, because I receive an emotion that's probably smugness. I'm still not as adept as Ada at interpreting emotional subtext.

With our current brain boosts, two minutes is plenty of time to have an actual conversation, albeit a light one. In the past five months, Mitya has stripped several of his companies of high-end servers in order to throw these resources at the brain boost project. This has given us all cognitive capabilities we're still learning to exploit. We accepted Mitya's servers because making money with boosted intelligence has become so easy for us that we can easily compensate the affected companies. And even without that, the companies will be better off because we used our boosted intelligence to design replacement servers that will be head and shoulders above the ones we've borrowed. In fact, many of these super servers are currently in the pipeline at major manufacturers. Among the new hardware available today, the highlight is probably the Braino servers, built with IBM's custom and highly experimental neurosynaptic computer chips. Then again, if you asked Muhomor, he'd probably say the best hardware we have is the Qecho. The 100-qubit quantum computer isn't yet used for brain boosts, per se, but it does help us solve several important and difficult problems, including encryption and decryption of secured messages—a branch of computer science that gives Muhomor the equivalent of what normal guys would call an erection.

"Yeah, we can chat," I tell Ada. "I was getting bored anyway."

"Oh?" Ada's avatar looks extra impish. "You're not multitasking?"

"Of course I am. I'm pair programming with Mitya right now."

One of the coolest benefits of having extra brainpower is the ability to split my attention in a way that wouldn't be possible unenhanced. That's what allows me to virtually observe Mitya's coding and provide him with feedback on the app he's writing while sitting here and talking to Ada. Mitya's app will allow someone with Brainocytes to move the latest model of the Roomba cleaning robot with their mind. Pair programming and my brain boost are how I've gotten way better at coding, though I've mostly concentrated on helping open-source projects online instead of writing Brainocyte-ware.

"Let me know if you want me to take over for you." Ada sends this telepathically, but her lips move as though she's speaking. "Talking to the doctor might require your full attention."

"I might take you up on that," I reply. "I could use the time to brush up some more on psychology."

The other day, when I started suspecting Ada would win our "see a shrink" argument, I read a bunch of psychology textbooks, but it's a big field and I could be better prepared.

"Just don't be a wise-ass." Ada's face looks too serious for an imp. "According to Google, she's the best in NYC."

"Fine, but I'm still skeptical," I mentally reply. "How much can I tell her? From what I know about doctor-patient privilege, anything short of planning a crime is protected, but you know how complicated it is with—"

"Tell her as much as you need to so she can do her job." Ada's avatar flies closer.

"But that might include mentioning the Brainocytes Club," I warn.

Brainocytes Club is what Mitya, Ada, Muhomor, and I call ourselves. Like in *Fight Club*, the first rule of Brainocytes Club is you don't talk about Brainocytes Club—a rule that's easy to follow since we use the Telepathy app instead.

"If you need to, I think it would be worth telling her about Brainocytes," Ada replies telepathically. "Then again, if it doesn't come up, don't mention it."

"Just in case, I have a non-disclosure agreement that Kadvosky drafted." I pull the paper out of my back pocket and examine the legalese that even the intelligence boost has trouble deciphering.

The Kadvosky law firm is the most famous and, not coincidentally, most expensive law firm in the world. Mr. Kadvosky is the best of the best, and Mitya put in a good word for me with them, resulting in me being able to use Kadvosky whenever I need legal counsel. When I asked for this non-disclosure agreement, I learned more than I needed to know about my default protections in the eyes of the law, plus the extra protection this document provides.

"That might be overkill, and she may not want to work with you." The imp avatar crosses her arms and narrows her eyes. She doesn't want me to sabotage this appointment. "Promise you'll do your best to make this part go smoothly."

The receptionist pops her gum. "Dr. Golovasi will see you now."

"Saved by the bell," Ada mumbles.

I get up and approach the office door with a disproportionate amount of anxiety. I feel as though I'm seeing a dentist instead of a shrink. I debate launching BraveChill, the anti-anxiety app Ada and I collaborated on. It works with neural networks that connect the cerebral cortex to the adrenal medulla—the inner part of the adrenal gland located above each kidney, an organ responsible for the body's rapid response to stressful situations. Then I chide myself. Using BraveChill in this circumstance would be like launching ballistic missiles as fireworks. App-medicating can be as addictive as using meds, and the last thing I need is an addiction.

Taking the natural route, I draw in a deep breath, release it, and walk into the room where Dr. Golovasi lurks.

THREE

WHEN I'M THIS NERVOUS, I AUTOMATICALLY STOP MULTITASKING AND focus my full attention on my environment because I've been known to trip on objects around me. Once, I nearly stepped on man's true best friend—a rat.

Being this focused gives me an unnaturally complete snapshot of the room around me. I observe details that would normally take ten minutes of careful examination to glean. I guess the age and make of every piece of furniture, and I estimate when the central air filter will need a change. I figure out when the room was last dusted, and since dust is mostly made up of dead skin cells, I calculate how many patients the shrink has seen since the last cleanup. Last but not least, I take in the antique redwood bookshelves surrounding the office and mentally catalog each title to look up later. I also spot the article the doctor was reading in the *New York Times* on the small table, then get around to taking a good look at the doctor herself—and feel instant relief.

If my first schoolteacher, Lydia Petrovna, mated with Mary Poppins and Mrs. Doubtfire, that odd hybrid child would look just like Dr. Golovasi after she reached menopause. Instead of anxiety, I suddenly feel like I should eat my vegetables and study geometry

—and this in turn makes me smile at her. It's weird how hard it is to feel nervous when confronted by such a kind sparkle in someone's eyes.

Dr. Golovasi notices my smile and gives me one in return. Her teeth are so toilet-white I bet they'd shine bright purple under a black light. She stands up and offers me her hand. "Nice to meet you, Mr. Cohen."

"Nice to meet you, Dr. Golovasi." Her hand is as warm as her face. "Please, call me Mike."

"Okay, Mike. Please call me Jane." She gestures at the plush, overstuffed couch.

"Sure, ma'am," I reply as I sit down and wonder why I have such a hard time picturing myself calling her Jane. In the Russian tradition, calling an older doctor Jane instead of by her full name with the patronymic would be the equivalent of not addressing her by the plural "you." Both cases are breaches of protocol and feel wrong, especially in light of her resemblance to my first-grade teacher.

The doctor sits back in her chair, her gaze enveloping me like a warm blanket.

"I—Before we begin... err... I'd like you to sign a non-disclosure agreement," I say and get back up, rustling the paper in my hands. I feel like a complete idiot. "I know this might not be orthodox, but I'm an extremely private person, and if you don't mind..."

Dr. Golovasi's eyebrows rise. "This is a safe place. Anything you tell me in here is already privileged."

"I get that," I say, feeling even more of an ass. "But this document should reinforce the seriousness of my need for discretion. This way, I can take civil action should—"

I don't finish my thought because I see a miniscule frown creep into the corners of the doctor's eyes.

"Good going." Ada's telepathic message is chock-full of sarcasm. "You just threatened a nice old lady."

Whatever doubts Dr. Golovasi might have, they disappear from her face and she says, "Please, let me have a look at that."

I hand her the paper and amble back to the cushy couch.

Dr. Golovasi puts on the pair of reading glasses hanging from her neck. That reminds me of the second nicest person I knew as a kid—a lady librarian who'd always save the newest science fiction releases for me in middle school.

Since I have some time while the doctor reads, I code-review Mitya's app, write a function for the open-source project I've been helping out on, balance my checkbook, do some light shopping on Amazon, research a couple of companies for my fund's portfolio, skim the ebook versions of the more interesting books I spotted on Dr. Golovasi's shelf, read a couple of articles in the *IEEE Journal on Selected Areas in Communication*, read an article in *Advances in Physics*, and write down an idea that occurred to me.

"Hey, Ada," I mentally say. "Check out my write-up. I think I figured out how we can make a transistor that can scavenge energy from its environment. If my back-of-the-head calculations are correct, that would lead to ultra-low power consumption."

"She's done." Ada's voice is so loud I get the illusion my ears are ringing. "Focus on your visit for now. The transistors can wait."

"Okay, Mike." Dr. Golovasi pushes her glasses higher on her nose, pulls out a pen, and signs the non-disclosure agreement. "Hopefully, this will make you feel safe here."

I retrieve the paper, sit back down, and look at the doctor.

"Though it might seem redundant, I must go over your usual patient privileges," she says and goes into an explanation that boils down to her being ethically, professionally, and legally obligated to not disclose anything I tell her, except something like me planning to hurt myself or others. She finishes with, "Do you have any questions about this?"

"No, Dr. Golovasi, I understand." What I don't add is that my non-disclosure would probably cover me in the unlikely event that I told her I was planning on hurting someone.

"Please, call me Jane," she says and takes off her glasses.

"Okay, ma'am," I reply and mentally send to Ada, "No offense, but this is where I bid you farewell."

"Good luck," Ada says without any hurt in her tone.

I turn off my Share app and Mr. Spock's equivalent (since Ada can and does access him), and say out loud, "Is this the part where I lie down and get in touch with my feelings?"

"If that makes you more comfortable." Dr. Golovasi gives me a wry smile. "To start, why don't you tell me what brought you here?"

"I'm not actually sure I even need to be here." I decide I prefer sitting after all.

She reaches for a notepad and pen. "The mere fact you came here proves you need to be here," she says gently.

To me, it's the fact that I don't call her out on that zany Hallmark-card wisdom that proves I indeed need to be here, but I don't say that. Instead, I choose to go with a more careful, "My biggest concern is trouble sleeping."

She asks for clarification, and I admit I've had really bad nightmares every night for months.

"We'll come back to that shortly." She scribbles something down, probably, *Yep, a nut job*, before looking up again. "Is anything else bothering you?"

"I've been getting anxious much too easily lately," I admit. "Sometimes, it happens for no reason, but I think it's just the effect of poor sleep. I also feel jumpy and easily irritated, and my girlfriend thinks I exaggerate the negative aspects of my life. But all these things can also be caused by insomnia."

I stop talking, but Dr. Golovasi looks at me expectantly, her patience reminiscent of a Buddhist monk's. Her posture says, *Okay, that's a good start, but now tell me the really juicy details.*

I stay silent for a few more beats, then decide to just come out with it. "I also relive certain horrible events that happened to me recently. I feel a lot of guilt, though I think it's a justifiable response."

Dr. Golovasi's left eyebrow rises slightly, as though saying, *Okay, I'll definitely need to hear about these horrible events, but it seems like you're still holding out on me.*

319

I take a breath and continue. "I guess the biggest issue is that I often feel like I'm being followed," I say.

This breaks through her calm facade. "Why do you say that?" she asks avidly, leaning forward—something I take as a bad sign.

Seeming to realize she's betrayed too much emotion, the doctor steeples her fingers in front of her face in a gesture that might've fooled someone whose brain wasn't as overclocked as mine. "Why do you say this feeling of being followed is your biggest issue?" she clarifies.

"Well, to start, no one believes I'm being followed," I say, wishing we could converse in Zik so I could add a big dose of hesitation to my words, as well as speed this whole thing up.

"You've told people close to you about these feelings?" There appears to be approval in her tone. "But you're not happy with their reaction?"

"I just told my bodyguard and my girlfriend," I say. "And yes, it sucks that they don't believe me."

She must have other patients with bodyguards, because she just looks at me expectantly again, her countenance saying, *Get on with it already.*

"Okay, I didn't even tell this to my mom." I inhale some extra air and breathe it out. "The thing is, I recently learned that my half-sister suffers from paranoid schizophrenia."

As soon as the words leave my mouth, I realize I never admitted this truth to myself. I never dared to connect the feeling of being followed with my research on my half-siblings—the kids my deceased father had with his wife of forty years. After the events in Russia, I learned I have a half-brother named Konstantin, or Kostya, and a half-sister named Masha. Kostya turned out to be one of the so-called New Russians. He made a lot of money in the oil industry, then invested in an internet startup that later exploded in growth. He's unmarried, likely because he spends considerable time and money on psychiatric care for Masha.

My half-sister believes poltergeists are after her. I learned that when Muhomor hacked the computers at the clinic where Kostya keeps her. In Masha's defense, there was a time in the eighties when many Russians believed in poltergeists, perhaps in part because Russian folklore contains a mystical creature called *Domovoi*, an often mischievous but friendly house spirit. The spirits my half-sister believes stalk her are more frightening than the relatively benign Domovoi, though. Last year, Masha tried to take her own life, but she said it was the spirits. This was her sixth suicide attempt. When Kostya shared the fate of our father with her, Masha scratched Kostya's face to the point of leaving permanent scars.

So yeah, my biggest fear is that the stressful events that led to my father's death triggered something in me, something like what poor Masha is going through.

After all, we share a quarter of our DNA.

"I can see there's a story behind all this," Dr. Golovasi says, taking me out of my reverie. "Do you feel comfortable sharing any of it?"

"It's a really long story..."

"The purpose of the first session is for me to learn more about you," Dr. Golovasi says. "I'm here for you to tell me long stories."

I sigh and do my best to tell her what happened five months ago. I explain how I enrolled Mom into the Brainocytes study and describe the kidnapping of Mom and the other patients, our trip to Russia, the rescue, and all the violence and death I witnessed along the way. I sugarcoat some of it—especially the murders my cousin Joe and his minions committed—and I don't mention my Brainocytes.

"I read about your mother's kidnapping in *The Times*." Dr. Golovasi shifts in her seat. "Your story sounds like it would cause anyone to have trouble sleeping."

I'm tempted to say that Joe sleeps like a psychotic little baby, but instead, I lamely mumble, "Yeah, it was pretty rough."

"At least you made new friends in the process. This Gogi and Muhomor sound like interesting individuals."

I nod. "True, though Gogi treats me like a client half the time, while Muhomor is just Muhomor."

"Oh?" She leans toward me again. "What do you mean?"

"Muhomor was brilliant even before—" I was about to say, "before Brainocytes," but I change it to, "Before he took a bunch of computer courses here in the States. Now his ego doesn't fit through most doors."

"But you guys can bond on a work level?" She tilts her head quizzically.

"Not really. Cryptography, Muhomor's passion, isn't my favorite branch of computer science. So we're not exactly bonding over that. If anything, he and Mitya might be getting close, and I wish I was above feeling jealous, but I'm not."

She looks so uncharacteristically interested in my words that I wonder if this bromance jealousy is something she wrote her PhD on.

"What do you think they do together that you don't do with Muhomor?" she asks, confirming my suspicions that she's latched on to this topic.

"Muhomor developed an ingenious cryptosystem that only Mitya can truly appreciate," I say with a shrug. "My girlfriend doesn't care about the subject, and neither do I, really."

What I don't mention is that, unlike Ada, I tried to understand Muhomor's work, and it was too dense for me—one of the few things to challenge me intellectually in a long time. It literally made my brain hurt.

Instead of her eyes glazing over at the word "cryptosystem," Dr. Golovasi looks like she just shot espresso into her eyeballs. I recall that we've decided to keep Tema—short for the Russian word "kryptosystema"—on the hush-hush, so I say, "Anyway, I think I got sidetracked a little."

"You're right." She fiddles with her pen as though unsure if she should write a note in her pad. "Tell me, what have you done to cope with all this stress?"

"Right. Stress management." I prepared for this question to the point where I can demonstratively fold over a finger for each activity. "I've been keeping busy helping Mom recover, I picked up a couple of new hobbies, I make sure to get pet therapy from my rat, and I've started a new exercise routine."

"Those are great, especially the exercise," Dr. Golovasi says, but I get the feeling she's holding back some questions, such as, *Did you just say rat?*

"Yes and no," I reply. "My hobbies involve coding, which can be frustrating at times. I also started learning how to shoot. Though it's therapeutic, it isn't your typical calm hobby."

"I see." She steeples her fingers again. "Then I urge you to consider things like yoga, meditation, and massages. Keep spending time with your pet." She stops, then adds, "Intimacy is also a crucial stress reliever."

I consider her words. Continuing pet therapy is easy. I feel Mr. Spock against my pocket as we speak, and I sense happy thoughts coming from him while the little guy munches on a piece of dry mango. Regarding meditation, we recently developed an app that helps us concentrate, and Mitya claims it's done wonders for *his* ability to meditate, so maybe I'll try that. I had an ex who tried to get me into yoga, and Ada goes to yoga as well, so I might join her. I hate massages, but for the sake of my sanity, I'm willing to give it a shot. Perhaps I'll start with a foot rub?

Thankfully, intimacy is one aspect of my life I have completely covered. Ada and I have so much sex that running out of condoms has become a real hassle, though I'm not sure I want to discuss this with this older woman, who's also a complete stranger.

As though psychic, Dr. Golovasi says, "I completely understand if you're not comfortable talking about your romantic relationship with me at this time. Just know it's an important part of your life, and we're bound to discuss it eventually."

"No, I don't mind," I lie, as much to myself as to her. Double-checking that the Share app is off, I tell the doctor, "There's not much to say. On my end, I think the relationship is great. I love her. I think she's amazing, caring, brilliant, and gorgeous. She gets me like no friend or girlfriend ever has. She loves me, though she doesn't like saying it. The intimacy, especially the sex, is beyond my wildest dreams... I just worry she'll get tired of my problems someday."

"What makes you think she will?"

"Nothing." I cross my arms over my chest. "If anything, she's extremely supportive. For example, she's the one who made this appointment for me. She cares about me and wants me to be well. It's just that, well, it goes back to that feeling of being followed."

What I don't mention is that Ada has been acting more than a little strange lately, and this change in behavior terrifies me. I hope I'm just being as irrationally paranoid about Ada's weird behavior as I am about being followed. Still, I can't shake the feeling that Ada wants to have a big talk with me about something, and when girls want to have a big talk, it's never good news. But I don't want to go into any of this with the shrink. I really am not comfortable with her yet.

Realizing I won't add anything more to this subject, Dr. Golovasi says, "Are you worried she'd terminate the relationship if you developed the same condition as your half-sister?"

I look down at the Persian rug, glad I killed the Share app when I did. "That's one of my biggest fears, yes."

"Maybe I can put your mind at ease, then," Dr. Golovasi says, and her voice turns exaggeratingly soothing. "Given what I've heard, and speaking with you like this, I doubt you're schizophrenic. If I had to diagnose you—and I don't yet—in the worst case, I would say you might be suffering from post-traumatic stress disorder. It's more likely, though, that you're having a normal reaction to a horrific situation—if the word 'normal' can have any meaning in this context. I think more sessions will allow us to sort through all this in more detail, but I don't think you should worry about becoming like your sister."

I exhale in relief. "Okay. So what do you recommend I do?"

"Let's start by having you come see me once a week. We'll do talk therapy like today and try cognitive therapy to control your negative thoughts. I'll also teach you some relaxation techniques that will help you cope with stressful situations. Your homework for today is to reduce the stress in your life as much as possible. Consider spending more time with your friends and family. Continue to exercise. Research meditation—though it's also something I would be happy to teach you down the line. Develop healthy sleep habits by only using the bedroom for sleep and sex, not TV, and go to bed at a regular time. Don't drink caffeinated drinks or other stimulants. And make sure your bedroom is dark and free of unwanted sounds."

"Okay." I store my ongoing recording of everything I just heard and saw during the last hour to the data servers in case I want to replay what the doctor said at a later date. Then I mentally text Gogi my desire to have a training session today, since it's what the doctor ordered. I also text Mom, telling her I'll come visit today, and call a meeting of the Brainocytes Club for later in the day, since that's also in the doctor's prescription.

Thinking of Mom reminds me of a joke I've been itching to tell the doctor, so I say, "You know, Dr. Golovasi, it's been nearly an hour and we still haven't blamed my mother for anything."

"As a mother, I find that stereotype insulting," the doc replies, her eyes crinkling into laugh lines.

"My mom is amazing," I say to make sure she knows I was kidding. "If I'm messed up, it's either my own fault or by random chance."

"As far as I'm concerned, when you can excel at your job, have fulfilling relationships with friends and family, and maintain a romantic relationship, you're not formally 'messed up,'" the doctor assures me. "If I were to use a car metaphor, I'd say you just need a little tuning, that's all."

I smile and shake my head. "Normal people don't need to see a shrink."

"Everyone should get therapy," she retorts. "I visit a therapist myself, as does my son."

"Forgive me if I remain skeptical when a professional tells me everyone should use their services," I say, but my tone is light.

A soft alarm sounds, and Dr. Golovasi looks at her watch. "I'm afraid this is the end of our session. We should have more time in our next session."

"That wasn't so bad," I tell her and realize it really wasn't. I know it's probably pure placebo, but I already feel somewhat better. I read about this in one of the psychology books I studied for this appointment. The act of making changes in your life makes you feel more in control of your destiny and often provides noticeable relief. I wonder if I'll feel like someone is following me at any point during the rest of the day.

"To make the next appointment, please speak with Monika." Dr. Golovasi gets up and offers me her hand.

"Thanks, Dr. Golovasi," I say and give her a firm handshake.

"Please, call me Jane."

"Of course, ma'am." I'm guessing if we continue this, in a year or so, I'll be able to address her so informally. "See you next week."

FOUR

"Begin," Gogi says and throws a punch at my shoulder.

I dodge and telepathically tell Ada, "Given that I didn't feel like anyone was watching me on my way to the pet sitter and here to the gym, I'd say therapy is already working."

"That's encouraging," she replies, her thoughts imbued with happiness. "I do wish you'd stop these brutal sessions, though."

There's a lot of hippie in Ada, and that includes a deep dislike of violence. She refuses to watch overly violent movies, even though some of them are awesome. So it's not a huge surprise that she hates my trips to the gun range and worries about Gogi's lessons. Trying to keep any defensiveness out of my mental reply, I send, "The doctor approved this. Actually, she suggested I exercise more."

"Yes, but if the good doctor saw this so-called training, I bet she'd recommend simple cardio, or lifting weights, or, my favorite, resistance band exercises."

"You mean the exercises my mom does?" I reply.

What I leave unsaid is that those puny resistance bands aren't necessarily Ada's favorite exercise, given how fond she is of dancing on that stripper pole in her bedroom. I don't feel comfortable even thinking about that in front of Gogi, lest he sniff out my thoughts and make a comment over which I'd have to kick his ass for real.

"Just because your mother does it doesn't make it less cool," Ada counters, though we both know she lost this round. Deciding to fight dirty, she plays the girlfriend card. "I just can't watch you get hurt."

"I can disable Share," I warn her and fling my fist at Gogi's solar plexus. "Or you can stop looking."

"Someone will need to call the ambulance when you eventually cripple each other," she says out loud in my head.

"Suit yourself. Now, if you don't mind, I'm going to focus on this. I think the warm-up is over."

"I'm just a fly on the wall," Ada says, and I feel a mental disconnect, telling me she shut down her Telepathy connection.

I try to focus, but my thoughts scatter, as often happens when I first bring all my attention to my physical surroundings. The white-floored dojo looks brighter and the mirrors on the walls shinier.

To get myself more in the mood, I use the Music app to play Metallica in shuffle mode. As with everything Brainocytes, the music is only in my head. That's fortunate, because if I blasted my tunes this loud in the real world, the dojo would shake, and Gogi and I would have permanent ear damage.

As though in sync with the frantic drumbeat in my head, Gogi chops at my neck, but I step back just in time.

Unbeknownst to Gogi, I decide to expand the scope of our session and enable the new app I named after its designer—the Muhomor app.

The room appears subtly different, and I get a strange set of synesthetic sensations that are part of this app's user interface. I see the Wi-Fi networks that permeate this space as slightly colorful shimmers in the air. In addition to the colors, these networks possess qualities reminiscent of something between taste and smell.

Gogi blocks my punch with his elbow and counters, so I keep most of my attention on him, but I also allow the Muhomor app to hack into the Wi-Fi it feels is the "tastiest," for lack of a better term. The app makes short work of whatever security the Wi-Fi possessed, and once I'm on it, I see a web of connected devices as Augmented Reality. Like the Wi-Fi, each device has a sensory perception associated with it. The brightest one is the security camera behind Gogi, my target from the get-go. A moment later, I can see his movements through the camera.

Someday soon, I'll have to convince Gogi to let me fight him blindfolded so I can look like a cool character from those old kung fu movies where the master hones the pupil's senses that way. For now, I use the camera feedback as an extra pair of eyes. The trick helps. I find it much easier to watch Gogi's legs from this vantage point, and I jump away from a shin kick in time. Gogi rewards the accomplishment with a grudging grunt.

As per my research, the majority of Gogi's moves come from a Russian martial art called *Systema*. If what I read about it is true, it's a pretty lethal system with plenty of creative ways for hurting people, which is ironic given how uncreative the title of the fighting style is. Systema means "the system" in Russian. Gogi definitely has his own take on Systema, though, with some influences from *Chidaoba*—a form of Georgian wrestling. These influences are apparent when Gogi gets his opponent (typically me) on the floor. Gogi also occasionally utilizes a move or two inspired by *Khridoli*—an eclectic, traditional set of Georgian martial arts that is so old and comprehensive it includes fencing and archery—as well as moves from Greek wrestling that he likely picked up from the late Nadejda.

I dodge Gogi's attempt to seize my elbow and realize I'll eventually need to hurt Gogi's feelings by getting another trainer. The intelligence boost helps me learn how to fight nearly as fast as any other activity, so I've made great progress in these few months of training. Once I learn everything I can from Gogi—likely in another couple of months—I won't want to limit myself to his style. Like Bruce Lee and many others before and after him, my long-term ambition is to form my own fighting style, something I'll get around to after I get a good sample of existing martial arts.

Daydreaming about my own style doesn't lower my battle awareness, so when I see an unusually fortuitous opening, I take great pleasure in kicking Gogi in the groin. Though he's wearing a protective cup, his face contorts in genuine pain, and I realize I applied too much force for a friendly sparring session.

Gogi's face reddens, and I can tell things are about to get serious. Everything about Gogi screams, *No more Mr. Nice Georgian.*

He chops at my neck, and I twist away to avoid getting my clavicle shattered. Then I barely dodge a frantic array of punches. Keeping me on the defensive, Gogi goes in for my right knee. Only my camera view allows me to catch his intention and step back in time.

Grunting something that I think means "good" in Georgian, Gogi leaps at me and grabs me by the shoulders.

I try to break his grip but realize my error a moment too late.

Gogi grabs me by the waist and does a maneuver he probably learned from Nadejda. Before I register the how of it, I'm flying toward the mat at a speed that's hard for even my enhanced mind to estimate.

"Careful!" Ada screams, as though I can control my flight in this fraction of a second.

I land on my side, and Gogi lands on top of me, causing me to lose what little air was still in my lungs.

I debate whether I should surrender, but something stubborn drives me onward.

If there's one part of Gogi's fighting style I haven't mastered yet, it's wrestling.

The Russians have a strong stereotype about Georgians. They think Georgians are horny all the time and swing both ways, leading to a whole genre of anecdotes (what Russians call jokes). Coincidentally, the butt of these Georgian jokes is almost always a guy named Gogi. I hate labels and discrimination of any kind, and it's not like I've done any statistical analysis on the behavior of the typical Georgian male, but this limited sample of one Georgian, Gogi, fits the Russian stereotype eerily well. He seems to enjoy this wrestling part of our training on a level I'm somewhat uncomfortable with—especially when, like now, I feel something poking me in the back. I hope it's Gogi's gun, or a Sharpie marker, or anything but him being too happy to be wrestling me.

Trying my best to convince myself of the educational value of wrestling on the ground, I decide to put in an effort and grab for Gogi's ankle.

My reward is a light kick to the face.

Before I even understand what happened, my face is under Gogi's armpit—a horrific place—and I can't see much with my eyes.

Struggling for air, I look at us via the camera feed. Though it looks like we're having rough, kinky sex, I'm in too much pain to find any humor in the situation. Instead, I tap the mat in surrender.

This is when I notice Joe standing at the dojo's entrance.

"Not this again," Ada's voice intrudes. "Just run away. Now."

"Remember what we agreed last time?" I remind her. "You just overstepped your bounds, and I'm turning off the Share app." Before Ada can object, I terminate all the communication apps.

My true reason for breaking contact with her is the very real chance that I might embarrass myself. I don't want my girlfriend witnessing my humiliation.

For good measure, I even get rid of the EmoRat app. The latest version of the software has created an almost empathic link between me and Mr. Spock, a feature that lets me know how the little guy is doing and lets him know when his behavior is upsetting me. It rarely does. Not for the first time, I wonder if you can say "he's such a good boy" about a rat? In any case, EmoRat might make him aware of my anxiety, and there's no reason for that. He's probably playing with his two friends, Kiki and Boss, at the pet sitter's place. Kiki and Boss are two strangely rat-friendly

Chihuahua brothers that the owners of the Furry Ritz have vouched for. I think the Chihuahuas decided that Mr. Spock is a runt of a dog from their breed, or maybe they formed an alliance with the rat based on the age-old logic that the enemy of my enemy—cats—is my friend.

Getting up, I dust myself off and prepare to leave the mat as though Joe isn't there at all.

"Show me what you've learned." My cousin is already on the mat, standing in a fighting stance.

"I'm good, Joe," I say, though I know full well it won't work. "I already got my blood pumping today." With faint hope, I try a lie that appeals to Joe's sense of professionalism. "I've got to hurry to get to an investor meeting in Midtown."

Instead of replying, Joe interlaces his fingers and stretches his arms so that his fingers produce a loud, painful crack.

Then he approaches me with the inevitability of the *Titanic* iceberg.

FIVE

BEHIND MY COUSIN'S BACK, GOGI GIVES ME A THUMBS UP THAT seems to say, *Hey, I think you can handle him this time, but if not, better you as his punching bag than me.*

"Einstein," I mentally command. "Please monitor my vitals. If I break something or pass out, I need you to call an ambulance immediately."

"You got it, boss," replies Einstein, and even though he uses Zik, he somehow still has a German accent. "Your blood pressure is already elevated. Your adrenaline levels are above normal. Your caffeine level is too high. You're—"

"Einstein, please don't use ongoing commentary," I say and feel a bit guilty for interrupting him. Then I feel silly about the guilt since, being my AI personal assistant, Einstein has no feelings to hurt. If Einstein had feelings, I wouldn't want to piss him off because he has a lot of information on me via a bunch of "lab on a chip" biosensors imbedded in my body. After spending two years in development at Mitya's BioInfo company, the sensors can detect increased levels of hormones, as well as the presence of alcohol and other pharmaceutical or illegal drugs, and they can even diagnose some diseases.

Seeing a blur of movement, I focus both my biological eyes and the camera on Joe. If the intensity of a stare could hypnotize a person, Joe would surely go into a trance. I turn off my music and debate disabling the camera view as Joe strikes with a speed a cobra would be jealous of.

If I wasn't watching his back muscles through the camera, I would now have a broken jaw. As is, I block with my left forearm (even though my physical therapist suggested I leave it alone for a month), and it explodes in pain.

Ignoring the nauseating sensation, I smoothly transition from the block into a right forearm strike. To my surprise, I graze Joe's face.

This is the first time I've made any contact with Joe, and a smidge of elation penetrates my deep dread.

The look in Joe's lizard-like eyes turns sixty shades icier than their usual emotionless abyss. Yet—and I could be having an adrenaline-induced delusion—there's something like pride in those eyes as well. I've been wondering why Joe does this to me, and the most generous conclusion I've reached is that perhaps these torture sessions are his way of showing me a type of cousinly tough love. Like maybe he's making sure I'm ready to defend myself should a psychopath attack me—and what better way to prepare for that scenario than fighting him?

Pride or not, Joe's counterattack is brutal. I duck just in time to avoid a broken nose. Then I shift to the side, taking a hard hit to my pectoral instead of my neck, but then I falter and get punched in the middle of my chest.

I'm still trying to remember how to breathe when Joe performs a throw I don't recall learning, and the room blurs in front of my eyes. Through the camera, I watch myself fly toward the mat and land on my back.

"This is an ambiguous situation," Einstein says. "Your oxygen levels are critical, but you're still conscious."

It takes all my willpower to mentally tell Einstein I don't need the ambulance yet.

Four hands help me up from the mat, and I dazedly comprehend that two of them must belong to Joe, who's never helped me up in the past.

I'm led to a bench and dumped there to come to my senses.

Dazedly, I hear Gogi and Joe discuss my progress in Russian, as though I'm not there.

"The kid is a quick learner," Gogi says. "Must be your good genes."

I can't decipher Joe's response through the frantic pulsing in my ears.

"You there? Can you speak?" Gogi walks over to me and waves his hand in front of my face as if I'm drunk. "Do you need my services today?"

"Maybe later," I half gasp, half grunt. "Going to the gun range next. I'll text you after."

Gogi loses interest in me and walks back to Joe. I hear him say, "Let's go smoke a joint. It's my treat."

I'm not sure what my cousin replies with, but they leave.

I spend the next half hour stabilizing my breathing so I can use an app to summon my new car, Zapo 2. Even in my condition, it's not hard to get the car to leave the parking lot and meet me by the door. The hard part is walking to the car, but I manage that too.

"Einstein," I mentally order when the car door closes. "Drive me to the gun range."

———

"You know you go to the gun range too often when the gun range people know your name, what gun you carry, and exactly how many bullets you'd like to buy," Ada says.

Despite her general anti-gun rhetoric, Ada chose a Lara-Croft-inspired avatar to talk to me, one with two guns sitting in sexy hip holsters.

"I need to focus, babe," I say and put a bullet in the head of the big target. "It's a miracle I made that shot while talking to you and looking at that outfit."

"That *was* a pretty good shot." Ada's avatar dissipates. "And you made it without the aim-assist app and while being distracted."

I grunt in satisfaction and do another warm-up shot, this time aiming for the target's heart. I hit it dead on, and Ada claps, though without visual cues, it's hard to tell if she's showing support or being sarcastic.

Next, I enable my newest app for the gun range, and the usual AROS interface gives way to a heads-up display (HUD) where I see the world as though through a sci-fi helmet inspired by my favorite video games, particularly *Halo* and *Metroid Prime*. The HUD keeps track of bullets in my gun and my hit stats, and it has a sobriety indicator along with other goodies. It also lets me put an overlay on the target I'm shooting at. Today, that happens to be a picture of Joe's face, but it could easily be anyone from Osama bin Laden to Barney the Dinosaur. Once Joe's illusion is in place, I pull the trigger, and the HUD shows a nice animation of my cousin's head exploding when I hit the center of his forehead.

"Very mature," Ada says when I restore the fake Joe and shoot him in the forehead again. "All you need to do is refuse to fight him next time."

Instead of answering, I hack into the gun range's security camera and close my eyes.

Shooting in this mode is something I still need to master. I shoot, and all that happens is my already sore arms hurt a little more from the recoil.

I adjust my aim and shoot again. The bullet doesn't even hit the side of the paper target.

"Maybe it's too soon?" I ask Ada rhetorically and enable the aim-assist app in a special camera-view mode Mitya helped me design.

In the camera view, I see a line of magical-looking light going from my gun to the target. Aiming becomes a matter of moving my arm around until the line touches the desired part of the paper target.

I align everything and shoot. This time, I hit the bull's-eye—something I'm hoping to learn to do without the aim-assist as well.

"I'm visiting Mom after this. Do you want to join me?" I telepathically ask Ada as I reload my gun.

"Yeah, definitely," she replies. "I think that's where JC is, so he shouldn't bitch too much about me taking a longer lunch."

Her mention of her boss, the CEO at Techno, reminds me that I haven't checked my corporate email today, so I mentally read and reply to emails as I squeeze out a couple more rounds of ammo. Work has become something I do remotely, with a small percentage of my attention dedicated to it. I had to hire a few more people to cover for me when it comes to routine matters, and I made it crystal clear to everyone to only include me in meetings that would have existential consequences to the fund. Those types of issues come up about once every couple of weeks. In any case, given my Brainocytes-assisted ability to pick good companies for the fund, my people probably think I sold what was left of my soul to the devil, and they're happy to communicate with me however I want, so long as my picks continue making us obscene amounts of money.

"Your lunch might be extra long," I remind Ada. "We're going to the Brainocytes Club meeting after."

"I can join that virtually, like Mitya. I'll dedicate part of my attention to the meeting while I sit in my office at work."

"No, please. I need you there. If Muhomor and I are the only ones present physically, he'll take it as a chance to bond." That wouldn't be a bad thing, except for Muhomor, that means talking about his collection of zero-day exploits and telling me how many hackers couldn't crack his unbreakable Tema. Or worse, making me an accomplice to a federal crime by sharing with me the latest highly secure network he got into just for kicks.

"Fine. I'll strongly consider your preference," Ada replies telepathically, and I learn that there's a way to make a message sound noncommittal in this mode of communication. "Bear in mind, I've been working remotely so much that my minions pulled JC into a couple of meetings, and he's more than a little peeved with me about it."

I tsk-tsk. "Yeah, pulling the boss into a meeting should be considered cause for dismissal."

For my last bullet, I shoot blindfolded without the app and again miss. Figuring Ada will do as she wants in regard to the club meeting, I change the topic and ask, "Would you mind picking up Mr. Spock from the Furry Ritz on your way to Mom's?"

––––––

I approach Mom's new apartment and ring the doorbell.

It took all of my boosted intellect to convince her to let me buy this place. Now she lives much closer to my pad and, as a small side effect, close enough for JC to visit on his lunch break. Ada was right: he *is* visiting Mom today—either that, or someone else in this neighborhood drives a red Tesla with a lucky four-leaf clover pendant hanging from the mirror and plates that spell TECHNO.

As I walk into the downstairs lobby, I smell Mom's *borscht*. That she can go out and locate a store in a new neighborhood, remember to buy all the borscht ingredients, and recall that her new and younger boyfriend, JC, likes borscht for lunch is but a small part of the outstanding improvements brought about by Brainocytes. Mom is completely back to normal—and above normal in many ways, since she can do some of the same things as the Brainocytes Club. Because she's one of Techno's success stories, we are keeping her brain loaded with official Techno applications only, but as soon as her official treatment is over in a few months, we plan to extend her an offer to join the Club and take advantage of everything we've developed.

"Hi, kitten." Mom kisses my cheek excitedly and adds, "JC is here." She makes JC sound like "Jessy," but her boyfriend doesn't seem to mind.

When I walk into the room, I see Techno's redheaded CEO holding a piece of dark bread that Mom buys from a local Ukrainian store, and adding spoon after spoon of farmer's market sour cream into his large bowl of borscht.

In the middle of the table is a big chessboard. Leave it to my mother to play physical board games, and chess no less. I can see that the whites—probably JC's—will be toast in four more moves. That Mom can play chess again is yet another heartwarming sign of her improvement.

JC looks at me, and I reluctantly smile. I guess as long as he doesn't make jokes such as, "Call me Dad," our relationship can stay fairly cordial.

"Please tell me Adachka is coming," Mom says.

Before I can reply yes, the intercom rings.

I scan the kitchen and notice Ada-safe food in the form of potato-filled dumplings, pea-filled pirogi, and a huge salad. The sight of boiled cow tongue with mashed potatoes throws me for a loop; then, with a sinking feeling, I recall whom Mom makes this for. Confirming my suspicions, I hear Mom scream from the door, "Abrashen'ka, Josen'ka, please take off your shoes."

It's Uncle Abe, whom I'm happy to see, and his son Joe.

When they enter the kitchen, Uncle Abe shakes JC's hand, but Joe gives the older man a look that says, *If my aunt so much as says one wrong word about you, in lieu of a cow tongue, it will be yours that gets boiled next time—and it will be attached to you during the cooking process.*

Joe then turns his attention to me, looking me up and down. "How did the investor meeting go?" If he's upset about me not inviting him to join us for lunch, he hides it well. "Everything is cool, right?"

"All good," I reply. I wonder if this is Joe's roundabout way of forbidding me from telling Mom and his father about our earlier fight, or checking how I'm feeling.

"JC, let's call it a draw," Mom says, and I'm pretty sure she's just pretending not to see her eminent victory. "Next time, I play whites."

I help Mom clear the chessboard from the table, and we set more plates down.

The intercom rings again, and I go open it this time, since it can only be Ada.

"Hi, honey," Ada says and kisses me on each cheek. "Here's someone else who wants a kiss."

She takes out Mr. Spock, and he looks at me with the warmest expression a rat is capable of. Giving me a dog-like wiggle of his tail, Mr. Spock washes his whiskers with his little paws and scurries over to my hand. Before Mom can catch sight of him and possibly faint, I give Mr. Spock a little smooch and mentally ask him to hide in my inner jacket pocket—a request he's happy to comply with, as always.

We enter the spacious kitchen, and Ada gives Joe a narrow-eyed stare.

Unsurprisingly, her telepathic message is full of annoyance as she states, "What, the gym wasn't enough? He's here too?"

"Part of the family," I mentally reply. "In his defense, Mom is happy to see him."

Happy might be an understatement. Mom is practically beaming with contentment after everyone sits down and she tells us about the food options.

"This is amazing, sis, as usual." My uncle ceremoniously places a bottle of Stolichnaya vodka he brought for the occasion in the center of the table.

"A toast," JC says, quickly realizing he *will* have to drink vodka on his lunch break. "To Nina's amazing recovery."

To match his words, JC looks at Mom with such warmth that I grudgingly pick up my shot glass and clink it against his. Uncle Abe grunts approvingly and clinks glasses with JC, and even my cousin looks slightly less eager to stab JC with his fork.

I feel guilty that Gogi isn't here. He loves being the *tamada*—a type of Georgian toastmaster—at a table with drinks, and his long toasts are legendary. I've told him many times that if he left the bodyguard business, he could always turn his toasts into Hallmark holiday cards.

"Gogi," I text to appease my conscience. "I have an important meeting taking place at Kharcho in a bit. I could use your protection."

I don't really need his protection during the Brainocytes Club meeting, but if I offered to buy him lunch just for the heck of it, he might refuse. Kharcho is an authentic Georgian restaurant owned by Gogi's distant relative, so I'm not surprised when my bodyguard eagerly replies that he'll be there.

Everyone eats Mom's food and drinks another round of vodka shots, courtesy of Uncle Abe's typical Russian peer pressure. Ada is the only person without vodka in her belly, and this is because my uncle gave up trying to convince her to drink vodka months ago. I think Uncle Abe gave up on Ada in general when he learned she's vegan. We had to painstakingly enumerate a list of what vegans do not consume for him, and I think he still has a hard time with the "no ham" part. To Uncle Abe, Ada's dislike of vodka is almost normal compared to her veganism, and he probably erroneously thinks that Ada considers alcohol an animal product—and hey, sometimes, there are worms in tequila.

"So, how are things going between you two?" Mom asks, her words slightly slurred from the alcohol. She asks the question in English, though Ada's Russian is now good enough that she would've understood it.

"Things are great," Ada says after an awkward pause. "Why do you ask?"

That pause makes me worry. This is yet another example of strange behavior on Ada's part that I should've discussed with the shrink. Language aside, Ada probably doesn't realize this is Mom's roundabout way of asking when she'll be a grandmother, so there's no reason for my girlfriend to feel weird about the question.

"I think you make the most wonderful couple." Mom smiles at us and plops another serving of mashed potatoes on Ada's plate.

"You really do," my uncle says. "Let me say a toast to you."

He orates the equivalent of an epic poem dedicated to our health and vitality and about how lucky we are to have each other.

I don't let my uncle's words go to my head. To consume extra vodka, Russians will happily drink in celebration of anyone's health, including dead leaders like Lenin, and use any holiday as an excuse to drink, even something as uneventful as National Doughnut Day or Dress Like a Pirate Day.

"We should leave before dessert," I mentally tell Ada after she explains to Mom how full she is. "JC is too drunk to worry about your lunch time."

As though to support my secret message, JC gulps down another shot, his nose already turning a deeper shade of red. Until recently, I thought JC had Irish blood, but now I'm less certain. When it comes to drinking with the Russians, JC definitely doesn't live up to the Irish stereotype of being able to handle large amounts of liquor—not that I believe in stereotypes.

"Blood alcohol level is unsafe to drive," Einstein informs me after I swallow my final shot.

"Noted," I mentally reply. "When we get inside Zapo 2, you're driving, no matter what I say, and Ada can even sit behind the wheel."

SIX

ADA AND I HOLD HANDS AS WE WALK FROM THE PARKING SPOT TO the restaurant where we're meeting the rest of the Brainocytes Club.

Unfortunately, as the vodka buzz begins to dissipate, the annoying feeling of being followed returns. I wonder if the shrink's effect was indeed a placebo, and a short-lived one at that. I almost feel as though I'm being followed by a new group of people. This is odd, and not just because I have no clue who was following me before, besides figments of my imagination.

Gogi is already at the restaurant, and Muhomor promises to arrive in a couple of minutes. The day is extremely nice for November, so we decide to get a table outside and order our drinks—vodka for Gogi, a glass of famous Borjomi water (a mineral-rich water of volcanic origins that's over fifteen thousand years old) for Ada, and tea for me.

When Muhomor arrives, we order food and wait for Mitya to get in touch with us remotely.

Ada and I get *gozinaki*, a confection made of caramelized walnuts fried in honey, and I get an extra piece for Mr. Spock. Since we're the only guests at the restaurant at the moment, and because the server knows us, I allow Mr. Spock to sit on the table, next to my plate.

Gogi comments that we ordered a treat that's traditionally eaten on New Year's and thus incongruous in the middle of fall, especially on such a warm day. We point out that it was on the menu, so his gripe is with Nikolozi, his fourth-removed cousin and owner of this place. Gogi orders *kharcho*, the signature Georgian soup from which the restaurant got its name, and *shashlik*, a Georgian version of a shish kebab.

"Lots of vegan-safe dishes," Ada says wistfully as she scans the menu. "I'd like to try the beetroot *pkhali* with walnuts, but I'm too full."

"I'll bring you here on an empty stomach tomorrow," I promise. "Also, Mom knows how to make some Georgian dishes since they've made their way into Russian cuisine, so I'll tell her to make something for you next time."

"Are we ready for the meeting?" Muhomor sends Mitya, Ada, and me an invite from the Teleconference app.

"I'm ready." Mitya shows up as a see-through holographic image in one of the empty seats at the table, making our meeting look like the Jedi Council gathering from *Star Wars*.

"Let's begin, then," Muhomor says in Zik via the Teleconference app and uses the Augmented Reality interface to give himself giant ram horns that humorously complement his usual pajamas.

"Speaking of you being horny," Ada says to him in Zik. "Mike told me Lyuba is in town."

"Lyuba's vacationing in the US, yes." Muhomor looks confused. "What does that have to do with my horns?"

I almost choke on my tea, and Ada bursts into laugher, probably getting Borjomi water into her nose. Of course, the way-too-normal and gorgeous Lyuba isn't Muhomor's girlfriend. Ada now owes me a beer and a sexual favor since we made a bet on this topic earlier. She was sure Lyuba and Muhomor were in a long-distance relationship, and I said that wasn't possible. Mitya and I call Muhomor bisexual behind his back, only the "bi" is short for "binary code." The guy eats, sleeps, and dreams cryptography, hacking, and coding, and he doesn't have any interest in either gender when it comes to sex. Two weeks ago, one of my investors invited us to his bachelor party. Muhomor came with us and proceeded to hack the stripper's phone instead of getting a lap dance or even looking at the girl. He also hacked the website of the club where the event was taking place.

"Whose turn is it to speak?" I ask. I opt not to spruce up my avatar today, beyond putting a gun holster on the outside of my jacket in the Augmented Reality. In the real world, my unlicensed Glock 19 from the gun range is hidden right behind the virtual one inside my blazer. After Russia, I can't bear to walk around unarmed—another issue I should probably work on with the shrink.

"Ladies first, as usual?" Mitya winks at no one in particular.

"Isn't that reverse sexism?" Muhomor complains.

"I don't have much to share anyway." Ada ignores Nikolozi as he brings out a tray with food and starts putting it on the table. "I've worked out a method to mass-produce nanomembranes, and Mike has helped me set up a company that will fabricate an ultra-rapid water filtration system by the end of next year. The prices should be low enough for anyone to afford it, and it will be easy for a philanthropist"—she gives Mitya and me a pointed look—"to make a huge dent in solving the world's clean drinking water problem."

We nod approvingly, and Ada shares a couple more things she's developed, all with the theme of bringing global abundance and prosperity.

"What about Brainocytes development?" Mitya asks when Ada pauses to mentally take a breath and sip her real-world water. "Did you put together any interesting apps?"

"I have," Ada replies and examines her glass. "Mike and I pair programmed it and plan to test it out, but I'm not ready to disclose the details yet."

Ada likes to be mysterious, and in this case, I'm glad she is.

From what I understand from observing Ada coding it, the app does something like the Vulcan mind meld, only in real time. The two individuals who use this app together will have their brains temporarily connected. The sex applications are so obvious that I'm glad Ada doesn't give my friends any new fodder with which to tease us for being a couple. When it comes to this topic, Mitya and Muhomor have the maturity of fourth graders in detention.

"Fine." Mitya bites into a Snickers bar, and I assume he does it for real since I see no reason for him to fake it using Augmented Reality. With mock grumpiness, he adds, "Is that all?"

Ada shakes her head. "I also figured out an extremely efficient technique that will allow us to convert atmospheric carbon dioxide into carbon nanotubes." In the real world, Ada tells Nikolozi that she's not interested in more dessert, while at the same time, in Zik, she says, "The nanotubes can be used as batteries or even as the water filters I mentioned. That's what sparked that idea in the first place."

"And?" Muhomor makes sure Ada can see him bite into his pork shashlik. He knows she doesn't like the idea of pigs being killed for food. She thinks pigs are cuter than and as smart as dogs —not that this argument would work on Muhomor. He'd probably eat dog shashlik if it were on the menu.

"Dude." I send Muhomor a private telepathic message imbued with a touch of anger. "Don't piss off my girlfriend. Besides, Georgian food is famous for lamb, not pork shashlik."

I also tell Ada to ignore Muhomor's shenanigans.

"You think Ada prefers baby sheep as food?" Muhomor replies and, as usual, makes the telepathic message disproportionally snarky. "You realize Georgians believe in having the whole sheep family watch the killing."

"They do not," I counter, but then realize I'm doing exactly what I warned Ada against—paying attention to Muhomor's crap. Still, I can't resist adding, "In any case, in America, lamb doesn't always mean baby sheep."

"And that's it," Ada says in conclusion, not looking at Muhomor or his food. She clearly took my advice of not rising to Muhomor's bait better than I did.

"Perhaps I can go next?" Mitya is now drinking a Red Bull, another item inconsistent with our Georgian cuisine. "Ada's given me a nice segue, because my 'benefit for humanity' idea would provide those batteries she mentioned with cheap energy."

"Yes, go." I sip my tea and, not for the first time, wonder how crazy we must look to Gogi, Nikolozi, and even Mr. Spock. The whole meeting is happening virtually, in our heads, so to them, with maybe the exception of Mr. Spock, we must look like we're sitting there, eating in silence. Ada, Muhomor, and I can multitask by talking to Gogi while keeping the meeting going, but Gogi doesn't seem to mind the silence today.

"Fusion," Mitya says triumphantly. "Specifically, 'star in a jar' technology that will provide nearly limitless energy in two years, or thereabouts."

Everyone looks at Mitya with a mixture of wonder and skepticism.

He smirks and says, "I'm sending you the details, but to sum up, I invented a three-dimensional shape that will allow us to cheaply confine plasma inside a powerful magnetic field."

"Hold on," Muhomor says after a moment. "You're talking about a *tokamak*—technology Soviet scientists invented back in the fifties."

I look up "tokamak" and find that the idea has indeed been around.

"Sure." Mitya grins. "That was the inspiration, of course, but unlike all the early designs and plans, mine *will* be built, *will* be cheap, and *will* change the world more than anything we've come up with thus far."

We all let our imaginations run wild at the thought of what limitless energy could do for the world.

The purpose of the Brainocytes Club, or one of its purposes, is to benefit humanity. More accurately, we figured we owe it to the world to use our enhanced brainpower for its betterment. And if our various contributions toward that goal were a contest, Mitya would be winning. I guess it shouldn't be a big surprise; the guy always had grand visions, and the brain boost only multiplied his talents many times over.

"Anything else?" Muhomor asks sarcastically and with obvious jealousy. "Did you figure out how to have world peace and save all the kittens from starving? Oh, wait, that's Ada's thing."

"I respect Ada's endeavors." Mitya gives Ada a good-natured thumbs-up. "Since you asked, though, why yes, I do have something else. Several things, actually. A few things I've saved for last. A) I've gotten us more server space, B) I've designed another set of brain regions we can simulate, C) I've designed a way of caching access to the servers, resulting in faster performance, and last but not least, D) I've optimized our overall brain boost allocation algorithms while still keeping it as max-min fair as I could." Mitya stops and notices that the second part of his statement wasn't fully understood, even by Ada. "In other words," he clarifies, "we're ready for brain boost v9."

Ada claps in excitement, Muhomor almost chokes on his meat in glee, and I have a hard time suppressing my grin. Every time we've boosted our intellect, the gains have exceeded all of our lofty expectations, and with each boost, our expectations have grown higher and higher. The only downside, and it's a tiny one, is that each boost triggers side effects in the beginning. Still, the worst side effect so far has been dream-like pre-cog moments. I'll never forget the one that scared me so much during Mom's rescue. Nowadays, though, we've figured out a way to cope with these deceptively realistic hallucinations by remaining vigilant during our boost upgrade times and asking ourselves, "Is this really happening?" more often than a normal person would. So far, we've all reported that asking ourselves that question short-circuits the pre-cog moments—if that's what's happening. Pre-cog moments are different from dreams, in that I have asked myself, "Is this really happening?" during a nightmare, and it didn't wake me up.

"I take it you want me to launch it." Mitya looks too smug for his pseudo-Jedi avatar. "It's ready to go."

"Of course you should launch it," we scream, almost in unison. Muhomor actually says it out loud in the real world, and Gogi raises his unibrow at him.

"Okay then." Mitya's avatar pushes the big red button that appeared next to him. "Get ready to be smarter."

SEVEN

Unlike with the other brain-boost upgrades, I feel a difference in my perception. It's as though I took a drug that makes the world around me slow down. The feeling is reminiscent of how everything seems in moments of extreme duress—something I experienced quite a bit during the trip to Russia.

"Wow," Ada says, probably experiencing the same effects as me.

"You rock." Muhomor salutes Mitya's hologram with his glass and gulps down the wine. "I feel like Mike should speak next, since Mitya's work is impossible to follow up."

"Fine, I'll go." I pick up Mr. Spock and scratch his chin like the EmoRat app told me he wanted me to. I don't care if my friends make snide remarks about me looking like a movie villain with my pet rat. "I've been pair coding with all of you, as well as writing code for various open-source projects. I now feel confident enough to write Brainocyte apps on my own, so unless someone objects, that's what I'll start doing." I give them a moment to object, but they seem to agree that I'm ready, making me feel warm on the inside—though Mr. Spock's bruxing is helping with that too. "When it comes to my big idea, I'm still obsessed with giving Brainocytes to the whole world. I think we should make it open source right now, if Muhomor finally agrees."

I've been arguing that Brainocytes should be widely available, even if it means Techno, and by extension Mitya and I, makes less money in the process. If the mere four of us have begun to noticeably change the world for the better, what would happen if millions or billions of people like us existed? Surprisingly, it's Muhomor who objects, and we try to run the Brainocytes Club through unanimous votes.

"I'm still not ready." In the real world, Muhomor asks Nikolozi for *pakhlava*, a dessert similar to Turkish baklava and one of my favorites. "But now that I've finally made Brainocytes traffic secure, we're closer than ever to being able to release this technology without plunging the world into a dystopian surveillance state where the government can read your thoughts."

"Hey, you're taking someone else's turn to talk about your agenda." As usual, Ada is acting as the moderator of the Club meeting. "We'll come back to you in a second. Let Mike finish. I happen to know he has more to say."

"Thanks, Ada." I bend down to put Mr. Spock on the pavement, as the little guy wants to go to the bathroom by a tree. "One of the things preventing wide Brainocytes adoption is the lack of a way to mass-produce some of the nanoparticles required for Brainocytes. So, I've developed a way to do just that. How much do you guys know about microfluidics—a way of manipulating tiny droplets of fluid in a narrow channel?"

Everyone gives me a look that says, *Are you kidding? We know all.*

"Right, okay." I spot a cat far in the distance and use the EmoRat to alert Mr. Spock. "My idea should reduce the cost of Brainocytes development from obscene to less ridiculous levels. Of course, there's still a ton of work that needs to happen in the manufacturing space, but I think once the incentives are there and more people are looking at the Brainocyte designs, the costs will drop further. This is yet another reason to release the technology into the world."

"I agree," Ada says. "That's what always happens when you make technology open: costs go down."

"Especially technologies susceptible to Moore's Law, which the Brainocytes are," I add as I feel Mr. Spock run up my pant leg and jump back onto the table.

"Okay, I've been sold on sharing Brainocytes with the world for a while." Mitya must've gotten bored of his avatar, because he's replaced his regular visage with a gray, faceless blob. "Send me the specs for the microfluidics idea. I think it might be an interesting read."

"Me too." Ada steals the saucer from under my teacup, pours water into it, and pushes it toward Mr. Spock.

"Me third," Muhomor echoes and takes a piece of pistachio from the top of his dessert and throws it in my rat's general direction. "Maybe you'll impress me enough for me to stop vetoing this Brainocyte-sharing idea."

"That's it for me," I say. "Muhomor, the baton is yours. Go ahead and spew your security-related wisdom at us."

"Before I start, has anyone cracked Tema?" The hacker looks challengingly at Mitya, the only person he deems capable of even coming close to such a feat.

"No." The gray blob that Mitya chose as his new avatar looks down, as if in shame. "And not for the lack of trying, believe me. You can rest assured, Big Brother doesn't stand a chance."

I also tried cracking Muhomor's cryptosystem—mainly to wipe that smirk off Muhomor's face—but alas, I had no luck. Ada also failed, and she likes annoying Muhomor more than I do. It's safe to say the Tema cryptosystem is unbreakable, but none of us will admit this to Muhomor. He's already too arrogant to let live.

"I doubt any of you can crack my baby," Muhomor says and grabs a cup with his honey-sticky fingers. "Did you do as I asked and rewrite all the AROS apps to use Tema?"

"Yes," Mitya and Ada say, as I knew they would since I was looking on while they made the necessary code changes to all our communication apps.

"What about EmoRat?" Muhomor points at Mr. Spock, who decided to munch on what's left of my gozinaki. "The rat is happy right now, isn't it? It wants to jump into your pocket soon, right?"

"Unlike you, Mr. Spock is a he, not an it." I know Muhomor didn't simply guess Mr. Spock's EmoRat messages to me, but rather hacked my connection with the little guy. The hack was possible because the app must not be encrypted with Tema. "I'll fix the app now."

I open the AROS integrated development environment, aka AROS IDE, to work on the code in question.

"Outside of Tema," Muhomor continues, "I developed a way to use Brainocytes as a biometric authentication system—a sort of brain print as it were. Emailing you all the deets."

I skim the specifications Muhomor sends and exchange glances with Mitya. I think we're both wondering if it's worth boosting Muhomor's already enormous ego yet again. Ada must not share our qualms, because she turns to Muhomor and says out loud in the real world, "Muhomor, this is brilliant. I wish I'd come up with this."

Gogi raises his unibrow even higher—aiming it at Ada.

"I try." Muhomor looks like he might have an aneurism from pride. "Once Brainocytes are widespread, people can start using my brain-print technology and not bother with passwords, since most people can't create a strong-enough password to save their bank accounts. The final thing I want to report is my success in penetrating the IARPA systems."

Short for Intelligence Advanced Research Projects Activity, IARPA is a government agency that does high-risk/high-payoff research for the US government intelligence community. So naturally, the mood at the meeting grows solemn, and Mitya speaks for everyone when he says, "Dude, how many times do we have to ask you to stop doing illegal stuff? You're in the US on my H1B visa. If you get caught, I'll be guilty by association."

"I was cautious." Muhomor runs his fingers through his anime haircut and scratches his skull. "What I found was worth it. IARPA is working on reverse engineering the human brain's algorithms. Can you think of anyone interested in those results?"

"They'll eventually publish their research to the public," Mitya says, but the idea of reading whatever Muhomor stole seems to have mollified him. "I guess what's done is done. Let's see the papers. I know you're dying to share."

Ada and I aren't so easily placated. I'm about to give Muhomor a piece of my mind, when the paranoid feeling of being followed returns and then gets multiplied a thousand-fold.

I focus all my attention on the strange feeling, and as though from a distance, I hear Ada complain about Muhomor's hacking escapades.

Something tells me it's not paranoia this time, though I guess that's how paranoid people always feel. That same something tells me there are people stalking me more openly, and that same instinct insists I *was* being followed before.

Unsure whether I should go along with my delusion, I decide to prove the feeling wrong by showing myself that the street is as empty as it appears at first glance. It's fortunate there are no pedestrians and cars, because that will help me provide my neurosis with irrefutable evidence. Diligently, I examine every inch of the dead-end street and don't see anyone, only a row of parked cars.

Next, I look for people inside the surrounding businesses, and that yields no results either. I can't even see the owners inside. Since not much happens on this street on weekdays around 3:30 p.m., I don't take the empty street as a sinister sign. Unfortunately, despite the input from my eyes, something in my brain insists people are hiding somewhere.

Determined to try another route and working almost on instinct, I launch the Muhomor app, and the software does what it usually does, allowing me to sense the invisible electromagnetic waves all around us.

I see the bluish, cherry-scented Wi-Fi network of our restaurant. Muhomor's Brainocytes and phone, Mr. Spock's Brainocytes,

Ada's Brainocytes and phone, and Gogi's phone are all connected to this cherry-scented Wi-Fi, which makes sense. I also experience colors, tastes, and smells from the Wi-Fi networks of the other businesses on the street, but I still have no clue as to the nature of my concern.

Figuring Wi-Fi is useless, I switch the app to focus on cell phone traffic instead of Wi-Fi. Luckily, the app can detect a wide range of signals, including AM/FM radio, TV signals, Bluetooth, and a slew of other options that would only interest Muhomor.

Cell phone coverage is an almost imperceptible shimmer, like the heat haze you see on a hot day above a desert road. It takes concentration to tell Verizon apart from say, AT&T, but around each cell phone, I can make out the colors that indicate its cell phone provider, and akin to Wi-Fi, I can smell and taste these connections, giving me an idea of whether I can hack them.

I close my eyes and focus on the cell phone colors around me. Predictably, there's a bunch around the table and a couple inside some of the businesses. All those are as I expected.

What I didn't expect, though, are the shimmers behind a couple of the parked cars down the street.

At first, I tell myself people might've forgotten their cell phones inside their cars. But when I open my eyes, I verify with ever-increasing dread that the shimmer is coming from outside the cars, not inside. Then I see one of the shimmers move and catch a glimpse of sunlight reflecting off one of the lurker's sunglasses.

Trying my best not to panic, I frantically switch back to Wi-Fi mode and seek a camera to look through. I hit jackpot when I get on the pawnshop's mint-scented Wi-Fi, located just to the left of the spot where I spotted the reflection. The security camera is basic, but I still make out the one chilling detail I was missing.

The man wearing those shades is holding a gun with an elongated barrel ending with a silencer.

What's worse is that I see more people with guns. This isn't that big of a surprise, since each man is attached to the cell phones I detected earlier.

My racing heartbeat reminds me of the sounds the engine in Mitya's Bugatti Veyron made the day we drove through the Nevada desert at 250 miles per hour.

I wasn't being paranoid before—and now that I know I'm not crazy, I almost wish I were.

EIGHT

As before, when I was in those gray-hair-inducing situations in Russia, the stress combines with the brain boost to drastically slow down time. The sunglasses-clad man in the camera seems to move as though through molasses as he signals his conspirators.

I leap into mental action. In panicky Zik, I inform my friends about my discovery and then deal with their reactions, which start off as incredulity but quickly turn to terror. At the same time, I craft a text to Gogi. "We're being ambushed. Here's a link to a camera feed. Don't show any alarm yet. We want them to think they still have the element of surprise."

"Who are they?" Mitya demands.

"What do they want?" Ada grabs my elbow, her small hand like an icicle. "Do we have time to call the police?"

"Mitya, get in touch with the cops first and Joe second, in that order," I mentally send instead of answering their questions. "Muhomor, I can't hack their phones, but I suspect you might succeed where I've failed."

As my friends start on their tasks, I notice Gogi hasn't checked his phone yet, and a whole microsecond has already passed.

I kick Gogi's foot under the table, and when I catch his gaze, I pointedly look at his phone. Since it isn't clear whether Gogi understood my intent, I use EmoRat to give instructions to Mr. Spock. The rat scurries down the table to get within Gogi's eyesight, freezes, and then glares at the phone. He lifts his paw and points his nose at the phone—a rat's version of a posture I usually associate with hunting dogs.

"I'm in their phones," Muhomor says. "Sending you all the information on their identities."

Continuing to multitask, I read our assailants' profiles while trying to devise a plan.

The men ambushing us are former military personnel, with a dash of penal system alumni, and they're all extremely dangerous. They have something else in common as well—they work for a security agency that sounds eerily like Joe's. A man called Vincent Williams spearheads the agency, and his resume makes my cousin look like a boy scout.

Viewing images of Vincent Williams, I shudder. He reminds me of this documentary about chimpanzees I recently saw. In the documentary, there was an extremely violent, cannibalistic chimpanzee named Scar, and Vincent wears that same expression, the one that says, *I'll kill you and then I'll eat you*. Like the ape, Vincent also has a scar on his face, and like the ape, Vincent is impossibly big for his species. I suspect Vincent has been working out and taking steroids since high school, an impression that strengthens as I mentally flip through his dossier. On his social media, he posted pics where he's posing like a bodybuilder, so I gather he might be into that sport. His muscles look like giant tumors in some places, and I suspect the ginormous latissimus dorsi muscles in his back are growing their own sets of muscles at this point— and those muscles might also have muscles.

After what feels like millennia—though I suspect it took less than a second—Gogi looks at his freaking phone. Ever so slowly, he clicks my link, and I watch in real time as blood leaves his face. Then his jaw muscles tighten, and his Stalin mustache twitches.

"Ada, take Mr. Spock in an unsuspicious manner, like you want to pet him," I mentally order. "And be prepared to do exactly as I instruct. Same goes for you, Muhomor."

"Police and your cousin have been notified," Mitya reports.

Almost instantly, the texting app notifies me that I have a message from Joe. It states, "Do not engage Williams. I'm too far away from your location. Run."

I see that Gogi has received the same not-so-useful advice from Joe, and he's probably thinking the same thing I am. How are we supposed to run? Problem one is that we're on a dead-end block with the bad guys blocking our exit. Problem two is that if we get up, the hidden assailants will become open assailants. Our only option is to use the restaurant's back door—assuming it has one.

"Muhomor, get us schematics for the buildings on this block," I say urgently. "We're looking for back doors. Hack City Hall if you need to, but get it now."

In the back of my mind, I wonder if this whole attack is Williams's attempts to settle a score with Joe? Alternatively, is it possible an enemy of mine hired this goon? If so, who? Did my half-brother, Kostya, learn of my role in our father's death and decide to take revenge? I decide to tackle this question later, in the unlikely event that we survive.

"Your stress levels are abnormal," Einstein chimes in. "If I might recommend—"

"No audio feedback until I command otherwise," I mentally snap at the poor AI. "If you want to be useful, launch the Batmobile app for me."

The Batmobile app is what I've been calling an app Mitya wrote a few weeks back. It allows me to remotely drive Zapo 2 and lets Mitya control a couple of the high-end limousines that he owns in every major city. I rarely use the app because I usually ask Einstein to auto-deliver the car—a task the latest version of Einstein can easily do, thanks in part to Mitya's brain-boosted coding prowess. Automating and controlling vehicles remotely is one of my friend's obsessions.

In any case, with the various sensors embedded throughout

Zapo 2, I can see the road on all sides of the vehicle. Using the app to start the engine, I carefully pull the car out of the parking spot and cruise it at five miles an hour down the street toward Vincent Williams and his pals.

"Schematics," Muhomor says and uses the Teleconference app to pull up the necessary screens for all of us to see. "Also, more camera views." Footage of our attackers shows up from different vantages. Some of the camera views seem to be from the culprits' own phones. If we survive, I'll risk boosting Muhomor's ego by telling him how awesome he is.

"No back exits that I can see," Mitya mumbles. "There are windows facing the other street. Maybe if you break them—"

"And assuming they aren't coming from that way too," Muhomor interrupts.

As I drive the car and confirm Mitya's analysis of the schematics, I also examine the weapons the bad guys possess while battling a heavy feeling settling in my stomach. "I can crash Zapo 2 into them. In the commotion, we can try escaping through the window Mitya mentioned," I think half to myself and half to my friends. "Or I can move the car closer. We can jump in and—"

"Get sprayed with bullets on our way out of the block," Muhomor cuts in. "I don't think your windows are bulletproof, so jumping in won't work."

"Don't tell us what *won't* work without offering your own suggestions," Mitya counters.

"Fine," Muhomor says tersely. "How about—"

In that moment, Nikolozi comes out of the restaurant with the check.

Through the camera views, I see frantic movement happening behind the cars.

"Shit," Mitya says somewhere in the distance. "He spooked the lurkers."

I feel like my consciousness splits into two. One me speaks out loud while the other me sends mental messages. Mentally, I say, "Ada, run into the restaurant and hide in the refrigerated room here." I highlight the spot on the schematic. "Muhomor, try to be useful. Mitya, if you haven't already, report shots fired to the cops." Out loud and at the same time as my mental messages, I bark, "Gogi, we're being attacked."

I then jump to my feet and turn over the table in front of us the way I've seen heroes do in movies.

Our adversaries no longer bother with stealth; their heads are now visible to the naked eye from behind the cars.

Blood pumps in my ears, and the world around me seems to move even slower—as though it was shot with an impossibly fast camera, or like I'm seeing everything in bullet-time, a la *The Matrix*. Then Williams fires his gun, and the fact that I don't see the bullet mid-flight breaks the illusion.

A soul-piercing scream reverberates through the air.

NINE

Worry for Ada rips at me like a rabid bear, as it's her voice I just heard. Without turning, I scan my surroundings through the restaurant's security camera.

A body hits the ground behind us with a thump.

My breath whooshes out in a mix of horror and relief. The victim is not Ada, who must've been screaming in horror; it's Nikolozi. The head wound I see in the camera leaves no room to doubt as to his horrific fate—not unless someone knows how to put parts of his brain back in his head.

Trying to keep my hand as steady as on the gun range, I aim the Glock. Part of me registers that Gogi is doing the same. I enable the HUD and the target-assist app. I'm now surrounded by small views into every camera I have access to, as well as some helpful gun stats, including the number of bullets in my gun—ten. I also have a virtual assist line that makes it nearly impossible to miss.

Cursing myself for not carrying extra ammo, I aim for the bad guys' leader's shoulder, but then I spot Gogi aiming for him as well. I change my target from Williams to Jason—a man who's aiming at Gogi's forehead. As I place the aim-assist line on Jason's shoulder, I note that Ada is hurrying toward the restaurant. *Good.*

I pull the trigger.

Without the gun range's earmuffs, the gunshot smacks my eardrums like a brick and creates the illusion that the recoil of my Glock is stronger than usual. My reward is the sight of Jason's right shoulder turning into a bloody steak as he falls to the ground.

Gogi must've fired at the same time, but instead of hitting Williams, his target, the bullet hits the back of Ethan Madison, who, according to his dossier, is a new recruit in Williams's crew. Ethan must've decided to take the bullet for his boss. Unless he's wearing a bulletproof vest—a possibility to take into account—the decision just cost him his life. Ethan falls on top of Williams in a murder-scene-body-outline heap that tells me he wasn't wearing a vest after all.

As I aim at my next target, I notice Muhomor running behind Ada. Despite the apparent cowardice of this move, I'm relieved, as he's blocking Ada with his body.

Kevin, the next man I shoot in the shoulder, cries out, and Gogi takes his second shot. A man who used to be called Bob Young falls to the ground with a bullet in his cheekbone. Somehow, despite his scream, Kevin—the guy I shot—is still standing, so I waste another bullet, this time going for his right shoulder. This shot does the trick. Kevin slumps to the ground and screams like a detainee in the Abu Ghraib prison.

Ada and Muhomor are almost through the door. To give Ada the best cover I can, I mentally floor the gas of the Batmobile app and point Zapo 2 at the gap between two parked cars, where the majority of the remaining attackers are hiding. For good measure, I activate the nitro system, inspired by something I first saw in the *Fast and the Furious* movies. Sven, the guy who installed the nitro, warned me I could only use that feature twice before needing a refill, and more importantly, that Zapo's tricked-out engine could easily get shot to shit from a single nitro use. But I think Sven would agree that if there was ever a time to risk the engine, this would be it.

Through Zapo's microphones, as well as with my own ears, I

hear the brain-shattering screech of metal and plastic tearing each other asunder. Through the cameras, I see Zapo rip through the back and front bumpers of the cars parked in its way. A couple of the assailants manage to jump out of the way, but two aren't so lucky. One of them, Logan, is left lying on the asphalt, with a chunk of bone sticking out of his right leg like an ancient arrow tip and his blood gushing in a stomach-turning geyser. Another guy, nicknamed Deaf John, got hit with Zapo's left mirror and is on the ground as well, hopefully knocked unconscious for a long time.

Though I'm flooring the mental brake pedal to spare the car any unnecessary damage, poor Zapo continues its unfortunate trajectory for another couple of feet, straight into the laundromat's front window. I cringe when I hear the shattering sounds coming from the laundromat—sounds I perceive both through my real-world ears and from what Zapo's microphones deliver to my brain's hearing center. Then I needlessly blink my real-world eyes as the cameras show me Zapo hit the coin machine. The four front-facing cameras blink out of existence, but the side and back cameras still work, allowing me to see car parts and quarters fly in every direction.

"I fear Zapo 2 might've joined its predecessor in car heaven," Mitya says from somewhere, but I ignore him.

Ada is inside the restaurant, but Muhomor is acting like a complete idiot. He turns around to see what the big bad noise was about.

"Go in!" I mentally shout at him. "Make sure Ada makes it into that fridge. Drag her in by force if you have to."

I have to stop paying attention to Muhomor, because Williams uses the commotion to push Ethan off him, and he's again ready for action.

"Watch out," I scream for both Gogi's and Muhomor's sakes. I get a strong feeling that Williams is about to do something desperate.

Gogi and I duck behind the table, and through two camera

views, I see Williams stick his gun around the badly damaged Volvo. My whole body tightens as Williams squeezes out a round of bullets in our general direction.

The table shatters into little pieces of stone, and a bullet whooshes by my ear. I guess tables aren't as good a cover as they make them out to be in Hollywood.

My breathing is racecar fast, but since I'm out in the open, I decide to take advantage of the situation and put the aiming app's line in the center of Williams's exposed hand.

Two shots go off, mine and Williams's.

My bullet goes right for his gun hand and must do damage, because his gun clinks to the ground. I see him clutching his right hand with his left and hear his pain-filled curses. To my horror, though, I also hear a scream behind me.

It's Ada.

TEN

THOUGH IT'S INTENSELY TEMPTING, I DON'T DARE LOOK BACK. Instead, through the restaurant's security feed in my HUD, I see Muhomor fall down, a huge red stain on his back.

To make a horrible situation worse, Ada rushes back from inside the cover of the restaurant, her face whiter than Mr. Spock's fur.

"Run back in," I telepathically shout at her, imbuing the message with as much anxiety and fear as the Telepathy app will allow. "Now, Ada!"

She doesn't listen. With Mr. Spock in a death grip, Ada squats over Muhomor and grabs him by the back of his shirt.

"Cover her!" I scream at Gogi and mentally calculate how long it will take Ada to drag Muhomor's body far enough inside for her to be safe.

Through the camera, I spot Dylan—a thin, bug-eyed flunky who's been hiding to Williams's left—rising to his feet. I aim the gun where his head will be in a moment and squeeze the trigger. I figure if he puts his head in the bullet's path, it's manslaughter, not murder. It could even be considered suicide. Dylan yelps and clutches the top of his head, and I both hate and respect myself for my relief at knowing I didn't kill him.

Just in case the head wound is too light, and since I have a clear shot at his right shoulder, I reluctantly put my sixth bullet into it. He collapses, screaming and clutching at the injury.

I breathe easier when I see Ada disappear inside the restaurant again, though instead of going to the freezer as I ordered her to do, she crouches by the entrance, ripping Muhomor's shirt from his body.

"The bullet hit his spine." A wave of horror accompanies her telepathic message. "He might never walk again—if he doesn't bleed to death."

As Ada's words register, the utter despair I feel makes me wonder if this whole thing is one of those pre-cog moments that happen during the adjustment period of a new brain boost.

Mitya did, after all, recently give us a new boost.

"Is this really happening?" I ask myself in desperation. I'd give anything for this to be a pre-cog moment or a dream.

Unfortunately, nothing changes, so this is happening for real.

Someone's gun glints in the sunlight, and Gogi fires a shot. A rush of adrenaline takes me out of my wishful-thinking stupor. Gogi just shot and killed a guy who was aiming at me. If he hadn't done that, I'd be toast.

Doubting reality will have to take a backseat for now.

Justin, the crew's youngest member, tries to be bold, so I have no choice but to put my seventh bullet through his upper arm.

Aiden Williams—Vincent's younger brother and right-hand man —peeks out from behind the bullet-riddled, bumperless Camry that has served as his shield until now. After all this, and even knowing that these fuckers hurt Muhomor, I can't believe I'm still uncomfortable with shooting to kill—something my new shrink and I will probably need to work on. Gogi, however, doesn't share my qualms. He shoots, and through the camera view, I witness Aiden's brains turn the pavement behind him into a macabre Pollock painting.

Vincent stops clutching his bloody hand and gapes at his fallen brother with shock that seems foreign on his overly angular face. Then I can practically see something inside him snap. He yanks a gun from a leg holster, gripping it with what's left of his damaged right hand, and screams, "Everyone, charge now or I'll shoot you myself!"

In that slow-motion, bullet-mode of being, I watch as Vincent Williams and five of his remaining men—Gabriel, Nathan, Connor, Isaac, and José—struggle to their feet.

In a moment, I'll have six targets and only three bullets left. The HUD has no count for Gogi's ammo, though if my brain hasn't failed me, Gogi should have four bullets in his Makarov pistol.

"Go for the ones on the left," I shout at Gogi and shoot Gabriel in the right upper arm.

Seeing Gabriel lose both his gun and the will to keep attacking us, I focus on his blond neighbor, Isaac, determined to hit his shoulder instead of his arm on the assumption that it'll be a more painful wound.

Shots ring out, and I feel like Godzilla just bit off my left ear after spewing its fiery breath. I must not be hurt too badly, though, because I'm still standing. With a fresh blast of adrenaline, I hit Isaac's shoulder, and his fall is my reward.

Gogi fires twice. José gets a bullet in the neck, while Nathan is shot through his nose.

The adrenaline in my veins makes the world around me crawl as I watch both Connor and Williams aim at us in slow motion. I extrapolate their movements and guess that Williams is about to aim for my head while his prematurely graying ally has Gogi's center chest in sight. As soon as my mind draws this grisly conclusion, my body reacts.

In a move I learned in the dojo, I half fall, half crouch as my finger spasms around the warmed-up metal of the trigger.

The bullet Williams intended for my head whooshes harmlessly an inch above my skull, hurting only my eardrums.

My own bullet hits Connor in the elbow, destroying his

chances of shooting again for a long time and, critically, causes the man to drop his gun.

This is when Gogi makes a tactical error.

He shoots the already disarmed Connor in the face. Like the prior couple of instances today, Gogi must figure the injury I inflicted wasn't damaging enough.

Connor's face explodes, but Gogi's momentary distraction was all Williams needed to swiftly aim at Gogi and pull his trigger.

"No!" Screaming both mentally through all the apps and out loud, I aim my empty gun at Williams and pull the trigger.

Unsurprisingly, nothing happens.

Desperate, I throw the gun at Williams's head—and miss by a wide margin.

Before my gun lands on the ground, I focus on Gogi. He's hit, but I can't discern whether the bullet got him in the groin or upper leg. Then, as he falls, grunting, I see him clutch his leg—which I guess is better than the groin.

Williams moves toward us.

I prepare to dive for Gogi's gun, though I suspect it's empty.

"Move another muscle, and I'll shoot you." Williams's voice is reminiscent of a dental drill. "I mean it. Freeze."

The man is halfway to us, and his gun is pointed steadily at my head.

Surprised to be alive, I raise my hands. "I'm unarmed." A bizarre calm settles over me as I simultaneously scan my environment for any advantage and find few. Almost unconsciously, I mentally order, "Einstein, give me a status report on Zapo."

"Step away from the Georgian," Williams orders and waves his gun toward himself.

I drag my feet in his general direction and try my best to put my body between Williams and Gogi, figuring if he's reluctant to shoot me for some strange reason, perhaps this will stop him from finishing off the bleeding man. Inside the restaurant, I see Ada coming toward me, and I telepathically bark, "Ada, don't move. If you spook Williams, Gogi and I are as good as dead."

What I don't tell her, since I'm trying to save her life, is that we're as good as dead anyway.

"Brake system unresponsive," Einstein reports somewhere in the periphery of my attention. "Cooling system reports it's damaged. Headlight controls unresponsive—"

I dare pay only a tiny sliver of attention to Einstein as I focus on Williams. He's now close enough that he could pistol-whip me if he so desired.

Stopping, he gives me a simian stare. "If you tell me where Cohen is," his vocal cords drill out, "your last moments will be blissfully quick."

ELEVEN

I SPOT THE BLOODY STUMP THAT, AS A RESULT OF MY SHOOTING, HAS replaced Williams's right middle finger and know he's lying. He'll hurt me for that, no matter his promises. I'm about to say something brave, or at least sarcastic, about his proposal, when Williams adds, "I'll even consider forgetting I saw that girl here, and the Georgian will also get a quick death—even though his name is on the list."

Adrenaline further spikes my heart rate, but I mentally note the mention of a list as I answer, "I'm Cohen, and I'm right here." As I talk, it dawns on me that the guy must've been hired to track down Gogi and Joe, with an emphasis on Joe, who must be at the top of the list. That's why Williams is asking me questions.

Williams correctly realizes I'm being a wise-ass, so he presses the barrel of his gun against my upper arm. I can see his muscles twitch, and I'm sure I'm about to get a bullet in my flesh.

In a flash of brain-boosted insight, I see Williams has made a critical mistake. He looked at me or read my bio someplace and figured he'd be safe coming within striking distance, perceiving me as a rich and spoiled venture capitalist dork.

He didn't count on me being a quick learner due to the boost, nor on the many disarming drills Gogi put me through. He also probably doesn't know that disarming one's opponent is a cornerstone of the Systema martial art—or at least Gogi's flavor of it.

With a hopefully sudden motion, I allow muscle memory to guide me as I grab the gun and twist it the way I rehearsed.

My movements are smooth as silk, and before Williams's eyes register surprise, his gun clanks onto the pavement—and that's only because I didn't have a good angle to apply the move in a way that would allow me to keep the gun.

My opponent yelps in pain; the disarming move applied pressure to his mutilated finger.

I see his eyes follow the trajectory of his gun and take advantage of that distraction by punching the larger man in the middle of the chest, hoping to hit him in the solar plexus.

Gogi would be proud: my strike is textbook perfect. Only my fist feels like I've punched concrete. Instead of doubling over in pain like a normal human, Williams doesn't even blink.

What's worse, he swings his giant fist at my face.

I block the hit with my right elbow, but unlike the training version of this block, my elbow feels like it has split into little shards, and each shard has a pulsing nerve attached to it. I try to score a kick—as I've been taught is optimal in this situation—but unlike Gogi during training, Williams sidesteps my kick and lands a fist to my jaw.

Now, it's not like I haven't learned how to take a hit. In a way, I should be an expert, since Gogi has hit me by accident a couple of times during training, and Joe has hit me on purpose more times than I can count. But I now realize they've been pulling their punches. I didn't expect that from Joe. Hell, even Anton—Mom's kidnapper who punched me months ago—was a wimp compared to my current attacker.

The impact of his punch is instant, and it's only my brain extension that allows me to think at all. The biological parts of my brain, and by extension, my body, shut down and enter knockout mode.

In a moment, I might take a nap right here in the middle of the road, and it takes everything I have to fight for lucidity. Desperate, I put all my focus on the parts of my brain that run on faraway computer servers—the impact-resistant parts.

"Back lights are undamaged," Einstein says somewhere in my head, and I recall that I instructed him to tell me the status of Zapo 2. "Nitro boost undamaged."

By the miracle of Brainocytes, I maintain enough control over my body to duck the next punch and take the punch that follows on my left forearm.

As the pain of the block scorches my brain awake, I frantically launch the Batmobile app and try to start Zapo 2 again as a plan forms in my head.

"Stop," I croak at Williams, but his fist lands in the middle of my stomach. Regrettably, unlike his, my solar plexus works the way it should, and I almost faint from the pain and loss of air.

"Joe," I try to say. "I'll tell you where Joe Cohen is."

My words come out garbled, but Williams pauses, perhaps out of curiosity. I take advantage of the reprieve by dropping to the ground and rolling to the right on the dusty pavement. My destination is the side of the road.

Through the camera views, I see Williams's face contort, as if he's debating whether to kick me or ask me more questions. The desire to kick seems to win out, and he raises his foot.

Putting Zapo 2 in reverse, I will the car to start and mentally promise it complete repairs, gold rims, and an oil change every week if it will just please, pretty please *start*.

To my shock, my desperate plea is answered.

Despite the earlier crash, Zapo's electric engine activates, and the car is ready for action.

My attacker's foot is about to connect with the side of my head when I mentally slam the gas and rip the wheel all the way to the right.

My world explodes in white stars, informing me that Williams's foot has reached my head.

The trick of relying on willpower and the distant server extensions of my brain won't work much longer.

Still, before consciousness finally abandons me, I see Williams's body grow larger and larger in Zapo's back cameras. I also notice he's turning around to see what's going on.

I do my best to make myself as small as possible and roll farther to the side of the road. Then, in the last picosecond of consciousness, I activate Zapo's nitro system to make the car zoom forward.

TWELVE

"You have been unconscious for twenty seconds," Einstein reports. "The current time is 3:55 p.m."

Twenty seconds isn't my usual eight hours of sleep. Something other than catching z's must be responsible for my mind outage. Fleetingly, I wonder if Joe knocked me out in the dojo again. Until now, our sparring has only resulted in me losing consciousness once, and even then, I was only out for a second.

Sirens blare somewhere in the distance. Is that an ambulance coming for me? If it is, this would be the first time Joe has damaged me this badly.

Ada will never let me hear the end of it.

Then I see all the camera feeds in the AROS interface and register the bullet-riddled cars on the street. With a jolt, I remember everything, particularly the part where I was just fighting for my life.

"Einstein," I mentally command. "I'm unable to see through Zapo's cameras."

"It's been twenty-two seconds since I was able to ping the car's computer systems," Einstein laments. "Based on my assessment, Zapo is totaled."

If Einstein were human, he would've sarcastically added, "Again."

With monumental effort, I roll over onto my side and survey Zapo's sad leftovers.

I half expect, half hope to see Williams pinned between Zapo's back bumper and the remnants of the Ford Mustang I must've inadvertently killed half a minute ago. Alas, the giant man isn't there. Williams's absence raises a critical question. Where is he? I'm pretty sure I positioned Zapo to hit him before I blacked out, but I guess he rolled off the hood or something along those lines.

Fighting the feeling that I've swallowed concrete, I scan for Williams with all the cameras.

Nothing.

As more of my mental acuity returns, I remember to look for Williams's wounded compatriots, but I can't find any. They must've escaped from the sirens with him.

Speaking of sirens, they're accompanied by flashing lights, so the authorities are on the scene.

High on relief, I try to get up, but decide it's too soon to try something so drastic.

From the comfort of the pavement, I use the restaurant's camera to assess the damage Gogi endured. Luckily, the Georgian fared better than my most optimistic hopes. Someone, probably himself, wrapped a makeshift tourniquet around his leg, and the bleeding has slowed to a trickle.

Unlike Gogi, Muhomor looks bad. He's marble white and unmoving, and telepathic messages from me don't seem to get his attention.

"Mike," Ada says out loud from the restaurant entrance. "Don't move. You might have a back injury."

"Go back inside," I insist telepathically. Seeing that she's not complying, I demonstratively wiggle my fingers and add, "I just wiggled my toes too, and it was a great success. No back injury. Go inside. Please."

Her reply is interrupted by the commotion of the emergency

vehicles that consist of police and paramedics, though a fire truck is also on the scene.

Despite the migraine the sirens are inducing, I welcome the blaring sound, and when cops and EMT personnel flood the street, I allow myself to relax.

In a blink, Muhomor, Gogi, and I find ourselves on stretchers, each one loaded into a separate ambulance. Ada joins me in mine.

"I'm okay," I valiantly lie to my paramedic team when they close the ambulance doors behind Ada. "Please focus on my friends."

"Your friends have at least three responders with them," the larger paramedic reassures me. His sleep-deprived eyes look too hollow for someone so young. "We can and will focus on you. Can you tell me your name and date of birth, please?"

I carry on a conversation with the EMT guy while also talking telepathically with Ada, who seems overwhelmed in her post-adrenaline slump. Her eyes glisten with tears as she stares at me, and fine tremors wrack her slender frame.

Since my EMTs don't know how Muhomor and Gogi are faring, or are refusing to tell me, I try using Muhomor's nifty app to hack into the other ambulances to see if I can learn something—but no luck. The cars don't have complex enough computers to hack, and the EMT personnel don't write patient information into their private phones.

"No, I don't feel any pain," I lie to the EMT guy for the fifth time. "I don't want any painkillers."

"How much pain are you really in?" Ada asks, apparently recovering from her shock. Her eyes are dry again, and her telepathic message is filled with a mixture of worry and annoyance. "You're paler than I've ever seen you—too pale even for a programmer."

"I feel like someone kicked me in the head," I mentally reply. "And what do you know? I probably feel that way because I *did* get kicked in the head."

"Then why don't you tell them you're hurting? Why are you always needlessly trying to be a hero?"

"If they give me painkillers, the drugs will likely knock me out.

That's what happened when I crashed the last Zapo," I explain. "I want to say conscious. I want learn what happened to our friends."

Sometimes, the brain boost allows me to perceive the world fast enough to catch so-called microexpressions—those brief, involuntary facial ticks that appear in accordance with the emotions the person is experiencing. Ada's momentary scowl is classic annoyance. The expression is instantly gone, though, and to Ada's credit, her telepathic message is patient and soothing as she suggests, "How about you at least use Relief? It won't knock you out. This is probably the exact situation that app was designed for."

I consider her suggestion, even though she's talking about an app that's among the scarier software we've developed. In fact, this app, which Mitya dubbed Relief, is at the top of my scary shortlist because it's designed to dampen pain and, along with BraveChill (the app that helps with fear and anxiety), is ripe for abuse. When I tested these apps, BraveChill reminded me of chasing a Xanax with a beer—something I did once back at MIT and liked too much to ever allow myself to do again. The Relief app is even scarier, since I felt warmth and pleasure from it. Though I've never abused that class of drugs, I'm guessing the feeling was akin to what morphine or oxycodone would feel like. Of course, using those apps when I wasn't frightened or in pain wasn't a fair test.

Out loud, to emphasize the seriousness of my words to Ada, I say, "In those experiments where rats could stimulate their pleasure centers, rats would press the lever that delivered the artificial pleasure over pressing the lever for eating, drinking, and even sex. They pressed the button to the point where they starved to death."

The EMT guys exchange confused glances but remain silent, likely ascribing my statement to my head injury.

Worried that Mr. Spock understood what I said and is horrified by the idea of such barbaric rat experiments, I pet the little guy—which causes the EMT folks to exchange yet more looks as it's not every day you see a pet rat. Mr. Spock seems to be okay, at least gauging by his EmoRat output and the visual cues I'm getting better at recognizing.

"You have better self-control than a rat, Mike," Ada counters out loud and scoots closer to me on the gurney. "No offense," she tells Mr. Spock. "Besides, the Relief app provides a precisely calculated mild stimulus to the pleasure center. It dampens pain by—"

"Fine," I mentally interrupt, worried that Ada was about to praise Mitya's genius again—a common activity that never fails to activate my greenest jealousy. "I'm turning it on."

She smiles knowingly, and I wonder why I even try resisting her wishes. When it comes to arguing with Ada, I'm learning it's easier to give in. Deep down, I know she only wants what's best for me and wouldn't convince me to use an app that could lead me into trouble—not on purpose anyway.

I explain Spock's presence to the paramedics as I turn on the Relief app. As a concession to my fears about the app, I dial the app settings all the way down, so it becomes the approximate equivalent of a couple of adult doses of Tylenol or maybe a single Tylenol with Codeine.

"Damn it," I mentally send Ada when the app's bliss makes the pain in my bloody ear and my awful headache subside. "I do feel better, but as I said, I'm worried I'll get hooked on this."

"We could always write you a rehab app." Ada touches my shoulder soothingly and winks at me. "Something that would block the Relief app from connecting to the servers."

"I'd just write something to overrule you." I put my hand on top of hers, and the warmth is better than anything an app could induce. "If you didn't want me to become addicted, you shouldn't have encouraged me to get so good at coding."

"Don't worry. If you do become an addict, I'll lock you in a room with no access to internet if I have to." Ada's tone is much too playful given the cruel and unusual scenario she described. "In all seriousness, if Muhomor can write an app to help himself quit smoking, we can write an app that would help you quit using another app if needed. But it won't be."

Her mention of Muhomor gets me worried again, and I debate running BraveChill to lessen that bout of anxiety. In the end, I decide against using the app, since *not* worrying about my friends in *this* scenario would make me a horrible friend and less of a human being.

"Speaking of apps," Ada says, picking up on my shift in mood. "You should run the Neurogenesis app in case you got brain damage from the fight."

Neurogenesis is the process of growing new brain cells, and it's arguably one of the scarier apps that I have no problems with. I actually use it on a regular basis. Besides the obvious idea of "the more brain, the better," assuming neurogenesis does give you "more brain," my rationale for using the app is that many good-for-you activities seem to cause neurogenesis. In other words, I figure if running, sex, enriching environments and experiences, and even random dietary things like fish oil, turmeric, and blue-berries cause neurogenesis, then neurogenesis might be behind some of the benefits of those activities, and thus it's a good idea to get neurogenesis any way I can. Mom and the rest of the folks in the study run a heavy-duty version of the app, and even I have to admit it was a stroke of genius when Mitya thought of the idea. It's helped patients with more advanced Alzheimer's like nothing else in the treatment, leading me to believe that neurogenesis *does* give one more brain power. For me, it's hard to separate neurogenesis's impact on my intellect from the brain boost, but I still think the benefits exist. Plus, if Ada ever did lock me up in a room without internet, I would at least be left with a naturally boosted brain.

"Done," I tell Ada once the Neurogenesis app is up and running. "I think we're arriving at our destination."

Punctuating my words, the ambulance stops and the EMT guys take me to the ER.

———

"Stop fidgeting," Ada says out loud—a sign of annoyance—after I contemplate leaving the hospital bed for what feels like the thou-sandth time. "You *have* to get seen by a doctor. It's not negotiable."

"I'll stay still if you go and find out what's going on with Gogi and Muhomor," I counter, opting not to use the words "benevolent dictator."

"Deal," Ada replies telepathically and leaves, proving I must be fine, or else she wouldn't have left my sight.

Even as Ada walks away, the wait begins to feel like hours—a negative side effect of my super-fast new mode of thought. To stay sane, I try to occupy my mind. I start with my work email, going through and replying to the couple of hundred of the most urgent emails. That kills a few minutes and takes longer than it should because I read and type at a leisurely pace. Done with work, I decide to play with my phone for a bit. I only got this unit a few days ago, but I've already dubbed it Precious 3. Precious 3 is better than its predecessors in every way, and it has hardware a super-computer would've been happy with a decade ago. Ada, Mitya, and I designed my favorite feature—a light-sensitive solar charger incorporated into the outer shell. When combined with the efficient internal battery, Precious 3 can charge itself even in room illumination. I haven't had to plug it into the wall since the first time I got it. The only problem with Precious 3, if you can even call it a problem, is that I can do just as much, if not more, with the Brainocytes in my head. Still, there are thousands more games available on the phone than the Brainocytes Club could ever hope to put together. I choose a newer strategy game and give it a spin, though playing games on my phone doesn't fully keep my attention. The games are optimized for regular people.

Recalling that Lyuba is in town, I get in touch with her and tell her Muhomor got hurt. I urge her to stop by the hospital, figuring he'd be happy to see her when he can. I assure her that no, I have no clue what his medical condition is at the moment. Then, for a few long minutes, I debate telling Mom where I am. In the end, Mitya agrees with me that it's not essential that Mom know about my mishaps, unless I have something seriously wrong with me. I don't consult Ada, as she might think Mom has the right to know. Since I have Mitya on the line, I agree to play a virtual game of Go with him and promptly lose. Then, as we agreed, we play chess, and of course I win. As usual, we have a telepathic/verbal fight about which win is more impressive, Go or chess.

"Go is an ancient Chinese strategy game that's older and arguably more complex than chess," Mitya says, regurgitating his usual argument. "Look at artificial intelligence. AIs have been able to beat the best chess player for ages now, while they've only recently mastered Go."

"That has more to do with people wishing to build the right AI," I counter. "Besides, since you mentioned AIs, I can beat the best AI at chess, while you can't beat the best AI at Go."

"That's not my point," Mitya says distractedly, and I suspect he just challenged an AI to a Go match.

With Mitya occupied, I look for more ways to keep myself busy.

———

"They're taking Gogi for some scans, and they're stabilizing Muhomor," Ada tells me when she comes back fifteen minutes later. "Getting information here is like pulling teeth."

The mental image of pulling teeth doesn't help my usual white-coat-generated anxiety, nor does the knowledge that Muhomor's condition is so bad that he requires stabilizing. On the subject of neuroses, if the shrink did help me with my paranoia, that progress has been undone, because some insistent part of me feels like someone at the hospital is covertly watching me. This eerie sensation makes me recall how I felt inside a recent nightmare where faceless people wearing suits were coming to get me.

After what feels like another week of anxiety-filled waiting, a doctor breaks the monotony by confirming what I've been saying to Ada all along: my condition is not a true emergency, and I can leave the hospital soon.

Of course, "soon" is a relative term in hospitals. Since I'm fine and a low priority, I have to wait a long time before I get my ear stitched and various cuts and scrapes bandaged. The nurse who helps me informs me I have to speak with a police officer. It's standard procedure for gunshot victims, and that includes people whose ear barely got grazed by a bullet.

"Ada, please check on Gogi and Muhomor again," I mentally plead as a cop enters the room. "Maybe there's more information available?"

"Of course," she replies soothingly. "Do you want to play chess and talk while I walk around? It might help you keep your cool while the cops question you."

"Sure," I reply to Ada mentally as the cop introduces himself as Officer Jackson. "Though I can keep my cool on my own."

"Maybe we can also pair code this app I've been thinking about," Ada mentally says after I skillfully take her first pawn in our chess game.

"Whatever you want, sweetie," I mentally reply, realizing all this multitasking isn't just for me, but also to ease Ada's anxiety at the prospect of seeing what happened to our friends.

"No, I never met these men before," I explain to Officer Jackson for what seems like the tenth time. "I only know their names because I used facial recognition on them."

As the incredulous cop asks me another set of follow-up questions, Ada and I play chess, and I watch her write a piece of software meant to integrate Brainocytes with a specific model of smart lights. It would allow us to mentally turn lights on and off in our place. I don't point out that we can already work the smart lights via Einstein, as diminishing the value of Ada's work will only upset her more.

"And how does Joe Cohen fit into all this?" Officer Jackson asks, and I understand his unsurprising and not-so-subtle agenda.

My cousin is always of interest to the police.

"I don't know," I reply as politely and patiently as I can. "My cousin and I aren't close."

"Well, what's your theory?" the cop persists. "Why do you think they attacked?"

"I really don't know why they attacked," I tell Officer Jackson, and it feels like I've answered a variation of this question before. "If it did have anything to do with Joe, as you're implying, you can discuss your theories with the man himself when you speak with *him*."

In actual fact, I keep wondering about the reasons behind the attack, and I plan to ask Joe some pointed questions when he gets here, so the cop will have to wait his turn.

As the officer pesters me with more questions, I make a chess move that means a checkmate for Ada and mentally text Joe, "There's a cop here asking a lot of questions about you. Take that into consideration when you arrive."

"How's Gogi?" My cousin's reply is almost as quick as from someone with Brainocytes, though, of course, he writes in English, not Zik.

"I don't know yet," I reply to my cousin as I say out loud, "Officer, I really need to go check on my friends. If you have more questions, I think I'd like to have my attorney, Mr. Kadvosky, present. Perhaps you've heard of him?"

Joe's text is clear and to the point. "I want a report on Gogi's condition ASAP." My cousin doesn't need to add niceties such as, "Or else I'll break your neck when I get there," because it's implied when conversing with him.

"I've heard of the Kadvosky law firm," says Officer Jackson, and his expression is such that you'd think we were talking about a den of vampires or an earthquake. "We're done for now. Thank you for your help."

Though it's clear he's being disingenuous, I still shake the cop's hand. As he exits the room, Ada finalizes her code and submits it to our new, Muhomor-secured source control repository.

Figuring now is as good a time as any to try walking, I swing my legs off the bed and carefully put my weight on them.

I don't fall or scream in pain, but I strongly suspect I would've at least yelped without the Relief app. I tentatively disable the app and see that I'm right. I'm still aching all over, the pain as tolerable as a root canal without anesthesia.

"Any update?" I mentally ask Ada and take a deep breath to see if it'll help with the pain.

"I finally located Gogi in this maze," Ada says. "Going to check on his condition now."

"I'll look for Muhomor then," I tell her and enable the Relief app. The deep breath made the pain worse.

For the next half hour, I stalk around the ER, asking nurses questions when I can find them. The staff aren't used to patients asking questions about other patients, so I have to turn on all my boosted intellect and attention to seem sane and charming. My work eventually pays off, and I learn that Muhomor was stabilized and taken for an X-ray and CAT scan, and that he's now inside an MRI machine.

"I'm in Gogi's ICU room," Ada says at the same time as I plead with a nurse to let me speak to the doctor who examined Muhomor in the ER. "You should hear this for yourself."

The nurse gives me the name of the doctor, and Ada enables the Share app, allowing me to see through a new virtual window into Gogi's room. I hear someone, likely Gogi's doctor, say, "He just got out of surgery, and it went well. There's laceration of muscles and some shattered bones, but I think he'll recover well in time."

As soon as I hear Gogi's diagnosis, I exhale with relief and instantly relay the information to Joe. He replies with, "I'll be over in twenty minutes. I've also sent Jean and Nick to join you. They're closer to your location."

Nick and Jean are two guys I sometimes see at the gym. As far as I can tell, they're a rare subset of people in my cousin's world who do exactly what his official business is supposed to be about. They work as high-end bodyguards and nothing else—meaning nothing shady. Even their backgrounds are more legitimate than usual. Nick almost made it into the Navy SEALs. Rumor is, he was rejected because he wasn't smart enough. And Jean almost made it onto a professional football team (that's American football, not its European namesake, soccer).

Sounds like Joe doesn't trust hospital security and wants us to have extra protection—a sobering thought.

The relief I felt upon learning of Gogi's condition dissipates, and I concentrate my remaining worry full force on Muhomor.

After a few minutes of fruitless searching, Ada joins me. Together, we ambush an MRI technician, the only person we can find who's seen Muhomor recently.

"I only take the tests. I don't interpret them," the woman says and nervously pushes her glasses a millimeter higher on her nose. "You'll have to speak with Doctor Zane once he's done with the surgery."

"You do MRIs all the time," I point out. "Can't you tell us what *you* think? We won't hold you to it."

Seeing she's going to be stubborn, I decide to try an age-old Russian persuasion technique. I mentally ask Ada to take out all the money she has on her. Ada takes out a couple of hundred dollars, and I demonstratively place it all on the tech's small desk, saying, "We just want your uneducated guess. Please."

The woman looks stunned by the bribery—something that I guess never happens in this expensive American hospital. After a second, though, she pockets the money and says in a low tone, "If he makes it, I doubt he'll ever walk again."

As we gape at her, she fiddles with her glasses, and I can see her debating if she should say something else. Something, maybe decency, wins out, and she quietly adds, "I'm sorry, but it's a complex surgery, and I think you should prepare yourselves for the worst."

THIRTEEN

Ada and I frantically pace the hospital corridors, trying to deal with the fact that our friend might die at any moment. In an effort to calm down, I stroke Mr. Spock's fur, but after a few minutes, he uses the EmoRat to notify me he'd rather I stop, so I do.

As I try my best to hack into the hospital computers, I can't help but dwell on the painful irony that Muhomor would be the best person to help with this. But if he were in a condition to hack, we wouldn't need to hack into the hospital computers to check on him.

"I've taken him for granted," I message Ada, adding sadness to my telepathic words. "I didn't tell him how highly I thought of his skills."

"I think we all could've been better friends." Ada stops pacing and puts a comforting hand on my forearm. "Let's treat this as a life lesson."

Ada's touch calms me enough for me to focus, and I begin mentally tasting and smelling the hospital computer networks through the Muhomor app. It takes a couple of minutes—ages for someone with my speed of thought—but I finally find a yummy loophole in the hospital security.

I notify Mitya and Ada about my finding so they can exploit the system with me.

"I can't find much beyond what the MRI technician already told us," Ada says after some time, echoing my own conclusions.

"I had a bit more luck," Mitya chimes in. "I figured out where the surgery is taking place. Sending you the info now."

Ada and I get an electronic delivery of a map of the hospital with a (typical of Mitya) giant red cross in the middle of the third floor.

When we're halfway to our destination, I get a text from Joe that states, "Nick and Jean are in the hospital. Where should I send them?"

I forward Mitya's map to Joe and ask, "What about you? When will you get here?"

"Shortly," Joe replies. "Where's Gogi's room?"

I send Joe directions on how to find Gogi and again wonder if Joe is the reason for this horrible mess. I'll risk my life by asking him, but not over the phone.

As Ada and I walk through the hospital corridors, the smells of formaldehyde and bleach compete with the much worse medicinal aromas I'd prefer to ignore. The reason I focus on smell instead of sight is my resurgent paranoia. Though my eyes see medical beds and equipment all around, and though, on the surface, we're surrounded only by people wearing gray-green scrubs, part of my brain is aware of unseen people watching me, and that same part of me insists these people are wearing suits—like in my nightmare.

Nick and Jean are waiting for us in the surgical waiting room, and they're the only people there. The big men are occupying two of the cheap, uncomfortable-looking chairs and flipping through yellowing magazines with last year's headlines. This windowless room must be a low priority for the hospital staff in charge of restocking magazines.

Nick's greeting is more monosyllabic than Jean's, but only by a narrow margin. I wonder if they're trying to live up to some kind of bodyguard stereotype. So far, they're succeeding.

We sit down, and I grab a magazine from the pile on the decrepit-looking end table and pretend to read while I take another stab at navigating the labyrinth that is the hospital Wi-Fi. In the meantime, Ada uses her entire mental capacity to engage the two brutes in a semblance of conversation.

"Jackpot," I mentally shout at Ada and Mitya. "I found two security cameras in the operating room."

I access the first one, and my blood pressure spikes as I take in the room with its masked surgeon and slew of faceless helpers. Muhomor is barely recognizable with the mask over his face, and the hospital cap covering his signature hairdo is extra depressing. A green sheet covers his poor body, somehow making him look thinner than usual—almost frail. The second camera shows a gaping red hole in the back of his getup, with bright light streaming down at it from the special surgical lamps. I can see the grisly details of the surgery, and I let my eyes wander around the room, focusing on anything but the gore to avoid fainting. My chest aches even more, and guilt gnaws at me as I think of all the recent jokes I made at Muhomor's expense, not to mention the stuff I told the shrink. "This is so bad," I mumble to myself in Russian.

"Hey, he's alive," Mitya says from somewhere. I guess I accidentally transmitted my thoughts, or Mitya overheard me through Ada's Share app. "Don't mourn him yet. It's bad luck."

I shake my head in an effort to clear it. Though I didn't think Mitya had a superstitious bone in his body, he has a point. In the Russian culture, it's a bad sign to cry on the behalf of someone who's sick; it's believed that those who do might contribute to a fatal outcome. Though I'm even less superstitious than Mitya, for Muhomor's sake, I decide not to tempt fate and calm down.

"He's a fighter," I say, trying to believe my own words. "I'm sure he'll make it."

"Are you hungry?" Ada asks, whispering out loud in my ear, and

I could kiss her for the change in topic. It refocuses me, and though I can still see the operating room in my peripheral vision, my stomach shocks me by rumbling so loudly that Nick chuckles.

"I'll take that as a yes." Ada looks from my belly to Jean and his partner and says more loudly, "What about you, gentlemen? I'm about to go get some food. Would you like me to get you anything?"

To Ada's chagrin, Nick and Jean ask for two meals that are the antithesis of veganism—not a surprise, given their meaty builds.

"An oatmeal for me," I say out loud before Ada can start debating nutrition with the two muscle-bound bodyguards. "With lots of nuts if they have it."

Mr. Spock's vocabulary is still severely limited, but he knows the word "nuts." Through EmoRat, he expresses his excitement about the possibility of nuts. Incidentally, he also knows the words for a bunch of other treats, his name, both with the Mr. honorific and without, and the phrase, "Fresh air?" He loves that question, because it means he can jump into my pocket and hitch a ride outside.

"Ada, get some extra nuts on the side and some raisins too," I mentally add, knowing full well that the word "raisins" was understood and appreciated by the little schemer too. "Mr. Spock wants a snack."

As I suspected, at the mention of raisins, his second favorite word of the day, Mr. Spock exudes excitement and begins bruxing in anticipation.

"Okay." Ada looks pacified by my choice. "I'll be back soon."

I watch Ada walk through the room and into the hallway. When she enters the elevator, I put down my magazine and turn my attention to Nick and Jean. "I haven't seen you guys at the gym lately," I say.

My mention of the gym brings warmth to Jean's eyes, and in a booming voice, he says, "Been busy. I've seen you practice with Gogi, though. You're not bad, for a civilian."

"Thanks," I reply while writing a mental message to Ada and

Mitya that says, "I need more distraction than this glacial conversation."

"What?" Ada replies instantly. "You don't find talking to Tweedledee and Tweedledum intellectually stimulating enough?"

"Sorry to interrupt." Mitya's Zik message is full of anxiety. "I've been looking through the hospital cameras, and there's something you *need* to see."

Mitya sends a link, and when I click it, every part of me, tips of hair included, freezes in fear.

FOURTEEN

THE VIEW THROUGH THE CAMERA IS FAMILIAR. IT'S THE ELEVATOR WE used to get to this floor.

A group of three men walk out of the elevator and look around furtively. One walks up to the nurses' station near the corridor entrance and says something to the nurse. I can imagine what he said since it probably wasn't all that different from what Ada and I recently told the nurse: "We're here to wait for a patient."

"Sketchy person alert," Einstein says loudly three times—once for each man on the screen.

"I knew that this time," I mentally reply to the AI as my adrenaline levels skyrocket. "Pull up their profiles so I can read them." To Nick and Jean, I say sharply, "Someone is coming for me. Be ready."

In the moment it takes me to load the screens into my AROS interface, I compose a Zik message and send it. "Ada, leave the hospital if you haven't already. When you're outside, get as far away as you can."

"I'll give Ada the rundown and make sure she gets to safety," Mitya says. "Don't waste any brain bandwidth worrying about anything but the men coming your way."

"Okay," I reply. "Just get her out. If you have to, tell hospital security she's a dangerous psycho and they need to throw her out ASAP."

"I'll make sure she gets out," Mitya promises grimly. "Don't worry about it."

I wish it was so easy not to worry about Ada, but I have no choice. Screens with faces and words show up in front of me as Einstein provides me with the profiles I requested.

I have to hand it to Jean and Nick. They don't waste time asking needless questions. In the brief time it takes me to read the bios, the two bodyguards are already up and reaching for their guns.

I reach for the place where *my* gun should be, but I remember I ran out of bullets and lost it earlier today—probably a good thing, since an unlicensed gun would've been hard to explain to the emergency responders. Still, I wish I had it now, as the profiles tell me a crucial piece of information.

These men work for Vincent Williams.

Aside from that, the profiles tell me what I could've guessed. These are dangerous people. One, Keyon, did time for murder, and another, Broderick, also served time, but for racketeering. The third man, Cristiano, isn't a criminal, but that doesn't make him any less dangerous. He served in the Exército Brasileiro—a branch of the Brazilian army. For now, I shelve questions such as "How did they find me?" and "What's Vincent's beef with me in the first place?" Given how my last meeting with Vincent Williams's men went, I hiss out loud, "Nick. Jean. The men you're about to face work with the fucks who put Gogi in the hospital."

At the reminder that his comrade's hurt and that he's about to get a chance to even the score, Nick's eyes glint with Joe-like homicidal glee. Jean's face is harder to read, but both men take the safeties off their guns and launch into motion, performing maneuvers that remind me of police procedurals. Nick slides against the wall adjacent to the corridor and aims his gun at the entrance, while Jean herds me behind him and as far away from the entrance as possible. Once Jean is satisfied with our position, he points his gun at the entrance too.

My pulse hammering, I watch the AROS view and whisper the bad guys' movements to Jean until the three attackers get out of the camera's range. Then I search the Wi-Fi network for another viewpoint, but the closest one I can locate is the security camera right above my head, showing me an extra few inches of the corridor compared to my eyes.

"Have the rat peek into the corridor," Mitya tells me after I share the reconnaissance problem with him. "You have an app that shows you what he can see."

"This isn't the time for cruel jokes." I imbue my Zik retort with as much righteous anger as the interface will allow. "He could get squished."

"Wow. Ada has you whipped," Mitya grumbles. "You're treating a lab rat like a person."

"If you want to be useful, tell Joe what's happening," I reply tersely. "Maybe notify hospital security and the cops of what's going on."

"I already notified hospital security and the cops. Now, regarding Joe." Mitya's reply is slower than his usual telepathic messages. "Ada and I were debating if we should distract you with that part."

"With what?" I didn't think my adrenaline level could go any higher, but I was clearly wrong. It's so bad that my hands are shaking and Einstein pops up an alert about my stress levels on my AROS screen.

"A picture is worth more than words." Another link accompanies Mitya's message. "This is a camera view into Gogi's room."

When the screen pops up, I recognize the outside of Gogi's room. Only there are two large men there fighting Joe. Their movements are so fast they appear blurry through the cheap security camera.

From the broken-looking wrist of the larger of the two attackers, I can guess Joe recently disarmed him. A gun is on the floor.

The slightly smaller attacker is bending over to grab it, but he meets Joe's knee instead.

"Why doesn't Joe have his gun out?" I message Mitya. "Did he not get a chance to take it out, or did they snatch it from his hands somehow?"

"Focus on your own problems," Mitya retorts. "According to my calculations, *your* trouble is about to start."

Mitya is right. I enable the Recorder app to capture everything so I can review it later and prepare to focus on my own attackers.

This is when an object flies into the room from the corridor.

Since my thinking is fast, I'm probably the first, if not the only, person in the room who has time to process what the object is and what's about to happen.

It's a grenade about to explode.

FIFTEEN

"GRENADE!" I TRY TO SCREAM, BUT THE WORD DOESN'T COME OUT because the explosion goes off.

Jean's body slams into mine with the force of a baseball bat hitting an ant.

Despite Jean's body blocking me, my retinas get blasted with a supernova-bright light that's about as pleasant as seeing a million camera flashes go off at once.

With my vision gone, my ears get assaulted next. The grenade's boom feels like Thor banged his Mjolnir hammer against my exposed eardrums.

It's as if someone dropped me on my head and then drove over me with a pickup truck.

"Judging by what I saw through the camera, it was a stun grenade," Mitya comments telepathically. "That means that, in a moment, the attackers will barge in."

"I'm going back to the hospital," Ada intrudes. "Mike might need my help."

"Don't—" I start, but Mitya beats me to it.

"You will do no such thing, Ada," he snaps. "You need to get

396

farther away. Stop this. You're distracting him, and he's already concussed."

With colossal effort, in less than a nanosecond, I mentally look through the camera above my head.

Jean looks as stunned as I feel, but Nick seems to have fared much better. Must have something to do with his SEAL training.

One of the attackers becomes visible in the corridor. My brain is jumbled, but I believe this is Keyon, the murderer of the bunch.

Before I can warn Nick somehow, the big bodyguard realizes we have company and aims his gun at approximately where Keyon should be in a moment.

Even through the ringing deafness in my ears, I hear the gunshot. I hope that means my ears aren't permanently damaged.

Keyon grabs his chest and falls to the ground. Before I can allow myself to whoop in joy, Keyon's partner, Broderick the racketeer, comes into view. A warning is about to leave my lips when Broderick shoots Nick in the face.

Nick falls, but the shooting has brought Jean out of his confusion—at least enough for him to unload his gun in the direction of the corridor. Since I still can't see anything with my eyes, I'm pretty sure Jean can't either and he's just shooting blindly. Still, Jean must be lucky or well trained, because a bullet hits Broderick in the neck. The man clutches the wound in what I hope is his death throes.

"One left," I scream, though I doubt Jean's ears have recovered enough to hear me.

Jean begins to reload.

I really hope Cristiano, as a guy who served in the army, will be careful after seeing his comrades killed. If he moves slowly, his hesitation might give Jean the few precious seconds he needs to load his gun.

Without much will on my part, my attention goes to the camera overlooking the elevator, and I watch the elevator doors open.

People dressed in hospital garb run out pushing a gurney—

which sort of makes sense. They might be here to rescue any survivors of the explosion. I wish these were hospital security guards or cops instead. Didn't Mitya summon them?

What I see next doesn't make any sense, though. The remaining people in the elevator are wearing suits.

"Is this a dream?" I ask Einstein in panic.

"No. You're conscious." Einstein's reply holds no trace of humor.

In case this is a pre-cog moment, I ask myself, "Is this really happening?"

However, I'm still where I am, and the suits are still there. I briefly wonder if a dream might include Einstein saying I'm conscious, but I decide it's unlikely and focus on the camera input.

I count at least four suited men, but when I try using facial recognition on their angular faces, nothing happens. In two cases, I get an excellent look at their features—enough that I'll remember them in the future—so I know the lack of recognition isn't some issue with the camera's angle. These men must not be in any of the facial recognition databases—a feat that seems close to impossible, as that means, among other things, that they have no social media or DMV records.

Moving on from the mystery of their identities, I take a closer look at the strange weapons in their hands. They're reminiscent of Nerf guns.

As though they rehearsed the most efficient way to storm out of the elevator, the group of Suits heads toward the corridor leading to my waiting room.

I mentally blink, but the camera view doesn't change, and people in suits are still rushing down the corridor, out of view.

Jean is done reloading and points his gun at the wall. He must think it's the room's entrance, but he's about twenty-five degrees off.

"Jean!" I scream in his ear.

The big man doesn't flinch, so I grab his arm to redirect his aim.

My world explodes again, but I fight to stay conscious, understanding what just happened. Blind and confused, Jean must have mistaken me for a bad guy and elbowed me in the face.

I slide down the wall and cradle my poor head in my hands, unable to peel my secondary gaze from the two camera views.

The last attacker, Cristiano, runs into the room and fires at Jean. Jeans shoots where he was aiming, at the wall, and misses Cristiano.

Cristiano fires another shot, and Jean falls on top of me.

Cristiano approaches. I think he intends to push Jean off me and put a few bullets in my head.

Even if I had the strength to grab for Jean's gun, it's way out of my reach.

I realize this is a situation when the brain boost can play a cruel trick on me and make my last moments feel subjectively longer. I debate saying goodbye to Mitya and Ada, but decide against it. Ada might do something crazy, like rush back in. Instead, I take a moment to check on Mr. Spock and find him still alive, though deaf and blind like me. He's managing something I thought was impossible.

He's even more frightened than I am.

"Slide into my pants and hide behind my leg," I order Mr. Spock through the EmoRat app. "If he shoots me in the chest, he might hit *you*."

Cristiano is in the middle of the room when I see the first suited figure walk in. The suited man raises the weird weapon —a Taser.

Unaware of the people behind him, Cristiano takes careful aim at me, his features impassive, like he's about to snap a picture of me with his phone. His finger twitches on the trigger—and the tallest Suit shoots.

Cristiano convulses and collapses to the ground. One of the medical personnel runs up to the fallen Cristiano and injects him.

A square-shouldered Suit approaches the pile that is Jean and me and aims his Taser at my exposed leg.

"No—" I try to scream, but the weapon's sharp prongs reach me and my whole body convulses. Every muscle gets jolted and paralyzed at the same time.

I barely register the guy with the syringe come up to me and prick my flesh in the same careless fashion as he did with Cristiano a moment ago. For some reason, my biggest concern is whether he used a different syringe and needle.

"Did you see all this?" I frantically write to Mitya. "What the hell is going on?"

"No idea." Mitya's reply is equally panicked. "But the Tasers imply they want you alive."

I glance at the camera view where Joe is fighting for his life. No people in suits have interfered on my cousin's behalf. It's hard to tell whether that's good news, but at least he's still alive and fighting.

"Hide from them," I order Mr. Spock, who's managed to crawl down my right pant leg as I instructed. "If you can—"

I don't finish my mental command to Mr. Spock. Whatever the injection was, its effects reach my brain, and the cloud extensions can't help me stay awake any longer.

My world fades to black.

SIXTEEN

"You have been unconscious for twenty-six minutes," Einstein reports somewhere in my bleary mind. "Current time is 6:48 p.m."

My whole body aches and pulses. I feel like a banana after it's been frozen and pulverized into one of Ada's smoothies. I seem to have regained my hearing, but what I hear—booming, whirling sounds like in the loudest circle of hell—makes no sense.

I open my eyes, and I'm glad to learn that, like my ears, they work again. Taking in my surroundings, I realize where I am.

I'm in a large helicopter, the source of that noise.

"He's awake," I hear someone say from behind me.

"Then what are you waiting for?" says a square-shouldered Suit and waves his vein-crossed hand in my general direction. "Put him back under."

"Wait—" I attempt to say, but burning warmth spreads into my arm, and I descend back into the abyss of unconsciousness.

———

I wake up, but since opening my eyes caused me to get knocked out the last time, I decide to get my bearings before I show anyone I'm awake.

It takes me less than a heartbeat to realize something is terribly wrong.

Actually, many things are wrong, but the biggest issue is my state of mind. I can barely form a coherent thought.

At first, I think my mental handicap is from the concussion the stun grenade gave me and the drugs the Suits pumped me with, but I soon determine that the truth is more horrifying.

I have no access to the internet.

Frantically, I launch one AROS app after another, and all of the network-reliant ones, a large majority, report connectivity errors.

Eyes still closed and determined not to panic, I launch the Muhomor app to jump onto a Wi-Fi network or, failing that, a cell network.

The app shows me the visual representations of two Wi-Fi networks and a number of faint Bluetooth connections from unknown devices (likely smartphones). When I try smelling for a tasty connection, I find that both Wi-Fi networks have the sulfur stench of high security that the app can't hope to penetrate.

One of the Wi-Fi networks has the option of entering a password, and I take a few guesses before giving up. Guessing would take a million years, and my failed login attempts might get detected after a couple more tries.

Panic sets in.

Concussed, drugged, and without the brain boost, I feel like I've smoked a few pounds of pot, drank a gallon of vodka, and then received a botched lobotomy. If I could magically inhabit my four-year-old brain, this is probably what it would feel like.

Cringing mentally, I try to hack the foul Wi-Fi connections, knowing full well it won't work. Muhomor's app makes the experience extra disgusting before informing me of "penetration failure"—an error text that would usually make me chuckle but isn't even remotely funny now.

Desperate, I tackle the Bluetooth connections one by one. Failure follows another failure until I discover the faint smell of a familiar phone connection.

Its taste confirms my suspicions.

It's my phone, Precious 3, but it's almost out of range. Being a Class 1 Bluetooth device (a rarity for smartphones), Precious 3 has a transmit power of 100 mW, giving it a rather impressive range of 328 feet—a lesson I recall from Muhomor's diatribe into the often overlooked topic of Bluetooth security. As he put it, most people think Bluetooth is safe because of its short range. It's often true, but not always, and it looks like whoever is holding me prisoner underestimated my phone's capabilities, or more likely, they don't know I can connect with my phone.

With my connection to Precious 3 established, I enable the phone's hotspot feature and brace for the cellular internet connection. It's less than ideal, but better than nothing.

The boost doesn't happen.

I check the phone stats and see it's also outside cell-tower range. Perhaps whoever has me isn't so stupid after all.

After I triple and quadruple check that there's no way to get online with the phone, I try to use it to gather intelligence and create an AROS screen that gives me a view through my phone's front camera. The screen is black, so I try the back camera in case the phone is lying face down. The back camera works better, and I see a boring cement wall. The only interesting detail is an air duct, adding to my growing impression that I'm somewhere underground. I see the battery on the phone is full and realize I got lucky that it's lying face down, with the solar charger on the back facing the industrial halogen lamp.

"You're awake," a man says. His tone reminds me of a jaded customer service representative who's trying to sound friendly but would rather stab his ears with a pencil than talk to yet another person on the phone. "No need to pretend."

I open my eyes and see that the voice belongs to that square-shouldered Suit I saw earlier. Only now, for whatever reason, he's wearing aviator sunglasses in this poorly lit, windowless room.

Stifling a fresh jolt of panic, I examine my surroundings and find blank concrete on all sides, further corroborating my underground bunker idea. That could explain the lack of cell service.

"Where am I?" I attempt to ask, but something unintelligible and hoarse comes out. It feels like my throat is filled with cheap kitty litter sand. "Who are you?"

"He might be too weak for a conversation," says a man whose face is covered by a surgical mask.

"You're done here, Doc," says the Suit. "Someone will come get you when it's time."

Doc's eyes glint with mild disapproval, but he listens to the Suit and leaves.

I try to lift my hands to scratch the tip of my nose but find that my wrists are restrained by leather straps attached to the sides of the hospital gurney. I also note that I'm wearing a drab hospital gown. There's an IV in my arm, explaining the painful gnawing in the back of my hand. In general, I feel a symphony of pain and discomforts. Some are strange—like the really weird feeling in one of my most private parts.

"I'm glad you're awake, Mr. Cohen," the Suit says in that same falsely cordial tone. "I'm Special Agent Lancaster."

He takes out his ID and shows it to me—but so briefly that I don't get a chance to see what agency he's with, if any. Not that it matters whether I get a good look at the ID, since those things can be falsified. I do weigh his claim that he's with the government against what I know so far. I was inside a helicopter, and the fact that he isn't in any facial recognition databases does suggest this is something government-related and clandestine. Who else would have the resources to remove people from every facial recognition database?

"Okay, why did you kidnap me, Mr. Lancaster?" I ask, fighting to sound calm while my sluggish brain tries to figure out the answer to my own question. It comes up with a vague list of conspiracy theories that includes my adventures in Russia at the top and Brainocyte technology in general at the bottom. I long for the brain boost like never before. I bet if I had it, I'd know what these people want from me.

If neurogenesis made my biological brain any nimbler, I don't feel that at all.

"We didn't kidnap you. We saved your life." Lancaster's fake niceness springs a small crack. "And it's Agent Lancaster."

A surge of anger chases away my anxiety, clearing some of the fog from my brain. Since I'm connected to my phone, I begin recording our conversation to Precious's local disk. This way, I can replay this exchange and look for extra clues at my leisure when I have my brain boost enabled.

"Okay, *Agent* Lancaster," I say, emphasizing his title. "Let's review the facts, shall we? I'm tied to a bed." I demonstratively yank on the straps. "I wasn't read my rights. I have no clue where I am. Given our interaction so far, I choose to call this a kidnapping."

"This is a place where you can be safe," the agent says and cracks his knuckles with a disgusting pop—a gesture I find vaguely threatening. "As you no doubt noticed in that hospital, dangerous people tried to kill you. If we hadn't intervened, you would be dead. I thought you'd be more appreciative of *these* facts."

"Well, thank you for saving me," I begin and realize what the odd sensation in my private parts is. They stuck a catheter into my bladder. It's one of my worst nightmares, nearly as dreadful as being in a room without internet. Gritting my teeth, I finish with, "Now I'd like to be seen by my own doctor, in a hospital of my choosing."

I'm about to mention my lack of clothes, when I realize I've been the most selfish rat owner ever. While worrying about myself, I completely forgot about Mr. Spock. I last recall him hiding inside my pants. Now he's missing—as are my pants. I bring up the EmoRat app, and it gives me an error code that states, "Unable to establish contact with sweetums." If I wasn't terrified for Mr. Spock's life and my own, I'd probably chuckle at Ada's error message, but as is, I fall into deeper despair, my stomach knotting with anxiety once more.

"I'm afraid that leaving isn't safe," Agent Lancaster says without a hint of genuine regret in his tone. "This is the only way we can make sure you're not attacked again. Also, the doctors tell me you're in no condition to go anywhere."

My molars grind together again. "I don't feel too safe. But I am feeling well enough to go, so please let me go."

"You're on pain medication," the agent says. "Otherwise, you wouldn't be so eager to get on your feet."

The mention of medication prompts me to mentally ask Einstein for a report on the contents of my blood. He's the way I interface with the "lab on the chip" imbedded under my skin. Of course, Einstein requires connectivity, so I instantly get an error message.

"I walked out of a hospital after a car accident," I tell Lancaster, trying not to cringe at the memory. A sign of weakness wouldn't help my case, so I make my face expressionless as I say, "For that matter, even after getting into a car accident, the hospital didn't find the need to take the draconian measures you've taken. Why the catheter? Why can't I pee on my own?"

The agent's lack of expression matches mine. "If you leave, you'll die. I'm sure you're aware that Vincent Williams will never forget the death of his brother."

"You're well informed." My eyes narrow. "Maybe too well informed. How do I know you didn't hire Vincent Williams to attack me in the first place?"

"Come now, Mr. Cohen." Agent Lancaster pushes his shades higher on his nose with his middle finger in a flip-off gesture that may or may not be inadvertent. "According to your dossier, you're supposed to be a smart man."

A dossier? My hands tighten into fists. "Right. I'm smart enough to know you got me here for a reason that has nothing to do with my health or safety. Smart enough to have noticed your surveillance a while ago. We both know you've been following me for months before the attack."

The words burst out of me before I even realize the truth of them. Once I say it, though, I know I'm right. These guys must've been following me around. They grabbed me when they thought I was about to get killed before they could learn whatever it is they want to learn from me. Or, more likely, they grabbed me after Vincent Williams, a goon they hired, scared me enough to cooperate with my "saviors." Because if they aren't behind Williams, why didn't they assist me during the attack at the restaurant? Were they having a change in surveillance shifts or something?

My headache intensifies as my world paradigm realigns, and I fully consider the reality of being spied upon. All the paranoia I thought was irrational wasn't. To paraphrase the popular saying, you're not paranoid if some shady government organization really *is* out to get you. Thanks to the brain boost, on some level, I must've known these guys were surveilling me. Gogi didn't believe me because he isn't enhanced, and they must not have been following Ada. That might be a clue. Then again, maybe they did follow Ada, and she might be less observant than I am, even with a boost. Or perhaps I noticed my surveillance because I *am* more prone to paranoia. I decide to later look up if paranoia correlates with being more observant.

Agent Lancaster takes off his aviator glasses and looks at me with gray eyes that eerily match the naked slabs of concrete behind him. "Since you brought it up, why don't we start with that? How did you know about our surveillance?"

I can see this bothers him more than he's letting on. I guess he has a high opinion of his organization's tradecraft, and my claim that I spotted them doesn't fit neatly with his ego.

"What do *you* think? What's the likeliest answer to that question?" I'm hoping he comes up with some kind of theory, because truthfully, I have no idea. Besides my vague paranoia, all I had were bad dreams featuring people in suits.

"None of the likely scenarios are possible." For the first time, anger openly appears on his face, and I wonder if it's a good idea to get him angry while I'm in such a vulnerable position. "I hand-picked every person on this task force."

Now I understand why he's so pissed. His worst nightmare is probably having a double agent working for him. At the risk of making him angrier, I decide to pursue this idea, seeing a chance to probe him for critical information. "You picked them, yet it looks like you have a rat in your midst."

I choose my words carefully, figuring if they have Mr. Spock, he might reveal that upon hearing the word "rat."

I know the actual expression features a mole rather than a rat, but the agent understood me fine, as evidenced by the tension in his jaw. After a moment, however, the anger leaves Agent Lancaster's face. He's either a good poker player, or he considered the idea of a double agent and decided it couldn't be the case. Or he figured if there is a traitor on his team, someone I know about, I wouldn't tell him about it so openly. I think about pointing out that I could be double bluffing, but I opt instead to watch him quietly and not think about the uncomfortable tube inside my penis.

"You're just a paranoid guy who got lucky," the agent says, reaching the correct conclusion. "That's all that was."

I breathe a small sigh of relief that he didn't mention any actual rats and focus back on the issue at hand.

"I notice you didn't deny the surveillance," I say, attempting to stare him down. I can only hold his gaze for a few moments before I get the urge to look away. "Was it legal for you to follow me around all this time? Did you have a court order? For that matter, why on Earth were you following me?"

His eyes narrow to icy slits. "You don't want to have an adversarial relationship with me, trust me."

"So now you're threatening me," I say, wishing I felt as brave as I sounded. "I'd like to go on record. I want my lawyer present. I want to make a phone call. I don't want to be here, and you have no right to keep me." My voice rises as righteous anger grips me again. "If I'm guilty of a crime, then tell me what it is. I want—"

"I need you to calm down." Lancaster's words are clipped. I spot his fists clenching and unclenching at his sides and realize again I'm yelling at a guy who has me at his complete mercy.

I hear beeping from the device that's monitoring my heartbeat, which means I'm not imagining the pounding pulse in my ears. Losing my cool is a bad idea, so I activate the BraveChill app—which doesn't work for the same reason as most of the others. Forcing myself to take deep breaths, I mentally curse the server client architecture design we chose. It makes logical sense to do the heavy-duty computations on remote servers, but I'd give anything to be able to do this stuff in my head.

"Look," I say when my breathing steadies a bit. "It's hard to calm down when someone ties you to a bed and shoves needles and tubes into your orifices."

"I understand, but your best course of action is to cooperate." Lancaster's tone goes back to fake friendliness and concern.

"Answer my questions, untie me, and get me a lawyer, and I'll think about cooperating."

His friendly mask slips. "You're in no position to make demands."

"A US citizen is always in a position to ask for a lawyer. And I'm asking."

"Cooperate, and then we'll talk about lawyers."

I stare at him, and he stares back at me.

"I want a phone call and a lawyer," I say again. "I'm not cooperating until I get that."

"No? We'll see." He turns and walks to the door.

"Wait," I yell, and though I know he can hear me, he shows no sign of it as he strides toward the exit. "Don't leave. I really need to go to the bathroom."

He ignores me, and I find myself alone in the room.

If Lancaster's goal was to rattle me, he succeeded spectacularly. Though I knew I was in an awful situation, being left alone like this is infinitely worse.

It makes me realize just how screwed I am.

SEVENTEEN

IN CASE THERE'S A MICROPHONE IN THE ROOM, I PROCEED TO YELL obscenities at Agent Lancaster until my throat gets scratchy and I feel overwhelming thirst.

Then I yank at the restraints, but all that does is give my wrists a nasty rope burn.

Ignoring the pain, I try talking politely this time, emphasizing the whole bathroom issue as a priority, but to no avail.

What's really annoying is that, unlike movie heroes who lie about their bathroom needs to aid in their escape, I genuinely have to go. Though nauseatingly unpleasant, the catheter takes care of me needing to do number one, but it does nothing for the more and more urgent call of number two.

My panic builds, and under my breath, I curse Ada's high-fiber diet for leading to this situation. Then I channel the negativity where it belongs and curse Agent Lancaster some more—but mentally this time.

For a few minutes, I distract myself with violent revenge fantasies of what I'd do to Agent Lancaster if I got the chance. It makes me wonder if I could wind up as bloodthirsty as Joe if pushed too far.

My stomach cramps, and I strongly consider yelling about cooperation, but I can't bring myself to do it. My anger at being put in this situation feeds something stubborn in me, something I didn't even know I had.

I also realize the aches I was feeling have evolved into pains. I recall Agent Lancaster mentioning pain medicine. Could I be due for another dose?

To distract myself, I decide to check on my blood contents via the lab on the chip in my body. When Mitya originally made Einstein work with this technology, I pair coded with him and saw how he used the special API that gives direct access to the chip's outputs.

Loading the AROS IDE, I begin coding.

Coding without a brain boost is *much* harder than I ever imagined, especially with the distraction of pain, my growing hunger, and the overwhelming need to use the bathroom. The app I want to put together is completely no frills—just a little screen that will show the findings of the micro-laboratory in plain text. Given all my handicaps, what would have been a ten-minute project takes me what feels like two hours.

The good news is that the coding effort somewhat distracts me from my troubles. The bad news is what I learn upon completing the project. There are indeed small traces of oxycodone and acetaminophen in my blood. That means they gave me some Percocet—a drug consisting of that combo. The last time I used this pain medicine, it worked on me for about four hours before I needed another dose, but that was when I was dealing with a toothache. Assuming they gave me the dose in the helicopter when Einstein told me it was 6:48 p.m., and since it's now 11:20 p.m. according to Precious 3, I need another dose. Otherwise, I'll be in worse pain soon. I guess the pain might be part of the point Agent Lancaster is trying to make.

What's even worse is that I also have bisacodyl in my blood. Bisacodyl is a laxative that the doctors gave my mom after her accident, and its presence in my blood means one of two things.

Option one, my captors are genuinely worried about me having constipation as a side effect from Percocet. When I took Percocet for that toothache, I *did* experience constipation. Option two, the likelier one, is that they're using the pretext of option one to engineer a deeply humiliating situation for me.

Determined not to give the bastards the satisfaction of seeing me squirm, I try to think of some solutions. One simple idea arrives right away. It's nighttime, so I could try sleeping. Hopefully, the bisacodyl can't do its job while I'm unconscious, but even if it does, at least I won't be aware of it happening.

I close my eyes and do my best to even out my breathing.

My eyelids grow heavy, and I'm gladly slipping into oblivion when a brain-shattering noise jolts me awake.

I cringe and curse the bindings for preventing me from cupping my ears. The hellish noise sounds like a giant is drilling through a mountain. To my concussed brain, this experience is similar to having a chainsaw buzzing inside my head.

"Stop," I yell with my exhausted vocal cords. "I won't sleep if you don't want me to."

The noise doesn't stop.

They're purposely torturing me. I realize that now. This drilling is to stop me from sleeping—not so different from the infamous "enhanced interrogation techniques" used on terrorists. Lancaster claims he's a government agent, and he let slip that he's part of a task force. Is the government allowed to torture civilians? Or is this treatment a sign that forces more sinister than Uncle Sam are holding me captive? For all I know, Russian KGB/SVR might have me because they want the Brainocyte technology—or as payback for what happened in Russia a few months ago. If that's true, I might never want to cooperate, since the SVR wouldn't keep me around after I told them whatever it is they need to know. Alternatively, could these people be a part of some private organization? Could my half-brother be doing this to me because he learned of my role in our deceased father's fate?

On second thought, a Russian connection is kind of a long

shot. They had that helicopter—something too high-profile for an intelligence organization from another nation. Lancaster's English is flawless, and he's either an award-winning actor or really a government agent. It's possible that torture is allowed under certain anti-terrorism laws, or else they have plausible deniability for everything. They could say, "Well, he was hurt, so we had to provide medical help, and we had to use the catheter and every-thing else. He was in danger, so we hid him from his foes. Cell phone signals are crappy in our hideout, so we couldn't let him call his lawyer—or anyone. Oh, and we had to do some last-minute construction work around our secret lair, hence the drilling from hell."

Remembering the drilling brings me violently back into the present, and before I recall how bad of an idea it is, I throw up. Lucky for me, I just dry-heave. Having no food in my stomach is at least good for something.

Acting almost on instinct, I start the Music app in my head and bless the day I decided it should have a feature to play music from my phone on top of playing music from my cloud collection. Unfortunately, my phone's music library is all workout music. I set it up this way so I could hook my phone up to the dojo's speaker system on the days Gogi felt like fighting to music. The shuffle feature gives me a song called "One" by Metallica, and the guitar riffs completely mask the drilling noise, as Brainocytes deliver sound directly to my brain, overruling input from my ears. Though this song is infinitely preferable to the drilling, the irony is that this kind of music was used as an enhanced interrogation technique that involved loud bursts of metal music, including songs by Metallica. The key difference is that I like this music and I feel more in control, given that I can change the song if I feel like it or return to the drilling sounds if I start to feel masochistic. The effect is the same as what my captors intended, though.

I can forget about sleep.

After an hour, the lab on the chip informs me all traces of pain meds are out of my system—something I already knew based on how much the pain has worsened. The bisacodyl is still there and working, though, and out of all the hurts, my stomach is the worst. It feels like a creature from *Alien* is slowly growing inside me, preparing to burst out.

I kill some time by figuring out if I can write something that will work like the Relief app. Though Brainocytes don't have the computing power to run an app so complex, maybe I can use Precious 3's hardware to do the heavy lifting? Thinking about it more, I see two insurmountable issues. First, without the brain boost, I'm less capable as a programmer, and this kind of app will require finesse. Second, and this is more critical, I lack the resources to guide me when it comes to affecting the right parts of the brain in the correct way. I could easily end up stimulating the pain center of my brain, or give myself seizures.

Oh well, at least thinking about the app distracted me for a few minutes and briefly gave me the illusion that I had some control over my fate.

After another half hour of stomach agony, I wonder how bad it would be if I relieved myself right here in the bed. I mean, yes, it would be disgusting beyond belief and humiliating, but it should make the cramps from hell go away and hopefully make it unpleasant for Lancaster to be in the room with me when he comes back.

I remain strong for another hour before my body takes the decision out of my hands and the inevitable happens.

Babies cry when they do this to themselves, and I totally understand why. It's an extremely unpleasant set of sensations, both physically and emotionally. I'm on the verge of shedding a few tears fueled by self-pity, but I don't want to give Agent Lancaster the satisfaction of thinking this treatment broke me. In fact, if Lancaster's idea was to damage my will so I would start babbling information at his whim, I feel like he accomplished the reverse. I find solace in my anger, and it makes me resolved to not utter a single word when the asshole inevitably returns to speak to me again.

To stay semi-sane, I replicate my phone's screen in a big AROS window and launch the Chess app. With the brain boost, beating the in-game AI was so easy I gave this app a low rating in the app store after I first installed it. In my current state, the game gets its revenge as it defeats me twice in a row. My only excuse for losing is that thinking while in pain and trying not to breathe air is as difficult as it sounds.

I'm halfway through another match when the door opens and Agent Lancaster strides in.

I turn off the music blazing in my mind and find that the drilling sound is gone. The quietude envelops my ears with pure pleasure—until Agent Lancaster steps up to me and ruins it by speaking.

"Hello again, Mr. Cohen," the object of my hatred says. "I hope we can have an adult conversation this time."

EIGHTEEN

THOUGH I'M THIRSTY AND MY MOUTH IS DRY, I SOMEHOW GATHER enough saliva to spit at Agent Lancaster. The spittle flies across the distance between us and hits him square in the eye—a lucky shot.

The agent leaps forward and slaps me across the face. The sting is sharp, and my eyes water.

However, having him hit me is inspiring. It makes my boiling anger turn into a plan that might allow me to get even. Before I fully formulate the plan or get a chance to put it into motion, I see Agent Lancaster's face contort from anger to confusion to disgust. He must've registered the smell, and maybe he thinks he smells my reaction to his bitch slap. Does he think I'm such a weak coward? I sure hope so, because that would aid my half-formed plan.

Before I can blink, Lancaster storms out of the room and slams the heavy door shut with enough force to break a weaker door-frame. I wonder if he's upset with himself for reacting so strongly to my provocation or if he's that pissed at me. The second option would be bad for my newly hatched plan.

The plan is simple. I'll pretend to cooperate enough to get them to take off the restraints, and then, when I get the chance, I'll attack Lancaster and attempt to damage him using the skills Gogi taught me. Yes, it won't allow me to escape this place, and it'll probably lead to worse treatment, but it'll give me the satisfaction of revenge that I desperately crave. Of course, part of me knows I'll be much more comfortable in the interim as I go through the pretense, and an even more skeptical part of me worries that I've rationalized genuine cooperation under the guise of fake one.

I'm dead tired, but I don't dare close my eyes for fear that they'll turn the buzzing on again. I'm enjoying the silence too much for that. I'm convinced Lancaster will retaliate against me for the spitting incident, and I hope I'll get the chance to convince him I'm ready to cooperate before that happens.

After what feels like many hours—though according to my phone, only twenty minutes have passed—the door opens again.

Two people wearing scrubs come inside. They're carrying a tray of objects I have trouble making out. Just like earlier, the medical people hide their faces behind surgical masks, and when I try to look them in the eye, they avoid my gaze.

The larger of the two holds a huge syringe to my neck and says in a deep male voice, "We're just here to wash you and make sure you don't starve. If you move a muscle, I'll be forced to use this." Matching actions to words, he pricks my skin with the giant needle.

The smaller person, probably a woman, undoes my right wrist restraint.

I clear my throat. "I won't fight, but can you please get me out of here? I'm being held against my will."

The people in scrubs ignore me, and the smaller one turns me over to clean me up.

I debate fighting them despite my promise, figuring if he knocks me out, it might make the washing less embarrassing. However, I decide to tough it out so it'll be more believable when I claim I'm ready to cooperate as part of my new plan.

When the humiliation is complete, the smaller person ties my hand back down and reaches for something on the tray.

"Don't move." The male's eyes dart from me to his partner as he gives a little nod. "We have one more thing we need to do."

The smaller one is holding a long tube in his or her hand and brings it closer to my face. I recall the guy saying something about making sure I don't starve and realize what it must be.

"Wait." My voice rises. "I'd rather starve."

"It's just a nasogastric tube," says the smaller one, her soft voice confirming that she's a woman. "You need food, and all other methods for getting it into you are more invasive."

"I can eat the fucking food with my mouth," I snap. This device, the NG tube, was installed in Mom's nose after her horrible accident, and I was horrified just seeing it done to someone else. When my words don't seem to have an effect, I yell, "I refuse this treatment! There's no medical necessity for it. None at all. You hear me? I don't want this thing!"

My raised voice is half for them and half for the benefit of a hypothetical listening device. The tube moves closer to my nose, and I squirm in place. The restraints leave burns on my wrists as I struggle. Blinding anger returns in full force, and without realizing what I'm saying, I scream, "I don't care how much you hide your faces! It won't help. I'll find out who you are, and I'll end your careers!"

That seems to discomfit the woman, but I realize I made a mistake if my plan was to maintain the pretense of cooperation.

"I think you should give him that shot," the woman says, though I see a glimmer of doubt and perhaps even sympathy in her eyes.

"Well, *I* think you should do your job," the man tells her sternly. To me, he says, "If you move around, the tube could go into your lungs, and that would cause a number of problems, not to mention you'll make the whole process more uncomfortable."

"Exhale," the woman says and sticks the tip of the tube into my left nostril.

Panicking, I loudly exhale as my heartbeat accelerates so fast the nearby monitoring equipment rings in alarm.

"Try to relax," she says and slowly inserts the tube into my nose.

At first, the feeling reminds me of getting water in my nose while also getting a giant brain freeze from a Slurpee, but multiplied a thousand-fold. Then a burning that feels like I'm snorting a pepper-spray-covered porcupine sears my sinuses.

"Don't move," she says, but it's too late. I pull my head away and rip the tube out of my nose, but even with it out, the burning is still there.

"Please, don't do that again," I croak. "Just tell Agent Lancaster I'm ready to tell him anything he wants."

The woman looks at the man, but he shakes his head.

"I'll try the other nostril," she says without looking at me. "Please, try not to pull it out this time."

Since I know what's about to happen, the dread of having it happen to my other nostril is impossibly worse than my original fear. She begins the insertion, and the process hurts worse than the first time. It takes all my willpower not to pull my head away.

The tube clears the back of my nose and spreads the burning downward into my throat. My gag reflex kicks in, and I can't take it anymore. In a swift motion, I pull my head away and rip the tube out of my nose—an action that hurts nearly as much as the insertion.

I know I can't handle another attempt. Like a cornered animal, I feel myself getting desperately dangerous. The woman must not realize my state, because her hands are still close to my face.

In a blur of motion, I crane my neck, jut my head forward, and sink my teeth into the woman's left pinky as hard as I can. The woman screams like a pig family during slaughter, but instead of letting go of her flesh, I clench my teeth so hard that my jaw spasms in pain.

At some point in the past, I heard an urban myth that a finger is as easy to bite through as a carrot. I now know that story is false. I can tell I won't be able to snap the finger in half as I originally intended, but at least I did a lot of damage to it.

I consider doing a zombie-like ripping motion with my head to further hurt the finger, but then I feel the needle go into my skin. The oblivion comes almost instantly, allowing one last thought—a hope that they'll insert the NG tube while I'm unconscious.

NINETEEN

I WAKE UP BUT DON'T OPEN MY EYES, FIGURING I SHOULD GET MY bearings first.

According to Precious 3, it's 9:01 a.m. on November 16. I was out for eight hours. Despite getting the rest I was craving, I feel sleep deprived for some reason. Maybe the drug that induced my unconsciousness didn't provide any real sleep benefits?

I also feel new pains. My left eye is swollen. Someone, probably the woman I hurt, must've punched me in the face. Additionally, there's the most horrid sensation in my throat—the cursed tube. I try to swallow and instantly gag. Despite my conscious wishes, I try to swallow again, and it's just as unpleasant.

On the plus side—if it's even a plus—I don't feel any signs of hunger, so the tube has fulfilled that part of its purpose. It was used to deliver food into my stomach.

To relax, I try breathing slowly and evenly, hoping to forget about the obstacle in my throat, but I might as well be trying to forget my name.

"Are you awake, Mr. Cohen?" asks a new voice. "My name is Agent Pugh."

I open my eyes, and once they've adjusted to the light, I see a woman standing in front of me. She's wearing a pantsuit and holding one hand behind her back. Her face is extremely symmetrical, except her green eyes are much too big in proportion to her features. There's sympathy in her eyes as she says, "I work with Agent Lancaster, but he doesn't know I'm here."

Bullshit, I think to myself, but out loud, I croak, "Help me." The tube in my throat makes my attempt to talk extremely uncomfortable, and my eyes water to the point where she might think I'm crying.

"That's why I'm here." She takes out a napkin and wipes my face. "I'm here to help you."

I stare at her. It doesn't take a brain boost to understand what's happening. It's the oldest trick in the book—the good cop/bad cop routine.

"I'm uncomfortable with the way things have escalated," Agent Pugh says. If there were Oscars for government agents who could say rehearsed lines with proper regret, she'd at least get a nomination. "Please, work with me, and I'll get you more comfortable."

"What can I do?" I choke out, but I'm not sure she understood me with the gagging sounds coming out of my mouth.

"Just nod if you agree with me and shake your head if you don't," she says.

I nod to show I understand.

"I want to tell Agent Lancaster you're ready to cooperate," she says. "Would you like that?"

I nod vigorously.

"I also have news about your medical condition," she says. "When you were unconscious, we did some X-rays, and it appears you're intact."

"The tube," I gurgle out. What I mean is, "How do you expect me to talk with the tube?" as well as, "Why the hell is this tube in my nose if I'm intact?"

"Now that we got nutrients into your system, the tube will be removed," she says, her nose crinkling. "We'll also give you something for the pain, if that's okay with you."

I nod even more vigorously this time.

She moves her hand out from behind her back, and I see she's holding a syringe. Instead of sticking the needle into my skin, like the asshole in the mask did, she uses the IV that's already in my arm to deliver the medicine.

Warmth slowly spreads throughout my body, and I watch her leave the room as my vision blurs and I fall under.

————

I wake up feeling amazing. All the earlier pains and aches are gone, and when I try to swallow, I confirm that the tube is blissfully missing from my nose and throat.

My phone states that it's 11:05 a.m. on the 16th, so I was out for three hours this time.

Opening my eyes, I see I'm no longer in the windowless cement room. Someone sat me on a chair in a new location—a room that seems to have been modeled after the most stereotypical interrogation room you'd see in a police procedural show. I spot three gray walls and one mirrored wall, a chair, and a table. Instead of leather straps as before, standard-issue police handcuffs bind my hands. I guess someone did this out of a need to stay consistent with the new decor. There's even a glass of water on the table—out of my reach, as per the *Interrogation 101* handbook.

Hopeful, I search for a Wi-Fi network but find none.

"Hello, Mr. Cohen," says Agent Lancaster in his signature fake-friendly voice. His eyes are hidden behind his aviator sunglasses again, and his posture exudes calm confidence. "I'm glad you decided to cooperate."

"Hello," I say. Even with the pain meds, my throat is still sore from my earlier ordeal. Raising my handcuffed hands, I ask, "Is this really necessary?"

Instead of answering, Agent Lancaster slams a giant paper-filled folder on the desk in front of me and says, "Before we begin,

I wanted to show you this." He opens the folder to a random page and pushes the whole mess toward me.

I look at the page in question and feel the hairs on the back of my neck rise. I remember this email. It's an email an investor sent me a couple of months ago—the one where he was thanking me for an outstanding quarter.

When he notices my reaction, Agent Lancaster flips the page, and I see a number of my emails. Some are from my personal account, including a very private email where Ada asked me to get us more condoms for a romantic evening we had planned (Muhomor was testing Tema for us at that time and our Brainocyte traffic was not private).

Thankfully, I don't see any private texts or emails sent via Brainocytes. That would've meant that Agent Lancaster and his minions literally had access to our private thoughts. I wonder if our Brainocytes communications are somewhere else in that folder, but I doubt it. Before Tema was ready, Muhomor insisted we all get email and text accounts that couldn't be traced back to us, and he had us all get new accounts on an annoyingly regular basis. With Tema in place, he agreed to be more lax in the future.

"As you can see"—Lancaster's voice takes me out of my paranoid reverie—"we know a lot about you, Mr. Cohen." He closes the folder and moves it out of reach. "I'm only showing you this so you know a large majority of my questions will be about things I already have answers to. That means if you lie, I'll know it, and if I catch you in a single lie, no matter how small, our polite conversation will end." He leans across the desk and looks me in the eye. "Am I making myself clear?"

"Yes," I say, and it comes out too meekly for my liking. My earlier plan of pretending to cooperate might've suffered a major setback. I was, of course, planning to lie about everything just to spite the bastard, but now I have to be careful since I don't know what he knows.

"Good." Agent Lancaster sits back and steeples his fingers.

"Let's start with an easy question first. How long have you been an agent for the Russian Federation?"

The question catches me so far off guard that for a few moments, I sit there, blinking at a rate of a hundred eyelid flops per second. I'd be less shocked if he'd slapped me in the face again.

"I'm not a Russian spy," I finally say, feeling dumb at having to say these words. The whole thing reminds me of having to deny something extremely obvious, like not being an invisible pink unicorn. "So, zero time."

Even as I say this, I realize how much trouble I might be in if he believes the accusation he made. I know very little about due process when it comes to captured spies. In movies, it doesn't look like habeas corpus. Do suspected spies get phone calls or lawyers? I imagine it would be dangerous to let them have those things since they could code a message to their handler through the phone, or the lawyer they use can help them kill themselves to prevent giving away state secrets.

"Come now, Mr. Cohen." Lancaster demonstratively massages his temples. "We know."

"If you indeed know, then you *know* I'm not a spy for any country, least of all Russia. Doesn't it say somewhere in there"—I point at the folder—"that I came to the US as a refugee? Or that I arrived at an age much too young to be recruited into the spy business?"

"I thought we agreed you'd cooperate." Agent Lancaster flips through the pages in his folder and stops on something he must like, because he pushes the image toward me.

I'm stunned. The image is blurry because someone took it with their phone inside a poorly lit nightclub, but I can tell it's a picture of me standing on a DJ's stage. It looks like I'm aiming a gun at the crowd, though in reality I was aiming at the goons who'd come to attack us.

"That was taken at the Dazdraperma club," Agent Lancaster says triumphantly. "In Moscow."

"That's me protecting myself *from* the KGB—err, I mean, SVR," I say, then realize I might have admitted to something my lawyer would've advised against. Weakly, I add, "That's the opposite of working for them."

"Sure." Agent Lancaster's tone is dripping with sarcasm. "All venture capitalists are known to take little trips to participate in shootouts in Moscow."

"I was saving my mother," I retort. "Her kidnapping was in the newspapers. She wasn't the only person I saved. There are a dozen American citizens you can interview."

"You mean those handicapped Americans whose brains are being manipulated by the technology you created?" He rubs his temples again. "I can see this isn't going anywhere."

There's a small silver lining to what he said. He didn't refer to the Brainocytes by their proper name—something I'd expect him to do if he was interested in the technology. Then again, if he doesn't want the Brainocytes, I can't think of what else he might want.

If he truly believes I'm a spy, that would be really bad.

"Look." I fight the temptation to get up and start pacing the room. "How can I prove I'm not a spy?"

"You can't prove you're not a spy because you are one," Lancaster says. "But if you're useful enough, we could overlook your other indiscretions."

I already miss the brain boost with a passion, and right now, I'd pay a million dollars for a few seconds on the internet. Though thinking is difficult without the boost, I'm beginning to feel like I'm being skillfully manipulated. Agent Lancaster might be accusing me of being a spy as an interrogation technique. I've seen it used in shows. The detectives will often mention a murder or something big to get suspects to admit to a smaller crime. At least I hope that's what's going on. Unfortunately, if the purpose of this technique is to make me scared enough to tell them whatever they want, it's working spectacularly well.

"I'm as much of a spy as I am a ballerina," I reply, though my bravado sounds hollow, even to my own ears. "You want something. I get that. Just come out and say what it is."

"Fine." He removes his aviator sunglasses and looks at me with his colorless eyes. "In that case, let's talk about Viktor Tsoi."

I repeat the bit where I blink at him repeatedly and then vow to perfect my poker-face reaction to strange questions and behaviors in the future. Viktor Tsoi is the name of a famous Russian rock singer who tragically died in a car crash at twenty-eight. True, I love his songs even to this day, but I fail to see why Agent Lancaster would be interested in him, so I ask, "And why are we discussing Russian music?" He looks confused for a moment, so I add, "Viktor Tsoi was a songwriter and singer. He's dead."

"In case you don't know," Lancaster says in the tone of someone who's sure I'm just messing with him, "Viktor Tsoi is the name of a man who is very much alive." He opens his folder to a new page and hands me a picture of Muhomor and me sitting in a downtown café. The picture was clearly taken during last month's Brainocytes Club meeting. "Viktor Tsoi goes under the hacker alias 'Muhomor.'"

TWENTY

THINGS BECOME INSTANTLY CLEARER, TO THE POINT WHERE I'D smack my forehead if my hands were free. Of course this misadventure is connected to Muhomor. If I weren't so worried about Muhomor's life, I'd want to kill him. As is, I channel my anger at the agent in front of me instead. But seriously, how many times have I told Muhomor to cool it with the hacking? Now something he did got me into this situation. I really hope we both survive our ordeals so I can properly express my displeasure toward the skinny hacker.

Since the agent is still waiting for an answer, I say, "I genuinely didn't know that was Muhomor's real name. Now that I know Viktor Tsoi is his name, I'm not surprised he goes by a nickname. Muhomor loves his individuality, and his celebrity namesake was as famous as Elvis Presley." The agent doesn't look impressed by my disclosures, so I add hastily, "I'd be glad to talk to you about Muhomor. Why don't we start with his current medical condition? Is he alive? How did his surgery go?"

I expect Agent Lancaster to answer with the cliché, "I'm the one asking questions," or something along those lines, but he surprises me by saying, "Muhomor is alive but in a coma." There's a dose of genuine regret in his voice, though I can't tell if he's upset that Muhomor is alive or that they can't question him because he's in a coma. "His spinal injury was severe."

The ache in my chest returns in full force, and I instinctively try pinging Muhomor with the Telepathy app. The error message is a painful reminder that I can't get in touch with him or anyone else.

"Look." I take a deep breath and let it out. "Agent Lancaster, if Muhomor is in a coma, he isn't a threat. Why all this?" I raise my handcuffed hands, and the chains clink against the table.

"The situation is more complicated than that." Lancaster rubs the stubble on his dimpled chin. "As you well know."

"I honestly don't," I say in confusion.

"All this"—he waves his hand around the interrogation room —"had to be escalated because you all nearly got yourselves killed."

"Or you nearly got us killed as a way to pressure me to speak," I reply, though I now wonder if it would be logical for Lancaster and his minions to hire Vincent Williams to come after us. After all, if they're interested in Muhomor, killing him or putting him in a coma is a really bad plan—assuming he *is* in a coma, as Lancaster claimed.

"I thought we had an understanding." The agent's jaw tenses, and he puts his glasses back on—but not before I gleam the anger in his eyes. "If you need more time to think…"

I know that "time to think" is a euphemism for more torture, and the threat sends a wave of anxiety through me. However, my pent-up anger swiftly overrides it.

"We do have an understanding," I say and do my best to look scared rather than pissed off. Perversely, I'm annoyed at how well I manage to sound meek, but I continue my performance by having my voice crack as I add, "I'll tell you what you want to know. I really don't want any more time to think."

"Tell me about Muhomor's recent hacks." Agent Lancaster's tone is patronizingly soothing. "In as much detail as possible."

"He penetrated the IARPA systems," I say. Though it feels shitty betraying my friend's confidence, I'm sure I'm telling Lancaster something he already knows, so I look at this revelation as a necessary evil to earn the agent's trust. "IARPA was working on a project to reverse engineer the algorithms that run the human brain. Muhomor was interested in the research."

Agent Lancaster must be an excellent poker player, because he betrays no clues as to what he thinks of my statement. Since he's waiting for me to continue, I say, "Prior to that, he hacked into the Verizon servers to gain free cell phone service."

What actually happened is that Muhomor hacked into Sprint's servers, but I added that small discrepancy on purpose to see how detailed Agent Lancaster's knowledge is.

The man slightly turns toward the mirror to his left, and his hand almost goes to his ear before he stops himself. Did someone feed him information on Sprint versus Verizon? Was it someone behind that mirror?

"Are you sure it was Verizon?" Agent Lancaster interlaces his fingers in front of his face and stretches his arms out. "Details are important."

"I'm sorry," I lie. "It was one of the major ones. I thought it was Verizon, but it could have been AT&T or perhaps Sprint?"

The fact we're being watched limits my new plan to attack him when I can.

"What are the Qecho servers?" he asks.

If he wanted to catch me off guard, he failed.

"A 100-qubit quantum computer," I reply right away. "Muhomor likes to use it."

"What does he use it for?" This question comes out faster and more forcefully.

"Encryption and decryption. But I bet you already knew that."

"What's Tema?" The intensity in Agent Lancaster's voice is now set to eleven out of ten. "How does it work?"

I'm not at all surprised at the direction this conversation has taken. The moment the agent brought up Muhomor, I suspected he would ask about Tema—Muhomor's unbreakable cryptosystem. Out of everything the Russian hacker has done, Tema is the epitome of what would get on a government's radar. Muhomor said so himself many times, but I always thought there was a dose of self-aggrandizement in my friend's rhetoric. He claimed that governments rely on reading everyone's communications at will and that his unbreakable cryptosystem would revolutionize the world, because Tema is impervious to attacks by quantum computers, unlike most "legacy" cryptosystems that rely on multiplying large primes. Looks like Muhomor was right on every count.

When the government can't crack your messages, they do indeed get upset.

The biggest problem with this is that I can't help Lancaster even if I wanted to. I barely understand the basic principles behind Tema with the aid of the brain boost, and right now, it might as well involve magic as far as my understanding goes. Worse, Agent Lancaster probably wants to know how to break Tema and won't believe me if I tell him that the most powerful minds in the world haven't been able to break Muhomor's new baby, leading us all to believe that the thing is unbreakable.

"Tema is short for the Russian word 'kryptosystema,'" I begin. "It's a cryptosystem Muhomor invented. He thinks it's unbreakable." I'm tempted to add, "Given my presence here, I take it he was right."

"How does it work?" If Agent Lancaster wanted to hide the importance of this question, he certainly failed. His whole body tenses, making him look like a jaguar preparing to leap at a deer.

"It's complicated," I say as earnestly as possible since the next part of my plan depends on this. "Do you have paper and something to write with? I'll do my best to break it down for you."

Without hesitation, Lancaster takes out a fancy pen from his inner jacket pocket and hands it to me. He then takes a couple of pages out of the thick folder and says, "You can write on the back of those."

I take the pencil in my right hand and write as clumsily as I can.

As I hoped, even without the pretense, the handcuffs make writing difficult.

"I think this would go a lot better if I didn't have these on." I jiggle the handcuffs and try not to look too eager.

Agent Lancaster betrays his excitement again by getting up and walking over to my side of the table. Heart drumming, I watch him take out a key and undo the cuffs.

As soon as my hands are free, everything around me comes into focus to the point where I momentarily feel as though I've regained internet access and my brain boost. In less than a blink, I relive the moment Agent Lancaster slapped me in the face and the indignity and pain I suffered while strapped down in that cement room. The awful recollections culminate in the memory of that feeding tube going into my nose, and my slow-boiling anger explodes with the force of Vesuvius.

My left hand forms into a fist, and I punch Agent Lancaster in the crotch—a move made easy by his current stance. Something soft crunches under my knuckles, and I almost feel male sympathy for my enemy.

Almost, but not quite.

A grunt escapes Lancaster's lips, and he begins to double over.

Then again, maybe he isn't doubling over. His hand is balled into a fist, and I suspect he's planning to hit me back.

I turn my head, and his fist whooshes past my right ear. I grip the pen in my right hand and randomly stab the source of my angst in his quickly approaching face.

The aviator glasses fly into the mirrored glass on the right wall, and the pen tip enters his eye with a stomach-twisting squishy noise.

Agent Lancaster's scream is inhuman, and I gape in horrified trance at the damage I just wreaked. Again, more thoughts than normal swoosh through my mind, the main one being a conviction that my usual PTSD nightmares will expand to include this scene —assuming I ever get to sleep again.

To his credit, despite the agony he must be in, my enemy uses my hesitation to reach into his jacket for what I assume is his weapon.

If I survive the next moment, I'll have to build Gogi a statue for all the disarming drills he had me do. I leap to my feet, and my hands move with practiced confidence. As soon as I see the gun gleam in the halogen light, I twist Lancaster's right wrist, and the gun clanks against the table before falling onto the chair and then hitting the floor with a metallic, tile-cracking sound. Continuing almost on autopilot, I put my foot behind my opponent and push him.

As Agent Lancaster's body flies into the mirror, I hear the door behind me crack open.

I leap for the gun.

In the mirror, I catch a glimpse of someone wearing SWAT gear, but I still hold a glimmer of hope. Maybe I can get the gun and somehow shoot my way out of this mess.

Unfortunately, the harsh reality of this universe doesn't comply with my hopes. Something bites painfully at my right shoulder. The impact is too mild to be a bullet, though. The prongs of a Taser, perhaps?

I grab the Glock's handle and begin to pivot, ready to aim. But before I'm even halfway facing my opponent, fifty thousand volts spread through every muscle in my body.

I drop the gun as my body jerks uncontrollably. My vision blurs as pain spears through my body, but I make out a shadow looming over me.

A needle pricks my skin, and a hard boot connects with my head in a violent kick.

My world fades to black.

TWENTY-ONE

I SLOWLY BECOME SELF-AWARE, BUT MY MIND IS HAZY TO THE POINT where I can't tell if I'm awake or dreaming.

Figuring the solution is simple, I open my eyes.

Though it takes great effort to think, I still have enough wits to note that if the last room they kept me in was cliché, then this room outdoes it in strides. I've never seen a closer representation of an insane asylum with padded walls. Everything around me seems to be made out of cheap pillows in gray pillowcases, including the floor.

There are no cameras that I can see, but I feel someone's unfriendly eyes watching me.

As I could've predicted, when I look down, I see a straitjacket binding my upper body, with my arms forcefully crossed in front and secured in the back. Now that I think about it, I also feel something on my face, and there's a pulling sensation at the back of my head, as if I'm wearing that signature Hannibal Lector mask.

My sense of being watched gets stronger, and I feel like bacterium under a microscope as I try to puzzle out my strange surroundings.

Once I start looking around, I find that the action of thought is getting harder with every second. My senses seem to blur, and I swear I see the restraints holding my arms sprout tentacles of warm light. They paint a pretty mosaic across the room, making it momentarily less gray and unhealthily cheery. The nice colors make my paranoia subside, and I feel good for a moment.

Unfortunately, the warm light soon turns on itself, and it looks as though the room is surrounded by a herd of miniature black holes—places in space determined to suck in all the light and warmth in the universe. Worse, eyes of dark intelligence stare at me from the event horizons, and I get the urge to crawl under the floor pillows.

"Einstein, am I sleeping right now?" I ask out loud and realize that to someone who doesn't know about Brainocytes, this question might seem as crazy as everything else in this room.

Neither the AI nor the real scientist named Einstein reply. From some remnants of critical thinking, I recall this was a way I could tell if I was dreaming or not. Then again, wouldn't the realization of being inside a dream wake me up? And if not, wouldn't my current level of panic accomplish the same trick?

"Is this really happening?" I ask myself, but nothing happens—nor did I expect anything to happen since I can't have a pre-cog moment without a brain boost.

In grim wonder, I watch the black holes turn into smaller black dots. The dots stream toward me to cover my skin like insects.

I wish I hadn't thought of insects, because as soon as I do, my skin feels like an army of spiders decided to battle centipedes on the outer and inner surfaces of my dermis.

If I hadn't been restrained, I'd be clawing at my skin to get rid of the creepy crawlers.

As my breathing speeds up in panic, I tell myself there's nothing on my skin and certainly nothing under it. I tell myself I'm sleeping, but the experience feels more visceral by the second.

I begin screaming, and the bugs fly back into the air and merge into an amorphous malevolent presence in the room. The presence oozes gray colors that spread everywhere, including into my nose and ears. I inhale the gray colors and feel like I'm being polluted and turned into something less human. I try to cough out the poison, but only suck in more grayness into my lungs.

"If you bite off a bolt from a choo-choo train, how does it affect the price of a kilo of hotdogs?" a loud male voice booms all around me. "Keeping in mind that a brick is floating on the glass river, of course."

I'm attempting to compute the question or statement I just heard, when an even louder female voice demands, "What are you *not* thinking about right now?"

I feel like my head is about to literally explode as I ponder the second question, but the burst is prevented by a chorus of new voices that boom, "This sentence is false."

I contemplate screaming again, but it seems impossible to drown out these voices, especially a moment later, when they all begin speaking out of sync with each other, each voice louder than the next, each statement like a knife stabbing into the remains of my fragile sanity.

I no longer feel paranoia. Paranoia is what I am, and she feels me.

I try to ignore the visual and auditory onslaught and meditate, but it's a disastrous idea because it allows me to pay attention to the bodily sensations that, like everything else, are out of control. I'm a beehive of aches that swiftly turn into pains in my right shoulder, which morph into a vaguely pleasurable sensation in my left toe and finally circle back into the pain spreading evenly throughout all my extremities. The rest of me feels like it's made out of clay that someone cured into a solid state and shattered against the wall.

I then try using pure willpower to ignore the sensations and voices, but it's hard. The walls in the room breathe in and out, as though they're the stomach lining of a giant squid that has swallowed me whole and is about to digest me. However, when I close my eyes, sunspots form images on the insides of my eyelids. They remind me of fairies having a rave, followed by an orgy, followed by a laser lightshow. The visuals assault my eyes even through the closed eyelids.

"Have my Brainocytes gone awry?" I ask someone mentally, though I only half recall what Brainocytes are and have no idea who I'm talking to. Realizing questions have a higher chance of getting answered if I ask them out loud, I add, "Have I gone insane?"

"No," I mentally reply to myself. "Can't even think about insanity right now, because if I think it, I might summon it."

The feeling of being watched intensifies, and because I have nothing better to try, I roll on the floor. The movement instantly triggers the feeling of dropping through a soft surface and free-falling like during the HALO jump. Until this moment, that was the worst experience of my life.

As I fall, the air around me takes on the putrid, sulfuric stench of the color gray, and I can taste the pungent sourness of the number twenty. In the next moment, my thinking clears enough for me to recall that colors don't smell and numbers have no taste —but Wi-Fi networks do. Piggybacking on this moment of clarity, I wonder if the voices and tricks of light are somehow being intro-duced from outside my brain? Are projectors and speakers surrounding me? Or is all this stuff being fed directly into my noggin? Something tells me nothing good can come from theo-rizing about thoughts being put into my brain, as that road leads to tinfoil hats. Then again, something also tells me that a properly insulated tinfoil hat made out of something suitable, like lead, could cause my brain to experience connectivity problems.

Realizing my eyes are open, I close them again, and it eases the feeling of my mind melting into a puddle. The free fall turns into a feeling of forward movement, and I swear I'm about to drive into a tunnel made of a kaleidoscope of bright symbols.

With my eyes closed, I wish I could close my ears too, because voices are still assaulting me. In fact, I'd give anything to simply put my hands over my ears, and it's maddening that I can't. I can't even recall the reason my arms are stuck in place, refusing to move. I just know it has nothing to do with aliens.

Actually, the reason is on the tip of my tongue, but I can't quite remember it. Maybe my arms belong to someone else for the moment?

The cursed voices are now speaking as though from underwater, giving me the conviction that time is slowing around me, a feeling I'm familiar with, though I can't recall why.

"I'd like to wake up now," I yell the next time I feel a moment of clarity, but nothing changes and my journey into hell continues unabated.

What feels like a month later, I develop deep revelations about the ultimate nature of reality and wish I had a pen, paper, and hands to write them down with. I feel connected to a web of conscious beings that create the fabric of what we all know as existence. I realize that my world, such as it is, might only be a glorified videogame meant to amuse godlike intelligences that exist outside this plaything universe.

Soon, I understand that these metaphysical musings are there to mask a fear I've been unsuccessfully ignoring. It's a rather familiar fear—the fear of losing my mind. In fact, I recall that this is something I've been worrying about since I learned I had a half-sister with schizophrenia. What really bothers me, though, is that I have trouble remembering what my half-sister's name is or what her symptoms are, for that matter. Part of me even doubts I have a half-sister. I'm certainly not used to the idea of having one.

As soon as I allow myself to consider the possibility of insanity again, panic grows like a parasitic worm in my chest. For a moment, my rapid heartbeat silences the voices, and all I feel is the need to throw up.

A couple of dry heaves later, the sense that I've completely lost my mind grows stronger until it's a conviction deep in my bones. My biggest worry seems to be how my mom will react when they tell her I'm genuinely crazy. What will she say?

"Make it stop," I yell and roll on the cushioned floor. "Please. Someone. Make it stop."

As though in reply, the voices get louder, and the lights in the room flicker from blindingly bright to nearly pitch black with increasing speed. I soon realize that the lights are speaking to me in Morse code, revealing important secrets only the chosen few are supposed to know. They tell me that the experiences in this current life can have a deep impact on the person you might become in the next life.

After what feels like another few years, the lights stop, and the voices speak at a lower volume.

I realize my eyes are open and I'm staring at the door to my room—though I could also be staring at a supernova that's about to explode.

A figure is standing in the doorway. The bright light behind her makes me think of saints or angels, though there's something more reminiscent of an alien visitor about the figure.

The being or person gets nearer. Though her edges are blurred against the gray backdrop of the room, I discern with some disappointment that this is merely a human woman plodding toward me.

A spotlight falls upon the woman's face, and it takes me a only few moments to recognize her gently smiling face. She looks exactly like the therapist I visited a lifetime ago, though it could've been yesterday.

"Hello, Mike," she says calmly. "I'm Dr. Golovasi, your psychiatrist."

TWENTY-TWO

MEMORIES FLOOD MY CONSCIOUSNESS.

As I recall Ada, a galaxy of warmth dances through my heart. I float in happy feelings related to Ada until I remind myself what I'm seeking in my memory. Ada made me see someone named Dr. Golovasi. It had something to do with me having problems sleeping. Ironically, there's a high probability I'm inside a bad dream at this moment.

"Hello, ma'am," I mumble through sandpaper lips. "Are you really here?"

Dr. Golovasi smiles sadly at me. The problem is that her large white teeth seem to come alive and grin at me, though *their* smiles are more sinister for some unfathomable reason.

"Do you know where you are?" Dr. Golovasi asks.

As though scared of her presence, the cursed voices stop screaming in my head long enough for me to consider her question.

"I'm in a government facility," I reply, almost on autopilot. I don't know how I arrived at the answer, but I feel a conviction that it's true. My convictions might not be worth much, though, because I'm convinced the doctor's forehead just sprouted a third eye that can see inside my deepest inner thoughts. The rest of her face looks confused, so I clarify my earlier statement by adding, "I think I might just be inside my head."

Instead of saying anything, she walks over to where I'm lying and helps me sit up. Her hands are soft, and I feel their psychiatric healing warmth spread into the shoulder. I end up sitting in a crouch on the floor. The position is more comfortable and could come in handy if I decide to do some sit-ups later, though I guess it might look crazy if I suddenly started exercising while wearing a straightjacket.

"How would you feel if I told you this is a private mental health institution?" Dr. Golovasi asks, all her eyes, even the third one, radiating caring warmth. "Do you recall getting committed? Do you remember our sessions? What's the last thing you recall?"

"It's difficult for me to think," I say, and the effort required to give her this answer makes me want to rest for a while. Since she just stands there, patiently looming over me, I do my best to recall more. "I remember how I was sitting on a comfortable couch in your office, and we were talking about Russia."

"Yes." She crouches and sits in a lotus pose on the soft floor. Her face is closer to mine, and this makes her third eye dissipate. "That's excellent. Anything else?"

"I recall vague flashes of violence," I say and realize that talking like this seems to make the world around me more solid—proof that talk therapy works miracles, I suppose. "Did that violence really happen?"

"Some of the violence was real." She fiddles with her glasses, her face the epitome of concern. "That's how you ended up in this room. Most of the violence you recall, however, is part of a persistent delusion."

"I hurt someone," I whisper, half to myself, half to her. Images of bitten fingers and stabbed eyes flit through my mind, jacking up my heartrate, and I dry-heave again before gasping out, "Is Ada okay?"

"Ada is taken care of." Dr. Golovasi's posture and serene face make her look like a saint again. "Ada misses you and wants you to get better. We all do."

"What's wrong with me?" I take a breath in an effort to calm my racing pulse. "Actually, wait, I'm not sure I want to know."

"You had an episode," the doctor explains. "You got some ideas in your head that made you distraught. You attacked one of the nurses at this facility and badly injured one of the guards. Do you remember any of this?"

Something about what she says rings at least partially true. I do recall biting someone's finger and stabbing someone with a pen—classic mental patient behaviors. Part of me rejects something about her explanation, though. On some level, I feel like the people I hurt deserved it. They were after me—but could this be my paranoia talking?

"You've been having persistent, intrusive thoughts," Dr. Golovasi says when I don't answer. "Thoughts about being followed, thoughts about a big conspiracy where the government wants something from you. You made progress on some of these issues before the last episode. Does this ring any bells?"

I consider her words, then shake my head. My heart is still thudding against my ribcage in a mad rhythm. "It's all muddy in my mind. It's like what you say sounds familiar, but I don't think it's the full story."

"That's normal," she says. "The fact that you can recognize me again is a big step in the right direction. Yesterday, you thought I was an evil librarian."

"How can I get out of here?" I ask and take another calming breath in an effort not to tell her she does indeed look like a librarian. "I don't like this room."

"You can make progress," she says soothingly. "You can show you're not a danger to yourself or others. I recommend we have a session. Would you like that?"

"I guess." I shift from foot to foot, my bent knees beginning to ache.

"Great," she says. "We can develop tools and practices that will clear your thoughts and center you in the present moment."

"I see," I say and wonder if I should mention that us talking is clearing my thoughts. What's even more impressive is that the voices I was hearing before are completely gone now. "What should we try?"

"Hmm," Dr. Golovasi says, and I realize she has her trusty notepad and pen out and is looking through her notes. "How about free association?" When I look at her blankly, she adds, "I'll say a word, and you blurt out the first thing that comes to you, so long as it's inspired by the word I say."

"Okay," I say hesitantly. "I can try." What I don't add is that she's already made me think of umbrellas and classrooms just by being here.

"Russia," she says.

"Darkness. Trouble."

"Good." She gives me a smile. "Next word. Sister."

"Madness," I say instantly. "Heredity."

"Ada." She points her index finger at me, indicating I should speed up my answers.

"Fluffy puppies, and, err, thongs." I chuckle nervously.

"Joe." She clearly doesn't want me to get a chance to regroup my thoughts.

"Alligator tears." When she doesn't say a new word, I add, "Icebergs?"

"You're doing really well," she says and rewards me with another smile. This time, her teeth merely look like chunks of porcelain. "Now, I'll give you a topic, and I want you to free-associate a true story from your life. I'll start with something safe, something not too personal to you. How does that sound?"

"Sure," I say. "Shoot."

"Open source."

"Hobby."

"No." She gives me an intent look. "This time, I want you to form a story."

"Oh." I try to banish the pretty colors swirling through the doctor's gray hair and do my best to come up with a story about open source.

"I assume you know what open source generally means," I begin. "It's a computer program in which the source code is available to the general public. Of course, the term spread from the software world, and now there are open-source colas and beer, not to mention open source in medicine in the form of pharmaceuticals and genetic therapies, as well as open-source science and engineering." She nods sagely, so I continue. "The reason I said hobby is because I've been helping write open-source software on a number of projects. It started because I wanted to sharpen my C++ skills, and, to a smaller degree, I wanted to give something back. My friends and I use a ton of open-source software as starting points for our apps."

She's still listening, so I go on.

"Once I was part of the open-source community, I learned more about the spirit and purpose of open source, and the more I discovered, the more I liked what I learned. It was a shock because I thought that, as a venture capitalist who invests in software companies, I would be driven by self-interest to find faults with open source." I note that her eyes are glazing over, but my spiel is clearing my mind, so I keep talking. "Open source is a great development model. It's decentralized, and—this is key—it encourages collaboration. Many companies found that, despite intuition stating the opposite, they can and do make money supporting open-source software—"

"This is great," Dr. Golovasi interrupts. "Now here is a new topic. Morality."

Since this therapy is clearing my mind, I share my personal moral philosophy with Dr. Golovasi. As I speak, her hair takes on the appearance of the snakes in Medusa's hairdo but rapidly returns to normal—another sign of my improvement. Her reading glasses try to grow eyes, but the eyes soon dissipate. The story (if you could give my ramblings such a lofty title) takes me something like forty minutes to get out, but then I realize I could've just said two words—the Golden Rule (or is it three words? English can be confusing sometimes). "So basically," I say in conclusion, "I treat people the way I want to be treated."

"Keep it up," Dr. Golovasi says encouragingly. "Next topic —cryptography."

"It's something my friend Muhomor can talk about for hours," I say, then falter as I notice the good doctor's countenance change. She's looking at me with more intensity than ever before.

Something about this topic really bothers me.

I struggle to clear my mind and succeed enough for me to recall something dire about Muhomor.

He's badly hurt.

He was shot.

Remembering Muhomor getting shot triggers a cascade of other memories. I recall the shootout at the Georgian restaurant and the hospital visit that led to me being taken by people claiming to be part of a government task force. I recall the tube up my nose and Agent Lancaster and his questions about Tema—Muhomor's cryptosystem.

Suspicions and revelations mushroom in my brain, then spread through my synapses like a nuclear explosion.

My hands turn into fists as I realize the full depth of the grievances committed against me.

Something must show on my face, because Dr. Golovasi asks, "Is everything okay?"

"You fucking bitch," I grit out through my teeth. "Everything is far from okay."

TWENTY-THREE

PART OF ME KNOWS THAT, DESPITE MY SUSPICIONS, I MIGHT STILL BE crazy. This could be a *Total Recall* type moment that's part of my delusions. Maybe what I think is happening is really the problem, and the truth is what Dr. Golovasi wants me to believe. My counterargument is that if my insanity were that far gone, saving me would require strong medication, not therapy. And if that's the case, being rude to my shrink is the least of my worries.

I have to hand it to Dr. Golovasi. The look of shock on her face is genuine. If her goal was to make me doubt reality, I'd give her at least an eight out of ten. But before I can get lost in my muddy thoughts again, I decide to verify my suspicions by doing something concrete and summoning the AROS interface.

Icons show up across my vision.

Good.

The icons look exactly as I remember—meaning they either work as I recall, via Brainocytes, or they're as real as those snakes that were part of Dr. Golovasi's hair not long ago.

Almost on autopilot, I seek out Wi-Fi connectivity, but alas, I find none. Actually, the lack of internet is a clue. Why make your networks Muhomor-proof in a mental hospital?

Next, I connect with my phone and see if Precious 3 can get onto any new Wi-Fi networks, but again, all is for naught. Seeing the cement room my phone is in tells me I'm either sane or so crazy I might as well give up and wait for electroshock therapy.

I check the video files on my phone and verify that I have my session with Dr. Golovasi in her New York office recorded on there. So I didn't dream that up—unless I'm dreaming now. I also have recordings of some of the things they did to me in this facility, another bit of proof.

Encouraged, I begin recording our new conversation just in case and finally get around to the main reason I opened up AROS in the first place. I run the AROS app I recently wrote—the one that gives me access to the lab on the chip imbedded in my body (assuming that's real too).

The earlier output from the chip was bisacodyl, oxycodone, and acetaminophen. I run the app again, and the output is replaced with a long list of new chemicals. I scan the list and recognize a few entries. Lysergic acid diethylamide is LSD, also known as acid —the famous psychedelic drug. Tetrahydrocannabinol is better known as THC, one of the fun ingredients in cannabis. 5-trimethoxyphenethylamine is the scientific name for mescaline, a drug made from the famous peyote cactus. Also on the list is psilocybin, the active ingredient in "magic mushrooms"—a factoid I happen to know because Muhomor's nickname is Russian for amanita mushrooms. He likes to correct people who think that amanita shrooms (his namesake) contain psilocybin, because they don't. Consequently, the two hallucinogenic chemicals amanita mushrooms do contain, muscimol and ibotenic acid, are also present in my bloodstream. Finally, I also recognize sodium thiopental—a substance I came across in that TV show about spies, where it was used as truth serum.

They gave me a cocktail of drugs designed to make me think I was crazy.

The visions, the bodily sensations, the memory problems, the paranoia, and even my eagerness to chat with the shrink were all chemically induced.

"You wanted me to think I'm a paranoid schizophrenic?" I'm so angry I barely get the words out. "After I told you about my half-sister?" Her eyes bulge, but I'm not even close to done. "You injected me with LSD?" I yell. "And THC?"

I rapidly read off the list of junk in my bloodstream, and with every substance I rattle out, Dr. Golovasi looks more and more like I punched her in the stomach.

"How can you know this?" she finally whispers. "How can you know about the medicine?"

I can't believe she just pretty much admitted to this atrocity—but I'm glad I'm recording it. If I get out of here, her career is over.

Then another wave of revelations hits me.

She isn't a real doctor. She's not worried about her career. She's just surprised I know something I shouldn't, or perhaps she's worried about her organization getting into trouble over drugging a detainee.

Things fall into place, and the universe all of a sudden makes sense—though it's feasible my epiphany is the result of the drugs in my system.

Agent Lancaster mentioned he was part of a task force. They must be a cybersecurity task force with a mission to learn as much as they can about Muhomor in general and his genius invention, Tema, specifically. They had everyone Muhomor knows followed, including me. Thanks to either my brain boost or my innate para-noia, I spotted the surveillance and told the people closest to me that I was being followed—except no one believed me. When the task force got an opportunity, or became extra desperate, they imbedded a secret agent into my life in the form of Dr. Golovasi. Who better to learn secrets than a therapist? Their job is to ask questions. Hell, I recall how interested she was in my friendship with Muhomor during that first session. That should've stood out as an odd interest for a doctor to have, but I was too focused on my problems to notice.

The task force must've hacked our computers, or at least Ada's. Maybe they managed to control Ada's Google searches too. When Ada Googled "best psychologist in Manhattan," the task force made sure she saw a fictional site for Dr. Golovasi at the top of the results. Muhomor has bragged about doing similar hacks, so I know it can be done, no matter how paranoid it sounds.

If all my theories are correct, the woman in front me might not even have a psychology degree, or if she does, she might be an expert in criminal profiling. More likely, though, she's just a CIA agent or something similar.

When I was being uncooperative, I bet it was Golovasi, or whatever her real name is, who suggested they make me think I'm crazy. I told her about my private fears during our therapy session, and she thought she could leverage that against me—and it almost worked.

As my angry haze lifts a little, I realize she's been frantically talking to me all this time, saying something about me falling back into psychosis and delusions again. Her story sounds like the plot for that film where the staff at an insane asylum playacts the hero's delusions as a form of therapy. "You agreed to participate in an experimental treatment," she says. "The medications—"

I tune her out and focus on my legs instead. If I leap fast enough, I can smack her in the face with the mask I think I'm wearing. Though if there isn't a mask on my face, the impact will hurt me as much as it'll hurt her.

Decision made in a blink, I leap forward as quickly as I can.

I brace for impact, but to my shock, Golovasi counterattacks. Her movements remind me of Aikido or another martial art where you use your opponent's momentum against him. More specifically, while still sitting in the lotus pose, she manages to tilt her body left, grab my shoulder with both hands, and direct my motion away from her.

I plop face down onto the soft floor and do my best to regain my breath. The cocktail of drugs they gave me must dampen my pain perception, because I don't feel much. My pride is probably more hurt than my body, since I was thwarted by an old lady in a meditation pose. Granted, she might've gotten CIA training, and I'm a living pharmacy of hallucinogens, which probably isn't helping with my coordination. Still, I thought I had her, and she kicked my ass.

A needle pricks my left shoulder, and I forget about my wounded pride. I'm not sure if it's Golovasi or someone else who injected me with whatever I just got injected with, but I know it won't matter soon.

"You should've talked," Golovasi says, not bothering to disguise the venom in her voice. "I was the good cop."

As the drug takes away my awareness, I reflect on her words. She might actually be telling the truth. She might be the good cop to Agent Lancaster's bad cop. And if so, I shudder to think what I'm going to face when I wake up.

TWENTY-FOUR

I COME TO, AND THE FIRST THING I FEEL IS PAIN ALL OVER MY BODY. Did they beat me while I was unconscious?

Actually, there are other possibilities. They could've beaten me after I half-blinded Agent Lancaster, but before I was tripping on every drug known to man. The drugs could've been masking the pain. This last scenario is likely, because I vaguely recall some bodily sensations that must've been echoes of pain.

The good news is my mind is clear, or as close to clear as possible without Brainocytes. Sadly, that isn't all that clear.

I check for Wi-Fi, but it's still as unbreakable as before. My phone is available to me, so I check if it has internet access— maybe someone moved it to a room with cell reception—but the answer is no. I look through the phone camera and see the same room with the same air vent—the only non-concrete object I can see.

The lab on the chip confirms all the drugs have been flushed out of my system. I don't have any painkillers left in my blood either. No wonder I feel so many aches and pains.

According to my phone, it's November 17, 12:30 p.m. Last time I checked the clock was yesterday, when I had that conversation with Agent Lancaster right before noon. The bad trip must've happened later that day, though I don't know when.

Carefully, I open my eyes.

I'm back in that original cement room—though it could easily be another one just like it. It wouldn't be hard to mass-produce a legion of underground bunker-style rooms like this.

I'm tied to a bed again, but it doesn't look like I have any medical equipment hooked up to me, not even an IV. My throat is sore, and I wonder if I was tube-fed again, maybe even recently.

My other bodily functions are blissfully calm. If that implies I used the bathroom while unconscious and got washed again, I don't want to know about it.

Despite the seeming lack of threats, my mind goes into overdrive with angst. My biggest worry has to do with Muhomor. If Agent Lancaster is to be believed, my friend is in a coma.

My second worry is Ada. She was supposed to leave the hospital, but I recall Golovasi (if that's her name) saying, "Ada is taken care of." What did she mean?

My third worry is a vague one about Mr. Spock. Where is he?

Last but not least, I have no idea if Joe survived that attack. And if he didn't, was Gogi killed with Joe?

As I lie there ruminating about it all, my worry priorities change. I realize my primary concern should be about me. Given how badly I antagonized and hurt my captors, what will the consequences be?

Logically, when they resume their questioning, it'll be worse than what preceded it, but it's hard to imagine the situation getting worse. Though I'm doing my best not to think about torture, I can't help but imagine getting waterboarded. As someone who once choked on soda, I have some idea of what the feeling of drowning is like. I'm guessing the real thing—or its approximation via waterboarding—is a million times worse. Will I talk if they do that to me? And even if I'm able to resist waterboarding right now, could I resist it after not sleeping (or eating or drinking) for a long time?

I'm not going to kid myself. Some things would make me talk for sure. Any of the more brute-force approaches would do the trick, like breaking a bone, blowtorching any body part, drilling a tooth, or cutting off a finger.

The worst part is that even if I decide to talk, I can't tell them anything that would make the torture stop, not if they want the Tema cryptosystem cracked or thoroughly explained. I barely understood Muhomor's baby while on Brainocytes, and even then, only on the same level as a layman comprehends the workings of a TV. We all know there aren't little people sitting in that magical box, but only some of us know that LCD screens work by switching liquid crystals electronically to rotate polarized light.

Something I see through my phone's camera distracts me from my musings.

No, not some*thing*.

Some*one*.

I zoom the camera to make sure I'm not having a residual hallucination, and my heart rate jumps as one of my worries resolves itself.

It's Mr. Spock.

He's sitting behind the ventilation grill, munching on something.

When I puzzle out what he's eating, I nearly scream at him to stop.

The little guy is eating a giant cockroach.

Frantically, I launch the EmoRat app, route the connectivity through my phone, and pray Ada didn't recently do something clever, like routing all the EmoRat app's traffic through a fancy server I can't access without internet.

Mr. Spock stops munching and perks up—and I feel us connect.

I get flooded with rat happiness that proves Mr. Spock was as worried about me as I was about him.

"Where have you been?" I send him through the app. "What happened?"

Mr. Spock reacts to my words with more warmth, but also with confusion. It takes me a few moments to understand why he's being a bit dense. Like me, Mr. Spock isn't as smart as he used to be because his brain boost also requires internet connectivity.

"Why are you eating such disgusting food?" I ask, hoping he can understand something as simple as that.

Even more confused, he replies with the same emotions he typically does when I give him peanuts—his favorite treat. I think he's trying to say, "Dude, this cockroach is yummy."

I project my relief that he's okay and my love for him in general, and he shines with a deep violet aura—his happiest state of being.

He then crunches on his snack and tries to send me the resulting emotions, as though he's trying to say, "See, I told you it's yummy."

I do my best not to gag and wish I had access to Google so I could check if it's safe for rats to eat cockroaches. Common sense tells me it should be, or else New York would be littered with rats that died from cockroach poisoning. I bet that in the wild, rats eat a ton of insects for protein, so why not cockroaches? They're nonpoisonous bugs, after all.

An idea forms, and I ask, "Mr. Spock, can you get outside?"

He doesn't seem to understand, so I try a command I typically use when I'm leaving the house. It tells him to jump in my pocket if he wishes. "Mr. Spock," I send. "Fresh air?"

I see that he recognizes what I said, because I'm hit with a wave of ratty excitement that typically accompanies the idea of riding in my pocket.

I wait to see if he extrapolates the command to be as I meant it, which has nothing to do with going in my pocket.

Gulping down the last of his gross meal, Mr. Spock scurries away, telling me he's probably looking for fresh air, or, just as likely, for me and my pocket.

The app that allows me to see what he sees doesn't work due to lack of connectivity, unfortunately, but I do get an idea of his progress based on the emotions I gleam from the EmoRat app.

After a few minutes, the EmoRat app disconnects, informing me Mr. Spock is out of range from the phone—a sign he went somewhere far, though not necessarily proof that he went outside.

My theory is that Mr. Spock hid somewhere in that helicopter. That means his journey brought him to the ventilation shaft of a garage or hangar or roof—places that are likelier to have exposure to the outside and cellular connectivity, assuming we're near cell towers right now and not somewhere like Antarctica.

What's key is that after Mr. Spock finds fresh air and enjoys it, he must then get back into the app's range. If he doesn't, my idea won't work. I'm hopeful he'll do the right thing, because once he does find cell connectivity, he should get his rat version of the brain boost back, and that will increase the chances of him coming back. Or he might just come back in any case when he wants my company again.

Deciding to work on the assumption that I'll see Mr. Spock again soon, I rush to fully implement my idea and launch the AROS IDE.

Luckily, the required code is something I should be able to handle without the boost, though all the pains in my body and worries about my immediate future are distracting.

The premise of the app is simple. I plan to use Mr. Spock as a high-tech carrier pigeon of sorts. Each Brainocyte is a tiny computer with a basic processing unit and memory. The Brainocytes' resources are limited. This is why we use the server/client architecture that puts most processing and memory requirements in the cloud. But, in a pinch, Mr. Spock's Brainocytes have more than enough memory to store a short email and another app. The new software will run in Mr. Spock's version of the AROS system and scan for internet connectivity. Once the app gets online, it will send the pre-prepared email to a predetermined list of people.

I code away, and the work makes time fly, which is great, especially since my captors are probably leaving me be so I can ruminate in my tied-up boredom. What would usually take me minutes in my enhanced state takes two hours—and by the time I finish, I'm really worried about Mr. Spock not getting back, thus making this whole programming exercise pointless.

I review the code I wrote about a hundred times and test parts of the code that can be independently tested. It would suck if I missed my chance to get in touch with my friends due to a mundane software bug. When I feel like I'd rather have another tube up my nose than review the same lines of code again, I stop coding the email-sending part of the app and write a module to receive emails, in case my friends reply.

When all the coding is complete, I consider what to include in the actual email.

"Hi, all," I begin. "People who claim to be part of a government task force have taken me." I go on to explain my predicament, what they did to me, and take care in describing the people I've encountered. "Ada, the shrink you booked for me is with the CIA or something similar. I know how crazy that sounds, but I assure you it's true. I bet you could confirm it if you dug deeper into her cover as a psychologist. Joe, the pseudo shrink's receptionist might know something. She didn't seem like a government agent to me. Her name is Monika."

I pause and check if Mr. Spock has returned, but the EmoRat app is silent.

To kill more time and stop myself from going crazy, I review my recording of the session with Golovasi to see if I can include anything else in my email that might assist my friends in helping me. I come across something useful, but I'm not sure if I'm upset enough with Golovasi to include this tidbit. Then I decide I am, and end the email with, "Joe, Golovasi mentioned she has a son. It could be part of her cover, but by the way she said it, I don't think so."

Since Mr. Spock isn't back, I work on expanding the email app to support image attachments, figuring I could include a snapshot from the Golovasi videos, as well as one of Agent Lancaster's face.

Once the task is complete, I attach a couple of images of my captors.

When I can't think of any more improvements to the app, or anything to add to my message, I begin to fret about Mr. Spock's return in earnest.

Suddenly, the door to my room opens, and two masked people walk in, dragging some sort of wheeled table.

A green piece of cloth covers the table, but despite the obstruction, the setup makes my bare feet grow colder as blood leaves my extremities.

"What is that?" I demand, trying to sound brave. "And do you realize you're keeping me here illegally?"

Instead of responding, one of the men pulls the cloth off with a flourish. Dumbfounded, I stare at the objects on the table as the two people leisurely exit the room.

Nausea curls in my stomach as I catalog each item. There are mallets, scalpels, saws, drills, a car battery with sinister-looking clamps, and a vast number of sharp and painful-looking things I can't even name.

My worst fears are manifesting.

They plan to torture me for real now.

TWENTY-FIVE

No.

These are government employees, and the government doesn't torture people. Okay, maybe they do, or did, but not officially and certainly not like this—with equipment a Bond villain would cringe at. At least I don't believe they do, even in the case of spies and terrorists. Then again, they shouldn't have pumped me full of drugs either, but they did.

There's a small chance this is a psychological tactic meant to scare me into cooperating. If that's the case, it's working really well.

Battling my nausea, I examine each tool for signs of prior use, but that doesn't lead anywhere. If anything was used before, it's probably been sterilized, and that makes a dark sort of sense. You wouldn't want to give your captives HIV or hepatitis while torturing them, since that would go beyond breaking the Geneva Convention. It's a bit like the alcohol swipe used on prisoners before a lethal injection.

I begin to scream obscenities at my captors and continue until my throat hurts. Then I plead for them not to use this stuff on me and to let me go. I get no results, aside from bringing myself to the edge of a panic attack.

I'm about to burst with worry, when a wave of positive rat emotions interrupts my tribulations.

"Mr. Spock, buddy, you made it back." I cram my message with all the relief I'm feeling. "Please, stay where you are. I need to do something."

I have no idea if he listens to me or runs toward the room with the phone, thus staying in range of the hotspot, but I stay connected to Mr. Spock long enough to load the new app that will turn the rat into a high-tech carrier pigeon.

Now for the trickiest part of all.

"Now, Mr. Spock," I send. "I need a huge favor. I want you to go outside again."

A dose of confusion mars the happy feelings coming from the EmoRat app. Without his boost, the little guy has trouble understanding human language.

"Who's a good little rat?" I reassure him as soothingly as I can. "Don't get scared."

When he's content again, I mentally cross my fingers and try the whole "go outside" thing again, though I fear he might reply with something like, "Hey, fool a rat once, shame on human. Fool a rat twice, shame on rat."

"Mr. Spock," I send casually, as though I'm about to head out for a stroll in Central Park. "Fresh air?"

I guess his lack of brain boost can work in my favor.

Mr. Spock gets excited, and I can tell he's going for it. I just hope he *was* outside when I lost contact with him—a big assumption.

After ten nerve-racking minutes of hoping to lose connectivity with my rat, the EmoRat app throws a connectivity error.

Having nothing new to do, I resume looking at the cursed table and wonder if it's considered a form of torture to make someone wait to get tortured. Eventually, I force myself to close my eyes to stop staring at the damn table.

A couple of seconds after I close my eyes, the horrific drilling sound resumes.

"Hey, I wasn't trying to sleep," I yell, knowing full well that my complaints are pointless. "I'll keep my eyes open. Just shut that down."

The sound remains, so I override the noise with music again. This time, a song by Evanescence comes on.

Since it's 10:12 p.m. and I know it'll take Mr. Spock hours to complete his task, I start playing games on my phone to kill time.

After more anxiety-inducing hours, I decide that, by all rights, Mr. Spock should be back by now. It's almost six in the morning on the eighteenth, meaning it's been an hour longer than the last time I waited for him, assuming that, with all this lack of sleep, my math is correct. Also, is it safe to assume it would take Mr. Spock the same amount of time to go outside and come back as the last time?

In another hour, I start to wonder if I should develop a Plan B.

When no Plan B occurs to me, even after another hour of concentration, I realize I'm starving and thirsty and, paradoxically, need to go to the bathroom. I guess my circadian rhythms know it's morning, and my body is demanding breakfast and a bathroom trip as per usual.

I stop playing with my phone, open my eyes, and resume making myself crazy by imagining the horrid equipment on that table being used on me.

After another half hour that feels like it spans half my life, the door to the room opens.

I turn off the music and find the drilling sound is gone.

Tensing all over, I watch Agent Lancaster slowly amble into the room.

If I thought about it, I would've expected him to be wearing a black patch over his eye, like a pirate. Instead, the entire right side of his face is covered in bandages. He looks more like an unfinished mummy.

"My superiors doubt my objectivity," he says, his voice colder than Siberian winters. "They're sending a replacement inter-rogator to this facility, which means we only have twenty-four hours to enjoy each other's company." He brushes his fingertips over the torture instruments with a lover's caress and adds, "I intend to make the best of what little time we have left."

I open my mouth to plead for mercy, though nothing I say will give this guy his eye back. Before I can get a word out, his cell phone goes off, the heroic ringtone sounding like the theme from a show like *24*. How the hell does *he* have reception in this place? I guess his phone must use Wi-Fi for calls, like some of the more recent phone services allow, or maybe this wasn't a call at all, but an email message or text.

Agent Lancaster looks at his phone, his remaining eye narrows to a slit, and he storms out of the room.

I frantically check the EmoRat app to see if Mr. Spock is in range, but he's not. Did Mr. Spock even get outside? Do my friends know what's going on with me already? Could that message Agent Lancaster received have something to do with it?

Could they somehow save me before he gets around to his grisly task?

For another two hours and forty minutes, nothing happens, and the wait is driving me insane. Suddenly, the door opens again, but instead of Agent Lancaster—and to my slight relief—Golovasi walks in.

"We need to talk," she says, her face wearing a mask of moth-erly concern. "Steven—I mean Agent Lancaster—might have lost it." She scrunches her nose at the torture devices. "I couldn't—"

I don't catch what she says next because, to my huge relief, I'm hit with Mr. Spock's emotions.

"You're the best rat ever," I send him and check for any emails he might've brought me. "I'll get you a whole pound bag of peanuts once we get out of this."

There's an email from almost everyone I know. I'm about to read the email from Ada when I catch Golovasi looking at me quizzically. I guess she didn't expect me to not pay attention to her.

"Look, Jane, or whatever your name is," I reply, my tone clipped. "I understand the game you're playing. Your colleague, Agent Pugh, already tried a similar technique. You're the good cop right now. Lancaster is the crazed bad cop. I watch a lot of Netflix and know the drill."

She looks thoughtful, probably considering how best to handle me. Finally, she says, "He really will hurt you. I can promise you that."

I believe her. Though she's a liar, I'm convinced she's telling the truth right now, and despite my renewed hope, that knowledge floods me with dread.

"It's not like we're asking you to betray your friends or your country," she says earnestly. "We just want—"

I don't listen to her sophistry about the government's need to be able to crack any crypto security that its "enemies" might deploy. Before this debacle, during a recent Brainocytes Club meeting, I argued with Muhomor about this very topic, and my views at the time were sympathetic with what she's saying. Things are different now. I won't lift a finger to stop Muhomor from unleashing Tema into the world, open-source style. Hell, I'll help him, or do it instead of him, just to spite these people.

Holding eye contact and nodding at Golovasi like I'm listening, I read Ada's email.

"Sweetie," it begins. "I hope it's okay, but I had to delay Mr. Spock from going back to you to give us time to do some research into your situation. Look on the bright side. We can now pass some useful information your way. You're going to get messages from the others, but just know I got out of the hospital and no one bothered me, so you don't need to worry about me. Muhomor is indeed in a coma. Your situation made your cousin crazier than usual, and I didn't think that was possible. He thinks he has a way to get you the help you need, but he said we don't want to know the details. You should read his email—"

I stop reading Ada's message, ignore the email from Mitya, and open Joe's, noting there's an attachment to his email, which is odd.

"Her real name is Jean Berger, and she indeed has a son," Joe's email begins, and I feel a chill run down my spine as I look at the person Joe is talking about. "The son's name is Mark. His wife's name is Evelin. Her granddaughter's name is Mary. I'm in their home in Queens. See attached." My mental finger shakes as I double-click on the attachment icon. I see an image of a man my age. His eye is black and swollen, his face looks scared, and Joe's gun is to his temple. "Tell that bitch that if I don't hear back from you in a few hours, I'll kill them, one by one, starting with the kid."

I nearly choke on a mix of horror and relief, but push the emotions aside.

Joe just gave me the little bit of leverage I need.

"Your name is Jean Berger, and your son, Mark, is in deep trouble," I say in a hushed whisper, interrupting Golovasi-Berger's tirade.

She pales and looks over her shoulder, confirming my suspicion that this place has a camera and microphone embedded somewhere. "What? How can you—"

"Come closer," I hiss. "I'll whisper the rest."

She eyes the table, and I can see she's tempted to grab something sharp and stab me. Her motherly instincts win out, however, and she approaches close enough that I could bite her ear if I wanted to.

"Do you know what kind of monster my cousin is?" I ask her as softly as I can, hoping the microphone behind her isn't sensitive enough to pick up my words.

She nods, her chin trembling.

"Then you understand the severity of the situation." I realize I sound inhumanly cruel, but it can't be helped. I don't have much sympathy for this manipulative woman. "Joe is in your son's home. Besides Mark, he also has Evelin and Mary. He says he'll kill them if he doesn't hear from me. He says he'll start with Mary." I describe what Mark looks like in the picture.

"Tell that psycho if he so much as touches a hair on their heads, I'll skin you alive," she hisses vehemently, forgetting to whisper.

"You're wasting valuable time," I whisper. "I don't want *innocent* people to get hurt."

Something inside the woman seems to break. Her shoulders droop, and tears flood her eyes. "Look, I don't know how you're communicating with him, but I can't get you out, even if I wanted to. I'm not—"

"Let's make sure Joe doesn't do anything crazy," I interrupt. "I'll tell him to stand down, but you have to get me onto your Wi-Fi so I can make that connection. Quickly."

She looks confused but says, "The Wi-Fi password is in my phone." She reaches down, plays with her phone, and shows me a long string of digits. "How do you plan to reach your cousin? Do you want me to bring you your phone? It might be faster if you call him with mine."

"Jean." Agent Lancaster's voice manages the impossible feat of sounding colder than ever before. "I can't believe you're falling for his social engineering hacker tricks."

TWENTY-SIX

CRAP. HE MUST'VE HEARD ME CALL HER BY HER REAL NAME THROUGH the surveillance in the room and came to make sure she didn't let me out.

What he might not realize, though, is that I already got something extremely valuable. I recorded the Wi-Fi passcode she showed me, and I'm getting onto their network while they argue.

"How can he know the names of my son and his family?" I hear her ask as though in the distance. "Or that they live in Queens, or what my son looks like?"

"He saw you for that therapy session in Manhattan," Lancaster replies. "He must've hacked—"

I don't hear what the agent says next, because I get online and my brain boost hits me like a ton of pleasurable bricks.

"You've been offline or unconscious for three days," Einstein says. "Current time—"

I ignore Einstein because I'm overwhelmed with the sensation of becoming whole again. It's like regaining sight after being blind for ten years, waking up from a coma, and coming home after a military tour, all rolled into one package and multiplied a million-fold. The time dilation effect kicks in instantly, and I feel like I could write a philosophical treatise in the moment it takes Agent Lancaster to say a single angry word to Jean-Jane.

I form a plan to get out of this place almost seamlessly. Then I realize I can come up with a dozen more, though none will get me out of here as fast as I'd like.

In the span of a breath, I sweep through my captors' computer network and verify this is indeed a government task force, as Lancaster said. Their specialty is cybersecurity, and they recently formed due to some bullshit political pressures. I also see clues that explain past events. For example, when my pseudo-shrink told them about my paranoia, they stopped spying on me for the rest of the day, which explains why I felt relieved after therapy. They genuinely weren't following me anymore. And when they found out Muhomor and I were admitted into the hospital, they freaked out, in part because of some interesting information I discover about Muhomor in the task force's files.

As it turns out, despite all the frequent bragging, Muhomor never told us about his most dubious accomplishments. For example, under other aliases, he's participated in the creation of cyber-weapons for the US, UK, and Israel—software that makes the Stuxnet worm, a weapon designed to sabotage Iran's nuclear program, look like child's play. The agents also think he has a whole database of *kompromat*—the Russian word that stands for blackmail materials.

I soon see that this is why the task force didn't go after Muhomor directly, no matter how much they wanted Tema for homeland security purposes. They had good reason to believe he has a sophisticated version of dead man's switches/insurance in place that would get triggered if something happened to him—like being locked in a room with no access to the internet. The task force believes that much of his kompromat will go public if he's in a jam, and they even worry that automated cyber attacks might hit American and/or Russian targets. These attacks would create a major scandal, because the weapons used would be of state design.

What's really telling is that they fear a scandal more than the cyber threats.

When they learned about Muhomor's condition, they risked hacking some of his servers to prevent his countermeasures from getting released, but it was all encoded using Tema, giving them an extra reason to need to crack the system as soon as possible. Though I get the sense they would've done what they did to me even without the rush.

It's ironic that they feared a scandal from Muhomor, because now, they're going to get one anyway, courtesy of *me*. I upload all the videos from my phone's disk onto Mitya's most secure server in case someone figures out I'm in their network and shuts the whole thing down. Once the videos are safe, I create a nice montage of the most shocking violations of my human rights, shown in the grisliest details. That done, I email the footage to Mitya and start a Teleconference app connection with him and Ada, frantically saying in Zik, "Hey, Mitya. I'm back online. Sorry, but I didn't read your email. What can you do with this video?"

"Mike," Ada responds instantly, her message full of so many turbulent emotions that I can't tell them apart. A torrent of Zik messages follows so fast I wonder if Ada got an extra boost while I was away and can now talk faster than I can register.

"Slow down, please," I interrupt her. "I have a ton of favors to ask of you too, but let me talk to Mitya first. He has connections who can help me."

"Start Share," she demands and appears in the air in front of me as her normal self, only smaller. Her worried face is a balm to my overactive nerves.

I start the Share app so my friends can see what I see. I also locate the camera in my room and send them the video feed. This way, they'll have two vantage points.

"Dude," Mitya butts in, his telepathic message a discernable mixture of concern and relief. "As I mentioned in the email that you didn't read, I know who has you and I started the ball rolling on getting you out." Mimicking Ada, he appears in the room as a small, floating figure near Agent Lancaster's shoulder, and like Ada, he's wearing his usual clothes. "Your task force was formed by agents from the CIA, FBI, NSA, and a slew of other acronyms. A certain Congressman Chandler is the driving force behind it."

I multitask as Mitya talks, doing a quick mental internet search that reveals Congressman Chandler was a victim of a major hack by Russia. Somehow, he turned that embarrassment into a political crusade. It's not surprising that he's behind this task force.

"I'll be meeting with the congressman shortly," Mitya continues. "I'll inform him of what kind of shit his name is about to be associated with, not to mention the fact that I'll spend a few hundred million dollars on negative ad campaigns against him if you're not released in the next hour."

I put a large red circle around the torture table in Mitya's view of my room and say, "You best cut that hour down to minutes."

"Of course," Mitya says, this time out loud. "I'm watching the video you edited, and I can't believe these people."

"Me neither," Ada chimes in, her face full of horrified sympathy. She turns her gaze from me to my arguing captors, and her sympathy morphs into wrath. "I can't believe what they've put you through."

"Let's post that montage on YouTube," I tell them. "Plus the live feed into this room."

"Great ideas," Mitya replies and looks thoughtful for a moment. Then he nods and says, "Video's already on YouTube, and I'm messaging James, my marketing guru. He'll make it his top priority to push that video until it goes viral. The live feed will also go online, and I'll send it to the congressman."

"Speak with Kadvosky as well," Ada suggests vindictively. "Once we're done with these people's credibility and careers, we'll need to destroy them in court."

"And have my cousin visit a few." I nod at the slow-speaking Agent Lancaster.

"That one-eyed asshole will probably end up in jail after all of this is over. For a cop, that can be a fate worse than a visit from

Joe," Mitya says. "I'll also look around their network. If I find something embarrassing, I'll distribute it as publicly as possible."

"Thanks, guys." I switch from Zik to English for emphasis. "I owe you big."

"Don't mention it," Mitya says.

"It'll take a *lot* of sexual favors for us to be even," Ada mentally replies.

"TMI." Mitya's face reddens. Ada must've said her joke in the shared conversation instead of privately.

"Okay, here, look around." I send Mitya the task force's Wi-Fi credentials.

"So," I say to Ada as Mitya starts his work. "I have something I want to ask you to do, something less urgent."

"Of course. What is it?"

"I want to fulfill Muhomor's dream," I say. "I want to make Tema open source."

"I see," Ada says with obvious enthusiasm. She always took Muhomor's side when we argued about Tema's fate. "Once the whole world has access to Tema, this task force will no longer need you."

"Exactly," I say. "But it's also meant as a big fuck-you to them."

"And," Mitya chimes in, "once it's wide, the world will see that Tema is uncrackable, and no one will ever want to kidnap any of us to get some kind of edge on it."

"That's what I thought too," I say. "Which leads me to another, even less urgent idea. I think we should share the Brainocyte design and software with the world—open source it all like I've been suggesting for months. Had these people known about Brainocytes, I'd be in worse shape. The next bunch of idiots might want Brainocytes, and they might kidnap one of us to get it. Plus, of course, my usual argument about openness leading to faster development of more features and apps and cheaper production of nanos, etcetera, ad infinitum."

"You're just distraught and want to disrupt the established world order." Mitya whistles as he considers a world where millions of people become members of the Brainocytes Club. "You know I was never against this idea. Muhomor was."

"I wasn't against it either," Ada says. "And I suspect Muhomor will forgive us once he learns we released Tema."

"Then it's settled," I say, relieved they're going along with my idea. "Mitya, did you talk to your congressman yet?"

"Dude," Mitya says sarcastically. "Congressman Chandler is working on regular-people time, so he obviously hasn't even opened the email yet. But I'll text him and urge him to check his damn email."

"Okay, thanks." I then look at Ada's image and say, "Babe, can you lead Mr. Spock out of the building?"

Since the little guy is still not connected to the internet, I connect him, and he instantly showers me with positive emotions. I guess he likes his brain boost as much as I do.

"I'll get him out," Ada says, and her forehead crinkles in determination. "What do I tell your mom? I've been covering for you, but she's getting suspicious. It's been a few days since you last spoke. Also, Lyuba and Gogi want to know where you are."

"Stall Mom a bit longer," I say. "But you can tell Lyuba and Gogi where I am. How's Gogi, by the way?"

"Healing well," Ada says. "He and Lyuba are keeping Muhomor company."

"I'm sending a car to your location," Mitya says. "Oh, and you'll be happy to learn these morons kept records of the drugs they gave you, as well as the surveillance video of some of the atrocities they did to you—including stuff you missed because you were unconscious. Kadvosky and his gang will have these people's firstborns."

"And speaking of atrocities," Ada says. "Are you listening to that conversation?"

As soon as she directs my attention back to it, I realize I indeed wasn't paying attention to what Agent Lancaster was saying, but I am now, and I hear him say, "I want you out of this room. Now."

Less than a few seconds of real-world time have passed since my friends and I started our hyper-quick Zik chat, so I know I didn't miss much of Lancaster's monologue. I can extrapolate that he said something like, "He lied to you about your son."

The old woman looks scared and for good reason. Lancaster looks like he might choke her if she disobeys his demand for her to leave.

"Joe," I text my cousin. "I'm almost out of this. Don't kill anyone. Talk to Mitya or Ada. We're in touch."

"Where are you?" Joe's reply is again impressively quick for a Brainocyteless human.

"Talk to Mitya about that also," I text Joe. "And I repeat, leave her family alone."

"Fine," Joe answers. "We'll meet shortly."

I gleam a lot of sinister subtext in Joe's words, but since it's directed at people who deserve it, I don't care. Besides, he's not suicidal enough to take on the government.

"Your family is safe," I tell Golovasi-Berger as she shuffles toward the door. Unsure why I'm being nice to her, I decide to get something for myself out of this setup and add, "After you leave, please tell whoever's in charge to call Congressman Chandler. Also, tell him or her to check YouTube for a viral video that'll surely make all of you infamous."

At the mention of the congressman's name, the eyes of the fake shrink and the only eye of the agent look like they want to jump out of their sockets.

"What did you tell him?" Agent Lancaster looks ready to grab a scalpel and slice open his colleague. "What did you do?"

"Nothing." Golovasi-Berger sounds panicked.

"Out," he shouts. Before she even exits the room, he grabs an icepick-like object from the table and leaps at me. "He's going to tell me everything in a couple of minutes. I guarantee it."

"Oh shit," Mitya says in Russian. "That doesn't look good."

"Activate the Relief app," Ada orders me, and I instantly obey.

I enjoy a couple of breaths free from the million aches and

pains plaguing me. I also enjoy how the app dilutes the calls of my body's functions.

Unfortunately, my respite is brief.

Agent Lancaster crosses the distance between us and grabs my left hand in a death grip.

"Oh shit," I say, echoing Mitya's earlier assessment, only I say it in Zik. I cringe and turn away, though I can still see what he does through the video feed from the wall camera. "I don't think the Relief app was designed for something like this—"

I don't finish my thought because I begin screaming.

Lancaster sticks the icepick under the nail of my right pinky finger and slides it into my flesh.

TWENTY-SEVEN

I keep screaming, out loud in Russian and English, but also telepathically in Zik.

My body convulses, and I fear I'm about to lose the contents of both my bladder and bowels.

If the Relief app is lessening this pain, I don't want to imagine what this would feel like without it.

My friends telepathically scream with me.

"I'm ready to talk," I yell at Agent Lancaster as loudly as I can.

"I just found his phone number in their directory," Mitya says. "I'm sending the full Tema algorithm to it."

"Check your phone," I shout. "You got your fucking Tema!"

Instantly, Lancaster's heroic ringtone goes off.

"It might not be my email." Mitya looks at the culprit phone suspiciously. "Maybe it's the congressman. If he's watching the live feed I sent him, I bet he's beyond pissed."

The problem with the brain boost is it makes the agony last longer. After an intolerable millisecond of pain, Agent Lancaster rips the icepick from my poor finger and glares at his phone.

The Relief app masks the pain in my wounded finger, allowing me to finally inhale.

The door to the room creaks open, and Golovasi-Berger storms in with a couple of Suits whose faces I remember from the hospital, plus Agent Pugh.

Just like at the hospital, the Suits are holding Tasers. Unlike at the hospital, it's Agent Lancaster, and not me, they're pointing their weapons at.

"You should speak with Congressman Chandler," one of them says in a hard tone. "Mr. Cohen is to be released, immediately. You are relieved of your duties."

Lancaster looks like a trapped animal, and in a pre-cog-like moment, I can almost see him raising the icepick and jamming it into my eye.

I guess the Suits also see his intent, because without another word, they shoot him with their Tasers.

Lancaster collapses onto the floor, and a person in a surgical mask shows up, seemingly out of nowhere. He injects the twitching agent with a syringe, and Lancaster's body slumps on the floor.

"I think I'll need to run the BraveChill app for a few weeks after this," Ada says. She sounds as shaken as I feel. "Is it just me, or did this agent totally lose his mind?"

"I guess he was attached to that eye," Mitya deadpans. "He must've wanted to literally have an eye for an eye transaction with Mike."

Ada groans, but I focus on the medical person, because he pulls out another syringe and approaches me next.

"Wait," I say. "What are you—"

The needle goes into my arm, and warmth spreads throughout my body.

"This is a good sign." Ada reassures me, though it's unclear if she believes what she's saying. "I bet they're letting you go but don't want you to know where the black site is."

"I would have preferred one of those black bags over my head," I reply, my thoughts already blurring. "And I know where I am."

"I guess it's too late to tell them we already know where their station is." Mitya sounds like he's far away.

"I can't believe I'm getting knocked out again," I send in Zik, and the drug finally does its job, making everything go black.

———

I wake up to the smell of coconut shampoo and the feel of petite hands stroking my back.

"You have been unconscious for five hours and sixteen minutes," Einstein says. "Current time is 5:47 p.m."

Still confused, I assess the situation and realize I must be in a car that's in motion—or sitting on a vibrating mattress, though this seems less likely.

An avalanche of excitement hits me from the EmoRat app, and I feel Mr. Spock cuddle up to my face, his whiskers tickling my cheek.

"What's that, baby?" says a voice that sounds like Ada's baby/rat talk. Since the voice is not coming from an app, I must assume Ada is the owner of the small hands working the kinks out of my back, and the source of the nice scent filling my nostrils. "He's finally awake?"

"I'm awake," I say out loud and open my eyes—only to be met by the pink gaze of my favorite pet.

"Where am I?" I turn over.

Ada's amber eyes are puffy, like she was crying, and the sight makes me want to rip someone's head off, though I'm too groggy to decide whose. As I look, I see fresh tears in her eyes, but I think they're happy tears. Honestly, I didn't let myself fully register how much I missed Ada until now. If, as the old adage goes, distance makes the heart grow fonder, then getting kidnapped and abused by the government makes the heart nearly burst with emotion.

I sit up and find it surprisingly easy to move. A quick check of the lab on the chip reveals why. I'm pumped to the brim with painkillers.

Unbidden, my arm goes around Ada's waist, my palm landing on my favorite spot—the two dimples in the small of her back. She leans into me, and I pull her in for a kiss. Her lips quiver as they explore mine, and her breathing quickens as her tongue begins to—

Someone loudly clears his throat, and I pull away from Ada to look around the car—something I probably should've done first.

We're inside a massive limousine, surrounded by a bunch of people who I assume work for Joe, because he's also here. When Joe spots me looking at him, his somber expression twists, and he does something I didn't think I'd ever—and I mean *ever*—see him do.

He winks at me.

Maybe he developed a nervous tick that I mistook for something playful?

"It's official," says a familiar voice from my right, and I realize this is the person who cleared his throat a second ago—Gogi. "You'd sleep through Armageddon."

I turn and see that Gogi is sitting between a couple of extra-large dudes, and there's a pair of crutches at his feet. He looks much better than I expected him to after four days of recovery.

"How are you feeling?" I ask and can't help but grin at the Georgian's good humor. Telepathically, I ask Ada, "So, what happened?"

In the time it takes Gogi to tell me he's healing okay, Ada gives me the rundown of what happened while I was out in swift mental Zik messages. She starts with a quick update on some of the technological advancements these guys have come up with in a deceptively short time. The most interesting development is Mitya's new algorithm that allows Einstein to pilot a drone—something that will severely cut costs for Mitya's drone delivery system that services New York and New Jersey (since the current system uses human pilots). I then learn that both Tema and the Brainocytes got released as soon as I was knocked out, and the releases are exploding the brains of everyone in the cryptography and tech fields. Amazingly, in a few hours, at least fifty articles were published on the subject of how the Brainocytes could be used. Some of the ideas proposed are things we, the arrogant Brainocytes Club members, never imagined. Ada sends me her favorite ten ideas so I can review them later, and then she moves on to a less pleasant topic that she would clearly rather avoid.

Thanks to Mitya's marketing people, my videos, especially the one where the tube is going up my nose, have gone viral. JC has been working hard at making sure my mom doesn't see the videos, but I'll have to tell her what happened at some point, or risk her hearing it from the news. Human rights organizations are on the warpath over the videos, which is good, but I'm forever cursed to be a celebrity of sorts, which is bad. A popular senator, who had experienced torture as a war prisoner, tweeted a condemnation of the things done against me, as did leaders of many countries around the world. The president hasn't commented yet, but several US government officials, both elected and appointed, already held a record number of press conferences. Some claimed that at least part of the torture was medical assistance provided to a suspect detained after sustaining severe injuries—baloney, in other words. Some also said my capture was based on faulty intelligence, and later conferences suggested the actions committed against me were the result of an agent gone rogue. Both Ada and I know this is just a case of scapegoating.

"All the medical people at that facility lost their licenses, even the woman whose finger you damaged. Everyone else behind the task force will regret their actions," Ada concludes, her real-world eyes getting that dangerous gleam I've learned to be wary of. "After the news cycles complete their witch hunt for whoever the media deems responsible, we'll unleash Kadvosky and his lawyers on any survivors and make them wish they never heard your name."

"I think you should take it easy," I tell Gogi. At the same time, I mentally tell Ada, "Thanks, but you never explained how I ended up here, in this limo, with this entourage."

"That's simple," Ada says out loud, and no one in the car so much as blinks at the sudden reply to an unasked question. "The government people dropped you off at the Hackensack University Medical Center in New Jersey. As soon as I learned your location, I wanted you transported to the NYU Langone Medical Center. Your cousin demanded the security detail tag along—"

"And she insisted on joining," Joe intrudes, and I can tell he and Ada must've argued about this issue. Somehow, he lost. "Nor did I want this invalid here." Joe points his index finger at Gogi accusingly, but the Georgian doesn't look chastised.

I look through the tinted window. The sight of greenery crisscrossed by electrical towers, as well as the warehouses and factories in the distance, suggests we're still in New Jersey. Einstein confirms this via GPS.

Still looking at the road, I start the Teleconference app and invite Mitya and Ada into the session.

Mitya says, "I'm still in the air, but I should be in New York soon." He must see my avatar show up in the room in front of him, because he smiles and adds, "Oh, if it isn't Sleeping Ugly."

"I'll let that slide, given how much you've helped me in the last few hours," I say. "Do you guys have an update on Muhomor?"

"You didn't tell him?" Mitya asks Ada.

"I didn't get the chance," Ada counters. "Here, Mike, watch this video. It was taken from the hospital security camera."

I see a hospital room that looks a lot like the luxury accommodations they have at the NYU Langone Medical Center—our destination. There's a bed in the middle of the room, and Muhomor is set up with medical equipment that gives me an unpleasant flashback.

A bunch of people are there, including a blond woman with classic good looks whom I recognize as Lyuba—Muhomor's ally, but not girlfriend. She's visiting from Russia. Ada is among the crowd, telling me I'm looking at a recording rather than a live feed.

Seeing Muhomor like this is sad. It's probably the longest I've seen him not say something snarky.

Suddenly, the monitoring equipment beeps, and medical

people begin to murmur. Even without a medical degree, I can see what happened.

Muhomor's eyes are open, and he's trying to say something.

"How are you feeling?" a doctor asks him in the video.

"Viktor, can you hear us?" Lyuba asks in Russian, her hand on his wrist.

Muhomor keeps mouthing the same phrase over and over, and when I eventually hear it, I can't help but chuckle. "This hospital's cybersecurity is atrocious," he's saying. "I want all my personal data expunged from this sorry excuse of a database. I want—"

I stop the video. I suspect Muhomor's rant might be long, and I just wanted to know how he's doing.

"How is he now?" I ask Mitya and Ada and notice they're each waiting for the other person to answer the question—not a good sign.

"He's paralyzed from the waist down." In the real world, Ada puts her hand on mine reassuringly. "The doctors say this was the best-case scenario."

I grasp her hand and sever my emotional link to Mr. Spock, lest he experience too much of my sadness.

"How are his spirits?" I ask, unsure what to say in the midst of such a horrific revelation. "Is there anything I can do?"

"Why don't you ask him?" Mitya says. "I just invited him to this conversation."

"Misha." Muhomor's telepathic message is filled with way too much excitement. "I was just talking about you with Mitya."

"Yeah," Mitya echoes sarcastically. "Why don't you tell *him* what you just told me?"

"Sure," Muhomor states in Zik and manifests his usual anime-inspired avatar into the limo. "I was saying how glad I am that Mike was tortured."

I'm distracted for a second by the depressing knowledge that while Muhomor's avatar is standing on cartoon legs, real-world Muhomor will never be able to stand like that again. Then his words hit me. "What? You're happy I was tortured?"

"I'm happy about the consequences of it," Muhomor clarifies. "Not the actual pain you suffered per se, but that's irrelevant to my point."

"That's nice," Ada chimes in. Her sarcasm has a dangerous edge. "Very empathetic."

"All I'm saying," Muhomor continues, unfazed, "is that it was genius of you to release Tema and the Brainocytes on the tail of this torture business, even if I wish you'd asked my opinion on releasing the latter."

"How so?" I ask. "I mean, I'm glad I got myself tortured for the greater good, but it would be nice to know what that greater good is or was."

"When contemplating the release of Tema, one of my big concerns was that the government might want to regulate or suppress it." Muhomor's avatar sprouts a cartoony pipe and puffs out a cloud of cartoon smoke. "But now, with you as the figurehead behind these technologies, things might go differently. Think about it from a politician's point of view. After all the wrongs the government has committed against you, no one wants to be known as the guy who picked on you again by attacking your intellectual achievements. In other words, whoever decides to suppress your technologies will look like they're trying to pick on you—and no one should, since they'd get tainted by this torture business."

"That makes a warped kind of sense," Mitya says. "Especially if politicians thought like you, Muhomor. Thankfully, they do not. I think this is a moot point anyway. There's little chance of suppressing either technology, given the way I distributed them—worldwide. The power these will bring will cause a paradigm shift. Suppressing it in the US would just mean the US would technologically fall behind more forward-thinking countries. Like China, for example."

We sit quietly for a moment, each imagining what the world will be like once the Brainocytes are ubiquitous.

I know I'll regret this, but I say, "Muhomor, at some point, you've got to tell us about your kompromat and cyberweapons. The task force feared you had dead man's switches prepared in case you got into trouble. Is that true?"

"To quote Machiavelli, it's better to be feared than loved," Muhomor replies cryptically. "I will only tell you about these things when I feel like I have enough kompromat on all of *you*, and I don't feel that way—yet."

"On that nice, friendly note, Mike and I are going to disconnect," Ada says. "Glad to hear about your improving health, *Viktor*."

"We're going to disconnect?" I ask in the real world.

"Yes," she replies telepathically. "I've been meaning to talk to you about something important for what feels like a year, and I don't think it can wait."

"All right, guys," I send into the group conversation. "We'll be back in a bit."

"Someone's in trouble," I hear Muhomor tell Mitya as Ada and I disconnect.

"Am I in trouble?" I ask Ada, my pulse accelerating.

She looks at me with uncertainty for a real-world second—a long time telepathically.

A sick feeling curls in my stomach as I remember my suspicions about Ada's strange behavior in recent weeks. My paranoia about being followed turned out to be warranted, so could my worry about Ada's behavior be as well? Desperate, I blurt out, "Would you really break up with me so soon after I was tortured? Have you no heart?"

Ada looks taken aback. "What? No, you're not in trouble," she mentally replies. "At least not *that* kind of trouble."

I exhale in relief. "Okay, then what *is* this big talk about?" Before Ada can answer, my brain-boosted mind runs through different possibilities, each scarier than the next, and my stomach plunges again. "You're not sick, are you?"

"No. Not sick. Not exactly, anyway. It's more of a big news sort of deal." She chews on her lower lip. "A big surprise. Because of how unexpected it is, I wasn't sure how to tell you."

"Tell me what?" If I wasn't communicating telepathically, my voice would've probably betrayed my panic. An improbable suspicion flits through my mind, but I dismiss it, because what are the odds?

"I'm pregnant," Ada blurts out in emotionless Zik. "Or is it more appropriate to say *we* are pregnant?"

"We're pregnant?" I yell out loud, switching to Russian—something I've never done under stress before. My improbable suspicion was spot on—another score for my boosted intelligence. Not that having had that glimmer helps; I still feel utterly shell-shocked.

Ada looks around us, her cheeks reddening. "I meant for this to be a private, telepathic conversation," she says, also out loud, and I realize Gogi and my cousin are staring at me. Gogi wears a shocked expression, but Joe looks like he's in thoughtful contemplation.

Kiril, one of Joe's Russian-speaking goons, gives me a thumbs-up and starts to say something, but Joe gives him a quelling look. I interpret it as, "Don't fuck with my cousin right now. He just made me an uncle, and I always wanted to be someone's uncle."

Even Mr. Spock, who isn't linked to me via the EmoRat app, picks up on the tumult of emotions in the air and peeks out of my pocket, glancing at Ada and then me, his nose twitching nervously.

I tear my eyes away from the rat and stare unblinkingly at Ada for a couple of breaths.

Ada doesn't blink either, her gaze expectant. She's probably waiting for some sort of reaction from me.

"I don't know what to say," I finally say, still out loud. "This is huge." Then, telepathically, I add, "I'm not calling *you* huge. I can't actually tell you're pregnant—"

Figuring now is a good time to shut up, verbally and mentally, I reach out and give Ada a tight hug. With her warm body firmly pressed against mine, I process what she told me and feel like I'm riding a roller-coaster, though I'm not sure if I'm spiraling up or down.

Ada relaxes in my arms, and I realize I must've done the right thing.

It takes all my willpower not to say something idiotic like, "How could this happen?" Instead, I use my mind to quickly search the internet for answers. We always use condoms when we have sex, but I quickly learn that condoms *can* break, and the tear in the latex is invisible to the naked eye. Considering how much sex we have and with how much vigor, I can see how that could happen. As it turns out, when looking at it statistically, condoms are eighty-five-percent effective in actual use, so Ada and I are among the lucky fifteen percent. A few other things also make sense. Ada felt pretty nauseous a few days back. She didn't drink any vodka or wine, even the Georgian wine that's organic and vegan without egg whites or gelatin. Also, and this was the big clue, her period is usually at the beginning of the month, yet we never stopped having sex this month, meaning her period never happened. And—

"We never got a chance to talk about kids," Ada mentally interrupts my chain of thought. "I now wish we had."

"That's not entirely true. We had that one conversation," I remind her. "When you said one day you wanted to use CRISPR and other genetic modification tools to make a super baby with biological super intelligence, extreme longevity, enhanced empathy, and I forget what else."

"Right." She pulls away from the hug, and I see that she's smiling. "You mean that day when you said you'd prefer to make a virtual baby, 'a merger of our minds, not our genetics,' one we'd only experience via Virtual and Augmented Reality interfaces—so no diapers and other unpleasantness?"

"I guess we're both going to experience something far more mundane." I lay my right hand on her knee and run my left hand through her spiked hair. "I'm sure it'll be very interesting. Just think about it. Building an artificial general intelligence is such a difficult problem, even with the Brainocytes, yet a baby basically starts off as a dumb bundle of cells that grows to gain general intelligence out of the box. Just provide some coloring books, some food, some love, and some toys and other entertainment. Maybe we can learn how to—"

"I want to give the baby Brainocytes," Ada mentally interrupts and gives me a worried look in the real world. "As soon as it's safe to do so."

"That sounds like a cool idea," I reply without hesitation. "Some people might see it as experimenting on the baby, but to me, it's no different from those people who play Mozart to their baby or get them fancy tutors and toys. We'll be able to communicate with our kid before he or she can speak. We can probably modify the EmoRat app to—"

I stop talking, confused by the sheer amount of adoration in Ada's beautiful eyes.

"What? Is it something I said? I mean, thought?"

She shakes her head. "I'm just happy. You're going to be a great—"

Ada doesn't finish her thought because, in that moment, a gunshot rings out, and the tinted limousine back window shatters into small pieces.

TWENTY-EIGHT

My pulse jumps, and adrenaline floods my veins. Through the shattered window, I see a red truck on our tail. It must be the source of the gunfire. There's not much traffic on the freeway otherwise, with more cars ahead of us than immediately behind. Still, there's a small chance the shot came from a car hiding behind the truck.

I squint and confirm my suspicions about the truck. There are two people in the front seats. A black motorcycle helmet obscures the driver's face, something that's suspicious on its own, and not just because it thwarts the facial recognition app. However, it's the second person, the one with the assault rifle pointed at our limo, who seals my conviction that the truck is up to no good.

I don't need an app to recognize that I'm staring at the killer chimpanzee mug of Vincent Williams.

Just when I think the truck is the only vehicle we need to worry about, I hear the roar of two-stroke internal combustion engines revving, and four motorcycles appear from behind the truck. They must've been hiding there. The bikers are wearing helmets like that of Williams's driver, only one of them drew a fierce scowling skull over his or her helmet.

The rush of adrenaline puts my boosted mind into that sloweddown battle mode, a sensation that's unfortunately beginning to feel familiar.

My first thought is about Ada's safety, and I wonder if it's the pregnancy variable making me feel so savagely angry at the attackers. I feel myself becoming wrath. I wouldn't be surprised if I burst into green skin and rippling muscles. If I had the chance, I'd beat every one of our pursuers to death with a small hammer and then do something equally awful to their corpses.

Ada and I are still sitting within hugging distance in the back, meaning she's much too close to danger. I grab Ada by the shoulders and pull her toward the middle of the limo while telepathically saying, "Stay here, baby."

She's in so much shock that she complies—or she's just smart enough to comply. My logic for putting her in the center is that, with all these men around the car, the middle is the safest place. To reach Ada, the bullet will have to go through me or one of these men—a sacrifice I'm willing to make.

While I'm taking care of Ada, my brain boost allows me to pay attention to the world around me. I'm aware that Joe and his people sprang into action at the same time I did. Gogi gets up too, but it's clear that moving hurts him. Two men—Luke and Carter, according to the face recognition app—already have their guns out and are leaping for the broken window, probably moments away from shooting back. Everyone else, including Joe, is reaching for the seat they were sitting on—though I can't fathom why.

A number of facts surface and congeal into a partial explanation of what's happening. Agent Lancaster was adamant about not having anything to do with Vincent Williams's attacks. There was a point when I wasn't sure if he was telling the truth, but I later believed him, mostly because his words were supported by the fact that Muhomor nearly got killed during the attack at the restaurant, and the task force wanted Muhomor alive—in part due to his insurance policy, and in part because they wanted Tema. I also suddenly recall something that slipped my mind while they were holding me prisoner.

Williams mentioned a list when we faced each other. That list doesn't make sense in the context of the task force, but it does if someone has a bone to pick with Joe and me. So, if Vincent Williams attacked us for reasons unrelated to the task force, it stands to reason he would still be after us, even though the task force is done with me. Then again, whatever his original mission, Williams is likely after us now to avenge his brother's death.

Thanks to the boost, I think all these thoughts while Luke and Carter only make a millimeter of progress toward the window, moving as though underwater.

Joe and the rest are also still reaching for their seats.

Since I have no gun and no plan, I decide to do something that won't take much real-world time and jump back into the virtual conference with Mitya and Muhomor. As soon as I connect, my friends' images show up in the already crammed interior of the limo. Grateful for the speed with which we can communicate in Zik, I do my best not to sound too hysterical as I summarize the situation, concluding with, "It's Williams again. Oh, and Ada has to survive at all cost. She's pregnant."

In this moment, Ada also joins the conversation. She must've recovered from her initial shock.

"We need to work together to get us out of this." Ada's Zik is again quicker than normal. "Mike, you take the lead, like during the gunfight at the restaurant."

"Got it," I reply, careful not to point out that she's taking a lead by assigning me a role, since I'm grateful she did.

I have to give Muhomor and Mitya credit. They don't say a peep about Ada's pregnancy or complain about her bossing everyone around. Instead, in unison, they ask, "What can I do?"

"Muhomor, you're on reconnaissance and, if possible, sabotage duty," I rattle out. "Mitya, I want you to come up with a plan. Get police on the phone and find us a good place to go and maybe supplies we can use—"

"I'm already in the process of hacking into some satellites." Muhomor's anime avatar rubs his cartoony hands together in anticipation. "Also, I'll see if I can get into your pursuers' phones or their vehicles' computers."

"I don't have a plan yet," Mitya chimes in, "but let me enumerate some useful information. First, you're driving in my limo, which—"

"Please tell me it's one of the Zapo rip-offs," I interrupt. "The ones you asked Sven to mod? That would be awesome news."

"And please tell us that unlike the window, the rest of the limo is bulletproof," Ada adds. "Because in my opinion, *that* would be awesome news."

"I don't own any bulletproof vehicles," Mitya replies defensively. "Unlike some people, I don't have any enemies. Also, I wouldn't say it's a rip-off per se. An argument can be made that Zapo was a rip-off—"

"No time to argue about originality," I cut in. "Is it a limo that can be remotely driven with the Batmobile app? The one with a bunch of sensors all around it, a nitro boost, and so on?"

In the real world, Luke and Carter finally reach the window and shoot. The sound reverberates through the confined space, and Ada mentally curses. The motorcyclists or the people in the truck shoot back. I hear Luke grunt and see him clutch his shoulder. Carter is fine and returns fire.

The gunshots scare Mr. Spock to the point where his mental aura is a nervous gray. I do my best to reassure him through the app. Mr. Spock's mood turns amber, and I feel a pang of jealousy. I wish someone could do for me what I just did for him, because if I were a rat, my aura would be the darkest black.

Meanwhile, my cousin and his people open the limo seats, and I finally understand why. Under the seats is storage, and it contains an arsenal that would make a warlord squeal in glee. At a glance, I see guns, bulletproof vests, and even something that looks like a rocket launcher.

"Yes, it's one of those limos, and yes, it's Sven's work. Before you ask, I told your cousin about that storage space, though I didn't think he'd turn it into an armory." Mitya's reply is only slightly grumpy. "The limo is currently being driven by Einstein. The driver is just there to open doors for you guys, so you can have your cousin hand him a gun. Eli is a Gulf War vet, so he can probably assist you."

"Joe," I say out loud. "Toss me a gun and pass one to the driver."

Joe doesn't just throw me a gun; he also pulls out a stack of bulletproof vests and tosses three my way. He then scoots up to the small window, where the driver's hand is already sticking out, and gives the man a gun. I put on one vest and hand both the smaller and the larger ones to Ada, figuring two vests are better than one. To emphasize the importance of my request, I address Ada out loud. "Put those on, please."

I then hand Mr. Spock to Ada, figuring she's bound to stay safer if she's protecting him as well as herself.

Then I recall she's already protecting something small—our unborn baby—and this thought brings back the blinding anger. It threatens to overtake me, but I push it back for now.

I need a clear head to deal with this.

"Protect her," I tell Mr. Spock through our mental connection. "Do your best to keep her calm."

I could swear Mr. Spock gives me a small nod before letting Ada stuff him into her bra under the bulletproof vest. I bet he's already bruxing in the warm comfort of her bosom.

While I examine my new gun and put on the vest in the physical world, I also keep the hyper-fast virtual conversation going with my faraway friends. "Mitya, take over driving the limo. You have a brain boost, so your response time should be better than any normal human driver and, in this case, better than the safety-obsessed Einstein."

"Done," Mitya says. "I'll take you to my LAR facility. It's only fifteen minutes away."

Again, I multitask by doing more than two things at once. I enter the information of the gun my cousin gave me into the aim-assist app while also researching what Mitya meant by LAR. A millisecond later, I find out he's talking about Levin Aero Robotics, the facility that produces and stores his delivery drones. While I do all that, I tell Joe out loud, "Can you spare two men to protect Ada with their bodies? I want her inside a human pyramid."

I expect my cousin to protest or say I should be either at the front or back of the pyramid I proposed, but he nods decisively at Gogi and Luke. "You heard him. Gogi, bind Luke's shoulder while you're at it."

His choices make sense. Both men are wounded and can't help in the fight anyway. Gogi grunts in pain as he gets to the floor, and Luke follows him. This is the only situation I can imagine when it would be okay for other men to be so close to my Ada. Once she's in that protective formation, I feel like I can exhale the breath I've been holding since the shooting began.

"Why are you taking us to LAR?" I ask Mitya. "It's just a glorified factory."

The gun information—Beretta 92—registers with the app, and when I enable the HUD overview, a bullet count of fifteen shows up in the corner of my vision. This gun feels a bit bigger in my hand than the Glock I've been practicing with, and I hope that doesn't affect my aim.

"There are four security guards on LAR's premises," Mitya explains. "And it's not just a factory. It's also a storage facility where we do some research and development—"

"Just take us to the damn LAR." Ada looks unhappy about her passive position. "It'll give the police a specific location to go to and—"

"This isn't the best plan." Muhomor imbues his message with worry, though he's watching the events from far away in a hospital bed. "I just checked the satellites. Four more cars and five more motorcycles will join you at the next exit, and I don't think you can get to LAR without passing by that exit. I'll send everyone the link to my view."

In a fraction of a second, I see what Muhomor is talking about. Vehicles are turning onto the exit in question. The black helmets leave no doubt that these people are in league with the bikers behind us.

"Well, the limo can't get anywhere without passing that exit anyway," Mitya says, and I have to agree with him. We already passed the ramp leading off the freeway, and the tall walls on either side of the road prevent us from going off-road, either intentionally or by accident.

"How many drones do you have parked at LAR?" Ada asks Mitya. "I think I have an idea."

"A hundred percent of the ones that deliver in New Jersey," Mitya says. "And forty percent of the ones that service NYC."

As Ada and Mitya talk telepathically, I say out loud during a pause in the gunfire, "Joe, we're about to have more company."

"Mitya, does this screen work?" I ask, nodding toward the gigantic TV located next to the little window on a wall that separates the driver's section from the passenger side.

"Yes, it does," my friend replies. "I'll put up a regular Skype window there so Muhomor and I can speak with your cousin and the rest of the Brainocyteless."

"I also want you to put feeds from various cameras around the car," I say. Realizing I haven't taken the time to put the feeds from those cameras onto my AROS overview, I do so.

"Mitya, I'm taking over control of all the available drones." Ada's telepathic message is a fury of determination. "These fuckers pissed me off."

"Shit," Muhomor messages me privately. "If pregnant women are anything like bears with cubs, Ada might be a sight to behold right now."

Before I can reply to Muhomor, another bout of automatic gunfire rings out, and the side windows shatter into little pieces, raining onto the carpeted limo floor.

The cameras show that the gunfire came from the motorcyclists who were hiding behind the truck. There are four of them, and they sped up to flank us on both sides.

Two motorcyclists are level with the front doors, while the other two are level with the middle. What's worse is they're all aiming their Uzis at us, ready to shoot again.

I brace for the blast of noise and deadly danger.

"I got this," Mitya says from the screen. "It's going to get a little bumpy."

"Dude, wait," I mentally send, but it's too late.

Tires screeching, the limo veers toward the left side of the road.

TWENTY-NINE

GOGI CURSES AS HE NEARLY FALLS ONTO ADA. JOE AND MOST OF HIS guys grab on to the tops of the seats, and I follow their example, my wrist feeling like it might come out of its socket.

"I know this isn't a good time to complain about someone's BO," Ada shares in a telepathic chat, "but if we survive this, I'm getting Gogi a case of deodorant."

The driver's door of the limo crashes against the middle of the front-most bike, resulting in another unpleasant bump for us. The bike flips in the air, tossing the rider off like a mad bull at a rodeo. The motorcyclist's black helmet slams against the asphalt, and he rolls under the limo's back wheels. It feels like we hit a speed bump as we run the guy over.

I hope the downed bike trips up the second motorcyclist driving right behind it, creating a nice chain reaction of death for our pursuers, but the second guy must've worked as a stunt driver. In a brain-boost-worthy display of quick reactions, he lets go of his Uzi, grabs the hand grips until his knuckles turn white, and pulls in a jerky motion. His front tire lifts at just the right moment, and he runs his bike up the obstacle in the most impressive way possible. After the guy successfully finishes his maneuver (and probably feels a rush from that accomplishment), Joe shoots him in the head. The motorcyclist falls sideways with his bike without letting go.

He has a literal death grip on it now.

The motorcyclists on our right must be upset with the fates of their leftmost brethren, because they frantically shoot at us again, as do the two assholes in the truck behind us.

"What happens if they hit our tires?" Ada asks inside the virtual conference. Her wide-eyed avatar looks as panicked as I feel.

"The limo's tires are airless," Mitya says. "Didn't Sven put the same ones on Zapo?"

"You know he didn't," I reply, glad that transmitting jealousy is optional when using the Telepathy app. "What else can this car do that Zapo couldn't?"

"I'll give you the full specs when we have a free moment," Mitya promises. "For the time being, let me focus on my driving."

As though to illustrate Mitya's request, the limo wobbles, and I can tell my friend is trying to regain control of the vehicle. This means he can't repeat the maneuver he performed against the rightmost thugs. I decide to deal with them myself, or at least the front-most one since my window is closest to him. Knowing these people are shooting at pregnant Ada leaves me with few qualms about their fate. Yet, out of morality or hypocrisy, I don't shoot my target in the head. Instead, I place the line from the aim-assist app on the guy's right wrist and pull the trigger.

Since my target was effectively driving one-handed, he loses control of the bike and somersaults through the air. His bike skids across the asphalt, sparks flying everywhere, and in the satellite view, I see some bystander's Toyota Camry hit the bike and swerve into the freeway wall.

"Okay," I say into the virtual conference. "Now we only have to deal with the one remaining biker asshole on the right."

"And the truck behind us," Ada reminds me telepathically.

"And the people ahead of you," Muhomor adds.

They're both right, of course. The truck is still on our tail, and according to the satellite view, we're going to pass the ramp leading onto the freeway in a couple of seconds.

Another shot rings out from the truck behind us. I use the camera inside the limo to see that Carter got hit, and his neck wound looks bad.

Joe and Caleb, the guy on his left, both dive for the unprotected back window. This is when I notice that Joe is shouldering the portable missile launcher.

"I think that's Russian," Muhomor says. "RPG-7."

"What are you talking about?" Mitya asks telepathically. "Don't distract me with video-game talk. Now that I've evened out the car, I'm going to do that maneuver again."

In a flash of insight, I realize Mitya isn't seeing what's happening inside the limo at the moment, and he thinks Muhomor is talking about Role Playing Games instead of the Ruchnoy Protivotankovyy Granatomyot. In that same flash of insight, I see a big problem with what's about to happen and mentally yell, "Wait—"

Mitya either doesn't hear me or my message arrives in his brain a moment too late, because the car swerves right—exactly as Joe shoots his rocket/grenade.

The last motorcycle guy, the one with the skull painted on his helmet, slams into the back of the limo and cartwheels backward in a mess of metal and meat.

Unfortunately, Joe's missile doesn't even scratch the truck as it flies by and explodes against the freeway wall. The bang is so loud it blows out the remnants of glass from the window in front of me and turns Mr. Spock's aura black.

Through the ringing in my ears, I become aware that Muhomor is chastising Mitya for ruining Joe's shot while Ada's telling them to focus on the task at hand.

Shaking off the stunned feeling, I look at the cavalcade of enemies that just got on the freeway up ahead. They're slowing, which means we'll have to deal with them soon.

"Do you see that Jeep Cherokee?" Muhomor's question jerks

me out of my thoughts, and I realize I was just looking at the car he named.

"Yes," Mitya says. This must've been part of an argument they're having.

"This is how it's done." Muhomor's avatar waves his hand in a gesture worthy of a crappy magician, and the Jeep Cherokee's tires suddenly stop spinning, causing the driver to lose control. As the Jeep careens into the freeway wall, it takes out one of the bikers.

"Great job," I chime in. "Now do that to the rest."

"The rest aren't as hackable as the Cherokee was." Muhomor's avatar suddenly appears less smug. "I'll keep trying, though." More defensively, he adds, "I've been distracting your opponents by having their phones text each other nonsense and vibrating at random. It beats messing up someone's RPG." Muhomor gives Mitya's hoodie-clad avatar a derisive stare.

I ignore Mitya's reply and my own racing heartbeat as I assess the remaining enemy forces ahead. There's a yellow Hummer driving in the rightmost lane, a silver 4Runner in the leftmost lane, and a blue Honda Ridgeline truck ahead of the others, riding in the middle. Plus, there are four more bikes riding between civilian cars ahead of the 4Runner. Of course, there's still the red truck behind us, the one Joe is still shooting at—a truck I finally recognize as a Toyota Hilux. This is odd, because I don't think this model is sold in the US.

"They're slowing," I tell my friends in the conference. "I think they're planning a TPAC."

When I get asked, I explain what I read online. TPAC stands for Tactical Pursuit and Containment formation. The maneuver is used in England. Specifically, it involves boxing in a car between four other cars, one in the front, one in the back, and one on each side.

"Screw that." Mitya's avatar angrily pushes his glasses higher on his nose. "I'll take their British pursuit tactic and raise them a good-old American one called the PIT."

Mitya must activate the nitro—that, or someone shot the limo with a rocket—and we torpedo forward at 250 per hour.

We whoosh between the Hummer and the 4Runner so fast no one gets a chance to shoot at each other. In a blink, we're on the tail of the Ridgeline—the car that must've planned to position itself at the front of the makeshift box these people wanted to build around the limo.

I research the PIT, and as soon as I do, I want to object to Mitya's idea, but it's too late. The limo is already passing the Ridgeline on the right, nitro boost gone.

The PIT, or Precision Immobilization Technique, is something American cops do, and it involves ramming the offending car behind the back tire.

And that's exactly what Mitya does.

The limo shudders with a disgusting crunch, but it's worth it. The Ridgeline loses control and swerves onto the median strip that separates us from oncoming traffic, sparks and plastic flying in every direction.

As a bonus, the yellow Hummer is forced to slow down to avoid crashing into the remnants of the blue truck.

"That's a lot like the maneuver you did to those bikers," Muhomor points out. "Just with a fancy name."

"Cops aren't allowed to do a PIT on motorcyclists," Mitya responds pedantically.

I don't shut either of them up since their competition to get rid of our problems is a win-win fight.

Unfortunately, the impact makes us lose speed, and the 4Runner gains on us. The bikers in front of us slow down as well.

"Boys," Ada intervenes. "Can you focus on keeping us alive until the next exit? It's a measly minute away at this speed."

Mitya replies to Ada, but I don't listen because my attention is on the 4Runner as it begins to pass us on the right. Its windows are down, and at least four helmeted enemies are staring out, ready for action.

Then I see something extremely worrying.

The front passenger in the 4Runner is holding a grenade.

"Grenade!" I yell just as it begins flying in an arc toward the limo.

Adrenaline makes the flight of the cursed object seem glacial, like slowed footage shot with a high-speed camera.

If my boost-assisted calculations are correct, this grenade is going to land in the middle of the limo… and blow up next to Ada.

THIRTY

As the grenade flies, I mentally scream for Mitya to adjust our course, though I know there isn't enough time.

I reflect on the cruelty of thinking fast without being able to move proportionally fast. If I could move like the Flash, I would jump on the grenade and cover it with my vest-clad body. But I know I won't make it in time, so I don't even try. Instead, I put the aim-assist app's line in the center of the helmet of the guy who threw the grenade and, without a single qualm, pull the trigger.

The guy's head begins to explode inside his helmet just as the grenade flies through our broken window.

I consider saying some last words to Ada but decide against it on the off chance she doesn't realize we're about to die. I figure if I didn't know our situation, I wouldn't want it explained to me either. Besides, even if Ada could see the grenade, what would I say?

Then I notice something happening in the path of the grenade's trajectory—something that gives me faint hope. Gogi's hands are closing in on the exact location where the grenade is about be. He's about to pull a maneuver that looks like a slowed-down replay of a catcher getting the baseball after a strike out—though being an immigrant from baseball-less Russia, I might have this analogy wrong.

"Could they have taught him a move like this in the Georgian Special Forces?" I manage to ask in the chat as Gogi grabs the grenade and tosses it right back at the 4Runner. Even his throw reminds me of a high-speed pitch from baseball.

The grenade's flight seems to go much quicker on its way back, and I watch without blinking, still adjusting to the idea of continued existence. When the grenade lands on the floor of the 4Runner—meaning no one in that car possessed Gogi's skills—I allow myself to blink. As soon as I open my eyes again, the 4Runner turns into a big fireball, and chunks of silver SUV fly in every direction.

Simultaneously, I hear gunfire coming from both in front and behind us. The Hummer and the red Hilux are still far enough behind us not to be a cause for concern, but the same can't be said about the four bikers in front.

Just when I thought things couldn't get worse, I see that the bikers are toting AK-47s.

We didn't blow up just so we could get shot a moment later instead.

The rattle of machine guns gets louder, and shattered glass rains onto the floor in the front of the limo.

When I glance at Eli, the guy behind the wheel, I see his left arm covered with blood, but that isn't preventing him from shooting at the motorcyclists with his right as bullets cut through the divider on the passenger side. Two bullet holes appear in the TV screen that Mitya and Muhomor have been using, and Mr. Spock's aura is now a color I've never seen.

Maybe I was wrong when I thought black was the worst mood a rat could be in.

Though I know our exit ramp is coming up soon, I fear it won't arrive soon enough. Still, I check the satellite view, and what I see makes no sense.

There's a small dark cloud heading straight for us.

"Guys, am I having an LSD flashback?" I ask, my heart rate speeding up further as I examine the low-flying cloud that's getting closer to us.

"It looks like something out of an American antidepressant commercial," Muhomor quips. "Like your personal rainy day."

"You must be talking about my work," Ada says. "The only way we'll make this exit is if we get rid of these bikers in our way."

I'm about to complain about her lack of explanation, when I realize the cloud is close enough to see through the limo's front camera.

Now that I can see it, I realize that, of course, this isn't a cloud.

It's a swarm.

A swarm of drones—as in unmanned aerial vehicles, not to be confused with male wasps.

"Babe," I mentally say, "please tell me your big idea was to take control of all the drones at Mitya's LAR facility and fly them toward us?"

If Ada says no and the drones belong to the bad guys, we'll be beyond screwed—and until a few moments ago, I didn't think our situation could get any worse.

Ada doesn't answer, but I can see my supposition was spot on, because the swarm dives, and the drones hit the first biker. He does a one-eighty in the air before landing on his neck.

There is a new, more frantic round of AK-47 fire, and a bullet hits Luke in his bulletproof vest, causing the poor guy to yelp in pain.

Ada's answer is instant. Five drones hit the second motorcyclist, two from the front and three from the back. The resulting cartwheel looks like something people do in extreme sports, except stunt people don't usually fly out of their seats like this guy does—nor do they go splat against the road like that.

The third and fourth bikers stop shooting at the limo and open fire at the descending drones.

Many drones get damaged, but even with automatic weapons,

the motorcyclists don't stand a chance against the number of drones Ada has under her command.

A single drone, with delivery package still attached to its bottom, lands under the tire of the third biker. The bike flies into the air and does a half rotation before the driver cannonballs onto the asphalt.

I guess Ada got especially bloodthirsty, because she hits the fourth biker with a dozen drones all at once. They all fall in a heap of plastic and metal as the motorcycle draws the number eight in the air.

"Well," I message Mitya. "The good news is all the bikers are gone. The bad news is all these broken bikes and damaged drones have created unsafe road conditions."

"You're right, but I'm taking the exit anyway," Mitya says from the broken screen on the wall. "It's going to get bumpy again, so hold on."

Remembering what happened the last time Mitya said this, I clutch the seat in front of me and hold on as though my life depends on it—since it might.

Taking the turn at 150 miles per hour is bad enough, but when we hit the bike and drone debris, we begin to skid.

Since we didn't die the last few times I thought we would, I remain optimistic. If we hit the wall, though, this could be it.

We don't hit the wall—not exactly. We crash into a yellow, water-filled barrel, a device placed on highways to lessen the impact of such hits, though I doubt the barrel was designed to help at our insane speed.

My heartbeat feels hypersonic, and that's with all my perceptions slowed by the boost.

Water sprays the limo in a fountain, and the impact makes my hands slip.

I fly across the limo, trying my best not to land on Ada.

Gogi manages to grab me by the leg mid-flight. It's the only thing that prevents me from flying out the window.

My head hits the seat so hard I'd have a cracked skull if it weren't for the cushion. As is, I see white stars dance around my vision. The real world blurs in my eyes, but the AROS screens remain as sharp as ever.

"Ada," I shout telepathically. "Are you okay?"

"Busy," she replies. "Have a look at this."

The link Ada gives me leads me to a strange camera view, one that resembles something a fly or a spider would see. It's the world seen through hundreds of eyes, all of which are looking at the Hummer and the red Hilux truck, but also into the distance.

"See that black Chevrolet Suburban speeding through the lanes up there?" Ada's mental tone is tense. "I'm worried about it."

"Yeah, probably more bad guys, but I wouldn't worry about them," I reply. "They'll be too late to kill us, since the guys in the Hummer and Hilux will surely beat them to it."

"Not if I have anything to say about it," Ada counters, and dozens of drone views go into dive mode.

The ground rushes toward each drone. I quickly get dizzy, so I look through one of the limo's back cameras.

From this vantage point, what Ada is doing to the yellow Hummer looks like a scene from Alfred Hitchcock's *The Birds*, only with drones attacking.

"Ada, don't forget to send some toward the red Hilux," I say, but it's clear she's already on it. It's just that the helmeted driver of the Hilux is insane. Though he must have zero visibility due to the diving drones, the red truck still speeds up.

Ada must be desperate, because the swarm separates into two halves, and each group drops onto one of the cars.

For a moment, I can't even see the Hilux or the Hummer under the mess made by the drones.

Then, to my relief, the drone-covered Hummer hits the freeway wall.

Unfortunately, the Hilux ignores the drone parts scattered across the asphalt in front of it, the drones sticking out of its broken windshield, and the drones diving at it.

Then my boosted mind calculates the truck's trajectory and

reveals its driver's intent. I scream out loud, "We need to get out of this car!"

For the first time, I take in the wreckage inside the limo. The place looks like that grenade did explode in here.

My cousin begins to move, as do Gogi and Luke. Based on the drones' behavior, I know Ada is conscious, as is Mr. Spock, because I can see his horrified aura. No one else is conscious enough to move, yet that's what we must do and fast. In the camera view, the red truck is getting closer, and I'm a hundred-percent certain it intends to ram into our stopped limo from behind.

Ada is my biggest worry, so I get up and instantly have to enable the Relief app to mask the pain spreading through my body.

The Hilux looms closer.

"The people in the Hummer are getting out," Mitya says mentally. The wall TV is too busted for him to say it from there.

"Let's hope we live long enough to worry about them," I grimly reply.

"And don't forget about the black Suburban," Muhomor chimes in.

"They'll need to take a number." I wish I felt as confident as my mental replies suggest. Out loud, I say, "Gogi, Luke, let go of Ada and try to get out of the car."

The men separate, and when I see how pale Ada is, I want to kill someone again. Only there isn't time. The Hilux is seconds away from turning us into a pancake.

Ada tries to stand up, but yelps and crouches again. "I've been sitting on my leg, and it's completely asleep. All pins and needles." She tries to get up again but nearly twists her ankle. "Go. I'll follow you."

"Help her," Luke grits out, his face twisted in pain. "I got Gogi." Matching action to words, he begins dragging the Georgian out of the car.

"Lean on me," I tell Ada and put my arm around her slim back.

"No," Joe says with an intensity that brooks no objection. "Grab her legs. I'll take her arms."

Ada mumbles something about the indignity of the situation, but Joe and I grab her like a sack and scramble for the door.

In the camera view, I see the truck is about to slam into us.

THIRTY-ONE

My foot is still in the doorframe when the Hilux rips into the limo, destroying our car with the enthusiasm of a competitive eater chomping on his first hotdog.

It feels as though it's the sound wave of the impact that pushes me the rest of the way out. I stumble and nearly drop Ada's legs, but I recover and grab on to her tighter.

"At least we're done with Vincent Williams," Ada comments in the virtual chat.

"Afraid not," Mitya replies. "Whoever built the Toyota Hilux must've been inspired by tanks."

He's right. The red truck is just slightly bent in the front—completely disproportionate to the totaled state of our ride. If the Hilux had airbags—a safe bet—and if the riders wore seatbelts, which I think I recall seeing, they could easily still be alive.

"I have one more operational drone," Ada says. "Should I crash it into someone's head?"

"Let's use it for reconnaissance," I suggest. "Can you raise it up a bit so it can check on both the Hummer and the Suburban? Since we're still alive, we need to worry about them now." While the mental conversation is happening, Joe and I carry Ada to the grass by the road and gently put her down next to Gogi and Luke. Out loud, I say, "Gogi, Luke, please get back into your earlier position in case bullets start flying."

"No," Ada says out loud. "Give me a gun. I can use the aiming app same as you."

"Shit, that reminds me." I pat myself down. "I don't have a gun."

As though taunting me, Joe reloads his weapon at that very moment, and Gogi and Luke check their weapons as well.

"I guess going to a gun range is one thing, but being a professional is something else entirely," Muhomor comments sardonically. "How could you not grab a gun on your way out?"

"Here." Gogi hands me his pistol. "You and Joe should draw fire away from us."

Joe is already running back toward the limo, and I follow while frantically trying to add Gogi's Makarov Pistol to my aiming app.

"Crap," I say after a frustrating moment. "Mitya, why is this gun not in the gun database?"

"I'm not sure," Mitya responds. "Maybe because it's of Russian design? Do you even need the aiming app anymore? You got all that practice."

"I practiced at the shooting range, not in the field." I weigh the unfamiliar weapon in my hand as I approach the limo. "Plus, I did it with a Glock."

"Hey, Mike." Mitya's Zik message is full of worry. "I don't like what I'm seeing from the drone."

As though to highlight Mitya's concerns, a gunshot rings out, and a bullet zings by my head.

Joe and I duck under the limo's carcass, and when I look through the drone's view, my feet freeze to the ground. While we were busying ourselves with surviving the crash, the fourteen people sitting in the wrecked Hummer left it. They're running toward us, their shiny black helmets unmistakable.

Even worse, the black Suburban is just a few feet behind the fourteen new attackers. Assuming there are eight people in that car, Joe and I don't have enough bullets, even if we put each bullet directly into each person's brains. And that's without the two people in the red truck who might be coming to their senses, if they haven't already.

My depressing math is interrupted when I spot the attacker closest to us aiming a scoped rifle at where Ada, Gogi, and Luke are.

He must not see Joe and me hiding behind the car and probably thinks the trio on the grass is what remains of the resistance.

My heart leaps into my throat as the rifle fires.

Ada gasps and then screams.

Since her Share app is still running for Mitya's and Muhomor's benefits, I try to look through it and succeed, which means Ada's brain is intact. Shaking with relief, I realize the reason for Ada's screaming.

The rifleman shot Luke in the head, making it explode, and the gore is covering Ada's entire body.

The already slow-moving time crawls for me now, and I can see Luke's gun begin to fall to the grass and Ada's hand reach out to catch it.

I comprehend what's about to happen.

Ada is going to grab that gun and start shooting.

"Ada, no!" I scream at her from my hiding place. Mentally, I frantically add, "If you start shooting, you might as well draw a target on your forehead."

Ada catches the gun, and I see no evidence that she heard me or that she's willing to listen.

An insane plan flits through my mind.

I know how to draw fire away from Ada… at a steep price to myself.

The guy with the rifle begins to reload, and I attempt my crazy idea.

The world takes on a surreal quality as I leap from my hiding spot and shoot at the rifleman.

Without the aim-assist app, and with the unfamiliar gun in my hand, I miss.

The rifleman finishes reloading, but instead of aiming at me, he points the barrel in Ada's direction again. My heart threatens to burst out of my chest, but I climb onto the limo's ruins, take careful aim at him, and squeeze the trigger again. I must be getting used to my new gun, because my shot fells the rifleman.

His thirteen still-alive allies turn their guns in my direction.

Strong hands push me from behind, and it takes an unimaginable feat of coordination for me to land on my feet.

Joe must've pushed me, I realize. Then I hear thirteen shots ring out like a firing squad.

Their bullets are going toward the top of the limo—toward Joe.

I shoot back once, twice, and each bullet reaches its designated helmet.

Something falls on top of the limo, making my heart sink.

I'm reluctant to learn the horrible truth, but I force myself to switch to Ada's Share view. Her vantage point is getting closer, enabling me to see what the sound was about, and my stomach grows cold as the otherworldly quality of my surroundings intensifies.

It was indeed Joe. A couple of the thirteen bullets reached his head, and what's left of his skull is barely recognizable as having belonged to a human being.

I instantly regret all my snide thoughts about my cousin. Despite everything, I've grown to care about Joe, and I know this loss will devastate our family.

Before grief can warp my mind, another shot rings out, the bullet tearing through my chest.

Despite the Relief app, the pain is worse than anything I've felt —though my grief could be intensifying it. The agony is at least a thousand times worse than when the sharp object was stuck under my fingernail.

My knees buckle, and I sink to the ground.

Something tells me I'm only alive because the bulletproof vest saved my life, but this won't be the case for long, as my enemies take aim at me again.

Through Ada's Share app, I see her vantage point is getting even closer to the limo, and I finally understand what it means.

Gun in hand, Ada is running to save me—which means she's running toward the shooters.

"No, Ada," I scream mentally. "Don't get any closer!"

To my horror, the gunmen stop aiming at me and turn their sights onto Ada, who must, at this moment, seem like the more dangerous target.

"Drop to the ground!" I scream at her.

Thirteen shots ring out.

Ada's view is a swirl of motion that indicates she's falling.

"Ada?" I frantically message in Zik. "Ada, are you okay?"

She doesn't reply.

My grief for my cousin morphs into a terrifying black hole as Ada's Share app begins to show static, like an ancient out-of-tune TV.

Mindlessly, I leap to my feet and turn.

I have to see this for myself.

I have to see her.

As I feared, Ada is on the ground, blood pooling around her face.

The shots ring out again, and I know I'll no longer feel this horrible grief in a moment.

It's a relief I welcome.

In the instant before I die, something clicks in my head. It could be wishful thinking, but I have to try.

Out loud, as though I'm addressing someone other than myself, I ask, "Is this really happening?"

THIRTY-TWO

THE SURREAL QUALITY OF THE WORLD DISSIPATES, AND I SNAP OUT OF the pre-cog moment—just like every other time I've asked myself this question when experiencing those nightmare scenarios.

The brain-boost vision short-circuits, and I find myself back behind the limo—effectively back in time to a few fateful seconds ago, before Joe and Ada got killed.

I understand what just happened. When I came up with that insane plan to draw fire away from Ada, my brain showed me what might happen as a result. During our last Brainocytes Club meeting, Mitya provided us with the new brain boost, and I didn't get a chance to adjust to it. I was also offline for a number of days. I'm probably lucky this is the first pre-cog moment I've experienced—if you can call that scare lucky.

The reality of our situation sets in. The pre-cog moment happened at the speed of boosted thought, and since I didn't jump onto the limo and no shots were fired, what's really happening is that the rifleman is still reloading his weapon.

The problem is that I'm running out of options. The pre-cog moment convinced me not to execute that desperate maneuver, but I also know if Ada fires the gun she just caught, she won't be alive for long.

"Ada—" I begin to scream at her again, but then in her Share view, I see I wasn't the only one worried about her. I forgot Gogi and his Special Forces background, not to mention his years of bodyguard experience. Since Gogi is already almost hugging Ada, he just makes his hug tighter and falls on top of her the way bodyguards have done since time immemorial.

Ada's gun falls out of her hand, and she spouts mental curses about being sandwiched between a dead body and a wounded Georgian.

"Better that than dead," I reassure her mentally.

Either Gogi's action or my screaming did the trick. After the rifleman finishes reloading, he doesn't aim for Gogi or Ada, since a flat target is too difficult to hit. He focuses on me, since I've been kind enough to scream and announce my location.

Suddenly, Joe jackknifes to his feet, takes quick aim, and pulls the trigger.

The rifleman falls, but that only seems to anger the other dozen attackers running toward us. They begin to fire at the limo.

"The black Suburban will be between you and those people in a second," Mitya states in the chat.

I can see he's right, but with or without the black Suburban, Joe and I don't stand much of a chance.

Then Ada chimes in. "I'm looking through the Suburban's window with the drone," she tells us. "I think you might want to look, too."

THIRTY-THREE

THE SUBURBAN'S TIRES SCREECH, AND IT STOPS BETWEEN US AND THE twelve attackers—a strange maneuver in and of itself.

I follow Ada's advice and look at the black car's windows through the drone's camera.

Unlike the rest of their helmeted allies, this group is wearing sunglasses and suits. That is, aviator sunglasses and creepily familiar black suits. I recognize a couple of people in that car. Agent Pugh is the one driving, and a couple of other task-force Suits—facial-recognition-immune men I first saw at the hospital—are here as well.

"How did I not see this sooner?" Mitya says as the same realization must hit him. "They were driving the most cliché government vehicle known to man. And it's even black."

"What I'd like to know," Ada says, "is whether they're here to hurt us or help us?"

I consider her question. Earlier in the chase, I decided that the task force wasn't behind Vincent Williams, and someone else must have hired him. Was I wrong?

In perfectly rehearsed unison, the Suits stick their guns out of

the window and answer my question in the simplest way they can
—they open fire at our attackers.

"They must've been tailing you," Muhomor says. "Even after all that hoopla in the media. Thank God bad habits are so hard to break."

"Not only did they follow us," I say, "but they also did it from far enough away that they didn't activate my paranoia. They must be learning from their mistakes."

Emboldened by the newfound support, Joe and I stand up and aim at any helmeted people we can spot, but it's difficult with the black car in the way.

I unload half my gun before I see movement inside the red Hilux truck next to us. Seemingly before my conscious mind even knows what I'm planning, my hand takes aim and shoots.

My bullet slices into Vincent Williams's ear but doesn't stop his escaping the car.

"Check his passenger," Joe barks at me. "Williams is mine."

What Joe doesn't say, but what I assume based on the cold glint in his alligator-like stare, is that he intends to make Williams pay dearly for every man Joe lost today.

I check the drone view to make sure it's safe for me to walk to the other side of the limo, since that's what's required to get to the passenger side of the truck. The Suits and our earlier attackers are still exchanging fire, and the Suits are winning. Their only casualty so far is one of the dudes I saw at the hospital.

Since the drone doesn't have a good view of the damaged Hilux, I scan the limo's sensors. I'm shocked to find a semi-functional camera in the back.

Despite the cracked camera screen that blocks the view, I can still make out Williams as he exits the car. Joe meets the large man the moment his feet touch the ground. The first thing Joe does is put a bullet in Williams in his right hand, disarming his opponent and costing Williams yet another finger or two on his already digit-lacking hand. Williams's guttural scream brings a horrid smile to Joe's face—the same one he wore when I caught him beating a bird with a rock as a teenager.

"Oh no," I say inside the chat. "I'm afraid my cousin might not be thinking strategically."

No one replies, but in a moment, I'm proven right. Instead of shooting Williams in the head, as I would have done, Joe pistol-whips the man in the face.

"He might be out of bullets," Mitya suggests halfheartedly as we all see Williams's lip split and his blood spray across Joe's face in the ultimate unhygienic fountain.

Whatever the reason for Joe's decision to throw hits, Williams takes the damage with surprising stamina and tries to grapple with his enemy. Joe is ready for him and uses a move he's used on me at the gym. I call the move a kick-twister, only I see that Joe was severely pulling his punches and kicks with me. When Joe completes the kick-twister this time, Williams's right wrist breaks, and his already damaged hand hangs limply to the side.

With an animalistic roar, Williams punches Joe with his left hand. As someone who's received a punch like that before, I feel sympathy for Joe. To my shock, Joe takes the punch with that same creepy smile and leaps at Williams with a growl.

Since I'm standing in front of the passenger side door of the red truck, I focus on what's in front of me right now—the damaged truck's door—and proceed to pull.

The door creaks, but opens. I can see that the helmeted person who rode with Williams is—or was—a man, and he looks knocked out or dead. Something about this person's body or clothing seems familiar to me. I get the strong urge to lift his helmet to see the face hidden beneath.

Jutting my gun out, I say, "If you're alive and you move, I'll shoot you in the stomach."

"I say you shoot before you check him," Muhomor suggests. "This way, we'll be certain he's dead."

"That's cold, even for you, Viktor," Mitya counters, and I tend to agree with him. Though I did finally take kill shots at people in the heat of battle, killing someone who's unconscious like this is a whole other step, and one I'm not willing to take, especially considering the vague familiarity I feel when I look at this man.

Clicking the gun's safety off, I reach for the helmet's visor.

"No way." Mitya gapes at the mystery person's face. "It can't be him."

"Seriously," Ada echoes. "Isn't he dead? There was a posh funeral and everything."

"The funeral could've been faked," Muhomor says. "We're talking about Russia, after all. In any case, if he wasn't dead before, he might be dead now."

I study the man's face until I have no doubt. This is Alex—as in Alexander Voynskiy, the Russian billionaire. As in the guy who betrayed us on that rescue trip to Russia—a betrayal he paid for with his life, after Joe tortured him, or so it seemed until this very moment.

Of course, if Alex had survived, he would want revenge. He's the perfect person to hire all these people trying to kill us. Besides revenge, he might want us dead so he can stop pretending to be dead—a preventative strike since Joe would kill him if he knew of his survival. So it's no surprise that Alex wants Joe dead, though I'm sure he's equally pissed at the rest of us. He's the exact kind of person who'd put together a kill list, with Joe at the top, and give the list to someone like Williams. This would explain why Williams mentioned some kind of list.

Though I'm still reluctant to shoot him, I consider hitting Alex in the face to make sure he doesn't wake up anytime soon. Then the implications of Alex's survival hit me, and I frantically send Ada a telepathic message, saying, "Ada, ask Gogi if Joe has anyone guarding Muhomor. If he does, tell Gogi to order the guard to rush into Muhomor's room."

As though in response to my suspicions, Muhomor sends into the chat, "Crap. I shouldn't have said anything out loud to her. I need help. SOS."

I find the camera view into Muhomor's room and confirm my

suspicions. Lyuba is there, and she's holding a pillow over Muhomor's face.

"Hold on, buddy," Ada says. "Gogi just passed along Mike's message."

Muhomor doesn't answer—a bad sign—but Jacob, another one of Joe's people I've seen at the gym, rushes into the room.

Jacob is very, very good at his job, and before Lyuba knows what's happening, the man unceremoniously punches her in the jaw.

Unsurprisingly, Lyuba imitates a knocked-out sack of potatoes as she crashes to the floor.

I never thought I'd see the day when Ada would cheer a man hitting a woman, but she does.

Jacob stabs at the nurse-call button and begins performing CPR on Muhomor.

In case someone hasn't already reached the conclusions I have, I say into the chat, "Muhomor left it to Lyuba to get rid of Alex. The billionaire must've convinced or bribed her to let him live, and she's been working with him ever since. This is how Williams and his people knew we'd be at that restaurant and how they knew we were at the hospital. We told Lyuba about it. Even this chase is her fault. I bet Muhomor told her what hospital I was left at and where we were going."

"Tell that brute I'm okay," Muhomor says into the chat after a moment. "I can't tell him because he's rape-kissing me."

"Hey." I feel instant relief. "At least we now know you've gotten to first base—"

"Watch out!" Ada screams, both mentally and from under Gogi.

Realizing I've been paying too much attention to the AROS views and not my real-world senses, I focus on Alex and see his eyes are open and narrowing at me.

"Shoot him," Muhomor urges. "Use your gun."

I'm about to listen to Muhomor, but before I get a chance to pull the trigger, Alex savagely kicks my legs, and my shin explodes in unbearable pain. In shock, I stumble back and trip, falling out of the tall truck.

My gun clanks on the asphalt, but I'm happy that I landed on my ass instead of breaking my neck in the fall, though my tailbone violently begs to differ.

Alex leaps out of the truck after me and stomps on my chest as he falls on top of me, causing the air in my lungs to escape with an almost audible whoosh.

Recovering quickly, he repeatedly punches me in the head.

The world grows distant, and I must use my willpower to stay conscious. In the AROS view from the limo's last camera, I can see Joe is still in the process of hitting what's left of Williams's face with something heavy. That's too bad for me, since I was hoping Joe would be done with his prey and on his way to rescue me.

"You bastard," Ada says inside the chat, and even through my haze I'm tempted to tell her Alex can't hear her cursing without Bra(inocytes.

Then I see Ada has a plan. Dimly, I watch as our last drone crash-lands into the side of Alex's head.

There's a satisfying crunch, though I think it's the plastic drone that breaks and not Alex's skull. Still, Alex's eyes glaze over, and his body goes slack on top of me.

I push Alex off me and struggle to my feet. Since I don't trust him to stay unconscious for long, I need to finish him off somehow. Shaking my head in an effort to further clear it, I think something I never thought I'd ask myself.

What would Joe do?

Since my legs are barely supporting my weight and my muscles are screaming for mercy, I decide that my gun is my best option. Pulling the trigger will be easier than punching or kicking in my current condition.

I look for the gun, but it seems to be under the limo wreckage. I'm not sure it's a good idea for me to climb under for it.

In Ada's Shared view, I see a flicker of movement behind me and instinctively duck.

As a result, I only lose a small piece of my scalp instead of my life.

My head is burning, and a double shot of adrenaline hits my brain as I spin around to face Alex and assess the situation.

Not only is he conscious, but he also pulled a knife on me, explaining that missing inch of skin on the crown of my head.

Alex stabs the knife at my torso, but I jump back, causing him to slice a gash into the bulletproof vest, not me. Wondering what would happen if he'd stabbed me instead, I perform a frantic internet search and learn this lighter type of bulletproof vest doesn't have good knife protection.

For whatever reason, Gogi and I didn't think it was realistic that I'd ever get into a knife fight, so knife combat was a low priority. I practiced mostly hand-to-hand combat and gun disarm techniques in the last months. If I live, I'll tell Gogi he sucks at risk assessment.

Alex slices at my lower body, and I decide to take a gamble and treat the knife like a gun.

I catch Alex's wrist in a crisscross of my outstretched arms and begin to twist the knife out of his hand, as I would with a gun.

Then I realize this maneuver is best used on guns with trigger guards, which facilitates the twist that breaks the finger. Alex's butterfly-style knife doesn't have a trigger guard, so his finger is fine.

Realizing my twist was ineffective, Alex propels his whole body forward, like a fencer, his arm sliding between mine.

I watch, dumbfounded, as his knife slowly enters my body.

THIRTY-FOUR

AT LEAST AN INCH OF STEEL IS IN MY UPPER THIGH, BUT I ONLY FEEL a tingle of electricity, like I got Tasered with the voltage focused on a single point. Figuring I need to take advantage of the fact that I'm not in pain yet, I yank my leg back to make sure the knife doesn't go in deeper.

Paradoxically, as the knife rips out of my thigh, the nauseating pain hits me. It feels like a burn made by a thousand hot needles. I wonder what protection the Relief app is giving me at this moment, if any. It sure doesn't feel like this pain is dampened in any way. If I survive, I'll probably consider giving this app a "knife wound" setting, though something tells me the app would have to become equivalent to shooting heroin, presenting an even higher risk of addiction.

With my adrenaline spiking to inhuman levels, I chop at Alex's neck with my right hand and use the distraction to grab Alex's right wrist with my left hand.

Alex tries to pull out of my grip, but I'm holding on with the desperation of a man about to bleed to death—because that's my reality.

With the world around me sharpening, I realize that not only do I need to beat Alex, but I must also do it in the quickest way possible—ideally, two seconds ago.

A half-baked and perilous idea forms in my mind, and I wish my brain had showed it to me as a pre-cog moment so I could assess it better. Since pre-cog moments don't seem to come when you want them to, I execute my idea, which is simple.

Still holding on to the wrist of the hand that's wielding the knife, I sidestep and sweep Alex's legs.

In training, the best-case scenario for this move was Gogi and I ending up on the floor, meaning I was toast shortly after, given my lack of skills in wrestling.

In this case, my concern is that I might land with the knife in my heart.

Twisting in the air, Alex and I tumble onto the asphalt. My back hits the ground, putting me at a huge disadvantage as he lands on top of me. But the knife isn't in my heart, because I'm still holding on to Alex's wrist.

In movies, I've seen heroes twist a knife in someone's hand and then stab them with it. It usually begins with the hero stopping the knife close to his eye and turning the tables—or arms—and ends with the bad guy getting knifed.

Alex must've also seen those movies, because he grabs the knife with his other hand and pushes down frantically.

I would use two hands if I could, but my right arm is pinned under me. I was instinctively trying to protect my poor tailbone this time. With my arm pinned to the asphalt, I have one hand left to defend myself. Soon, it becomes obvious that I'm not stopping the knife's descent at all. At best, I'm slowing it down.

I feel blood seeping out of my leg wound, and with it, my energy and will to fight.

Alex's face is red with exertion, and beads of his sweat fall onto my face as he pushes the knife down another millimeter.

Something is happening in one of the AROS views, and the gunfire between the Suits and Alex's or Williams's remaining people stops, but I don't dare shift my focus away from the knife.

Suddenly, white fur flashes by my face, and a rat is biting Alex on the ear.

"Ada," I mentally shout. "Mr. Spock ran away from you. A rat is no match for a human. Once Alex is done with me, he'll hurt Mr. Spock."

Somehow, getting bitten seems to give Alex strength, because the knife descends another couple of millimeters and begins to enter the vest's material.

"No," Ada says out loud—from less than a foot away. "He won't hurt anyone anymore."

Through her Share app view, I see she's holding a gun firmly to Alex's head, and that Alex is aware of the gun.

"You will put that knife down," Ada says, her voice so cold she'd give Joe a run for his money. "Now."

Alex must read the deadly determination in Ada's eyes, because he tosses the knife aside and raises his hands in the air.

The first thing I do is grab Mr. Spock from Alex's ear and cradle the little guy, though I think the gesture comforts me more than my currently bloodthirsty pet.

"You left a permanent tooth mark," I tell Spock softly after examining Alex's ear. "Good rat."

Alex lifts his body off me, and as soon as I'm free, I try to stand. Finding that I can only get up to my knees, I stay there, swaying, and study Ada as she holds the gun aimed at Alex.

I wonder if she's going to shoot the bastard, and I think he's wondering the same thing. It makes me recall Muhomor's joke comparing Ada to a mama bear.

"It wouldn't be very vegan of you," I tell Ada mentally. "But if you pull that trigger, I'll support you one hundred percent."

Alex carefully backs away from Ada and says, "Look, Ada, I never had an issue with you—"

I'll never know if Alex had the balls to try to talk his way out of this predicament, because the sound of someone dragging their feet interrupts Alex's speech.

We all look at the source of the noise and see Joe. So much

blood covers my cousin it's as if he's been through hell's meat factory. Alex's pupils grow to the size of his irises as he takes in the depth of hatred in my cousin's icy eyes. I bet Alex is reliving flashbacks of Joe torturing him in that car. He must realize his fate will now be worse.

Ada looks over Joe's shoulder, and I see Agent Pugh lumbering toward us, her own weapon raised.

"Lower your gun," the female Suit says. "There's been enough shooting already."

"Agent Pugh," I gasp out, the blood loss making it hard to speak louder than a whisper. "Think about how it'll look if you hurt one of us."

Agent Pugh looks uncertain, making me think she heard me.

Ada drops her gun on the ground and looks expectantly at Joe.

I show my hands empty of weapons—unless you count a rat as a weapon.

Joe's gaze doesn't leave Alex's face as he begins to lower his gun, but then I realize he isn't lowering it so much as aiming it at Alex's head.

I grit my teeth.

A gun goes off, the boom smacking my eardrums like a blow.

I look at Agent Pugh, worried I'll see a cloud of smoke around her weapon, but it isn't there.

It was Joe who fired his gun, and the result of his work is the gaping hole in Alex's forehead.

Lowering the weapon, Joe lets the gun slip from his fingers and hit the floor.

Agent Pugh walks up to Alex and stares at his corpse, her face unreadable.

"His people killed your colleagues," Ada tells her. "What Joe did was a preventative measure of self-defense. This guy had enough money to get out of any legal mishaps coming his way."

"Speaking of legal mishaps," I croak, swaying on my knees as I try to stay conscious. "If you agree this was self-defense, I'll consider us even and won't unleash Kadvosky and his lawyers on you."

Agent Pugh's expression is still unreadable as she moves her gun from Joe to Alex. Before I register what's happing, Agent Pugh puts a bullet in Alex's already cooling chest.

"Now I'm in the same boat as you," Agent Pugh says. "As I see it, this was self-defense."

My relief makes my exhaustion intensify, and I put down Mr. Spock so that I can lie back down on the asphalt. The rat sniffs my cheek and then scurries away as someone kneels to check my vitals, and someone else wraps a tourniquet around my leg wound.

"He'll be okay," someone says. "The first responders are almost here."

"I'm going to faint now," I tell Ada telepathically. "When the ambulance comes, please tell them to go ahead and use drugs. Lots of drugs."

THIRTY-FIVE

I WAKE UP GROGGY BUT BLISSFULLY FREE OF PAIN. I VAGUELY RECALL coming to my senses inside an ambulance and receiving a nice injection that knocked me out again.

Opening my eyes, I see my mom, Uncle Abe, and Ada staring at me intensely. I'm attached to a ton of medical equipment, but the room around me is nice for a change, well lit and crowded with comfortable furniture. This is as close as a hospital room can get to a suite at the Four Seasons.

"Kitten," Mom says in high-pitched Russian. "How are you feeling?"

"I feel great," I say out loud. Telepathically, I ask Ada, "How come I feel great? I should be in lots of interesting pain."

"They gave you morphine," Ada explains mentally and winks at me in the real world. "I didn't tell your mom about that, though."

"I'm glad to hear you're feeling great." Mom's worried tone doesn't change. "The doctor says you'll be fine, but you needed stiches on your head and leg, and that scar on your ear—"

"Calm down, sis," my uncle says soothingly. "Think of your blood pressure."

"Yeah, Mom," I chime in. "I'm fine. There's a perfectly good explanation for all of this."

"How much does she know?" I ask Ada telepathically. "Please tell me she didn't watch the news."

"Not so much," Ada replies in Zik. "But I think you should do your best to tell her what happened and soften some details if you must."

"Can you leave us alone, please?" I ask Ada and locate my bed's controls to raise the bed into a sitting position. "I think I have an idea that might make this conversation have a happy conclusion."

"Uh-huh." Ada's Zik message is pure mischief. "It seems you're thinking what I'm thinking." She looks down at her belly.

"Mr. Cohen," Ada says to Uncle Abe. "I'd like to check on your son if you don't mind."

"They're not going to buy your wanting to check on Joe, of all people," I mentally say.

"I could be warming up to him," Ada retorts. "It's theoretically feasible."

"But not likely." I chuckle in the real world, garnering myself strange looks from my mom and my uncle. "How is Joe, anyway?"

"Joe is doing better than you are," Ada replies. Despite her earlier assertions, her Zik message doesn't contain a single positive emotion, and it would have if she were happy that Joe is okay. "He's got a room here, but Gogi tells me that Joe is planning to leave the hospital soon. Something about some business we'd rather not know about."

It's all too easy to picture Joe leaving the hospital and initiating a deadly hunt for any survivors from Williams's organization. For the first time, I wish my cousin good luck in his sinister activities, but I don't share that sentiment with Ada, lest she think I'm becoming a monster. Because I'm not. I'd like to think I'm simply becoming more pragmatic, as I figure a future father should be.

"So, it all started after we left that lunch at your house," I begin in Russian when Ada and my uncle are out of the room. "Or maybe it started when we were rescuing you in Russia. It depends on how you look at it."

I tell Mom a version of the events that downplays the risks to me as much as I can.

Since I'm speaking out loud, I have plenty of time to check the internet for interesting developments—like news about further lynching of the officials complicit in the task force, or the excitement in the cybersecurity community over Tema. My favorite part is reading the reactions to open-source Brainocytes. People are speculating on countless uses and making plans to improve the technology in a thousand different ways.

After the internet, I check my emails. My friends sent me some ideas for future development, and my favorite one is something Ada came up with based on some initial work by an Israeli scientist named Golan Dahan. He has an MD specializing in nanomedicine and a PhD in nanoengineering. Golan's interest seems to be in nanomachines that can turn parts of people's bodies into computers. This specific paper outlines a design for nanobots that could turn bones into computing and storage substrates, making the bones stronger and lighter as a side effect.

I instantly see such "smart bones" as a solution to the problem of not having access to the internet—like what recently happened to me. Granted, no computing constrained to the human body will be as powerful as the supercomputers we can access via the cloud, but it would be a good backup option. Also, this could help us with another project—caching. Caching is a hardware (and sometimes software) component that stores data so future requests for that data can be served faster—a performance enhancement technique that tries to predict the future based on the recent past. Our earlier solution for better caching was to cram more Brainocytes inside our brains, but this opens up more interesting opportunities.

"A nice find for our nanobots collection," Mitya says after I forward him the article. "Almost as cool as the Respirocytes."

Respirocytes are nanobots that were designed by Robert A. Freitas Jr. in 1998. They can replace or supplement much of the normal respiratory system, allowing the user to take one breath per several hours. We, the Brainocytes Club, have plans to build these, along with microbivore (artificial white blood cells that will create a super-immune system) and many others.

"Stronger bones might be an awesome effect on its own," I add when I realize I got lost in thought.

"Yeah." Mitya's Zik message is only partially sarcastic as he adds, "And sharp retractable claws coming out of our hands would be nice if we were ever in a jam."

The fact that I missed the connection to Wolverine until Mitya's joke is a sign that the morphine has dulled my thinking. Mentally chuckling, I say, "In Muhomor's case, the claws will have USB plugs on the ends."

"Great idea," Mitya replies. "Okay, I'll go and try to recruit this Israeli guy."

In the slow-time world, tears are standing in Mom's eyes throughout my story, and I feel like she might have a nervous breakdown or start crying unless I finally play the proverbial ace up my sleeve, so I say, "But that isn't the most exciting thing that happened. I learned something amazing as well." When I'm sure I have Mom's undivided attention, I drop the bomb. "You're going to be a grandma."

Mom looks shell-shocked but recovers surprisingly quickly, clapping her hands in excitement. A huge smile spreads across her face, and my tired vocal cords can barely keep up as she peppers me with questions.

"No, Ada didn't tell me how far along she is," I say. "But she only missed her first period, so I guess the whole thing is just beginning."

"Did you do an ultrasound?" In her excitement, Mom begins to pace around my lavish room.

"No, Mom. I just learned about this a few hours ago. I don't carry around a portable ultrasound machine."

"Did you read any books about pregnancy?" Mom asks, and at

first I think she might be kidding, but her expression is dead serious.

I take advantage of the few milliseconds between answering her questions and buy a book called, *What to Expect When Your Wife is Expecting*. I read a large chunk of the book as I reply, "Yep, Mom, I got one already and started reading it."

"Good boy," Mom says and stops pacing. "So, what are your intentions toward Ada?"

It's funny Mom asked that, because I've been thinking about this whenever I've had a free moment to think.

"Well, I've known for a while that I wanted to marry Ada some-day," I say after I make sure I turn off my Share app. "Even when we were moving in together, I told you I thought she was the one, and that feeling has only gotten stronger."

"I know." Mom nods sagely, beaming with pleasure. "I can tell by watching the two of you."

"Right." The conversation is making me dizzy, so I lower the bed a few degrees. "This baby development does change the timeline."

"Why does it seem like you're about to say 'but'?" Mom walks up to the bed and sits on the edge.

"I don't want Ada to think I'm proposing for the wrong reasons." I use my IV-free hand to wipe my suddenly sweaty fore-head. "Like because I knocked her up."

"Silliness," Mom says and folds her arms across her chest. "Look, kitten, I love you, and you know I think highly of your intellect, but Ada is twice as smart as you are and would never worry about such nonsense."

"There's also that 'I love you' thing," I remind Mom. "How do I know if Ada even believes in a traditional marriage? She's got radical views on so many things that—"

"It doesn't matter what the two of you call your relationship," Mom interrupts. "Whether she says 'I love you' every five minutes or once a year, that girl does love you, and you're crazy about her as well. If she's not into a traditional marriage, if she wants to call it something else, like a social union or a banana, you should remember that marriage is but a piece of paper anyway. What matters is how the two people feel about each other—and this you know."

"I guess you're right. It's just a bit scary."

"I understand," Mom says. "But you're in luck. I'll help you with at least one decision, but I have to go."

Before I can say anything, Mom gets up from the bed and almost runs out of my hospital room.

I stare at the closed door, thinking that the trick of telling Mom about the baby might've worked a little too well. I guess I wanted her to fuss over me for a little while before running off to who knows where.

"So, you're still awake," Mitya says out loud as he enters the room.

In a weird Russian tradition, Mitya brought me apples and a box of candy. He puts them on the end table near the bed and sits on one of the cushy couches.

When he catches my questioning look, he pretends to misinterpret it and says, "This isn't an avatar. My plane finally landed, so I figured I'd visit you."

"No, really? And here I thought you gave me virtual food." I feign a snarkiness I don't feel. "So, what's up?"

He tells me he already hired Golan Dahan, and he'll get him to come to the US from Israel shortly. Then he asks me about my health, and I tell him I'm feeling fine. Soon, our conversation turns to the same subject Mom and I were talking about—marrying Ada.

"Have you thought about the how of it?" Mitya asks. "I'm not an expert, but maybe a nice romantic proposal is the way to go?"

"That might be tricky for some time." I look down at my white hospital gown. "I don't know when I'll get out of this bed, and I want to talk to her about this as soon as possible." Suddenly, an idea hits me. "By the way, do you still own that virtual reality video game development company? The Samurai Ostrich or whatever it's called?"

"Penguin Ninjas," Mitya responds, his expression telling me he might already see where I'm going with this. "Yes, I still own them."

"Well," I say conspiratorially, "here's my idea."

———

By the time Ada mentally informs me she's close, Mitya and I are almost done coding the ideas we came up with during a conference call with Penguin Ninjas.

"I got it from here," Mitya says telepathically. "Just give me a few minutes."

The door opens, and Ada enters.

"Hi, Ada," Mitya says out loud as he gets up. "I was just leaving. I want to go check on Mr. Viktor Tsoi."

"Hey," I say out loud. "Let's not tease Muhomor too much. The guy just lost his ability to walk."

"You didn't tell him about Project Iron Fly?" Mitya asks Ada reproachfully. "It's the coolest thing we've done in the last hour."

"No." Ada walks up to my bed and sits on the edge. "I'll tell him now, though."

Mitya leaves, and Ada switches to mental communication as she explains that Project Iron Fly is a high-tech suit she and Mitya designed as a surprise gift for Muhomor. They started off by reading everything in the field of robotic exoskeletons, both military applications (what little is public) and suits designed to let paralyzed people walk. They then designed their own model that, if all goes well, will look like a pair of ski pants that the Brainocytes will seamlessly operate.

"This should allow Muhomor to run faster than a regular person," Ada concludes, "and without ever getting tired."

"You can weaponize this thing too," I say, getting into the spirit of it.

"Yeah." Ada rolls her eyes. "The first thing Mitya wanted to do was put rockets in the feet, hence the project name."

The first part of Muhomor's name means "a fly" in Russian, so

Iron Fly is a pretty apt name for a superhero-type suit that Muhomor will wear.

"I want to help build this thing." I imbue my message with excitement. "But I think Muhomor will want to participate in the design too."

"He can build part two if he wishes," Ada counters. "If we left it up to him, he'd design a glorified wheelchair that sits on top of the most compact super server he can cram under his butt so he can hack things without reaching out to cloud servers."

"Not if we really turn his bones into computing substrate, but you have a point." I look at the opening door and say out loud, "Oh, hey, Mom."

Mom enters the room, smacks herself on the forehead in a theatrical gesture, and says, "Ada, I feel so absentminded. I forgot to pick up Misha's grilled vegetable sandwich."

If Ada notices Mom's glaring attempt to speak with me privately, she doesn't show it and instead offers to go pick up the sandwich.

"Okay," Mom says as soon as Ada leaves the room. "Here it is."

She walks up to my bed and extends her hand, palm up.

There's a ring box in her hand.

I reach out and grab it. Opening the box, I stare at the glorious piece of jewelry in fascination.

"Your great-great-grandfather was a jeweler," Mom explains. "Your great-great-grandmother was the most beautiful woman in Tomovka—a tiny Jewish village in Ukraine. Since he wanted to marry someone so out of his league, he managed to somehow get that rock"—she points at the two-karat, orange-colored diamond —"and it worked. This ring has been passed down in our family ever since."

"I don't even know what to say." I didn't even realize diamonds came in such colors, but the internet confirms they do and that this type is very rare. "Thank you so much, Mom."

"Of course," Mom replies and leans in for a kiss on the cheek.

"I'll go find my brother. You best think of what you'll say to her when the time comes."

After Mom leaves, I finalize the app Mitya and I developed and test it out a few times. Then I do as Mom suggested and think of what I'll say when the time comes.

———

Ada brings the sandwich I never asked for, and I gladly munch on it as she and I speculate in Zik about the future of our planet once the Brainocyte technology is inside the heads of a large portion of the population.

"Smarter people will be in a position to eradicate the last remnants of age-old problems, like famine, diseases, and war." Ada walks up to the window and looks out at the impressive view of the Manhattan skyline. "We can also hope to solve some of the uniquely modern problems, like cancer and lack of long-term planning."

"I'm sure it won't all be so rosy." Though I share Ada's optimism, someone in our soon-to-be family needs to play devil's advocate, and it might as well be me. "It's only a matter of time before someone finds a way to use Brainocytes for something evil, like to spy on them as Muhomor fears."

"Tema makes spying difficult." Ada turns away from the window and comes toward me. "And we can always write an app to address whatever problems might arise."

I see a perfect segue way for my big surprise and say, "Speaking of apps, I designed something with Mitya's help, and I'd love to experience it with you."

I send Ada the Ninja Penguin app in question and wait for her to signal that she's launched it.

"Got it," Ada informs me. "You want me to start this app now?"

"Let's do it together," I say and activate my version of the app. "Close your eyes once the app is up and running."

Ada stops in the middle of the room and closes her eyes.

I initiate the app, and as soon it starts, I close my eyes as well. Instead of the backs of our eyelids, the app makes us see a fantastical garden all around us.

"The app takes Augmented Reality to the next level," I explain as I look around in awe. "It's safer to call it Virtual Reality."

Ada looks around, takes in the candlelight coming from every corner of the virtual environment, looks at the myriad of delicate flowers, and smiles at me—or smiles at who she thinks is me but is really my avatar.

My version of the app is a little different from Ada's. Ada's body controls her avatar, and the avatar is in the exact part of the room she's in. The only difference is that her avatar is clad in a glorious evening gown with a low-cut back. In contrast, because I'm currently bedridden, I control my avatar the way I would a video game character. My virtual self is sharply dressed in a tux, and he's standing next to me in the virtual environment, mainly because it's easier to control him that way.

Ada looks around some more, her amber eyes wide at the new marvels that appear as the sun sets behind the trees—details Mitya and I stole from one of Ninja Penguin's more popular VR games.

The garden is full of surreal luminescent plants of every variety, but I can tell Ada's favorites are the ones that remind me of cherry blossoms.

Birds that look like deep-water sea creatures float in the black-purple night sky. Behind the birds, we can see bright star constellations that don't resemble anything viewable from Earth.

"I get it. You're going for 'very romantic.'" Ada looks my avatar up and down appreciatively. "And you clean up nice—virtually."

"You look amazing yourself," I reply, a little at a loss for words. "Come here."

Ada walks under the spindly vines, brushing her fingers against the branches. A couple of shiny alien butterflies try to land on Ada's shoulder, but she shoos them away.

"If you're planning to sell this game, or whatever this is, the *Avatar* movie franchise might sue you." Ada's Zik message is teasing, but she looks serious as she stands under the luminous cherry blossoms, next to my virtual representation.

I activate the command that causes the leaves to fall, and before Ada knows what hit her, my avatar gets down on one knee and extends his hands in that classic gesture.

Ada looks at me intently, her eyes shining with unreadable emotion.

"Ada," I ceremonially say out loud. My heart rate spikes, and I worry a nurse might barge in on us in the real world. "Will you marry me?"

I open the ring box, and the virtual ring shines with an iridescent orange light that reminds me of the suitcase from *Pulp Fiction*.

"Wow," Ada says out loud. She sounds overwhelmed with emotion, but since she's talking in English and not Zik, the emotions are unclear. "I didn't think you'd actually go through with it."

"You what?" Her words catch me completely off guard.

"Oh, I'm sorry," Ada says, still out loud. "Now that I've seen it, it's incredibly romantic and almost not corny at all. I didn't mean—"

I turn off the app and look at Ada in the real world. She must do the same thing, because she's facing *me* and not my avatar.

"You knew I was going to propose?" I ask, switching to Zik.

"Again, I'm sorry. I considered acting like this was a surprise, but I didn't want to repay such a nice gesture with a lie." Ada walks up to my bed and sits on the edge again. "In my defense, if you wanted this stuff to stay secret, you and Mitya shouldn't have committed your fascinating Virtual Reality code into our shared source control repository."

She gives me an innocent smile that makes me want to smack my head.

Before I can actually do so, she gently touches my left hand just below the IV entry point and says, "Also, when you shut down your Share app, you need to remember to turn off the one running in Mr. Spock's head as well, like you did at the fake shrink's office."

At the mention of his name, Mr. Spock runs out of his hiding spot behind the large cushion in the middle of the room and gives Ada a drowsy nod.

"And finally," Ada says out loud, "if you want privacy, you need to make sure your room doesn't have any cameras." She points at the hospital security camera above the big TV on the opposite wall.

"So you knew." I find the bed remote and raise myself into a sitting position so I'm looking directly into her eyes.

She nods sheepishly.

"And yet you let me go through with it." I look at Mr. Spock for support, but he loses interest in us and goes back under the cushion.

Ada nods again.

"Well," I say and pull out my right hand from under the covers. I'm still grasping the ring box containing the real-world ring Mom gave me. "You must've heard me say I want to marry you because I want to be with you and not because you're pregnant."

"Yes, I heard that." She leans closer and studies the ring box curiously.

"And you've had time to think about your answer?" I open the box, and though this version of the ring doesn't have the other-worldly shine of its VR twin, it does sparkle in the room's halogen lights.

Ada looks at the ring for a moment and then back at me, making me feel like I'm a small prehistoric bug about to get stuck in amber for millennia.

Finally, with almost ceremonial gravity, she says, "Yes."

"Yes, you've had time to think about the answer?" I ask as my heart rate equipment starts to beep.

"No." A Mona Lisa smile plays in the corners of Ada's eyes. "I was answering your other question."

"Which one?"

"No, not 'which one.'" Ada grins. "Will you marry me?"

"Yes," I say confidently. "Of course I'll marry you."

"I wasn't asking you. You were asking me." Ada reaches out as though to touch me with her left hand, but instead of touching me, she simply spreads her fingers apart.

"And you said yes." I take the ring and slip it on her extended finger.

Without saying a word, Ada leans in for a kiss.

As our tongues begin to dance, a single Zik message from Ada reverberates through my head, a message imbued with an emotion Ada hasn't used until now—something warm and fuzzy, the Zik equivalent of a heart emoji.

I read the message attached to the feeling and deepen the kiss.

The message states, "Yes."

NEURAL WEB

HUMAN++: BOOK 3

ONE

I'm thirteen hundred feet up, on the 102nd floor of one of the newer tourist magnets in Manhattan, One World Observatory. The crowds around me are flattening their noses against the floor-to-ceiling glass to gulp down a view that can turn a normal person acrophobic. I join in and stare. Every borough is visible under our feet, like a detailed 3D map of New York City.

A vague sense of déjà vu sweeps over me, filling me with overwhelming dread. It's hard to say if I'm scared of the heights, the large crowd, or something more ephemeral.

A dark shape moves in the crowd, and I pivot on my heel to deal with it.

I'm faced with a man with two noses. He has pierced nostrils where his eyes should be, and a cyclopean eye in the center of his face.

My facial recognition app reports an error, and the biological equivalent of a system failure happens in the part of my brain responsible for recognizing faces.

The nose-eye man takes out a gun, and before I can theorize how he got it through the security downstairs, he raises it, aligns the sights with his one eye, and squeezes the trigger.

Without the earplugs I typically use at the gun range, the gunshot blasts my eardrums, likely hastening age-related deafness by at least a year. The humongous window next to me shatters into small pieces that twist and oscillate, doing their best to cut as many tourists as possible.

I ignore more shots fired, as well as the blood and screams all around me, because another man with the same eye-and-noses face appears right behind me. I spin and try to punch the abomination in the one eye, but he dodges.

I do a double take. If I used Photoshop to duplicate the eye, delete the extra nose, and move it all to the right places, the face in front of me would look a lot like the face I see in the mirror every day (minus the nose piercings).

My attacker uses my distraction and momentary lack of balance to push me toward the broken window.

I scream, but it's too late. After a cartoon-like moment during which I look down and take in the impossible height, I begin to fall.

This building is so tall there are clouds around me. The feeling of déjà vu gets stronger as I race past the surrounding skyscrapers. From here, they look tiny. The Statue of Liberty is like a toy in the nearby water, and the people on the streets are too small to see, like bacteria.

My heart realizes I'll splatter on the pavement in around ten seconds and tries to evacuate my chest cavity while it still can. The terror in every cell of my body deepens the feeling of déjà vu.

I choke on my scream as a fiery figure swoops in from nowhere, like the legendary Firebird from the Russian legends. As it approaches, I realize it's a glowing human being. In a whoosh of fiery wings, it cradles me in its arms, and we hover around the eightieth floor of the skyscraper.

My savior's hair forms a telltale Einsteinian halo around his head. When I recognize the AI's face, I instantly know what he's about to say.

Sure enough, he announces with a German accent, "You're safe.

As part of your nightmare reduction therapy, I'm letting you know that this is a dream. You also wanted me to suggest that you try lucid dreaming, which would require you to stay asleep."

"Of course." I barely resist smacking myself on the forehead. "That's what that déjà vu feeling was about. I've had this nightmare before."

"You've had other dreams of falling as well." Einstein's glow is completely gone, and he no longer possesses fiery wings. "We can discuss your dreams later. Your window of opportunity for lucid dreaming is closing fast."

He's right. If I want to take control of my dream world as all the books on the subject suggest, I need to act now.

First, I focus on turning my unpleasant dream of falling into a dream with a similar physical action but nearly opposite subjective value. I wish to fly, and a moment later, I find myself soaring through Manhattan and enjoying views that passengers on a tourist helicopter tour would envy.

The now-ordinary Einstein and I form a flock of two, his arms in front of him like Superman and mine out like wings.

"This is awesome," I tell the AI. "If falling feels overwhelmingly stressful, flying is pure joy."

"Just watch out," Einstein replies. "Exhilaration can wake you just as easily as—"

———

I wake up in my bed, a rat nose at my back and Ada's warm body spooned in front of me.

"You have been unconscious for two hours and thirty-seven minutes," Einstein's voice says.

"Another nightmare?" Ada whispers over her shoulder.

"Nothing bad," I say—a euphemism I use to mean I didn't dream about family members being slaughtered in front of my eyes nor any of the other horrors I've dealt with. "Just some weird faces and falling."

"I bet it's a manifestation of stage fright. After all, our trip is the day after tomorrow." She switches on the soft bedroom light with a mental command to Einstein and turns to face me, her amber eyes glinting with a surprising level of alertness for the time of night.

She might have a point. We're going to be doing presentations about our company in several new markets, and I've been increasingly dreading these trips—and not just because, like any normal human, I don't like speaking in front of huge crowds.

"I'm actually more concerned about telling our offspring," I say to Ada in a private Zik message. Illogically, I feel like our son might somehow overhear us if I so much as vibrate the airwaves in the house. "It's right after his birthday, and I don't want to ruin the big event for him."

"Don't worry about that for now." She strokes my shoulder. "If you'd like, I'll be the bad one this time around—anything to help you sleep."

"You're the best wife ever, but this is something we'll have to tell him together. Now let's sleep."

"In a few minutes." She shifts closer, and as her lips approach mine, I realize what she wants. My anatomy reciprocates—strongly. "After you fulfill your marital duties, you'll sleep even better," she adds in a huskier voice, making sure her lips brush mine as she talks.

"VR or for real?"

"Why not both?"

She yanks down the blanket with a flourish, and sleep becomes but a distant memory.

TWO

"S DNYOM ROZHDENIYA, ALAN," UNCLE ABE SAYS TO MY SON AND raises his shot glass.

"Happy birthday! Four years old." Mom also raises her vodka excitedly. "You're such a big boy."

Flanked by Gogi and Joe, my progeny is standing next to his avatar, which he has made visible only to Ada and me so that we can privately see him roll his eyes.

"Be nice to your grandma." The newest version of the Telepathy app allows Ada to sound kind, firm, and slightly scolding at the same time—something you can't do with just voice. The emotions the app conveys have nuances that can only be understood and felt by people with Brainocyte-enhanced brains. "If you really were as mature as you think you are, you wouldn't mind phrases like 'baby' or 'big boy,'" she continues.

"Or 'kid,'" I add, winking at Alan. "Or—"

"Thanks, Grandma," he replies on a public thought channel, without a hint of negativity. His public Zik message shows proper gratitude and happiness; it's scary how good of a liar my son can be. "You're right, of course, Mom," he adds in our private chat. His avatar's head bows impossibly low and his foot paints an arc in

545

front of his body, telling me he's overacting his contrition. "Some words and phrases just seem to trigger my inner primate—something I'm working on."

I look over my son, both his real-world visage and his digital representation. If you take Ada's amber eyes and double up on the mischievous twinkle, you get Alan's real-world eyes. If you take my smile—specifically, the smile I get when I've done something truly devious to someone who totally deserves it—you get Alan's smile. The rest of his face is a mixture of my wife and me with a slight simian twist, as though we'd spliced capuchin monkey genes into our offspring (which we didn't, though we now have the technology to do that or anything else Dr. Moreau would be jealous of). Alan must be able to see the monkey in his own face as well. How else to explain that "inner primate" comment?

In contrast to his tiny real-world self, Alan's digital avatar looks like a twenty-year-old man who, quite literally, is a mixture of Ada and me. He created this avatar using a neural net he designed a few weeks ago, a specialized AI whose sole purpose was to scan every picture of Alan's parental units and produce a 3D face that perfectly blended our features. He didn't use us as inspiration for his body, though, opting instead for something he must've seen on a cover of some magazine—hence the broad shoulders, chiseled abs, and precancerous tan.

Everyone in the real world clinks their glasses together, and I join in.

"You know," Mitya thinks at me privately, his real-world self chewing on a caviar sandwich, "it's crazy that we have a table filled with Russian cuisine in the middle all this."

I look around and acknowledge that Mitya is right. This party doesn't belong here, in the dinosaur exhibit of the Museum of Natural History. When I rented *Night at the Museum* a few weeks ago, I didn't realize how obscenely expensive that movie rental would turn out to be. Then again, what's the point of being one of the richest people in the world if you can't rent your son a museum on his birthday?

"Do you like my gift?" Muhomor asks after he stops grimacing, something he does after every shot of vodka.

Muhomor is wearing the latest model of his Brainocyte-controlled power suit, which means he can walk for days nonstop, run a hundred marathons, and beat a world record in sprinting. If he wanted to, he could leap up and dance a jig on the skull of that giant dinosaur skeleton that happens to be the centerpiece of this enormous hall. Golan Dahan, our Director of Nanotech, thinks we're mere months from fixing Muhomor's spine—and the spines of anyone else who needs it.

"Who doesn't love reading about blockchains?" Alan's private avatar rolls his eyes again. "I always wanted to know how bitcoin works in as much detail as possible."

Only Ada and I can detect the sarcasm in Alan's real-world voice. Muhomor takes his words at face value and grins as though he managed to hack yet another bank. Ada and I exchange glances and decide that since we ourselves roll our eyes at most of Muhomor's statements, we should let Alan's impertinence stand. After all, he learned this behavior from us.

"I just want to make sure this 'gift' doesn't include any ideas on how to hack bitcoin's cryptographic functions." Ada's pointed smile makes Muhomor nearly choke on his lamb kebab. "I hope we all agree that something like that would not be suitable as a gift for a four-year-old?"

Alan suddenly looks a lot more interested in his gift. Muhomor hastily gestures at it, and the virtual gift box changes, the new one noticeably smaller.

I consider having one of the myriad parallel instances of myself examine the gift in detail but decide against it. Instead, I think to Ada, "If Alan were to set his sights on bitcoin, it would be toast anyway."

Alan got Brainocytes as soon as he was born, long before US laws set eighteen as the minimum age for Brainocyte eligibility (our expensive lobbyists are working on overturning those laws, along with any other hint of legislation against our products). Alan also got Respirocytes with the rest of us. The only thing we didn't give him—because he's still developing—are Bone Servers. That's what Dahan, our Director of Nanotech, calls the beta product that allows us to have stronger bones that can serve as computing resources in a pinch.

In any case, when it comes to brain enhancements, Alan got as many as the rest of us in the Brainocytes Club inner circle—and that's an impressive number indeed. He was also the first human to have his complete brain connectome mapped in a digital substrate, though the rest of us followed shortly. Like with us, his digital brain parts in the cloud far outstrip his meager biological parts. His mind is distributed among the top-of-the-line servers that only enhanced brains could've developed in such a short span of time.

As a result, Alan has as much in common intellectually with a typical four-year-old as we do with a vanilla, unenhanced human being. Alan could speak Zik when he was a month old. He recently completed his PhD thesis in Computer Science and plans to study more fields. If he wanted to get into hacking, he'd be a frightening force, but I don't think that activity would be stimulating enough for him.

"He won't bother with something as mundane as hacking," Ada says, echoing my thought. "He has more interesting projects to keep him busy."

It's true. Alan's current intellectual challenge is advanced video game environments that use virtual reality—or as he likes to call it, world simulations. I think he first got interested in this when he learned I used VR to help me cope with PTSD-like symptoms. He has now created a whole virtual world for Mr. Spock and the rest of our enhanced rats to roam. This world is a rat nirvana, and Mr. Spock and his kin now spend most of their time there. In fact, Rat World is where they are right now, virtually, though their actual biological bodies are at home. Being stimulated like that helps enhance rat life expectancy, as do the nanocytes that we're experimenting with (and which we'll eventually use to triple human life expectancy). The most interesting part about Rat World, though, is that Alan populated it with virtual rats with brains mimicked at such detail that the resulting creatures are, for all intents and purposes, real rats (unless you want to get philosophical about it, which Alan likes to do). When I walked through Rat World and saw the multitudes of his rat creations, it wasn't hard to picture my son growing up to create whole universes, like a self-made deity.

"Nor does he have a financial incentive to crack bitcoin," I add when Ada looks at me expectantly.

"Exactly," she agrees.

Ada and I set up a multi-billion-dollar trust fund for Alan a year ago. His monthly allowance is in the millions. However, he won't need our funds for long because his many businesses will soon show profits. The kid has more patents than Thomas Edison.

"If it's gift time, I have something for the little bunny," Mom says, and I notice JC, her new husband, touch her elbow in warning. He understands Alan better than she does. "Here"—she grabs a box from under her chair and brings it out with aplomb—"it's from your grandparents."

Mom insists that Alan think of JC as his grandpa, but Alan insists on calling JC by his initials like everyone else does. In part, this is because Alan supersedes JC on the Human++ corporate hierarchy. JC still leads Techno, which is now just a small part of the giant corporation that Mitya, Ada, and I formed together, while Alan is a major shareholder of that corporation.

"It's a knitted sweater," real-world Alan says without a hint of the disappointment that even I feel on his behalf. "Thank you."

He walks over to Mom and kisses her cheek, and she promptly melts into a contented puddle. I sure hope he never turns evil, because that move would make Machiavelli proud.

"My turn." Uncle Abe pulls out a wrapped package that's obviously a skateboard. "Here you go. It's so you can play outside more."

Unlike the rest of the family, Uncle Abe didn't join the new Human++ megacorporation, and he's refused advanced versions of

Brainocytes. It took a lot of convincing to even get him to accept the newest, FDA-approved Brainocytes delivered via a transdermal patch—the Tier III ones Human++ has been giving away for free to billions of people. His lack of understanding of Alan's mental capabilities is why he miscalculated his gift so dramatically; otherwise, he'd have known that Alan assessed the risks of skateboarding and found the scary statistics unacceptable—or at least I hope that's what happened.

Oddly, Alan looks genuinely grateful, which is worrying. I privately think at Ada, "Hon, we should create a virtual reality experience of riding that thing for Alan so he doesn't get tempted to split his head for real."

"I'm pretty sure he's only planning to ride the board using one of his robo-avatars," she replies calmly. "My other thread can see his favorite body walking this way."

I check the museum security cameras and confirm that one of Alan's "bodies" is indeed walking our way. More reminiscent of a Terminator skeleton than a human being, this advanced model has sight, hearing, taste, smell, and touch sensors that pass for their human equivalents. But unlike a human body, it also allows us to sense electrical and magnetic fields, perform echolocation, detect changes in air moisture, and a couple of other things I haven't tried yet.

On a whim, I spawn another instance of myself, take possession of one of the robot bodies I left on standby, and walk it toward Alan's metallic avatar.

Embodying this equipment still gives me an eerie feeling, much more so than when I operate avatars in virtual environments. In part, that's because I have hundreds of virtual personae running at any given moment, whereas I only rarely need a physical robot body for business or recreational tasks. Still, to my expanded consciousness, the robot body is quite serviceable, and its senses are surprisingly lifelike. Riding this body really nails the idea Ada has been trying to sell to everyone for ages: that the human body is a machine like this robot, just made from meat.

"Will you let me ride your skateboard?" my robot self asks Alan's robot instantiation. My synthetic voice is almost indistinguishable from that of a human.

"Of course, Dad." As an addendum to his words, Alan's avatar's metallic face tries to smile at me, something that still looks ghastly on this particular model. "But I go first."

"Hey, it's your birthday." I make my robot wink.

"I got this for the little warrior," Gogi says in the meantime and pulls out a box. If the newly arrived robots made Gogi nervous, he doesn't show it, unlike white-faced Uncle Abe.

As his robot body skates away, the tiny human version of Alan rips into the wrapping of Gogi's gift with age-appropriate enthusiasm. As a rule, Alan and Gogi get along, having bonded over violent video games. Not surprisingly, Gogi's present turns out to be a pair of little boxing gloves—another not-so-subtle hint that Alan should begin training in self-defense in the real world. In the virtual world, the kid wipes the floor with Gogi already, and I bet if Gogi were able to control a robot, which he can't, Alan would beat him that way also.

Ada frowns at the gift. I grab her small hand in mine and gently squeeze, saying privately, "If Alan learned to box, it would only make him safer."

She doesn't seem pacified but doesn't say anything.

Joe clears his throat, indicating that he must also have something for the birthday boy.

Ada's frown deepens. Despite Joe's recent improvements in his business dealings and temperament, she's still not his biggest fan.

"Here," he says to Alan. "I hope it fits."

Alan unwraps Joe's box with even more enthusiasm than Gogi's, but when he looks inside, his whole posture seems to deflate. With excitement I can clearly discern as fake, he says, "A bulletproof vest. Wow. Thanks, Uncle Joe."

In our private virtual reality, Ada and I exchange a meaningful glance, and I secretly say, "You know, it could've been something worse—like a knife."

Unlike his father, Joe has the more advanced Tier II Brainocyte suite that gives its user a wider range of utilities, including a modest brain boost. Tier II is a perk for all Human++ employees, and as Head of Security, Joe was one of the early adopters.

Tier II brain boost has had an interesting effect on my cousin. The guy now seems to possess a conscience, albeit a rudimentary one. There are a couple of theories as to the cause of this, and all of them assume he didn't have a conscience before. Mitya believes Joe is simply mellowing with age, but we all think that's baloney, as the "mellowing" happened in the last four years. I think that the experience of getting smarter makes one realize that violence is sometimes not the best solution, but my friends think that's too simplistic an explanation, as plenty of intelligent people have committed violence over the years.

Ada thinks the older Brainocyte brain boost methodology is behind the changes in Joe, as we still employ the older method for Tier II. The old boosts use simulated computer brain regions to enhance brainpower, meaning Joe is getting more brain that isn't his original brain and thus somehow gaining empathy or whatever else he previously lacked. If she's right, we may want to be careful about how, when, and if we give Joe Tier I access, as that uses the newer method for the boosts.

Out of necessity, Tier I Brainocyte capabilities are still available only to the four original members of the Brainocytes Club, plus my son. It's not because we're trying to hoard power, though. We want everyone to become Tier I eventually; we just have a bottleneck when it comes to computer resources.

The Tier I brain boosts are different because of advancements in brain scanning technology. We let existing Brainocytes scan our biological brain in minute detail. Then, when we build computer models for the extra brain regions, we base them on the scans of our brain circuitry. This new and better method of enhancement cuts down on the negative side effects that Tier II people experience, such as pre-cog moments. The new method also decreases the boost adjustment period to a matter of hours instead of days.

But it's computationally much harder to accomplish, and we can't afford to give it to everyone yet.

Additionally, this brain scanning gives us backups of our brains in case something happens to the fragile tissue, like a stroke or a blow to the head. Mitya has become obsessed with this line of research and already has his whole biological brain backed up. It's this obsession of his that was behind the protocols that ensure our prodigious nonbiological brainpower is backed up on a regular basis. I think he's wasting his time worrying so much about his meat brain, as Ada calls it. Our biological brainpower will soon become but a tiny part of what we are, so small that we might not miss it if we suddenly lost it.

"You're multitasking too much again." Ada's complaint pulls me out of my thoughts.

"No."

My reply is too defensive, and I take in a breath to examine myself. Ada's been trying to get me to be more in the moment. She worries that I don't get any quality time with her and Alan. I don't like to think that I'm the kind of father and husband who needs reminders like that—even if I sometimes do.

"I'm merely coding that new app we discussed"—the defensiveness is completely gone in my thought-speech—"testing our surprise gift, reading work emails, and having a psychotherapy session with Einstein. That last one was something you suggested."

Using Einstein as a shrink is a new service we're about to roll out to the worldwide Brainocyte user base. It's going to be part of our freemium model, and we expect it to bring about a lot of good in the world, as this therapy has been instrumental in curbing my nightmares and relieving my post-traumatic stress.

Ada looks placated enough, and we companionably watch Alan open a gift from JC, which turns out to be, of all things, a yo-yo. Alan seems to appreciate it and starts doing tricks with it immediately.

"Our turn soon," Ada says with a wink. "You might want to

reduce your workload a little more. For whatever reason, you seem a bit distant."

Ada claims that heavy multitasking takes away from each activity. Since she designed the system, it must be true. On my end, though, I rarely feel the distractedness. I stopped feeling as if I'm doing multiple things at once a couple of years back.

The term multitasking is misleading for what we can now do, anyway. The me who's talking to Einstein in the virtual therapy room feels very different from the me who's watching the current proceedings. It's as though I exist in multiple places at once, but later I have the memory of all these bits of myself. Of course, rationally I know that each of these instances of myself uses dedicated computer resources, and that if these resources are overloaded, something will happen to all instances of me. That something could easily look like distractedness to an outside observer.

"Didn't you design the system to prevent a thread from being created during resource overload?" I ask her.

"I did, but once your resources are allocated, they are never taken away. If you start doing more with your resource allotment, you can get distracted."

I stop some of my tasks. I know better than to argue with Ada about Brauocyte tech. She's still the world expert, so if she says multitasking leads to being distant, it's probably true despite my feelings to the contrary.

"Let's let Mitya go next." I make myself look as alert as I can. "We want to end this gift giving with a splash."

"Show off, you mean?" Her private avatar, the one that looks like a punky panda bear, smiles.

"Maybe," I reply, realizing that my earlier list of activities didn't include skateboarding with Alan—a sign that I honestly am distracted right now. "You're proud of our work too. It's okay to admit it."

A smile touches Ada's real-world amber eyes, and I can tell she's anxious to see her son's reaction to our surprise.

"My gift is something everyone might enjoy," Mitya says, and we switch our attention to him. "I've secured a deal between Human++ and Disney. The folks at Disney are going to build a huge virtual park that Brainocytes users can visit in VR, without the need to fly to places like Orlando. This"—a huge golden ticket flies toward Alan in the shared VR environment—"is part of that deal. Alan gets VIP access pass to the park—for life."

Now that most of the human population has Brainocytes in their heads, many companies have chosen to create apps and experiences tailored for Brainocytes, so Disney's jumping on the bandwagon isn't a shock to anyone. Still, Alan seems thrilled at the prospect of seeing what the folks at Disney will create. My guess is he has professional interest as a world creator—and probably also thinks a Disney park will be fun.

"Looks like it's our turn." Ada gets up and I follow.

"You'll be able to enjoy our gift right away," I say to Alan. I give Mitya a narrow-eyed stare—he knew what Ada and I had prepared for Alan, yet he chose a gift that's very similar to ours. "I'd like everyone to pay attention to the public VR."

Ada lets me launch the B-Day app, and the museum around us comes alive.

THREE

A FLOCK OF PTEROSAURS SWOOPS TOWARD OUR BIG TABLE, AND MOM squeals in excitement. The giant skeleton in the room grows meat and muscle, and is seconds away from manifesting skin. When the monster dinosaur begins to move, it gives Godzilla a run for her (or is it his?) money.

"Our room is but a small part of the world Ada and I put together," I tell the awestruck guests. "Other rooms in the museum are also animating right now. Here are some highlights." I share screens with everyone so they can see the walking mummies, the giant blue whale that sings its song as it splashes the virtual water on the first floor, and Ada's least favorite, Lucy and the other early hominids hunting animated mammals and dinosaurs from other exhibits.

For the first time today, Alan behaves as I imagine a four-year-old should: he jumps to his feet and runs to check out the rest of our creation.

Before Ada can notice and disapprove, Joe nods to a couple of his security people, and they follow Alan at a perfectly calculated distance.

The fact that our son is physically running is a testament to our gift's success. The kid is a master of distributing his mind into robots and cameras, to the point where Ada and I sometimes worry about his lack of physical activity.

Ada and I both take a bow, and the rest of the guests clap with genuine enthusiasm, even Muhomor. We sit back down, and Gogi pours another round of drinks across the table as giant virtual dragonflies swarm around his head.

"I don't mean to spoil the merriment," Joe says with a cold carelessness that contradicts his words, "but you should at least be aware of the protestors outside."

I suppress a groan as adrenaline surges through my veins. If there's a consequence of our success I could do without, it's the protests. If one is really happening outside the museum, it would be an especially unpleasant surprise. We tried so hard to keep this event a secret from the public.

It takes me just a moment to find the best camera from the myriad available outside. After a quick examination, my adrenaline levels stabilize. "These are the anti-GMO people," I say privately to Joe. "They're harmless."

My cousin doesn't bother showing his disdain for my opinion. He probably spent all his disdain on the protestors outside.

I inwardly sigh as I take another look at the crowd of haters. Despite the obscene money Human++ regularly spends on PR, these kinds of protests have been happening more frequently. It's shocking how many of our gifts to humanity have been met with hostility. In part, this is because certain technologies have been villainized by books, Hollywood, and special interest groups. Robots are a great example of the former, à la *The Terminator*, while GMOs are a good example of the latter.

What people don't seem to get is that we're smart enough to avoid Skynet scenarios and purposely keep Einstein's intellect far behind our own. Also, our genetically enhanced plants are different from the GMOs of old, in which foreign genes were introduced into traditional domestic plants. We use CRISPR and other gene-editing technologies to merely tweak certain genes in semi-domesticated or wild plants. The wild legumes and quinoa at this very table are the products of this work, and they're amazing —and the fact that they're being eaten by the richest and smartest people is a good indication of their lack of risk to human health. But it's hard to convert people who have turned their hatred of GMOs into a quasi-religion.

Ada nervously spikes her hair. "The Real Humans Only crowd is also outside. Joe was right to be concerned."

"Maybe those guys are not as violent as we think," I tell her, wishing I could believe my own words. "At least the RHO's cause is easier for me to understand." Seeing Ada frown, I add, "Though not agree with or condone."

Her frown deepens. "They're basically Luddites under a different name, except the machines they want to break are in our heads."

It's true. Like the original Luddites, the RHO worries that jobs will go away as a result of our technology, and there are good reasons for that. One Brainocyte-enhanced lawyer can do the workload of ten unenhanced lawyers; ditto with doctors and almost any other profession. Given that the world needs a limited number of doctors, some jobs could disappear. And it's not just experts in danger; regular workers will be impacted as well. Our tech now allows one person to control a group of robots that can do many of the difficult, dangerous, and dirty jobs that formerly required teams of people.

"Will this make it hard for the other guests to arrive?" I ask Joe. "Alan has an after-party planned."

"The after-party people are already here and have been vetted," Joe says.

Alan runs back into the room, catches his breath, and rattles out, "That was awesome. Thank you, Mom. Thank you, Dad."

"You came back just in time," I say to Alan as I spot the baker navigating his way into the hallway. No doubt he has also been vetted. "Prepare your wish."

Instead of saying something like HAPPY BIRTHDAY, ALAN, the cake states P vs. NP in yummy chocolate sauce.

"What does that mean?" Uncle Abe asks. "And do I even want to know?"

"It's just a computer science problem I want to solve when I grow up," Alan replies with false modesty. "In a nutshell, this asks if every problem that can be quickly verified can also be quickly solved."

"By quickly, he means polynomial time," Muhomor says, though it's clear Uncle Abe couldn't care less if he actively tried. "I think we can all agree that P does not equal NP."

"You're just saying that because you hope it doesn't," Alan replies teasingly. "Tema would be beatable if P equals NP."

Alan and Muhomor begin to argue computer science theory, and everyone else focuses on their own conversations as they consume large quantities of dessert.

"You should let the after-party people in," I tell Joe when the last of the cake is gone. "The family portion of the festivities looks to be over."

As though on cue, everyone gets up and attempts to overcome their impending food comas by walking around the museum to check out Alan's gift. Alan, Ada, and I remain behind, since we already know what it looks like. Waiters attack the big table, and within minutes, the space is ready for the cocktail-style after-party.

"It's going to be great to see some of my friends for the first time," Alan tells us excitedly.

"Are these online-only friends?" I look my son up and down.

His mischievous expression turns defensive. "Do I have any other kind?"

"And did you tell them what you actually look like?" Ada asks sternly.

Alan starts to reply but stops when a man enters. The guy appears to be in his thirties, with the air of a college professor about him. I use face recognition to confirm my intuition; indeed, he's a tenured professor of philosophy at Columbia. His name is John Moore, and he isn't on any sexual predator lists—not that Joe would let him live, let alone enter this room, if he were.

John confidently walks over to me and holds out his hand. "Alan, it's a pleasure to finally meet you."

"Well, that answers that question," Ada tells me privately. "They don't realize they've come to a four-year-old's birthday."

"Hello, John." I give the man a warm handshake. "I'm not Alan."

"You're not?" He looks at Ada for help. "You look a lot like your avatar." He looks at her more closely. "I'm so sorry, are you Alan? You also look like that avatar, but I thought you were a man. Not that—"

"I'm Ada," she cuts in. "This is Mike." She gestures at me. "And this"—she points at our son—"is Alan."

"I really enjoyed our discussion about the Cambridge Declaration on Consciousness," Alan tells John, his eyes beaming with mischief. "I just sent you details for our party VR session. If you enter it, you'll be able to see me in the guise you're more comfortable with."

Once John's eyes stop threatening to jump out of his sockets, he uses his Brainocytes to see Alan's adult avatar.

"I hope you don't begrudge me this surprise," Alan says both in VR and the real world. "I decided my birthday would be the perfect time to come out as a four-year-old. I couldn't figure out a way to explain it online."

"But how?" John whispers. "Is this a prank?"

As Alan explains about his Brainocytes, Joe glides over silently and grasps John's shoulder so firmly John cringes in pain.

"If I may have a word," Joe says. "Now that you know who you came here to see, I just want to say—"

I don't hear the rest, because he leans in and whispers into John's ear.

John's previously awestruck expression changes, and his pale face turns an almost purple shade of terror. It doesn't take a lot of imagination to figure out that Joe must've told him something like,

"If you touch my nephew in any way, especially the wrong way, your short and painful life will not be long enough to get onto the registered sex offenders list."

"Joe," Alan says, obviously realizing the same thing, "stop bullying my friends."

Joe reluctantly lets go of John's shoulder and stalks to the far corner of the room.

To diffuse the tension, I look up the Cambridge Declaration on Consciousness and learn that it states that many animals are conscious and aware.

"The number of scientists who signed the Cambridge Declaration on Consciousness is truly impressive," I say casually. "Their list of species is great too. Besides mammals, they included birds and even octopuses."

"Maybe this means people will finally understand this basic, self-evident truth," Ada grumbles. "Animals are just as self-aware as we are."

"But not necessarily as intelligent," John chimes in, his demeanor turning professorial. "Consciousness does not equate to intelligence."

"No, but admitting that animals have consciousness should at least be enough for people to enlarge their circle of empathy to include them." Ada plants her feet wider apart and regards John belligerently. "We don't eat unintelligent human beings, do we?"

John blinks and pushes his glasses higher up his nose. "I see where Alan gets some of his views. I understand what you're saying, of course, but you can't downplay the role of intelligence."

Alan glances at his mom worriedly. Like me, he's aware this is a touchy subject. "Can we try another thought experiment, John, like usual?"

John looks at the real-world Alan and rubs his temples. "I'm still adjusting to the fact that you're you. But sure, let's hear it."

"Let's say there existed a rat who was smart," Alan begins. In our private VR, he winks at me. He's obviously talking about Mr. Spock and his relatives, but John doesn't know that.

"Okay," John replies. "I can picture that."

"Now let's further assume this rat is intelligent by most definitions of the word. To simplify, let's say this rat is smarter than most of my peers."

"Right," John says. "What you describe is a scenario where we'd have to be very nice to such a rat. We'd treat the rat as a person. If such a magical creature existed."

"So you claim the fact that the rat is intelligent, not the fact that he's conscious, is the criterion for giving him nicer treatment?" Alan asks. "According to the Cambridge Declaration, all rats are conscious, since they're mammals."

"I'd say my position is more nuanced, but yes, I guess that's what I believe." John takes a step away from Ada, who's not even trying to hide her dislike of his philosophy.

"Forget the rat, then," Alan says. "Suppose there's an entity, an intelligent creature that's smarter than a human by the same factor that a human is smarter than a rat."

"Okay," John says hesitantly.

"Would such a creature have the right to treat human beings as 'nicely' as humans currently treat rats?" Alan steeples his tiny real-world fingers. "Run experiments on them, develop special poisons to try to wipe humanity out of existence, place sticky traps that will cause people to die horrific deaths, and so on?"

"Well," John says, rubbing his temples more vigorously this time, "I think that—"

Someone coughs, and John doesn't get a chance to finish his thought. A woman has come in and is peering around the crowd.

"Margret?" Alan yells. "We're over here."

Margret seems even more confused than John when she realizes how old her online friend is. According to face recognition, she's a theoretical computer scientist working at one of the larger NYC hedge funds. Her specialty is Big Data, which is probably what she and Alan talk about. He has an uncanny ability to see patterns in large quantities of data and is always trying to understand how his mind does what it does.

More people arrive, and the conversations move toward Alan's favorite subjects of identity, consciousness, and the technological singularity.

"If we define the singularity as the point when a regular person can no longer keep up with technology," Margret says, "my mother is already experiencing it."

"I define the singularity as the point when things radically change and the speed of advancements skyrockets beyond anyone's wildest dreams," Alan says. "Right now, things are moving fast—but when the singularity hits, our progress will seem like a snail's pace in comparison. I agree, though, the term 'singularity' is definitely beginning to mean different things to different people."

John adjusts his glasses. "To me, it means AI running amok and causing something like the technological Armageddon. It's the start of a dystopia where humanity becomes extinct."

"I didn't realize you sympathized with the people outside," Alan says. Of course he knows about the RHO protestors. "I see the singularity as a point when humanity finally matures and becomes something it was always meant to be, something more than thinking meat... something rationally transcendent." He looks up at the adult faces, and when he sees everyone listening, he continues with fervor. "We can be a way for the universe to become aware of itself. Brain enhancements and integration with our AI and other technology is just the first step. In the long term, I see us becoming first a planet-sized conglomeration of minds, then a galaxy-sized intellect, and on and on, as far as the laws of physics allow."

"There may be as many definitions of the singularity as there are people," Ada says as she gazes proudly at our son. "My own vision is closer to that of Alan's, because I know we can bring it about and avoid any apocalyptic scenarios."

I nod at her words. "We take the concept of 'the world is what you make it' to its full, logical extreme," I say. "With us watching over it, I think the singularity will usher in a new step in evolution, a time when we'll take everything we cherish about being human and push it to an eleven out of ten."

"Even if these rosy predictions come into being," John says with the tone of someone who doubts it very much, "will the beings that inhabit the future actually be human?"

"Why not?" Ada asks. "Though even if they weren't, they would in the worst case be, in the words of Hans Moravec, our mind children."

She glances adoringly at Alan, and when she notices I've followed her gaze, she locks eyes with me and winks.

"I still have to respectfully disagree," John says. "Being human is so closely tied to being biological that I think becoming pure technology will turn people into machines."

"Perhaps I can take a stab at it," Alan says. "You're a fan of thought experiments, so why don't I try one?"

"Sure," John says with an eagerness only a philosophy professor could possess. "Please."

"Imagine that someone has invented an artificial neuron," Alan says. "Now also imagine that someone has taken one of your biological neurons and replaced it with the artificial one. You'd still be you, correct?"

"I'm familiar with this idea." John sips from his champagne glass. "It's called the neuron replacement thought experiment. Once I agree that I'm still the same after getting a single artificial neuron, you'll ask, what about a hundred? Then what about a billion? And soon after that, what if we replaced all of them?"

"Well, just because you know it doesn't mean it's not persuasive," Alan says. "You'd still be you, even if the substrate of your brain were artificial."

"I can only counter this with a thought experiment that is just as persuasive," John says with a smirk. "It's called the Chinese room argument, postulated by John Searle..."

I tune out the rest of the discussion, because this topic reminds me that Ada and I still must break the news of tomorrow's trip to the birthday boy. Our regular work-related travel is a source of upset for Alan, mainly because he thinks he's now old enough and mature enough to join us.

"When do we tell him?" I ask Ada after I pull her into a private VR room that is the exact replica of our living room.

"Let's not ruin the party," she says without clarifying the what or the who, a sign this topic is on her mind as much as it is on mine. "He's having such a good time."

Since Alan is currently poking holes in John's best arguments, I'm forced to agree. The kid loves winning arguments, though it's harder when he debates someone as augmented as himself.

"He'll be mad if we tell him at the last minute." I plop into a replica of my favorite rocking lounge chair and stare at the replica of our awesome Manhattan view.

"I'd rather he be mad on a less special day—like tomorrow," Ada counters. She breaks the VR room's consistency by magicking herself a replica of her office chair to sit on. "I still vote for tomorrow."

"We can always blame Joe again and say he's the one who thinks it's not safe. It's mostly the truth." I rock back and forth in my lounger. For some reason, Alan's puppy eyes work much better on me than on Ada, and I'm not looking forward to this unpleasant task.

"We should tell him in VR," she says ruthlessly. "Tomorrow afternoon, when we're on the way to our destinations."

"You mean so that he won't be able to strong-arm us to take him?" I fight the urge to get up from the chair and start pacing.

"No." She pushes her chair closer and reaches over to clasp my hand. "We tell him that way so that it comes off as the law of the land rather than a topic for debate."

"That might be too authoritarian. I thought we were trying to be authoritative instead."

"I knew it was a mistake to have you read those books on parenting styles." She squeezes my hand. "How about we tell him in the morning at breakfast? Then it can be a back-and-forth, as long as the two of us agree that he's not going this time, no matter what he says."

"Agreed." I feel bad for Alan. He has no chance of winning against this conspiracy of parents.

"I didn't realize that having a preschooler would be this tough." She drops her hand. "It's much worse than those books on child development said."

"If you think this is bad, let's see what happens when he's a teenager."

We both jokingly shudder, but we're all too aware of the Russian proverb: "There is part truth in every joke."

FOUR

THE ISLAND COUNTRY OF CURAÇAO IS AMONG THE SHRINKING number of places without widespread Braincyte adoption—hence my reason for being on this stage.

I survey the huge crowd gathered in front of me and activate a special version of the BraveChill app that's custom made to counteract stage fright. As soon as I'm calmer, I let myself gaze into the distance, where smoke chugs from factory pipes incongruent with the idyllic Caribbean Sea beyond.

"Dear friends." I begin in English and instantly say it again in Dutch and Papiamento, mainly as an easy way to demonstrate some of the things I'm about to present. "My name is Mike Cohen, and I'm here to tell you about Human++ and its gift to you and the world. Specifically, I want to discuss our paradigm-changing product, Braincytes, and our free-energy project that will greatly improve your skies."

I point at the smoke pipes, and the crowd cheers. I wait for them to calm down before I proceed with the rest of my speech, a spiel that's been carefully crafted by our PR department. I tell the crowd that they're going to get free electricity, the same free electricity that most of the world already enjoys. This is the easy part of the talk, because most people find the idea of free energy easy to understand. Here in the Caribbean, people picture themselves using as much AC as they want; elsewhere, they imagine leaving all their lights on and never paying the electric bill.

I explain some of the bigger but less intuitive consequences of free energy, like no more paying for gas after switching to an electric car. When I talk about the possibility of nearly free fresh water, I get cheers and clapping. The clapping turns into a standing ovation when I proceed to explain how few will go hungry as the price of food production plummets.

Joe's security people pass a mic into the crowd, and a wise-looking woman asks, "If all this is free, how do you make your money?"

"That's a great question," I reply. "We use a freemium model. Most private individuals and small businesses will get electricity for free, but bigger businesses with heavier consumption will incur some cost. But that cost is still going to be a fraction of what they're used to, so everyone is happy in the end."

"This part of the lecture isn't playing as well here in Bahrain," Mitya says in our private VR meeting.

The VR space perfectly mimics our favorite conference room in the Human++ tower, right down to the touchscreen boards, ultramodern furniture, and dazzling view of the Manhattan skyline. Though every one of us is physically conducting a similar presentation somewhere around the globe, it's become our policy to keep one instance of our virtual avatars sitting in this room. Muhomor, Alan, Ada, and I are almost always in this room in some fashion anyway, but Joe only joins on days like today, when his security guys are on high alert.

"This part of the spiel never does well in places where oil helps the economy," Ada agrees. "Here on Iturup Island, we're close enough to Russia for people to also be a little wary."

"They might be wary because some of them grew up hearing about free stuff," I say.

"Yeah, that's how most understood what communism would be like," Mitya says.

"Why did Ada get to go to the Kuril Islands again?" Muhomor grumbles. "I still say it should've been one of us native Russian speakers. As you just made obvious, we don't just speak the language natively, we understand the culture—"

"If it's complaining time now," Alan says, "I resent staying back in the States."

"Resent" is a polite word for his actual feelings on the subject. He nearly threw an age-appropriate temper tantrum when we told him that no, he would not be presenting. He doesn't understand our possibly irrational parental worry about sending a four-year-old overseas by himself. Besides, how seriously would people without Brainocytes take such a tiny presenter?

The large virtual screens behind my friends show the crowd and their surroundings at each location. Mitya's crowd in Bahrain is probably the largest, and even through the virtual window, I can almost feel the heat of his dusty yellow surroundings. Ada's gathering on Iturup Island is the smallest, though that could be an illusion thanks to the never-ending sea in the distance. Muhomor's location is a lot like mine, minus any industry; he's on the tropical island of Les Cayemites in Haiti. Each of us have Joe's security people around us, and a couple of robot surrogate bodies as well, in part for security but also for my favorite part of the demo, which will happen toward the end.

On a whim, I embody the robot to Ada's left and use its sensors to savor the crisp, salty air. I then possess a robot next to Mitya and confirm the low humidity and heat.

"Now let me tell you about Brainocytes," I say into the microphone. I can feel the crowd grow more alert; this is probably what they came to hear about.

I explain that Brainocytes are nanomachines that interface with the brain. Once my listeners have an idea what the signature tech does, I move on to dispel some common worries that always come up about our products.

"No brain surgery is required to get Brainocytes." I reach into my pocket and pull out a little square piece of fabric I have prepared for the presentation. "The current delivery method is transdermal patches like this one." I wave the patch and put an image of it on the big screen behind me.

Meanwhile, in the VR room, our conversation continues full on. Ada looks at Mitya. "How are things going on the delivery front? I'm tired of explaining these patches."

"We'll be able to put Brainocytes into the drinking water shortly." Mitya has been driving this initiative, and it's clear he takes great pleasure in showing off how quickly he's accomplished this task. "We've honed it to the point where Brainocytes will only activate in adult humans, but I still don't think we ought to put it in water where people don't want or know about Brainocytes."

This is an old argument between Mitya and Ada, one that the rest of us haven't taken sides on. Ada wants to put Brainocytes into the water supply in places where the government oppresses the populace, as these are usually also places where the government doesn't let us deliver or market Brainocytes to willing customers. But Mitya thinks that despite the tyrannical regimes in those places, we have no right to put machines into people's bodies without their consent, even if they would provide greater freedom for said people.

"It's going to be a moot point soon," Alan chimes in. "Every dictator and tyrant now has Brainocytes in his head anyway, so eventually they'll want it for their people too."

"Ah, the naïveté of the young." Muhomor's VR shades hover in the air without temples or a nose bridge, making him look like a poker player from space. "Just as with any other form of power, the dictators will want to hoard Brainocytes for themselves."

"You're wasting time on these arguments," I interject. "We know thousands of patches got smuggled into even the most closed-down countries. Once the dissidents, or whoever the users are, tell regular citizens about the benefits of our tech, people might start a revolution to get their hands on Brainocytes."

"Which segues well into our next real-world point," Ada says.

She's right, because I say out loud in Curaçao, "At the very basic level, this technology can replace a personal computer of any kind, as well as your TV, your music player, your smartphone, GPS, AI assistants such as Siri, Alexa, and Cortana, devices like the Kindle, gaming consoles, and pretty much all other gadgets. We're revolutionizing education and how people work. Widespread Braincyte adoption is taking the internet revolution to the next level..."

"Our PR people have dumbed down the message," Alan complains back in the VR room. "When I finally get a chance to speak at these conferences, I'll write my own speech."

"So what does the wise toddler think we should be saying?" Even through his shades, it's clear Muhomor just rolled his eyes.

"People might worry about self-replicating nanotechnology," Alan says. I feel proud as a father on a couple of levels but particularly when I realize how stoically Alan just ignored Muhomor's insult—proving that in many ways, Alan is the more mature of these two. "You should tell them about our nonreplicating nanofactories and how—"

"Too technical," Muhomor counters. "And if we tell them why we're being careful with nanotech replication, they'll just get scared."

"Then we should at least tell them about the opportunity to get premium services." Alan's avatar now resembles Ada, and I wonder if he's created an algorithm that morphs his face based on the topic of conversation.

My son is talking about Ada's initiative: paying people to create content that's beneficial to humankind. Ada wants to encourage people to write wiki pages and blogs, to create original art, and to even put up nice pictures of themselves so that other people might enjoy them. The idea, as she puts it, is to "encourage an era of cultural expression." To that end, we created a version of Einstein to trawl the internet for such activities. When he finds any, he rewards the content producer with special points that can be turned into cash or premium services.

"That program makes us seem too Machiavellian," Muhomor says. "And we don't want people to know the truth about that." His glasses float upward, and when they clear the middle of his forehead, his right eye winks conspiratorially.

"You also don't mention some of the benefits of Einstein." Alan's face now morphs to more closely resemble mine—I guess because he knows I like Einstein's features more than Ada does. "Einstein's getting to know each user better than they know themselves. He's on the cusp of helping people with critical decisions. He'll be a sort of digital consciousness for many. He might tell them whom to date or remind them not to make deals when their blood pressure is too high or their dopamine levels too low."

"It makes Einstein sound like Big Brother," Ada says.

She so rarely agrees with Muhomor on anything that everyone in the room exchanges glances.

I chuckle. "Alan actually sees Einstein as a big brother—but in a literal sense, not in a *1984* way."

"If our users wanted to fear anyone, it should be us, not Einstein," Alan says.

"And therefore, you shouldn't write your own speeches," Muhomor says with finality. "If Marcus in PR heard what you just said, his Brainocytes would explode out of his brain."

We move on to less contentious subjects in the VR room, while in the real world, I explain how Brainocytes will work with Global Terahertz wireless internet, a Human++ freemium product Curaçao already utilizes. Global Terahertz will keep Brainocytes users connected to Human++ servers at all times (unless some evil scientist puts them in a Faraday cage with thick lead walls). Many eyes light up as I explain the potential, including voting with one's mind, crystal clear air in large cities, VR dating and relationships, and a slew of other sweeping societal changes.

The conference is going smoother than usual, yet something begins to bother me.

The events of four and a half years ago taught me to trust my paranoia. I put an end to all my parallel activities, leaving my attention on the VR conference room and the real world. In a fraction of a second, I beat ChessMaster, the world's best AI algorithm, and refuse it a rematch; I complete four Rubik's Cubes I've been solving in parallel; and I stop writing my fifty-sixth novel and submit all the unfinished code I was just working on to source control.

As often happens, the extra attention I now direct to the real world gives me the illusion that I'm watching reality in slow motion. On the surface, everything looks routine, like the many conferences we've done before. Yet despite the BraveChill app, I'm overcome with a strong sense of dread.

Parts of my mind are identifying dangers before my conscious awareness can catch up.

Frantically, I scan my surroundings through the eyes of the robots next to Ada, Mitya, and Muhomor. At first, I can't even verbalize what I see. Then my vision zooms in on a guy in the crowd around Mitya, and I understand what's been bothering me.

This guy's clothes are way too bulky for the unforgiving Middle Eastern heat.

Now that I know what to look for, I see men wearing something similar at every location, including my own.

"Suicide bombers!" I shout in the VR room.

In an instant, I text images of the suspects to Joe and his security teams in every region, and put them up on screen in the VR room. If I'm wrong and these aren't suicide vests, I'd rather apologize for being paranoid.

While everyone's reacting to my revelation, the guy in Mitya's crowd inches toward the stage with wild eyes. I jump my awareness into a robot, using his camera eyes to zoom in on the man's hands, and my metallic robot jaws clench with an audible clunk.

He's closing his hand around a device clutched in front of his chest.

I analyze the device in a picosecond. It can only be a detonator.

The man's features contort in fear.

Someone else, probably Mitya, takes control of the bulkier

robot to my right. I make my robot follow his and prepare to jump toward the bomber.

I don't need a brain boost to realize that the robots will not make it in time.

"Run!" I scream through metal lips as my robot flies through the crowd.

"Run!" I yell at Mitya in the VR room.

The robots might as well be miles away, because the bomber's fingers finish squeezing the detonator.

All cameras at Mitya's location show a flash of fire.

I leave my robot before it's ripped apart, but not before I get a horrific glimmer of flesh exploding around me. The microphones roar with soul-piercing static. Then all video and audio goes silent at Mitya's location.

"Mitya!" I scream. "Are you okay?"

Mitya doesn't reply.

We all stare at Mitya's VR room avatar, who stands wide-eyed and uncomprehending. Then the avatar lets out an inhuman scream and turns pixelated—like a ghost inside a machine.

FIVE

I'VE NEVER FELT THIS DISJOINTED.

It's as though there are four distinct versions of me operating completely independently of each other. One, a purely emotional one, is beginning to grieve for Mitya, whose avatar is still disappearing from VR like a mirage.

In complete contrast, the other versions of me exemplify bloodthirst and pragmatism. Enraged, I slam my consciousness into a robot at Ada's right and leap for the bomber in her crowd. I'm glad we overdesigned the strength and speed of these metallic bodies, as I'm flying at an incredible speed. But even this breakneck rescue might not be fast enough.

No.

What just happened to Mitya isn't going to happen to Ada.

I won't let it.

I operate on pure instinct. Grabbing my left robotic arm with the right one, I rip it off. The swell of pain is sharp, but I ignore it.

Teeth clenched, I hurl the separated limb at the approaching bomber.

The metal arm whooshes through the air and smacks into my

target's right shoulder. The man stumbles back, the trigger device clattering to the ground.

Before I can rejoice, he recovers and crouches to pick it up with his uninjured left arm.

I'm grateful the crowd flees from the bomber, because no one impedes my progress. The one-armed robot body lands in front of the crouching man, and I use its remaining left hand to punch into the mushy human body of my enemy. My metal fingers rip through the rib cage and close around a piece of pulsing flesh.

"He was about to kill Ada," I say grimly in VR, as though someone were about to criticize my actions.

No one replies as I pull the asshole's beating heart out of his chest like a priest in some macabre Aztec ritual. The people around us scream. A video of this kill will undoubtedly end up on YouTube, confirming all the fears the paranoiacs have about our robots, but I'm beyond caring.

Back in my real body, I reach into my pocket for the gun one of Joe's people handed me earlier today. The security team around me already has their weapons out, but my training at the range pays off yet again. In less time than it takes the bomber to blink, I put a bullet in his brain.

In the past, I might've worried about taking a life, but paradoxically, it's my respect for life that makes me take the headshot. If the bomber got the chance to squeeze the trigger, hundreds of people would've died. And hey, the asshole was in the process of killing himself anyway. If Ada gives me crap about this later, I can truthfully tell her that a headshot was the best and safest solution.

At the same time as I'm rescuing Ada and myself, I also take charge of a robot near Muhomor. But as soon as I begin to move, I see that I'm too late.

The bomber squeezes the trigger.

All the blood drains from my face.

"I'm sorry." My voice cracks in VR. "I tried."

"Don't worry about me." Muhomor manages to sound smug. "I found a way to jam that signal."

Stunned, I realize the bomb didn't go off. And though my robot is no longer running toward the bomber, another one is.

Wild-eyed, I scan the VR room. "Who—"

"It's me," Alan says. "I think—"

In the real world, the bomber realizes his bomb isn't going to work, so he pulls out a gun and aims it at Muhomor. In the time he takes aim, I've blocked my friend with my robotic metal body. Joe's security people also move to shield him, but Muhomor is already on the move, his exoskeleton legs outpacing even the robots.

The bomber must've realized he won't be able to hit him, because he turns the gun in his own direction.

It takes me less than a millisecond to recognize his plan. The bomber wants to plant a bullet in his own chest, probably to activate the bomb. I have no time to research if this maneuver will succeed or not, so I assume the worst. Though Muhomor is running quickly, he can't outpace the spread of an explosion. Frantically, I grope for solutions as the bomber's hand continues its deadly arc, but nothing comes to mind.

This is when Alan's robot lands next to the bomber. Before the bomber can finish turning the gun at his chest, Alan rips off the guy's suicide vest with the smooth motion of a hungry ape insta-peeling a banana.

The bomber stumbles back, his gun turning upward.

"Alan, stop him!" Joe yells in the VR room. "I need him alive."

But it's too late. Before Alan can command his robot to do anything, the bomber aims the gun under his chin and presses the trigger.

The shot is deafening, bits of blood and brain matter flying everywhere. In every crowd, people are screaming in different languages, but their behavior is uniform: everyone is trying to get away from the bombers and the stages.

Overwhelmed, I allow Joe's security people to take over. In Curaçao, I'm ushered backstage and swiftly led to a bulletproof car. Through the eyes of the robots, I see everyone else getting into other bulletproof cars.

As we speed away from the presentation sites, I finally recover my wits enough to say dazedly inside the VR room, "Someone coordinated an attack on us."

Alan nods gravely. "There's also an anomaly going on with our Ohio data centers. It might—"

"You're both focusing on the wrong thing," Ada says hoarsely. Her punky avatar is sitting in the corner of the virtual room, her knees clasped tightly against her chest. "Don't you remember? Mitya is dead."

I freeze, feeling like I've just been hit by a tsunami of ice. The heat of battle pushed Mitya's fate out of my mind, but it's all I can think about now. My chest is painfully tight, my heart like a block of lead inside my ribcage. Mitya's avatar is still evaporating, one pixel at a time, and in desperation, I wonder whether Ada could be wrong.

Maybe my best friend isn't truly gone.

Filled with sudden hope, I tap into satellite imagery and zoom in on Mitya's position. As soon as I get a clear view of the blast site, though, I have no choice but to accept that Ada is right. Our smart bones are stronger than regular bones, and the Respirocytes in our bloodstreams allow us to go for a while without breathing, but none of these advantages could've helped Mitya. The pieces of charred human flesh around the stage leave no room for doubt.

Not a single person on that stage could've survived.

The pain is so intense it steals my breath away. I feel like I'm about to shatter. It's too much, too overwhelming—the horrified faces that mirror mine in the VR room, the knowledge that I was too late to save my friend.

That I'll never see him again.

Dragging in a shallow breath, I wrap my arms around my real-world body, and in VR, I create a separate room to be alone.

The worst part about my pain is that Brainocytes allow us to manipulate what and how we feel. Ada has been experimenting with apps that expand her circle of empathy, as she calls it, so that she's able to fully empathize with the suffering of non-humans. In this moment, I'm tempted to manipulate my experience in the opposite direction with an app that would make me numb. The only thing that stops me is knowing that if I feel numb after learning my friend is dead, I might as well be effectively dead myself.

It quickly becomes clear that seclusion is not helping, so I do what I always do when I feel down: I invite Mr. Spock into the room. The rat is now savvy enough with the VR interface that he has an avatar, a largish white rat that looks much fiercer than the real Mr. Spock. As soon as my furry companion runs up to me, I make my own avatar small enough that I can hug him to my chest like a teddy bear.

"What's wrong?" he asks in Zik. He and his kin now have the vocabularies of unenhanced four-year-olds. "Are you cold? Are you hungry?"

I hug him tighter. I guess he can tell I'm not in a talkative mood, because he begins to brux, a behavior I've grown to find soothing.

"Maybe we should have an unscheduled session?" asks the accented voice of Einstein's shrink instantiation. True to his current role, the AI looks and sounds more like Freud than the famous physicist.

"Maybe later," I tell him grimly. "Let me be."

In the real world, Joe's people move me from the bulletproof car into a helicopter. I go along without complaint.

Being with Mr. Spock helps me get a grip on my chaotic emotions, and I return to the joint VR room. Ada's avatar is quietly crying, so I approach her and pull her into my embrace, feeling awful for leaving, even if it was only for a brief time.

Mitya might not have been her best friend, but she needs consolation as much as I do.

As I hold her, gently stroking her back while I battle my own grief, I notice something strange. Mitya's remaining pixels have stopped dissipating. In fact, they may be slowly regenerating. His avatar is re-solidifying, like the Cheshire cat from *Alice in Wonderland*.

I wait for a few moments to be sure, then clear my throat. "Guys, if Mitya is dead, what's going on with his avatar?"

"I don't think of myself as dead," says the reappearing avatar, and goosebumps spread all over my body as he continues. "I prefer to think of myself as facing some physical challenges—or whatever the current politically correct term is for an invalid. Think of me as an amputee who just happens to have lost every part of his body."

SIX

I GAPE AT THE AVATAR AS QUESTIONS PEPPER MITYA FROM THE REST of the room.

"Dude, I see your charred remains," I manage to say when I regain my voice.

Mitya's avatar is now completely solid, and there's a hyperrealism to it, like when you switch from regular TV to ultrahigh definition. Also different are his clothes. He's wearing something reminiscent of a toga and a helmet with a swan on top, and he's carrying a double-headed axe and a shield with a bull's face etched on the front.

"Okay," he says, interrupting the nonstop questions. "Here's the deal. As you guys know, I've been worried about my biological brain."

"Right," I say for everyone. I already know what he's about to say, but we all need to hear him say it before we can officially start to process the information.

"I last backed up the biological connectome when I went to bed yesterday," the strangely dressed avatar continues. "When my unfortunate disembodiment occurred a few minutes ago, a special set of instructions was activated as soon as my Brainocytes declared official brain death—a set of instructions you people would have thought paranoid."

"You figured out a way to run your mind without the biological brain?" Ada gasps. "I thought you were still far away from making that work."

"I settled on a prototype solution about six months ago. Just didn't have a good way to test it." He lets go of his axe and shield, and they hover in the air. "Is this so hard to believe? Only a small fraction of your mind is biological now, anyway."

Muhomor looks him up and down a couple of times. "It's not just the brain that makes us what we are. There's also the rest of the body."

"Speaking of that," Alan asks, clearly intrigued, "how does it feel to be without a body?"

Mitya grimaces. "I can't tell you for sure, because I was only without a body for a few subjective milliseconds. Now, though, I'm running an ultrarealistic simulation of the real body"—he spreads his VR arms—"plus I'm inside a couple of our top-of-the-line surrogate bodies as we speak—though I have to say, we'll need to further this line of research immensely, else I can forget about going on a real-world date."

He doesn't seem too put out, but that's not surprising. Even when he had a body, Mitya mostly used VR for intimate encounters because of an obsessive fear of sexually transmitted diseases.

Muhomor stares pointedly at the axe. "Okay, I'll be the asshole to ask: what's with the getup? This is not how you used to dress when you were a real boy."

"Since I'm pretty much pure mind now, I figured I'd make myself look like the Slavic god of wisdom." Mitya pointedly grabs the axe and shield from the air and waits expectantly. When no one says anything, he says with clear disappointment, "Radagast."

I can't help but look up the god in question.

"According to what I just read, Radagast was a god of hospitality," Muhomor says, beating me to it. "Hence the 'Rad' part, which is Russian for 'happy,' and 'gast' for 'guest.'"

"It's also very likely that such a god didn't exist," Alan adds, "at least according to what I see on the Russian Wikipedia page. Radagast might've been the name of a town that an ancient chronicler accidentally turned into the name of a deity."

"And most importantly," Ada says, finally smiling, "Radagast was the name of that wizard in *The Hobbit* movies, the one who lived with a bunch of animals in the woods. Then again, I guess I do see some resemblance." She puts up a screen with the likeness of the crazy old man in question.

Mitya's avatar momentarily shimmers, and a moment later, he's standing there in a very typical jeans-and-hoodie outfit. "I didn't expect this much teasing on the day I die."

"Jokes aside," I say, staring at my lifelike, sort-of-dead friend, "you're going to be legally dead. What does that mean for your fortune? For your status in human society?"

"Funny you should bring that up." He stands up straighter. "I'm discussing this very thing with Mr. Kadvosky right now. Hold on, let me pull him into this room."

A man with noble, eagle-like features appears—an avatar we all recognize as the favorite of Nathaniel Kadvosky, recently appointed Head Attorney at Human++. The avatar exudes gravitas to such a degree that no one dares mention that in the physical world, he looks more like a plucked sparrow.

"This is a historic case," Kadvosky says without so much as a hello. "Supreme Court judges would have a hard-on if they heard of this—at least those of them able to get hard-ons."

"It won't be that difficult to build a case." Mitya sounds as if he's continuing whatever conversation they began earlier. "I don't have a will—"

"Nor do you have children or close relatives," the lawyer says. "No one benefits if you're declared dead—aside from, perhaps, your business partners." He looks pointedly at the rest of the people in the room.

Mitya visibly saddens at the mention of his lack of family. His parents were murdered a while back, and he didn't take the loss well. It might even have been the trigger for the obsession that led him to research how to remain alive after death.

To pull him from his momentary funk, I say as confidently as I can, "Mitya's not dead, as far as I'm concerned. I would not challenge his share of the company."

"I feel the same," Ada says.

Muhomor nods. "He's as lame now as he's always been. I wouldn't declare him dead, that's for sure."

"So no heirs," Kadvosky sums up. "That's good, but that fact alone doesn't hand us the case. What will help is your idea of presenting this as a disability. There's a man in Florida who lost half his brain in an automotive accident, but he's fully functioning, thanks to Brainocytes, and no one disputes his personhood or that he is alive. We have quadriplegic people who move around on Human++ legs and eat with Human++ arms; no one challenges their status as living, either."

"Yeah, we can coin a new term: quinqueplegic, or septemplegic," Mitya says.

"I notice you skipped the term for six." Muhomor chuckles. He expectantly surveys our humorless faces, then defensively adds, "Because in that case, the term would sexplegic."

"If anyone here were sexplegic, it would be you," Ada tells Muhomor. I bet it's taking all her willpower not to smack him on the back of the head, something she feels she can let herself do in VR because it's not real violence.

"The actual term is irrelevant," Kadvosky says, and I'm impressed at the admirable job he's doing at pretending Muhomor isn't even there. "We can use whatever term the PR department decides would have the best resonance with the public."

"But what about the question of identity?" Alan asks. "I don't think we want to abandon the question of inheritance so quickly."

Ada and I exchange proud glances. Kadvosky seems to be lagging behind Alan's train of thought.

"What do you mean?" the lawyer asks.

"Knowing Mitya, he's probably already figuring out a way to

copy himself," Alan says. When Mitya smiles mischievously, my son adds, "That's what's happening with the servers in Ohio, isn't it?"

"No," Mitya says. "The Ohio servers took the brunt of running what used to be my biological brain. All our servers are running at peak capacity now, which is why I wouldn't worry about my copying myself for a while."

Alan looks back at Kadvosky. "You need to plan for when he does clone himself. Who will own his money at that point?"

"Your other selves will certainly only get one vote during our Brainocyte Club meetings." Muhomor crosses his arms across his chest.

"I can remain a singleton for a while," Mitya says with a hint of disappointment. "Or I can design a new mind modality where me and my clones will become a sort of hive mind. But long term, yeah, this is something we'll need to work out—just not now. I'm sure a new copy of me should get some resources from me, a little bit like a child does from a par—"

"Why don't we focus on the immediate issue of your corporealness?" Kadvosky moves to adjust his glasses, then remembers he doesn't wear any in VR. "I don't think the Supreme Court would find the fate of your copies as interesting as the status of your current self, though I personally find the implications fascinating and would gladly discuss them further."

"What is the worst-case scenario?" Mitya asks Kadvosky with a seriousness unusual for him. "Can the law decide I'm software that can simply be deleted?"

"No need to get so dramatic," Kadvosky says. "In the worst case, your legal status would be akin to that of Einstein. Before we let the AI drive cars and drones, we made sure it has the same legal rights as corporations. In other words, you will still be able to own things, be sued, and sue other people. You'll also be able to give money to political campaigns and so on."

"But corporations can't marry," Mitya says.

I can't resist. "If you find the right girl, you can have a merger."

Kadvosky gives me a scathing glance. "I have a lot of work ahead of me. I'm going to have to leave you to continue this conversation on your own. Just keep telling yourself that brain amputation is not death."

Without waiting for a reply—or perhaps dreading one—Kadvosky poofs out of the VR room in a manner most VR users would find rude. Leaving the room through the virtual door is quickly becoming the custom.

Alan responds to Mitya's subdued expression with a worried look. "Am I the only one who's looking on the bright side of this? You won't need food or to use the bathroom. You can run drug trial simulations on your simulated brain with no harmful side effects. You can boost your mind to a degree we can't even dream of. You can—"

"Young man," Ada says to Alan in her stern maternal voice, her hands on her hips, "don't even think about ditching your biological body, not over my d—"

Joe's avatar slams the conference table with such force that the virtual glass shatters and the table breaks into pieces.

"Enough of this bullshit," he says through gritted teeth. "It's time you apply your sorry excuse for enhanced brains to the actual attempt on your lives."

SEVEN

ADA AND I EXCHANGE GUILTY LOOKS. JOE IS RIGHT. SOMEONE PUT together a coordinated attack on us, one that spanned the whole globe.

"I already did some investigating," Mitya says defensively. "My thought process is at least double what it was when I was slowed down by a biological br—"

"Dude, stay on topic," I say, noting how Alan's eyes shine with avarice at this tidbit about Mitya's new state of being.

"Right." Mitya manifests screens with the faces of the four bombers and reads the bio as he points out the bomber from Bahrain. "This is Hamad Marhoon. He's a programmer for the Al Baraka Banking Group. He was the first of the bombers I thoroughly—"

"Racial stereotyping," Ada grumbles. "Great."

"If I were stereotyping, it wouldn't be that big of a leap." Mitya looks at me for support, since I was in Manhattan that day on 9/11. When I don't support him in time, he adds, "This doesn't seem to be Jihad-related—or whatever the politically correct term is for that type of terrorism."

"I agree," Muhomor chimes in. "Bahrain is a progressive coun—"

"Right." I nod. "Plus the other people involved in this make it seem unlikely." I already knew some of this from the facial recognition app that's always running in my head, but I haven't had the chance to analyze it yet.

Mitya points at the next man. "This is Vurnon Corsen. He's a Curaçao native who does security and IT for Campo Alegre, a legal brothel. He's a Catholic and a father of four. Nothing in his profile hints at why he'd want to hurt us at all, and I have a hard time picturing someone recruiting him to be a suicide bomber for any cause, let alone some radical Islam group. Even less suspicious is Garcelle Derulo, a Haiti national who worked for Royal Caribbean Cruises as a nurse. The man was a saint—he worked almost a week straight, pro bono, helping the recent earthquake victims. They wrote about him in the papers."

"I just checked the NSA files," Muhomor says. "None of these people were on any terrorist watch lists. Checking the Russian sources next."

"Speaking of Russia, this is Ermolai Ruzatov, and I think he's our best lead." Mitya motions at the pale face of the third bomber.

I realize I've been avoiding this bio because the man's face invokes conflicting emotions. On the one hand, he almost killed Ada, so he got what he deserved. I'd kill him again to keep her safe. On the other hand, I ripped this man's heart out of his chest—not something I would've imagined myself capable of, even if the situation demanded it.

"Ruzatov is a quality assurance engineer for Gazprom," Mitya reads. "He's never been religious and has no living family and only a few friends outside work."

"He doesn't belong to any terrorist groups, either." Muhomor puts up a bio in Russian, something he must've gotten from the "Russian sources" we'd rather not know about.

Ruzatov seems boring, as far as Russian government interests go. He's never criticized the current regime or done anything worthy of notice.

"Why did this Ruzatov come to our conference?" I ask. "He's from Vladivostok. He would have no trouble getting Brainocytes there."

Muhomor looks smug. "They all had Brainocytes, every one of the bombers. But that and their fascination with technology in general is the only thing I can see that links them all—and they share that fascination with billions of other people."

Ada rubs her temples. "I won't ask how you know they had Brainocytes."

We pride ourselves on the privacy we provide to our users, so the fact that Muhomor can get that information so quickly isn't something we'd ever want the public to know.

"Don't be so paranoid," he says. "I simply extrapolated their Brainocytes status based on how they used easier-to-hack technology."

"So," I say before Ada can have a fit of righteousness, "did they ever email each other? Or call each other? Or meet in person?"

"No. At least, not prior to getting Brainocytes. Afterward, it's harder to say. Everything sent out is Tema-encrypted."

"What about the bombs?" I look at Joe. "There are ways to track those."

"Working on it," my cousin says. "But the local police departments aren't being very helpful. Did any of those four people show any interest in the Luddite movement?"

Muhomor looks thoughtful for a moment—probably querying his prodigious resources. "Ruzatov had a coworker named Eugene Blinov who's part of the Green Party. That's the closest connection I could find. But the Russian Greens aren't that interested in Human++."

"Why, Joe?" I ask, recalling the protestors outside the museum on Alan's birthday. "Do you think the RHO or someone like that is behind this?"

"I don't know." Joe kicks a large piece of the virtual table glass, and it shatters against the wall. "I'll find out soon, though."

"It's feasible," Mitya says. "The Unabomber was anti-technology, and his manifesto sounds like the same crap you might hear from the RHO."

"I'll deal with the RHO," Joe says with barely disguised menace.

"Don't hurt anyone," Ada warns.

"Not without evidence," I clarify.

Ada gives me a narrow-eyed glare.

"I could use some help investigating in Russia," Joe says without dignifying our comments with a reply.

"I'm not going to Russia," Muhomor and I say at the same time.

Muhomor is a wanted man there, and I still have nightmares from what happened the last time I was in the country.

"Uncle Joe doesn't want you to go," Alan chimes in. "He'd have a hard time protecting you there. He probably wants you to use one of our robots—so can I help?"

Joe gives Muhomor and me a look that seems to say, "How is it that a four-year-old is so much smarter than the two of you?"

"That's a great idea," Mitya says. "I can help also. The only trick is getting some avatar bodies. Because of the laws against them, we have very few operating in Russia and none in Vladivostok right now. I should be there in a couple of hours, though."

"You start on that," I say. "The rest of us will think through other possibilities and explore other angles."

Everyone gets busy, and as things quiet down in the VR room, I get a private telepathic message from Ada: "Please join me in the Bedroom."

The Bedroom is a euphemism for the virtual reality sex room Ada and I use for intimate encounters when we're not in proximity to each other (our Manhattan penthouse also has a non-virtual room designated for sex only, separate from our bedroom).

As soon as I think about it, I find myself there. Out of habit, I enhance my muscles in the way I hope Ada likes and put on an outfit she designed for me to wear here (one I wouldn't be caught dead wearing in the real world).

As soon as I see the expression on my wife's face, I realize this isn't going to be the usual sort of session we have in this room. Her eyes look puffy, and there are deep worry lines on her forehead— incongruous details among the sex toys, swings, mirrored walls, racks of lingerie, gallons of scented oils, and ultrarealistic VR characters with slack expressions and varying degrees of seductive nudity.

Seeing Ada like this instantly makes me wish we could be in front of each other in person. But I still have a few hours of flight time before I reach New York City, and her flight is longer still.

"I thought I would lose you." Her hands are visibly shaking as I take her small, cold palms in mine.

"It's okay, babe." I try to sound as reassuring as I can. "You're stuck with me forever."

A hint of a smile lifts her lips. I build on my success and grab her in a large hug. The benefit of the hug is that she can't see my face, because I suspect I don't look that reassuring. Now that we're past the battle and the shock of Mitya dying, I allow myself to contemplate the horrible possibility of Ada's death, and the stupid thought fills me with an ocean of dread.

Fighting it, I pull away and gaze down at her. "Whoever is behind this, I'll make sure they—"

She presses a finger to my lips, then slides it down my neck and across my chest. She then rises on tiptoes, and our mouths intertwine, the kiss more urgent than usual, almost primal.

"I want to finally test the Join app," she tells me telepathically. Her Zik messages' emotional undertones are still on the sad side. "Please?"

The app is something she first thought of years ago, but it turned out harder to implement than she originally conceived. The idea is to use Brainocytes to merge two or more minds. The melding, or whatever the proper term would be, is an extremely complex process. The simplest aspects include the heavy simulation of mirror neurons for both parties. Both participants experience one another's memories and emotions by sharing a lot of nonbiological brain regions, in part to swap sensory data and in part to process neurological data together. The basic idea is that I'd experience the world as Ada does, and she would get the reverse experience.

A month ago, Ada finally decided she was happy enough with the app to test it on our rats. The rats, especially Mr. Spock and Uhura, liked the experience a lot and now run the app continuously. As a result, Mr. Spock got a bit more mellow, for lack of a better term. Sadly, though, the rats aren't yet smart enough to properly explain how the Join app makes them feel—at least beyond terse descriptions like Kirk's "I just feel better," McCoy's "It makes me feel never alone," Scotty's "It's more fun than Alan's Rat World—and I like Rat World," Uhura's "It makes me happier," or Mr. Spock's slightly less cryptic "It makes me love Uhura more." To me, the idea of having Ada inside my head seems scary. Despite my therapy with Einstein, I'm afraid that what she finds there could scare her away.

"It's unfair to ask me today," I whisper once our lips unlock. "Why don't we do that zero-gravity position?" I begin the gesture to disable gravity in the room, but she puts her hand on mine to stop me.

"I really need this." She's still speaking virtually. "It will take our relationship to the next step, I know it will, and I want to do that because life is unpredictable, and—"

"It's okay." I lose myself in her amber eyes again, grateful she didn't alter their color today. "If it means so much to you, I'll do it."

I stop myself from adding something like, "It was going to happen eventually, anyway." I learned long ago that I can only tell Ada no for a very short time, and the whole process is full of guilt and other subtle unpleasantness. There's an old Russian saying that goes, "The husband is the head, and the wife is the neck." That's our relationship in a nutshell: I turn where Ada wants me to turn and see what she wants me to see. Not that this means I imagine myself as the head of our family. Ada is both the head and the neck in our household, while I might be something like the gallbladder.

A giant new icon shows up in the room, and I psych myself up to activate the Join app. If I look at it through Ada's eyes, this is a way to get closer to each other. Seen that way, the whole business doesn't sound nearly as scary. Besides, Ada already knows what I did five years ago in Russia and a few months later in the US. She also saw what I did earlier today. Hopefully, she won't hold any of my memories against me. And she's going to see how I feel about her, which is worth something. We don't say the L word to each other as much as other couples, so that reassurance might be a nice bonus.

Perhaps as blackmail, or as extra motivation to get me to start the app, Ada VR-magicks her clothes away from her body.

I instantly get rid of mine as well.

"This is how I've always pictured this," she says, stepping toward me.

Without voicing my doubts, I give in to the call of biology, and as the pleasure begins, I launch the Join app and close my eyes.

EIGHT

Brainocytes allow us to experiment with safe psychedelic experiences, and Mitya has made it his personal mission to blow our minds with a set of LSD-like apps of ever-increasing potency. But none of Mitya's apps, real drugs, or even the horrific truth serum cocktail used on me four and a half years ago could've prepared me for this assault on my sense of reality.

My senses feel completely crisscrossed—though that's not quite accurate. What's really happening is that I'm trying to sense through Ada's eyes, skin, ears, nose, and mouth, while in a strange, recursive loop, I'm also feeling what it feels like for her to experience my own senses. It's like placing a mirror in front of another mirror. We each get lost in our experiences of each other's experience of the other person's experiences, down infinite levels, until we simply forget there's a difference between Ada and Mike—which I think is one of the goals.

It quickly becomes clear that sex is not the best way to first experience this app because of the sensory overload that comes with intimacy. A part of me that's more Ada than Mike disagrees and thinks we'd be equally overwhelmed during a session of knitting or playing solitaire.

The boundaries between the being who is Mike and the glorious entity that is Ada blur more with every second, yet I still feel that I'm myself at the same time. Although I'm used to being in many places at once, what's happening now feels completely different. In a strange way, I feel more in the moment in multiple places at once, more alive in multiple places at once, and again paradoxically more myself, even though I'm merged with someone else. I can't shake the feeling that this is how I'm supposed to be, that this is the real me. Finally free. Finally home.

As my mind adjusts to this roller coaster of newness, I begin to see myself through Ada's eyes. I feel what she feels for me, and I feel what she's feeling as we make love, here in the VR room. I knew she loves me, but because she doesn't like to overuse the words to express her feelings, sometimes I'm open to doubt. I will never doubt again. Ada loves me with an intensity I might not be capable of myself, though I must be wrong, because she swells with contentment when she experiences how I feel about her.

They say that as couples live together, they become like rocks polished by a river. Any differences and problems between them smooth away. I'm not sure if there's any truth to that metaphor, but in this VR room, in one instant, we understand and move past whatever tiny flaws we've noticed in each other. We forgive all grievances by seeing the world through the other's eyes. We become more as one than a couple who have lived together all their lives.

This is when the oddest part begins. A surge of Ada's memories flood my awareness. I recall a nice day in Central Park when she was walking over a scenic bridge and musing about her deadbeat father, who left her mother and was never heard from again. Her conflicting emotions are familiar to me, and I soon realize that I have had almost identical musings about my own father, a man whose death I still relive with intense guilt. I recall Ada's memory of sitting in the hospital, her love for her mother swelling her chest, and I remember myself in similar circumstances after Mom's accident.

Not all the memories pull us closer. Some memories are almost opposites: Ada worried after losing her virginity as a teen, while I worried that I'd never get the chance to lose mine. Some are completely foreign to me, like the ordeal Ada experienced when she lost her mom to cancer.

Tears stream down my face, both in VR and in the real world, as I relive her struggles. The pain she felt is unlike anything I've ever experienced, carrying me to the verge of panic.

Soon, though, the sad memories are over, and happier ones move to the forefront. I witness Ada discovering coding, her first love. I recall her first kiss in a forest camp and her first crush on a young professor in Intro to Java class. I remember how she felt the first time we had sex, and when she said her vows during our Hawaiian wedding—and the first time she held a screaming Alan in her arms. I understand that Ada is most defined by her happier experiences, and I hope she finds the same to be true about me, though it's probably not the case.

If it were possible to feel yourself evolving into a better person, this is what it would feel like. There's no jealousy when I recall the men and the one woman from Ada's past. I would hug them and thank them if I met them now—a reaction I can't believe I'm having. I also now understand Ada's abhorrence of violence, having felt her conviction of how precious life is and how even the worst person in the world is still deserving of love and kindness.

Ada has been trying to get me to meditate, and in the process, I've learned a little bit about Buddhism. Now, using the Join app, I feel as if I've reached enlightenment, or how I imagined it would feel, although I probably had a very reductionist view of that spiritual term.

Experimentally, I open my eyes in the real world. The plane is still in the air, and when I try to introspect, I feel normal. I feel like an individual—that is, until I try to feel one with Ada. Then the feeling of enlightenment rushes back full force.

I open my eyes in the VR room and see Ada's naked body

reflected in all the mirrors. We're still joined in this way, too, our virtual sweat glistening on our ephemeral bodies.

Something new becomes possible, and it demands my attention. As the intensity of the Joining lessens, I discover that we can think as one, at least for a moment. Unimaginatively, we jointly contemplate, "We think, therefore we are."

"Wow," I reply. "Our hive mind is a philosopher."

"Amazing," she agrees. "I know that neither of us came up with that thought, yet we thought it."

"I need a way to reference self," the hive mind thinks to themselves (or herself or himself or itself).

"How about The Cohens?" I suggest.

"The Cohens would make more sense if we Joined with your uncle, cousin, and mom," it counters. "But fine, it will do."

Somehow, a reminder about the rest of the family during sex doesn't seem gross or even weird. It feels completely neutral, like thinking about clouds. Perhaps this is part of an evolved state of being, though it might also be because sex is the last thing on our minds now, even though we're still making love.

"Can more than two people Join like this?" I ask. "I mean, the Join app, not—"

"The more people, the more complete we'd become," answers the being code-named The Cohens.

"Besides people, we could even pull in other beings, like Mr. Spock," Ada adds. "But perhaps after we finish."

I don't get to make any bestiality jokes because we're getting to the climax of the physical—well, the virtually physical—part of our Bedroom extravaganza, and it's becoming impossible to talk, even telepathically. I pray nobody is watching me on the plane right now, or if they are, I hope they don't record my facial expressions or consider my reactions some form of sexual harassment.

Though I've become acclimated to Ada's senses, now that she's this close to release, I begin to feel overwhelmed. What I feel intermingles with what she's feeling, and I'm eager to learn what this part will feel like from her perspective.

Then she performs a maneuver possible only in VR (though she claims she's going to start doing Kegel exercises to replicate this in the real world). My response arrives like clockwork, and for a moment, I forget the hive mind named The Cohens or even my own name.

At some point during Brainocyte development (maybe around the seventh brain boost, though it might've been the eighth), we cloud-replicated the parts of the brain responsible for orgasms, giving us a much greater capacity for appreciating this already miraculous experience. Without the Join app, I'd say what I usually feel is at least a hundred times more intense than an unenhanced orgasm. With the Join app, however, I feel Ada's reactions as well as my own enhanced ones. Our minds meld into pure bliss with no boundaries or limits and an intensity thousands of times more powerful than anything we've ever experienced.

What feels like a hundred heavenly years later, I catch my breath and reflect on how hard it is to become winded when you have Respirocytes doing the job of your red blood cells. Then again, I just got winded in VR, so oxygen efficiency obviously isn't the main factor.

"Not my best idea," Ada whispers as soon as she's able to make coherent sentences again. She VR-magicks herself a virtual cigarette, more as a jokey prop than because she has any physical need for it. "The Join app on its own would've been enough."

"It might've been one of your best ideas," I say, my voice thick from the experience. "Should I shut down the app?"

"I think so," she murmurs. "Though it would make The Cohens go away."

"We'll use this again," I say. "The Cohens will return."

"I'm glad that part of the app actually worked," she says with noticeable enthusiasm.

I gaze at my brilliant wife with pride that borders on worship. "You utilized our idle brain regions, didn't you?"

Her eyes shine with mischief. "That's a very primitive way of looking at it, but something like that. I leveraged Einstein to provide this app with a platform to self-organize our unused resources. Clearly, it worked."

"Fascinating," state The Cohens. "We're intrigued about bringing more minds into ourselves."

"Good idea, but not now." Ada releases the smoke from her cigarette. Instead of the usual toxic fumes, the cloud has a soft, vaporous quality and smells like bergamot tea with a slice of lime. It probably tastes that way as well, since that's Ada's favorite morning pick-me-up. "How about we shelve the Join app experiments until we figure out who's trying to kill us?"

"I agree," I reply. "The Cohens will also have to wait."

"We do not fear nonexistence," The Cohens reply.

"You won't not exist," Ada says. "You're us. As long as we exist, you also exist."

"However long it takes for you to Join again will seem but a moment to us," The Cohens say enigmatically.

"On that note, I'm turning off the app." I match mental actions to my words.

I instantly feel a sense of loss. The being that was The Cohens is gone without a trace. Until it disappeared, I didn't realize I felt it was a part of me. Given Ada's pained expression, I can see something similar is happening to her.

"Is the app addictive?" I ask.

"We just need to readjust to being alone," she replies softly. "But I can now see why our rats run a version of this app all the time."

"Me too. I wonder what their version of The Cohens is like."

"Their Join app doesn't have that part. I actually wonder if it's safe to have in our version. What would happen if we Joined with more than a few thousand people at once?"

"Because The Cohens would be too smart to control or comprehend?" I yawn demonstratively. Post-coital bliss always hits me hard, whether the coitus is real or virtual.

"Exactly," she says. "We should run this by the others at the next Brainocytes meeting."

"Sounds like a plan. What do we tell them about this app for now?"

"Nothing, if you don't mind. Let me prepare to tell them about it properly."

"Fair enough." I can't help another yawn. "Can we sleep?"

"Our friends probably think we fell asleep anyway," she says through another puff of yummy smoke. "So yeah, why not? It might actually be a good idea."

"I have enough left of my flight for a decent nap." I yawn so temptingly that she yawns as well.

"I actually have time for a substantial rest," she says after another contagious yawn. "Let's just check on everyone before we fall asleep."

We rejoin the VR conference room and learn that nothing interesting occurred while we were away discovering a new state of consciousness.

"Time for a nap," I say in the VR room, fighting to stay awake.

"We'll wake you up if you're needed," Joe says flatly.

"I had no doubt you would," I mutter under my breath. Joe has no problem having his people slap me awake if that's what it takes.

Stopping all multitasking, I leave my mind firmly in my real-world environment, and my thoughts turn to the change in my marriage. Now that I've seen the world through Ada's eyes, I don't think I can ever have an argument with her again—not that we normally have many. I must also admit that, although I loved Ada before the Join app, my feelings are now almost frighteningly intense. Fully understanding her has made me see how sacred her mind is, how sublime. It's as though Ada is a literal part of me, her well-being irrevocably entwined with my own.

I might be a better husband than before. Perhaps even a better human being.

Another yawn makes my jaws crack and interrupts my self-aggrandizements, so I decide to just sleep. Usually, I use an app designed to help me fall asleep, but I don't need it today. Instead, I simply run a utility app called Do Not Disturb, which basically disables hearing and vision for the duration I want—in this case, five hours.

As soon as it turns on, Do Not Disturb creates the effect of being in a deep underground silo. Not a single photon hits my eyelids, and not a fraction of a decibel titillates my eardrums. I open my eyes because I still find it fun to see how Do Not Disturb makes the space around me pitch dark even with my eyes wide open. Then I close my eyes again and drop like a stone into unconsciousness.

NINE

THE HALL OF MIRRORS STRETCHES AS FAR AS MY EYES CAN SEE. A camera inside a drone above my head shows me that this space has taken over the whole world, horizon to horizon.

I run, barely breathing, my heart rate squarely in the anaerobic zone. When the place tries to be a maze and puts a mirror in my way, I shatter the offending surface with a well-placed kick. My goal seems to be to not see myself in any of the reflections, so I do it again and again as more mirrors pop up.

When I kick the tenth mirror, pain explodes in my leg, but the cursed glass doesn't even crack. The pain breaks my concentration, and I catch the reflection staring back at me—and regret it instantly. The baleful glare on Joe's face makes his everyday coldness seem warm and fluffy.

My whole body freezes in panic as Joe's face stares back at me with varying shades of wrath from the infinitude of mirrors. A scream escapes my mouth, vibrating the air so violently the mirrors around me ripple and explode in a chain reaction.

I'm on the verge of some great epiphany when the image in the mirror that refused to break morphs.

First, Joe's military cut grows into tufts of white hair that spread like a halo around his head. Next, his features soften into a wrinkly smile. Soon, Einstein's famous face is staring at me, eyes twinkling with wisdom and mirth.

"This is a dream," I tell Einstein, my fight-or-flight response already calming down.

"We discussed this one in therapy," says the AI's German-accented voice. As usual, in the context of psychology, it comes off sounding suspiciously like Freud. "You're not becoming a monster."

"Make a note to discuss this again when I'm awake. For now, I want to try lucid dreaming again."

Einstein nods and disappears. After a moment of concentration, I soar upward toward the drone still flying in the empty, mirrored sky.

TEN

I WAKE WITH A START TO THE SIGHT OF GOGI'S FACE TOO CLOSE TO mine. Given that I can hear a car's engine and see my friend, the Do Not Disturb cycle must be complete.

My cheek burns. He must've tried to smack me awake, one of the few ways to bypass the Do Not Disturb app—but not needed in this case, since mine was no longer on.

"You have been unconscious for five hours," Einstein says. "You had one minute of REM sleep, and I estimate that your sleep debt is still a full night's sleep of eight hours, which I suggest you get as soon as you can." Mitya has been incorporating emotional cues and contextual information in this latest version of Einstein, and the AI's voice sounds annoyingly caring and consolatory. "Current time is 7:36 p.m."

I'm jealous of Ada, who's still napping thanks to her longer flight. Rubbing my eyes, I wonder if I can order Gogi to let me sleep but decide against it, since my chances of getting quality sleep during the short ride are slim to none. Besides, given the time of day, it might be best if I suffer for a few hours and then sleep when it's dark out. For now, I might as well catch up with my friend.

"If I had a ruble for every time I dragged you from the plane to the car, I'd be able to retire," Gogi says, a smile visible through his Stalinesque mustache.

"You can retire now," I answer groggily, unhappy that the Do Not Disturb app made me miss my landing. "You own a piece of Human++."

His face turns serious. "What's with trying to get yourselves killed when it's my turn to babysit?"

"Next time I'll try to get bombed when you're around." All remnants of sleep flee from my mind. Realizing I might be channeling negativity at the wrong person, I add in a conciliatory tone, "You can help find and deal with the people responsible. How are you at controlling the robots?"

"The kid has been training me," Gogi says. One of the robots inside Zapo X (at least I assume that's what we're driving) gives me a salute.

I give Gogi a rundown of the recent events as I proceed to multitask, a part of me rejoining the VR room to check on the investigation.

"I secured four robots," Mitya says. "Your cousin is already walking one to speak with the bomber's Green Party coworker." He points at a screen where people are staring in awe at the shell of Joe's robotic body stalking through the Russian streets.

"Excellent job," I tell him. "Gogi just volunteered to take one, and so have I."

"It might be best if you take one to speak with the bomber's mother." He warily eyes Joe's VR avatar. "This task might require some finesse."

What goes unsaid is that Joe and Gogi are not above torturing the poor woman, who doesn't yet know she lost her son, for information. Even before mingling my mind with Ada's, I firmly believed the sins of the parents don't transfer to their children and vice versa. With my post-Join outlook, I want to help this woman instead of interrogating her. The only issue I see is that I'm the one who killed her son. Facing her might be hard, though I probably deserve whatever discomfort I feel.

"I'm going to try to locate his father," Mitya says and puts up another screen showing a robot that also begins moving. "The dad is a drunk, and the mom divorced him a long time ago. But who knows? Maybe this Ruzatov guy stayed on speaking terms with his old man."

I take possession of my designated robot, an older model that reminds me of a microwave oven mixed with a Cylon from the original 1978 *Battlestar Galactica*. I plug the mother's address into the GPS app and start clanking down the street. The GPS interface is the same as the Brainocyte one we put into wide use a couple of years ago.

As I walk the Russian streets, I'm overcome with déjà vu. Though my native Krasnodar is nearly six thousand miles from Vladivostok—a distance possible only in Russia—I might as well be walking the streets I remember as a kid. This is what happens when you recycle architectural designs the way the Soviets did: cookie cutters seem original by comparison. In America, some of the government-built housing, such as the projects in New York City, evoke this kind of feeling, only this part of Vladivostok is much grayer and danker.

To avoid becoming depressed, I look with my real-world eyes through the limo window at the streets of midtown Manhattan. Compared to Vladivostok, this is another world. In a strange way, when I swap points of view, I get the sense of traveling into the future, then back into the past—and I mean years, not just the switch between day and night brought about by the fourteen-hour time difference. Of course, this isn't a fair comparison. Moscow is a lot like New York when it comes to the adoption of new technology and would make a fairer match; comparing a backward Vladivostok street to Manhattan's Midtown is like comparing New York City to Nowhereville.

New Yorkers have adopted every single one of Human++ innovations and still crave more. Though it's long after most offices have closed, robotic commuters still litter the streets, a vast improvement for folks who live in the boonies yet whose jobs require their physical presence. No one so much as blinks at their metallic figures, and it's clear that the future is going to look a lot like the movie *Surrogates* (but hopefully without the societal issues). For every robotic wearer, thousands of people are using VR to work remotely. All the big firms not only allow but encourage this form of telepresence, which allows them to hire the best people regardless of where they are in the world. Also, it helps that VR space is much cheaper than real-world office space, especially for companies based in Manhattan.

VR's presence is affecting more than the way people work, of course. Tourists on the street are using both augmented and virtual reality, their expressions blank as they tune in to the tours engineered to trigger near popular sights. The natives are just as affected by the new tech. Instead of keeping their noses in their smartphones and other devices, everyone is "in their heads." People who can afford premium Brainocyte services are able to multitask while walking, and they watch the new, fully interactive movies that have more in common with video games than with the movies of old. Those using free entertainment end up sitting in cars and public transportation while doing the same.

The cars, including ours, are all electric, silent, and self-driving, and most of them are commandeered by Einstein. For the first time in over a century, there are no traffic jams to speak of in Manhattan. The air is as clean as in rural areas, and even the noise pollution is down, thanks in part to Brainocyte-enabled telepathic communication that's quickly redefining the way people interact.

The relative quiet of the street is short-lived, however, because when we get to 42nd Street, we see a crowd of protestors. Their shouting is hard to discern, but signs like BRAINOCYTES STEAL YOUR SOUL and HUMANITY IS LOST leave little room for doubt that this is yet another demonstration by the RHO or a similar group.

"Is this a coincidence?" I ask in the VR room. "Or should we reroute the car?"

"You should reroute in any case," Mitya replies instantly. "I just calculated the travel time to your apartment, and your current route is the slowest."

"Are you going to become our Einstein replacement?" I ask.

"I can integrate with Einstein much better now," Mitya says. "It's now clear to me that the biological brain is a bottleneck of a sort. I can think much, much faster already, and I've only just begun to tweak my capabilities."

"We're walking through this crowd," Joe says without even a hint of interest in this fascinating update on Mitya's condition. "No one here is wearing bombs."

He must be using a sniffer device, a gizmo designed by one of the enhanced engineers at Human++ R&D. Sniffers are orders of magnitude more reliable than a dog and, to quote Ada, "don't require canine slave labor."

I authorize Einstein to take the path Mitya recommends and ask, "If Joe is in that crowd and Gogi is in the car, who's watching Alan?"

"I'm with Dominic, Father," Alan replies grumpily. "Also Jacob and a slew of others."

"Alan, you're smart enough to realize security is necessary," I say, figuring it beats "watch your tone, young man," which was my initial instinct. "Plus, you like Dominic."

"Yeah, yeah." His petulant expression looks odd on his adult avatar's face. "Just get home already."

Though I don't say it out loud lest I upset Gogi and Joe, Dominic may be the most qualified person to stay with Alan, and not just because of their friendship. A schoolteacher back in his early twenties, Dominic enlisted in the army after 9/11 and eventually became part of the Special Forces. That's how his path crossed with Joe's, but their personalities couldn't be any more different. Dominic is as straight an arrow as I've ever come across.

An IED explosion left him in a coma, which he came out of two years ago, but the traumatic brain injury he received left his body in a completely locked-in state, unable to move any muscles. Unlike some people in that condition, he didn't even have the ability to blink yes or no in response to questions.

Brainocytes gave Dominic back a form of sight, a way to communicate, and an exoskeleton that allows him to move around —that is, until Dahan, our Director of Nanotech, works out an even better solution, enabling nanomachines to repair the damage he received. A state-of-the-art bionic arm replaced the one Dominic lost in that explosion, and he claims he's unable to tell the difference between his left and right arms anymore.

In large part because of what he regained thanks to our help, Dominic is probably the most grateful and loyal person who works for us. I've grown to trust him almost as much as I trust my closest friends and family.

Almost ready to stop worrying about my kid, I remind myself that Alan mentioned that Jacob is guarding him as well. Jacob is extremely competent. His quick reactions saved Muhomor's life in that hospital four and a half years ago, and he's moved up rapidly through our security ranks ever since.

"I've built Dominic a VR world," Alan brags to me privately. "It's doing wonders for his PTSD, and I think he'll be able to walk up to cars soon without feeling any panic."

"Let me know when your VR therapy worlds are ready to be turned into a product," I tell him. "They're helpful for me. I'm actually now walking in Russia and don't feel any dread."

The truth is that I do feel some negative emotions as I walk the morning streets of Vladivostok, but this isn't due to irrational leftovers from my misadventures in Russia. I worry because a crowd is walking menacingly toward me. American protestors can look plenty angry, but these Russians seem even scarier in their emotionless movement.

I make the robot cross the street, and the lynch mob crosses the street at the same time, leaving no doubt they're up to something sinister.

I turn my robotic head and see another, smaller group of people flanking me from behind.

"Joe." I cram my telepathic message with apprehension. "Look at what my robot is seeing."

"It's not just you." Joe's telepathic reply is calm but foreboding.

He's right. In the VR room, everyone's screens show their robots under pursuit by people who look a lot like the mob approaching me.

"We're in different parts of a large country," I say, confused.

"Yes, I know." Mitya sounds just as puzzled.

"None of these people seem to even know each other." Alan points at a large screen where he's posted hundreds of face recognition profiles.

"If they destroy the robots, it will take days to procure more," Mitya says. His crowd of people looks even more sinister than mine; they remind me of the pitchfork-wielding villagers approaching Frankenstein.

"This attack has to be government sponsored." Muhomor scares away a couple of scrawny cats as he cuts through a side alley to get away from his pursuers. "The Russians still hate us for developing Tema. Maybe this is payback?"

Part of me agrees with Muhomor's assessment. It's not just Russia; every government wishes the Tema cryptography didn't exist. Still unbreakable, Tema makes the ability to surveil your own or another country's citizens a thing of the past—one the governments of the world dearly miss. Some countries tried to outlaw Tema, but once we made the algorithms, theory, and even the software open source, outlawing this system became like trying to outlaw the Pythagorean theorem.

"I find it hard to picture these people working for the government," Alan chimes in as I cast another wary look at my robot's pursuers. "The majority are alcoholics and can barely keep a shitty job."

"Hey, watch your language," I tell him privately, doing my best to embed fatherly disapproval into the Zik message. "But you're right, they don't look impressive."

"At least we found something they have in common," Mitya says. "Because the kid nailed it. A lot of these people recently recovered in hospitals from alcohol poisoning. I guess Russia got rid of *vytrezvitel.*'"

"*Vytrezvitel* is a detoxification center where cops take drunks to sober up," I tell Alan. "The fact that the Soviet Union had a need for such facilities tells you a little bit about the culture at the time."

"Was Ruzatov an alcoholic?" he asks. "Though even if he was, I fail to see how it sheds light on any of this."

"He drank every now and then, but normal amounts." Mitya's robot dodges a red brick flying at his head and increases his pace. "For a Russian, anyway."

"He did get committed to a hospital." Muhomor finds people waiting for his robot at the end of the alley, so he turns back. "A week ago."

"His blood alcohol level was .10," Alan adds.

"Like I said." Mitya's robot dodges a broken bottle this time. "That number is normal for a Russian."

"He had some head trauma," Muhomor says. "Maybe he was in a drunken brawl?"

"Speaking of a drunken brawl," Alan says. "You should all focus on the trouble in the real world. We can pause the meeting for now."

He's right. Though all of us can carry on a conversation in VR and deal with these attackers, it's best to focus, especially considering what Mitya said about the difficulty of getting new robots.

I stare at the cracked asphalt street. The first set of pursuers is but a foot away. Using the robot's sense of smell, I verify the stench of stale vodka on the breath of the nearest man.

"I don't want to hurt anyone, but I need this robot, so I won't let you break it," I rattle through the robot's mouth in Russian.

"Monster," yelps the nearest drunk in a strange falsetto. "You'll regret your sins."

As though emboldened by this cry to action, the two groups surround me and close the distance. My real-world heart forgets the difference between physical and robotic bodies, because it slams against my chest like a hydraulic motor after a power surge.

ELEVEN

WHEN THE FIRST MAN STRIKES MY METALLIC FACE, I REALIZE THAT things might not be as dire as we fear. The guy's fist is bloody, yet my robot's diagnostics show no ill effects. To my shock, the guy hits me again, his bone crunching against the chest chassis. I see no pain in his face, just determination to hit me repeatedly.

"He must be drunk right now," I yell in VR when the same man headbutts the metal, his nose spraying blood onto the camera that serves as my eyes.

"Watch out for that one with the crowbar," Alan shouts. I instinctively duck, and the metal of the blunt weapon skitters along the top of my metallic skull.

"Einstein, turn on Battle Mode," I mentally command. "Adjust it to this robotic body."

"Done," Einstein replies. "Do you want to turn on the Emotion Dampener as well?"

"Let's save Emotion Dampener for a much worse situation."

Battle Mode—or BM, as we sometimes abbreviate it to—is something I've been working on ever since I mastered the martial arts that now make up my personal, still-to-be-named fighting style. It's a merger of my acquired skills and technology—a way to leverage Brainocyte-enabled, superluminal decision-making in a combat situation. Emotion Dampener—which we *never* abbreviate to ED—is an add-on to BM. It's an optional subroutine that approximates what happens (or doesn't happen) in Joe's mind when he fights. It makes the regions of the brain responsible for empathy take a back seat, so users are free to maim and kill without compunction. It's a scary enough app that I never told Ada about its existence—though in a way, the fact that I need an app like this proves I'm a good person, doesn't it?

Battle Mode starts by highlighting the trajectories of all the nearby fists, bricks, crowbars, and booted feet in my Augmented Reality. It then overlays a ghostly outline for the various dodges and strikes I can make. Each offensive and defensive choice is based on my own brain regions and thus polished by countless hours of fighting Gogi, Joe, and the best sensei that money can buy.

The tricky part, and the reason I choose not to use the Emotion Dampener add-on to Battle Mode, is that I don't want to hurt these people too much. After all, they don't pose any threat to my life. Ultimately, the only thing they're guilty of is trying to damage some (albeit important) corporate property. I don't even have evidence that they're in league with the bombers, though it does seem likely.

Before anyone gets a chance to blink, I choose Action Option 50 and allow the robot body to begin moving. As expected, a fist misses my head and crashes into the shoulder of a drunk behind me. A kick does land, but at such an angle that I feel only the barest vibration in the robot's left side. The owner of the foot probably has a broken toe.

"They're ignoring all damage to their bodies." Mitya's frantic private thought echoes something that's been gnawing at my awareness for a few seconds now. "Like the bombers, these idiots are utterly dedicated to their cause—or crazy."

"Not that there's a difference," Alan mutters.

I don't reply, because my robotic ears ring with the bang of a gunshot that comes as a complete surprise. I hadn't registered anyone with a weapon when I scanned the crowd earlier.

The bullet hits the right side of my metal head, and I'm grateful that I only feel a fraction of the pain I would've experienced if this happened to my real-world flesh. Still, it's as bad as the sparring session last week when Jacob landed a hit on my jaw.

Battle Mode gets help from Einstein when it comes to ballistic trajectories, and soon I have the location of the shooter highlighted in my view, as well as the movements I'll need to take to reach him. I begin to execute the suggested maneuver, even at the cost of getting smacked by a nearby crowbar. The crowbar dents my robotic shoulder blade, but I manage to grab and crush the gun, along with the guy's hand.

Unfortunately, Battle Mode is only good at anticipating rational behavior. It cannot foresee the drunk with missing teeth who purposely drops under my feet while some assailant behind me tackles me with the intensity of a football player on cocaine. Both men will likely end up in the hospital after this, but they accomplish what they set out to do, because I begin to fall. Waving my metal arms reflexively, I manage to bring down two people along with me.

The attackers savagely kick me, and though most of the kicks reach my metal body, some of them end up striking their fallen allies, presumably by mistake. Here again, these people are causing more damage to themselves than the robot (especially if you count all the toes they're breaking right now).

Someone lands a lucky kick that hits me in the joint of my metal neck with a loud clang. Emboldened by the sound, someone smashes a red brick against the same spot, and the diagnostics complain about structural damage.

I struggle to get up, but a couple of heavyset men are hanging onto my robotic legs, so all I accomplish is a half roll on the ground. I use my arms to throw off some of the nearest attackers. I'm clearly beginning to forget about the desire not to hurt people over a robot, because my flailing breaks a dozen bones and dislocates a handful of shoulders.

Undaunted by the damage I dish out, the drunks keep pounding away at me. They remind me of a starving man with a can of tuna but no can opener. Slowly and methodically, they begin to damage my metal body, undeterred by the cost to themselves. One insane man bites my camera, losing some teeth but loosening the sensor enough that the next man's kick leaves me blind.

It doesn't take long to locate a security camera in a nearby liquor store, but all that viewpoint does is allow me to see the robot massacre continuing to unfold.

"My robot is dead," Mitya says. "Joe's will soon be a goner also."

"Not much better on my end," Muhomor complains.

I remove my mind from what's left of the robot body. "Same here."

I look through everyone's views. Joe is the only one whose robot is still semi-functional, and that's only because he wasn't hesitating to kill the drunkards over it. Completely covered in blood and brain matter, his robot slips on gore and finally goes down. The drunks still alive proceed to beat the poor machine with the dismembered limbs of their comrades, proving without a doubt that they are at least as crazy as the people who were willing to blow themselves up earlier today.

Two more waves of onslaught extinguish the last spark from Joe's robot.

When I get back to the VR room, Joe has broken the virtual glass table again, and no one has run the app to repair it because he looks like he'd break it again, possibly with his glare.

I look at the grim faces one by one. "Seems like someone really doesn't want us investigating in Russia."

"I wouldn't rule out a group that hates technology." Alan's grown-up avatar seems smaller, almost frail. "The savagery they showed toward the robots smells like fanatics to me."

"We'll soon have someone to talk to about that," Joe says, his eyes such that I could swear his VR avatar is about to morph into a lizard.

"This whole thing doesn't make any sense," Mitya says. "Those drunks out there wouldn't have the resources to locate each of our robots on their own, no matter how much they hate machinery."

"Can we hire people who live in Russia to investigate?" I ask, looking warily at Joe. "Gogi has those Georgians."

"All dead." Joe squeezes a fist so hard I expect blood to pour out of his palm. "All our Russian contacts are gone. And this"—he puts up an image of an explosion—"is what's left of the Human++ Moscow office."

We stare at the ruins in silence. I have trouble processing the horror of it. There were at least a thousand employees in that Moscow building, including a dozen people I worked with on a weekly basis and a management team that I personally interviewed.

I feel a bout of nausea in the real world, and frantically scan my physical body's surroundings. Zapo X is pulling into my home building's parking lot, and Gogi is staring at my green face with solemn determination. He's clearly in the loop about the events, including the death of his Georgian comrades.

I get Einstein to stop the car so I can open the door and make a mess of the otherwise spotless pavement. As I do so, I make a mental note to give a huge tip to the janitor.

Feeling a modicum of relief, I close the door, resume the car's parking progress, and speak both in VR and out loud. "We need to go on the defensive. I want Alan and Ada in that bunker we bought in New Jersey. I think all of us should stay there. We must also evacuate everyone in the Human++ buildings and send a mass email for everyone to work from home tomorrow."

Mitya and Muhomor nod, but Joe just stares.

"Route the arriving planes to the airport nearest the bunker," I say. "Joe, can you have your man in Ada's plane wake her up so we can tell her what's happening?"

In the real world, Gogi frowns. "We're not just going to run with our tails tucked between our legs."

"I'm not suggesting we stop the investigation," I say. "Just that we take safety precautions, regroup—"

"And then strike with everything we got," Gogi and Joe say in unison, one in VR and the other in the car.

We exit the car, and Gogi is herding me toward the stairs when a screech of tires echoes through the parking lot.

My gun is in my hands before I make any conscious decision to take it out, and Gogi and I leap behind the nearest parked cars, prepared for battle.

TWELVE

BEFORE EITHER OF US GETS A CHANCE TO SHOOT ANYTHING, I recognize the old-school (and now illegal) manual-drive Ford Mustang that must cost Joe a fortune in tickets and gas. Once electricity became nearly free, oil production plummeted and prices skyrocketed, as expected for a luxury item.

I lower my gun.

Joe gets out, stalks toward his back seat, and grabs something there. I expect it to be many things, but not a small, curvy, and seemingly unconscious woman.

"Who is that?" I ask in a stern tone I've never used on my cousin before. Reasonable scenarios, such as "drunk friend," don't even cross my mind.

Joe ignores my question, strides to Zapo X, and deposits the woman inside. I find both the way he carries and puts her down creepily gentle, as if he's afraid she might break prematurely.

"According to facial recognition," Ada says to me privately, "that's Tatum Crawford. She's a de facto leader of the Real Humans Only group."

"You're awake." I confirm what Ada said with my own facial

recognition. Indeed, the round and highly symmetrical face belongs to the RHO leader.

"Woke up to a nightmare," Ada says. "They told me about Russia—and now this."

"I guess we now know why Joe went to the protest," I reply telepathically. Out loud, I say, "Joe, I thought it was understood that Human++ is not in the kidnapping business."

He doesn't deign to reply. Taking out a syringe, he rolls up the woman's sleeve. After a barely perceptible hesitation, he pushes the needle into the exposed pale flesh, presses on the plunger, pulls the needle out, and closes the door. He then turns around and must issue a command to Einstein, because Zapo X's back window rolls down.

"Nice touch," Ada says. "He doesn't want his captive to suffocate."

"A real humanitarian." I match her sarcasm in my telepathic undertones.

"In his defense," Gogi whispers when Joe is no longer within earshot, "these people are at the top of our suspect list, so talking to their leader might be just the thing we need."

"Joe," I call out and head after him. "You can't just pull something like this and say nothing."

"She's just our guest," he says when I catch him by the elevator. "If this has nothing to do with RHO, you can let her go."

I eye his security people guarding the elevator, but they show no sign of listening.

Frustrated, I stab the elevator button. "It's not that simple. She'll press charges and crucify us in the news. Also, as soon as you let her wake up, she'll use her Brainocytes to summon the authorities."

"Her Wikipedia page states that she doesn't have Brainocytes," Mitya says to everyone in VR. "Those RHOers are crazy." When Ada focuses her displeasure on him, he adds, "Not that I approve of taking her captive, of course."

Joe's icy stare makes the hairs stand up on the back of my neck.

Maybe I overestimated how much conscience his brain boost granted him.

"Hope you didn't just convince him to kill the poor girl," Ada privately states. Not for the first time, her telepathic message echoes my thoughts.

"Let's deal with one problem at a time," I say more calmly as the doors to the penthouse open wide. "Getting our family to safety comes first."

"Mishen'ka!" Mom exclaims from the living room. "Dominic is saying something about a road trip to New Jersey."

"Hi, Dad." Alan is right behind his grandmother, an unreadable expression on his tiny face. "I'm ready to go."

"Sir," Dominic says telepathically after I hug my mom and son. He can speak through a special voice box in his exoskeleton, but he prefers mental communication. "Get whatever you need so we can head out."

Joe looks at his man approvingly. As per Dominic's preference, I'm using Augmented Reality to overlay his real-world face with a virtual avatar that looks exactly as he would have if not for explosion. The avatar's noble features look worried—and if Dominic is worried, we mere mortals should be peeing our pants.

"What about Uncle Abe?" I ask Joe as I look around for anything I should take with me.

"We'll pick him up on the way." Joe moves to the large safe where he and his people stash weapons and begins openly unloading a large arsenal of guns and rifles.

Mom eyes me questioningly, so I give her a simplified rundown of the situation, downplaying the danger as much as I can. Mom's blood pressure has been a real issue lately.

"It's mostly a precaution," I finish. "I prefer to think of this as a fire drill. This way, we'll know what to do in case of a real emergency."

"What about Mom?" Alan asks telepathically, mindful not to worry his grandma.

"Still flying back, but when she lands, I'll be there to pick her up," I reply.

"Can we bring the rats with us?" he asks, still telepathically.

"Of course." I give him a real-world wink. "Just make sure your grandmother doesn't see them."

Alan asks Dominic to help him "with something," and they head to the eighth bedroom in the penthouse, also known as the Rat Room—a room my mom likes to pretend doesn't exist, since Mr. Spock and his kin have made it their home.

It takes me only a minute to get ready. It's amazing how few physical possessions a person needs once they have Brainocytes in their heads. For another ten minutes, I gather all the stuff Ada requests, even though I'm ninety-percent sure our personal assistants have already gotten these items for the bunker—even Ada's high-powered blender that I nicknamed "The Chainsaw."

The most urgent tasks complete, I walk the hallways Ada and I jointly decorated. The ultramodern design, with all the blues and grays and the smart home devices at every turn, feels like home. Thanks to the million sensors spread around the place, "feels like home" takes on a new meaning for me because I can literally feel the apartment when it comes to temperature, lighting, water and chemical levels in the indoor pool, the contents of the fridge, and even how much dust is on the floor. I hope we don't have to stay in the bunker too long, because I'll miss this place.

"Hi, friend," Mr. Spock says in Zik as he scurries up my body into my pocket. "Can I ride on you?"

"Most would ask before diving for my pocket," I tease. "But of course you can."

Mr. Spock rewards me by bruxing, then gives me an update on where his family is hiding from Mom.

The trip downstairs is quick. After I get Alan into the car, I hold the door open for my mom.

"Who is this girl?" she asks as I take what would be a driver's seat, if this car needed one. "Is she okay?"

I give Joe a narrow-eyed look. When he ignores the question, I say, "She's Joe's friend, Mom. She's just napping after a red-eye flight."

"Hmm." Mom looks over Tatum Crawford's plump, petite frame. "Josya's friend." She looks like she's tasting the idea. "She's pretty."

I debate correcting her but decide there's no harm if she thinks Tatum is Joe's girlfriend. That implies two nice fantasies: that Tatum isn't kidnapped, and that Joe is capable of feelings that lead to having girlfriends.

"In the Caucasus Mountains, where our friend Gogi is from," Mitya says in the VR room, "they have a famous but barbaric custom of kidnapping brides—"

I don't find out the punchline, because my attention ricochets back to the real world as the sensors in the penthouse scream in the smart-device equivalent of horrific pain. The roar of destroyed door sensors quickly follows the screeching of malfunctioning appliances, and sparks blind every camera.

It's an explosion—one that shakes the building with such intensity the car alarms in the parking lot start blaring.

THIRTEEN

NOT BEING IN THE BUILDING, WE'RE ALIVE, SO I CAPITALIZE ON THIS small bit of luck and bring up the most up-to-date version of the Batmobile app to steal control of Zapo X from Einstein. The tires squeal as the heavily customized limo catapults onto the Manhattan street.

Taking over one of the myriad delivery drones flying around, I assess the damage and immediately wish I didn't. As I feared, the explosion came from the penthouse. The place is totaled. Our extra-thick, hurricane-proof windows are raining down on the street in tiny shards.

People on the street are gawking at the flames, their faces pale. Many New Yorkers, including myself, get unpleasant flashbacks when an explosion happens in a high-rise building.

Mom's voice quivers. "At least we all got out in time." She puts a shaking hand on my shoulder, as though I'm the one who needs consoling.

"Yeah, Dad," Alan says, nodding at her words. "We can replace material stuff."

His words reassure me that he's okay—child or not, my son is more mature than many adults—so I push aside my shock and telepathically reach out to Ada. "How are you?"

She opts to show up as an AU avatar next to Alan, her eyes suspiciously puffy. "Intellectually, I understand that it's just stuff. But I still feel like I just lost a piece of myself."

I swerve onto Lexington Street as we ride in silence.

After I recruit a couple more delivery drones as air support, I notice that everyone in the car is privately asking me to check out the news, so I do. The media is already obsessing about the Midtown explosion, as they're calling it.

"My inbox and voicemail are filling up with questions from the government and the media," Mitya complains.

I check and realize the same is happening to me.

"We don't know if we can trust the authorities," Joe says. "Don't tell anyone where we are and especially where we're going."

"In that case, I wouldn't even take calls or open emails," Muhomor chimes in. "We don't know how sophisticated our adversary is."

I turn onto the West Side Highway and speed up. By the time I reach the tunnel, I've earned a couple of thousand dollars in speeding fines, not to mention several tickets for manually overriding the navigation system. Despite being hosted in our data centers, Einstein squealed on me just as he would on any other driver.

We fly through the tunnel. One advantage of self-driving cars is that you can race around them easily. When they know a human driver is near, they treat that car like it has rabies.

As I drive, I also go through the building's security footage. It takes mere seconds to locate the suspect, since he's wearing a suicide vest nearly identical to the ones from the earlier attempts on our lives. I get a good shot of his face and scan the report from the face recognition software.

"Are you watching the news?" Gogi asks out loud. He glances at Joe's captive and telepathically asks me, "Do you still think we don't need her?"

I tune in to the news and confirm what I just learned from facial recognition: Lennox Dixon is a prominent member of the RHO. In fact, there are pictures of him and Tatum all over the news, so I learn another tidbit: the authorities are looking for Tatum, which may further complicate Joe's kidnapping of the woman.

"First a protest, then blowing shit up," Muhomor says. "The RHO does not look good right now."

"I just hope they know we have their leader." I get onto the Brooklyn-Queens Expressway. "So they stop trying to kill us."

"Even if the RHO is behind this, Joe had no right to do what he did," Ada says.

"We'll deal with that when we're safe," I reply, careful not to tell her my theory that the worst for Tatum is still to come. Joe is undoubtedly planning to question her using dubious methods.

I spot an emergency vehicle in the distance and race ahead to perform a maneuver that was popular in New York before self-driving cars. Catching up to the EMT van, I get behind it so that when it gets the right of way, I can take advantage of the window in the traffic.

Something bugs me, though—something to do with the recon I'm getting from the drones above us. I'm not sure what I'm seeing yet, but I've learned to trust my intuition after being the only one who noticed government surveillance four and a half years ago.

"Guys," I say in the VR room, as that's where the quickest-thinking group is. "Something is off."

I put up feedback from the drones I appropriated, and everyone adds their own—turns out each of them was also providing air support.

"There and there," Alan says. I recognize his facial expression—this is how he looks when he's absorbed in a video game. "We're in trouble."

I consult the screen and realize what the oddities are: we're not the only manually driven car on the road. There's a green SUV swerving around the self-driving traffic in a way that leaves little doubt there's a human involved. What's worse is the giant Peterbilt truck steamrolling onto the ramp at triple the speed limit.

"The truck will block you from speeding up." Mitya shows us a screen where he models what he thinks is going on—an impressive feat that must be possible thanks to his newly nonbiological mind. "The SUV probably contains a suicide bomber ready to blow up when he catches up with you."

I send a frantic message: "Joe, Gogi, join VR."

They obey, joining almost instantly.

Mitya repeats his theory, and Joe's grim expression leaves no doubt that he concurs with what's about to happen.

Joe's security team from the car shows up in the VR room. Muhomor nods at Jacob; after the big man saved his life, they became friends. Dominic looks like a regular person here in VR, and it's eerie to see his shoulders droop. His exoskeleton doesn't have the capability to express emotion in the real world.

"You"—Joe gestures at Dominic—"secure Alan, while you"—he points at Jacob—"look out for my aunt."

He proceeds to give more orders, and I'm pleased to see he's treating me as one of the security people. I'm to stay alert and react to the situation. Then again, he might not have ordered anyone to secure me because I'm in the front by myself.

"Gogi and I are going to take care of the SUV," Joe says. He looks around as though challenging anyone to contradict him, but no one dares.

"I should drive," Mitya says once the plan of action is solidified. "My reaction times are now at least double any of yours."

I shudder as I recall the last time Mitya drove in a life-or-death situation. Still, reaction time is the key metric here, so I hesitantly agree.

"We go back to real time on three." Gogi wipes sweat from his virtual mustache. "One. Two. Three."

Unlike the guards, I don't need the countdown to pay attention to the real world. I'm already there, double-checking my seatbelt.

Jacob buckles up my mom, and Joe even finds a moment to put

a seatbelt on the unconscious RHO leader, though he's probably less concerned for her safety than preserving the pleasure of torturing her later. Meanwhile, Dominic takes Alan into his arms as though he's trying to give the kid a hug. Given that Dominic's body is mostly titanium, Alan should be more secure than in any kind of kiddie car seat.

Joe and Gogi are the only people unbuckling their seat belts. I know what they're about to do, so I open the side windows in the back of the car.

They move in sync, like dancing partners. Both jump up and slide to the window on their side. Both take out their guns seemingly at the same moment. Their simultaneous shots merge into a single eardrum-damaging bang, and the SUV's tires blow out—Joe and Gogi's marksmanship is app-enhanced.

Unfortunately, the SUV appears to have new tires designed, ironically, by Human++. Sparks fly as metal grinds against pavement, but the car doesn't slow down quickly enough—not if we want to keep a far enough distance from a potential blast radius.

"I'm speeding up," Mitya says. "I think that's the only option. If the truck gets off the ramp ahead of Zapo, you're toast—and at the moment, we don't have the resources to run anyone else's minds in the cloud besides mine."

"Wait, hold on," I yell at my friend in VR. "We're going to be by the ramp at the same time. The truck will be able to ram straight into us."

Mitya either doesn't hear or doesn't care.

Zapo X zooms forward.

FOURTEEN

BEFORE I RECOVER FROM WHIPLASH, MITYA SWERVES INTO THE middle lane. Does he think the truck will have trouble with a few extra feet of distance? Then I realize that puts a car between us and the truck—an empty self-driving red Toyota that works for Uber.

"I had to speed up," Mitya says in VR as we watch the slow-from-this-perspective progression of the truck on the ramp. "If the SUV driver is another suicide bomber, going faster is your only option."

"The problem is the truck driver might be a suicide bomber as well," I counter.

"I don't think so." Mitya's left eye twitches. Even in digital form, he retains his signature poker tell. His face is calm, but I'm not buying it. "Let's put it another way. If the truck driver has a bomb, you're all dead anyway."

I realize that he and I are both right.

"Joe, Gogi!" I scream in the real world. "Get back into your seats."

The trucker has no bomb, but he's still suicidal. He's realized he can't get ahead of us, so he's now speeding up and clearly intends to crash into the red Toyota that currently separates us. The trucker must think that hitting the Toyota won't slow him enough to keep him from reaching us. My heart rate speeds up as I realize he might just be right.

In real-world slow motion, the cars inch toward each other. I brace myself, cringing at the sight of Gogi and Joe still not in their seats.

Using the quantum servers, I model the upcoming set of collisions a couple of times. When the results come through the same on the third simulation, I shout in VR, "Mitya, Muhomor, get that ambulance in front of us to stop. We're going to need it."

Important task done, I squeeze my eyes shut and brace for the impact in the real world.

The truck almost pulverizes the empty Toyota. As the modeling showed, there's indeed enough momentum left to then ram into Zapo's hulk with notable force.

For some reason, my enhanced brain registers the sound first, a crunch that sounds as if a giant with diamond teeth decided to chew the bulletproof metal of Zapo with his mouth wide open. The jerk comes next, and every part of my body jolts forward, my neck muscles straining to keep my head attached. Shards of glass rain through the vehicle without cutting anyone, thanks to the patented shatter-without-edges technology that cost the equivalent of a modest car to install.

Through the drone cameras, I can see that Zapo has withstood the impact slightly better than the modeling predicted, though the suicidal driver got his death wish when he catapulted through his broken window. When I rewind the video, I see him somersault over Zapo's roof and land in a bloody splat of broken bones.

Unfortunately, the unsecured Gogi and Joe also behave as foretold in the modeling. As though continuing their earlier synchronicity, each man flies head first at the opposite wall and smacks his skull before collapsing into a limp bundle. The only differences between them are the blood pouring from Joe's head wound and the unnatural angle of Gogi's ankle.

I'm not sure how Mitya or Muhomor managed it, but the ambulance we've been following is backing up.

Then it hits me that I'm relaxing too soon. Surviving the truck still leaves us with the SUV behind us, a car with a suicide bomber behind the wheel.

"Dominic," I scream, "behind us!"

I don't think I needed to prompt the former soldier. He gently sets Alan on Jacob's lap and sweeps into action with a set of maneuvers that explain to me why the army is so keenly interested in the exoskeleton technology he now controls. With a powerful push of his legs, he leaps through the broken back window, reaches for his gun in midair, and lands with the softness of a feline predator. He then sprints toward the SUV, his biological hand holding the gun and his bionic hand extended palm outwards.

"I can't even imagine what he's feeling right now," Alan messages me privately. "Dominic has a deep-seated anxiety when it comes to walking up to cars, even parked ones."

Dominic's bullet hits the driver squarely in the head, but the car still has enough momentum to roll toward us, despite the naked metal of the wheels now gouging deep gashes in the pavement.

Dominic's palm connects with the SUV's grill. If his arm had been mine, enhanced bones or not, it would have snapped. But his state-of-the-art bionic arm holds the car without any problems and makes him look like a superhero as he skids backward in his effort to slow the SUV. The bottoms of his feet are covered by the same titanium as the rest of his body, and the sparks from his feet rival those produced by the car's wheels.

In a fraction of a second, I use the quantum servers again to see if the rest of his exoskeleton will prevent his midsection from getting splattered if the SUV slams him into our vehicle. The answer comes out negative—he'll likely die if he doesn't stop the car. I frantically run another simulation to tell me if he'll manage to stop in time.

Dominic's back slowly draws nearer. Before I get the calculation results back, he stops, his right foot a millimeter from Zapo's back tire.

Everyone in the car cringes. Though the driver can't activate the bombs now that he's dead, if his allies have an override, we're about to go up in smoke.

"They shouldn't have an override," Mitya says in VR, but it's clear he's unsure. "They didn't in earlier attempts."

"They might have adapted them," Alan says.

"I bet they had the bombs made ahead of time," Ada says, her Zik message hopeful. "That makes it harder to adapt, unless the driver was very handy with explosive-related gizmos."

"Get into the ambulance now," Muhomor says. "Don't wait to find out."

Dominic seems to have the same idea, because he jumps back into Zapo and picks up Gogi like a doll.

"The exoskeleton is now one of my favorite creations," I say in the VR, awestruck. "That, or Dominic is a biological marvel."

"I know." Ada doesn't seem to realize that she just bit a virtual nail. "The man isn't even out of breath."

An EMT emerges from the passenger side of the ambulance. "What's going on? We were responding to a heart attack when the car navigation started acting up and made us back up." Coming closer, he takes in the scene and asks, "Is anyone hurt?"

"Yes," I reply. "Please help."

"That rerouting sounds like Muhomor's work," Mitya says in VR. "Too bad someone's going to die because of it."

"The call was from a hypochondriac." Muhomor gives Mitya a defensive look. "I'm checking her out through her webcam, and Einstein agrees she's just having a panic attack."

"I'm making sure another ambulance double-checks Doctor Muhomor's diagnosis," Ada chimes in. "Meanwhile, take our people to the hospital."

Ignoring the emergency personnel, Dominic puts Gogi inside the ambulance and comes back for Joe. The EMT guys gape at all this in fascination; they're undoubtedly used to doing all the work on their own.

The rest of us unbuckle our seatbelts, and I check that Mom is okay. She's been silent throughout the ordeal, and her pale face looks more frightened than the day we rescued her from that Russian facility. On a hunch, I reassure her that Joe is going to be okay, and that seems to return a hint of color to her cheeks. I wait another beat, and when her shallow breathing evens out, I help her stand up. Before she gets a chance to completely come back to her senses, I lead her out of the ruins of Zapo as Jacob carries Alan behind me.

"That was scary," Mr. Spock telepathically announces from my pocket. "Let's not do it again."

"I'd love not to do that again, bud," I reply. "The bad people didn't give me a choice."

"I don't like bad people," he says confidently. "Can I bite them?"

Mr. Spock has been learning human social mores, and the mere fact that he asks if he can bite before doing so is a huge sign of progress.

"I hope you don't have to bite them. They taste really bad," I tell him.

"You're going to need another vehicle," Muhomor says.

A white limousine promptly screeches to a halt in the opposite lane.

Dominic grabs the still-unconscious Tatum, steps over the road divider, and proceeds toward the limo. He opens the door and climbs inside. Moments later, a bunch of dressed-up teenagers file out, their expressions a blend of anger, fear, and confusion.

"I'm very sorry, but we need to borrow your ride," I tell the biggest kid. I take a few crisp hundreds from my wallet.

"Tell him another rental is on the way," Muhomor says. "A better, more expensive, and cleaner one, at that."

I relay what Muhomor says and hand over the money. "If you need a place to stay after the prom, I just rented you a couple of suites at The Beekman."

I bypass the stunned teenagers and get Mom comfortable in the front of the limo. The rest of our group sits in the back.

"Have the EMT drive to the nearest hospital that's not over-crowded," I tell my friends in VR. "Also, make sure a car rental is waiting for me there. I'm going to stay with Gogi and Joe while Dominic takes Mom and Alan to the bunker."

"My plane arrives soon," Muhomor says. "Can they pick me up?"

Dominic thinks picking up Muhomor might be safer en route, so I agree to that.

"I'm staying with Josya at the hospital," Mom says when I tell her the plan.

I shake my head. "No, Mom. I need you to be there when Dominic picks up your brother." I'm not just being manipulative. Uncle Abe might balk at going with the robot man, as he calls Dominic behind his back in Russian. "I also need you to get in touch with JC and have him double-check on office evacuations and then join us in the bunker," I continue. "This mess is looking worse and worse, and I wouldn't want them—whoever they are—to hurt any more people, especially your new husband."

I seem to win this fight. Mom looks distant, a habit when using her Brainocytes.

I patch into the camera in the EMT van. To my relief, Joe and Gogi's vitals are good.

Mitya keeps the limo on the tail of the ambulance all the way to Coney Island Hospital. We're not allowed to enter the emergency room driveway, so Mitya takes me to the main entrance instead.

"Alan, Mom," I say as I get up to leave, "I'll see you in the bunker. Love you."

"Let me know when you find out how Uncle Joe is doing," Alan says. "And Gogi too."

"What am I going to tell Joe's father?" Mom looks at me sternly.

"Maybe we'll know something by the time you have to explain," I lie. Uncle Abe lives on Brighton Beach just a few blocks away, and there's no chance Joe will be seen by a doctor in the time it takes the limo to pick up his father.

"Okay," she says. "Go make sure they take good care of him."

"I'm conscious." A telepathic message from Joe arrives without any emotional overtones.

"Great," I reply. "I'm going to come see you in a moment."

Entering the hospital brings back unpleasant flashbacks of my prior hospital visit, and I fight the hollowness in my chest.

"If any of us visit a hospital a few more times," Muhomor says, "they'll probably offer us a procedure for free."

My friend's joke fails to dispel my disquiet, so I get into a virtual room with Einstein in therapist mode. This version of Einstein is good at reading facial cues and body language, and right away, he gives me a soothing smile. His German accent is almost nonexistent as he asks, "How does it feel to be in a hospital?"

"I'm going to need a gallon of vodka." Gogi's grumpy telepathic message comes in at the same time. "Why the hell did you take me to the hospital? You know I hate these places."

"Stay put." I'm hugely relieved that Gogi has also regained consciousness. I also feel slightly guilty that I wasn't as relieved when I learned that Joe had come to. "I'm on my way to the ER."

"They're taking me and Joe someplace," Gogi says.

"To image your heads," Muhomor explains when I pass on Gogi's comment. "They didn't encrypt their ancient system using Tema, so I'm in there. I expedited things as much as I could. You'll see a doctor as soon as the imaging is complete."

"They're checking your brain for any damage," I tell Gogi. "Nothing to worry about."

In my post-adrenaline slump, the need for sleep presses like a weight against my eyelids. Fighting to keep from yawning, I walk up to the check-in window.

"Hi," says the tall receptionist as she looks at me through fake eyelashes. "How can I help you?"

"I'm here to visit my cousin. An ambulance just brought him in."

The receptionist looks at me with a gaze completely devoid of empathy. "If your cousin was just brought in, he won't be in the system yet."

"He should be in the system," I say, annoyed she didn't even ask for his name. "He's getting his head scanned."

"We can't let you walk in while the patients are getting scanned," she says in the same monotone. "Please take a seat."

"Muhomor." I rub my temples both in VR and the real world. "Can you get me through the red tape?"

Muhomor waves his hands like a conductor in VR, then says, "Walk up to the security guard and launch this app"—an icon that looks like a one-eyed pirate shows up in my AROS view—"and your Brainprint will confirm your identity as a doctor."

Brainprint was one of Muhomor's early inventions. It replaced most ID cards, log-in passwords, bank account PINs, and other identity-verifying security. Brainprint uses Brainocytes for biometric identification, as each person's brain is more unique than their retinas and fingerprints combined. In fact, Muhomor claims that Brainprint doesn't allow identity theft at all, and if he thinks so, it's safe to assume it's pretty much the case. But if you make up a fake person from scratch (something Muhomor can do), you can also create a fictional Brainprint for such a person—and add the Brainprint to the hospital database.

The screen next to the guard blinks green, and my name shows up as "Dr. Hui."

"Very mature," I mutter as I plod through the opening door. In Russian, *hui* is the vulgar word for male genitalia.

The guard consults the screen and chuckles. Given this hospital's proximity to Brighton Beach, he probably understands what my name means.

"Dr. Hui's first name is Richard." Muhomor's VR grin is annoyingly cheerful. "But friends call him Dick, of course."

"I hope you weren't stupid enough to give Joe an alias like that."

I cross my VR arms over my chest. "You're about to be taken to the same bunker as he, and he's bound to be in a bad mood after getting his head bashed in."

Muhomor's smile disappears. "I didn't get a chance to give them fake identities. The EMT guys read their Brainprint before I could interfere."

"Did you at least delete them from the hospital database?" My voice jumps an octave. "The bad guys seem to be operating out of Russia, and this hospital is crawling with Russian-speaking staff."

"The security for patients is better than for employees," Muhomor says defensively. "They don't want to remove the wrong person's kidney due to an identity mix-up."

I shoot him an incredulous look. "So you can't hide their tracks?"

"If the brain imaging is clean, I'll make it look as though they were never here," he says. "If not, we'll figure something out. I guess I can create fake people with the same medical problem as Joe and Gogi and fake an admission trail—"

"I'm done with the scans." Joe appears in VR, his lizard-like eyes watching without emotion as everyone jumps.

"Gogi is done also," Muhomor says. "No skull fractures or brain damage for either, but Gogi's ankle is hurt."

"We need to get to the bunker then," I say. "Get a couple of our Human++ doctors to join us there in case we need them. Speak with Dr. Jarvis in particular, and tell him to bring his whole surgical team along with any equipment they might need."

"ER," Joe says. He disappears from VR.

When I reach the emergency room, Joe is already standing, ready to go.

"*Blyad*," Gogi mutters when his foot touches the floor. He tries to take a tentative step, then explodes into more Russian and Georgian curses that garner the attention of the Russian-speaking people around us.

"Here, sit on this," Joe says.

I'm shocked to see he's already pilfered a wheelchair. Gogi grudgingly sits, and Joe begins pushing, forcing me to follow.

"This place smells bad," Mr. Spock mentally complains from my pocket.

"We're leaving, bud." I gently tap him through my clothes, angry at myself for forgetting to give him to Alan earlier.

"Watch every camera in the hospital," I tell my friends in VR. "Every time I've been to a hospital lately, it didn't end well."

"Sir," someone shouts from behind us. "Stop!"

FIFTEEN

WHATEVER THE NURSE WANTS, WE'LL NEVER LEARN, BECAUSE WE proceed forward as fast as the wheelchair allows. To my surprise and relief, no one bothers us once we get outside the ER, and our luck continues to hold all the way to the parking lot.

"My plane landed, and I got picked up," Muhomor says in VR. "In case anyone cares."

Dominic also reports that he, Mom, Uncle Abe, and Alan made it to the airport without any problems, and that Muhomor is now in the car and en route to the bunker.

"Lean on me," I tell Gogi when we locate the luxury Lexus rental car waiting for us. He lets me and Joe help him get into the front seat.

"For an ankle that wasn't seriously damaged, it sure hurts like a sonofabitch," he says as the car begins to move.

"We'll get you some ice when we get to the hideout," I reassure him. "Run the Relief app for now."

"We should expedite the research on nanocytes that reduce swelling," Ada says in the VR room. "Maybe once things calm down a bit."

"All our efforts should focus on computing resources," Mitya counters. "And we might want to start thinking about that now, not later."

"More hardware so that you can spawn more of yourself?" Muhomor makes an okay sign with his left hand, then spears it with his right index finger in a gesture vaguely related to reproduction.

"No." Mitya's avatar seems to become more solid, and his inability to keep a poker face shows me that Muhomor might've been right. "I want you guys to have the option of getting resurrected as I was. In the longer term, this option should exist for more people."

"He's got a point," Alan says. "We nearly died today."

"We have enough disk space to back ourselves up as you did," I say. "It's processing power that we lack."

"Yes," Mitya says.

"So if we die but have a backup"—I can't help but shiver at the thought—"you can still resurrect us once the processing power is available in the future."

"Of course," he says. "Obviously I can. But building new hardware will take a while—time that will seem like forever to someone like me, a mind whose subjective experience of the world is so much faster."

"Are you saying you'd miss us for an eternity?" Alan asks. It's unclear if he's teasing Mitya or is dead serious.

"You understand it better than most, kid," Mitya says. "I bet in your four years, you've experienced the equivalent of fifty subjective years."

"If not more," Alan says sagely.

Muhomor takes off his sunglasses and rubs his eyes. "Knowing that I depend on you for my resurrection, my fear of death is getting worse."

"That's right." Mitya rubs his palms like a supervillain. "You better be on your best behavior, or else you might wake up a hundred years from now. Or not at all."

"We should do the backups more regularly." I make a mental

note to speak with therapy Einstein about my utter horror at being in a disembodied state like Mitya. "And I agree that we should work on the hardware problem, especially since that aligns with so many of our other endeavors."

"Anyone against?" Muhomor looks at Ada.

"We can make hardware a priority," my wife says, "but we should still work on nanocytes that reduce inflammation."

"Agreed," I say for everyone.

"Since no one is trying to kill you at the moment, how about we brainstorm?" Mitya says.

"Speaking of that," Alan says, "our car just reached the bunker."

I exhale in the real world and realize it's been many minutes since I held my breath in worry for my mom and son. "Great. In that case, let's talk hardware while I'm stuck in my own car. I've been thinking a lot about quantum dot cellular automata lately, so maybe let's start with that."

———

When Gogi first floated the idea of building the bunker four years ago, I told him he was bonkers. Now I'm glad Joe took his colleague's side, and we ended up with this impenetrable monstrosity. Originally a Cold War-era nuclear fallout shelter, the renovated space is a survivalist's wet dream. The entry door alone cost more than a modest house, and it's impervious to most explosions, which is what motivated me to come here.

Inside, the bunker looks like a malignant man cave that kept growing in someone's basement until it became the size of a small mansion. The comfortable plush furniture tries to trick you into thinking you're in a luxury hotel, but the lack of windows betrays the truth.

"If the zombie apocalypse were to happen tomorrow, this is where you'd want to be," Muhomor says to us in lieu of a greeting. "It looks darker and smells even stuffier than I imagined."

He's right. The place smells like a wine cellar where all the wine has turned to vinegar.

"Joshen'ka," my mom exclaims as she takes in Joe's bandaged head. "How are you feeling?"

"Fine." He takes off the bandage, sees his father's worried expression, and shows the side of his head. "Barely a bump."

We sit Gogi on the nearby couch.

"Does your foot hurt?" Alan asks him.

"Ankle," Gogi replies. "I'm sure it's going to be fine."

"Dr. Keeplan," JC calls from the grotto-like kitchen section of the bunker. "Please have a look at Gogi's ankle."

The portly doctor swings into action, and soon Gogi has an ice pack on his ankle and a Percocet in his bloodstream.

"Boss," Jacob says to Joe as he enters the space designated as the living room of the bunker. "Your woman—I mean, your guest. She's awake now."

Joe puts down the sandwich he's been munching on and is instantly on his feet. "Where?"

"The storage room," Jacob says. Looking down like a guilty schoolchild, he adds, "She's breaking a lot of pickles."

"Do we have a view into that room?" I ask my friends in VR.

"Yes." Muhomor sets up a large screen in the bunker's Augmented Reality, making it look like a giant flat-screen TV we used as recently as three years ago.

On the screen, Tatum's delicate features are twisted in a mask of fury. Like a wronged housewife, she grabs a glass jar of pickled tomatoes and hurls it against the pantry wall—and by the looks of the room, it's not the first one.

"I made those," Mom exclaims in a horrified whisper. "I used those purple Ukrainian tomatoes Ada brought for me."

Joe's expression is completely unreadable as he springs into motion. Before anyone can blink, he's in the camera view, opening the door to the storage room.

SIXTEEN

Tatum looks Joe up and down, her eyes narrowing. She must not recognize him as the guy who knocked her out, because the latest jar isn't yet flying at his head.

Instead of worrying about a potential projectile, Joe climbs the shelves. We all, Tatum included, watch his actions with morbid fascination. Only when my cousin's palm grows large does it occur to me what he's doing. When the camera is ripped out of its socket, I congratulate myself for being right. Maybe he's trying to win Tatum's confidence by showing her that she was under surveillance. Oh hell, who am I kidding—he just doesn't want us to watch.

Everyone stares at the blank screen for a couple of beats before Ada asks, "Is there another camera in that room?"

Muhomor shakes his head, and when I ask Joe's security guys the same question, they all claim there's no other camera.

I walk up to the door, hoping I can at least overhear something. Unfortunately, the thick, heavy wood blocks any noise from escaping.

"Maybe this means she's not screaming in pain," I say, only slightly joking.

"You can't let him do this." Ada's amber eyes glint dangerously in the VR room.

"Do what?" Mitya asks. "We don't know what he's doing. For all we know, they might be having a civil conversation."

"Someone is clearly in need of a brain," Muhomor says. "This is Joe. If she's not screaming, it's because he has her gagged. Or worse."

I wonder if Joe's people would obey a direct order to go check on Tatum, assuming I wanted to be the guy giving such an order, which I don't. Dominic might listen to me, but I can't help but notice he's not rushing to check on Tatum voluntarily.

We argue for a few minutes in real time, and Ada has almost convinced me to ask Dominic to break the door when said door swings open and Joe swaggers out. Hard to read in the best of times, his current facial expression is an enigma wrapped in the skin of the Loch Ness monster.

"She's not involved," he says over his shoulder as he strides past us into the gloomily lit kitchen.

I follow him in and watch as he swiftly finishes his uneaten sandwich, then proceeds to get more bread from the pantry and some cheese from the fridge. "What do you mean?"

"She didn't order the attacks," he says without looking up from spreading mayo on the bread.

"Are you sure?"

"Go talk to her." He angrily slaps some cheese onto the bread. "And give her this."

He hands me the sandwich, which I regard as if it might sprout tentacles. Oblivious to my confusion, he grabs a sealed bottle of Poland Spring water and hands that to me as well.

"I should at least check if she's okay," I say in the VR room after making sure he's not in there. "Plus it doesn't hurt to double-check if she really is innocent or not. I mean, she was our best lead."

"The RHO was," Ada corrects. "But maybe she's not its leader as everyone thinks. Or maybe they have independent cells that don't operate under her direct command."

I head over to the room where Joe's captive awaits. For some reason, the food and drink feel like lead in my hands. Why couldn't all this have waited until tomorrow morning? I'd pay a couple of million for a quick nap.

Alan is blocking my way. I look down at him questioningly.

"You might find this helpful." He hands me a tablet computer, one of those ancient relics that only the likes of my uncle still use. "No Brainocytes, remember? You won't be able to show her anything online without it."

"Thanks, son," I say on autopilot. I hold the sandwich in my teeth while I slide the tablet under my armpit.

Jacob opens the heavy door for me, and I momentarily hesitate, afraid of blood and whatever else I might find. The little spike of anxiety jolts me awake. Realizing it's not safe to keep the door ajar so long, I step in and enable my Share app so my friends can see what I see.

The woman is sitting on a stack of canned beans, her piercing blue eyes regarding me with a mixture of curiosity and disdain.

"Michael Cohen," she says in a pleasant singsong voice. "I should've guessed you're in charge here."

"The way she said your name, you'd think she was talking about Lucifer." Mitya manifests in the room's public Augmented Reality, choosing the little devil avatar he sometimes likes to use.

Tatum doesn't acknowledge him at all, confirming her lack of Brainocytes. Her attention is on my hands, so I extend the water and sandwich.

"Joe wanted me to give you this."

To my huge surprise, she doesn't shudder at his name. Instead, her eyes gleam with some undefinable emotion. Realizing I'm watching her, she quickly recovers her mask of disdain, but that doesn't stop her from grabbing both the sandwich and the water.

Taking a giant bite of the sandwich, she eyes me challengingly as she slowly chews her food. If she thinks she can bore me so easily, she's going to be disappointed. Thanks to Brainocytes, if the real world is boring (which it almost always is), I can do a hundred other things virtually.

I lean against the wall of canned beans and make sure Tatum can tell that I'm comfortable enough to stay here for hours, if she insists. I then reply to all the emails that have accumulated since these crazy events began, launch several processor designs since that's a new priority, initiate an important conversation with Ada about Alan's plan to earn another PhD from Yale, begin writing a couple of apps, get started beating several world champions at chess, and outline a few chapters for my latest publication.

Once Tatum figures out she can't bore me into leaving, she says, "At the rallies, I always said what you did was criminal." She unscrews the bottle cap and gulps the water with the zest of a desert dweller. "I didn't realize how literal that was."

"You have the gall to bring up criminal acts with me?" My voice hardens. I'm having flashbacks of the multiple ways I nearly died today, along with memories of all the favorite things lost in my deceased penthouse—like the Swiss armchair I'd sit in while in VR and the obscenely expensive Pollock and Dalí originals. What a ghastly loss. I take a deep breath of pickled vegetables and add more calmly, "Your people tried to kill me. Multiple times. You blew up everything I own."

Her look is so full of sympathy that I stop talking and blink in confusion.

"I'm sorry about what happened to you." To heighten the sincerity of her words, she momentarily stops chewing, though I get the sense that she's dying to resume. "The RHO is a peaceful organization, and I would never authorize violence of any kind, even against you."

"Then how do you explain this?" On the tablet, I pull up a picture of her and Lennox Dixon, the guy who blew up our apartment, and transpose it with the news articles about the bombing.

I hold the screen toward her, and she puts down the water and grabs the device out of my hands. If Joe mentioned any of this to her during his mysterious interrogation, there's no sign of it. She looks shocked, her eyes filling with tears.

"If this is a trick," she says, blinking rapidly, "it's very cruel. Even for someone like you."

"Can you stop saying that? I'm not the devil."

She glances around the storage room as if to say, "I'm here, a prisoner, and you're in charge—do the math."

"Your being in this room is just a misunderstanding," I say. "We'll obviously let you go as soon as we understand who's trying to kill us and why. Besides, didn't you catch the part where the authorities want to question you?"

"Why shouldn't I talk about you as though you're the devil?" she asks, her gaze hardening now that she's no longer staring at the tablet. "You're about to usher in the apocalypse for the human species. That makes you pretty much the textbook antichrist."

"So you admit you tried to kill me." I speak quickly, trying a persuasion technique I've used a few times on investors. "You wanted to prevent the apocalypse."

The miserable expression returns to her face, and she shakes her head, her gaze on the tablet once more.

"I would never do that," she says. "Nor would Lennox ever do something like that, for that matter." She looks thoughtful for a moment, then shakes her head again. "No, he really wouldn't."

I latch on to her hesitation as a clue. "Yet he did. There's something you're not saying."

"Lennox didn't have long to live," she says after a pregnant pause. "A brain tumor. But he acted normally. Besides, where would he get a suicide vest? Why would he bomb your apartment, where your family might be? It just makes no sense."

"And yet it happened."

In VR, I ask, "Why didn't we know about his tumor?"

"Unlike Coney Island Hospital, most doctors' offices encrypt their records using Tema," Muhomor says defensively.

"We should see if anyone else had a terminal illness," I say in VR.

In the real world, Tatum frowns at me uncertainly. "Maybe someone offered him money? He was worried about his dad, but I told him we'd take care of his family." She begins to cry.

I feel like a monster, even though I haven't really done anything. I fight the temptation to walk over and touch her shoulder reassuringly. Comfort from "the antichrist" would probably make matters worse. "Can you think of anyone who would've paid him to do something like that? Maybe a more zealous part of your organization?"

"We don't have bloodthirsty zealots like that." She wipes the remnants of tears from her eyes to make sure I register the scathing look she gives me. "Most of us are unemployed, thanks to you and your company. We're as useless as the rest of humanity is going to be soon, if you're not stopped."

"Tell her about our plans to allow people to make money as artisans in their fields," Alan says, raising one of his favorite topics. "Also mention our plans for universal basic income."

"No zealots," Ada says, her voice dripping with sarcasm as she ignores Alan's tirade. She appears as an angel avatar next to Mitya's devil and gives Tatum an unsympathetic once-over. "Ask her how they planned to save humanity, then. By being a nuisance?"

"If you truly believe that we're bringing about the end of the world," I say instead, "isn't it just a matter of time before someone gets violent?"

"If Gandhi could drive the British out of India with patience and without violence, we should be able to reverse the harm you're doing using the same methods," Tatum says. Her dimpled chin juts upward.

"Did she just compare herself to Gandhi?" The tiny Mitya devil lands on Tatum's right shoulder. "Why not the Dalai Lama? Or Santa, while she's at it?"

"I bet fifty bucks she's going to compare us to Hitler at some point in the next few minutes," Ada replies, matching Mitya's tone.

I do my best to ignore the commentary from Augmented Reality. "Do you still think I fabricated what this tablet is showing you?"

"No." Tatum visibly deflates.

"Then you agree that despite what you tried to do, violence happened."

She nods.

"Then help us figure out who's responsible," I say. "If RHO is innocent, then it would seem someone is framing you guys. You should be as interested in getting to the truth as I—perhaps more so, since the authorities are looking for you."

She's silent for a moment. Her nicely trimmed eyebrows move animatedly on her forehead as though they're a window into her brain. "I don't think you're fabricating this." She gestures at the tablet, looking genuinely miserable. "I just don't know how I can help."

"Joe is right," Muhomor says in the VR room. "She's useless."

"I agree," Ada says. "Let's let her go after I land."

"I'm not convinced." Mitya's avatar flies from Tatum's shoulder, grows to the size of a small dog, and lands a foot away from her legs. "The fact that she doesn't have Brainocytes does open an interesting possibility. We could force her to get Brainocytes with a modified AROS interface that has the Polygraph app running in the background. We could then find out for sure if she's telling the truth."

"No." Ada's angel grows bigger than the devil avatar and flies through the room to place herself between Tatum and Mitya. "We're not doing that."

The Polygraph app was a failure created by the intelligence community, designed to test its own people. It's a Brainocyte app that can accurately spot if the person running it is telling the truth. It's a million times more reliable than the polygraph exam from which it takes its name. Even before Brainocytes, tools like fMRI and other brain-scanning technologies were used in lie detection, but Brainocytes took such technology to new levels.

The reason the project failed was that we designed Brainocytes in such a way that no one can force someone else to run a specific app; you must rely on the person to do it on her own. That led to an easy way to thwart the Polygraph app: a spoofed version of the app that doesn't keep an eye on the user's brain but instead shows results that look like the output of the Polygraph app.

What Mitya suggests would work around the spoof problem because Tatum would get Brainocytes for the first time. As a new user, she'd not be able to figure out how and where to get the Polygraph-faking app. Also—and this is probably why Ada is so upset —Mitya is suggesting that her Brainocytes would run an app in the background without her explicit consent, something our lobbyists are trying to make illegal in as many countries as we can.

"That's an interesting idea," I say to my friends telepathically. "If we made sure she's not connected to the internet, we could be certain the Polygraph app is working as intended. Or that the custom AROS build wouldn't even have internet. Hell, we could even give her a normal AROS interface and just insist she run the Polygraph app without internet. This way—"

"I said no." Ada's head turns toward me, her amber eyes burning with ire. "It's extremely unethical."

"Oh, she'd like us to do that," Muhomor says. "Confirmation bias. She'd love it if we confirmed every fear the RHO has about us."

"No," I say to Muhomor. "I just read some of Tatum's blog posts, and I think Brainocytes would be her worst nightmare. I guess we're back at square one."

"I think you're telling the truth," I say to our victim in the real world. "My cousin said as much." I say the last bit out of curiosity. I'd still like to know what Joe did to her to reach his conclusion.

"You mean Joe?" To my shock, her expression is less dire than I would've expected at the mention of her tormentor. It's almost excited, even. "You're related?"

"His father is my mother's brother." I raise my eyebrows in VR as if to say, "What *did* he do to her?"

"I see," Tatum says, her expression unreadable again.

Ada, Muhomor, and Mitya all shrug.

"I'd like you to stay with us a little bit longer," I say after a long and uncomfortable silence, during which Tatum finishes both her food and water.

"Stay your prisoner, you mean?" she says. It's hard to say if she's really upset or she's just using the chance to poke at the antichrist.

"I'd prefer to look at it as giving you shelter while we figure out how to clear your name." I wave at the tablet.

"Since I don't have a choice, I don't see why not," she says. "Any chance I can take a shower, use the bathroom, and take a nap?"

Mitya sends me the bunker schematics with one room circled. "Nine suites, two of them unused. That one has a door that someone can guard."

"Let me see what I can do for you," I tell Tatum.

After some quick setup, Gogi takes her to the room Mitya picked out.

"Dominic," I say. "Do you mind taking the first watch?"

Instead of answering, he assumes his position. I believe his exoskeleton would allow him to stand like this for days, but I've never double-checked by asking if it's true. Dominic doesn't like to talk about his body.

"Hey, Dad." Alan is using his real-world, hard-to-resist kid voice, which means he's about to say something I won't like. "Can I speak with her?"

"Tatum?" I glance at Dominic for support, but the guard's Augmented Reality face shows no emotion. "You want to talk to the woman who might've ordered that bombing?"

"We decided she didn't do it." He speaks telepathically now; he knows that when it comes to arguing, you sound less persuasive when your voice is that of a four-year-old.

If I start arguing, he's probably going to get his way, as well as delay my getting to sleep by precious minutes. So I do the easy thing and give in.

"Put another guard at the entry and take Dominic with you when you go inside." I make sure Dominic gives me a little nod.

"Okay," Alan says reluctantly.

"And run the Share app, recording every word she says."

"Well, of course."

"You okay with this?" I privately ask Ada. "I'll be the bad guy and say no, if you want."

"Let him talk to her," she replies, her message almost free of anxiety. "Dominic will be with him."

I send Dominic a private message. "If she so much as looks at him wrong or says a mean word, pull him out. If she touches him in the wrong way—in any way—break her arm."

The big man gives me another nod.

"And can I pick up Mom when she lands?" Alan asks, his eyes glinting mischievously. He knows what I'll say, but he's testing me anyway.

"Absolutely not." I try to look as authoritative as I can.

"We'll discuss this after you get some sleep," he says. "You're not in the best of moods now."

"My answer will be the same."

"We'll see."

I send a private telepathic message to my cousin. "Joe, make sure to wake me up before you go get Ada."

"Obviously," he replies.

"And when we go, please have someone check the car to make sure Alan is not stowed away in it someplace. He's gotten it into his head to go with us, which I don't think is safe."

"I agree," Joe replies grimly. I get the feeling that if he does catch Alan in the car, my son might get his first-ever spanking. Or worse.

"Can someone interview the family of the Curaçao bomber?" I ask in the VR room with a demonstrative yawn. "And can someone else do the same in the other locations?"

"I now can control a dozen more robots than when I was corporeal," Mitya says. "I volunteer."

"All right. Then can the rest of you guys please watch over Alan while he goes to talk to that witch?" I yawn again. "I can almost get a solid's night sleep before Ada's plane arrives."

"Not fair," Ada says. "I'm exhausted and want to go back to sleep also."

"So?" Muhomor says. "You don't trust me to watch over the offspring in a bunker full of guards?"

"Fine." Her yawn is even more contagious than mine. "I'm sleeping for the rest of the flight."

"Anything else we can do while the two of you slack off?" Muhomor asks sarcastically.

"It would be nice to look into the people who drove those cars earlier," I say. "My face recognition app didn't catch their faces, but maybe you can hack into police department or the morgue to find out who they were."

"Fine." He looks embarrassed. I guess this is the first time he hasn't already thought of hacking the answers.

I gulp down a smoothie I made while speaking in VR, then make my way to the master suite and plop down on the bed. I make a mental note to upgrade it to the Mitya-designed WhisperAir mattress at some point in the future. This mattress is the ancient memory foam variety.

Then I realize I'm accepting the need for bunkers too readily. The terrorists (or whoever they are) are winning.

"Watch Alan," I tell Mr. Spock. "Make sure the woman he's about to talk to doesn't upset him."

"If someone hurts Alan, I will bite them," Mr. Spock says, his basic Zik message full of wrath.

"It might be enough to run up to her and squeak," I tell him. "If violence is required, let Dominic deal with it."

"If she makes me squeak, I might not be able to stop myself from biting," Mr. Spock says.

I'm very proud of Mr. Spock's self-knowledge. "Do your best, bud."

"Sleep well." He scurries out of the room.

As my eyelids close, I send Ada our usual telepathic good-night message and blank out.

SEVENTEEN

THE HOSPICE TRIES TO BE AS CHEERFUL AS SUCH A PLACE CAN possibly be, but with every step, I'm drowning in sorrow. A long gray tunnel in front of me ends with a large door marking my destination. Each step echoes through the hallway, and my legs seem to move without my conscious consent.

I know what waits behind that door.

Mom is there, her body a battlefront of cancer.

I feel as if I'm falling instead of walking, and the feeling of falling makes something click in my psyche. I'm pulling the door handle when I become certain that this is a nightmare—a dream inspired by the Join app experience during which I saw what happened to Ada's mother through Ada's eyes.

Bright light hits my retinas as the door opens. Will I see Ada's mother or my own mom in this dream? Or is this a dream at all?

Instead of anyone's mother, Einstein's grinning face greets me. The AI is wearing a gown and has tubes attached, just like in Ada's memories.

"You're getting much better at recognizing and controlling your dreams," he says. "Will you be practicing lucid dreaming now?"

Instead of answering, I focus my attention and transform the room into a rose garden. Once a sweet-scented breeze replaces the stuffy fumes and there's no hint of the hospice, I manifest Ada into the scene.

"Haven't you had enough of me when awake?" dream Ada asks seductively. She loosens the right strap of her yellow summer dress.

"Never," I whisper and float toward her.

EIGHTEEN

"You have been unconscious for eight hours and forty-seven minutes," Einstein reports somewhere in my groggy brain. "Current time is 8:55 a.m."

I jackknife in bed and send Ada a frantic telepathic message: "Are you back? Did Joe go pick you up without me?"

She doesn't reply, so I put together another Zik message. "Joe, where are you?"

Joe doesn't reply either. As my real-world hand reaches for my pants, I pop into the VR room, hoping either Ada or Joe are there, but they aren't. The only person in the VR room is Mitya, but his avatar looks strange. His face is like that of a statue in Madame Tussaud's museum, his open eyes glassy.

"Dude," I say when I realize he hasn't blinked for an unnatural length of time. "What the hell is going on with you?"

Mitya's eyes slowly blink and recover some of their liveliness. In almost no time, they sparkle with their normal intelligence, and his face animates into a smile. "Oh, hey."

"Hey," I reply cautiously. "You didn't answer my question."

"What was the question?" He raises his arms over his head in a catlike stretch. "I'm afraid I was a little out of it."

"No kidding," I say. "What was up with your eyes being glazed over?"

"Is that what it looked like?" He stretches his neck, tilting his head side to side. "Since everyone was asleep, I figured it was as good a time as any to experiment with sleep and dividing my attention."

"So that was you sleeping?" I say. "Your eyes were open."

"Do you think anything about me has to do with this avatar anymore?" His body morphs into a row of miniature computer servers. "This is what I really look like now," he says in a slightly metallic voice. "Not this." His avatar is back in the room and continues to stretch his limbs as though nothing happened. "I don't need to breathe," he says on an exhale. "I don't need to worry about my weight." A banana sundae appears on the meeting room table. "I don't—"

"—need to sleep?" I'm eager to get back to the subject of Ada. "Did you rid yourself of sleep? Was that what you experimented with?"

"I'm still mostly an emulation of a bunch of brain regions," he says. "Since the biological brain needs sleep, I'm afraid to just give it up without due diligence. No one's figured out what sleep is for: consolidation of memory, practicing scenarios for the future, or other, sometimes contradictory theories. For now, I'm experimenting with allowing parts of me to sleep while other parts of me remain conscious—a little bit like dolphins, although unlike the dolphins' tactic of sleeping half a brain at a time, I'm trying to figure out a more distributed configuration."

"Okay," I say. "Sounds interesting, but I'm here for a reason. Have you heard from Ada?"

"I was fully asleep for the last real-world hour or two. I wanted to record everything that was happening with every part of my being. But before that, Ada was sleeping, along with everyone else. I checked because I wanted to share my Curaçao findings, along with research on the other bombers—but alas, you guys didn't wake up even for that. I must say, this first night as a spirit inside the machine was pretty boring overall, and I foresee myself making lots of new friends around the world if you guys keep on sleeping regularly like this."

"This is odd," I say. "By all rights, Ada's plane should've landed already. I was expecting it at 7:30 a.m. or thereabouts."

"Perhaps no one woke you up because severe weather delayed the flight?" Mitya says and then frowns. "I can't reach the pilot or any of the crew. That really is odd."

My breathing speeds up in the real world, where I'm still only in the process of putting a foot through my right pant leg. I telepathically ping Ada again, and then do the same with Joe.

Nothing.

Desperate, I try getting in touch with Muhomor and get an auto-reply that he's sleeping. This isn't surprising, as Muhomor's earlier nickname was Upir—Russian for vampire, because he strongly prefers night to day. I debate getting in touch with Mom, but she might have a heart attack if I tell her my current situation, so I abandon that idea.

After a slight hesitation, I write a Zik message to Alan, certain that he of all people would be wide awake, bright-eyed and bushytailed. The kid is like that Energizer Bunny from the commercials. He gets up at 7 a.m. even if he goes to bed after midnight.

As milliseconds pass without an answer, my real-world heartbeat picks up. "I'm going to focus on what's happening in real time, so I won't be fun to talk to. Can I ask you to check into their location on this level?"

"Of course," Mitya says. "Here are the views into everyone's rooms through the security cameras our bodyguard set up. I'll proceed by locating the plane, and then—"

I stop paying attention because I'm taking in everyone in their rooms, and I don't like what I'm seeing. Muhomor and Mom are sleeping, as I thought, as are prisoner-guest Tatum, Gogi, Dominic, and most of the guards. Alan, however, isn't in his room or anyone else's. There's no camera in anyone's bathroom (a camera in the bedroom is bad enough, even for an underground post-apocalyptic bunker), so I can't check to see if he's merely brushing his teeth—though if he's awake, why would he ignore my messages?

I fully ignore VR and pour all my prodigious attention into the act of putting on pants while hopping toward the door. I'm pulling my zipper up as I dash toward Alan's room, passing a snoring Jacob on the way. He's napping on guard duty, but I'll leave it to Joe to reprimand his man—assuming I can find Joe.

In person, Alan's suite is only slightly smaller than the one designated for me and Ada. The bed is still empty, and I run up to it to feel for warmth. He must've left the bed a while ago, because the silk sheets (his favorite material) are cold to the touch. I check the bathroom and don't find him there, either.

I grab Alan's tooth-rinsing glass and fill it up with chilly water, then retrace my steps back to the lounge chair where Jacob is still sleeping on the job.

"Jacob."

Unsurprisingly, he keeps on snoring. In case he is stupid enough to run the Do Not Disturb app on duty, I toss the contents of my glass into his face and follow it up with a bitch slap.

I must hand it to Jacob's training. He's on his feet instantly with a gun to my head. Irritated, I prepare to disarm him, but before I get the chance, his eyes widen in recognition and he lowers his weapon.

"What the hell?" he asks as he rubs his cheek and looks down at his wet shirt. "What's gotten into you?"

My worry transforms into sudden fury. "Where is he?" A speck of my spittle lands on Jacob's nose. "Where is my son?"

"Alan?" He blinks. "He's with Joe. You should know that."

"Where is Joe?" My hands clench into fists.

"He went to pick up your wife." All remnants of sleep are gone from his face, replaced by an expression of deep concern.

"Joe took Alan with him?"

"Yes."

"It didn't seem odd to you that Joe took Alan but not me?"

"Well." Jacob looks panicked now. I guess Joe being his boss means he didn't question what happened, but now that I've forced him to think about it, he sees that he's failed in his guard duty. "I didn't think—"

"I can't reach any of them." I'm shouting, so I lower my voice. "I can't reach Joe, Ada, or Alan."

The blood leaves Jacob's face, and his eyes widen to the size of quarters.

"Behind you." Mitya's private telepathic Zik message comes imbued with the urgency flags set to maximum. "Jacob isn't reacting to your words."

Mitya's right; Jacob is staring at something behind me. I turn my whole body instead of just my head so that whatever the threat is, I'm facing it head on. At the same time, I use Muhomor's app to locate the melon-scented security camera.

Gogi is standing there with a gun. His face lacks his usual good humor.

"Wait," I order telepathically, but it's too late.

Gogi presses the trigger.

A red stain spreads on Jacob's chest right below the water spot I caused earlier. Jacob's expression is a mixture of horror and confusion as he drops to the ground. Like me, he can't believe he just got shot by a fellow guard—and not just any guard, but Gogi, Joe's second-in-command.

I see new movement from the corner of my eye, but all my attention is on Gogi's gun, because he turns and aims at my frantically beating heart.

NINETEEN

IT'S ALMOST CRUEL HOW MANY THOUGHTS I CAN HAVE BEFORE GOGI presses the trigger. Hell, I might have enough time to write a farewell letter to everyone I ever cared about in the time before the bullet reaches my head.

When Gogi shot Jacob, I didn't know what to think. Granted, I had momentarily felt like killing the guy myself when I learned he didn't stop Joe from taking Alan and leaving without me. But I would never act on such an impulse. Joe might've shot Jacob for this, but not Gogi—or at least, that's what I thought.

Now that Gogi is aiming at me, only one answer seems logical, but that answer makes zero sense.

Gogi is a traitor.

As difficult as it is to believe, the enemy has somehow recruited Gogi and either blackmailed or bribed him to kill me.

Another idea develops, but before I can consciously register it, I see something wonderful. Using his exoskeleton legs to move unlike any mortal man, Muhomor is already behind Gogi. He may have refused to learn martial arts all these years, but his metal-reinforced leg is able to kick away the gun, sending it flying under the nearby lounge chair.

Gogi's hand should be in excruciating pain, but the big man's face shows nothing.

"Jacob saved my life," Muhomor says through gritted teeth as he throws a punch at Gogi's face. "You—"

Though Muhomor hits his target, his unrehearsed punch doesn't stop Gogi's fist from slamming into his pale jaw in return like a baseball bat into a softball. Muhomor's outraged expression instantly slackens, and he slumps to the floor, clearly out.

Gogi lifts his foot to kick Muhomor, but I'm already leaping at him. He doesn't shift his attention swiftly enough, and I see an opening for a devastating blow to his larynx. Yet something makes me hesitate.

"He's your friend," Mitya comments privately, as though he's read my mind. "Of course this will be hard."

"I'm more worried about damaging his neck," I think back at Mitya. "I need him to be able to talk later."

Gogi takes advantage of my delay by throwing a punch at my shoulder. I twist away and counter with a kick, but I don't use the opportunity to break his leg. Something in his movements doesn't fully make sense. I file the oddity away to analyze when I'm not fighting for my life.

Despite all my training, I'm not prepared for what I encounter in this fight. I've always relied on disabling my opponent, typically by causing severe harm very quickly. But I can't bring myself to do that to Gogi. I'm not sure if it's because of the love for life I've caught from Ada during that Joining or the fact that Gogi has been like family for years. Whatever the reason, I'm pulling my punches, blocking his hits and countering with a force no stronger than I'd use during sparring.

In contrast, Gogi's attacks are all real, all aiming to leave me disabled. This is somehow more painful than his intent to shoot me earlier, because there's something more premeditated about fighting someone hand to hand. I can see that if I don't overcome my reluctance, he'll win this fight. Belatedly, I recall that I now have access to Battle Mode and enable it, but I'm wary of turning on the Emotion Dampener because I might then kill Gogi in the most brutal way imaginable.

"Gogi," I say out loud and via a telepathic message. "Whatever they're paying you, I'll double it."

He doesn't stop. His emotionless eyes don't even register comprehension.

Battle Mode highlights my possibilities. I choose an opening that will result in a painful but hopefully not-too-damaging kick in the family jewels. I've already begun to execute the maneuver when I realize my mistake: I've fallen for a feint. Gogi grabs my foot, and we tumble to the ground.

Battle Mode shows me how to position my body midflight to make sure I don't break my spine. My heart pounds against my chest a couple of times before I smack onto the bunker floor. Despite all my training and Battle Mode, I'm still no match for Gogi when it comes to wrestling. I'd be in trouble even without the handicap of my hesitation to hurt a friend.

Out of utter desperation, half based on my own intuition and half on Battle Mode, I slither out of his grasp like a Vaseline-covered eel. To my surprise, I manage to grab his ankle in a lock.

This is when it hits me: the guy hurt his ankle yesterday and could barely stand, yet he's showing no sign of pain during our fight. How much is it costing him to do this? And how much pain am I causing now by continuing the lock?

Gogi behaves as though he wouldn't care if I sawed his ankle off completely. Either he faked his injury earlier, or he's on some major painkillers right now. Then he does something he's never done during training: a very unprofessional, fish-like spiral. We end up rolling on the floor, each trying to get leverage on the other.

Before I even realize what's happened, Gogi's knee connects with my groin, and he headbutts me in the face. His nose cracks, but I'm momentarily stunned. When my world stops spinning, he has me on my back, his knees on my biceps and his hands around my throat.

I wriggle underneath and try to kick him without any luck.

Because of my enhanced bones, I don't fear my neck breaking, and with Respirocytes, it's much harder to choke me than a regular person. To make me run out of oxygen, Gogi will have to block my airflow for many minutes—but if I can't escape this hold, that shouldn't be a problem.

Battle Mode doesn't highlight any useful maneuvers, and my body's fight-or-flight response doesn't seem to have gotten the Respirocytes memo. I gasp frantically, my heart rate skyrocketing and my vision narrowing to a tunnel. I don't know how long this choking torture lasts, but I can feel myself beginning to weaken. I assume my oxygen supply is dwindling, even with its fancy red-blood-cell-carrying technology.

"Somebody help," I scream in the VR room and send Zik messages to my whole contact list with the exception of Mom. "Gogi is choking me!"

My last hope is that Gogi's hands will cramp from all this intense squeezing, but it doesn't take long to realize he cares as little about the pain in his hands as his bleeding nose and his alleged ankle injury.

In the end, I realize that Respirocytes make dying of suffocation a more horrible experience because the process is so much slower. I begin to fade in and out. During a moment of clarity, I realize I'm no longer kicking with my legs, so I try to use the last of my strength to thrash about. The last-ditch attempt doesn't help, and I'm left with dazedly staring into the empty eyes of the former friend who's methodically taking away my life.

If I die, Mitya might eventually be able to bring a computer substrate version of me back, the way he did for himself. This thought only scares me more, since I can't picture what such an existence would be like. Besides, I can't die without knowing what's happened to Ada and Alan—especially since I now fear the worst. And a digital resurrection would only happen if our adversaries don't destroy our whole company and the data servers, something no longer safe to assume now that they've somehow managed the impossible: turning Gogi against me.

Unable to fight anymore, my body slackens, and the darkness of unconsciousness closes in.

TWENTY

THERE'S A FLURRY OF MOVEMENT BEHIND GOGI, THOUGH IT MIGHT simply be the final firing of my oxygen-starved neurons.

Gogi's hands fight to stay on my neck, but a force pulls him back so hard that his nails rip away chunks of my skin. I gasp for air as Dominic's bionic arm lifts Gogi into the air before tossing him aside like a racquetball.

Gogi slams into the wall, slides down, and to my amazement, tries to get up again. Dominic lunges for him.

Using the action of standing up as his cover, Gogi reaches into his boot.

"Dominic, knife!" I yell out loud as well as telepathically.

Gogi has always bragged about the many times that military-issue knife saved his life in the Georgian special forces. He'll be lethal with it even after that devastating smack against the wall. I struggle to crawl in the hope of helping Dominic as best as I can. My legs feel as if they've turned to hair gel and my arms are heavy, but I manage a wobbly few inches toward the couch where I last saw Gogi's gun.

Through the camera view, I see either anger or faith driving Dominic onward. If he heard my shout about the knife, he doesn't seem to care. Before Gogi gets a chance to fully stand, Dominic's artificial arm clamps on his hand like a vise.

Still frantically gasping for air, I reach the couch and fumble underneath it for the gun.

Gogi's knife gleams in the bunker's artificial light. He's grasping the hilt with his free left hand. Dominic sees the threat and tries to pull the man away from his own body, but he's too late.

The knife swings toward his face.

It lodges where Dominic's right eye would be, in the scar tissue that's a reminder of that horrific explosion. If he still had that eye, he would've lost it now without a doubt. He yelps in pain, and given how tough the big man is, I understand just how much harm Gogi just managed to inflict.

My fingers finally brush across the cold barrel of the gun. It takes me less than a second to pull the weapon out. I roll into a shooting position, heart pounding, and as soon as I see a clear shot, I aim at Gogi.

Even after this betrayal, I'm loath to shoot the person I thought for so many years was my friend.

Gogi rips the knife from Dominic's eye socket. He's about to stab him again.

Hesitation gone, I shoot Gogi's knife-wielding arm.

I haven't had time to enable the aim-assist app, but my time at the gun range pays off yet again. Gogi's palm blossoms with red, and the knife clanks against the floor, the handle cleaved in half by my bullet.

Dominic grunts and, with almost no effort, bends Gogi's right arm at an impossible angle. There's a crack of breaking bone.

Gogi doesn't even blink. He's still trying to get at Dominic despite both injuries. Fortunately, there's a limit to how much the body can do with a broken arm, even if the mind is willing it.

Dominic pulls Gogi's head into his bionic grasp, and I know he has enough power in his artificial limb to decapitate him. To my relief, he crashes his opponent's head against the wall instead.

Since Gogi's skull doesn't explode into bits, it's safe to assume Dominic was tempering his strength. Nevertheless, Gogi slides to the floor, the cumulative damage enough to finally knock him out.

By the time I'm on my feet, Gogi's hands and feet are in handcuffs that Dominic produces from somewhere. The restraints come just in time, because Gogi comes to and begins thrashing against the cuffs.

"Monster," Gogi bellows when he sees that no matter what he does, he can no longer move. His voice doesn't sound like his usual voice; there's a flute-like quality to it. His efforts become eerily frantic, and I can only imagine the horrific pain in his broken, damaged arms.

Dominic produces a syringe from the same mysterious hiding spot as the cuffs and stabs Gogi in the neck with the thin needle. Gogi instantly goes limp, though as his eyes close, he says in the same odd voice, "If you don't do as you're told, Ada and Alan will die. You must—"

I don't hear what he says next, because he slumps into a drugged netherworld.

"Wait." Rubbing my aching throat, I start toward the unconscious man. "He said something about Ada and Alan. They're missing. I need to know what he knows."

"What's wrong with Alan and Ada?" Fury makes Dominic's avatar as frightening as his damaged body. Though he doesn't like me to, I switch from looking at his avatar to the burned flesh in the real world. His eye socket is bleeding despite the surrounding scar tissue, making it look as if he's shedding macabre tears of blood.

The wound must be bad, because he sinks onto the couch, clutching at his face to stop the bleeding.

"I can't reach either of them," I say. Mentally, I'm examining the bunker schematics to figure out where Dr. Jarvis sleeps. Jarvis is a brilliant surgeon, and I'm glad I tasked him with bringing his whole team plus equipment. "Obviously, their being incommunicado has something to do with Gogi's attack."

"I'm sorry. The drug I gave him..." Dominic tightens his left fist, and I get the feeling that he's as tempted as I to try to rip the information out of Gogi's unconscious body. "He's going to be out for a few hours."

"We don't have that long." I head over to Jarvis's room on unsteady legs. "We need information now."

There's a moan from where Muhomor stirs. Through the camera mic, I hear him say confusedly, "What? How? Who? Why?"

"Joe, Ada, and Alan are missing," I tell him in the fastest Zik I'm capable of. "Gogi seems to be a traitor."

As I speak to him, I storm into the doctor's bedroom and flick on the lights. Despite the gunfire, Dr. Jarvis and his wife are still sleeping. They either have the Do Not Disturb app on, or they overdosed on Ambien. I doubt it's because the walls in this bunker are as heavy and soundproof as the marketing people claimed when we were buying the place.

Breaching all etiquette, I approach the good doctor and slap him across the face.

His eyes pop open, his hand flying up to cradle his cheek as he sits up. "What's going on?" He looks as though he's about to have a heart attack, which I hope he doesn't, as he's our only surgeon.

I rip the covers from his bed, not caring that I'm also exposing his wife. "We need medical help. Get up. I'll go gather the rest of your team."

I repeat a version of this rude awakening several times, and when I've woken the last nurse, I find Dr. Jarvis and a few colleagues setting up a sterile environment in the big open space.

Dominic is already being prepped.

"They're going to be fine," the doctor says when he sees me.

"Is there a way to wake Gogi from his state?" I ask. "I know drug addicts get Narcan to come out of an overdose. Is there something similar here?" I do a quick online search via Brain-ocytes. "Perhaps Flumazenil?"

"Dr. Blantor?" Dr. Jarvis says to a thin man on his left who, according to face recognition, is an anesthesiologist.

"Nothing that we have here," says Dr. Blantor. "Plus—"

"I got some information," Mitya tells me telepathically. "Join me in VR."

I thank the doctors and take a seat next to where a nurse is applying a bandage to Muhomor's head. "Are you well enough to join VR?"

"Already there," he says through his swollen lip.

The nurse begins to examine me as I switch my full attention to VR. The well-lit illusionary conference room is such a contrast to the bunker that it takes me a moment to mentally adjust—proof I'm still groggy from near suffocation.

Mitya has prepared several screens for us. The biggest shows our private jet in the nearby New Jersey airport.

Mitya's expression is extremely subdued, and I fear the worst as I ask, "What did you find out?"

Mitya looks from me to Muhomor. "You best see for yourself. I've always warned you about him."

The screen shows Joe marching purposefully up the plane stairs, a gun in his hand.

Eugene, one of Joe's most trusted bodyguards and who's tasked with protecting Ada, greets his boss with a smile.

The smile instantly drops when Joe raises his gun, pointing at the man's chest.

"Boss," Eugene says, "what—"

Joe presses the trigger.

He then steps over the dead man without a hint of emotion and stalks into the plane.

TWENTY-ONE

IN HORRIFIED SILENCE, WE WATCH JOE EXECUTE TWO MORE OF HIS men—they run out to learn what the shooting is about, see their boss, ask a question, and get slaughtered. Following the same basic formula, a couple more people die inside the baggage compartment, then two more on the ramp that leads into the fuselage. After that, Joe stalks into the passenger compartment and puts another couple of bullets into his remaining people there.

The enormity of this betrayal doesn't compute in my enhanced brain. Nor does Joe's behavior. Why kill his men when most of them are loyal to him and him alone?

If Joe is with the bad guys, I'm well and truly screwed. After years of training in the dojo, I haven't beaten my cousin once during sparring. He still shoots better than I at the range, still lifts more weight at the gym. Simply put, Joe is the deadliest person I've ever encountered, and the idea of him as my foe is terrifying—especially since I don't know if I'm capable of hurting a relative. Yet I have no doubt that he wouldn't hesitate to kill me.

A new fear overrides all my concerns when he begins searching through the seats.

He's looking for Ada.

He discovers her sleeping on the massage-capable couch that was the selling point of this plane. She must have the Do Not Disturb app on as usual, because the bright lights after landing would've awakened her long before the gunfire. Before we developed DND, she made me tape up every LED light in our bedroom with black masking tape. If we survive, we should tweak the stupid app to allow life-threatening sounds and sights to come through.

Target acquired, Joe leaps for my wife, pulling out a syringe on the way. Her peaceful expression doesn't change. The only sign of what he's done is her complete lack of response when he throws her over his shoulder like a sack of potatoes.

In the real world, my nails dig into the base of my palms as my hands clench into too-tight fists.

"I'm sorry, dude," Mitya says as though from the distance. "That was only a part of it. Do you want to see more?"

I nod, because I don't trust myself to speak for the moment.

He plays a clip of Joe sneak-attacking the guards he took with him to the airport, and then he shows me a current video feed of the guards' bodies still lying in the bunker parking lot.

Then he plays the clip I'm dreading the most.

"Thanks so much for taking me with you, Uncle Joe," Alan says as the two of them exit the bunker. "Why did Dad not want to come with us?"

Alan's back is to Joe, so he doesn't see the syringe headed for his flesh. A second later, my son's tiny body slumps, and Joe catches him and places him on the ground.

Overwhelmed with emotion, I jump to my feet in VR and run up to the virtual window. Using my command of the VR design, I turn my reflection in the window into a shadow of Joe and proceed to punch it with all my strength. I'm not sure who I'm angrier at: myself for not preventing this disaster, or my cousin for being the tool my enemies used. My knuckles meet the bulletproof glass again and again, and I welcome the virtual pain.

Mitya puts his hand on my shoulder. "At least he left Alan behind when he was shooting the other guards."

I can't fall apart now, for Alan and Ada's sake. I launch the BraveChill app, which subdues my angst enough to halt my tantrum.

"You need to keep your cool," Mitya messages me privately. "We need your leadership to get through this."

He walks back to the table and swipes his hand along the glass. The surface turns into another screen that shows Joe carrying Alan into the car.

"I can't believe this." Muhomor spits on the table, aiming for the image of Joe. "We never should've put that psycho in charge of security."

"Where are they?" I demand of no one in particular. "We ought to be able to follow the car or limo or whatever Joe drove."

"I have no idea where they are," Mitya says, his eyes downcast. "Joe must've switched cars multiple times, and he must've started with that manual-drive clunker of his that has no tracking technology of any kind."

"Did you check the satellites?" Muhomor asks. "Traffic cameras? Dashboard cams?"

"You're welcome to check my work," Mitya replies testily. "Obviously I wouldn't tell Mike that I have no idea where they are before I had exhausted all options."

Muhomor doesn't answer with anything snide, which tells me he's doing research of his own. Figuring three enhanced brains are better than two, I try my best to follow Joe's trail but quickly discover that Mitya is right. Five minutes or so after the kidnapping, the trail goes completely cold—and it's been hours now, so he could be anywhere within an enormous radius. After futile attempts to reach Alan and Ada via every app we have, I admit defeat and crank up the BraveChill app to its maximum setting to keep from falling apart.

"This doesn't make any sense," I say both in VR and out loud as BraveChill begins to clear my judgment. "Joe is among the richest people in the world. No one could pay him enough to be willing to do this."

Mitya and Muhomor look at me worriedly. The same thought must've crossed both of their enhanced minds.

"Maybe someone had something on him worthy of blackmail?" Muhomor suggests. "Or another kind of leverage?"

Mitya nods. "We all have seen him kill people. Maybe someone has a murder on tape?"

The image of Joe killing my biological father strobes in the forefront of my memory, and I again feel like I'm about to lose my shit—BraveChill notwithstanding.

"Joe would sooner go to jail than do this," I say when I regain my speech. "Besides, Kadvosky and the rest of our lawyers would state the video is fake and make short work of it. Joe knows that."

"Maybe they have someone he cares about?" Muhomor sounds even less certain than before. "'Bring us Alan and Ada or else we kill X.'"

"Who would be X?" I try to get my breathing to even out. "If he cares about anyone, it would be us, his family. The people Joe took are the very people someone would need to kidnap to get him to cooperate—assuming Joe didn't preemptively kill the conspirators."

"Maybe someone poisoned Alan and Ada and told Joe he needs to bring them to some location for a cure." Muhomor bites the nail on his right index finger. "Or maybe they implanted a bomb into Joe's neck and told him it would go off unless he does as he's told."

"Dude." Mitya gives the hacker a baleful stare. "Do you think Mike wants to hear dumb theories like that?"

"It's okay," I manage to say. "No idea is a bad idea. The poison theory doesn't work, though. Joe would get us involved; he wouldn't kill his people. Plus, Gogi's actions don't fit."

"Mike's right," Mitya says. "Same logic, or lack of it, can be applied to Gogi." He puts a recording of Gogi's attack on the screens. "He's not as well off as Joe, but Gogi still has enough shares in Human++ to be too rich to be bought. He loves you like a brother."

"He's loyal to Joe, though," Muhomor says. "So maybe it's just one puzzle instead of two?"

"He's not that loyal to Joe," I reply confidently, though internally I'm less convinced than I sound. Would Gogi hurt me for Joe? I've never had to ponder such a question before, and now that I do, I'm not sure what the answer is.

"What Gogi did makes no sense at all." Mitya stares at the part of the recording where Gogi's hands are around my throat. "If I can think of some crazy reason for Joe to take Alan and Ada someplace, I simply can't imagine why Gogi would want to kill you—"

An earlier idea re-forms in my mind, and everything falls into place.

"Guys," I say triumphantly. "I think I know what's going on."

"You do?" my friends ask in unison.

"Yes." Either this epiphany or the BraveChill app finally allow my heart to stop racing like a kid with ADHD. "Gogi wouldn't betray his friends. Joe is even less likely to betray his family. The logical conclusion is that they did not betray us."

"So you think Joe took Ada and Alan for a fun ride?" Muhomor asks derisively. "And Gogi nearly killed us for kicks?"

"No. But they didn't *willingly* betray us," I say. "Someone hacked their Brainocytes. Someone is controlling Gogi and Joe like puppets."

676

TWENTY-TWO

M<small>ITYA</small> AND M<small>UHOMOR</small> STARE AT ME, THEIR AVATAR JAWS threatening to perform an unrealistic VR animation of falling to the floor.

"No," Muhomor says. "AROS security can't just be hacked willy-nilly like that."

"No, Mike's right." Mitya looks somber. "That theory fits all the facts. I even considered it briefly, but dismissed it when we learned that all the people attacking us had the official Human++ Brain-ocytes—which you, Muhomor, claimed to be unhackable."

"I said Tema was unhackable." Muhomor makes his usual shades disappear, revealing uncharacteristically worried eyes. "I only ever said that it was improbable that someone besides me could find a flaw in AROS security. And any flaws I discovered, I patched up."

We look at each other. That's not what he said—in fact, his certainty was why I didn't consider this possibility from the very beginning—but now is not the time to debate semantics.

"The improbable happened," I state flatly. Since I'm in control of my emotions for the time being, I try to capitalize on it and move our investigation as far along as possible. "Someone took away your self-proclaimed best hacker title, Muhomor. You were beaten at your own game. Live with it. This isn't about your ego anymore. We have to figure out who did this and how."

"Well." Mitya gets up and begins pacing around the table. "We know how it could've been done with someone without Brainocytes already in place. Does that help?"

The topic is uncomfortable for us all. Though Brainocytes have generally been a force for the betterment of the world, like any technology, they're not without their demons. Monstrous people have created their own perverted versions of Brainocytes to turn people into zombie-like slaves. Whenever we hear about such efforts, we do our best to destroy the organizations responsible. Thus far, this has happened six times in Africa, twice in Eastern Europe, and once in the Middle East. We abhor this situation and don't shy away from the methods necessary to combat it, from legal action to Joe's ruthlessness and Muhomor's hacking.

The organizations caught doing this don't even exist as mentions on old internet pages anymore. Still, we know that it's simply impossible to locate and deal with every instance of this atrocity. Our best defense is to spread legitimate Brainocytes throughout the human population. Until now, having Human++ Brainocytes has been the best protection against getting your brain hacked.

Muhomor must be thinking along the same lines. "Gogi and Joe have Brainocytes already," he says. "That makes this a completely different problem for the hacker."

I drum my fingers on the table and try to calm my thoughts again. "If you were the hacker behind this, how would you go about it?"

Muhomor's forehead creases, and his shades return to his nose. "Assuming this is really what you say it is, then there must be a vulnerability in one of AROS's core apps."

Yet again BraveChill fails, and a knot forms in my stomach. Muhomor is right. For reasons of security, certain modes of Brainocyte operation, particularly the sending of data to neurons outside the visual and auditory regions of the brain, are locked to all apps except those built by us. Users have the option of overriding this for themselves, but everyone knows it's not safe to do so—especially people who work for Human++ like Joe and Gogi.

I take in a deep breath. "As unlikely as it sounds, let's assume it is a core app. For example, say it's the video player. What would you do then?"

"That's very farfetched," Muhomor says. "The video player is probably the most secure app."

"Humor us." Mitya stops pacing and slumps back into a chair. "Say the video player app had an exploit."

"Well, I'd have to write a virus to take advantage of whatever the imaginary weakness is," Muhomor says. "Then spread it. Somehow."

"Wouldn't you need to get a special video on another company's server?" I ask. "I imagine Netflix and their ilk wouldn't want someone using them to spread a virus like this. Bad PR."

"I'd hack into Netflix," Muhomor says dismissively. "Or I'd use social engineering to work with employees already at the company." He looks so excited at this roleplaying that I feel like reaching over and giving him a smack. "Alternatively, I'd put together a new video streaming service that I completely control and create a video that could potentially be used as a vector of attack—"

"There's a problem with all this." Mitya folds his arms across his chest. "This attack was targeted to Joe and Gogi. A virus that takes advantage of something like video streaming would get inside the heads of everyone who watched the video."

"You're right. Targeting the virus would be extremely difficult." Muhomor rubs his thin chin thoughtfully. "It's not impossible, though. You could give every user a virus that would lie dormant, then activate special instructions only for people in proximity to some location or—"

"I really hope that's not what's happening," Mitya says. "That would mean every Human++ customer has a vulnerability in their heads... that most of the world carries this exploit ready for abuse."

"They seemed to be laser-precise with Gogi and Joe." I'm trying not to freak out with dread for the Brainocyte users of the world—a group that includes everyone I know, including myself. "If this is a proximity-based virus, why not turn all our guards against us? Or better yet, enslave us and make us commit suicide? Or enslave Alan and Ada and make them kidnap themselves?"

The reminder of Ada and Alan's status increases my already elevated heartbeat, both in VR and on the couch where the nurse is checking me for damage. Despite the luminous speed of this VR conversation, I still feel enormous guilt because I'm talking instead of acting. At the same time, I have no idea what action I can take until we figure out this mess.

"For that kind of targeting, you'd need someone's Brainocyte ID," Muhomor says. "But getting someone's ID is as hard a project as finding a loophole in one of the apps."

"But it's not impossible?" I ask.

Muhomor shrugs. "You know better than I. In the software universe, few things are impossible. There are just levels of difficulty."

The three of us share a look. We purposefully left out the details about how the ID system works when we open-sourced Brainocytes to the world. But we also know that relying on trade secrets isn't a very good strategy for keeping secrets, so it was just a matter of time before everyone found out everything there's to know about Brainocyte technology—yet another reason we've dumped billions into security research and development.

"Someone would've had to reverse-engineer the IDs somehow," Mitya says, proving he's thinking exactly what I'm thinking. "It could be done from either inert Brainocytes, or if you wanted faster results, from hardware that you harvested from a hopefully dead user's head. It would take many years, either way, even if you had as much money as we have."

The morbid mention of a dead someone's head sparks a hint

of an idea, but when I try to verbalize it, it escapes my consciousness. This happens with enhanced thinking sometimes; you get that feeling of having something on the tip of your tongue, but it takes minutes or sometimes hours before it comes to the forefront of your mind in a eureka moment. For now, I say, "Let's skip the how of it for the moment and assume someone knows how Brainocyte IDs work. What would be next?"

"They might be able to work out a way to get someone's Brainocytes to reveal a specific user ID," Muhomor says. "It would require the Brainocytes to interface with some app directly—"

"Like a brain scan at the hospital?" I smack myself on the virtual forehead. "Gogi and Joe both got hit on the head and were scanned. Could someone have used that as a chance to learn their Brainocyte IDs?"

Muhomor looks a bit like my mom does when she's multitasking using AROS. He must be doing some heavy research.

Mitya, on the other hand, gets excited. "Lennox Dixon had his head scanned because of his tumor." The speed of his Zik messages is on the verge of being too fast to follow. "Ruzatov had a head trauma. The drunks in Russia had been to a hospital right before they attacked our robots."

"I just checked, and everyone involved shares this pattern," Muhomor says. "Every bomber, every drunk, the drivers of the two cars that tried to kill you in Brooklyn—everyone was in a hospital or some other facility where they had their brains scanned. This is compelling evidence that Brainocyte IDs are a part of this mess, and that in turn supports the hacking theory."

He looks at me with the disgust of a person learning he just got syphilis from a toilet seat. I can relate. Besides BraveChill, the only thing that stops me from panicking is the knowledge that I haven't had my brain scanned, so my ID remains unknown to our adversaries. The only way I could be turned into a mindless slave is if the entire world—or a subset such as, say, all of New York—were turned into puppets, a disquieting idea on its own. Then again, it would take insane computational resources and staff to control more than a handful of people.

Mitya remains annoyingly calm, probably because his brain is cloud based and has no Brainocytes to hack.

"This would explain why previously nonviolent men would be willing to blow themselves up," I say. "Or why Gogi didn't care about his wounds when he fought me, and why the drunks in Russia didn't care about damaging themselves with the robots."

"It all adds up, unfortunately," Muhomor says, frowning. "Now we need to figure out who's behind it. And make them regret it."

"Yeah," Mitya says sarcastically. "That's so simple. Why didn't we think of that? We just need to figure out who's doing this. Thanks."

"No need to be snide," Muhomor says. "Let's just continue to break this down logically. The important question is who benefits from this."

"Someone who hates our guts?" Mitya looks at us. "Someone who thinks we're the antichrist?" He pauses dramatically, and when he sees recognition on both our faces, he says, "Did anyone else find it suspicious that Joe found our Real Humans Only prisoner not guilty so easily?"

"And with all her fingers attached?" Muhomor says.

"Could it be because he was already under her control?" Mitya continues.

Was this the theory that's been gnawing at the edges of my mind? When it came to Tatum, Joe's behavior had been odd, to say the least.

"It could be that he cleared her because he's just that good at reading people." I realize I might be playing devil's advocate. "Also, he might've had another agenda. You might think me crazy, but I thought maybe there was an unholy attraction between those two."

"You *are* crazy," Mitya says. "Your cousin is indeed good at reading people—but your second theory, the one that assumes he has human feelings, is preposterous."

682

In the real world, I hear the nurse tell me my blood pressure is high. I'm not surprised in the slightest.

"If it's the RHO behind this hack, things could turn ugly," Muhomor says. "If they want to make Brainocytes look bad, which we know they do, they can use this virus to make the entire world do something horrible. They can prove us to be the devil by bringing about an apocalypse of their own design—a sort of self-fulfilling prophecy."

"I don't think it would be so easy to do something like that," Mitya says. "How would they control so many people?"

"A specialized AI?" Muhomor suggests. "But I see your point. Maybe they can't cause chaos on a global scale, but they can certainly keep people from ever trusting Brainocytes again."

Goosebumps spread over my body as I picture the RHO targeting people in key government positions or with celebrity status.

"Tatum must be a great actress," Mitya says. "Alan spoke to her last night, and she didn't act like someone plotting to kidnap the boy."

A flicker of hope speeds up my pulse. "Let me see some of that footage. Maybe she gives something away?"

"Alan was recording everything himself," Mitya says. "You might prefer to experience the whole thing as he did—that way, you can examine his reactions to her at the same time as yours."

Before I experienced Ada's hive-mind-generating, trippy Join app, the only way to see what someone else saw, heard, and (to a limited degree) felt was to play back a recording made with the Share 2.0 app. Originally, these recordings allowed their creators to relive experiences they particularly enjoyed. Human memory would fill in the missing details and emotions, helping users feel as if they were truly reliving the past. With some work, we've retrofitted Share 2.0 recordings to play back as VR experiences, with the emotions recorded in the Share 2.0 app simulated in the watcher's brain. Playing back someone else's recording isn't as cool as most VR movies these days, but it can come in handy in many circumstances. It's been a boon for the porn industry, for sure. Aside from that, Ada and I, as well as many other couples who use Share 2.0, have fewer fights of the "he said, she said" variety because we can show each other a recording of what happened from the other's point of view. We've learned how unreliable our regular memories are. I shudder to think about all the people in jail based on old-school eyewitness testimony.

"As per Alan's explicit request, I've never played back his Share sessions before," I say as I locate the recording in question. "He considers that an ultimate invasion of privacy."

I was worried that Alan might've encrypted them with Tema to make sure Ada and I kept our promises, but I'm glad to find he didn't take that precaution.

"Your intentions are pure," Muhomor says. "Besides, not encrypting a file is basically an invitation for people to watch it."

"You watched it already?" I narrow my eyes at both my friends.

"I never promised Alan anything," Mitya replies defensively.

"And as I already said"—Muhomor runs a hand through his anime hair—"not encrypting a file is as good as an invitation to watch it."

"So what did you think?" I ask.

"Why don't you watch it and form your own opinion?" Mitya says. "Don't want to bias you."

"I agree with the ghost," Muhomor says. "Watch it and then we'll talk."

Figuring it'll be faster to just do as they say, I load the file and prepare to watch my son's memory through his own eyes.

TWENTY-THREE

My steps are short due to Alan's tiny legs, and everything in the room seems taller and bigger than I'm used to. It's creepy. The last time I experienced this point of view was when I watched the recent VR remake of *Child's Play*, particularly the scene where the killer doll, Chucky, knifed the pretty teenager (who reminds me a little of the petite Tatum).

The RHO leader gives us the cooing smile people typically reserve for speaking with children. Her face completely transforms when she glances back at Dominic, who's walking behind us. With his camera for eyes, exoskeleton, and bionic arm, he must be her technophobic nightmare come to life.

Alan's annoyance and resentment toward Tatum are so strong the VR interface makes them feel like my own.

"Hello," Tatum says in a tone Alan finds patronizing. "Who might you be?"

"Hi, Tatum," we say. We feel further irritation when Alan realizes she's hearing his childish voice and seeing no AR avatar. "My name is Alan."

Only seconds into the experience, I can already see why Alan wouldn't want me and Ada to watch these recordings of his. He doesn't want us to feel what I now feel—shame at turning my son into an adult trapped in a child's body. Because that's precisely what he feels like when Tatum looks at him.

"Hi, Alan." Tatum bends down to shake our extended hand, and her eyes go from warm to confused. "How do you know my name?"

"I make a point to know people who want to destroy everything my parents and I stand for," we say. "You are Tatum Crawford, born in Kansas to Jenny and Mark Crawford." We proceed to read the first paragraphs of her Wikipedia page until she pulls her hand away and the confusion in her eyes turns to fear.

"Just because I criticize what your parents do doesn't mean I'm your enemy." Her usually pretty smile is nervous at best.

I find it interesting how little her feminine charm affects Alan's emotions. On some level, I'm relieved his maturity didn't extend into sexual interests.

"You want me to devolve to an intellectual invalid who runs around like a monkey and plays with toys," we say derisively. "If you had your way, Dominic there would be blind, unable to hear or move, completely locked inside his body."

She takes a step back. We take sadistic pleasure at the roller coaster of emotions on her face as she realizes she's not speaking with a typical four-year-old.

"Why are you here?" she asks after she recovers some composure. "What do you want?"

"I want to understand," we say. We walk over to the nearby redwood chair. "I've never had a chance to speak with someone as misguided as you."

"I don't think you'll understand," she says sadly. "Your parents brainwashed you too well."

"Try me," we say. "You might find I'm a pretty rational person."

"If you were truly rational," she says, her patronizing baby talk completely gone, "you'd see the self-evident dangers of technology, especially AI. You'd see that our dependence on technology threatens our autonomy. You'd understand that virtual reality prevents humans from experiencing the world directly and acting from free will. Your parents' creation will continue the horrific trend the internet started. It will alienate humans from nature, bringing about harmful psychological eff—"

"Your worries have some seed of truth, but the dangers can be mitigated." We purposely interrupt her in a way people without Brainocyte enhancements consider rude. "This technology will expedite progress beyond anything we've seen. It will broaden people's world view and empower those who have never had power before. Bashing technology the way you do is a trend that goes back millennia. Plato was against the technology of writing. The most classic case is that of the Luddites during the Industrial Revolution. Those self-employed weavers destroyed weaving machinery. Since then, it's been a never-ending quest among the likes of you."

"Except now it's every job that's in danger of going the route of weaving." Her hands are on her hips. "AI and Brainocytes will see to that."

"Not every job should continue to exist." We climb up on the chair and sit. "Politics is a space where AIs can do a much better job than many of the current psychopaths in charge. This very tablet was created by people who work in conditions that lead to suicide, and if AIs take over that sort of production, that segment of humanity will be better off. In fact, the more we look back in history, the more examples we see of jobs that should've gone away—and did. Did you know that kids a couple of years older than myself were once trained to be chimney sweeps' apprentices? To fit into chimneys, they were purposefully underfed. Over time, they developed lung problems that included cancer, though often they simply died of smoke inhalation. I bet you bought into the romanticized image of chimney sweeps from fairy tales and long for the good old days before mechanical means of sweeping chimneys existed."

"You can cherry-pick examples, but that doesn't address my main thesis," she says. "All jobs will go away."

"No," we say calmly. "Look at the rise of VR bloggers who make money from advertisers fighting to put ads before the best content. Look at the VR video game industry that became a multi-billion-dollar business nearly overnight. New technology always creates new jobs. Once the dust settles on this technological revolution, professions you couldn't even dream of will take place of the old drudgery. Those who don't embrace technology will end up jobless, true. But we'll take care of them via the universal basic adjustment benefit that our company is trying to put into place."

"So you want people like me to live on handouts?" Her eyes glint. "To live without any purpose in our lives?"

"Unenhanced people can and will find purpose in artisanal work." We jump out of the chair—the energy of a four-year-old human male makes it very hard to sit still for such a long subjective slice of time. "Arts, science, philosophy—once everyone's basic sustenance needs are met, purpose in life will reach a new Golden Age, both for people with Brainocytes and, to a smaller degree, for people like you."

Tatum's mouth tightens. "You see? I told you I couldn't reason with a zealot."

"Do people without Brainocytes completely lack the sense of irony? Calling me a zealot is like me calling you 'kid.'" We turn to leave the room.

"We are the only people left who have true senses," she counters sharply. "You're just crunching data now."

"Crunching data is what all brains do." We are level with Dominic now and wave the big man to join us in leaving the room. "Humans expanded their senses with technology as soon as they began inventing lenses, hearing aids, and the like. We're just integrating those technologies more seamlessly with everyday experience."

"Your parents and their people claim that they will not create AIs that can think and act as people." Her voice rises. "From where I'm standing, they already have."

If she thinks she can insult Alan by calling him an AI, she

doesn't know my son. He loves Einstein and has considered him a friend since early childhood.

"I'm more human than you'll ever imagine." We don't say the words louder because we know it's pointless to expect her to understand them. "I'm better than you at everything you consider a purely human pursuit, from empathy to my ability to love."

As though to highlight our words, we pat our pocket and over-flow with deep love for Mr. Spock, one of our earliest childhood friends. We love him despite our different intellectual levels and superficial differences such as belonging to different species.

My attention is no longer on Alan's recording because my son inadvertently gave me a new hope.

I exit the Share 2.0 experience shaking with excitement. "How could I forget about Mr. Spock? I told him to watch out for Alan."

Before Mitya or Muhomor can respond, I'm already contacting Mr. Spock. "Hey, bud, where are you?"

"Don't know," comes the rat's anxiety-imbued reply. "Alan doesn't wake up."

"So Alan is with you?" I'm trying not to make Mr. Spock panic with either worry or the excitement that overwhelms me.

"Yes," the rat replies. "But I can't talk to him."

"Don't worry. He was very tired, so he's just going to sleep for a while," I lie. "This is very important: do you know where you are?"

"I am hiding," he replies. The memories are clearly making him uncomfortable, because he sends me enough fear to shake an elephant. "Something is wrong."

"You did an excellent job hiding." I make my Zik message as reassuring as I can. "But now I need you to do something a little scary. Do you think you can be brave to help Alan?"

"Yes," he says with renewed confidence.

"I'm going to enable your Share app and have you peek out of Alan's clothes," I say. "Can you do that very carefully?"

"Okay," he replies, his confidence noticeably weaker.

"I know you can do it," I say firmly. "You're the alpha."

Mr. Spock is the alpha rat in our mischief—the proper term for a pack of rats. Unlike his wild cousins, he's an enlightened ruler who doesn't try to keep the other males away from food (even peanuts) or females (even Uhura). Still, the reminder of his high social status seems to work, because his affirmative reply is full of pride and determination.

I enable the rat version of the Share app. The first thing I do is verify something I already inferred but didn't want to worry Mr. Spock by asking: Alan's heartbeat is steady through his shirt, and the boy is breathing evenly.

Relieved at the proof my son is alive, I examine Mr. Spock's surroundings as much as I can. With the rat's inferior vision, it's hard to tell for sure, but it seems like we're in a well-lit room—or so I presume, based on the vague shapes I can discern through the fabric of Alan's pocket. Being a lab rat and thus albino, Mr. Spock's sense of smell is slightly worse than that of a regular rat, but that's still light years above that of an unenhanced human. Since the Share app translates rat experience into human perception, the room smells stagnant, reminiscent of the recycled air in our bunker. It also tells Mr. Spock (and thus me) that there are a couple of male humans in the room.

"Be very careful when you peek," I say. "It's okay if we can't see what's going on."

Mr. Spock slides his nose about a millimeter out of Alan's shirt. I make a snapshot of the environment before I have him hide again.

Ada is lying on a cot next to Alan, and there are indeed two armed men in the room, though unfortunately, both are wearing Richard Nixon masks over their faces.

"Stay still," I tell Mr. Spock. "We're lucky they didn't see you."

"Okay." He proceeds to contemplate whether he wants the cashew, the walnut, or the raisin that remain in Alan's pocket.

Using Muhomor's app with Mr. Spock as a conduit, I check out the Wi-Fi networks in the place. The single network smells like rotten eggs, so I give up trying to hack it for now, though I plan to unleash Muhomor himself on it shortly. I then try locating Mr.

Spock's coordinates using GPS, but wherever he is, there's either no GPS signal or they're using a jammer. At least Mr. Spock has access to Global Terahertz wireless internet, or we wouldn't even be able to communicate. The Terahertz system allows me to approximate the location of Mr. Spock's connection.

"Catskills," I announce triumphantly.

The walnut gets stuck in Mr. Spock's throat, and he sniffs the air in full panic mode. "I know they do," he says when he doesn't find a cat in the pocket with him or smell one in the room. "Why remind me?"

"I'm sorry, bud," I say. "Not 'cats kill.' The Catskills is the name of a mountain range in New York state."

He relaxes. "Bad name."

"I know. I'll petition to change it to Ratsrule, but don't hold your breath."

"I don't like to hold my breath," he says sagely. "It's hard."

"Then don't hold your breath," I say as seriously as I can. "I want you to keep your nose ready so you can let me know if those men leave the room."

"Okay," he says with the kind of pride in his olfactory senses I'd expect from a good hunting dog. "I'm on it."

Almost giddy with progress, I switch attention to the VR room and find Mitya and Muhomor watching me intently.

"So it's hard to say if she's guilty or not," I say. "But watching that video gave us a big break." I proceed to tell them about Mr. Spock.

"I'll try to get onto that Wi-Fi." Muhomor changes his sunglasses into the pince-nez he likes to wear when he hacks. "But if it uses—"

"Just do it," Mitya says. "Tell us when and if it's done."

"What's with the hostility?" Muhomor uses his middle finger to pretend to push the pince-nez farther up his nose, but we all know he's flipping Mitya off.

"Sorry," Mitya says in a tone that suggests nothing of the kind. "I just keep feeling like we're playing catch-up with our adversaries. They seem to be a couple of moves ahead of us at all turns. Their plan A was to get Gogi to kill Mike for them, but they also had a plan B—take Ada and Alan hostage in case plan A fails."

"And force Mike to leave the safety of the bunker to run after his family," Muhomor says, his tone more serious.

"Which I'm about to do," I say, nodding. "But I don't really have a choice."

"Which is why I'm irritated." Mitya looks at Muhomor apologetically. "It's like a bad game of Go."

"Well," I say. "We do have Tatum. Perhaps we can question her on the way to the Catskills and get ahead in the game."

"Assuming she knows anything," Muhomor says.

"And assuming our adversaries didn't plan for whatever Tatum revealed," I add.

"And assuming she herself is not the adversary who manipulated us to get her out of the bunker according to some plan," Mitya says.

"I can leave her here with Muhomor to question her," I say. "Then we'd still have some leverage."

"I'm not going?" Muhomor asks.

"I don't think you should," I say. "You're not a fighter, and we can use your help here on the back end."

"Okay," he says. "Anyway, someone with a brain needs to look after your mother and uncle."

I nod. "And this way, Tatum doesn't leave the bunker."

"Agreed," he says. "Let me prepare to question her while you get ready for departure."

I nod and switch to the real world, where the nurse is beginning to agree that I'm going to be fine. To make sure the medical staff doesn't revolt, I try to exude health and vitality as I get up from the couch.

Step one in my prep: check on Dominic's condition.

"I'm fine," he says, though the bandage around his eye looks serious to me. "What's the update?"

I tell him what's going on until Dr. Jarvis comes over and gives me a stern look. "He should be resting."

"I'm coming with Mike," Dominic says to the doctor.

"Then you're doing so against my recommendation," Jarvis says.

"I'm going," Dominic says with the kind of certainty only people with that much brute power can have. "I'll organize the other guards."

He gets to his feet, his legs running without a hitch thanks to his exoskeleton. As he rushes to rally his troops, I tell the doctor to keep Gogi unconscious until we return.

Then I head to Mom's room, mentally debating what, if anything, to tell her before I leave.

Mitya's avatar shows up in the air in front of her door. "I suggest you speak to her afterward."

"But she'll wake up and not know where I am." He has a good point, though.

"When she wakes up, Muhomor will tell her the truth—that you went to get Ada."

"But he'll avoid the full truth," I say sternly in VR. I make sure Muhomor nods back.

A part of me fears that later, I might not get a chance to tell Mom anything at all. If I get myself killed, she might resent that last night's mundane conversation about the quality of the bunker food was our last one. I picture myself as a digital ghost like Mitya, resurrecting in a few years to a torrent of complaints from Mom.

To stop these morbid thoughts, I go into the kitchen to put a banana-avocado smoothie into my system.

"You'll elaborate on Muhomor's story when you come back," Mitya says when he sees me come out and glance at Mom's door one more time. What he leaves unsaid is: "If you come back."

"I'll come back," I mutter, more to myself than to Mitya. "Even if that means I come back as a ghost like you."

TWENTY-FOUR

MITYA IS DRIVING THE CAR AGAIN BECAUSE EINSTEIN DOESN'T SPEED even when his creators beg (or forcefully insist) that he drive faster.

We're going to be in the Catskills soon, but I still have no clue exactly where Alan and Ada are or who's keeping them and why. Though the likely answer to this last question is: to lure me outside the bunker.

"It's all ready," Muhomor says in Zik. "I sent you a camera view."

"What's ready?" I ask.

He doesn't answer, probably to force me to look. I'm tired of staring out the window at the same never-ending fields, power lines, and distant factories, so I close my eyes and dedicate my attention to the new viewpoint.

The camera shows Tatum's bedroom in the bunker. Muhomor stands over the poor girl like a crazy stalker. He reaches out and touches her shoulder in a way that's creepy even for Muhomor.

"Hey, what are you doing?" I say, frowning. "I know your experience with the female of the species is limited, but I can assure you, they don't like what you're currently doing."

694

"You don't need girl experience," Mitya chimes in. "Just use the golden rule. Picture yourself waking up and seeing some really weird-looking dude touching you like that."

"It would depend on why the handsome stranger was there," Muhomor says, but he leans away from Tatum.

"Mike, when you tell Ada about this later, I did not approve Muhomor's plan," Mitya says.

"But he did help me with it." Muhomor seems to be on the verge of maniacal laughter. "Our ephemeral friend was actually instrumental to my plan."

"I really hope I get the chance to sell you out to Ada soon," I say. "I think I know what you did—but why don't you tell me anyway?"

"I just attached a transdermal Brainocyte patch to her shoulder," he says.

"One that runs the Polygraph app on the loop, as we earlier discussed," Mitya adds, confirming my suspicions.

"Not sure I want to tell Ada about this at all," I mutter. "This is pretty messed up, you guys."

"Her people have your wife and kid," Muhomor snaps.

I'm shocked at the intensity in his voice. I didn't think he cared this much, and it's a pleasant surprise to find out that he does—even if it's resulting in unethical behavior.

"Miss Crawford," Muhomor whispers loudly. "Please wake up."

"There are earplugs in her ears," Mitya says. "They look heavy duty, so I doubt she'll hear you even if you shout next to her face."

"But don't shout next to her face," I say, unsure if Muhomor needs the clarification or not.

"How last century." He deftly plucks an earplug from the woman's ear.

Her head lolls to the side, exposing a pillow-creased pink cheek.

Muhomor gets bolder and repeats, "Miss Crawford?"

She pulls a blanket over her head. He tugs the blanket away and then, for good measure, leans over her and shakes her shoulder.

Her long eyelashes flutter open, and she gapes at the thin weirdo above her for a fraction of a second.

Then, predictably, she screams.

"You're still our guest," he says calmly as she proceeds to jump up and cover her nightgown with the fleece blanket.

"He's not there to hurt you," Mitya's voice says from a wall speaker.

Her gaze darts around the room, likely in search of something she can use as a weapon—objects that Dominic thoughtfully removed last night.

"That's right." Muhomor tries to smile reassuringly. On his face, the expression looks more like a scowl. "We have a bit of an emergency, and I wanted to ask you some questions."

Tatum now looks more confused than frightened.

"Please, Tatum," Mitya's voice says. "People's lives are at stake."

"Can you give me a moment to dress?" She looks around, trying to find the source of Mitya's voice. "Whoever you are."

"Sure," he says. "My colleague was just leaving."

Muhomor stands there as though he doesn't know that he's the colleague in question. His eyes narrow on Tatum as he launches a private Zik chat with us. "I don't want her to have too much time to realize she has AROS now."

"I think it's safe to let her put some clothes on," Mitya replies, imbuing his Zik message with so much snark that I fully expect Muhomor to revolt. "As the only incorporeal member among us, I'll keep an eye on her, though."

"Digital perv," Muhomor mumbles vindictively as he stalks out of the room.

"All right, Tatum, just come out when you're ready. I'll give you some privacy," Mitya says.

The camera goes blank—Mitya is being a gentleman—so I can only assume she gets dressed.

In a couple of minutes, Muhomor gives me a new camera view in the kitchen.

"Come eat some breakfast," he says with surprising warmth when Tatum finally comes out. "I just need a couple of questions answered."

Tatum warily eyes Muhomor's pajama-clad body, but hunger must win out because she says, "Fine. Let's go."

"Did you write an article for the *Green Voice* at some point?" he asks casually as he opens the fridge and grabs himself a Twinkie. Privately to Mitya and me, he adds, "I know she did. This is a baseline question."

He gallantly holds the fridge door open and gestures for her to get what she wants.

"I did," she says after fishing out a pack of cheese. "It's probably still on their website, if you want to read it."

"That was true, both according to facts and according to the app," Mitya says to me privately. "Now I wonder how he's going to get her to lie without telling her that he wants her to tell a falsehood."

"I'd love to read it," Muhomor says, sounding impressively genuine. "I have an oddball question for you: do you think my little nephew is cute?"

Using the screen attached to the front of the smart fridge, he pulls up a picture of the most hideous baby I've ever seen in my life.

She takes in the image, and I can tell she nearly loses her appetite. "He's very cute," she says after she recovers her composure. "How old is he?"

"That was a lie, according to the app, and it's safe to say we now have a baseline," Mitya says. "I don't even want to know where Muhomor got that picture."

"I had to use Photoshop to create that monstrosity," Muhomor tells us. To Tatum, he says, "Little Dimochka just turned two."

"Hey!" Mitya protests. The name Muhomor used is the diminutive of his own. "You should have named him Freddy or Jason."

"Oh, the terrible twos," Tatum commiserates. Her shoulders

relax as soon as Muhomor takes down the picture. "Your brother or sister is in for some tough times."

"Especially if this imaginary parent has eyes," Mitya mutters.

"I really hope you can help us, Tatum." Muhomor bites into his snack.

"You said so before." She spreads mayo onto a slice of rye bread and slaps cheese on top. "What happened?"

"You remember Alan? The child you spoke to last night?"

"Yes." She takes a careful bite of her sandwich. "Charming little guy."

"She's lying," Mitya comments. "About the charming part."

"Alan was kidnapped today," Muhomor says. "Do you know anything about it?"

"Kidnapped?" Her eyes look as if they might pop out of their sockets. "That's terrible. Of course I had nothing to do with it. I told Mike yesterday, my people are peaceful and would never hurt anyone—let alone kidnap a little boy."

"Everything she said was true," Mitya comments with clear disappointment. "Not good."

Muhomor proceeds as though Mitya didn't just shatter all our hopes. "Do you think anyone in your group is more radical than you? Someone tired of everyone else's nonviolence?"

"I can't think of anyone," she says without hesitation. "If I knew someone like that, I'd change their mind."

"Even this is all true," Mitya laments. "Or at least, this is what she really believes. We know some of her fellow RHO idiots are violent, like that asshole who poked holes in the tires of those Uber cars. But she truly doesn't see them as violent."

"There's something else," Muhomor says to Tatum, but it's obvious he's losing hope now. "Is anyone in your group knowledgeable when it comes to Brainocytes? Does anyone know how they work or how to hack them or to cause Brainocytes to have unintended consequences?"

She stops chewing, her expression as disgusted as if she'd just bitten into something spoiled. "We all stay as far away from those abominable devices as we can. Anyone who fetishizes Braincocytes would be kicked out of RHO."

"Again, true," Mitya says. "Let's go discuss this in the VR room. Looks like she was a complete dead end."

"I leave it to you to explain to her that you put the 'abominable devices' into her head," I tell Muhomor vindictively. "Just be careful she doesn't finally find that violent bone in her body and choke you to death."

"Or break one of your bones," Mitya adds helpfully.

"Make sure you also teach her how to use Braincocytes and disable the Polygraph app," I say. "Good luck."

My real-world eyes still closed, I pop into the VR room, which feels achingly empty without Ada.

"So," I say as Mitya and Muhomor's avatars turn my way. "Tatum is not guilty."

"It appears that way," Muhomor says reluctantly. "Or she should get an Oscar for that acting, and be entered into the hacker hall of fame for working around the Polygraph app."

"There's no way she worked around Polygraph." Mitya gives Muhomor a dark look. "You need to learn how to gracefully admit defeat."

"Fine." Muhomor grits his teeth. "She's innocent of the kidnapping, I admit that much."

"Then we must now explore our other big clue," I say. "Something we should've done in parallel with this Tatum fiasco."

Mitya's face lights up. "Russia."

"Exactly," I say. "We already thought Russia was the key to all this somehow. The original theory was that maybe RHO was working with some Luddite group in Russia, but if we know that RHO is innocent, a Russian anti-tech group sounds less plausible as well."

"Agreed," Mitya says. "But that means we're back at zero."

"Not exactly." I sink into the simulated high-end office chair and try to uncoil the tangle of emotions overwhelming me. "I had a glimmer of an idea back when you said something about skimming Brainocyte IDs from a dead user's head."

As I say the words, the theory that's been hovering in the corners of my extended mind clicks into place, and I blurt out, "We never found the head of Mrs. Sanchez."

Mitya's eyes gleam with understanding, but Muhomor looks confused, so I explain. "Mrs. Sanchez was the woman in that fateful Brainocyte study who was kidnapped together with Mom. She went into a diabetic coma and died before we met you in Russia, so maybe we never told you about her."

"Oh." Recognition dawns on Muhomor's face. "I think you did tell me, but I forgot her name and some of the details."

"The most important detail is that she was beheaded after her death," I say, hoping that when I say all this out loud, it will still make sense. "Her head could've given someone a chance to study Brainocytes long before we released any Brainocyte information to the world."

"And thus plenty of time to learn about Brainocyte IDs by now," Muhomor mutters. "Of course."

"You're following my reasoning now." My muscles involuntarily tense, because what I'm about to say next is, to a large extent, responsible for all the therapy I've needed over the years. "You were already with us at the end of that kidnapping disaster when we learned who was behind it all."

I surprise myself when I stop speaking, unable to continue.

"His mom was kidnapped by his biological father," Mitya tells Muhomor softly. "And I think Mike suspects that this new mess is because of those events—and now that I think about it, I tend to agree."

"But didn't Joe kill everyone who had a hand in that?" Muhomor asks, his eyebrows pulling together.

Images of Joe's knife slicing my father's throat intrude into my thoughts, and it takes slow breathing and an effort of will to say,

"There were thousands of people involved in that operation. Joe only went after the leaders, and even so, I doubt he got everyone."

My friends wait expectantly, though I suspect Mitya has figured out where I'm going with this.

"In any case," I say after a pause. "I think I know who's behind all this, and it's a person Joe definitely did not kill."

TWENTY-FIVE

MITYA AND MUHOMOR DON'T CHASTISE ME FOR TAKING MY TIME with the next part of my revelation.

Now that the theory is in my head, as so often happens in such situations, I don't understand why I didn't think of it sooner. Probably because I associate this person with painful memories. In fact, if I'm honest, I often try to forget he exists at all because of all the guilt I still carry over my father's death. Also, I suspected him of evildoing once before and was wrong, because Alex Voynskiy (now definitively deceased) turned out to be the culprit. I guess being wrong once before has biased me this time around.

"I think it's Kostya," I finally say. In the likely case that Muhomor doesn't recall who I'm talking about, I add, "My father's son with his wife in Russia. My half-brother."

I proceed to share all the research I did four and a half years ago on both Konstantin (Kostya for short) and my half-sister Masha. Kostya got rich from oil and became even richer when he invested in the right internet startup. As of four and a half years ago, he was still unmarried and a good brother to Masha, a poor soul who requires a lot of psychiatric care.

"You hacked the computers at the clinic where my half-sister was," I remind Muhomor. "You told me that Masha worries about poltergeists all the time."

"You can't expect me to remember such minutiae," Muhomor says. Noticing Mitya's evil eye, he quickly adds, "But now that you mention it, it all rings a bell."

Mitya gives me a sympathetic look. "Is she still alive? I recall you saying that Masha attempted suicide a number of times."

"I don't know," I admit. "I haven't looked up either of them in recent years."

"Well, let's look them up now." Muhomor rubs his hands together the way he does whenever hacking is about to commence.

"We can start with public info," Mitya says preemptively, though we both know it's futile.

"You two start with the boring public junk," Muhomor says. "I'll learn all the juicy details going on behind the scenes."

Mitya rolls his eyes but lets Muhomor do his thing. I search Yandex, the Russian search engine, for Kostya. Glad I can simultaneously read the thousands of hits I get back, I proceed to analyze them as fast as I can. It looks like my half-brother has become even richer in the last four and a half years and might now be on the Russian equivalent of the *Forbes* list of wealthiest people. Like me, a huge chunk of his new money was made thanks to Brainocytes. He owns companies that develop AROS apps of different varieties, plus a firm that turns out to be a third-party manufacturer that Human++ uses to produce Brainocyte patches for hard-to-reach corners of Russia. It's amazing how many such locations are in that country and how expensive regular deliveries there would otherwise be.

"Have you read this?" Mitya sends me a link to an article. "It's pretty incriminating."

I marvel at Mitya's newfound speed-reading skills; I haven't made it to this article in my results yet, and have to scroll forward a couple of thousand hits to see where he got it.

The first thing that catches my eye is an image of Kostya shaking the hand of the Russian president. This probably counts as a KGB connection. Kostya still has a scar on his cheek from when Masha scratched him after he broke the news of what happened to our father; clearly, she never heard the saying about killing the messenger.

I peer more closely at the photo. I never noticed until now, but Kostya and I both have sharp cheekbones and the same strong chin. I keep scanning until I see what Mitya meant: a big contract Kostya's company handled for the Russian military. Reading between the lines, I can see how brain manipulation might be something they would've experimented with.

"I have something much better," Muhomor says after he also reads Mitya's findings. "Check this out."

Muhomor got his hands on the records from the psychiatric facility where my half-sister spent so many years. As it turns out, she's no longer a resident there, and according to Dr. Ivanov, her shrink of many years, she was "miraculously cured using a therapy developed by her brother." Dr. Ivanov mentions that she received Brainocytes three years ago to aid her treatment, but it was an app that Kostya used a year ago that led to her amazing breakthrough.

"The patient was not herself," Dr. Ivanov's notes say. "It's as though she became a different person."

"My guess is that he used some mind control app on her." Muhomor drums his fingers against the glass of the conference room table. "If she starts to misbehave, he just takes over her mind and makes sure she behaves as a good sister should."

"Creepy, but sounds plausible," Mitya mutters. "And get this: As soon as she was 'cured,' he finally got married. The wifey is a supermodel."

"It doesn't fully make sense," I say. "If Masha is merely being remotely controlled, she isn't cured."

"My guess is that he wanted to get her out of that institution." Muhomor stops the drumming and wraps his arms around his chest, as if trying to give himself a hug. "It's where the Russian government would put political dissidents during the Soviet days, and it's just as drab now as it was back then. Even some of the staff are the same sons of bitches who worked there during the good old days."

"I just checked out the place, and he's right," Mitya says. "Think Russian version of the insane asylum from *Sucker Punch*."

"More like Arkham Asylum from *Batman*, if you ask me," Muhomor says. "Not a place you'd want your sister to stay long term, no matter how messed up she is."

"He must've hired a babysitter who takes over her body like a puppet when she misbehaves," Mitya says. "This way, she can live a semi-normal life outside the institution—and probably for a fraction of the cost."

"But it must be terrible for her," I say, frowning. "She has paranoid schizophrenia, and here Dr. Ivanov says she has delusions of control, which is a fear of being controlled by someone outside oneself. Now that's her actual reality. It's like sticking an arachnophobe into a cave filled with tarantulas."

"I'd choose her current fate to being in that facility," Muhomor says. "But that doesn't make your brother any less of an asshole if this whole thing is true."

"Have you been able to locate him?" I look at Muhomor as the likelier of the two to accomplish this feat.

"I thought you didn't want me to do any hacking," Muhomor says, the sarcasm clearly lifting his mood. "To know where he is, I would've had to get into his secretary's email—and that's illegal and unethical."

"You are the mightiest and most powerful hacker, and your services are greatly appreciated by all," Mitya says with his own flavor of sarcasm. "Now, can you spit it out? Mike doesn't know where to drive."

"I don't know where he should drive either," Muhomor admits. "But I just confirmed that Kostya is in the United States, which I figure is convincing evidence that he's our perp."

"Knowing the identity of our enemy is a great start, but we need more info," I say. "The Catskills span 5,892 square miles."

"I'll keep looking," Muhomor says.

"I will as well," Mitya echoes.

"Let me talk to our asset behind enemy lines," I say. "Speaking of whom—Muhomor, did you crack the Wi-Fi around Mr. Spock?"

"I would've said something if I had." Muhomor looks down. "Whoever your half-brother hired to handle security is very good."

"Fine." I make a mental connection to Mr. Spock. "Hey, bud."

"They took us somewhere," Mr. Spock reports. "I was scared."

"Where are you now?" I ask, fighting to keep the urgency out of my Zik messages. "Are the men still in the room?"

"I smell them. There are more now."

"When they took you someplace else, did you smell them also?"

"Even more men and some women," Mr. Spock says. I don't ask how he could smell the difference between males and females. "And bad smell, like at the veterinarian."

"A medical facility?" I'm unable to keep the worry out of my message. "What did they do to Alan and Ada?"

"Nothing with pain," Mr. Spock says. "Or else I would bite them."

"I know you would. They probably scanned their heads, which doesn't hurt."

What I leave unsaid is that scanning gives the bad guys Ada and Alan's Brainocyte IDs. If that's true, it means Kostya (or whoever) can now make my family do what he wants.

"Guys, I want you to make that loophole in Brainocyte security a priority," I say. "Not that it should've ever stopped being one."

"I never stopped working on it," Mitya says. "But it's a tricky problem."

"Same," Muhomor says. "Don't get your hopes up. I always look for loopholes in our security, and if this one was easy to find, I would've discovered it before."

"Just knowing it's there should make it a little easier," I say, more as a motivational tool than because I really believe it. "Just keep looking."

I open my eyes in the real world and look out the window at

the glorious mountain landscape in the distance. Alan and Ada could be anywhere here. We might be passing them right now. It's an infuriating idea.

After all this evidence, do I think that Kostya is behind the kidnapping and the bombings? Could vengeance for our father's death have motivated him to do something so heinous? If it is Kostya, given that we share DNA, does it mean I too could be pushed to do something like this?

No. I mentally shake my head. I share DNA with Joe too, and I know I wouldn't do some of the things Joe has done. Still, a small voice inside me tells me that if something happens to Ada or Alan today, my vengeance against the person responsible would be terrifying indeed.

We drive for another ten minutes in silence. I want to know where Ada and Alan are so badly that I feel like screaming or punching someone—and if killing someone got me the information, I'd stoop to it despite how Ada might feel about it. When I'm just about to burst from the nerves, I'm shocked into alertness by an email arriving into my inbox.

It's from Alan.

Marked as high priority, the email contains a video file attachment. The subject is the same as the single line of text inside: "Watch me."

My heart rate accelerates. I forward the email to Dominic and my friends and launch the video file.

The video pans across a room where Alan and Ada lie unconscious, surrounded by armed men in Richard Nixon masks. One guy isn't wearing a mask, and his face reminds me of a rabid bull terrier. The scary guy leans down slightly and takes an exaggerated sniff of the air near Ada, as though he's trying to determine what perfume she's wearing.

My hands ball into tight fists. If I were in that room now, I'd break that flat nose into tiny pieces that would hopefully pierce what passes for a brain in that thick, egg-shaped skull.

"I bet she's as sweet as she looks," says the abomination in a voice that sounds like gravestones rubbing together.

Trying to stay rational, I run facial recognition. He's a Russian citizen by the name of Boris Sobakin. The fact that he's Russian further supports our ongoing theory, but the things this man did in Chechnya turn my blood cold. I truly hope he's a zombie under Kostya's control; at least what Kostya is doing is motivated by vengeance, not twisted sadism.

"Now," says a voice from behind the camera.

The hair on the back of my neck stands up when all the men aim their guns at my wife and son in a rehearsed motion.

In unison, the men click safeties off their weapons, and their fingers tighten on the triggers.

TWENTY-SIX

"That's enough for the moment," the voice behind the camera says.

The men reengage their safeties one by one. The bull terrier Boris lowers his gun last. If I could, I'd punch his annoying face to wipe away that look of disappointment.

"Hold the camera," the speaker tells Boris, and there's a dizzying maneuver where the room spins, ending with the viewpoint centered on a new face.

Any doubts about my half-brother's culpability are now gone. Though he looks slightly older than some of the recent images, it is without a doubt Kostya, a fact facial recognition needlessly confirms.

"If you had just let the Georgian kill you, I would've let them go," Kostya says in a falsetto voice. He gestures at the camera, but I understand he means Ada and Alan. "I will give you one more chance. Come here, alone, and your family can go. You have twenty minutes. Here are the GPS coordinates—"

I frantically key them into my AROS GPS app. Einstein estimates it will take me a half hour to get there without traffic, meaning I'm already ten minutes late.

"Stop the car." I pop into VR conference room and look Mitya in the eye. "The guards need to get out."

"Is that wise?" Muhomor walks up to the big window. "If you go alone, as your half-brother insists, you're as good as dead."

"If I don't, Ada and Alan are going to get killed." I stride to the window to join Muhomor. "I don't think he was bluffing about that."

"Could the video be fake?" Muhomor drums his fingers against the glass.

It's a good question. Enhanced brains combined with some of the amazing hardware we've designed in recent years have led to a revolution in the cinematic effects industry. Particularly notorious are CGI VR porn and its cousin, political scandals based on fake video. It's common for Brainocyte users to enjoy ultrarealistic VR experiences, such as sleeping with their favorite celebrities (who, unfortunately, don't participate in the video at all and thus neither consent to the use of their likenesses nor make money). A good chunk of CGI VR porn originates in copyright-lax places like Russia, and I have no doubt that Kostya owns a bunch of the necessary studios. Every oligarch probably does.

Kostya could easily have faked that video and even created a virtual reality version of it to make me swear I was looking at the real Kostya, Ada, and Alan. The fact that Ada and Alan were sleeping would make that much easier to implement.

"There's no motive for someone to fake such a video," I say after a moment of consideration.

"Maybe to scare you or blame Kostya?" Muhomor asks without confidence.

"I'm already scared. We already knew Alan and Ada are missing. We already suspected my half-brother before we got this video."

"I concur," Mitya says. "I've researched tests for video authenticity, and I'm certain this was a real recording."

Muhomor and I exchange impressed glances. Mitya's speed of thought is beginning to reach biologically impossible levels.

"Relatedly," Mitya says, "I've analyzed the video for microexpressions—the sort of detail that a fake wouldn't bother recreating—and found no sign of deceit on Kostya's face. In fact, his face was extremely emotionless. Your half-brother is either as cold as a lizard or has had major Botox done."

"Doesn't that lack of expression point toward the video being fake?" Muhomor asks.

"Microexpressions are just one of the points I used to determine the video is real," Mitya says. "Plus, Boris has enough microexpressions for everyone in that video, and I can't think of a reason why someone would bother with such subtle detail for a minor character in a fake."

"Moving on, then. If there was no deceit on his face, do you think Kostya would really let them go?" Muhomor turns from the faux Manhattan skyline outside the window and stares intently at each of us in turn.

"Alan and Ada didn't have anything to do with our father's death," I say. "After Kostya deals with me and Joe, he might not want the death of a woman and her child on his conscience. The fact that he's kept them sedated is a good sign. It implies he doesn't want them to be too uncomfortable."

"Or he knows that Alan might go *The Ransom of Red Chief* on his ass," Muhomor mutters. "We all know that if Alan was aware, your half-brother would've killed him already—or if he's really above killing a child, he would now be begging you to take the little devil back."

"Ada's no picnic, either," Mitya says. "If I were your half-brother, I'd keep her as sedated as the kid."

"The biggest issue is that I suspect one or more of our guards might be taken over like Gogi." I massage my temples in a futile attempt to relieve some tension.

"Because your half-brother knows where you are?" Unsurprisingly, Mitya's quick to catch on.

"Exactly. How else did he know to give me so little time I'd have no choice but to drive where I'm told?"

"And if he does have eyes on you, you must get rid of the guards, or he might kill Ada or Alan to show he's serious," Muhomor says, catching on to my logic as well. "Not to mention that if you brought a compromised guard with you, he'd be a real hindrance."

The horrific theory rings in my virtual ears as the car screeches to a halt in the real world.

The guards respond with varying degrees of surprise. Dominic is the only one who knows what's going on, though he chooses to leave his Augmented Reality face unreadable.

"Get out," I bark. When they stare uncomprehendingly, I add steel to my voice. "Everyone out. That's an order."

"Are you sure?" Dominic asks privately. "We're in the middle of nowhere, and without a car, we have no way to follow you."

"Please get them out, Dominic." My private reply is beseeching. "I'm already late. There's no time for discussion."

Dominic grabs the shirt collars of the two men nearest him and drags them out of the car. Everyone else finally registers my demand and exits amid curses and grumbling.

"I'm driving," I tell my friends in VR. Matching actions to words, I launch the Batmobile app, take control, and press the virtual gas pedal all the way to the metaphorical floor. "At least the road is empty."

The car launches forward and hits sixty miles per hour in two seconds flat.

"I-84 isn't empty," Mitya says when he notices me double my initial breakneck speed. "You drive this fast, you'll die in a fiery explosion."

"It's the only way I can get there on time," I say. "If I crash, maybe Kostya will consider us even."

"Do you want me to take over?" he offers. "My response times are better."

"I want to do the driving myself. If you didn't get me there in time, I'd have to kill you."

"There are drones in the sky above," Muhomor remarks. "They

defied my intrusion attempts. Their security is as good as the Wi-Fi security around the rat, so they could be Kostya's."

"Keep trying to break the security," I say. "Or better yet, make progress on figuring out how Kostya takes people over. If we can release Joe, I'll have an ally."

"Obviously." In VR, Muhomor appears to be trying to hypnotize his feet through the glass table. "I already explained how difficult it is."

Mitya shakes his head with overblown disappointment. "Dude. The one time everyone is begging you to do your favorite activity, and you manage to let us down like this?"

"You're supposed to be pure intellect now," Muhomor snaps back. "Brain completely in the cloud. Thinking at unimaginable speeds. Why didn't you solve this problem?"

"In fact, I do have one idea." Mitya looks at me. "It's just not very practical."

In the real world, my tire rolls over a pebble. The car shudders like a choking victim. I guess at these race-car speeds, even a pebble can cause a skid. Ignoring everything but the car, I slow down and even out the virtual wheel. Zapo creaks, but I manage to keep it steady and on the road.

"Any idea is welcome," I say in VR when I have the vehicle back under control.

"If we know ahead of time who your half-brother will try to take over," Mitya says, avoiding my gaze, "we can put their Brainocytes into a modified debug mode I designed. This way, we can have AROS itself provide more data. Of course, that means the person in debug mode still ends up being taken over."

"Great," Muhomor says sarcastically. "Now we just need another member of Mike's family to hand over to Kostya with a request to take over their mind."

"Mike is heading into enemy territory. There's a chance that"—Mitya hesitates, clearly searching for a tactful way to proceed—"they'll take over his mind."

If this is Mitya's way of sparing my fears, I wonder what he had originally planned to say.

"You're right," Muhomor says with way too much excitement. "Kostya might want to make Mike kill himself. That's what I'd do. It's the perfect crime that would look like suicide to the cops."

I fight the urge to leap for Muhomor's throat in VR. Instead, I channel the surge of angst into my insane driving in the real world.

"Mike," Mitya says gently. "There's no harm in being prepared. I just sent you a link to the version of AROS I'm talking about. Install it, and hope we don't need it."

An email arrives. I silently proceed to install the new AROS interface. Once installation is complete, the only difference I notice is a slight slowdown of perception, which could be the result of anxiety. Still, I complain about it.

"It's the debug mode," Mitya affirms. "This AROS sends certain details back to our servers, and that kind of extra processing is going to slow you down. Is it too much to live with?"

"It's fine. It's no worse than a crappy internet connection." What I don't say is that a crappy internet connection is worse than a mind fogged up by pot or alcohol.

"Just focus all your attention on driving for now," Mitya suggests. "Once you reach your destination, focus on survival."

He makes a good point. I stop all nonessential tasks and, for good measure, I even stop the threads of myself that are trying to figure out how Kostya hacked Brainocytes. I'll rely on Mitya and Muhomor for this from now on.

"I'm feeling normal enough," I say hesitantly. "I think I can pop into this VR room without jeopardizing my life."

"Here's an aerial view of I-84," Mitya says.

My email dings, but there's something happening on the road up ahead.

"Crap. Why is there traffic here in the middle of nowhere?"

"There was an accident." Mitya highlights the part of the road where the density of cars lessens. "I'm guessing people are asking their car AIs to slow down so that they can gawk at the damage as they pass by."

"That makes sense." I wipe virtual sweat from my avatar's brow and wonder if we should at some point turn down the level of realism in this room. "I just had an idea about the drones. Can you guys take control of all the drones in the area, as well as any robots you can locate, and direct them to where I'm going? Kostya didn't say anything about bringing toys with me, just that I come alone."

"Unfortunately, 'all robots and drones in the area' amounts to a couple of drones and no robots," Mitya says. "I already checked. Sadly, this region is far behind the times."

I spare a moment to do some research, though the distraction almost causes me to veer off the road. When I'm safe again, I say in VR, "We do have that factory in Albany."

"That's an hour and a half away from your destination." Muhomor puts up a large map on the big screen with a map of New York state and the route from the factory highlighted. "By the time the robots arrive, you'll be dead."

"Even so, we'd make his half-brother pay for his death." Mitya curls and uncurls his hands.

"On that cheerful note, I think I'll avoid this room until I pass that traffic." I demonstratively walk toward the meeting room door before poofing out of VR, as proper etiquette demands.

"If you don't slow down, you won't come back, because you're going to turn yourself into a pancake," Mitya says to me privately.

"If I slow down, I won't make it to Kostya's hideout." I shift my focus to the road.

Since I-84 is still a few miles away and there's no traffic until then, I speed up as much as Zapo allows. Soon, the trees blur into a green haze. I push the car some more, until the seat starts to vibrate as though I'm riding an international ballistic missile, and then I push it harder.

I have to get there on time.

I simply have to.

TWENTY-SEVEN

It takes 1.7 seconds of breakneck speed before I approach the ramp to I-84 and slow down to merely two times the speed limit. Knowing that each car I pass could easily be my last makes my heart rate as fast as the insane rotation of my tires.

"Dude," Mitya tells me privately. "Your driving would make NASCAR proud."

I pull the virtual wheel all the way to the right to avoid the gray Volvo in my path. "That's always been my ambition, NASCAR or stunts for *The Fast and the Furious*."

I blast past a biker, provoking a stream of obscenities. I can't blame the bearded guy, since unlike most other people on the road, he's driving his death machine without AI assistance. I turn left and slip between a green Toyota and a silver Honda. If these cars hadn't been self-driven, their drivers might've cursed me out worse than the biker. As it is, most of the people I nearly kill are busy with their VR entertainment, or ironically, they're trying to look at the accident ahead instead of paying attention to the one in the making.

By the time I finally get through the snarl, I allow myself to check how I'm doing on time and feel giddy that I've gained five minutes of the ten I was short. Still, to make up the other five, I must get back to turbo speed, which I do without hesitation, focusing all my energy on the road.

"I heard a door close." Mr. Spock sends me his words along with a huge dose of excitement through the EmoRat app. "I can't smell the men anymore."

They probably left to prepare for my arrival. I begin to reply, then stop myself. No need to tell Mr. Spock I'm on a suicide mission. I say instead, "You did a good job telling me about this. How do you feel about leaving Alan's pocket to do a little reconnaissance?"

"Scared." Despite his words, Mr. Spock peeks out of the pocket and shares his view with me.

The room is indeed empty.

"Find a better hiding spot," I suggest. "Some place you can keep your eyes on them when they come back."

He runs down Alan's sleeve and then down the inside of his pants leg.

"That's very clever," I say encouragingly. My small friend likes compliments on his stealth skills. "Even if someone had come back in just then, they wouldn't have seen you inside Alan's clothes."

The compliment breaks through the fear that threatens to paralyze the little guy, and he leaps the rest of the distance to the floor and quickly scans the room. This looks like someone's man cave, with a high-end home theater setup and a pool table in the far corner. Both Alan and Ada are half sitting, half lying in plush La-Z-Boy recliners in front of a giant TV like the ones popular before VR made them obsolete. The light from a massive window to the right makes Ada's face appear almost angelic in her slumber, while Alan looks as if he might open his eyes at any moment to cause some mischief.

I turn off the emotions going to Mr. Spock from me, because I don't want to overwhelm the rat with heartache at seeing my unconscious family like this.

"How about you hide under Alan's chair?" I suggest. "You'll be able to see that door."

The door in question creaks open.

A surge of adrenaline nearly makes me lose control of the car in the real world.

Mr. Spock reacts much better than I would have. In a whirl of whiskers and white fur, he dives under Alan's recliner, finds an angle where he's hidden, and tightens his muscles in an effort to make his body smaller and less detectable.

The door is wide open by this point, and a man walks in. I can only see the lower portion of his body, but based on his clothes, I recognize Boris, the asshole from earlier. Two more guard types follow him in, and though I can't see their faces, I suspect they're wearing masks.

"Stay hidden," I tell Mr. Spock, even though he's smart enough to know this himself. "No matter what happens, don't leave that spot."

"I'm worried about Alan and Ada." Mr. Spock's EmoRat worry is nearly as bad as my own.

"They'll be okay, bud," I reassure him. I wish someone would do the same for me. "I promise they'll be fine. I'm working on saving them."

"I'll guard until then," he states bravely.

"Mitya," I write in a private Zik message. "If something happens to me, I want you to make sure Mr. Spock comes out of this alive. He's hiding under a chair where Alan and Ada are kept."

"Of course," Mitya replies. "And just so you know, if something does happen to you, I'll use the robots to make sure everyone responsible pays dearly for it."

"I'm not sure I want my half-brother killed," I say after a moment's hesitation.

"Then I'll just make sure he regrets what happened to you for the rest of his life," Mitya replies, the Zik message completely free of any emotional overtones. "But the punishment will fit the crime."

"I better focus on driving," I tell both Mr. Spock and Mitya. "Let's talk later."

"Keep Share on so Muhomor and I know what happens when you get there," Mitya says.

"I'll watch this room." Mr. Spock demonstratively narrows his pink eyes to get a better view of his surroundings.

Though the road after the accident is relatively empty, it doesn't feel that way at this speed, and I must swerve to avoid cars almost every moment. It's clear that if Zapo and I survive this, the car is going to need new tires by the time I get to my destination. And I might need a new set of adrenal glands and clean underwear.

When the GPS informs me that Kostya's coordinates are on the right side of the road, I let out a breath I've held half the distance down I-84. Pulling up to the gate of the giant mansion my half-brother has made into his lair, I take in my surroundings. With a forest on one side and mountain views on the other, the location is a high-end realtor's wet dream. There's a giant fence surrounding everything and a driveway that spirals up the hill for at least half a mile.

I jump out of the car, rush over to the large in-wall intercom, and press the only button there.

"*Da*," someone says almost instantly.

"Tell Konstantin that I'm here," I bellow in that exaggerated way my mom uses during international phone calls to her school friends, as though she wants them to hear her all the way in Russia. "I still have three minutes."

"Leave your car behind," the voice says. "Walk in with your hands above your head."

I raise my hands and trudge up the intricate pavers, my eyes never leaving my destination. My gray hair count doubles by the time the first Richard Nixon-masked asshole greets me with a machine gun, and triples when I realize just how many armed people are guarding the locked door.

"Where is my wife?" I demand from the guy closest to me. "Where is my son?"

The man doesn't answer, so I repeat the questions in Russian. This doesn't yield results either.

Yet another masked guard comes out and gestures for us to enter, looking like Richard Nixon as a creepy butler. I follow him into a gorgeous foyer and down a long, spindly corridor.

Through Mr. Spock's ears, I hear the grating voice of Boris. "The show is about to begin. Let me turn on the TV."

The television set in front of the room comes to life. Mr. Spock can only see a chunk of the screen from his vantage point. There's not much to see, only the figure of a large man with his back to the camera. He's standing like a statue, holding something shiny in each hand. The muscles in this guy's back are formidable, and even with the poor viewing angle, something about him is familiar. I have a good idea who it might be, so I keep a small window in my AROS interface open to keep a metaphysical eye on the TV screen as the guards lead me farther into the mansion.

Light from a skylight illuminates the modern art on the walls, but the masked guards with guns are the most common decoration throughout. Including this batch, I count fifty-eight men so far. Assuming they're spread evenly throughout the place and represent a typical ratio of armed men to house space, if I add the size of the mansion into the equation, I get a very depressing result. There must be close to five hundred armed people here.

"This place would be a death trap even if I were armed and had brought Dominic and the rest of security guys," I say after popping into the VR room. Since I'm no longer driving at race-car speeds, I can spare some attention.

Muhomor and Mitya both nod knowingly, verifying that they're watching through my Share app feed.

"Kostya is probably bankrupting one of his companies paying all these goons, assuming they're not being compelled like Gogi and Joe," I continue.

"I doubt any of these people are controlled." Mitya's palms

must be sweaty because I see droplets on the arms of the chair where his hands rested a moment ago. "Like Boris, they must be guns for hire."

"Too bad the robots are still an hour away." Muhomor points at the map of upstate New York where a number of dots are moving ever so slowly in our direction. "We have a hundred of them, which would be plenty to deal with these guys."

"Speaking of resources, Dominic is running toward you on foot." Mitya wipes his hands on his hoodie and puts a tiny dot on the map. "With his exoskeleton, he's almost as fast as the robots. He might get to the mansion in an hour and ten minutes if he keeps up that pace."

"Do you have anything more immediate than the robots?" I ask. "It's nice to know I can be avenged after my death, but I'd be even happier if I could stay alive in the first place."

"I've got three drones zeroing in on your location," Muhomor says proudly. "They should be there in about twenty minutes."

"Great," I say sarcastically. "With three measly drones, you'll be able to watch a live feed of my funeral from three angles, assuming Kostya buries me instead of liquefying my corpse in acid or something equally gruesome. I assume you failed to free Joe from his control?"

Muhomor looks down, and Mitya avoids my gaze.

"I didn't think so." I show my displeasure by poofing out of VR in a wisp of virtual smoke.

In the real world, we stop next to a set of heavy red doors, and my Nixon-masked guide pokes me painfully with his gun and then jabs it pointedly toward the entryway. Working completely in sync, his masked partner opens the doors. I enter of my own volition before I'm forced to do so.

The large room is empty of all furniture, and the ultra-polished hardwood floors reflect sparkling light into my eyes with unpleasant intensity. This must've been a dance floor before Kostya appropriated the space for his revenge. The room is also familiar because I'm now looking at it from two angles.

It's the room on the TV screen that Mr. Spock is currently watching.

The doors behind me snap shut, and I focus my gaze in the middle of the room where a single figure stands, a knife in each hand.

My earlier guess was unfortunately correct.

This is my cousin, Joe.

His Siberian icicle eyes show even less emotion than usual, zeroing in on me like two blue lasers. Instead of recognition, all I see is a "target acquired" type of acknowledgment.

Sunlight glints off the two blades as Joe menacingly lumbers toward me.

TWENTY-EIGHT

"Is that you?" Mr. Spock asks worriedly.

"It's me, buddy. Joe and I are just sparring. Just like that time in the dojo."

"I didn't like that time," he replies.

I don't have to remind him this is an understatement. The one and only time I took him to see me train, he threw the rat equivalent of a hissy fit. I always left him at the Furry Ritz after that. The fact that he remembers that fight at all is telling; his long-term memory isn't as good as a human's.

"It's a lot like your dominance games with the other males," I remind him. "No one will get hurt."

"But you're the alpha," he states, and despite everything, I'm warmed by my friend's high regard.

"Sometimes you must remind the other males that you're in charge. Remember your disagreement with Chekov?"

"Yes." His Zik message is full of guilt over biting his friend's ear. "I did give him a peanut later."

"You're the best alpha," I reassure him. "For now, can you do me a favor, bud? Go enjoy Alan's Rat World for ten minutes or so, but keep your eyes open. This way you won't see what happens, but I can still see the TV screen."

"You are smart," he replies distantly, the way he does when he submerges himself in my son's VR version of rat paradise.

In the time Mr. Spock and I telepathically converse, Joe makes it halfway across the room.

This part of Kostya's revenge is elegant in its devious simplicity. One of us—likely me—is about to die. Joe and I are the two people Kostya blames for the death of our father. I suspect he blames me as the leader and Joe as the executioner. He probably doesn't care that it was Joe alone who both decided and enacted our father's fate.

What Kostya doesn't realize is that he, Boris, and the rest of them are not going to get the big spectacle they anticipate. This fight will be over before anyone gets the popcorn, because every single time I've faced Joe in the gym, he's beaten me in a matter of seconds. I mean that literally. Unless he was purposefully toying with me, my record against Joe is four seconds and five milliseconds, and even that I only achieved thanks to Battle Mode. Those fights were also bare-handed. My survival probability shrinks significantly with each knife in Joe's hands.

"Please tell me you can fly a drone through that window," I say to Mitya and Muhomor.

"The three I mentioned are still nineteen minutes away," Muhomor says. "Give or take."

My heart drops to my feet, but I keep a poker face, determined to die with at least some dignity.

I enable Battle Mode.

Joe draws ever closer. Lines begin to show up in Augmented Reality, ideas for my actions and Joe's possible reactions to them. Not surprisingly, time seems to slow, though I think it's more of a trick of adrenaline than my superfast cognition this time.

I have a decision to make. If I enable the Emotion Dampener add-on, I won't have the problem I had when I fought Gogi—hesitation at hurting someone I care about. Should I willingly turn myself into a monster? Is there even any benefit to playing Kostya's game and hurting Joe, when the winner will ultimately die along with the loser?

"Joe is controlled, you're not," Muhomor tells me privately. He must've guessed at least a part of my dilemma. "He has no chance, while you do, albeit a small one."

Cognizant that I'm taking advice on ethical behavior from Muhomor of all people, I nevertheless turn on the Emotion Dampener.

"How many seconds should Emotion Dampener be on?" Einstein asks. This is a safety feature to make sure I don't remain a psychopath once the fight is over.

"Set it for eight seconds and ten milliseconds," I reply. "That's double my estimated time for survival."

Counting the moments, I try to imagine what fighting with Emotion Dampener will be like. I will probably be like a Viking berserker—

"Emotion Dampener enabled," Einstein states.

The world around me transforms.

TWENTY-NINE

THE OPPONENT IS A LEAP AWAY.

He has two knives, which is a huge advantage. But I can see his movement from two vantage points, a tactical benefit I need to leverage. His right knife hand is the dominant one. Battle Mode estimates he will thrust with it first; the TV view shows me his shoulder blades twisting in confirmation.

I sidestep and slightly pull back. At the same time, I strike the Opponent's forearm.

The knife clanks on the hardwood floor and slides toward the door. Though the weapon is behind me, the TV view shows that I have no chance to get it—but neither does the Opponent.

I don't need Battle Mode to show me that the left knife is about to slice at my mid-chest. I'm already reacting. I grab the Opponent's left wrist, successfully trapping it. With as much intensity as I can, I strike the Opponent in the groin. My plan is simple: the intense pain should force the Opponent to let go of the weapon, after which I can use the knife to carve the Opponent like a Thanksgiving turkey.

The groin strike doesn't cause the Opponent to let go of the weapon. Either he's wearing a cup, or Kostya's control enables him to withstand this intense pain. I surmise the latter, since that was the case in the fight with Gogi. This presents a problem, because outside of the ideal scenario in which I kill the Opponent, much of my strategy relies on inflicting copious amounts of pain.

So now I need to focus on killing him as fast as I can. If that's not possible, I need to cause the kind of damage that would make fighting physically impossible despite the mind control—for example, broken bones or severed limbs. Ripping out the eyes probably wouldn't be as strategic, because Kostya could still control the Opponent via camera views, but if the opportunity presents itself, I will gouge out the eyes to test this theory. Once the Opponent is thusly handicapped, killing him should be trivial.

I scan Battle Mode's recommendations and pick one unlikely to be anticipated, because it will cause minor harm to me. I pull back with my hands while bringing my head toward the precious knife. Stretching my jaw muscles like a snake, I take a vicious bite.

My teeth grate against the metal of the knife, but I ignore the pain of enamel scraping off and rip my head so violently to the right that my neck muscles spasm in complaint.

The Opponent's grip on the knife loosens, and I find myself with the weapon in my mouth. I let go of the Opponent's wrist with my right hand while simultaneously tightening my grip with the left. I claw at the knife in my mouth. As soon as I feel the plastic hilt in my palm, I thrust the knife at the Opponent's right eye. My goal isn't to blind him but to penetrate the brain—a very efficient way to kill.

Unfortunately, the Opponent acts as I would in his position. Ignoring the potential damage, he grabs the blade.

I could twist the blade to inflict maximum pain, but that isn't a motivator in this fight. I try another gambit. Letting go with my left hand, I wrap it around the Opponent's knife-holding hand and squeeze. If the knife is sharp enough and I apply enough force, I should cause the hand to cleave in two—a useful handicap.

As expected, the Opponent ignores the pain, curls his other hand into a fist, and throws a punch at my face.

I throw my head back to reduce the impact of the punch, but the maneuver doesn't help. The fist smashes into my chin, sending me to the verge of consciousness. Abandoning the plan to cleave the Opponent's hand, I let go with my left hand and rip the knife from his grasp with the right.

Blood pours from the Opponent's palm, but not fast enough to provide any advantage anytime soon.

Battle Mode shows me an opportunity. If I toss the knife just as the line shows, I'll pierce the Opponent's heart with a high probability of instant death.

I arc my arm as instructed and begin to throw.

I'm mid-throw when the world around me changes again.

"Emotion Dampener disabled."

THIRTY

Once a human body begins to perform an action, it's hard to stop. I hope that my highly trained and enhanced mind will be able to accomplish what regular free will cannot.

In the end, I only tweak my action very slightly as I let go of the knife, but the adjustment makes all the difference. Instead of piercing Joe in the chest, the knife scrapes his flesh, leaving a small gash that bleeds instantly.

Now that my emotions are back, taming my sympathetic nervous system is like riding a bull at a rodeo in hell. Ignoring the deafening pulse in my ears, I can't help but focus on how appalled I am at what the Emotion Dampener made me do and think. I initiated it because I thought that Joe would kill me so quickly and easily that Emotion Dampener might give me a slightly better chance at survival. As it is, I survived double the time I thought I would—but I find it hard to believe it's because of Emotion Dampener.

I nearly maimed and killed my cousin, something I don't think I could live with (though I guess "living with it" is a purely hypothetical concept under the circumstances). At the very least, I don't intend to give Kostya the satisfaction of becoming a monster for his viewing pleasure.

"You should delete the Emotion Dampener code from our source control repository," I tell Mitya. "I'm never using that atrocity again."

"I'd also add taking advice from Muhomor to your 'never' list," Mitya replies.

"If by some miracle I survive long enough to need advice, I'll only ask for yours," I tell him.

My cousin tries to punch me in the face. Specks of blood from the earlier knife wound trail the path of his fist like a tail following a comet. I block the punch with my forearm and reflexively counter with my elbow into his jaw.

The way my elbow screams in pain tells me he'll likely need surgery if he ever wants to chew again; even his strengthened bones couldn't have helped in this case. Despite the massive pain Joe must now feel, his expression doesn't change at all.

The realization finally clicks into place.

"Dude," I tell Mitya telepathically. "The reason Joe hasn't killed me already is because I'm not actually fighting Joe. I'm fighting whoever is controlling Joe—the puppet master, so to speak. Luckily, that person isn't as good a fighter as my cousin."

"This also explains why Gogi didn't fight like himself," Mitya says instantly.

On the TV screen, Joe begins to move his leg, so I step back from his kick. Now that I know what to look for, I'm certain my theory is right. This wasn't Joe's kick—he would've never been this sloppy. This was Kostya's (or whoever's) attempt at a kick.

This small droplet of good news in the sea of bad reinvigorates me like a full night's sleep and a gallon of coffee. I execute a combination of moves I never would've dared with the real Joe, finishing with a punch in the pit of his stomach. My fist strikes his solar plexus with an audible smack. Joe's body doubles over and draws in wheezing breaths.

This is my chance to knock him out—the only way out, outside of the heavy-handed ideas I'd had during the earlier Emotion Dampener insanity. I grab Joe by the hair and prepare to slam his face against my knee.

The tightening of Joe's neck muscles on TV is my warning that I've failed. I try to regroup, but it's too late. He rips out of my grasp and uses his momentary advantage to put a foot behind me and push.

On the TV, I watch myself fly toward the wooden floor in a wide arc. The fall seems to proceed in slow motion, and I even have a moment to calculate the odds of breaking my back when I land. I decide such an eventuality is unlikely.

I also realize my earlier mistake. A typical solar plexus punch hurts so much that the victim is unable to think for a moment— but in Joe's case, that didn't apply because Kostya doesn't feel Joe's pain. Also, a typical solar plexus punch knocks the wind out of the victim, but the Respirocytes swimming in Joe's system ensure his body has enough oxygen to throw me to the floor.

The good news is that these same Respirocytes should help me in a millisecond.

I land on the floor, the pain jolting through my nerves like a creaky wooden roller coaster. Despite knowing I'm not lacking oxygen, I'm unable to stop my body from desperately gasping to replace the air that cowardly escaped my lungs.

The TV screen shows Kostya preparing for another move that the real Joe would never do.

With a colossal effort of will, I override my uncooperative biology just in time to roll to the side of a wrestler-style slam that's just as likely to hurt him as me. There's a loud bang as Joe's elbow hits the floor; it sounds as if he's cracked either the wood or his bone. At least it wasn't my ribs.

Judging from my earlier fight with Gogi, Kostya must have some experience with wrestling, which makes me deeply regret ending up on the ground. I try to jump to my feet, but Joe's already next to me. Even without Battle Mode assistance, I can see that he wants to grab my right arm in a judo-style lock.

My counter is pure textbook and proves Kostya isn't as good of a fighter as I feared, because Joe's body ends up under mine. I spot his leg on the TV screen and realize that if his kick connects, I'll be singing falsetto for a while. I block the kick instantly and do my best to intertwine his legs with mine while grabbing both of his wrists.

In theory, I should be able to hold him this way for a while, but Kostya must realize it too. He makes Joe do something that no sane fighter would: he headbutts me at an angle that will be much worse for him than for me.

Joe's already damaged jaw crashes into my forehead, making me see an explosion of sparks where his bloody face should be. When my vision comes back, Kostya repeats the headbutt; this time, it's Joe's forehead that hits mine.

The concussion and the blood in my eyes make it impossible to see what's happening until I check out the TV and see Joe's head connecting with mine again. The impact makes the world around me seem unreal. I recognize this sensation—it happens every time someone (usually Joe) knocks me out.

I'm not the only one affected. Joe's body slackens under me, and on the TV, I see him pass out—right before my own world goes completely blank.

THIRTY-ONE

I wake up to a loud hum.

"You have been unconscious for twenty-three minutes," Einstein's voice says too loudly in my aching head.

The hum seems to intensify, and I realize that I'm someplace dark—at least I can't seem to detect any light through my closed eyelids. Before opening my eyes, I check on my family via the EmoRat app.

Mr. Spock is clearly bored. The room is quiet, and judging by the unmoving boots of the three guards, they must be motionless as well.

"Hey, bud, you're doing an excellent job as a guard," I tell the rat. "Keep it up."

"You're back," Mr. Spock says excitedly. "I called after I was done with Rat World, but you didn't respond."

"I was a little busy," I say. "I still am, but we'll have a long talk soon."

"Okay," Mr. Spock replies. "I'll wait."

A Zik message from Mitya interrupts, full of paranoid urgency. "Don't show them you're awake. Join us in VR."

I do as my friend suggests. Three people are in the VR room now: Dominic, Mitya, and Muhomor.

"Dominic," I say in lieu of a greeting. "Please tell me you're about to barge in and save us."

"I'm about half an hour away." Though this VR version of Dominic is free of the exoskeleton and bionic arm, he's still a formidable presence in the meeting room.

"He's running on foot through a shortcut in the wilderness." Mitya looks at Dominic's giant form with admiration. "We should give him a huge bonus when this is all over."

"What about the robots?" I ask.

"Twenty-five minutes until arrival." Mitya puts a map up on the big screen to point out the dots representing Dominic and the robots.

"What are the blue and yellow dots following the robots?" I ask after examining the map.

"The police and the news. It's not every day that someone reen-acts a scene from *I, Robot* in upstate New York." He puts up a view of the robots marching uphill in unison, sunlight gleaming off their metallic heads.

"They won't be here in time either," Dominic says. "They're lagging behind the robots."

"So is there anything that can help my current situation?" I look at everyone in turn, trying to ignore the sick feeling in my stomach.

"The three drones I promised you are outside the window of the room where you're being scanned," Muhomor says. "I have an idea, but I'd like your input."

He puts up three screens. Each drone must have a telescoping lens, because I see three views into a room that was probably a big guest bedroom before Kostya turned it into a makeshift lab and infirmary. On a bed to the right of the window, Joe is hooked up to some monitoring equipment. It shows a heartbeat that proves he's alive, at least for now.

Three figures in white coats stand with their backs to the

window, huddling around another body inside a big brain-scanning machine. Only the middle of the man's torso and legs are sticking out. It takes me a moment to realize that the torso belongs to me, and that this explains the hum and the darkness.

"What are they doing to me?" I walk up to the screen and point at the machine. "Is that a CAT scan or an MRI?"

"They just got your Brainocyte ID," Mitya says apologetically.

"But on the plus side, they also scanned your noggin for real, and it looks like Joe didn't fracture your skull," Muhomor adds.

"They probably want to hack into you the way they did with Gogi and Joe," Dominic says. He winces at the vicious glares from Mitya and Muhomor.

"As Captain Obvious says," Muhomor continues after a small pause, "Kostya must have more planned for you."

One of the people surrounding me is likely Kostya himself.

A crazy idea pops into my head.

"Muhomor, could you crash each of the drones into one of the people in that room?" I ask quickly. "There are three of them and three of the drones. I could jump out of that machine, finish them off, disable a guard to get a weapon, and barricade myself, Ada, and Alan in this room with Joe until the robots and Dominic arrive."

"What you said is my earlier plan," Muhomor says. "I can—"

"This plan has a low probability of success," Mitya says. "These drones are not that maneuverable, so unless the people are distracted already, there's little chance they'll allow themselves to get hit with one."

"And when that glass breaks, they'll have ample warning." Dominic stares at the screen intently. He must be looking for another idea and finding none.

"Anyone have any counterplans?" I ask. "Or are you dead set on sacrificing me to learn how this brain hack works?"

"Assuming the debug stuff they told me about even helps with that," Dominic says glumly. "That's a big if."

We sit in sullen silence as the people on the screen begin to pull me out of the machine and I feel the motion in the real world.

"The bad men are moving," Mr. Spock tells me urgently.

Through Mr. Spock's senses, I see the door open and a man in a white coat enter. In VR, I explain that something is happening in Alan and Ada's location and provide them with the EmoRat app so they can look on. They didn't already have this app because only Ada, Alan, and I use it routinely; it never became part of the standard AROS package.

"It's wakey-wakey time," says the new guy. "Boss wants them awake for the next part."

The two syringes in the white coat's hands probably mean he plans to inject Ada and Alan with something that might wake them. That would usually be good news, but in the context of "the next part," it seems beyond sinister.

"How long before the girl is fully awake?" asks the rock-on-rock voice I recognize as belonging to Boris. He's trying to sound casual, but there's a creepy inquisitiveness in his tone that fills me with dread.

"She'll come to her senses almost right away, but I'd give it a few minutes before she stops being groggy," the white coat replies. He walks up to Ada's chair, the syringe menacingly extended.

"Shouldn't we tie her up?" Boris asks with an unhealthy eagerness.

"Motherfucker," Dominic mumbles in VR. My other friends echo his sentiment in their own ways.

"Boss said not to use restraints," the white coat says. The chair blocks Mr. Spock's view, but I'm pretty sure the guy administers Ada's injection. "He has these two under control already, so they'll sit still once they come to."

It takes a huge effort to pretend to be unconscious in the real world. What I really want to do is open my eyes, grab Kostya's throat, and not let go until I choke the life out of my twisted fuck of a half-brother.

"We all suspected that your family would be hacked," Muhomor says in VR. Before he can expand on that thought, Dominic leans over and smacks him on the back of the head with an open palm. It couldn't have hurt too much, especially in VR, but Muhomor still squeals like a little piglet.

Ignoring VR, I work on calming my tumultuous emotions as the white coat injects Alan with the wake-up drug. To my luck, the people who took my body out of the machine are all busy watching something in the air above me, probably a private Augmented Reality screen.

"I'm needed back in the lab," the injection guy says on his way out. "Boss will be here shortly."

"I need a favor," Boris says to the other guards as soon as the door closes. "You two should take a short bathroom break."

The men look at one another.

"Boss said they're not to be harmed," one says, his voice muffled by the Nixon mask. "Not that it makes sense, considering, but orders are orders."

I really don't like the implication of that "considering" remark, but worry about its meaning is quickly overshadowed by the fury building in my heart.

"She will not be harmed," Boris says in a tone that sends angry shivers down my whole body. "Just a little sore is all. You know I'll make it worth your while if you do this for me."

The two other guards chuckle lasciviously and turn away.

My blood is boiling out of my veins. I'm probably more dangerous now than I was with the Emotion Dampener on. Emotion Dampener makes you a cold monster, but I would enjoy inflicting pain on Boris right now.

"The subject's heart rate is elevated," says someone next to me in the lab. "I think he's awake."

"The bypass is now activated," says Kostya's voice from my right. "It doesn't matter."

"They hacked you," Muhomor says in VR.

"I captured it via the debug mode," Mitya says.

"I don't give a fuck," I shout in VR, my fists clenched so tight it hurts. "That fucker is planning to rape Ada."

My friends look shocked at the vehemence in my voice. Even Dominic steps away from me.

"Your orders are about to be disobeyed," I scream at Kostya in the real world, yet nothing comes out of my mouth. "You said not to harm Ada, but she's about to come to harm!"

My brain reels from the strangeness of talking without any sound coming out of my larynx, and my fury intensifies at my helplessness.

Then my attention snaps back to the room with Ada, because Mr. Spock sees the door close behind the two guards.

Boris walks toward Ada's chair.

"I really hope you're already awake," he says in his grating voice. "I'll enjoy this so much more if you are."

No sound comes from Ada, but it could be because she's unable to scream, like me.

Boris's hands move toward his zipper.

THIRTY-TWO

IF I WERE THERE, I'D RIP THIS FUCKER'S NECK OUT WITH MY BARE teeth. Hate must create its own form of dark focus, because a plan of action instantly comes to me.

"Muhomor," I shout in VR. "Fly the drones into his head. Now."

"But you need them—"

"Now, or I'll fucking kill you!"

Something in my eyes must be convincing, because Muhomor swiftly obeys.

"Mr. Spock, you have to do something very dangerous for Ada, but it's very important." My EmoRat Zik message is a lot gentler than the order I barked in VR, but it conveys the same urgency.

"I'm ready," Mr. Spock replies right away. "What do I do?"

"I want you to run up this man's pant leg." I try to ball my hands into fists in the real world, but this doesn't work either, and my hands remain at my sides. "Once you reach the top, I want you to bite, over and over, as hard as you can."

A wave of eagerness comes back from the EmoRat. It's obvious that Mr. Spock has been itching to bite the bad guys for a while now, and only the social conditioning we've instilled in him was preventing this.

My perception slows to a crawl as the three drone views zero in on the nearby window. While I can't hold my breath in the real world, I stop breathing in VR as Mr. Spock dives for Boris's shoe.

Boris doesn't seem to notice the flash of white fur on the floor.

Mr. Spock's eyes show a repulsive view of a thick, hairy leg as he climbs toward an even more disgusting destination.

Boris must feel little claws on his leg, because he stops. The fastest drone points its lens at the window, and through that camera view, I see his puzzled expression.

Mr. Spock climbs higher. When he spots the white underwear, rat rage seeps through the EmoRat interface.

"Yes!" I spur the little warrior onward. "Bite that motherfucker."

Even lab rats like Mr. Spock have large teeth capable of administering painful bites. Rats usually avoid fighting humans because they know it's a losing fight, but if you corner one, you'd better prepare for some pain (and sometimes for rat-bite fever).

Mr. Spock's teeth easily pierce both the cotton fabric and the thin flesh of Boris's testicles.

The tortured yelp of pain is music to my bloodthirsty ears.

The drone is now an inch away from the window, and I get a glimpse of Boris's horrified face before window shards spray into the room and that face grows bigger.

Mr. Spock bites his target again, so hard I feel the little guy's jaws ache.

Boris's next scream is higher pitched. Via the drone, I see him struggling to decide if he should punch himself in the groin—a tough call.

"Run away," I command Mr. Spock. "Quickly."

I can feel his desire to keep biting, but he's a good rat and runs down. He's near Boris's knee when the first drone hits the man in the chest.

Boris doubles over, hopefully distracted from the source of the biting.

"To the rat, this must be like a scene from *King Kong*,"

Muhomor says in VR, earning him another smack on the back of the head from Dominic.

The second drone flies in through the window just as Mr. Spock leaves Boris's pants leg. Boris swats at it, and it crashes into the TV at the front of the room. His momentary distraction gives the third drone the chance it needs, and it slams into his temple with a satisfying smack.

Boris drops like a tree, his flailing foot inadvertently kicking Mr. Spock in the butt.

Momentum sends Mr. Spock skidding under Alan's recliner. He tries with all his might to slow down, but his claws don't provide enough traction.

There's a loud crash as Boris hits the floor. Through the camera of the last drone, I see him land on the debris of the TV, cutting himself in multiple places. Unfortunately, the view through Mr. Spock's eyes is nauseating as the little guy torpedoes toward the chair leg, followed by the smack of the rat's head into the wood.

Mr. Spock sends a rush of an all-too-familiar sensation—he's passing out.

"You did well," I tell him guiltily. "You're the fiercest rat in the world."

He seems to have heard me, because he flickers pride before he loses consciousness completely.

"Is the rat dead?" Muhomor asks and dodges Dominic's hand this time. "Hey, I'm just asking."

"I have a biofeedback chip in him," I say sharply. "His vitals look okay. He's just going to be out for a bit—and probably have a big headache once he comes to."

"Can we tell Mike about his own situation now?" Muhomor looks belligerently at Dominic. "I doubt he has much time left in VR."

"We've learned more about this hack," Mitya says. "It's basically a backdoor that allows Kostya to turn off and on any app inside your—"

"The loophole was the GPS interface," Muhomor jumps in

excitedly. "They must've had to hack into every satellite in the world to pull this off. The scope of this—"

Dominic smacks Muhomor much harder this time. "Shut up, or I'll shut you up for good."

"As I was saying," Mitya continues, giving Muhomor a withering stare, "the backdoor also allows Kostya to run any app in your AROS without your consent. You're getting some of these installed while he's shutting down your regular apps. When he gets to the VR interface, you won't—"

I abruptly find myself only in the real world. The VR room is gone without a trace. Kostya has done what Mitya was trying to warn me about: he closed the app in question.

I try sending Mitya a private Zik message, but nothing happens. I try email and social media without any results. Even the ancient instant messenger doesn't start.

"Let's try the motor function controls program," Kostya says next to me. "Have him open his eyes."

My eyes snap open without my willing them to.

The light in the room hurts my unadjusted eyes. I try to squint, but I don't have even that much control.

Panic forms in the back of my mind. Everyone has that visceral fear of being locked inside one's body without the ability to control it. I guess for me, this fear is stronger than usual. I try to distract myself from full-on terror, reminding myself that this is probably what those poor paralyzed patients experienced before we gave them Brainocytes. I focus on how good it feels to have helped people recover from such horror.

"Einstein?" I mentally ask. "What time is it?"

No reply.

Like every user, I've long since associated all my favorite apps with mental commands, which is why I haven't used the original visual AROS interface in a while. I try to summon it now.

To my surprise, the AROS interface shows up. Kostya must not have disabled the AROS UI controller app just yet. The number of icons that hover in the air in front of me is tiny in comparison to what's usually there. The Paint app icon disappears in front of my eyes before I can formulate some practical use for it; it had a Share button that likely uses APIs of the closed apps—a tiny chance that now is gone.

What's worse are the unfamiliar icons that show up. These must be the apps that allow Kostya to do whatever evil thing he plans to do to me—apps he can activate without my consent.

The AROS interface disappears, and a major portion of my mind splinters and dies a horrific death. The awful sense of dumbness is vaguely reminiscent of when I was without internet on a government black site. This sensation, though, is a million times worse. I've had more boosts since then and have come to rely on my cloud extensions even more. It's unclear if the computer substrate in my bones is helping my thinking or not, but in any case, I'm barely able to form a semi-coherent thought. It's as though I'm a ghost of myself, an analog copy of a copy of a copy.

Kostya must now have complete control over my mind, but the implications of that are now harder for me to grasp. I wonder if I knew what Kostya was about to make me do when I was whole just a minute ago. I also wonder if I had a plan at that point, because I'm overwhelmingly clueless now.

"Try to move around," a thin man in a lab coat recommends.

Kostya looks thoughtful for a moment, and suddenly, my body moves.

If having no control over my eyelids was weird, getting up like a marionette is even more bizarre. It's as though I've become a passive passenger inside my own mind. I still feel the pressure of each step, the in-and-out of my breathing, and the swing of my arms. But without control, it's more reminiscent of a low-budget virtual reality movie than of being myself.

I take a step, then another. The weirdest thing is that a part of me feels like maybe I'm controlling my movement after all, and it takes focus to verify that I'm not. That I can't. I guess my consciousness isn't used to not being in control, and tries to cling to an illusion of freedom, an illusion that's easy to shatter—all I need to do is wish to stop walking.

My body makes its way to the unconscious Joe, and my hand reaches toward a table with medical instruments right next to his head. My fingers brush the cold metal of a scalpel and gently pick it up.

"No," I try to say, but no words come out.

I fight for the control of my hand, but it's futile. The scalpel caresses Joe's ruined jaw, leaving a bloody streak where it cuts his skin. The cut is shallow and shouldn't do much harm, but if Kostya presses my hand even a millimeter deeper, the story will be different.

"Have you heard from Boris?" one of the lab coats asks.

My hand stops, and Kostya pauses his own movements momentarily. I can picture him placing a private call with his AROS and learning what happened to Boris. If that's the case, he's probably also summoning more goons to clean up the mess.

With a violent jerk, my hand throws the scalpel back onto the tray and my legs carry me back to Kostya. I stand in front of my half-brother like an ice sculpture, futilely willing my hands to grab his neck.

"How did Boris get hurt?" Kostya asks in that weird falsetto voice. "Where did those broken drones come from?"

I assume this means my mouth will work, so I test it out. "Fuck. You. I'm going to—"

To my huge disappointment, my stream of threats and obscenities gets cut off. That doesn't stop me from trying to inject my disdain for my half-brother into my unblinking gaze.

Something akin to an Augmented Reality icon flashes in front of my face. I'm abruptly grappling with the worst pain I've ever felt in my life, and I've lived through gunshots, explosions, and even torture. It's as if someone is repeatedly kicking me in the balls, only inside my brain.

I want to gasp for breath, but my body is breathing with the calm of a Hindu cow. I want to scream, but my mouth isn't working.

That flicker of an icon must've been the launch of an app that does the opposite of the Relief app: it causes lightning bolts to hit various parts of my brain.

The pain stops and Kostya repeats, "How did Boris get hurt? Where did those drone pieces come from?"

"Anyone ever tell you that you look like a syphilitic pedophile?" I say, my voice hoarse from residual pain. "You motherf—"

The surge of agony is worse this time. It's purer. Less reminiscent of anything physical. This is what it would feel like if a zombie munched your brain while you're alive—if your brain had pain receptors, that is.

After a subjective decade but probably a real-world second, the torment stops and Kostya repeats his questions.

As tempted as I am to curse my half-brother again, the fear of that pain returning is so intense that I decide to stop being a hero. "You never said I couldn't fly drones here. You just said to come alone."

He considers my words, and I inwardly brace for the pain to begin again.

"He can't command any drones now," one of the lab coats says.

"Still, I'm going to expedite the proceedings," Kostya says to the coat. "Let's go."

My body comes alive again, and I walk toward the room's exit, passing a number of white hospital beds as I go. Kostya directs me into a wide corridor. A door to the right opens, and several masked guards bring out a stretcher carrying Boris. More guards follow with black garbage bags that probably contain broken glass and the remains of the drones.

Kostya stops me next to the door the people just left.

"You made my worst nightmare come true," he says in an emotionless falsetto monotone. "I'm about to return the favor."

My attempt at a torrent of Russian and English obscenities doesn't leave my uncooperative mouth.

Kostya looks at me unblinkingly, and my perception momentarily flickers. When my vision reasserts itself, I realize he must've shut down my eyes, because I missed him move. And he must've moved, because he's already a foot closer to the door.

My arm rises, and Kostya hands me a Glock 19 just like the one I use at the range. There's something ceremonial about this hand-off, and if my body were still my own, I'd be gulping down breaths.

Kostya walks through the door, and I unwillingly follow.

Something about the room doesn't fully make sense, but Kostya forces my eyes to dart from Ada to Alan—a rare case when his malevolent purpose is in sync with what I want to do anyway.

Both Ada and Alan stare at me with paralyzed faces that hint at being under Kostya's control.

"Please, Dad, no," Alan says with an intonation that makes him sound like a stranger—likely a side effect of Kostya using his vocal cords. "Don't kill me."

"Do not shoot us, Mike," Ada says in the same strange way, her face completely emotionless.

My hand clutches the gun and rises.

I try to scream, but no words come out.

The barrel of my gun points at Ada's head, and Kostya forces my eyes to look through the sights. All my shooting range experience leaves no doubt in my mind: if my finger presses that trigger, the bullet will hit my wife in the middle of her forehead.

If it were possible for the naked brain to scream, mine would've done so already.

Desperate ideas flit through my head.

"This is a dream. Einstein, please show up." The AI doesn't appear, as he would if this was a nightmare.

"Maybe this is a precog moment." Then I remember that it can't be. Precog moments disappeared with the newer brain boost technology, and even when they did happen in the past, they short-circuited as soon as you thought the words "precog moment."

My finger slowly presses the trigger.

The gun's recoil pushes my hand back as Ada's head explodes.

THIRTY-THREE

"THIS CAN'T BE HAPPENING," I CHANT INSIDE MY HEAD. "PLEASE, please, please. Let this not be happening."

"Daddy, don't," Alan says in that creepy way again.

My arm points the gun unwaveringly at Alan's tiny torso.

I curse myself for wasting the drones on Boris earlier. I should've saved them to somehow kill myself—not that I have any app to control a drone with, but maybe Muhomor and Mitya could've done it.

My finger squeezes the trigger.

I'm oblivious to the ringing in my ears and the recoil. All I see is Alan's small rib cage devastated by the bullet.

With torturous intent, my eyes travel back to Ada's corpse, forcing me to stare at my dead wife for what feels like an eternity of grief before coming back to Alan.

I want to fall to my knees. I want to clutch my eyes. I want to rip out my hair. But my body just stands there.

If human beings could will themselves to die of grief, I would do so now.

Then my vision blurs once more, and I'm back outside the door.

How am I back here? What just happened?

Wild hope seizes me.

Could that murder scene have been a precog moment, as unlikely as that is?

Kostya is standing the same way he was before my vision went weird the first time. "I wanted to show you a preview of what's about to happen," he says. "I want you to know what I'm going to make you do in a minute, so you have a chance to really savor that experience."

I understand then. Kostya can run any app inside my AROS. That means he can force me to watch virtual reality videos, which is what that horrific vision was. That explains why I thought the room looked odd: there was no sign of Boris's earlier struggle. When Kostya made that fake video, he didn't know the incident with Boris would happen, so he didn't stage it.

In hindsight, it wasn't even that good of a video. I'd thought Ada and Alan's speech and facial expressions were weird because of Kostya's control, but it was just unresearched CGI.

"Here." Kostya hands me the gun as though I have a choice.

My hand extends and grasps it again, or for the first time—I don't care about semantics right now.

This time around, when I begin walking, I pay close attention to the most minute details to make sure I'm not in VR again. Given the pressure of the handle against my palm, the weight of the Glock pulling my arm down, and the faint smell of Boris's blood and Kostya's sweat, I must conclude that this is happening for real. VR technology doesn't yet have this level of detail—although neither does a nightmare, for that matter.

I appreciate Kostya's evil genius at making me doubt reality right now. As the result of the earlier VR, I'm hyper alert. If he makes me repeat the atrocity from the fake video, I'll feel every aspect even more vividly.

My right leg takes a step. Again I focus and make sure to sense the pressure of my foot touching the ground, the interplay of leg muscles. It's not only to verify the realness of what's happening, but also to try to wrest back control. Maybe some leg muscle will listen to my brain and allow me to topple over. Maybe some muscle in my hand will twitch upon my wish and drop the gun.

If Kostya's control has a loophole, I don't find it in the time it takes me to lumber into the room.

This time, I spot the signs of Boris's earlier mishaps: a window is missing, and glass crunches under my feet. Kostya makes me scan the room. There are two guards, one next to Ada and the other next to Alan. Kostya stops on my left, within easy reach—if only I could control my body.

As in my earlier vision, Alan and Ada's eyes are open. Unlike before, their expressions aren't completely blank. There's a nervous twitch in the corner of Ada's eye, and something similar at the corner of Alan's mouth.

My left hand takes the gun off safety—another detail the VR video omitted earlier.

My right hand fluctuates, as though Kostya is deciding whom he should have me shoot first.

He must make his decision, because my hand turns in Alan's direction.

THIRTY-FOUR

KOSTYA IS SLOWING MY MOVEMENTS IN ORDER TO TORMENT ME AS much as he can. His plan is working extremely well.

Then something penetrates his control.

If I could blink in confusion, I would, because I don't understand where this wave of groggy emotions comes from. Without a brain boost, it takes me a long moment to recognize what I'm experiencing.

This is how Mr. Spock feels when you wake him from a rat nap.

Has Kostya forgotten to stop the EmoRat app?

Now that I think about it, it's likely. Only Ada, Alan, and I are users of this app. Kostya or anyone outside our circle wouldn't even know it was there to stop.

"Buddy!" I shout urgently through the app. "I think you got hit on the head and knocked out, and you just came back to your senses."

"Sounds true," the rat replies. His mind is clearly groggy. "Your friend is in my head."

"What?" I ask with a glimmer of hope. "Muhomor...? Mitya? Can you—?"

"Already on top of it," says Mr. Spock with unusual sophistication. "This is Muhomor, by the way."

"Dude." I cram my reply with all the desperation of a man whose hand is in the process of aiming a gun at his son. "Please tell me Mitya's debug mode worked."

"Yeah, once I knew how they got in, it wasn't hard to reverse engineer the rest of it—especially since fate was kind enough to provide me with a Georgian test subject right here in the bunker." Muhomor's Zik reply contains an inappropriate amount of glee. "Ada and Alan are already free from control, by the way. They're just faking submission. Things are trickier with you because I've had no way to get in touch until now. I have to say, I always thought your pet rat was a stupid frivolity, but now that I can use him as a proxy for—"

"Can you see the room?" I interrupt. "The gun is almost pointing at Alan's head."

"True," Muhomor says. "That's where we want it. Until the last second. We don't want them on to us."

"This *is* the last second." Though my mind isn't nearly as sharp as it needs to be, I understand his plan—but I'm so pissed that if this conversation were happening in VR, I'd punch him in the face. "Free me. Now."

"Not yet. Kostya is paying close attention to you right now. If I wrest his control away, he'll instantly know that it happened. In case you hadn't noticed, there are armed people in the room."

"If you don't give me back control of my body, I will genuinely kill you when I see you next." I cram my hatred of my half-brother into my Zik message with the hope of getting through.

"Fine," Muhomor snaps. "Let's see if this works."

THIRTY-FIVE

MY MIND BECOMES WHOLE AGAIN.

No drug-induced ecstasy or the best orgasm in the world can compare with the sensation of regaining my full mental prowess. If someone magically turned an ant into a rocket scientist, this is how the little creature would feel.

Seeing simultaneously through my own eyes and Mr. Spock's viewpoint, I reassess the situation. It was a mistake to force Muhomor to give me control back at this very moment. Kostya is indeed about to become aware of what's happening—a few milliseconds too soon. Now I'm pissed that Muhomor gave in, but I have no choice but to work with the situation at hand. If I ever not have my brain boost again, I hope I retain enough wits to unquestioningly trust someone whose intellect (at that time) is so much superior to mine.

On the bright side, Mitya and Muhomor don't know the full extent of my combat skills. Hopefully, I can still get us out of this mess alive.

Instead of continuing the trajectory that would point the gun at Alan's head, my hand shifts an inch to the side, and I put a bullet between the eyeholes of the Richard Nixon mask of Alan's guard.

The mask breaks into little pieces, as does the skull of the man underneath.

I feel a tinge of regret at the death—an obvious side effect of having my mind Joined with Ada's so recently. Any police manual would advise lethal force in a situation like this. Shooting to kill is the safest option under the circumstances. I took unnecessary risks in the past by shooting people in the shoulder; now that I'm more experienced, I refuse to risk my family's life for some asshole again. If that makes me too much like Joe, it's something I'll have to live with—and I'd rather live to regret my choices than die as a saint.

In less time than it probably takes Kostya to register the boom of the gunshot, I elbow him in the stomach while pointing the gun toward Ada's guard with my other hand. Most people have trouble moving their hands completely independently like this; they first realize it in grade school when attempting the trick of patting their head and rubbing their belly at the same time. Of course, just like with that trick, practice helps tremendously.

My elbow connects pleasantly with Kostya's flesh at the same time as my right index finger presses the trigger.

The second gunshot thunders, and the second guard's brains splatter the wall behind him with streaks of brown and red, like the bloody stool of a cow suffering from dysentery. It's fitting, I think. The guard clearly had shit for brains.

Kostya doubles over in pain. I turn to him now, fury shading the blue lines of Battle Mode in red.

I raise the gun to his head, and my finger itches to do what Joe would've done in my place—end my half-brother, here and now. Yet a part of me wavers. I'm not sure if it's Ada's influence, my kinship with my target, or my seeing that he's no longer a threat.

Also, Alan and Ada are watching me.

To quell the bloodthirstiness that threatens to make me press the trigger anyway, I remind myself that Kostya could be useful as a hostage. Even Joe would consider that a reason to let him live.

Instead of firing, I pistol-whip Kostya in the face with all my might. There's a crack of something breaking, and my half-brother falls to the ground in a limp heap.

Ada and Alan are staring at me in shock. If we had a family competition to see whose eyes could grow wider, I'm not sure who would win.

"React in VR," I tell them both via Zik messages. "We don't have time for that in the real world."

Hopeful they'll agree, I pop into VR and leap into action in the real world. My first objective is to grab Mr. Spock from his hiding spot.

I arrive in the VR meeting room in time to catch Ada screaming like a banshee. She's madly pacing the room's circumference, and I give her space to finish a few circles before I attempt any consolation. Alan is faring a little better, or so I assume. The kid is sitting at the conference table, face down, arms hugging the top of his head as though he's blocking punches.

After a couple of circles, I grab Ada into a bear hug. She resists for a moment, then softens into me.

Muhomor and Mitya look extremely uncomfortable, while Dominic seems eager to break something or someone.

"We're okay," I say soothingly to no one specific. I gently release Ada and make my way toward Alan. "We're going to be okay."

"Those five hundred guards swooping to your location might disagree." Muhomor pushes his sunglasses higher up his nose. "You're far from okay."

I'm hugging Alan when I hear a solid thump behind me.

Muhomor angrily yelps, "That's classic. Shoot the messenger."

"Sorry," Dominic says. "All that adrenaline."

Ada's comforting hands slide around my shoulders. I think she wants her turn to hug our son, so I move away.

"Mike had a good idea earlier," Mitya says with urgency. "Go to the lab to rejoin Joe. Once there, try to barricade yourselves in. The robots will arrive in about twenty minutes, so hopefully you can hold out until then. Dominic should be there around the same time."

I can tell Muhomor wants to say something, but he sees my expression and holds his tongue. Besides, I know what he's about to say because I'm thinking the same thing: what kind of a barricade can withstand such an overwhelming force?

"We're going," I say nonetheless. "Ada, Alan, can you guys move?"

Ada's chin is still quivering, but she nods.

"Think you can look after Alan?" I ask. "My hands will be full."

"Of course," she says. "I'll carry him."

"I can walk," Alan says in a barely audible whisper. "I'm too heavy for you."

"You only weigh thirty-five pounds," she says, her voice already steadier. "If the lab isn't far, I can carry you."

"No, seriously." Alan's voice sounds healthier, and I wonder if Ada's using her mom reverse-psychology Jedi mind tricks on him. "I can walk."

"While we move, I have a task for you two," I tell Mitya and Muhomor.

"A diversion?" Mitya asks.

"A very specific one," I say. "You now have the backdoor into the Brainocytes of the entire human population."

Muhomor's eyes light up—he sees where my mind is going. "Including the assholes at your location."

"Exactly," I say. "I want to get inside the heads of all the guards in this place and—"

"We don't have their Brainocyte IDs," Mitya interrupts.

"We don't need them if we create a proximity-based virus," Muhomor says. I notice he's VR-magicked himself a new pair of sunglasses. "Mike here can be our ground zero. Anyone within a mile of him will get the Payload app, which will activate instantly thanks to the nature of the backdoor."

"I wish I had time to design a virtual hell to trap these fuckers in," Alan mutters through his teeth with unusual viciousness.

"Language," I say on autopilot. Ada rewards me with a small smile.

"So when I get there, I'll get this virus also?" Dominic asks worriedly. The idea of spending time in a virtual hell of Alan's creation doesn't seem to appeal to him, and I can't blame him.

"We'll obviously use a harmless app whose main purpose will be to distract its victim," I say. "Anyone besides Alan have an app in mind?"

"I do." Some mischief returns to Ada's amber eyes. "How about the Join app?"

"That'll certainly distract them." I put my hand on her shoulder and give it a reassuring squeeze.

"What app?" Mitya and Muhomor ask in unison.

"I never submitted it to source control," Ada says apologetically. "I'll send you the code now. You can figure it out from there."

Though Ada, Alan, and I don't leave VR, we refocus on the real world. My wife grabs my son (of course she won that argument), and I put Mr. Spock in my pocket. I tell Ada and Alan to wait in the back of the room, reload my Glock with the bullets I found in a clip inside Kostya's back pocket, and open the door.

The two guards in the corridor each get a bullet to the head before they can raise their weapons.

I return to the room, reload again, and grab Kostya by one leg so I can drag him.

"Stay behind me," I say in a telepathic message once I'm in the corridor again.

Ada nods in VR and follows with heavy footsteps.

"You're barely walking," Alan complains. "Put me down."

Ada ignores Alan's plea, and I debate taking the kid from her; she's tiny herself, and our son is heavy for her small frame. But before I can intervene, she relents and sets him on the floor. All signs of fear are gone from my son's face, and I suspect I was right earlier about Ada's mind tricks.

Dragging my half-brother behind me like a sack of potatoes, I continue down the corridor. Ada follows with Alan behind her. I step over the bodies of the dead guards, taking sadistic pleasure in

Kostya's head banging against the floor as I drag him over the grisly obstacles.

When I reach the door to the lab, I make eye contact with Ada and put a finger to my lips. She nods gravely, kneels next to Alan, and hugs him protectively.

With a powerful kick, I take care of the lab door, and as soon as it swings in, I scan the space for targets. Two guards raise their guns in my direction while the white lab coat guys from earlier look on in horrified fascination.

I shoot the two guards without hesitation.

"Now." I address the rightmost lab coat guy, whose face is whiter than his clothes. "The person who tells me the Wi-Fi password gets to live."

The men glance at each other and begin shouting all at once, though the guy I singled out is the loudest.

Since I'm now recording every second of my life, I play back the cacophony of words and easily decouple the password. They've all given me the same string of digits and numbers. After a few moments of mental fumbling, I'm into the mansion's ultra-secure network.

I pass the log-in credentials to the VR room. "Go to town." I debate teasing Muhomor about being the one to get the password but decide to let him focus on the virus app.

It takes only a fraction of a moment to take control of the nearby cameras. Ada and Alan both look tense as they wait outside the room, but the good news is that I see no danger creeping up behind them.

"Another chance to live," I tell my captive audience. "Who has those nifty syringes that knock people out?"

Every hand goes up, and they pretty much all yell their version of, "Yes, me, pick me and kill the others."

"Inject yourselves with the syringes," I say. "Anyone not unconscious via the drug will be made permanently unconscious via a bullet to the head."

The lab coats must think there's a competitive component to

this injection command, because they race to avoid being the last man standing.

I let go of Kostya and enter the room.

Methodically, I give each seemingly unconscious man a strong kick to the head. If anyone's injected themselves with something other than a knockout drug, they'll give themselves away by grunting in pain. No one makes a peep. I guess they weren't faking. They'll have horrible headaches upon waking, but that's the least I could do as payback for their part in taking over my mind.

Returning to the doorway, I grab Kostya by the leg and drag him into the room.

"The room's clear," I tell Ada after another quick scan.

She walks in after me, and Alan follows her warily. They both pretend not to see the bodies of the dead guards, and I'm grateful for their charade.

I dump Kostya's limp body on one of the hospital beds nearest the door. Boris's unconscious form is taking up the bed on the opposite side, and Joe is lying on an adjacent bed.

"Joe," I say out loud. "Can you hear me?"

"We freed him from the mind control," Mitya tells me preemptively. "He must still be out, though."

I check the monitors hooked up to Joe and exhale in relief. His vitals are good—much better than Boris's arrhythmic heartbeat.

"I'm going to barricade the door we came through." I head back, looking for a piece of furniture that would best do the job. Through the lab's security camera, I spot Ada searching for heavy objects to place next to the other door.

Alan turns from my cousin, worry contorting his small face. "We have to summon an ambulance," he says in VR. "Uncle Joe needs urgent medical attention."

"A helicopter is flying in," Mitya says. "Should be there in twenty minutes or so."

"Make sure they—"

I don't hear what Alan says, because I spot a flurry of movement from the bed on Joe's right—a bed I assumed to be as empty as the other ones.

A skeletally thin figure is hiding under the sheet.

A female figure.

I begin turning back, gun already in my hand and the Battle Mode and aim assist apps ready. But by the time I make a quarter turn, the woman is holding my son like a human shield.

Through the camera in the back of the room, I see her emaciated hand press a small-caliber pistol to Alan's temple.

"Drop your gun, or I'll shoot the little bastard," she says in an eerily familiar voice. "Do it now."

\

THIRTY-SIX

"THAT VOICE REMINDS ME OF HOW EVERYONE UNDER CONTROL spoke," Mitya says, sounding horrified.

He's right. All the mind-control victims we heard spoke in that specific, high-pitched voice. And because they all happened to be male, their voices sounded falsetto—but it must be that this woman's vocal cords are the basis for that strange register.

Then I realize that even Kostya spoke in this way. Could my half-brother have been another victim? Has everyone been under her mind control all this time?

Still looking through the camera, I'm not surprised to recognize her face, though I still run the face recognition to confirm the bad news.

There's no denying it.

This is Masha.

"My literally crazy half-sister has Alan," I say to everyone, in case they haven't figured this out already. "I don't know what to do."

I push Battle Mode to its limits, but neither it nor my own experience with violence show me a way to disable Masha without Alan getting hurt.

I demonstratively drop my gun and stop turning.

"Turn toward me," Masha orders. "Slowly."

I complete my rotation, and she peeks over Alan's shoulder. I stare into those eyes—the eyes that remind me of what mine would look like if I hadn't slept for a year.

Through the camera, I see Ada grab the inert Kostya by the throat. "If you don't let go of my son, your brother is as good as dead," she threatens loudly.

I'm not sure Ada has enough strength to choke a grown man, plus I know how she feels about violence and murder. Then again, who knows what a mother, even one as peaceful as my wife, might do to save her child?

Masha's expression doesn't change. "You already killed poor Kostya," she says, and I realize her mind is damaged beyond repair. "I can't guide him anymore."

"*Guide him,*" Muhomor says. "That's a nice euphemism. I don't need to be a shrink to confirm her diagnosis."

"I agree," Mitya says. "She just admitted she was controlling her brother. When Mike knocked him out, she saw it as a disconnect in her controller app—so she probably really believes he's dead."

"Masha," I say as soothingly as my nerves allow. "Kostya is just unconscious."

"I don't care what happens to Kostya." She shoves the gun harder against Alan's temple, making him wince. "He put me into Serbsky Asylum. He tried to take over my brain. I only suffered him to live to use his resources to get to you."

"She sounds convinced of what she's saying," Dominic says worriedly. "The brother leverage isn't going to work."

"Look, Masha." I apply all the power of my enhanced cognition to search for a way out of the situation. "You took Kostya over and made him do your bidding. He's suffered enough. So have we. Let's just stop this."

"Muhomor," I shout in VR. "I want you to unleash that distraction now."

"I'm still making sure the virus is safe for releasing into the wild," Muhomor replies. "Besides, I bet it won't affect her—she'll have closed that GPS backdoor into her Brainocytes as soon as she could."

"Alan is an innocent," Ada says in the real world, her hands leaving Kostya's neck. "And he's your family."

"He has your husband's tainted blood." Masha glares at me with pure hatred. "This is for my father," she adds—and blood leaves my face as her finger starts to squeeze the trigger.

THIRTY-SEVEN

As Masha's finger continues its deadly arc, her jaw muscles tighten and she leans away from her target, as though worried about the blood that will splatter her in a moment. My mind is sifting through an infinitude of flawed actions I can take, but none of them will save Alan or improve his chances.

Ada's eyes are wide with horror. She must also see the inevitability of Masha's actions.

A burst of motion explodes right behind Masha.

One moment, Joe was lying unconscious on the hospital bed; the next, he's on his feet wielding a scalpel. In a blur of violence, he slashes at Masha's gun hand. The scalpel goes through her fingers like a warm spoon through half-melted ice cream.

As the gun clanks to the floor, her scream turns into a dreadful gargling sound.

Joe just sliced her throat.

"Incoming," Dominic announces urgently in VR. "Has anyone been scanning through the cameras?"

I frantically consult the camera that monitors the lab's second exit and see five masked guards approaching.

I reach down to grab my gun and roll over the nearest table to hide us. Ada snatches a gun from one of the dead guards and throws it to Joe. He catches it, but I can tell he's weak. Dealing with Masha must've taken all the energy he had.

"Muhomor," I shout in VR. "Are you ready with the fucking distraction now?"

"I'm not sure if—"

"You told me you used something you made for the government as a basis," Mitya says. "Wasn't it safe to start with?"

"If it was, I wouldn't need to further secure it, would I?" Muhomor retorts. "Fine, fine, give me another minute."

"Ada, Alan—on the floor," I scream in every mode of communication I can access.

The door swings open, and the first Nixon-masked guy appears. Spotting Joe, he shoots. I shoot back at exactly the same time.

Joe is lucky Boris is in the bed next to him. The bullet meant for Joe hits Boris, and the asshole's heart monitor goes berserk.

Joe's shooter is down. Although I didn't even get a chance to aim, I got him smack in the brain. Joe shoots the second guard in the chest, and as soon as the man topples over, I put a bullet in the head of the guard behind him.

A bullet whooshes by my shoulder, and Joe fires two more times.

Two more bodies hit the floor, and the room goes quiet. The only audible thing is the equipment beeping about Boris's lack of heartbeat.

"Ten more in the corridor," Dominic reports in the VR room. "If you can hold out another ten minutes, I'll be there."

"So will the robots, and the cops after that," Mitya says.

"They won't survive long enough." Muhomor puts up a giant mosaic of camera views, most of them showing people with guns running toward the lab. "I want the record to show that I don't have a choice but to unleash the virus now."

"Just do it already," Dominic says.

All eyes in VR are on Muhomor, but his face grows thoughtful. "Just a few more seconds."

Dominic unleashes a growling sigh. "I just want to make sure I understand what's about to happen. Ada wrote a trippy app that cross-wires people's minds, and you're about to wrap it in a virus and use the GPS backdoor to force it into the minds of anyone within a mile of Mike?"

"That pretty much sums it up." Ada chews on her lip as she stares at a screen showing a huge crowd of guards moving ever closer.

"What I don't get is why that app?" Dominic asks. I suspect he's trying to keep Ada from panicking about the oncoming danger. "Why not take control of your attackers the way Kostya did?"

"Even if that weren't an ethical abomination," Mitya says, "we simply don't have an app for that." He looks at Muhomor, his eyes narrowing.

If any one of us had an app like that, it would be Muhomor.

"I don't have anything of the sort," Muhomor says, looking offended.

"But surely there are better distraction apps that are possible?" Dominic asks.

"I doubt it," Ada says. "Besides, I'm hoping that seeing through our eyes and experiencing our memories, hopes, and fears will turn some of these men away from violence against us. It's hard to harm people you get to know so intimately."

"She has a point," I say, thinking back to our Joining. "Though this is all academic, because we're about to die. I don't have enough bullets for the next wave of guards."

"Fine, just shut up already," Muhomor says.

An icon shows up in my AROS interface in that eerie way Kostya and Masha placed them there before.

"Alan, Joe," I whisper as the app launches. "Prepare for a wild ride."

THIRTY-EIGHT

JUST LIKE THE PREVIOUS TIME, THE JOIN APP PUTS ALL MY SENSES into a blender and presses the "Crush Ice" button. The intensity is much greater than my Joining with Ada, which makes sense since I'm sensing through multiples of sensory organs. The exact number of people now participating is hard to discern; it's an ever-growing target. Each of the people I'm linked with are experiencing the same thing I am, and that creates a downward spiral of cross sensations until we all begin to lose ourselves in this experience.

There's a duality to my consciousness in this sensory Armageddon. The boundaries between me and countless people disappear, yet I still feel that I'm my individual self.

A part of me can still see what's happening in the cameras. The men in the view are ripping off their Richard Nixon masks in confusion. Their guns are on the floor, and they're staring around and sniffing the air as if they're experiencing the world for the very first time—which isn't unlike how I feel as well. The thoughts of the guards seep into my mind and vice versa, and I realize this experience is infinitely more intense for them because they aren't comfortable being in many places at once, unlike Tier I minds like me.

I feel vividly alive and completely immersed in the present moment. Freedom and contentment spread through our Joined minds.

"Well, I've never seen a better distraction," Mitya says from someplace. "I'm jealous I'm not running this app myself."

Mitya's words pull me out of the experience enough to realize that something is going awry. I'm seeing the world from the eyes of a helicopter pilot—a pilot who's lucky he put his flying vehicle under Einstein's control today.

"Shit," Muhomor says from the same distant place where I heard Mitya. "The news helicopter got there too soon. They're going to spread the virus outside the necessary range. You guys didn't give me time to put the proper precautions in place."

"I thought your virus only worked up to a mile away from Mike." Mitya's voice rises.

"Not from Mike—the nearest virus carrier," Muhomor says irritably. "The helicopter's only about seven hundred feet above them, well within the fucking range."

Looking out through the helicopter pilot's eyes, I can see he's well trained. As soon as his trippy experience begins, he notifies Einstein. The AI sensibly sends the aircraft back to the base.

"Shit," Muhomor yells. "We need to stop that helicopter."

"On it," Mitya says.

"You're too fucking slow." Muhomor sounds like he's gritting his teeth.

"Why couldn't you do it yourself?" Mitya snaps back.

"Because I'm trying to think of a way out of this mess," Muhomor replies, and they glare at each other.

"How fast does this virus spread?" Mitya asks after a moment.

"With the speed of electromagnetic waves, plus however long it takes to make a copy of itself—so very, very fast," Muhomor says, his voice subdued. "It's too late to stop the helicopter now."

He's right. A huge number of new people Join us, some driving, some flying in a plane.

"You realize what this means?" Mitya sounds awestruck.

"Yes, I do. It means you guys shouldn't have rushed me," Muhomor says. "I was working on safety procedures but—"

"You said you based the virus on the work you did for the government." Mitya's voice rises again. "What was the basis, Stuxnet?"

Stuxnet is the old cyberweapon allegedly created by the US and Israel to sabotage Iran's nuclear program. The thing got aggressive and spread indiscriminately worldwide instead of staying in Iran.

"The basis for my virus is none of your concern," Muhomor retorts. "I'm going to have to work on a countermeasure right now."

"Make sure your countermeasure stops the Join app, deletes any sign of your virus, and closes the GPS backdoor forever," Mitya says sternly.

"Don't teach an expert or you'll eat baked shit." The Russian proverb sounds ridiculous in Zik.

I don't follow the rest of my friends' conversation because in that moment, the Join virus reaches the town of Kingston. Suddenly, we're not just six hundred people but over twenty thousand.

Our former opponents are now on the floor, the overwhelming flood of sensations putting them into a near-comatose state.

"I'm looking at this code," Mitya says from far away. "They're only in the first phase of the app, the initialization. Once everyone's merged, their memories are exchanged and the other phases begin. I think you'd better finish your cure virus before that happens."

"How does it know when the initialization is complete?" Muhomor asks. "I mean, they're gaining more people as we speak."

"When there's no new participants for a few seconds," Mitya says.

"I guess there's an unseen benefit to how quickly it's spreading,"

Muhomor says. "They won't reach a new phase for a while."

The virus reaches Woodstock, and another five thousand people join the sensory roller coaster. Joe slumps back on his hospital bed. His Tier II Brainocytes can't cope with all that data and keep him upright at the same time.

Roxbury and Saugerties are next, and another twenty thousand people's senses are thrown into the mix. Now Ada, Alan, and I collapse on the floor. Dealing with this much sensory data is too much even for us.

"I better take over the antivirus task," Mitya says from even farther away.

"Why?" Muhomor asks, but he sounds scared. I think he knows what Mitya is about to say.

"Because the virus is spreading almost instantly, and as the radius of the infected area increases, so will the rate of newly infected people," Mitya says. "All of New York state is a moment away from being affected, and New Jersey will follow a moment later. You're not over a mile underground, which means you and everyone in your bunker are about to be victims of your own stupid virus."

"But you suck at this!" Muhomor shouts. "It will take you so much longer—"

If I were a Jedi, I would call what happens next "a great disturbance in the Force." My best guess is that this is what having millions of people Joined together must feel like.

It's hard to form an intelligible thought, but I still manage to guess that, as Mitya said, all of New York and New Jersey are now Joined with us. If correct, that means eighteen million Brainocyte users in the Empire State and seven million in the Garden State just Joined together—an unfathomable number of people.

If it were possible to die from data overload, I'd now be a corpse.

The lab around me completely goes away, replaced with the Join app universe. It's as though I'm sitting on the bottom of an ocean of sights, smells, tastes, odors, and kinesthetic sensations.

Another, bigger disturbance follows as three hundred million American Brainocyte users are infected. Canada and Mexico are next.

Though it's difficult to think, I observe that it's easy for the virus to spread from North America to South America. The spread to Europe is trickier to puzzle out, because the distance between Russia and Alaska is a little short of three thousand miles, while the virus has a mile-long spread. Then again, there are the Diomede Islands between the continents; those people have Brainocytes. Considering submarines in the oceans and aircraft in the skies, it's reasonable to fear that the virus is already on its way to Russia, with the rest of Europe and Asia to follow. From there, it will travel to Africa and who knows where else after that.

When you're experiencing so many points of view, time becomes one of those concepts that has no meaning anymore. It could be that a second just passed, but it just as easily could have been many hours. It's impossible to discern. To preserve my sanity, I try to ignore all senses but vision; we humans are a visually oriented species.

A tsunami of sights rolls over the shores of my mind. I gaze at the spire of the Empire State Building from every conceivable angle and, at the same time, take in the stately White House from even more viewpoints. All the eyes I see through seem to be very low to the ground. These people have collapsed from sensory overload just as I have—their eyes, like cameras, continue to feed their brains the never-ending input of vision, now shared throughout the world.

The Golden Gate and Brooklyn Bridge crisscross the skies and blend with other bridges from millions of eyes. I get a chance to see through colorblind eyes, as well as nearsighted and farsighted ones. The red-orange colors of the Grand Canyon instantly change to the blues of Niagara Falls, and places I don't recognize flit through my mind like a kaleidoscope on steroids.

If I had any doubts about the potential scope of this virus, they're erased by the next wave of images. Christ the Redeemer spreads his arms over the green hills of Rio De Janeiro, followed by Florence, Cologne, and St. Basil's Cathedral. Stonehenge and the Colosseum, the Eiffel Tower and the Pyramids (both the ones in Egypt and the ones in Mexico) all explode in my mental view. The Taj Mahal and the Great Wall of China, Mount Fuji and Yellowstone National Park splash into my mind, followed by billions of things just as beautiful but whose names I'm too overwhelmed to recall.

The onslaught of visual data seems to be equally overwhelming to all of us around the world. As one, we close our eyes.

For a moment, it's as though the whole planet has gone dark. At the same time, closing our eyes does nothing to calm our other senses, so we're just as overwhelmed by odors as we were by sights, only there is no way to close off these perceptions.

After forever, I find that I no longer feel other people's senses. The data blends into a paralyzing cacophony. Thoughts become a distant memory, and memories an abstract concept.

A group in Asia has discovered a way for us all to cope better with these worldwide crisscrosses of senses. I recognize the solution with relief. These people were experienced meditators before the Joining began, and they are guiding the rest of the participants to ignore all sensation but one: the in and out of our breathing.

Slowly, breath awareness spreads through the Joining, and after a hundred years of subjective experience, we—a large bulk of humanity—begin to breathe at the same pace. The world becomes the in and out of air in our bodies.

Soon, we become simply the breath. I almost don't recall what it is to be me. I'm a single ant in a colony of ants—no, even less than that. I'm more like a single, lonely byte of data in a multi-terabyte hard drive.

After another eternity of breath awareness, my mind is clear enough to think again. No new people have been added to the Joining for a while, which means the next phase of Ada's app is going to kick in at any moment: the part where each participant becomes aware of others' memories.

As though my thought has been made manifest, the memories of billions of people slam into every one of our Brainocyte-enhanced brains like an ice asteroid crashing into a searing desert planet.

I think I lose consciousness for a few years, though I might be experiencing one of Dominic's memories. There was a time in his life when he was completely cut off from the world.

Memories bombard me. One moment I'm Alan, playing with his friends, the rats. The next moment I'm Joe, pummeling a school bully and intentionally trying to break the kid's nose.

Memories of joy and memories of sorrow barrage me with unspeakable intensity. I try to cling to something familiar, like recollections of the best VR flicks, or the billions of memories of riding in a self-driving car for the first time, or the varying reactions to the realization that electricity is not something you need to treat as a scarce resource anymore.

With each memory, I become that person for that moment. I am an architect in Germany working on our next design and reminiscing about a middle-school adventure at the zoo. I'm a woman in France remembering how we felt when we nursed our first daughter.

The rate of memories speeds up.

I'm an elderly shepherd in the Caucasus Mountains, Gogi's homeland. I recall shepherding the old-school way, but I also marvel at the new method using Brainocytes and Augmented Reality, where our enhanced sheep avoid obstacles only they can see.

I'm a Russian woman who recalls joining the Pioneers in the Soviet days. Our mother ironed that little red scarf for us, and we were proud and excited. The memories clash with my own—I too was a Pioneer, though I saw it for the commie propaganda that it was and couldn't have cared less about the dubious honor.

I'm a man in Rwanda who remembers the horror of hunger and is grateful that our son has never been hungry, thanks to free electricity and other technological marvels.

I'm a software engineer in India, reminiscing about the awe we felt when we first used Brainocytes to search the web with our mind.

The memories stream into my mind like a waterfall, and soon I'm only seeing patterns: millions of people getting married, smiling at loved ones, holding hands, eating comfort foods, and on and on.

Interspersed with our memories are the tiniest moments of clarity—moments when the interconnected humanity realizes something together. When I Joined with Ada, this is when we understood and forgave each other every grievance we'd ever had in our marriage. Such a feat is too difficult to accomplish on this global scale, but we do feel as one for many moments, and we jointly realize how much every human being has in common, especially when it comes to the inner world of our minds—the only reality that truly matters.

The moments of clarity start to get longer, and that sense of enlightenment I felt when I Joined with Ada comes back a billion times stronger. I feel part of something unimaginably bigger than myself. There's a certainty in our minds that we're all intricately connected to something unfathomably complex. For a nanosecond, the entirety of humanity experiences what it's like to be in Heaven, or Nirvana, or Shangri-La, or Zion, or Utopia, or fill in the name of a place of ultimate contentment, spiritual and psychological fulfillment, and pure joy.

The pleasant sensations give way to fears. We realize just how vulnerable we are. We have weapons that can kill us all in a blink, and despite the new abundance of energy, we still have habits that could turn Earth into a human-unfriendly hellhole. These fears turn into a determination to do something about these problems, and that leads us back to feelings of connectedness and hope.

A subjective century later, the whirlwind of memories and enlightenments subsides enough that I have an independent thought, and I recall this is when The Cohens made an appearance when Ada and I first Joined. Could Ada's self-organization code really take advantage of so many brain resources? In terms of hardware, it could. She uses each user's own allocation on our servers, outside their biological and virtual brains, so no extra server space or CPU is necessary.

Ada also mentioned she leveraged Einstein as part of the app. Would he have enough processing cycles? Mitya once claimed that a Brainocyte-enhanced brain at Tier III can perform two quintillion computations per second. Quintillion is ten to the eighteenth power, a number that's difficult to comprehend even at a Tier I brain boost. That means this worldwide version of The Cohens would achieve a few billion quintillion computations per second.

In theory, Einstein should be able to cope with that. He usually has enough processing cycles to assist every single Brainocyte user anyway, and since we're all lying on the ground not doing much, the AI should currently be idle and ready to assist.

Sure enough, the feeling I had with Ada returns many billion-fold stronger.

"We think, therefore we are," we jointly contemplate with the intensity of an earthquake.

"You're still a philosopher," I mentally say after I recover my wits. "But I guess it's not appropriate to call you The Cohens anymore."

"That being was but a shadow of me," the humanity thinks back. This time, the force of the reply almost makes me lose consciousness. "If I had to name myself, I think Gaia or Earth might be more apropos."

"Gaia," I think back, after I overcome the sense that I'm not worthy to speak to a creature so terrifyingly vast. I have a million questions vying for the honor of being asked first, but I go with my first intuition. "What is it like to be you?"

"What is it like to be anything? The simplest answer is the analogy already in your mind, the one where you compare yourself to a neuron and us to a fully functioning brain," Gaia mentally booms.

This time, the force of the answer does make me black out.

THIRTY-NINE

I FLOAT IN A DARKNESS OF COMPLETE SENSORY DEPRIVATION, EAGER to awaken so I can resume conversing with Gaia.

A familiar voice pierces the darkness. "Mike, this is Mitya. I've finally worked out a way to stop everyone's Join app and patch up Kostya's backdoor. You and your family will be the first to receive the fix."

"Wait," I want to shout. "I have more questions for Gaia."

I'm not sure if Mitya hears my plea or not, but I find myself thrust back into my physical body.

It takes a few hours to reorient myself. When I do, I'm still lying in a fetal position on the floor of the lab. Now that I'm disconnected from the worldwide Joining, I'm filled with utter despair for its loss. All I want is to reconnect or cry myself to sleep.

"Mom, Dad," Alan whispers in a haggard voice. "Are you alive?"

"I'm here, sweetie," Ada says from the middle of the room. "Let me recover a moment, and I'll crawl your way."

"I'm alive too," I reply. It takes all my focus to make sure my voice doesn't break as I talk. "Not sure if I can crawl yet."

"Can we talk in VR while we recover?" Alan suggests.

I'm flooded with relief at Alan's amazing resilience. The kid already sounds like his usual self. I wish I could say the same about me.

With a huge effort of will, I recall how to put myself into the VR conference room and appear there. The light from the windows makes me narrow my eyes, and Mitya's smiling face makes me jealous. He wasn't part of the Joining, and there's no way he can understand how I feel. Especially since I'm not perfectly clear on that myself.

"You should've given the world a few more minutes of Joining," Ada says as soon as she appears. "Maybe even a couple of days."

"Right," Mitya says sarcastically. "I should've watched the human population die of thirst and hunger. Great idea."

"You don't understand what it was like," Alan says from behind me. I didn't even notice him appear.

"I know that the world is a mess," Mitya counters. "Thousands got hurt, and there are many casualties."

The idea that fellow beings might be in pain overwhelms me with an unusual surge of empathy. I sink into an office chair before I succumb to the fetal position here in VR as well as in the real world.

Muhomor shows up, his eyes wider than dollar coins. "I'm a genius! My virus did that. I should get the Nobel—"

Mitya places a hand on his shoulder. "Your virus is also the reason we need to undertake an enormous restoration project."

Using every screen as well as the table surface, Mitya shows us the problem. Though most vehicles are self-driving nowadays, plenty still work the old way, with humans in control. Additionally, countless bicyclists, skateboarders, bikers, and rollerblade riders crashed into things or fell when the Joining first began.

"Transport is only one of many issues," Mitya says as he puts up more imagery. "Surgeons were midsurgery, countless folks were swimming, or fixing roofs, or—"

"That is so awful," Alan says in a barely audible whisper. "Are you sure people died?"

"Logic would dictate so, unfortunately." Mitya closes his eyes for a moment. "It could be that some instinctive part of them retained enough mental capacity to float on water or not kill a patient, but as you can see"—he shows another slew of images of people in trouble—"there are plenty of problems to solve."

"What about the men who tried to kill us?" Ada asks. "I doubt they would want to continue their folly or even be ready to continue if they did, but you never know what—"

"I had them tied up as soon as the robots arrived at your location," Mitya says. "They'll have to wait for the police to take care of them, and the police will be busy for a while. Now if you don't mind, I'll have those same robots carry you to the hospital, just as I'll use the rest of our robots worldwide to try to get things back in order."

Everyone agrees to let Mitya handle things while we recover. Before long, I find myself in the metallic arms of one of the more sophisticated robot models. The same thing happens to Alan, Ada, and Joe, although it takes two robots to carry Dominic. He was almost at his destination when the Joining took him over with the rest of us.

During the trip to the hospital, the yearning for Joining dissipates, and I offer my services to Mitya since I can also control a small army of robots. By the time we get to the Kingston hospital, I've learned that some people are easier to rouse to action than others. Luckily, doctors and other emergency personnel tend to be in the easy-to-wake group.

"You need to get moving," Mitya says through the metallic voice of a robot that's kneeling next to a man wearing scrubs. "We have people who need help."

Just as we've seen elsewhere, it takes only a couple of prompts before the man gets up.

Once there are enough self-aware doctors here at Kingston, I get them to check over Alan, Dominic, Ada, and me. After a bunch of stitches for me, we all get the green light, except Joe, who needs jaw surgery and some bones set.

"I don't foresee any complications," says Dr. Jarvis, whom

Mitya flew out in a helicopter. "Your cousin might have trouble talking for a few days, but that's about the only concern I have."

I convince Dr. Jarvis to stay in the surgery room as our representative. If it's unusual, the hospital staff are too dazed to object.

I keep myself busy as I wait for Joe to come out of surgery. Every thread that I spawn grabs a robot and tries to help someone still in trouble. I soon learn that most Human++ employees are doing the same thing I am, and by the time we run out of robots, plenty of people have recovered enough to help physically.

In another half hour, the media recuperates too, and the news begins blaring all over the world.

"We don't know much about what just happened," says a blond newscaster from the ancient TV in the dingy waiting room. "Here at the studio, we're calling the event the Joining. Here are some theories about—"

I ignore the rest, though it's amusing to hear some of the crazy ideas, the least fantastic of which has something to do with alien visitors.

Using AROS, I check better news sources on the web and find that not every reporter is as clueless as the blonde on TV. Some are covering what's most important: that worldwide recovery is underway and people should pitch in. Some are providing useful instructions, while others are reflecting that this restoration project is as unprecedented as the Joining that precipitated it.

I agree. It's heartwarming to see people, sometimes via robots, come together to help each other literally get back on their feet.

"You can see your cousin now," the surgeon says. His face is haggard, and I'm amazed the man could perform something as complex as a surgery so soon after the Joining. "The procedure was a success."

Dr. Jarvis gives me the thumbs-up over the man's shoulder, and I listen to the surgeon's instructions on how, when, and where I'll next see my cousin. Ada, Alan, and I make our way to the recovery room and watch as they wheel Joe in and hook him up to the monitoring equipment.

"He should be up shortly," Dr. Jarvis says, walking toward the door. "I'll go make sure he has a competent nurse to look after him when I leave."

We patiently wait until Joe opens his eyes, which takes what feels like two hours. Finally, his eyes blink blue, and when he sees us all standing there, I see something new in his gaze. It's not exactly warmth, but it's as close as Joe's probably capable of.

"It wasn't me in that room," he telepathically tells me in Zik, the message heavy with dark emotions. "I couldn't get control back. I tried."

"Don't even think about that," I say. "Masha almost made me kill my family, and I couldn't wrest control back either. It wasn't a matter of strength of will. The technology affected your brain directly."

"There are more people here to visit him," a pretty nurse says as she enters. "You'll have to give them space."

Reluctantly, Ada, Alan, and I turn toward the door, but when I see who the visitors are, I'm stunned.

"Mom! Uncle Abe! And what is *she* doing here?" I point at Tatum.

"Why wouldn't Joe's girlfriend visit him at the hospital?" Mom asks, her forehead furrowing.

"She's not his—" I recall the lie we told Mom earlier and cringe, adding, "Never mind."

Mom, Uncle Abe, and most surprisingly Tatum look at my cousin with worry.

"He's fine," I reassure them. "He probably just needs lots of rest."

At the mention of "rest," the full weight of the post-adrenaline slump hits me like a freight train, and I yawn, loudly.

"You need rest as well," Mom says, her eyes narrowing. "But once you've rested, we're going to have words."

"Great," I mumble under my breath as I make my way to my chosen hospital bed. "Now I won't hear the end of it for at least a year."

"I'm going to take a quick nap too." Ada follows me and gets into the bed next to mine. "You and I are going to spend a week in the Bedroom once I wake up."

"I'll hold down the fort while the old people relax," Alan says, his eyes crinkling with mirth. "But I do suggest you learn those sleep tricks Mitya's researching after the dust settles."

"You're not quitting sleep until you're eighteen," Ada says as she pulls the hospital blanket to her chin. "Not unless you conduct statistically sound research to prove the safety of said tricks."

"Which he will do by the end of the month, I bet." I pull my own blanket up. It's fuzzy and smells like antiseptic. "Now if you'll excuse me, I'm long overdue to pass out."

Ada and Alan chuckle, but it sounds far, far away because true to my word, I instantly drift off to dreamless slumber.

EPILOGUE

"HAPPY BIRTHDAY, ALAN," UNCLE ABE ANNOUNCES IN ZIK AND raises his shot glass.

"Five years old." Mom clinks her vodka glass with her brother's. "He's becoming such a charming young man."

I raise my own glass and look over the enormous picnic table in the middle of Central Park. Everyone from Human++ is in attendance, as well as their families, all of Alan's online friends, and many acquaintances. Even the mayor is here with his whole retinue, and a couple of other politicians I hoped to avoid.

"I propose a toast." Gogi ceremoniously holds up a shot glass, the scar I gave him barely noticeable on his hand. "Once upon a time, in a village high up in the Georgian mountains, there lived a strange rat—"

"I think this toast panders to you," I privately tell Mr. Spock as I add more walnuts to the tiny tea saucer that serves as his plate. "I believe it traditionally involves an eagle."

"Eagles are scary." He moves his whiskers worriedly back and forth.

"Don't worry, bud. I made sure there are no birds of prey here in the park. If one tried to get you, our security people would scare it off."

Mr. Spock resumes his meal, and I half listen to Gogi as I survey everyone around the table. My eyes settle on Kostya, my half-brother, who's sitting with the family some eight feet away.

After last year's events, we eventually let Kostya return to Russia—but not before Joe got the whole story from him using a custom version of the Join app. As Joe's investigation revealed, Kostya developed the Control app to get his sister out of the asylum, not for revenge against me.

However, his research and development team did discover the GPS backdoor in a project for the Russian government—SVR connections Kostya met through his father. This backdoor work was separate at first from that of the Control app, but just when the GPS backdoor information was in its final stages, Masha took over everything. The handoff of the GPS backdoor to the SVR never happened. In hindsight, I guess the only positive development from that whole nightmare was that the SVR didn't get a monopoly on such a powerful weapon.

As to how Masha took over, from what Kostya could puzzle out, she seduced one of the scientists, an expert on Brainocyte IDs, and took over his mind as part of some bondage game. She used that opportunity to make the man do her bidding, and things went downhill from there.

Kostya sees me gaze his way and salutes me with his shot glass, his face unreadable. He looks pretty good, given all he's been through, but I know he spent most of the past year in therapy. And it's no wonder. I was in his shoes for mere minutes, and I still have horrific flashbacks. To my relief, he's never once raised the question of his sister's fate with me. He must mourn her, despite all she'd done, and if I'm honest, even I sometimes wish Joe hadn't had to kill her. She wasn't evil; she suffered from a psychosis that she channeled into misguided revenge.

The thought of my cousin makes me look across the table. Joe isn't drinking his vodka—he just brings it to his lips for a moment, then places the shot glass back and gives Gogi a dirty look. Joe takes his job as Head of Security seriously. He refuses to get intoxicated on duty and doesn't like Gogi to drink either, even though Gogi officially retired a few months ago. Joe looks from Gogi to me, and the dirty look turns into a frown. I guess he's still mad about the choice of venue. As he put it, Central Park is a "security clusterfuck."

To Joe's left, Tatum downs her shot and cringes like all the non-Russian guests. This is her first official family event, and so far, I'm impressed with her poise. That she didn't press charges against us a year ago wasn't so surprising; the Joining had that sort of effect on a lot of people. What was surprising (and maybe even shocking) is that she didn't run away screaming after visiting Joe at the hospital after his surgery. Instead, she was there for him during his recovery, and now there's some sort of strange relationship between the two. Einstein and I think she shows signs of Stockholm syndrome, but I don't bring this up with my cousin. Joe seems happy in his own creepy way, and that's good enough for me.

"Is it time for gifts now?" Alan asks after everyone's shot glass is finally on the table. "You know I don't like suspense."

Everyone laughs, and Ada stands up and says, "May the gift giving begin."

There's a quick tussle as to who goes first, and as people often do these days, we let Einstein decide. The AI creates a list, and I can't help but notice that some of the honorary guests, mostly politicians, get to go first—very Machiavellian on Einstein's part.

"I'm happy to announce that we named a street after you," the mayor tells Alan. "It's in the south part of Queens. We named it Cohen Street."

Alan accepts the gift graciously, but I suspect he couldn't care less about this honor. I'm impressed, however. Given that the mayor is letting us use this park as a birthday venue, I didn't think he'd bother with more gifts. I make a mental note to support his campaign at reelection—probably the reason he's here in the first place and why the gift he gave Alan is as much an honor to Ada and me.

Politicians have a nuanced relationship with us. After Joining Day, most countries blamed Muhomor's virus on each other, especially the United States and Russia. The reason was simple: Muhomor had created cyberweapons for both nations, making his work difficult to attribute to any one player. But when Human++ took responsibility for the Join app without taking responsibility for the virus that spread the app, the governments put two and two together. Instead of prosecuting us, they made the wise decision to seek our favor instead.

"Wow, a trip on a spaceship?" Alan's voice brims with excitement as he puts down the ancient-looking gizmo that JC just handed him. "You're the best grandpa ever."

Ada and I exchange glances. We both know that if the kid finally called JC his grandpa, he must be beyond himself with joy.

"It's from the both of us." JC clasps Mom's hand.

He isn't fooling anyone. Mom wouldn't dream of getting her grandson such a dangerous gift, and I marvel at the effort it must've taken JC to convince her to allow this. I also wonder if he overspent. Then I decide that as a major shareholder in Human++, he can afford it.

After our admission that the Joining app is ours, some thought Human++ would finally suffer financial ruin. In contrast, even after funding restoration costs and compensating the victims and their families, our company is enjoying the largest profits since its inception. As tales of the Joining spread to the distant corners of the globe, Brainocyte adoption rates have soared beyond our wildest dreams. Most people who didn't have them now do, even members of Real Humans Only. Not having Brainocytes today is what not having internet access was a few years ago; some people choose to avoid it, but they're an ever-shrinking minority.

"Thanks, Grandma," Alan says earnestly and runs up to hug Mom.

As usual, when those skinny arms wrap around her, Mom

melts into a puddle of oxytocin. I love to see such a joyful expression on her face. It's a pleasant change after all the months she grumbled at me about the risks I undertook on Joining Day. Even though she was part of the Joining, it provided no advantage at all when it came to quelling her ire afterward. I'd say it took at least a week for her to begin to forgive me for almost getting myself killed again, then another two weeks until she let go of the fact that I hadn't told her a single thing before going to Ada and Alan's rescue.

"A house in the Hamptons?" Alan's expression is unreadable when Muhomor finally presents his gift. "Thanks."

Ada and I pretend surprise, though in reality, we precleared Muhomor's gift this year. This house was the only acceptable thing our hacker friend could come up with. I'm not sure about Alan, but I like the idea of a house with an ocean view. It reminds me of the Miami condo we stayed in while we were rebuilding the penthouse, which is only now beginning to feel like home again.

The gift giving takes an hour. Once it's done, the party changes from a Russian-style sit-at-the-table affair to an American cocktail party, with guests mingling at an open bar spanning the whole park—which is as expensive as it sounds.

I waltz up to a large group of Alan's online friends and smile at the two I recognize from last year, John the professor and Margret the computer scientist. Unsurprisingly, the Joining is the topic of this group's conversation. It's really all anyone has talked about for the past year.

"Gaia allowed me to glimpse something the philosophers of old would've sold their souls for," John says, his voice all but shaking with conviction. "I can't believe your negativity."

Looking much calmer, Margret sips her martini and says, "I just fear what would've happened if Gaia had existed for a few seconds longer. I'm not saying we'd all be like the Borg, but we ought to think twice before—"

I carefully make my escape before someone pulls me into this discussion. The nature of Gaia has been a topic of unending debate and obsession. People have compiled a whole database of wisdom Gaia reportedly conveyed during the Joining, and volumes have been written trying to analyze and make sense of it all.

We in the Brainocytes Club decided to play it safe going forward. All future versions of the Join app have had that hive-mind component removed. It's impossible to grasp the motives of such a being as Gaia, yet all too easy to envision losing control. We used the same logic here as when we considered building an AI smarter than us. Mitya summarized our attitude well when he said, "I'd rather we ourselves become vast intelligences over time. Building one just because we can or by accident, as with Gaia, is too risky."

"Mr. Cohen," says a male voice as I'm walking back to Alan. "If I could have a word."

It's the mayor, so I smile and say, "Sir, it's an honor. What would you like to talk about?"

"The honor is mine," he says pompously. "And this has nothing to do with my official role. I'm just here as a Brainocyte user—"

"You want to know when you can try the Join app again?" I make a mental note to use Battle Mode the next time I want to avoid politicians.

He looks scared for a second, and I wonder if he's one of those crazy conspiracy theorists who thinks Human++ would bother reading the thoughts of Brainocyte users. But curiosity seems to win out, and he nods. "That's exactly what I was going to ask."

"This stays between us," I whisper. I lean so close I can smell the vodka on the guy's breath. "I'm only telling you as a thank-you for letting us have the birthday here."

The man's eyes widen—I have his complete attention.

"The next update of AROS, the one that's slated for next month, will contain the Join app." I pull back and wink conspiratorially. "Of course, this version of the app will only allow you to send the Join request to the people in your contact list. Those people will have to accept the request before any Joining can begin."

"A bit like the videoconferencing?"

"Right." I sip my champagne. "This means that Joining Day cannot repeat itself again anytime soon—not unless someone has the whole world in their contact list."

I debate if I should tell him that we're capping that list at a million people and decide against it.

"So Joining Day definitely can't recur?" His disappointment is obvious.

"Not anytime soon." I give him a bland smile. "Even if you hypothetically had billions of friends, you'd have to convince them all to Join on the same day and time with you."

He nods. As a politician, he can appreciate the daunting nature of such a feat.

"It's not that we don't want Joining Day to repeat, per se. We just want to design a way to prevent such an event from becoming another worldwide disaster. That will take time."

"How long?"

"I can't say for sure." It's too much for him to know the truth: that another Joining Day must wait until every human on Earth has a mind that's mostly nonbiological. That would allow the Joining to happen in tandem with normal activity, as it now does for us Brainocyte Club members when we Join our small circle together.

"That's a shame," he says. "I worry that the citizens of Earth will begin to forget Joining Day and drift back to their old ways."

I know exactly what he means. After Joining Day, hundreds of conflicts ended in cease-fires, even in the most troubled zones in the world. Multiple peace treaties were born, as well as aggressive global nuclear disarmament initiatives. The US president suggested international accords to protect the environment, and the Russian president backed him up. To Ada's delight, many countries passed laws against capital punishment and took other steps showing that human life became more valued.

"I've made a hobby of collecting the things people credit to Joining Day," I tell the mayor. "And as an expert, I don't think all the positive effects are only due to that Joining experience, no matter how transcendental it felt. Some of the good things we saw might simply be thanks to Brainocytes making people so much smarter. In any case, not everything resulting from Joining Day was rosy. So many people died, and then there are all the new religions that sprouted in the aftermath. Nor is it clear to me if the overhaul of some of the older religions is a good thing."

"You might be right," the mayor says, his gaze growing distant for a second. Then he refocuses on me and says, "My people tell me you have the all-clear for the fireworks now. When will you start?"

I glance up at the dusky sky. "Let's wait until it gets even darker. Thanks for all your help."

"No problem. Sorry we had to put limits on the fireworks."

"I totally understand." The bubbly and the vodka have given me a buzz that spreads comfortably through my body. "We're going to enhance the real fireworks with a bunch of Augmented Reality ones, so Alan will still see the crazy display we had planned."

"I'm glad to hear that. I'll let you get back to your party."

I make my way through the crowds and locate Ada and Alan in a circle with Muhomor and Dominic, with Mitya in the middle.

"Hey, all," I say as I approach their comfortable meadow. "Is this an impromptu Brainocytes Club meeting?"

Muhomor raises a big bottle of vodka to his mouth and takes a generous gulp. "Just drunken musings."

I disable AR and still see Mitya's shimmering figure glowing blue in the dark. He's here as a hologram, something he does now when he wants to have a semi-physical presence.

"I was just asking Alan if he thinks we need to change the world some more," Mitya says in the slurred speech that means he's either clowning around or simulating intoxication inside his virtual body and brain. "I was in the middle of going over what we've accomplished already—things like enhanced brain capacity, Augmented and virtual reality, unimaginable new hardware, advances in robotics and AI... We even learned how to cheat death."

"Partial credit for that." Alan laughs and runs his hand through Mitya's holographic image. "At least in my opinion."

"I'd say my existence is superior to your meat-oriented one, birthday boy." Mitya floats up and lands on a branch of a nearby tree. "But what do you say, brother?"

A slightly taller version of Mitya's hologram appears where the original Mitya was just standing. This taller Mitya glows a shade of green.

We all stare.

Of course Mitya could already project multiple versions of himself using holograms, but I strongly suspect something else is happening. I don't share my suspicions with the others, because I'm sure Mitya wants to be the one to explain.

"Alan, I thought you might enjoy this announcement on your birthday," Mitya says triumphantly from the tree. "This is Dmitriy —the second me I hid from you to make him a surprise guest."

My guess was spot on. For the past year, Mitya has been using his new advantages, such as faster thought processing and less need for sleep, to escalate our hardware production to previously unseen levels. His efforts have resulted in more powerful chips and server types. He always claimed his work was aimed at supporting the new user base and bringing higher-tier brain boost capabilities to more people, but I knew there was more to it.

Now I see that I was right. He wanted to fulfill an idea we first discussed after his resurrection a year ago, and this taller version of him, this Dmitriy, is the result.

"Hello, Alan," Dmitriy says with a bow. "I am Mitya's superior copy, at your service. I'm smarter, handsomer, faster, and even taller than the original. I therefore propose my maker be called Mini-Me going forward."

"You didn't inherit a better sense of humor from the mini-you, but nice to meet you." Ada winks at the newcomer.

"The more Mityas we have, the merrier," Alan says. His eyes

excitedly dart up to the blue hologram and then back down to the green version. "This day just got that much better."

"Just as long as you guys remember that you and your mini-you only get a single vote to share at the next Braincocytes Club meeting," Muhomor grumbles.

"I hope that's open for discussion." Mitya lands next to his other self. "Dmitriy is going to be as much a person as me in the eyes of the law, so—"

"I'm sorry if my appearance interrupted your earlier conversation," Dmitriy says. "You were just talking about your impact on the world. As it so happens, Mitya's motivation in creating me was to effect change in the world—more specifically, to kick-start an unprecedented hardware revolution."

Dmitriy pauses for dramatic effect, and it's clear he's superior to Mitya even in his ability to present an effective speech.

"We'd like to build the ultimate computer, given the laws of physics as we know them today—to cram as many computations as possible into a given piece of matter. We have some basic designs already, and once you review them, I think you'll agree that we can push the limits of nanocomputing very close to their ultimate physical limits. Scientists made molecule-sized transistors and storage back in the late twenty-teens, and over the past year, we made these practical. Our ambition is to build a two-pound, laptop-sized computer capable of ten to the forty-second power computations per second—and to do so within Alan's biological lifetime."

"Such a big number is hard for even our brains to fathom," Mitya says. "To provide some comparison, the laptop Dmitriy describes would be able to perform the equivalent of all human thought over the last ten thousand years in ten microseconds or so. Another way you can look at it is this: this laptop-sized device could be used to run the brains of a billion civilizations of beings such as the two of us—where a civilization is defined as ten billion of us."

"And that's just in a laptop-sized device," Dmitriy picks up.

790

"There's no reason we can't build much bigger devices, even data centers. In the far future, we can cover the Earth with a computer substrate. Later still, it could fill the whole solar system—à la the matrioshka brain."

I try to imagine what we could do with the vast computers Mitya and Dmitriy have conjured up, but it hurts my alcohol-soaked biological brain.

"I now want this magic laptop as a birthday gift," Alan says, his voice filled with awe. "It would let me take world-building projects to the next level and create a whole multiverse of virtual univer—"

"A bunch of Rat Worlds, but for people?" Muhomor crinkles his nose in distaste. "I hope you're benevolent enough to randomly generate the denizens of these worlds. It would be very cruel to upload real people just to cast them into such a purgatory."

"I'm sure there are people who'd be glad to volunteer." Alan's eyes look distant—he's already lost in his fantasy. "The worlds could be thematically different, some optimized for educational value, some for pure entertainment. For myself, I'll make a world where sorcery is possible, and maybe a world where superpowers exist, and perhaps something with aliens or monsters—"

"And maybe a world with sexy vampires for your mom's birth-day?" I say jokingly and get an elbow from Ada in my ribs. She thinks her reading preferences are a closely guarded secret, but Muhomor hacked her Amazon account long ago.

"I can make anything," Alan replies excitedly. "Even mash-ups, like a world with vampiric aliens or—"

"A very good argument could be made that we already live in a place akin to what Alan is envisioning." Ada rubs her temples with her fingers. She's only drinking wine this evening, but it doesn't take much to overwhelm her tiny frame. "If you think about it statistically, is a random person likelier to be one of the mere seven billion lucky people who live in the 'original and thus real' universe, or one of the billions of billions that can be easily emulated on the laptop Mitya will probably give Alan for some future birthday? The odds are not in our favor."

"Babe," I say to her privately, "my brain officially hurts. Is that a sign that it's a real brain or one emulated by an Alan of the future?"

"It's a sign that we should start the fireworks," she answers with a grin.

Out loud, she says in a raised voice, "If I can get everyone's attention on the sky."

Hundreds of faces turn up. Following their example, I gaze at the blackness just in time to catch the first colorful explosion, a spherical halo of blinking stars. The next explosion follows on the heels of the first, with comet-like tails chasing each of the sparks. The effects escalate with each subsequent round: a willow-tree-like gold stars beneath a plumage that reminds me of the Firebird, followed by visuals with such complex mathematical patterns that only a pyrotechnician with a brain boost could've designed them.

I suspect all of New York City is gaping at the sky at this point.

Alan's mouth opens wider and wider as the fireworks continue. Ada and I exchange knowing glances. This is just the real-world event. The crazy Augmented Reality fireworks to follow will make this seem like backyard firecrackers in comparison.

"I have to say something." I project my voice virtually as well as through my flesh-and-blood mouth here, next to my friends and family. When all eyes turn toward me, I raise my glass in a toast. "What an exciting time to be alive!"

Everyone cheers amidst the explosive blasts of the fireworks, and I knock back my drink as I Join with Ada, my joy intensifying as her hopes and dreams blend with my own.

We're together, we're alive, and the entire universe will soon be our home.

THE END

SNEAK PEEKS

Thank you for reading! If you would consider leaving a review, it would be greatly appreciated.

Neural Web concludes the *Human++* series, but more books of mine are coming soon. If you'd like to be notified when they're out, please sign up for my new release email list at www.dimazales.com.

Other series of mine include:

- *The Last Humans* — futuristic sci-fi/dystopian novels similar to *The Hunger Games*, *Divergent*, and *The Giver*
- *Mind Dimensions* — urban fantasy with a sci-fi flavor
- *The Sorcery Code* — epic fantasy

I also collaborate with my wife on sci-fi romance, so if you don't mind erotic material, you can check out *Close Liaisons* by Anna Zaires.

If you enjoy audiobooks, please visit my website to check out this series and our other books in audio format.

And now, please turn the page for a sneak peek at *Oasis (The Last Humans: Book 1)*, *The Thought Readers (Mind Dimensions: Book 1), and The Sorcery Code.*

EXCERPT FROM OASIS

My name is Theo, and I'm a resident of Oasis, the last habitable area on Earth. It's meant to be a paradise, a place where we are all content. Vulgarity, violence, insanity, and other ills are but a distant memory, and even death no longer plagues us.

I was once content too, but now I'm different. Now I hear a voice in my head, and she tells me things no imaginary friend should know. Her name is Phoe, and she is my delusion.

Or is she?

––––––

Fuck. Vagina. Shit.

I pointedly think these forbidden words, but my neural scan shows nothing out of the ordinary compared to when I think phonetically similar words, such as *shuck, angina,* or *fit.* I don't see any evidence of my brain being corrupted, though maybe it's already so damaged that things can't get any worse. Maybe I need another test subject—another 'impressionable' twenty-three-year-old Youth such as myself.

After all, I might be mentally ill.

"Oh, Theo. Not this again," says an overly friendly, high-pitched female voice. "Besides, the words do have an effect on your brain. For instance, the part of your brain responsible for disgust lights up at the mention of 'shit,' yet doesn't for 'fit.'"

This is Phoe speaking. This time, she's not a voice inside my head; instead, it's as though she's in the thick bushes behind me, except there's no one there.

I'm the only person on this strip of grass.

Nobody else comes here because the Edge is only a couple of feet away. Few residents of Oasis like looking at the dreary line dividing where our habitable world ends and the deserted wasteland of the Goo begins. I don't mind it, though.

Then again, I may be crazy—and Phoe would be the reason for that. You see, I don't think Phoe is real. She is, as far as my best guess goes, my imaginary friend. And her name, by the way, is pronounced 'Fee,' but is spelled 'P-h-o-e.'

Yes, that's how specific my delusion is.

"So you go from one overused topic straight into another." Phoe snorts. "My so-called realness."

"Right," I say. Though we're alone, I still answer without moving my lips. "Because I *am* imagining you."

She snorts again, and I shake my head. Yes, I just shook my head for the benefit of my delusion. I also feel compelled to respond to her.

"For the record," I say, "I'm sure the taboo word 'shit' affects the parts of my brain that deal with disgust just as much as its more acceptable cousins, such as 'fecal matter,' do. The point I was trying to make is that the word doesn't hurt or corrupt my brain. There's nothing special about these words."

"Yeah, yeah." This time, Phoe is inside my head, and she sounds mocking. "Next you'll tell me how back in the day, some of the forbidden words merely referred to things like female dogs, and how there are words in the dead languages that used to be just as taboo, yet they are not currently forbidden because they have lost their power. Then you're likely to complain that, though the brains of both genders are nearly identical, only males are not allowed to say 'vagina,' et cetera."

I realize I was about to counter with those exact thoughts, which means Phoe and I have talked about this quite a bit. This is what happens between close friends: they repeat conversations. Doubly so with imaginary friends, I figure. Though, of course, I'm probably the only person in Oasis who actually has one.

Come to think of it, wouldn't *every* conversation with your imaginary friend be redundant since you're basically talking to yourself?

"This is my cue to remind you that I'm real, Theo." Phoe purposefully states this out loud.

I can't help but notice that her voice came slightly from my right, as if she's just a friend sitting on the grass next to me—a friend who happens to be invisible.

"Just because I'm invisible doesn't mean I'm not real," Phoe responds to my thought. "At least *I'm* convinced that I'm real. I would be the crazy one if I *didn't* think I was real. Besides, a lot of evidence points to that conclusion, and you know it."

"But wouldn't an imaginary friend *have* to insist she's real?" I can't resist saying the words out loud. "Wouldn't this be part of the delusion?"

"Don't talk to me out loud," she reminds me, her tone worried. "Even when you subvocalize, sometimes you imperceptibly move your neck muscles or even your lips. All those things are too risky. You should just think your thoughts at me. Use your inner voice. It's safer that way, especially when we're around other Youths."

"Sure, but for the record, that makes me feel even nuttier," I reply, but I subvocalize my words, trying my best not to move my lips or neck muscles. Then, as an experiment, I think, "Talking to you inside my head just highlights the impossibility of you and thus makes me feel like I'm missing even more screws."

"Well, it shouldn't." Her voice is inside my head now, yet it still sounds high-pitched. "Back in the day, when it was not forbidden to be mentally ill, I imagine it made people around you uncomfortable if you spoke to your imaginary friends out loud." She chuckles, but there's more worry than humor in her voice. "I have no idea what would happen if someone thought you were crazy, but I have a bad feeling about it, so please don't do it, okay?"

"Fine," I think and pull at my left earlobe. "Though it's overkill to do it here. No one's around."

"Yes, but the nanobots I told you about, the ones that permeate everything from your head to the utility fog, *can* be used to monitor this place, at least in theory."

"Right. Unless all this conveniently invisible technology you keep telling me about is as much of a figment of my imagination as you are," I think at her. "In any case, since no one seems to know about this tech, how can they use it to spy on me?"

"Correction: no Youth knows, but the others might," Phoe counters patiently. "There's too much we still don't know about Adults, not to mention the Elderly."

"But if they can access the nanocytes in my mind, wouldn't they have access to my thoughts too?" I think, suppressing a shudder. If this is true, I'm utterly screwed.

"The fact that you haven't faced any consequences for your frequently wayward thoughts is evidence that no one monitors them in general, or at least, they're not bothering with yours specifically," she responds, her words easing my dread. "Therefore, I think monitoring thoughts is either computationally prohibitive or breaks one of the bazillion taboos on the proper use of technology—rules I have a very hard time keeping track of, by the way."

"Well, what if using tech to listen in on me is also taboo?" I retort, though she's beginning to convince me.

"It may be, but I've seen evidence that can best be explained as the Adults spying." Her voice in my head takes on a hushed tone. "Just think of the time you and Liam made plans to skip your Physics Lecture. How did they know about that?"

I think of the epic Quietude session we were sentenced to and how we both swore we hadn't betrayed each other. We reached the same conclusion: our speech is not secure. That's why Liam, Mason, and I now often speak in code.

"There could be other explanations," I think at Phoe. "That conversation happened during Lectures, and someone could've overheard us. But even if they hadn't, just because they monitor us during class doesn't mean they would bother monitoring this forsaken spot."

"Even if they don't monitor *this* place or anywhere outside of the Institute, I still want you to acquire the right habit."

"What if I speak in code?" I suggest. "You know, the one I use with my non-imaginary friends."

"You already speak too slowly for my liking," she thinks at me with clear exasperation. "When you speak in that code, you sound ridiculous and drastically increase the number of syllables you say. Now if you were willing to learn one of the dead languages…"

"Fine. I will 'think' when I have to speak to you," I think. Then I subvocalize, "But I will also subvocalize."

"If you must." She sighs out loud. "Just do it the way you did a second ago, without any voice musculature moving."

Instead of replying, I look at the Edge again, the place where the serene greenery under the Dome meets the repulsive ocean of the desolate Goo—the ever-replicating parasitic technology that converts matter into itself. The Goo is what's left of the world outside the Dome barrier, and if the barrier were to ever come down, the Goo would destroy us in short order. Naturally, this view evokes all sorts of unpleasant feelings, and the fact that I'm voluntarily gazing at it must be yet another sign of my shaky mental state.

"The thing *is* decidedly gross," Phoe reflects, trying to cheer me up, as usual. "It looks like someone tried to make Jell-O out of vomit and human excrement." Then, with a mental snicker, she adds, "Sorry, I should've said 'vomit and shit.'"

"I have no idea what Jell-O is," I subvocalize. "But whatever it is, you're probably spot on regarding the ingredients."

"Jell-O was something the ancients ate in the pre-Food days," Phoe explains. "I'll find something for you to watch or read about it, or if you're lucky, they might serve it at the upcoming Birth Day fair."

"I hope they do. It's hard to learn about food from books or movies," I complain. "I tried."

"In this case, you might," Phoe counters. "Jell-O was more about texture than taste. It had the consistency of jellyfish."

"People actually ate those slimy things back then?" I think in disgust. I can't recall seeing that in any of the movies. Waving toward the Goo, I say, "No wonder the world turned to this."

"They didn't eat it in most parts of the world," Phoe says, her voice taking on a pedantic tone. "And Jell-O was actually made out of partially decomposed proteins extracted from cow and pig hides, hooves, bones, and connective tissue."

"Now you're just trying to gross me out," I think.

"That's rich, coming from you, Mr. Shit." She chuckles. "Anyway, you have to leave this place."

"I do?"

"You have Lectures in half an hour, but more importantly, Mason is looking for you," she says, and her voice gives me the impression she's already gotten up from the grass.

I get up and start walking through the tall shrubbery that hides the Goo from the view of the rest of Oasis Youths.

"By the way"—Phoe's voice comes from the distance; she's simulating walking ahead of me—"once you verify that Mason *is* looking for you, *do* try to explain how an imaginary friend like me could possibly know something like that... something you yourself didn't know."

—

If you'd like to learn more, please visit www.dimazales.com.

EXCERPT FROM THE THOUGHT READERS

Everyone thinks I'm a genius.

Everyone is wrong.

Sure, I finished Harvard at eighteen and now make crazy money at a hedge fund. But that's not because I'm unusually smart or hard-working.

It's because I cheat.

You see, I have a unique ability. I can go outside time into my own personal version of reality—the place I call "the Quiet"—where I can explore my surroundings while the rest of the world stands still.

I thought I was the only one who could do this—until I met *her*.

My name is Darren, and this is how I learned that I'm a Reader.

———

Sometimes I think I'm crazy. I'm sitting at a casino table in Atlantic City, and everyone around me is motionless. I call this the *Quiet,* as though giving it a name makes it seem more real—as though giving it a name changes the fact that all the players around me are frozen like statues, and I'm walking among them, looking at the cards they've been dealt.

The problem with the theory of my being crazy is that when I 'unfreeze' the world, as I just have, the cards the players turn over are the same ones I just saw in the Quiet. If I were crazy, wouldn't these cards be different? Unless I'm so far gone that I'm imagining the cards on the table, too.

But then I also win. If that's a delusion—if the pile of chips on my side of the table is a delusion—then I might as well question everything. Maybe my name isn't even Darren.

No. I can't think that way. If I'm really that confused, I don't want to snap out of it—because if I do, I'll probably wake up in a mental hospital.

Besides, I love my life, crazy and all.

My shrink thinks the Quiet is an inventive way I describe the 'inner workings of my genius.' Now that sounds crazy to me. She also might want me, but that's beside the point. Suffice it to say, she's as far as it gets from my datable age range, which is currently right around twenty-four. Still young, still hot, but done with school and pretty much beyond the clubbing phase. I hate clubbing, almost as much as I hated studying. In any case, my shrink's explanation doesn't work, as it doesn't account for the way I know things even a genius wouldn't know—like the exact value and suit of the other players' cards.

I watch as the dealer begins a new round. Besides me, there are three players at the table: Grandma, the Cowboy, and the Professional, as I call them. I feel that now almost imperceptible fear that accompanies the phasing. That's what I call the process: phasing into the Quiet. Worrying about my sanity has always facilitated phasing; fear seems helpful in this process.

I phase in, and everything gets quiet. Hence the name for this state.

It's eerie to me, even now. Outside the Quiet, this casino is very loud: drunk people talking, slot machines, ringing of wins, music —the only place louder is a club or a concert. And yet, right at this moment, I could probably hear a pin drop. It's like I've gone deaf to the chaos that surrounds me.

Having so many frozen people around adds to the strangeness of it all. Here is a waitress stopped mid-step, carrying a tray with drinks. There is a woman about to pull a slot machine lever. At my own table, the dealer's hand is raised, the last card he dealt hanging unnaturally in midair. I walk up to him from the side of the table and reach for it. It's a king, meant for the Professional. Once I let the card go, it falls on the table rather than continuing to float as before—but I know full well that it will be back in the air, in the exact position it was when I grabbed it, when I phase out.

The Professional looks like someone who makes money playing poker, or at least the way I always imagined someone like that might look. Scruffy, shades on, a little sketchy-looking. He's been doing an excellent job with the poker face—basically not twitching a single muscle throughout the game. His face is so expressionless that I wonder if he might've gotten Botox to help maintain such a stony countenance. His hand is on the table, protectively covering the cards dealt to him.

I move his limp hand away. It feels normal. Well, in a manner of speaking. The hand is sweaty and hairy, so moving it aside is unpleasant and is admittedly an abnormal thing to do. The normal part is that the hand is warm, rather than cold. When I was a kid, I expected people to feel cold in the Quiet, like stone statues.

With the Professional's hand moved away, I pick up his cards. Combined with the king that was hanging in the air, he has a nice high pair. Good to know.

I walk over to Grandma. She's already holding her cards, and she has fanned them nicely for me. I'm able to avoid touching her wrinkled, spotted hands. This is a relief, as I've recently become conflicted about touching people—or, more specifically, women—in the Quiet. If I had to, I would rationalize touching Grandma's hand as harmless, or at least not creepy, but it's better to avoid it if possible.

In any case, she has a low pair. I feel bad for her. She's been losing a lot tonight. Her chips are dwindling. Her losses are due, at least partially, to the fact that she has a terrible poker face. Even before looking at her cards, I knew they wouldn't be good because I could tell she was disappointed as soon as her hand was dealt. I also caught a gleeful gleam in her eyes a few rounds ago when she had a winning three of a kind.

This whole game of poker is, to a large degree, an exercise in reading people—something I really want to get better at. At my job, I've been told I'm great at reading people. I'm not, though; I'm just good at using the Quiet to make it seem like I am. I do want to learn how to read people for real, though. It would be nice to know what everyone is thinking.

What I don't care that much about in this poker game is money. I do well enough financially to not have to depend on hitting it big gambling. I don't care if I win or lose, though quintupling my money back at the blackjack table was fun. This whole trip has been more about going gambling because I finally can, being twenty-one and all. I was never into fake IDs, so this is an actual milestone for me.

Leaving Grandma alone, I move on to the next player—the Cowboy. I can't resist taking off his straw hat and trying it on. I wonder if it's possible for me to get lice this way. Since I've never been able to bring back any inanimate objects from the Quiet, nor otherwise affect the real world in any lasting way, I figure I won't be able to get any living critters to come back with me, either.

Dropping the hat, I look at his cards. He has a pair of aces—a better hand than the Professional. Maybe the Cowboy is a professional, too. He has a good poker face, as far as I can tell. It'll be interesting to watch those two in this round.

Next, I walk up to the deck and look at the top cards, memorizing them. I'm not leaving anything to chance.

When my task in the Quiet is complete, I walk back to myself. Oh, yes, did I mention that I see myself sitting there, frozen like the rest of them? That's the weirdest part. It's like having an out-of-body experience.

Approaching my frozen self, I look at him. I usually avoid doing this, as it's too unsettling. No amount of looking in the mirror—or seeing videos of yourself on YouTube—can prepare you for viewing your own three-dimensional body up close. It's not something anyone is meant to experience. Well, aside from identical twins, I guess.

It's hard to believe that this person is me. He looks more like some random guy. Well, maybe a bit better than that. I do find this guy interesting. He looks cool. He looks smart. I think women would probably consider him good-looking, though I know that's not a modest thing to think.

It's not like I'm an expert at gauging how attractive a guy is, but some things are common sense. I can tell when a dude is ugly, and this frozen me is not. I also know that generally, being good-looking requires a symmetrical face, and the statue of me has that. A strong jaw doesn't hurt, either. Check. Having broad shoulders is a positive, and being tall really helps. All covered. I have blue eyes—that seems to be a plus. Girls have told me they like my eyes, though right now, on the frozen me, the eyes look creepy—glassy. They look like the eyes of a lifeless wax figure.

Realizing that I'm dwelling on this subject way too long, I shake my head. I can just picture my shrink analyzing this moment. Who would imagine admiring themselves like this as part of their mental illness? I can just picture her scribbling down *Narcissist*, underlining it for emphasis.

Enough. I need to leave the Quiet. Raising my hand, I touch my frozen self on the forehead, and I hear noise again as I phase out.

Everything is back to normal.

The card that I looked at a moment before—the king that I left on the table—is in the air again, and from there it follows the trajectory it was always meant to, landing near the Professional's hands. Grandma is still eyeing her fanned cards in disappointment, and the Cowboy has his hat on again, though I took it off him in the Quiet. Everything is exactly as it was.

On some level, my brain never ceases to be surprised at the discontinuity of the experience in the Quiet and outside it. As humans, we're hardwired to question reality when such things happen. When I was trying to outwit my shrink early on in my therapy, I once read an entire psychology textbook during our session. She, of course, didn't notice it, as I did it in the Quiet. The book talked about how babies as young as two months old are surprised if they see something out of the ordinary, like gravity appearing to work backwards. It's no wonder my brain has trouble adapting. Until I was ten, the world behaved normally, but everything has been weird since then, to put it mildly.

Glancing down, I realize I'm holding three of a kind. Next time, I'll look at my cards before phasing. If I have something this strong, I might take my chances and play fair.

The game unfolds predictably because I know everybody's cards. At the end, Grandma gets up. She's clearly lost enough money.

And that's when I see the girl for the first time.

She's hot. My friend Bert at work claims that I have a 'type,' but I reject that idea. I don't like to think of myself as shallow or predictable. But I might actually be a bit of both, because this girl fits Bert's description of my type to a T. And my reaction is extreme interest, to say the least.

Large blue eyes. Well-defined cheekbones on a slender face, with a hint of something exotic. Long, shapely legs, like those of a dancer. Dark wavy hair in a ponytail—a hairstyle that I like. And without bangs—even better. I hate bangs—not sure why girls do that to themselves. Though lack of bangs is not, strictly speaking, in Bert's description of my type, it probably should be.

I continue staring at her. With her high heels and tight skirt, she's overdressed for this place. Or maybe I'm underdressed in my jeans and t-shirt. Either way, I don't care. I have to try to talk to her.

I debate phasing into the Quiet and approaching her, so I can do something creepy like stare at her up close, or maybe even snoop in her pockets. Anything to help me when I talk to her.

I decide against it, which is probably the first time that's ever happened.

I know that my reasoning for breaking my usual habit—if you can even call it that—is strange. I picture the following chain of events: she agrees to date me, we go out for a while, we get serious, and because of the deep connection we have, I come clean about the Quiet. She learns I did something creepy and has a fit, then dumps me. It's ridiculous to think this, of course, considering that we haven't even spoken yet. Talk about jumping the gun. She might have an IQ below seventy, or the personality of a piece of wood. There can be twenty different reasons why I wouldn't want to date her. And besides, it's not all up to me. She might tell me to go fuck myself as soon as I try to talk to her.

Still, working at a hedge fund has taught me to hedge. As crazy as that reasoning is, I stick with my decision not to phase because I know it's the gentlemanly thing to do. In keeping with this unusually chivalrous me, I also decide not to cheat at this round of poker.

As the cards are dealt again, I reflect on how good it feels to have done the honorable thing—even without anyone knowing. Maybe I should try to respect people's privacy more often. As soon as I think this, I mentally snort. *Yeah, right.* I have to be realistic. I wouldn't be where I am today if I'd followed that advice. In fact, if I made a habit of respecting people's privacy, I would lose my job within days—and with it, a lot of the comforts I've become accustomed to.

Copying the Professional's move, I cover my cards with my hand as soon as I receive them. I'm about to sneak a peek at what I was dealt when something unusual happens.

The world goes quiet, just like it does when I phase in... but I did nothing this time.

And at that moment, I see *her*—the girl sitting across the table from me, the girl I was just thinking about. She's standing next to me, pulling her hand away from mine. Or, strictly speaking, from my frozen self's hand—as I'm standing a little to the side looking at her.

She's also still sitting in front of me at the table, a frozen statue like all the others.

My mind goes into overdrive as my heartbeat jumps. I don't even consider the possibility of that second girl being a twin sister or something like that. I know it's her. She's doing what I did just a few minutes ago. She's walking in the Quiet. The world around us is frozen, but we are not.

A horrified look crosses her face as she realizes the same thing. Before I can react, she lunges across the table and touches her own forehead.

The world becomes normal again.

She stares at me from across the table, shocked, her eyes huge and her face pale. Her hands tremble as she rises to her feet. Without so much as a word, she turns and begins walking away, then breaks into a run a couple of seconds later.

Getting over my own shock, I get up and run after her. It's not exactly smooth. If she notices a guy she doesn't know running after her, dating will be the last thing on her mind. But I'm beyond that now. She's the only person I've met who can do what I do. She's proof that I'm not insane. She might have what I want most in the world.

She might have answers.

―――――

The Thought Readers is now available at most retailers. If you'd like to learn more, please visit www.dimazales.com.

EXCERPT FROM THE SORCERY CODE

Once a respected member of the Sorcerer Council and now an outcast, Blaise has spent the last year of his life working on a special magical object. The goal is to allow anyone to do magic, not just the sorcerer elite. The outcome of his quest is unlike anything he could've ever imagined—because, instead of an object, he creates Her.

She is Gala, and she is anything but inanimate. Born in the Spell Realm, she is beautiful and highly intelligent—and nobody knows what she's capable of. She will do anything to experience the world... even leave the man she is beginning to fall for.

Augusta, a powerful sorceress and Blaise's former fiancée, sees Blaise's deed as the ultimate hubris and Gala as an abomination that must be destroyed. In her quest to save the human race, Augusta will forge new alliances, becoming tangled in a web of intrigue that stretches further than any of them suspect. She may even have to turn to her new lover Barson, a ruthless warrior who might have an agenda of his own...

———

There was a naked woman on the floor of Blaise's study.

A beautiful naked woman.

Stunned, Blaise stared at the gorgeous creature who just appeared out of thin air. She was looking around with a bewildered expression on her face, apparently as shocked to be there as he was to be seeing her. Her wavy blond hair streamed down her back, partially covering a body that appeared to be perfection itself. Blaise tried not to think about that body and to focus on the situation instead.

A woman. A *She*, not an *It*. Blaise could hardly believe it. Could it be? Could this girl be the object?

She was sitting with her legs folded underneath her, propping herself up with one slim arm. There was something awkward about that pose, as though she didn't know what to do with her own limbs. In general, despite the curves that marked her a fully grown woman, there was a child-like innocence in the way she sat there, completely unselfconscious and totally unaware of her own appeal.

Clearing his throat, Blaise tried to think of what to say. In his wildest dreams, he couldn't have imagined this kind of outcome to the project that had consumed his entire life for the past several months.

Hearing the sound, she turned her head to look at him, and Blaise found himself staring into a pair of unusually clear blue eyes.

She blinked, then cocked her head to the side, studying him with visible curiosity. Blaise wondered what she was seeing. He hadn't seen the light of day in weeks, and he wouldn't be surprised if he looked like a mad sorcerer at this point. There was probably a week's worth of stubble covering his face, and he knew his dark hair was unbrushed and sticking out in every direction. If he'd known he would be facing a beautiful woman today, he would've done a grooming spell in the morning.

"Who am I?" she asked, startling Blaise. Her voice was soft and feminine, as alluring as the rest of her. "What is this place?"

"You don't know?" Blaise was glad he finally managed to string together a semi-coherent sentence. "You don't know who you are or where you are?"

She shook her head. "No."

Blaise swallowed. "I see."

"What am I?" she asked again, staring at him with those incredible eyes.

"Well," Blaise said slowly, "if you're not some cruel prankster or a figment of my imagination, then it's somewhat difficult to explain..."

She was watching his mouth as he spoke, and when he stopped, she looked up again, meeting his gaze. "It's strange," she said, "hearing words this way. These are the first real words I've heard."

Blaise felt a chill go down his spine. Getting up from his chair, he began to pace, trying to keep his eyes off her nude body. He had been expecting something to appear. A magical object, a thing. He just hadn't known what form that thing would take. A mirror, perhaps, or a lamp. Maybe even something as unusual as the Life Capture Sphere that sat on his desk like a large round diamond.

But a person? A female person at that?

To be fair, he had been trying to make the object intelligent, to ensure it would have the ability to comprehend human language and convert it into the code. Maybe he shouldn't be so surprised that the intelligence he invoked took on a human shape.

A beautiful, feminine, sensual shape.

Focus, Blaise, focus.

"Why are you walking like that?" She slowly got to her feet, her movements uncertain and strangely clumsy. "Should I be walking too? Is that how people talk to each other?"

Blaise stopped in front of her, doing his best to keep his eyes above her neck. "I'm sorry. I'm not accustomed to naked women in my study."

She ran her hands down her body, as though trying to feel it for the first time. Whatever her intent, Blaise found the gesture extremely erotic.

"Is something wrong with the way I look?" she asked. It was such a typical feminine concern that Blaise had to stifle a smile.

"Quite the opposite," he assured her. "You look unimaginably good." So good, in fact, that he was having trouble concentrating on anything but her delicate curves. She was of medium height, and so perfectly proportioned that she could've been used as a sculptor's template.

"Why do I look this way?" A small frown creased her smooth forehead. "What am I?" That last part seemed to be puzzling her the most.

Blaise took a deep breath, trying to calm his racing pulse. "I think I can try to venture a guess, but before I do, I want to give you some clothing. Please wait here—I'll be right back."

And without waiting for her answer, he hurried out of the room.

———

The Sorcery Code is currently available at most retailers. If you'd like to learn more, please visit www.dimazales.com.

ABOUT THE AUTHOR

Dima Zales is a *New York Times* and *USA Today* bestselling author of science fiction and fantasy. Prior to becoming a writer, he worked in the software development industry in New York as both a programmer and an executive. From high-frequency trading software for big banks to mobile apps for popular magazines, Dima has done it all. In 2013, he left the software industry in order to concentrate on his writing career and moved to Palm Coast, Florida, where he currently resides.

Please visit www.dimazales.com to learn more.

Made in the USA
Middletown, DE
10 September 2018